SCIENCE FICTION
AT ITS BEST

Here are sixteen stories chosen for the prestigious Nebula Award by the Science Fiction Writers of America.

The vast, star-spanning scope of the field is represented—such authors as Aldiss, Dickson, Leiber, Silverberg, Zelazny, and such unforgettable tales as Ellison's "A Boy And His Dog," McCaffrey's "Dragonrider," Moorcock's "Behold The Man," and Vance's "The Last Castle."

The Science Fiction Hall of Fame Volume I and Volumes IIA and IIB are already accepted in colleges, libraries, and by readers as definitive collections of science fiction's richest stories. Now the Science Fiction Writers of America creates a companion volume—the excellence continues.

Other Avon Books in the
Science Fiction Hall of Fame

THE SCIENCE FICTION HALL OF FAME

VOLUME III
Nebula Winners 1965–1969

Edited by
ARTHUR C. CLARKE
and
GEORGE W. PROCTOR

AVON
PUBLISHERS OF BARD. CAMELOT. DISCUS AND FLARE BOOKS

THE SCIENCE FICTION HALL OF FAME: VOLUME III, NEBULA WINNERS 1965-1969 is an original publication of Avon Books. This work has never before appeared in book form.

AVON BOOKS
A division of
The Hearst Corporation
959 Eighth Avenue
New York, New York 10019

First Avon Printing, March, 1982

ACKNOWLEDGMENTS

"Repent, Harlequin!" Said the Ticktockman, by Harlan Ellison, Copyright © 1966 by Harlan Ellison. Reprinted by permission of and by arrangement with the author and the author's agent, Robert P. Mills, Ltd., New York. All rights reserved.

The Doors of His Face, The Lamps of His Mouth, by Roger Zelazny. Copyright © 1965 by Mercury Press, Inc. Reprinted by permission of the Amber Corporation.

The Saliva Tree, by Brian W. Aldiss, Copyright © 1965 by Mercury Press, Inc. Reprinted by permission of the author.

He Who Shapes, by Roger Zelazny, Copyright © 1965 by Ziff-Davis Publishing Co. Inc. Reprinted by permission of the Amber Corporation.

The Secret Place, by Richard McKenna, Copyright © 1966 by Berkley Publishing Corp. Reprinted by permission of Mrs. Richard M. McKenna, author's widow.

Call Him Lord, by Gordon R. Dickson, Copyright © 1966 by the Condé Nast Publications, Inc. Reprinted by permission of the author and his agent, Kirby McCauley Ltd.

The Last Castle, by Jack Vance, Copyright © 1966 by Galaxy Publishing Corp. Reprinted by permission of the author and his agent, Kirby McCauley Ltd.

Aye, and Gomorrah. . . , by Samuel R. Delany, Copyright © 1967 by Samuel R. Delany. Reprinted by permission of the author and his agents, Henry Morrison, Inc.

Gonna Roll the Bones, by Fritz Leiber, Copyright © 1967 Fritz Leiber. Reprinted by permission of the author.

Behold The Man, by Michael Moorcock, Copyright © 1967 by Donald A. Wollheim and Terry Carr. Reprinted by permission of the author.

The Planners, by Kate Wilhelm, Copyright © 1968 by Damon Knight. Reprinted by permission of the author.

Mother to the World, by Richard Wilson, Copyright © 1968 by Richard Wilson. Reprinted by permission of the author.

Dragonrider, by Anne McCaffrey, Copyright © 1967, 1968 by the Condé Nast Publications, Inc. Reprinted by permission of the author and Virginia Kidd Literary Agents.

Passengers, by Robert Silverberg, Copyright © 1968 by Damon Knight. Reprinted by permission of the author.

Time Considered as a Helix of Semi-Precious Stones, by Samuel R. Delany, Copyright © 1969 by Samuel R. Delany. Reprinted by permission of the author and his agents, Henry Morrison, Inc.

A Boy and His Dog, by Harlan Ellison, Copyright © 1969 by Harlan Ellison. Reprinted by permission of and by arrangement with the author and the author's agent, Robert P. Mills, Ltd., New York. All rights reserved.

CONTENTS

INTRODUCTION

A cynic might argue that no art form can now be taken seriously unless it is honored by awards and award ceremonies so that the public can be reassured by some official certificate of excellence. ("And the name in this envelope is—LEONARDO DA VINCI! Better luck next time, Michelangelo!") In the science fiction and fantasy fields, we have the Galaxy, Jupiter, John W. Campbell, and International Fantasy Awards; but the best-known and undoubtedly most prestigious are the Hugo and Nebula.

The Hugo is named after Hugo Gernsbach (1884–1967), alternately praised and reviled as the father of magazine science fiction. Though many of his authors would have preferred the title Godfather, he was a great man and genuinely loved the medium; it wasn't his fault that he sometimes couldn't find the half-cent per word his rapacious writers demanded.

The Hugo Award is a finned, streamlined torpedo in the shape of a classic prespace-age spaceship. (I once had the challenging problem of carrying one aboard an airplane during a bomb scare.) It is presented annually at the World Science Fiction Convention, after a prolonged period of balloting and voting by the "fans." *Vox populi, vox dei;* the Hugo is the customers' token of gratitude to the books, short stories, and dramatic works that have given them the greatest pleasure.

The Nebula, on the other hand, is the tribute of the professionals to their peers. Titles are nominated and voted upon by the members of the Science Fiction Writers of America. It is thus the precise equivalent of the Oscar in the movie world, but is considerably more beautiful. (Sour grapes, perhaps; it's a harrowing experience to slink out of the Dorothy Chandler Pavilion with your undelivered speech of acceptance. I've never forgiven Mel what's-his-name for beating *2001* with *The Producers*.)

The Nebula is a block of transparent plastic, wherein are cunningly embedded various crystals and minerals to give it an astronomical motive; it puts on quite a display when you shine a laser into it. I am now the proud possessor of three (who was the criminologist who said, "Once is an accident, twice is a coincidence, but three times is a conspiracy"?) and won't be in the running for any more, so I can regard the entire Nebula voting system with detached complacency. Over the years the Award has been the subject of heated debate by the members of the Science Fiction Writers of America, some of whom have suggested its abolition altogether. They argue that it's meaningless to talk about a "best" in any category, and that no one can possibly read all the titles nominated in the final ballot.

They have a point. On checking the preliminary ballot for the 1979 Awards, I'm depressed to discover that I've read only six of the twenty-three novels nominated—and this includes one I'd written myself. In the other categories my record is even more deplorable: two of the eight novellas (17,500–40,000 words) and none of the twenty novelets (7,500–17,500 words) or twenty-six short stories. No wonder I had to disqualify myself from voting. . . .

Incidentally, the problem with the Oscars is even worse, except for anyone who lives in Hollywood. The Academy of Motion Picture Arts and Sciences used to send me lists of several hundred movies; I resigned the year I'd not seen even *one*.

I'd be surprised if even half the people who vote for the Nebulas have read a quarter of the stories nominated; most of them are too busy writing their own. But does it matter? Perfection is impossible in this world, and the laws of statistics usually even matters out. Rough justice is eventually done, and a really poor story seldom makes it to the finals.

And perhaps the most important function of the Nebulas is precisely that claimed for the Oscars. However worthy or unworthy the winners may be, the general ballyhoo (when will the Nebula dinners be televised?) creates interest and excitement that is good for the *genre*, as well as the writers, publishers, editors, agents, readers, and sales. Despite the tears and heartbreak (how many Kleenexes did Isaac use up before he finally made it?), *everyone* gains in the long run.

On looking at the contents of this volume, I'm happy to discover that I've met every one of the authors, and with a single exception, all are still very much alive. They and their stories can speak for themselves and need no words of introduction from me. Instead, let me talk about Richard McKenna (1913–64).

Last night by a weird coincidence, his name flashed on the ship's TV as we steamed through the waters he knew half a century ago. There was a screening aboard of the excellent movie made from his only novel, *The Sand Pebbles* (1962). To the five-hundred students of our floating campus, this saga of U.S. gunboat diplomacy in a vanished China must have seemed as remote as the Civil War. (I wondered, too, what our all-Chinese crew, from the captain on down, thought when they saw Steve McQueen patiently explain the mysteries of steam power to their primitive countrymen.)

Dick McKenna spent twenty years below decks in the U.S. Navy, then took his B.A. in literature at the University of North Carolina. Though his academic training must have been valuable, the magic of "The Secret Place" could have come only from his own subconscious. There are lines in this story that make my skin crawl; the voters for the 1966 Nebula knew what they were doing. But by then, the author was already dead.

I met him and his wife Eva at the Milford Science Fiction Writers' Workshop in 1958. Though it was our only encounter, I have never forgotten the impression of quiet power and integrity that he radiated.

There are many lessons to be learned from Richard McKenna's tragically brief career. He showed that a writer of real talent can emerge from any environment. In our own time, Alex Haley has also used the U.S. Navy as a launching pad, against even greater odds.

But perhaps the most important lesson McKenna can

teach us is one that we are only just beginning to learn. Science fiction *is* different from "mainstream" literature —but there are no barriers between them.

ARTHUR C. CLARKE
S.S. *Universe*
Krakatoa, Gt Basses Reef
October, 1980

THE NEBULA AWARDS—The Novels

1965   *Dune,* by Frank Herbert.

1966   *Flowers for Algernon,* by Daniel Keyes;
(tie)   *Babel-17,* by Samuel R. Delany.

1967   *The Einstein Intersection,*
      by Samuel R. Delany.

1968   *Rite of Passage,* by Alexei Panshin.

1969   *The Left Hand of Darkness,*
      by Ursula K. Le Guin.

1965

"REPENT, HARLEQUIN!" SAID THE TICKTOCKMAN

by Harlan Ellison

There are always those who ask, what is it all about? For those who need to ask, for those who need points sharply made, who need to know "where it's at," this:

> *"The mass of men serve the state thus, not as men mainly, but as machines, with their bodies. They are the standing army, and the militia, jailors, constables, posse comitatus, etc. In most cases there is no free exercise whatever of the judgment or of the moral sense; but they put themselves on a level with wood and earth and stones; and wooden men can perhaps be manufactured that will serve the purpose as well. Such command no more respect than men of straw or a lump of dirt. They have the same sort of worth only as horses and dogs. Yet such as these even are commonly esteemed good citizens. Others—as most legislators, politicians, lawyers, ministers, and officeholders—serve the state chiefly with their heads; and, as they rarely make any moral distinctions, they are as likely to serve the Devil, without intending it, as God. A very few, as heroes, patriots, martyrs, reformers in the great sense, and men, serve the state with their consciences also, and so necessarily resist it for the most part; and they are commonly treated as enemies by it."*

Henry David Thoreau,
CIVIL DISOBEDIENCE

That is the heart of it. Now begin in the middle and later learn the beginning; the end will take care of itself.

But because it was the very world it was, the very world they had allowed it to *become*, for months his activities did not come to the alarmed attention of The Ones Who Kept The Machine Functioning Smoothly, the ones who poured the very best butter over the cams and mainsprings of the culture. Not until it had become obvious that somehow, someway, he had become a notoriety, a celebrity, perhaps even a hero for (what Officialdom inescapably tagged) "an emotionally disturbed segment of the populace," did they turn it over to the Ticktockman and his legal machinery. But by then, because it was the very world it was, and they had no way to predict he would happen—possibly a strain of disease long-defunct, now suddenly reborn in a system where immunity had been forgotten, had lapsed—he had been allowed to become too real. Now he had form and substance.

He had become a *personality*, something they had filtered out of the system many decades before. But there it was, and there *he* was, a very definitely imposing personality. In certain circles—middle-class circles—it was thought disgusting. Vulgar ostentation. Anarchistic. Shameful. In others, there was only sniggering: those strata where thought is subjugated to form and ritual, niceties, proprieties. But down below, ah, down below, where the people always needed their saints and sinners, their bread and circuses, their heroes and villains, he was considered a Bolivar; a Napoleon; a Robin Hood; a Dick Bong (Ace of Aces); a Jesus; a Jomo Kenyatta.

And at the top—where, like socially-attuned Shipwreck Kellys, every tremor and vibration threatens to dislodge the wealthy, powerful and titled from their flagpoles—he was considered a menace; a heretic; a rebel; a disgrace; a peril. He was known down the line, to the very heart-meat core, but the important reactions were high above and far below. At the very top, at the very bottom.

So his file was turned over, along with his time-card and his cardioplate, to the office of the Ticktockman.

The Ticktockman: very much over six feet tall, often

silent, a soft, purring man when things went timewise.
The Ticktockman.

Even in the cubicles of the hierarchy, where fear was
generated, seldom suffered, he was called the Ticktockman. But no one called him that to his mask.

You don't call a man a hated name, not when that
man, behind his mask, is capable of revoking the minutes, the hours, the days and nights, the years of your
life. He was called the Master Timekeeper to his mask.
It was safer that way.

"This is *what* he is," said the Ticktockman with genuine softness, "but not *who* he is. This time-card I'm holding in my left hand has a name on it, but it is the name of
what he is, not *who* he is. The cardioplate here in my
right hand is also named, but not *whom* named, merely
what named. Before I can exercise proper revocation, I
have to know *who* this *what* is."

To his staff, all the ferrets, all the loggers, all the finks,
all the commex, even the mineez, he said, "Who is this
Harlequin?"

He was not purring smoothly. Timewise, it was jangle.

However, it *was* the longest speech they had ever
heard him utter at one time, the staff, the ferrets, the loggers, the finks, the commex, but not the mineez, who
usually weren't around to know, in any case. But even
they scurried to find out.

Who is the Harlequin?

High above the third level of the city, he crouched on
the humming, aluminum-frame platform of the air-boat
(foof! air-boat, indeed! swizzleskid is what it was, with
a tow-rack jerry-rigged) and he stared down at the neat
Mondrian arrangement of the buildings.

Somewhere nearby, he could hear the metronomic left-
right-left of the 2:47 P.M. shift, entering the Timkin
roller-bearing plant in their sneakers. A minute later precisely, he heard the softer right-left-right of the 5:00 A.M.
formation, going home.

An elfin grin spread across his tanned features, and his
dimples appeared for a moment. Then, scratching at his
thatch of auburn hair, he shrugged within his motley, as
though girding himself for what came next, and threw the
joystick forward, and bent into the wind as the air-boat

dropped. He skimmed over a slidewalk, purposely dropping a few feet to crease the tassels of the ladies of fashion, and—inserting thumbs in large ears—he stuck out his tongue, rolled his eyes, and went wugga-wugga-wugga. It was a minor diversion. One pedestrian skittered and tumbled, sending parcels everywhichway, another wet herself, a third keeled slantwise and the walk was stopped automatically by the servitors till she could be resuscitated. It was a minor diversion.

Then he swirled away on a vagrant breeze and was gone. Hi-ho.

As he rounded the cornice of the Time-Motion Study Building, he saw the shift just boarding the slidewalk. With practiced motion and an absolute conservation of movement, they sidestepped up onto the slowstrip and (in a chorus line reminiscent of a Busby Berkeley film of the antediluvian 1930s) advanced across the strips ostrich-walking till they were lined up on the expresstrip.

Once more, in anticipation, the elfin grin spread, and there was a tooth missing back there on the left side. He dipped, skimmed, and swooped over them; and then scrunching about on the air-boat, he released the holding pins that fastened shut the ends of the homemade pouring troughs that kept his cargo from dumping prematurely. And as he pulled the trough-pins, the air-boat slid over the factory workers and one hundred and fifty thousand dollars' worth of jelly beans cascaded down on the expresstrip.

Jelly beans! Millions and billions of purples and yellows and greens and licorice and grape and raspberry and mint and round and smooth and crunchy outside and soft-mealy inside and sugary and bouncing-jouncing-tumbling-clittering-clattering-skittering fell on the heads and shoulders and hardhats and carapaces of the Timkin workers, tinkling on the slidewalk and bouncing away and rolling about underfoot and filling the sky on their way down with all the colors of joy and childhood and holidays, coming down in a steady rain, a solid wash, a torrent of color and sweetness out of the sky from above, and entering a universe of sanity and metronomic order with quite-mad coocoo newness. Jelly beans!

The shift workers howled and laughed and were pelted, and broke ranks, and the jelly beans managed to work

their way into the mechanism of the slidewalks after
which there was a hideous scraping as the sound of a
million fingernails rasped down a quarter of a million
blackboards, followed by a coughing and a sputtering,
and then the slidewalks all stopped and everyone was
dumped thisaway and thataway in a jackstraw tumble,
still laughing and popping little jelly bean eggs of childish
color into their mouths. It was a holiday and a jollity, an
absolute insanity, a giggle. But . . .

The shift was delayed seven minutes.

They did not get home for seven minutes.

The master schedule was thrown off by seven minutes.

Quotas were delayed by inoperative slidewalks for
seven minutes.

He had tapped the first domino in the line, and one
after another, like chik chik chik, the others had fallen.

The System had been seven minutes' worth of disrupted. It was a tiny matter, one hardly worthy of note,
but in a society where the single driving force was order
and unity and equality and promptness and clocklike
precision and attention to the clock, reverence of the
gods of the passage of time, it was a disaster of major
importance.

So he was ordered to appear before the Ticktockman.
It was broadcast across every channel of the communications web. He was ordered to be *there* at 7:00 dammit on
time. And they waited, and they waited, but he didn't
show up till almost 10:30, at which time he merely sang
a little song about moonlight in a place no one had ever
heard of called Vermont and vanished again. But they
had all been waiting since seven, and it wrecked *hell*
with their schedules. So the question remained: Who is
the Harlequin?

But the *unasked* question (more important of the two)
was: How did we get *into* this position, where a laughing,
irresponsible japer of jabberwocky and jive could disrupt
our entire economic and cultural life with a hundred and
fifty thousand dollars' worth of jelly beans. . . .

Jelly for God's sake *beans!* This is madness! Where
did he get the money to buy a hundred and fifty thousand
dollars' worth of jelly beans? (They knew it would have
cost that much, because they had a team of Situation
Analysts pulled off another assignment and rushed to the

slidewalk scene to sweep up and count the candies, and produce findings, which disrupted *their* schedules and threw their entire branch at least a day behind.) Jelly beans! Jelly . . . *beans?* Now wait a second—a second accounted for—no one has manufactured jelly beans for over a hundred years. Where did he get jelly beans?

That's another good question. More than likely it will never be answered to your complete satisfaction. But then, how many questions ever are?

The middle you know. Here is the beginning. How it starts:

A desk pad. Day for day and turn each day. 9:00—open the mail. 9:45—appointment with Planning Commission Board. 10:30—discuss installation progress charts with J.L. 11:45—pray for rain. 12:00—lunch. *And so it goes.*

"I'm sorry, Miss Grant, but the time for interviews was set at 2:30, and it's almost five now. I'm sorry you're late, but those are the rules. You'll have to wait till next year to submit application for this college again." *And so it goes.*

The 10:10 local stops at Cresthaven, Galesville, Tonawanda Junction, Selby, and Farnhurst, but not at Indiana City, Lucasville, and Colton, except on Sunday. The 10:35 express stops at Galesville, Selby, and Indiana City, except on Sundays and holidays, at which time it stops at . . . *and so it goes.*

"I couldn't wait, Fred. I had to be at Pierre Cartain's by 3:00, and you said you'd meet me under the clock in the terminal at 2:45, and you weren't there, so I had to go on. You're always late, Fred. If you'd been there, we could have sewed it up together, but as it was, well, I took the order alone . . ." *And so it goes.*

Dear Mr. and Mrs. Atterley: In reference to your son Gerold's constant tardiness, I am afraid we will have to suspend him from school unless some more reliable method can be instituted guaranteeing he will arrive at his classes on time. Granted he is an exemplary student, and his marks are high, his constant flouting of the schedules of this school makes it impractical to maintain him in a system where the other children seem capable of get-

ting where they are supposed to be on time *and so it goes*.
YOU CANNOT VOTE UNLESS YOU APPEAR AT
8:45 A.M.
"I don't care if the script is *good*. I need it Thursday!"
CHECK-OUT TIME IS 2:00 P.M.
"You got here late. The job's taken. Sorry."
YOUR SALARY HAS BEEN DOCKED FOR
TWENTY MINUTES' TIME LOST.
"God, what time is it? I've gotta run!"
And so it goes. And so it goes. And so it goes. And so it
goes goes goes goes goes tick tock tick tock tick tock and
one day we no longer let time serve us, we serve time
and we are slaves of the schedule, worshippers of the
sun's passing; bound into a life predicated on restrictions
because the system will not function if we don't keep the
schedule tight.

Until it becomes more than a minor inconvenience to
be late. It becomes a sin. Then a crime. Then a crime
punishable by this:

EFFECTIVE 15 JULY 2389, 12:00:00 midnight, the
office of the Master Timekeeper will require all citizens
to submit their time-cards and cardioplates for process-
ing. In accordance with Statute 555-7-SGH-999 gov-
erning the revocation of time per capita, all cardioplates
will be keyed to the individual holder and—

What they had done was to devise a method of cur-
tailing the amount of life a person could have. If he was
ten minutes late, he lost ten minutes of his life. An hour
was proportionately worth more revocation. If someone
was consistently tardy, he might find himself on a Sunday
night, receiving a communique from the Master Timekeeper that his time had run out and he would be
"turned off" at high noon on Monday, please straighten
your affairs, sir, madame, or bisex.

And so by this simple scientific expedient (utilizing a
scientific process held dearly secret by the Ticktockman's
office), the System was maintained. It was the only expedient thing to do. It was, after all, patriotic. The schedules had to be met. After all, there *was* a war going on!

But wasn't there always?

"Now that is really disgusting," the Harlequin said
when Pretty Alice showed him the wanted poster. "Dis-

gusting and *highly* improbable. After all, this isn't the Day of the Desperado. A *wanted* poster!"

"You know," Pretty Alice noted, "you speak with a great deal of inflection."

"I'm sorry," said the Harlequin, humbly.

"No need to be sorry. You're always saying 'I'm sorry.' You have such massive guilt, Everett, it's really very sad."

"I'm sorry," he repeated, then pursed his lips so the dimples appeared momentarily. He hadn't wanted to say that at all. "I have to go out again. I have to *do* something."

Pretty Alice slammed her coffee-bulb down on the counter. "Oh, for God's *sake,* Everett, can't you stay home just *one* night! Must you always be out in that ghastly clown suit, running around an*noy*ing people?"

"I'm—" He stopped and clapped the jester's hat onto his auburn thatch with a tiny tingling of bells. He rose, rinsed out his coffee-bulb at the spray, and put it into the drier for a moment. "I have to go."

She didn't answer. The faxbox was purring, and she pulled a sheet out, read it, threw it toward him on the counter. "It's about you. Of course. You're ridiculous."

He read it quickly. It said the Ticktockman was trying to locate him. He didn't care, he was going out to be late again. At the door, dredging for an exit line, he hurled back petulantly, "Well, *you* speak with inflection, *too!*"

Pretty Alice rolled her pretty eyes heavenward. "You're ridiculous." The Harlequin stalked out, slamming the door, which sighed shut softly and locked itself.

There was a gentle knock, and Pretty Alice got up with an exhalation of exasperated breath and opened the door. He stood there. "I'll be back about ten-thirty, okay?"

She pulled a rueful face. "Why do you tell me that? Why? You *know* you'll be late! You *know* it! You're *always* late, so why do you tell me these dumb things?" She closed the door.

On the other side, the Harlequin nodded to himself. *She's right. She's always right. I'll be late. I'm always late. Why do I tell her these dumb things?*

He shrugged again and went off to be late once more.

•

He had fired off the firecracker rockets that said: *I will attend the 115th annual International Medical Association Invocation at 8:00 P.M. precisely. I do hope you will all be able to join me.*

The words had burned in the sky, and of course the authorities were there, lying in wait for him. They assumed, naturally, that he would be late. He arrived twenty minutes early while they were setting up the spiderwebs to trap and hold him. Blowing a large bullhorn, he frightened and unnerved them so, their own moisturized encirclement webs sucked closed, and they were hauled up, kicking and shrieking, high above the amphitheater's floor. The Harlequin laughed and laughed and apologized profusely. The physicians, gathered in solemn conclave, roared with laughter and accepted the Harlequin's apologies with exaggerated bowing and posturing, and a merry time was had by all who thought the Harlequin was a regular foofaraw in fancy pants; all, that is, but the authorities who had been sent out by the office of the Ticktockman; they hung there like so much dockside cargo, hauled up above the floor of the amphitheater in a most unseemly fashion.

(In another part of the same city where the Harlequin carried on his "activities," totally unrelated in every way to what concerns us here, save that it illustrates the Ticktockman's power and import, a man named Marshall Delahanty received his turn-off notice from the Ticktockman's office. His wife received the notification from the gray-suited minee who delivered it with the traditional "look of sorrow" plastered hideously across his face. She knew what it was even without unsealing it. It was a billet-doux of immediate recognition to everyone these days. She gasped and held it as though it were a glass slide tinged with botulism, and prayed it was not for her. Let it be for Marsh, she thought brutally, realistically, or one of the kids, but not for me, please dear God, not for me. And then she opened it, and it *was* for Marsh, and she was at one and the same time horrified and relieved. The next trooper in the line had caught the bullet. "Marshall," she screamed, "Marshall! Termination, Marshall! OhmiGod, Marshall, whattl we do, whattl we do, Marshall ohmigodmarshall . . ." and in their home that night was the sound of tearing paper and fear, and the stink of madness went up the flue and there was nothing, absolutely nothing they could do about it.

(But Marshall Delahanty tried to run. And early the next day when turn-off time came, he was deep in the Canadian forest two hundred miles away, and the office of the Ticktockman blanked his cardioplate, and Marshall Delahanty keeled over, running, and his heart stopped, and the blood dried up on its way to his brain, and he was dead, that's all. One light went out on the sector map in the office of the Master Timekeeper while notification was entered for fax reproduction, and Georgette Delahanty's name was entered on the dole roles till she could remarry. Which is the end of the footnote and all the point that need be made, except don't laugh because this is what would happen to the Harlequin if ever the Ticktockman found out his real name. It isn't funny.)

The shopping level of the city was thronged with the Thursday-colors of the buyers. Women in canary yellow chitons and men in pseudo-Tyrolean outfits that were jade and leather and fit very tightly, save for the balloon pants.

When the Harlequin appeared on the still-being constructed shell of the new Efficiency Shopping Center, his bullhorn to his elfishly laughing lips, everyone pointed and stared, and he berated them:

"Why let them order you about? Why let them tell you to hurry and scurry like ants or maggots? Take your time! Saunter a while! Enjoy the sunshine, enjoy the breeze, let life carry you at your own pace! Don't be slaves of time; it's a helluva way to die, slowly, by degrees . . . down with the Ticktockman!"

Who's the nut? most of the shoppers wanted to know. Who's the nut oh wow I'm gonna be late I gotta run. . . .

And the construction gang on the Shopping Center received an urgent order from the office of the Master Timekeeper that the dangerous criminal known as the Harlequin was atop their spire, and their aid was urgently needed in apprehending him. The work crew said no, they would lose time on their construction schedule, but the Ticktockman managed to pull the proper threads of governmental webbing, and they were told to cease work and catch that nitwit up there on the spire, up there with the bullhorn. So a dozen and more burly workers began climbing into their construction platforms, releasing the a-grav plates and rising toward the Harlequin.

After the debacle (in which, through the Harlequin's attention to personal safety, no one was seriously injured), the workers tried to reassemble and assault him again, but it was too late. He had vanished. It had attracted quite a crowd, however, and the shopping cycle was thrown off by hours, simply hours. The purchasing needs of the System were therefore falling behind, and so measures were taken to accelerate the cycle for the rest of the day, but it got bogged down and speeded up, and they sold too many boat-valves and not nearly enough wegglers, which meant that the popli ratio was off, which made it necessary to rush cases and cases of spoiling Smash-O to stores that usually needed a case only every three or four hours. The shipments were bollixed, the transshipments were misrouted, and in the end, even the swizzleskid industries felt it.

"Don't come back till you have him!" the Ticktockman said, very quietly, very sincerely, extremely dangerously.

They used dogs. They used probes. They used cardio-plate cross-offs. They used teepers. They used bribery. They used stiktytes. They used intimidation. They used torment. They used torture. They used finks. They used cops. They used search and seizure. They used fallaron. They used betterment incentive. They used fingerprints. They used the Bertillon system. They used cunning. They used guile. They used treachery. They used Raoul Mitgong, but he didn't help much. They used applied physics. They used techniques of criminology.

And what the hell: they caught him.

After all, his name was Everett C. Marm, and he wasn't much to begin with, except a man who had no sense of time.

"Repent, Harlequin!" said the Ticktockman.

"Get stuffed!" the Harlequin replied, sneering.

"You've been late a total of sixty-three years, five months, three weeks, two days, twelve hours, forty-one minutes, fifty-nine seconds, point-oh-three-six-one-one-one microseconds. You've used up everything you can and more. I'm going to turn you off."

"Scare someone else. I'd rather be dead than live in a dumb world with a bogeyman like you."

"It's my job."

"You're full of it. You're a tyrant. You have no right to order people around and kill them if they show up late."

"You can't adjust. You can't fit in."

"Unstrap me, and I'll fit my fist into your mouth."

"You're a nonconformist."

"That didn't used to be a felony."

"It is now. Live in the world around you."

"I hate it. It's a terrible world."

"Not everyone thinks so. Most people enjoy order."

"I don't, and most of the people I know don't."

"That's not true. How do you think we caught you?"

"I'm not interested."

"A girl named Pretty Alice told us who you were."

"That's a lie."

"It's true. You unnerve her. She wants to belong; she wants to conform; I'm going to turn you off."

"Then do it already, and stop arguing with me."

"I'm not going to turn you off."

"You're an idiot!"

"Repent, Harlequin!" said the Ticktockman.

"Get stuffed."

So they sent him to Coventry. And in Coventry they worked him over. It was just like what they did to Winston Smith in *1984*, which was a book none of them knew about, but the techniques are really quite ancient, and so they did it to Everett C. Marm; and one day quite a long time later, the Harlequin appeared on the communications web, appearing elfin and dimpled and bright-eyed and not at all brainwashed, and he said he had been wrong, that it was a good, a very good thing indeed, to belong, to be right on time hip-ho and away we go, and everyone stared up at him on the public screens that covered an entire city block, and they said to themselves, well, you see, he was just a nut after all, and if that's the way the system is run, then let's do it that way, because it doesn't pay to fight city hall, or in this case, the Ticktockman. So Everett C. Marm was destroyed, which was a loss because of what Thoreau said earlier, but you can't make an omelet without breaking a few eggs, and in every revolution a few die who shouldn't, but they have to because that's the way it happens, and if you make only a little change, then it seems to be worthwhile. Or to make the point lucidly:

"Uh, excuse me, sir, I uh, don't know how to uh, to uh, tell you this, but you were three minutes late. The schedule is a little, uh, bit off."

He grinned sheepishly.

"That's ridiculous!" murmured the Ticktockman behind his mask. "Check your watch." And then he went into his office, going *mrmee, mrmee, mrmee, mrmee*.

THE DOORS OF HIS FACE,
THE LAMPS OF HIS MOUTH

by Roger Zelazny

I'm a baitman. No one is born a baitman, except in a French novel where everyone is. (In fact, I think that's the title, *We are All Bait*. Pfft!) How I got that way is barely worth telling and has nothing to do with neo-exes, but the days of the beast deserve a few words, so here they are.

The Lowlands of Venus lie between the thumb and fore-finger of the continent known as Hand. When you break into Cloud Alley it swings its silver black bowling ball toward you without a warning. You jump then, inside that fire tailed tenpin they ride you down in, but the straps keep you from making a fool of yourself. You generally chuckle afterwards, but you always jump first.

Next, you study Hand to lay its illusion and the two middle fingers become dozen-ringed archipelagoes as the outers resolve into green gray peninsulas; the thumb is too short, and curls like the embryo tail of Cape Horn.

You suck pure oxygen, sigh possibly, and begin the long topple to the Lowlands.

There, you are caught like an infield fly at the Lifeline landing area—so named because of its nearness to the great delta in the Eastern Bay—located between the first peninsula and "thumb." For a minute it seems as if you're going to miss Lifeline and wind up as canned sea-food, but afterwards—shaking off the metaphors—you descend to scorched concrete and present your middle-sized telephone directory of authorizations to the short, fat man in the gray cap. The papers show that you are not subject to mysterious inner rottings and etcetera. He then smiles you a short, fat, gray smile and motions you toward the bus which hauls you to the Reception Area. At the R.A. you spend three days proving that, indeed, you are not subject to mysterious inner rottings and etcetera.

Boredom, however, is another rot. When your three days are up, you generally hit Lifeline hard, and it returns the compliment as a matter of reflex. The effects of alcohol in variant atmospheres is a subject on which the connoisseurs have written numerous volumes, so I will confine my remarks to noting that a good binge is worthy of at least a week's time and often warrants a lifetime study.

I had been a student of exceptional promise (strictly undergraduate) for going on two years when the *Bright Water* fell through our marble ceiling and poured its people like targets into the city.

Pause. The Worlds Almanac re Lifeline: ". . . Port city on the eastern coast of Hand. Employees of the Agency for Nonterrestrial Research comprise approximately 85% of its 100,000 population (2010 Census). Its other residents are primarily personnel maintained by several industrial corporations engaged in basic research. Independent marine biologists, wealthy fishing enthusiasts, and waterfront entrepreneurs make up the remainder of its inhabitants."

I turned to Mike Dabis, a fellow entrepreneur, and commented on the lousy state of basic research.

"Not if the mumbled truth be known."

He paused behind his glass before continuing the slow swallowing process calculated to obtain my interest and a few oaths before he continued.

"Carl," he finally observed, poker playing, "they're shaping Tensquare."

I could have hit him. I might have refilled his glass with sulfuric acid and looked on with glee as his lips blackened and cracked. Instead, I grunted a noncommittal.

"Who's fool enough to shell out fifty grand a day? ANR?"

He shook his head.

"Jean Luharich," he said, "the girl with the violet contacts and fifty or sixty perfect teeth. I understand her eyes are really brown."

"Isn't she selling enough face cream these days?"

He shrugged.

"Publicity makes the wheels go 'round. Luharich Enterprises jumped sixteen points when she picked up the Sun Trophy. You ever play golf on Mercury?"

I had, but I overlooked it and continued to press.

"So she's coming here with a blank check and a fishhook?"

"*Bright Water,* today," he nodded. "Should be down by now. Lots of cameras. She wants an Ikky, bad."

"Hmm," I hmmed. "How bad?"

"Sixty day contract, Tensquare. Indefinite extension clause. Million and a half deposit," he recited.

"You seem to know a lot about it."

"I'm Personal Recruitment. Luharich Enterprises approached me last month. It helps to drink in the right places.

"Or own them." He smirked, after a moment.

I looked away, sipping my bitter brew. After a while I swallowed several things and asked Mike what he expected to be asked, leaving myself open for his monthly temperance lecture.

"They told me to try getting you," he mentioned. "When's the last time you sailed?"

"Month and a half ago. The *Corning.*"

"Small stuff," he snorted. "When have you been under, yourself?"

"It's been a while."

"It's been over a year, hasn't it? That time you got cut by the screw, under the *Dolphin?*"

I turned to him.

"I was in the river last week, up at Angleford where the currents are strong. I can still get around."

"Sober," he added.

"I'd stay that way," I said, "on a job like this."

A doubting nod.

"Straight union rates. Triple time for extraordinary

circumstances," he narrated. "Be at Hangar Sixteen
with your gear, Friday morning, five hundred hours. We
push off Saturday, daybreak."

"You're sailing?"

"I'm sailing."

"How come?"

"Money."

"Ikky guano."

"The bar isn't doing so well and baby needs new
minks."

"I repeat—"

"—And I want to get away from baby, renew my contact with basics—fresh air, exercise, make cash. . . ."

"All right, sorry I asked."

I poured him a drink, concentrating on H_2SO_4, but it
didn't transmute. Finally I got him soused and went out
into the night to walk and think things over.

Around a dozen serious attempts to land *Ichthyform
Leviosaurus Levianthus,* generally known as "Ikky," had
been made over the past five years. When Ikky was first
sighted, whaling techniques were employed. These proved
either fruitless or disastrous, and a new procedure was
inaugurated. Tensquare was constructed by a wealthy
sportsman named Michael Jandt, who blew his entire
roll on the project.

After a year on the Eastern Ocean, he returned to file
bankruptcy. Carlton Davits, a playboy fishing enthusiast,
then purchased the huge raft and laid a wake for Ikky's
spawning grounds. On the nineteenth day out he had a
strike and lost one hundred and fifty bills' worth of un-
tested gear, along with one *Ichthyform Levianthus.*
Twelve days later, using tripled lines, he hooked, narco-
tized, and began to hoist the huge beast. It awakened
then, destroyed a control tower, killed six men, and
worked general hell over five square blocks of Tensquare.
Carlton was left with partial hemiplegia and a bankruptcy suit of his own. He faded into waterfront atmosphere and Tensquare changed hands four more times,
with less spectacular but equally expensive results.

Finally, the big raft, built only for one purpose, was
purchased at auction by ANR for "marine research."
Lloyd's still won't insure it, and the only marine research
it has ever seen is an occasional rental at fifty bills a day—

to people anxious to tell Leviathan fish stories. I've been baitman on three of the voyages, and I've been close enough to count Ikky's fangs on two occasions. I want one of them to show my grandchildren, for personal reasons.

I faced the direction of the landing area and resolved a resolve.

"You want me for local coloring, gal. It'll look nice on the feature page and all that. But clear this—If anyone gets you an Ikky, it'll be me. I promise."

I stood in the empty Square. The foggy towers of Lifeline shared their mists.

Shoreline a couple eras ago, the western slope above Lifeline stretches as far as forty miles inland in some places. Its angle of rising is not a great one, but it achieves an elevation of several thousand feet before it meets the mountain range which separates us from the Highlands. About four miles inland and five hundred feet higher than Lifeline are set most of the surface airstrips and privately owned hangars. Hangar Sixteen houses Cal's Contract Cab, hop service, shore to ship. I do not like Cal, but he wasn't around when I climbed from the bus and waved to a mechanic.

Two of the hoppers tugged at the concrete, impatient beneath flywing haloes. The one on which Steve was working belched deep within its barrel carburetor and shuddered spasmodically.

"Bellyache?" I inquired.

"Yeah, gas pains and heartburn."

He twisted setscrews until it settled into an even keening and turned to me.

"You're for out?"

I nodded.

"Tensquare. Cosmetics. Monsters. Stuff like that."

He blinked into the beacons and wiped his freckles. The temperature was about twenty, but the big overhead spots served a double purpose.

"Luharich," he muttered. "Then you *are* the one. There's some people want to see you."

"What about?"

"Cameras. Microphones. Stuff like that."

"I'd better stow my gear. Which one am I riding?"

He poked the screwdriver at the other hopper.

"That one. You're on video tape now, by the way. They wanted to get you arriving."

He turned to the hangar, turned back.

"Say 'cheese.' They'll shoot the close-ups later."

I said something other than "cheese." They must have been using telelens and been able to read my lips because that part of the tape was never shown.

I threw my junk in the back, climbed into a passenger seat, and lit a cigarette. Five minutes later, Cal himself emerged from the office Quonset, looking cold. He came over and pounded on the side of the hopper. He jerked a thumb back at the hangar.

"They want you in there!" he called through cupped hands. "Interview!"

"The show's over!" I yelled back. "Either that, or they can get themselves another baitman!"

His rust-brown eyes became nailheads under blond brows and his glare a spike before he jerked about and stalked off. I wondered how much they had paid him to be able to squat in his hangar and suck juice from his generator.

Enough, I guess, knowing Cal. I never liked the guy anyway.

Venus at night is a field of sable waters. On the coasts, you can never tell where the sea ends and the sky begins. Dawn is like dumping milk into an inkwell. First, there are erratic curdles of white, then streamers. Shade the bottle for a gray colloid, then watch it whiten a little more. All of a sudden you've got day. Then start heating the mixture.

I had to shed my jacket as we flashed out over the bay. To our rear, the skyline could have been under water for the way it waved and rippled in the heatfall. A hopper can accommodate four people (five, if you want to bend Regs and underestimate weight), or three passengers with the sort of gear a baitman uses. I was the only fare, though, and the pilot was like his machine. He hummed and made no other unnecessary noises. Lifeline turned a somersault and evaporated in the rear mirror at about the same time Tensquare broke the fore-horizon. The pilot stopped humming and shook his head.

I leaned forward. Feelings played flopdoodle in my guts. I knew every bloody inch of the big raft, but the feelings you once took for granted change when their source is out of reach. Truthfully, I'd had my doubts I'd ever board the hulk again. But now, now I could almost believe in predestination. There it was!

A tensquare football field of a ship. A-powered. Flat as a pancake, except for the plastic blisters in the middle and the "Rooks" fore and aft, port and starboard.

The Rook towers were named for their corner positions—and any two can work together to hoist, copowering the graffles between them. The graffles—half gaff, half grapple—can raise enormous weights to near water level; their designer had only one thing in mind, though, which accounts for the gaff half. At water level, the Slider has to implement elevation for six to eight feet before the graffles are in a position to push upward, rather than pulling.

The Slider, essentially, is a mobile room—a big box capable of moving in any of Tensquare's crisscross groovings and "anchoring" on the strike side by means of a powerful electromagnetic bond. Its winches could hoist a battleship the necessary distance, and the whole craft would tilt rather than the Slider come loose, if you want any idea of the strength of that bond.

The Slider houses a section operated control indicator which is the most sophisticated "reel" ever designed. Drawing broadcast power from the generator beside the center blister, it is connected by shortwave with the sonar room, where the movements of the quarry are recorded and repeated to the angler seated before the section control.

The fisherman might play his "lines" for hours, days even, without seeing any more than metal and an outline on the screen. Only when the beast is graffled and the extensor shelf, located twelve feet below waterline, slides out for support and begins to aid the winches, only then does the fisherman see his catch rising before him like a fallen Seraph. Then, as Davits learned, one looks into the Abyss itself and is required to act. He didn't and a hundred meters of unimaginable tonnage, undernarcotized and hurting, broke the cables of the winch, snapped a graffle, and took a half-minute walk across Tensquare.

We circled till the mechanical flag took notice and waved us on down. We touched beside the personnel hatch and I jettisoned my gear and jumped to the deck.

"Luck," called the pilot as the door was sliding shut. Then he danced into the air, and the flag clicked blank.

I shouldered my stuff and went below.

Signing in with Malvern, the de facto captain, I learned that most of the others wouldn't arrive for a good eight hours. They had wanted me alone at Cal's so they could pattern the pub footage along twentieth-century cinema lines.

Open: landing strip, dark. One mechanic prodding a contrary hopper. Stark-o-vision shot of slow bus pulling in. Heavily dressed baitman descends, looks about, limps across field. Close-up: he grins. Move in for words: "Do you think this is the time? The time he *will* be landed?" Embarrassment, taciturnity, a shrug. Dub something—"I see. And why do you think Miss Luharich has a better chance than any of the others? It is because she's better equipped? [Grin.] Because more is known now about the creature's habits than when you were out before? Or is it because of her will to win, to be a champion? Is it any one of these things, or is it all of them?" Reply: "Yeah, all of them." "—Is that why you signed on with her? Because your instincts say, 'This one will be it'?" Answer: "She pays union rates. I couldn't rent that damned thing myself. And I want in." Erase. Dub something else. Fade-out as he moves toward hopper, etcetera.

"Cheese," I said, or something like that, and took a walk around Tensquare, by myself.

I mounted each Rook, checking out the controls and the underwater video eyes. Then I raised the main lift.

Malvern had no objections to my testing things this way. In fact, he encouraged it. We had sailed together before and our positions had even been reversed once upon a time. So I wasn't surprised when I stepped off the lift into the Hopkins Locker and found him waiting. For the next ten minutes we inspected the big room in silence, walking through its copper coil chambers soon to be Arctic.

Finally, he slapped a wall.

"Well, will we fill it?"

I shook my head.

"I'd like to, but I doubt it. I don't give two hoots and a damn who gets credit for the catch, so long as I have a part in it. But it won't happen. That gal's an egomaniac. She'll want to operate the Slider, and she can't."

"You ever meet her?"

"Yeah."

"How long ago?"

"Four, five years."

"She was a kid then. How do you know what she can do now?"

"I know. She'll have learned every switch and reading by this time. She'll be up on all the theory. But do you remember one time we were together in the starboard Rook, forward, when Ikky broke water like a porpoise?"

"How could I forget?"

"Well?"

He rubbed his emery chin.

"Maybe she can do it, Carl. She's raced torch ships, and she's scubaed in bad waters back home." He glanced in the direction of invisible Hand. "And she's hunted in the Highlands. She might be wild enough to pull that horror into her lap without flinching.

". . . For John Hopkins to foot the bill and shell out seven figures for the corpus," he added. "That's money, even to a Luharich."

I ducked through a hatchway.

"Maybe you're right, but she was a rich witch when I knew her.

"And she wasn't blonde," I added, meanly.

He yawned.

"Let's find breakfast."

We did that.

When I was young, I thought that being born a sea creature was the finest choice Nature could make for anyone. I grew up on the Pacific coast and spent my summers on the Gulf or the Mediterranean. I lived months of my life negotiating coral, photographing trench dwellers, and playing tag with dolphins. I fished everywhere there are fish, resenting the fact that they can go places I can't. When I grew older I wanted bigger fish, and there was nothing living that I knew of, excepting a Sequoia, that came any bigger than Ikky. That's part of it. . . .

I jammed a couple of extra rolls into a paper bag and filled a thermos with coffee. Excusing myself, I left the galley and made my way to the Slider berth. It was just the way I remembered it. I threw a few switches and the shortwave hummed.

"That you, Carl?"

"That's right, Mike. Let me have some juice down here, you double-crossing rat."

He thought it over, then I felt the hull vibrate as the generators cut in. I poured my third cup of coffee and found a cigarette.

"So why am I a double-crossing rat this time?" came his voice again.

"You knew about the cameramen at Hangar Sixteen?"

"Yes."

"Then you're a double-crossing rat. The last thing I want is publicity. 'He who fouled up so often before is ready to try it nobly once more.' I can read it now."

"You're wrong. The spotlight's only big enough for one, and she's prettier than you."

My next comment was cut off as I threw the elevator switch and the elephant ears flapped above me. I rose, settling flush with the deck. Retracting the lateral rail, I cut forward into the groove. Amidships, I stopped at a juncture, dropped the lateral, and retracted the longitudinal rail.

I slid starboard, midway between the Rooks, halted, and threw on the coupler.

I hadn't spilled a drop of coffee.

"Show me pictures."

The screen glowed. I adjusted and got outlines of the bottom.

"Okay."

I threw a Status Blue switch and he matched it. The light went on. The winch unlocked. I aimed out over the waters, extended the arm, and fired a cast.

"Clean one," he commented.

"Status Red. Call strike." I threw a switch.

"Status Red."

The baitman would be on his way with this to make the barbs tempting.

It's not exactly a fishhook. The cables bear hollow tubes; the tubes convey enough dope for any army of hop-heads; Ikky takes the bait, dangled before him by remote control, and the fisherman rams the barbs home.

My hands moved over the console, making the necessary adjustments. I checked the narco-tank reading. Empty. Good, they hadn't been filled yet. I thumbed the Inject button.

"In the gullet," Mike murmured.

I released the cables. I played the beast imagined. I let him run, swinging the winch to stimulate his sweep.

I had an air conditioner on and my shirt off, and it was still uncomfortably hot, which is how I knew that morning had gone over into noon. I was dimly aware of the arrivals and departures of the hoppers. Some of the crew sat in the "shade" of the doors I had left open, watching the operation. I didn't see Jean arrive or I would have ended the session and gotten below.

She broke my concentration by slamming the door hard enough to shake the bond.

"Mind telling me who authorized you to bring up the Slider?" she asked.

"No one," I replied. "I'll take it below now."

"Just move aside."

I did, and she took my seat. She was wearing brown slacks and a baggy shirt and she had her hair pulled back in a practical manner. Her cheeks were flushed, but not necessarily from the heat. She attacked the panel with a nearly amusing intensity that I found disquieting.

"Status Blue," she snapped, breaking a violet fingernail on the toggle.

I forced a yawn and buttoned my shirt slowly. She threw a side glance my way, checked the registers, and fired a cast.

I monitored the lead on the screen. She turned to me for a second.

"Status Red," she said levelly.

I nodded my agreement.

She worked the winch sideways to show she knew how. I didn't doubt she knew how and she didn't doubt that I didn't doubt, but then—

"In case you're wondering," she said, "you're not going to be anywhere near this thing. You were hired as a baitman, remember? Not a Slider operator! A baitman! Your duties consist of swimming out and setting the table for our friend, the monster. It's dangerous, but you're getting well paid for it. Any questions?"

She squashed the Inject button, and I rubbed my throat.

"Nope," I smiled, "but I am qualified to run that thingamajigger—and if you need me I'll be available, at union rates."

"Mister Davits," she said, "I don't want a loser operating this panel."

"Miss Luharich, there has never been a winner at this game."

She started reeling in the cable and broke the bond at the same time so that the whole Slider shook as the big yo-yo returned. We skidded a couple of feet backward. She raised the laterals, and we shot back along the groove. Slowing, she transferred rails and we jolted to a clanging halt, then shot off at a right angle. The crew scrambled away from the hatch as we skidded onto the elevator.

"In the future, Mister Davits, do not enter the Slider without being ordered," she told me.

"Don't worry, I won't even step inside if I am ordered," I answered. "I signed on as a baitman. Remember? If you want me in here, you'll have to *ask* me."

"That'll be the day," she smiled.

I agreed as the doors closed above us. We dropped the subject and headed in our different directions after the Slider came to a halt in its berth. She did say "good day," though, which I thought showed breeding as well as determination, in reply to my chuckle.

Later that night Mike and I stoked our pipes in Malvern's cabin. The winds were shuffling waves, and a steady spattering of rain and hail overhead turned the deck into a tin roof.

"Nasty," suggested Malvern.

I nodded. After two bourbons the room had become a familiar woodcut, with its mahogany furnishings (which I had transported from Earth long ago on a whim) and the dark walls, the seasoned face of Malvern, and the perpetually puzzled expression of Dabis set between the big pools of shadow that lay behind chairs and splashed in corners, all cast by the tiny table light and seen through a glass, brownly.

"Glad I'm in here."

"What's it like underneath on a night like this?"

I puffed, thinking of my light cutting through insides of a black diamond, shaken slightly. The meteor-dart of a suddenly illuminated fish, the swaying of grotesque ferns, like nebulae—shadow, then green, then gone—swam in a moment through my mind. I guess it's like a spaceship would feel, if a spaceship could feel, crossing between worlds—and quiet, uncannily, preternaturally quiet; and peaceful as sleep.

"Dark," I said, "and not real choppy below a few fathoms."

"Another eight hours and we shove off," commented Mike.

"Ten, twelve days, we should be there," noted Malvern.

"What do you think Ikky's doing?"

"Sleeping on the bottom with Mrs. Ikky if he has any brains."

"He hasn't. I've seen ANR's skeletal extrapolation from the bones that have washed up—"

"Hasn't everyone?"

". . . Fully fleshed, he'd be over a hundred meters long. That right, Carl?"

I agreed.

". . . Not much of a brain box, though, for his bulk."

"Smart enough to stay out of our locker."

Chuckles, because nothing exists but this room, really. The world outside is an empty, sleet drummed deck. We lean back and make clouds.

"Boss lady does not approve of unauthorized fly fishing."

"Boss lady can walk north till her hat floats."

"What did she say in there?"

"She told me that my place, with fish manure, is on the buttom."

"You don't Slide?"

"I bait."

"We'll see."

"That's all I do. If she wants a Slideman she's going to have to ask nicely."

"You think she'll have to?"

"I think she'll have to."

"And if she does, can you do it?"

"A fair question," I puffed. "I don't know the answer, though."

I'd incorporate my soul and trade forty percent of the stock for the answer. I'd give a couple years off my life for the answer. But there doesn't seem to be a lineup of supernatural takers, because no one knows. Supposing when we get out there, luck being with us, we find ourselves an Ikky? Supposing we succeed in baiting him and get lines on him. What then? If we get him shipside, will she hold on or crack up? What if she's made of sterner stuff than Davits, who used to hunt sharks with poison-darted air pistols? Supposing she lands him and Davits has to stand there like a video extra.

Worse yet, supposing she asks for Davits and he still stands there like a video extra or something else—say, some yellow bellied embodiment named Cringe.

It was when I got him above the eight-foot horizon of steel and looked out at all that body, sloping on and on till it dropped out of sight like a green mountain range. . . . And that head. Small for the body, but still immense. Fat, craggy, with lidless roulettes that had spun black and red since before my forefathers decided to try the New Continent. And swaying.

Fresh narco-tanks had been connected. It needed another shot, fast. But I was paralyzed.

It had made a noise like God playing a Hammond organ. . . .

And looked at me!

I don't know if seeing is even the same process in eyes like those. I doubt it. Maybe I was just a gray blur behind a black rock, with the plexi-reflected sky hurting its pupils. But it fixed on me. Perhaps the snake doesn't really paralyze the rabbit, perhaps it's just that rabbits are cowards by constitution. But it began to struggle and I still couldn't move, fascinated.

Fascinated by all that power, by those eyes, they found me there fifteen minutes later, a little broken about the head and shoulders, the Inject still unpushed.

And I dream about those eyes. I want to face them once more, even if their finding takes forever. I've got to know if there's something inside me that sets me apart from a rabbit, from notched plates of reflexes and instincts that always fall apart in exactly the same way whenever the proper combination is spun.

Looking down, I noticed that my hand was shaking. Glancing up, I noticed that no one else was noticing.

I finished my drink and emptied my pipe. It was late, and no songbirds were singing.

I sat whittling, my legs hanging over the aft edge, the chips spinning down into the furrow of our wake. Three days out. No action.

"You!"

"Me?"

"You."

Hair like the end of the rainbow, eyes like nothing in nature, fine teeth.

"Hello."

"There's a safety rule against what you're doing, you know."

"I know. I've been worrying about it all morning."

A delicate curl climbed my knife, then drifted out behind us. It settled into the foam and was plowed under. I watched her reflection in my blade, taking a secret pleasure in its distortion.

"Are you baiting me?" she finally asked.

I heard her laugh then, and turned, knowing it had been intentional.

"What, me?"

"I could push you off from here, very easily."

"I'd make it back."

"Would you push me off then—some dark night perhaps?"

"They're all dark, Miss Luharich. No, I'd rather make you a gift of my carving."

She seated herself beside me then, and I couldn't help but notice the dimples in her knees. She wore white shorts and a halter and still had an offworld tan to her which was awfully appealing. I almost felt a twinge of guilt at having planned the whole scene, but my right hand still blocked her view of the wooden animal.

"Okay, I'll bite. What have you got for me?"

"Just a second. It's almost finished."

Solemnly, I passed her the wooden jackass I had been carving. I felt a little sorry and slightly jackass-ish myself, but I had to follow through. I always do. The mouth was split into a braying grin.The ears were upright.

She didn't smile and she didn't frown. She just studied it.

"It's very good," she finally said, "like most things you do—and appropriate, perhaps."

"Give it to me." I extended a palm.

She handed it back, and I tossed it out over the water. It missed the white water and bobbed for a while like a pigmy seahorse.

"Why did you do that?"

"It was a poor joke. I'm sorry."

"Maybe you are right, though. Perhaps this time I've bitten off a little too much."

I snorted.

"Then why not do something safer, like another race?" She shook her end of the rainbow.

"No. It has to be an Ikky."

"Why?"

"Why did you want one so badly that you threw away a fortune?"

"Many reasons," I said. "An unfrocked analyst who held black therapy sessions in his basement once told me, 'Mister Davits, you need to reinforce the image of your masculinity by catching one of every kind of fish in existence.' Fish are a very ancient masculinity symbol, you know. So I set out to do it. I have one more to do. Why do you want to reinforce *your* masculinity?"

"I don't," she said. "I don't want to reinforce anything but Luharich Enterprises. My chief statistician once said, 'Miss Luharich, sell all the cold cream and face powder in the System and you'll be a happy girl. Rich, too.' And he was right. I am the proof. I can look the way I do and do anything, and I sell most of the lipstick and face powder in the System—but I have to be *able* to do anything."

"You do look cool and efficient," I observed.

"I don't feel cool," she said, rising. "Let's go for a swim."

"May I point out that we are making pretty good time?"

"If you want to indicate the obvious, you may. You

said you could make it back to the ship, unassisted. Change your mind?"

"No."

"Then get us two scuba outfits and I'll race you under Tensquare.

"I'll win, too," she added.

I stood and looked down at her, because that usually makes me feel superior to women.

"Daughter of Lir, eyes of Picasso," I said, "you've got yourself a race. Meet me at the forward Rook, starboard, in ten minutes."

"Ten minutes," she agreed.

And ten minutes it was. From the center blister to the Rook took maybe two of them, with the load I was carrying. My sandals grew very hot and I was glad to shuck them for flippers when I reached the comparative cool of the corner.

We slid into harnesses and adjusted our gear. She had changed into a trim, one-piece green job that made me shade my eyes and look away, then look back again.

I fastened a rope ladder and kicked it over the side. Then I pounded on the wall of the Rook.

"Yeah?"

"You talk to the port Rook, aft?" I called.

"They're all set up," came the answer. "There's ladders and drag-lines all over that end."

"You sure you want to do this?" asked the sunburnt little gink who was her publicity man, Anderson yclept.

He sat beside the Rook in a deckchair, sipping lemonade through a straw.

"It might be dangerous," he observed, sunken-mouthed. (His teeth were beside him in another glass.)

"That's right," she smiled. "It *will* be dangerous. Not overly, though."

"Then why don't you let me get some pictures? We'd have them back to Lifeline in an hour. They'd be in New York by tonight. Good copy."

"No," she said, and turned away from both of us.

She raised her hands to her eyes.

"Here, keep these for me."

She passed him a box full of her unseeing, and when she turned back to me they were the same brown that I remembered.

"Ready?"

"No," I said tautly. "Listen carefully, Jean. If you're going to play this game, there are a few rules. First," I counted, "we're going to be directly beneath the hull, so we have to start low and keep moving. If we bump the bottom, we could rupture an air tank. . . ."

She began to protest that any moron knew that, and I cut her down.

"Second," I went on, "there won't be much light, so we'll stay close together and we will *both* carry torches."

Her wet eyes flashed.

"I dragged you out of Govino without——"

Then she stopped and turned away. She picked up a lamp.

"Okay. Torches. Sorry."

". . . And watch out for the drive-screws," I finished. "There'll be strong currents for at least fifty meters behind them."

She wiped her eyes again and adjusted the mask.

"All right, let's go."

We went.

She led the way, at my insistence. The surface layer was pleasantly warm. At two fathoms the water was bracing; at five it was nice and cold. At eight we let go of the swinging stairway and struck out. Tensquare sped forward and we raced in the opposite direction, tattooing the hull yellow at ten-second intervals.

The hull stayed where it belonged, but we raced on like two darkside satellites. Periodically, I tickled her frog feet with my light and traced her antennae of bubbles. About a five meter lead was fine; I'd beat her in the home stretch, but I couldn't let her drop behind yet.

Beneath us, black. Immense. Deep. The Mindanao of Venus, where eternity might eventually pass the dead to a rest in cities of unnamed fishes. I twisted my head away and touched the hull with a feeler of light; it told me we were about a quarter of the way along.

I increased my beat to match her stepped-up stroke and narrowed the distance which she had suddenly opened by a couple meters. She sped up again and I did, too. I spotted her with my beam.

She turned and it caught on her mask. I never knew whether she'd been smiling. Probably. She raised two fingers in a V-for-Victory and then cut ahead at full speed.

I should have known. I should have felt it coming. It was just a race to her, something else to win. Damn the torpedoes!

So I leaned into it, hard. I don't shake in the water. Or if I do, it doesn't matter and I don't notice it. I began to close the gap again.

She looked back, sped on, looked back. Each time she looked, it was nearer, until I'd narrowed it down to the original five meters.

Then she hit the jatoes.

That's what I had been fearing. We were about half-way under and she shouldn't have done it. The powerful jets of compressed air could easily rocket her upward into the hull, or tear something loose if she allowed her body to twist. Their main use is in tearing free from marine plants or fighting bad currents. I had wanted them along as a safety measure, because of the big suck-and-pull windmills behind.

She shot ahead like a meteorite, and I could feel a sudden tingle of perspiration leaping to meet and mix with the churning waters.

I swept ahead, not wanting to use my own guns, and she tripled, quadrupled the margin.

The jets died and she was still on course. Okay, I was an old fuddyduddy. She *could* have messed up and headed toward the top.

I plowed the sea and began to gather back my yardage, a foot at a time. I wouldn't be able to catch her or beat her now, but I'd be on the ropes before she hit deck.

Then the spinning magnets began their insistence, and she wavered. It was an awfully powerful drag, even at this distance. The call of the meat grinder.

I'd been scratched up by one once, under the *Dolphin,* a fishing boat of the middle-class. I *had* been drinking, but it was also a tough day, and the thing had been turned on prematurely. Fortunately, it was turned off in time, also, and a tendon-stapler made everything good as new, except in the log, where it only mentioned that I'd been drinking. Nothing about it being off-hours when I had a right to do as I damn well pleased.

She had slowed to half her speed, but she was still

moving crosswise, toward the port, aft corner. I began to
feel the pull myself and had to slow down. She'd made it
past the main one, but she seemed too far back. It's hard
to gauge distances under water, but each red beat of time
told me I was right. She was out of danger from the main
one, but the smaller port screw, located about eighty
meters in, was no longer a threat but a certainty.

She had turned and was pulling away from it now.
Twenty meters separated us. She was standing still.
Fifteen.

Slowly she began a backward drifting. I hit my jatoes,
aiming two meters behind her and about twenty back of
the blades.

Straightline! Thankgod! Catching, softbelly, leadpipe on
shoulder SWIMLIKEHELL! maskcracked, not broke though
AND UP!

We caught a line and I remember brandy.

Into the cradle endlessly rocking I spit, pacing. Insomnia
tonight and left shoulder sore again, so let it rain on me
—they can cure rheumatism. Stupid as hell. What I said.
In blankets and shivering. She: "Carl, I can't say it."
Me: "Then call it square for that night in Govino, Miss
Luharich, huh?" She: nothing. Me: "Any more of that
brandy?" She: "Give me another, too." Me: sounds of
sipping. It had only lasted three months. No alimony.
Many $ on both sides. Not sure whether they were happy
or not. Wine-dark Aegean. Good fishing. Maybe he
should have spent more time on shore. Or perhaps she
shouldn't have. Good swimmer, though. Dragged him
all the way to Vido to wring out his lungs. Young. Both.
Strong. Both. Rich and spoiled as hell. Ditto. Corfu
should have brought them closer. Didn't. I think that
mental cruelty was a trout. He wanted to go to Canada.
She: "Go to hell if you want!" He: "Will you go along?"
She: "No." But she did, anyhow. Many hells. Expensive.
He lost a monster or two. She inherited a couple. Lot of
lightning tonight. Stupid as hell. Civility's the coffin of a
conned soul. By whom?—Sounds like a bloody neo-ex. . . .
But I hate you, Anderson, with your glass full of teeth and
her new eyes. . . . Can't keep this pipe lit, keep sucking
tobacco. Spit again!

                              •

Seven days out and the scope showed Ikky.

Bells jangled, feet pounded, and some optimist set the thermostat in the Hopkins. Malvern wanted me to sit it out, but I slipped into my harness and waited for whatever came. The bruise looked worse than it felt. I had exercised every day and the shoulder hadn't stiffened on me.

A thousand meters ahead and thirty fathoms deep, it tunneled our path. Nothing showed on the surface.

"Will we chase him?" asked an excited crewman.

"Not unless she feels like using money for fuel." I shrugged.

Soon the scope was clear, and it stayed that way. We remained on alert and held our course.

I hadn't said over a dozen words to my boss since the last time we went drowning together, so I decided to raise the score.

"Good afternoon," I approached. "What's new?"

"He's going north-northeast. We'll have to let this one go. A few more days and we can afford some chasing. Not yet."

Sleek head. . . .

I nodded. "No telling where this one's headed."

"How's your shoulder?"

"All right. How about you?"

Daughter of Lir. . . .

"Fine. By the way, you're down for a nice bonus."

Eyes of perdition!

"Don't mention it," I told her back.

Later that afternoon, and appropriately, a storm shattered. (I prefer "shattered" to "broke." It gives a more accurate idea of the behavior of tropical storms on Venus and saves lots of words.) Remember that inkwell I mentioned earlier? Now take it between thumb and forefinger and hit its side with a hammer. Watch yourself! Don't get splashed or cut—

Dry, then drenched. The sky one million bright fractures as the hammer falls. And sounds of breaking.

"Everyone below?" suggested loudspeakers to the already scurrying crew.

Where was I? Who do you think was doing the loudspeaking?

Everything loose went overboard when the water got to walking, but by then no people were loose. The Slider was the first thing below decks. Then the big lifts lowered their shacks.

I had hit it for the nearest Rook with a yell the moment I recognized the pre-brightening of the holocaust. From there I cut in the speakers and spent half a minute coaching the track team.

Minor injuries had occurred, Mike told me over the radio, but nothing serious. I, however, was marooned for the duration. The Rooks do not lead anywhere; they're set too far out over the hull to provide entry downwards, what with the extensor shelves below.

So I undressed myself of the tanks which I had worn for the past several hours, crossed my flippers on the table, and leaned back to watch the hurricane. The top was as black as the bottom and we were in between, and somewhat illuminated because of all that flat, shiny space. The waters above didn't rain down—they just sort of got together and dropped.

The Rooks were secure enough—they'd weathered any number of these onslaughts—it's just that their positions gave them a greater arc of rise and descent when Tensquare makes like the rocker of a very nervous grandma. I had used the belts from my rig to strap myself into the bolted-down chair, and I removed several years in purgatory from the soul of whoever left a pack of cigarettes in the table drawer.

I watched the water make teepees and mountains and hands and trees until I started seeing faces and people. So I called Mike.

"What are you doing down there?"

"Wondering what you're doing up there," he replied. "What's it like?"

"You're from the Midwest, aren't you?"

"Yeah."

"Get bad storms out there?"

"Sometimes."

"Try to think of the worst one you were ever in. Got a slide rule handy?"

"Right here."

"Then put a one under it. imagine a zero or two following after, and multiply the thing out."

"I can't imagine the zeros."

"Then retain the multiplicand—that's all you can do."

"So what are you doing up there?"

"I've strapped myself in the chair. I'm watching things roll around the floor right now."

I looked up and out again. I saw one darker shadow in the forest.

"Are you praying or swearing?"

"Damned if I know. But if this were the Slider—if only this were the Slider!"

"He's out there?"

I nodded, forgetting that he couldn't see me.

Big, as I remembered him. He'd only broken surface for a few moments, to look around. *There is no power on Earth that can be compared with him who was made to fear no one.* I dropped my cigarette. It was the same as before. Paralysis and an unborn scream.

"You all right, Carl?"

He had looked at me again. Or seemed to. Perhaps that mindless brute had been waiting half a millenium to ruin the life of a member of the most highly developed species in business. . . .

"You okay?"

. . . Or perhaps it had been ruined already, long before their encounter, and theirs was just a meeting of beasts, the stronger bumping the weaker aside, body to psyche. . . .

"Carl, dammit! Say something!"

He broke again, this time nearer. Did you ever see the trunk of a tornado? It seems like something alive, moving around in all that dark. Nothing has a right to be so big, so strong, and moving. It's a sickening sensation.

"Please answer me."

He was gone and did not come back that day. I finally made a couple of wisecracks at Mike, but I held my next cigarette in my right hand.

The next seventy or eighty thousand waves broke by with a monotonous similarity. The five days that held them were also without distinction. The morning of the thirteenth day out, though, our luck began to rise. The bells broke our coffee-drenched lethargy into small pieces, and we dashed from the galley without hearing what might have been Mike's finest punch line.

"Aft!" cried someone. "Five hundred meters!"

I stripped to my trunks and started buckling. My stuff is always within grabbing distance.

I flipflopped across the deck, girding myself with a deflated squiggler.

"Five hundred meters, twenty fathoms!" boomed the speakers.

The big traps banged upward and the Slider grew to its full height, m'lady at the console. It rattled past me and took root ahead. Its one arm rose and lengthened.

I breasted the Slider as the speakers called, "Four-eighty, twenty!"

"Status Red!"

A belch like an emerging champagne cork and the line arced high over the waters.

"Four-eighty, twenty!" it repeated, all Malvern and static. "Baitman, attend!"

I adjusted my mask and hand-over-handed it down the side. Then warm, then cool, then away.

Green, vast, down. Fast. This is the place where I am equal to a squiggler. If something big decides a baitman looks tastier than what he's carrying, then irony colors his title as well as the water about it.

I caught sight of the drifting cables and followed them down. Green to dark green to black. It had been a long cast, too long. I'd never had to follow one this far down before. I didn't want to switch on my torch.

But I had to.

Bad! I still had a long way to go. I clenched my teeth and stuffed my imagination into a straightjacket.

Finally the line came to an end.

I wrapped one arm about it and unfastened the squiggler. I attached it, working as fast as I could, and plugged in the little insulated connections, which are the reason it can't be fired with the line. Ikky could break them, but by then it wouldn't matter.

My mechanical eel hooked up, I pulled its section plugs and watched it grow. I had been dragged deeper during this operation, which took about a minute and a half. I was near—too near—to where I never wanted to be.

Loath as I had been to turn on my light, I was suddenly afraid to turn it off. Panic gripped me and I seized the cable with both hands. The squiggler began to glow pinkly. It started to twist. It was twice as big as I am and doubtless twice as attractive to pink-squiggler eaters. I told myself this until I believed it, then I switched off my light and started up.

If I bumped into something enormous and steel-hided my heart had orders to stop beating immediately and release me—to dart fitfully forever along Acheron, and gibbering.

Ungibbering. I made it to green water and fled back to the nest.

As soon as they hauled me aboard, I made my mask a necklace, shaded my eyes, and monitored for surface turbulence. My first question, of course, was: "Where is he?"

"Nowhere," said a crewman. "We lost him right after you went over. Can't pick him up on the scope now. Musta dived."

"Too bad."

The squiggler stayed down, enjoying its bath. My job ended for the time being, I headed back to warm my coffee with rum.

From behind me, a whisper: "Could you laugh like that afterwards?"

Perceptive Answer: "Depends on what he's laughing at."

Still chuckling, I made my way into the center blister with two cupfuls.

"Still hell and gone?"

Mike nodded. His big hands were shaking, and mine were steady as a surgeon's when I set down the cups.

He jumped as I shrugged off the tanks and looked for a bench.

"Don't drip on that panel! You want to kill yourself and blow expensive fuses?"

I toweled down, then settled down to watching the unfilled eye on the wall. I yawned happily; my shoulder seemed good as new.

The little box that people talk through wanted to say something, so Mike lifted the switch and told it to go ahead.

"Is Carl there, Mister Dabis?"

"Yes, ma'am."

"Then let me talk to him."

Mike motioned and I moved.

"Talk," I said.

"Are you all right?"

"Yes, thanks. Shouldn't I be?"

"That was a long swim. I—I guess I overshot my cast."

"I'm happy," I said. "More triple-time for me. I really clean up on that hazardous duty clause."

"I'll be more careful next time," she apologized. "I guess I was too eager. Sorry—" Something happened to the sentence so she ended it there, leaving me with half a bagful of replies I'd been saving.

I lifted the cigarette from behind Mike's ear and got a light from the one in the ashtry.

"Carl, she was being nice," he said after turning to study the panels.

"I know," I told him. "I wasn't."

"I mean, she's an awfully pretty kid, pleasant. Headstrong and all that. But what's she done to you?"

"Lately?" I asked.

He looked at me, then dropped his eyes to his cup.

"I know it's none of my bus—" he began.

"Cream and sugar?"

Ikky didn't return that day, or that night. We picked up some Dixieland out of Lifeline and let the muskrat ramble while Jean had her supper sent to the Slider. Later she had a bunk assembled inside. I piped in "Deep Water Blues" when it came over the air and waited for her to call up and cuss us out. She didn't, though, so I decided she was sleeping.

Then I got Mike interested in a game of chess that went on until daylight. It limited conversation to several "checks," one "checkmate," and a "damn!" Since he's a poor loser it also effectively sabotaged subsequent talk, which was fine with me. I had a steak and fried potatoes for breakfast and went to bed.

Ten hours later someone shook me awake and I propped myself on one elbow, refusing to open my eyes.

"Whassamadder?"

"I'm sorry to get you up," said one of the younger crewmen, "but Miss Luharich wants you to disconnect the squiggler so we can move on."

I knuckled open one eye, still deciding whether I should be amused.

"Have it hauled to the side. Anyone can disconnect it."

"It's at the side now, sir. But she said it's in your contract and we'd better do things right."

"That's very considerate of her. I'm sure my Local appreciates her remembering."

"Uh, she also said to tell you to change your trunks and comb your hair, and shave, too. Mister Anderson's going to film it."

"Okay. Run along. Tell her I'm on my way—and ask if she has some toenail polish I can borrow."

I'll save on details. It took three minutes in all, and I played it properly, even pardoning myself when I slipped and bumped into Anderson's white tropicals with the wet squiggler. He smiled, brushed it off; she smiled, even though Luharich Complectacolor couldn't completely mask the dark circles under her eyes; and I smiled, waving to all our fans out there in videoland.—Remember, Mrs. Universe, you, too, can look like a monster-catcher. Just use Luharich face cream.

I went below and made myself a tuna sandwich with mayonnaise.

Two days like icebergs—bleak, blank, half-melting, all frigid, mainly out of sight, and definitely a threat to peace of mind—drifted by and were good to put behind. I experienced some old guilt feelings and had a few disturbing dreams. Then I called Lifeline and checked my bank balance.

"Going shopping?" asked Mike, who had put the call through for me.

"Going home," I answered.

"Huh?"

"I'm out of the baiting business after this one, Mike. The Devil with Ikky! The Devil with Venus and Luharich Enterprises! And the Devil with you!"

Up eyebrows.

"What brought that on?"

"I waited over a year for this job. Now that I'm here, I've decided the whole thing stinks."

"You knew what it was when you signed on. No mat-

ter what else you're doing, you're selling face cream when
you work for face-cream sellers."

"Oh, that's not what's biting me. I admit the commercial angle irritates me, but Tensquare has always been a
publicity spot, ever since the first time it sailed."

"What, then?"

"Five or six things, all added up. The main one being
that I don't care any more. Once it meant more to me
than anything else to hook that critter, and now it doesn't.
I went broke on what started out as a lark and I wanted
blood for what it cost me. Now I realize that maybe I had
it coming. I'm beginning to feel sorry for Ikky."

"And you don't want him now?"

"I'll take him if he comes peacefully, but I don't feel
like sticking out my neck to make him crawl into the
Hopkins."

"I'm inclined to think it's one of the four or five other
things you said you added."

"Such as?"

He scrutinized the ceiling.

I growled.

"Okay, but I won't say it, not just to make you happy,
you guessed right."

He, smirking: "That look she wears isn't just for Ikky."

"No good, no good." I shook my head. "We're both
fission chambers by nature. You can't have jets on both
ends of the rocket and expect to go anywhere—what's in
the middle just gets smashed."

"That's how it *was*. None of my business, of course—"

"Say that again and you'll say it without teeth."

"Any day, big man"—he looked up—"any place . . ."

"So go ahead. Get it said!"

"She doesn't care about that bloody reptile, she came
here to drag you back where you belong. You're not the
baitman this trip."

"Five years is too long."

"There must be something under that cruddy hide of
yours that people like," he muttered, "or I wouldn't be
talking like this. Maybe you remind us humans of some
really ugly dog we felt sorry for when we were kids. Anyhow, someone wants to take you home and raise you—
also, something about beggars not getting menus."

"Buddy," I chuckled, "do you know what I'm going to do when I hit Lifeline?"

"I can guess."

"You're wrong. I'm torching it to Mars, and then I'll cruise back home, first class. Venus bankruptcy provisions do not apply to Martian trust funds, and I've still got a wad tucked away where moth and corruption enter not. I'm going to pick up a big old mansion on the Gulf, and if you're ever looking for a job, you can stop around and open bottles for me."

"You are a yellow bellied fink," he commented.

"Okay," I admitted, "but it's her I'm thinking of, too."

"I've heard the stories about you both," he said. "So you're a heel and a goofoff and she's a bitch. That's called compatibility these days. I dare you, baitman, try keeping something you catch."

I turned.

"If you ever want that job, look me up."

I closed the door quietly behind me and left him sitting there, waiting for it to slam.

The day of the beast dawned like any other. Two days after my gutless flight from empty waters, I went down to rebait. Nothing on the scope. I was just making things ready for the routine attempt.

I hollered a "good morning" from outside the Slider and received an answer from inside before I pushed off. I had reappraised Mike's words, sans sound, sans fury, and while I did not approve of their sentiment or significance, I had opted for civility anyhow.

So down, under, and away. I followed a decent cast about two hundred-ninety meters out. The snaking cables burned black to my left and I paced their undulations from the yellow green down into the darkness. Soundless lay the wet night, and I bent my way through it like a cock-eyed comet, bright tail before.

I caught the line, slick and smooth, and began baiting. An icy world swept by me then, ankles to head. It was a draft, as if someone had opened a big door beneath me. I wasn't drifting downwards that fast either.

Which meant that something might be moving up, something big enough to displace a lot of water. I still didn't think it was Ikky. A freak current of some sort, but not Ikky. Ha!

I had finished attaching the leads and pulled the first plug when a big, rugged, black island grew beneath me. . . .

I flicked the beam downward. His mouth was opened. I was rabbit.

Waves of the death-fear passed downward. My stomach imploded. I grew dizzy.

Only one thing, and one thing only. Left to do. I managed it finally. I pulled the rest of the plugs.

I could count the scaly articulations ridging his eyes by then.

The squiggler grew, pinked into phosphoresence . . . squiggled!

Then my lamp. I had to kill it, leaving just the bait before him.

One glance back as I jammed the jatoes to life.

He was so near that the squiggler reflected on his teeth, in his eyes. Four meters, and I kissed his lambent jowls with two jets of backwash as I soared. Then I didn't know whether he was following or halted. I began to black out as I waited to be eaten.

The jatoes died, and I kicked weakly.

Too fast, I felt a cramp coming on. One flick of the beam, cried rabbit. One second, to know. . . .

Or end things up, I answered. No, rabbit, we don't dart before hunters. Stay dark.

Green waters finally, to yellow green, then top.

Doubling, I beat off toward Tensquare. The waves from the explosion behind pushed me on ahead. The world closed in, and a screamed, "He's alive!" in the distance.

A giant shadow and a shock wave. The line was alive, too. Happy Fishing Grounds. Maybe I did something wrong. . . .

Somewhere Hand was clenched. What's bait?

A few million years. I remember starting out as a one-celled organism and painfully becoming an amphibian, then an air-breather. From somewhere high in the tree-tops, I heard a voice.

"He's coming around."

I evolved back into homosapience, then a step further into a hangover.

"Don't try to get up yet."

"Have we got him?" I slurred.

"Still fighting, but he's hooked. We thought he took you for an appetizer."

"So did I."

"Breathe some of this and shut up."

A funnel over my face. Good. Lift your cups and drink. . . .

"He was awfully deep. Below scope range. We didn't catch him till he started up. Too late, then."

I began to yawn.

"We'll get you inside now."

I managed to uncase my ankle knife.

"Try it and you'll be minus a thumb."

"You need rest."

"Then bring me a couple more blankets. I'm staying."

I fell back and closed my eyes.

Someone was shaking me. Gloom and cold. Spotlights bled yellow on the deck. I was in a jury-rigged bunk, bulked against the center blister. Swaddled in wool, I still shivered.

"It's been eleven hours. You're not going to see anything now."

I tasted blood.

"Drink this."

Water. I had a remark, but I couldn't mouth it.

"Don't ask how I feel," I croaked. "I know that comes next, but don't ask me. Okay?"

"Okay. Want to go below now?"

"No. Just get me my jacket."

"Right here."

"What's he doing?"

"Nothing. He's deep, he's doped but he's staying down."

"How long since last time he showed?"

"Two hours, about."

"Jean?"

"She won't let anyone in the Slider. Listen, Mike says come on in. He's right behind you in the blister."

I sat up and turned. Mike was watching. He gestured; I gestured back.

I swung my feet over the end and took a couple of deep breaths. Pains in my stomach. I got to my feet and made it into the blister.

"Howza gut?" queried Mike.

I checked the scope. No Ikky. Too deep.

"You buying?"

"Yeah, coffee."

"Not coffee."

"You're ill. Also, coffee is all that's allowed in here."

"Coffee is a brownish liquid that burns your stomach. You have some in the bottom drawer."

"No cups. You'll have to use a glass."

"Tough."

He poured.

"You do that well. Been practicing for that job?"

"What job?"

"The one I offered you—"

A bolt on the scope.

"Rising, ma'am! Rising!" he yelled into the box.

"Thanks, Mike. I've got it in here," she crackled.

"Jean!"

"Shut up! She's busy!"

"Was that Carl?"

"Yeah," I called. "Talk later," and I cut it.

Why did I do that?

"Why did you do that?"

I didn't know.

"I don't know."

Damned echoes! I got up and walked outside.

Nothing. Nothing.

Something?

Tensquare actually rocked! He must have turned when he saw the hull and started downward again. White water to my left, and boiling. An endless spaghetti of cable roared hotly into the belly of the deep.

I stood awhile, then turned and went back inside.

Two hours sick. Four, and better.

"The dope's getting to him."

"Yeah."

"What about Miss Luharich?"

"What about her?"

"She must be half dead."

"Probably."

"What are you going to do about it?"

"She signed the contract for this. She knew what might happen. It did."

"I think you could land him."

"So do I."

"So does she."

"Then let her ask me."

Ikky was drifting lethargically, at thirty fathoms.

I took another walk and happened to pass behind the Slider. She wasn't looking my way.

"Carl, come in here!"

Eyes of Picasso, that's what, and a conspiracy to make me Slide. . . .

"Is that an order?"

"Yes—No! Please."

I dashed inside and monitored. He was rising.

"Push or pull?"

I slammed the "wind," and he came like a kitten.

"Make up your own mind now."

He balked at ten fathoms.

"Play him?"

"No!"

She wound him upwards—five fathoms, four. . . .

She hit the extensors at two, and they caught him. Then the graffles.

Cries without and a heat lightning of flashbulbs.

The crew saw Ikky.

He began to struggle. She kept the cables tight, raised the graffles. . . .

Up.

Another two feet and the graffles began pushing.

Screams and fast footfalls.

Giant beanstalk in the wind, his neck, waving. The green hills of his shoulders grew.

"He's big, Carl!" she cried.

And he grew, and grew, and grew uneasy. . . .

"Now!"

He looked down.

He looked down, as the god of our most ancient ancestors might have looked down. Fear, shame, and mocking laughter rang in my head. Her head, too?

"Now!"

She looked up at the nascent earthquake.

"I can't!"

It was going to be so damnably simple this time, now the rabbit had died. I reached out.

I stopped.

"Push it yourself."

"I can't. You do it. Land him, Carl!"

"No. If I do, you'll wonder for the rest of your life whether you could have. You'll throw away your soul finding out. I know you will because we're alike and I did it that way. Find out now!"

She stared.

I gripped her shoulders.

"Could be that's me out there," I offered. "I am a green sea serpent, a hateful, monstrous beast, and out to destroy you. I am answerable to no one. Push the Inject."

Her hand moved to the button, jerked back.

"Now!"

She pushed it.

I lowered her still form to the floor and finished things up with Ikky.

It was a good seven hours before I awakened to the steady, sea-chewing grind of Tensquare's blades.

"You're sick," commented Mike.

"How's Jean?"

"The same."

"Where's the beast?"

"Here."

"Good." I rolled over. ". . . Didn't get away this time."

So that's the way it was. No one is born a baitman, I don't think, but the rings of Saturn sing epithalamium the sea-beast's dower.

THE SALIVA TREE

by Brian W. Aldiss

> *There is neither speech nor language:*
> *but their voices are heard among them.*
>
> PSALM xix

"You know, I'm really much exercised about the Fourth Dimension," said the fair-haired young man with a suitable earnestness in his voice.

"Um," said his companion, staring up at the night sky.

"It seems very much in evidence these days. Do you not think you catch a glimpse of it in the drawings of Aubrey Beardsley?"

"Um," said his companion.

They stood together on a low rise to the east of the sleepy East Anglian town of Cottersall, watching the stars, shivering a little in the chill February air. They are both young men in their early twenties. The one who is occupied with the Fourth Dimension is called Bruce Fox; he is tall and fair, and works as junior clerk in the Norwich firm of lawyers, Prendergast and Tout. The other, who has so far vouchsafed us only an *um* or two, although he is to figure largely as the hero of our account, is by name Gregory Rolles. He is tall and dark, with grey eyes set in his handsome and intelligent face. He and Fox have sworn to Think Large, thus distinguishing themselves, at least in their own minds, from all the rest of the occupants of Cottersall in these last years of the nineteenth century.

"There's another!" exclaimed Gregory, breaking at last

from the realm of monosyllables. He pointed a gloved finger up at the constellation of Auriga the Charioteer. A meteor streaked across the sky like a runaway flake of the Milky Way and died in mid-air.

"Beautiful!" they said together.

"It's funny," Fox said, prefacing his words with an oft-used phrase, "the stars and men's minds are so linked together and always have been, even in the centuries of ignorance before Charles Darwin. They always seem to play an ill-defined role in man's affairs. They help me think large too, don't they you, Greg?"

"You know what I think—I think that some of those stars may be occupied. By people, I mean." He breathed heavily, overcome by what he was saying. "People who —perhaps they are better than us, live in a just society, wonderful people. . . ."

"I know, Socialists to a man!" Fox exclaimed. This was one point on which he did not share his friend's advanced thinking. He had listened to Mr. Tout talking in the office, and thought he knew better than his rich friend how these socialists, of which one heard so much these days, were undermining society. "Stars full of socialists!"

"Better than stars full of Christians! Why, if the stars were full of Christians, no doubt they would already have sent missionaries down here to preach their Gospel."

"I wonder if there ever will be planetary journeys as predicted by Nunsowe Greene and Monsieur Jules Verne—" Fox said, when the appearance of a fresh meteor stopped him in mid-sentence.

Like the last, this meteor seemed to come from the general direction of Auriga. It traveled slowly, and it glowed red, and it sailed grandly towards them. They both exclaimed at once, and gripped each other by the arm. The magnificent spark burned in the sky, larger now, so that its red aura appeared to encase a brighter orange glow. It passed overhead (afterwards, they argued whether it had not made a slight noise as it passed), and disappeared behind a clump of willow. They knew it had been near. For an instant, the land had shone with its light.

Gregory was the first to break the silence.

"Bruce, Bruce, did you see that? That was no ordinary fireball!"

"It was so big! What was it?"

"Perhaps our heavenly visitor has come at last!"

"Hey, Greg, it must have landed by your friends' farm —the Grendon place—mustn't it?"

"You're right! I must pay old Mr. Grendon a visit tomorrow and see if he or his family saw anything of this."

They talked excitedly, stamping their feet as they exercised their lungs. Their conversation was the conversation of optimistic young men, and included much speculative matter that began "Wouldn't it be wonderful if—," or "Just supposing—." Then they stopped and laughed at their own absurd beliefs.

"It must be nearly nine o'clock," Fox said at last. "I didn't mean to be so late tonight. It's funny how fast time passes. We'd best be getting back, Greg."

They had brought no lantern, since the night was both clear and dry. It was but two miles by the track back to the outlying houses of Cottersall. They stepped it out lustily, arm linked in arm in case one of them tripped in cart ruts, for Fox had to be up at five in the morning if he was to bicycle to his work punctually. The little village lay silent, or almost so. In the baker's house where Gregory lodged, a gaslight burned and a piano could be heard. As they halted smartly at the side door, Fox said shyly, "So you'll be seeing all the Grendon family tomorrow?"

"It seems probable, unless that red hot planetary ship has already borne them off to a better world."

"Tell us true, Greg—you really go to see that pretty Nancy Grendon, don't you?"

Gregory struck his friend playfully on the shoulder.

"No need for your jealousy, Bruce! I go to see the father, not the daughter. Though the one is female, the other is progressive and that must interest me more just yet. Nancy has beauty, true, but her father—ah, her father has electricity!"

Laughing, they cheerfully shook hands and parted for the night.

On Grendon's farm, things were a deal less tranquil, as Gregory was to discover.

Gregory Rolles rose before seven next morning as was his custom. It was while he was lighting his gas mantle, and wishing the baker would install electricity, that a swift train of thought led him to reflect again on the phenomenal thing in the previous night's sky. Mrs. Fenn, the baker's wife, who had already lit his fire, brought him up hot water for washing and scalding water for shaving and later a mighty tray full of breakfast. Throughout this activity, and indeed while he ate his porridge and chops, Gregory remained abstracted, letting his mind wander luxuriously over all the possibilities that the "meteor" illuminated. He decided that he would ride out to see Mr. Grendon within the hour.

He was lucky in being able, at this stage in his life, to please himself largely as to how his days were spent, for his father was a person of some substance. Edward Rolles had had the fortune, at the time of the Crimean War, to meet Escoffier, and with some help from the great chef had brought onto the market a baking powder, 'Eugenol', of which, being slightly more palatable and less deleterious to the human system than its rivals, had achieved great commercial success. As a result, Gregory had attended one of the Cambridge colleges.

Now, having gained a degree, he was poised on the verge of a career. But which career? He had acquired—more as a result of his intercourse with other students than with those officially deputed to instruct him—some understanding of the sciences; his essays had been praised and some of his poetry published, so that he inclined towards literature; and an uneasy sense that life for everyone outside the privileged classes contained too large a proportion of misery led him to think seriously of a political career. In Divinity, too, he was well-grounded; but at least the idea of Holy Orders did not tempt him.

While he wrestled with his future, he undertook to live away from home, since his relations with his father were never smooth. By rusticating himself in the heart of East Anglia, he hoped to gather material for a volume tentatively entitled *Wanderings with a Socialist Naturalist,* which would assuage all sides of his ambitions. Nancy Grendon, who had a pretty hand with a pencil, might even execute a little emblem for the title page. . . . Perhaps he might be permitted to dedicate it to his author friend, Mr. Herbert George Wells. . . .

He dressed himself warmly, for the morning was cold as well as dull, and went down to the baker's stables. When he had saddled his mare, Daisy, he swung himself up and set out along a road that the horse knew well.

The sun had been up for something over an hour, yet the sky and the landscape were drab in the extreme. Two sorts of East Anglian landscape met here, trapped by the confused wanderings of the River Oast: the unfarmable heathland and the unfarmable fen. There were few trees, and those stunted, so that the four fine elms which stood on one side of the Grendon farm, made a cynosure for miles around.

The land rose slightly towards the farm, the area about the house forming something of a little island amid marshy ground and irregular stretches of water that gave back to the sky its own dun tone. The gate over the wooden bridge was, as always, open wide; Daisy picked her way through the mud to the stables, where Gregory left her to champ oats contentedly. Cuff and her pup, Lardie, barked loudly about Gregory's heels as usual, and he patted their heads on his way over to the house.

Nancy came hurrying out to meet him before he got to the front door.

"We had some excitement last night, Gregory," she said. He noted with pleasure she had at last brought herself to use his first name.

"Something bright and glaring!" she said. "I was retiring when this noise came and then this light, and I rush to look out through the curtains, and there's this here great thing like an egg sinking into our pond." In her speech, and particularly when she was excited, she carried the lilting accent of Norfolk.

"The meteor!" Gregory exclaimed. "Bruce Fox and I were out last night as we were the night before, watching for the lovely Aurigids that arrive every February, when we saw an extra big one. I said then it was coming over very near here."

"Why, it almost landed on our house," Nancy said. She looked very pleasing this morning, with her lips red, her cheeks shining, and her chestnut curls all astray. As she spoke, her mother appeared in apron and cap, with a wrap hurriedly thrown over her shoulders.

"Nancy, you come in, standing freezing like that! You

ent daft, girl, are you? Hello, Gregory, how be going on?
I didn't reckon as we'd see you today. Come in and
warm yourself."

"Good-day to you, Mrs. Grendon. I'm hearing about
your wonderful meteor of last night."

"It was a falling star, according to Bert Neckland. I
ent sure what it was, but it certainly stirred up the animals, that I *do* know."

"Can you see anything of it in the pond?" Gregory
asked.

"Let me show you," Nancy said.

Mrs. Grendon returned indoors. She went slowly and
grandly, her back very straight and an unaccustomed
load before her. Nancy was her only daughter; there was
a younger son, Archie, a stubborn lad who had fallen at
odds with his father and now was apprenticed to a blacksmith in Norwich; and no other children living. Three in-
fants had not survived the mixture of fogs alternating
with bitter east winds that comprised the typical Cottersall winter. But now the farmer's wife was unexpectedly
gravid again and would bear her husband another baby
when the spring came in.

As Na cy led Gregory over to the pond, he saw Grendon with his two laborers working in the West Field, but
they did not wave.

"Was your father not excited by the arrival last night?"

"That he was—when it happened! He went out with
his shotgun, and Bert Neckland with him. But there was
nothing to see but bubbles in the pond and steam over it,
and this morning he wouldn't discuss it, and said that
work must go on whatever happen."

They stood beside the pond, a dark and extensive
slab of water with rushes on the farther bank and open
country beyond. As they looked at its ruffled surface,
they stood with the windmill black and bulky on their
left hand. It was to this that Nancy now pointed.

Mud had been splashed across the boards high up the
sides of the mill; some was to be seen even on the tip of
the nearest white sail. Gregory surveyed it all with interest. Nancy, however, was still pursuing her own line
of thought.

"Don't you reckon Father works too hard, Gregory?
When he ent outside doing jobs, he's in reading his pam-

phlets and his electricity manuals. He never rests but when he sleeps."

"Um. Whatever went into the pond went in with a great smack! There's no sign of anything there now, is there? Not that you can see an inch below the surface."

"You being a friend of his, Mum thought perhaps as you'd say something to him. He don't go to bed till ever so late—sometimes it's near midnight, and then he's up again at three and a half o'clock. Would you speak to him? You know Mother dassent."

"Nancy, we ought to see whatever it was that went in the pond. It can't have dissolved. How deep is the water? Is it very deep?"

"Oh, you aren't listening, Gregory Rolles! Bother the old meteor!"

"This is a matter of science, Nancy. Don't you see—"

"Oh, rotten old science, is it? Then I don't want to hear. I'm cold, standing out here. You can have a good look if you like, but I'm going in before I gets froze. It was only an old stone out of the sky, because I heard Father and Bert Neckland agree to it."

"Fat lot Bert Neckland knows about such things!" he called to her departing back. She had the prettiest ringlets on her neck, but really he didn't want to get involved with a nineteen-year-old farmer's daughter. It was a pity more girls didn't believe in Free Love, as did most of his male acquaintances.

He looked down at the dark water. Whatever it *was* that had arrived last night, it was here, only a few feet from him. He longed to discover what remained of it. Vivid pictures entered his mind: his name in headlines in *The Morning Post,* the Royal Society making him an honorary member, his father embracing him and pressing him to return home.

Thoughtfully, he walked over to the barn. Hens ran clucking out of his way as he entered and stood looking up, waiting for his eyes to adjust to the dim light. There, as he remembered it, was a little rowing boat. Perhaps in his courting days old Mr. Grendon had taken his prospective wife out for excursions on the Oast in it. Surely it had not been used in years.

He moved the long ladder over to climb and inspect it, and a cat went flying across the rafters in retreat. The inside of the boat was filthy, but two oars lay there, and it seemed intact. The craft had been hitched to its present position by two ropes thrown over a higher beam; it was a simple enough matter to lower it to the ground.

At that point, Gregory had a moment of prudence for other people's property. He went into the farmhouse and asked Mrs. Grendon if he might embark on the pond with it. That complaisant lady said he might do as he wished, and accordingly he dragged the boat from the barn and launched it in the shallows of the pond. It floated. The boards had dried, and water leaked through a couple of seams, but not nearly enough to deter him. Climbing delicately in among the straw and filth, he pushed off.

From here the farm, or such of it as he could see, presented a somewhat sinister aspect. The mill loomed above him, dismal and tarred black, only its sails white and creaking in the slight wind. To his other side, the blank-faced end of the barn looked immense and meaningless. Behind it he could see the backs of cowsheds with, beyond them, the raw, new brick structure of Grendon's machine house, where he made electricity. Between barn and mill, he could see the farmhouse, but the upper story only because of the lie of the land. Its decrepit humps of thatch and the tall stack of its chimney gave it a forbidding air. He mused on the strangeness that overcame one from looking at human works from an angle from which they were never designed to be seen, and wondered if there were similar angles in nature. Presumably there were, for behind him where the pond ended were only ragged willows topping reed beds. It looked as if there should have been something else—a little land at least—but no land showed, only the willows and the watery sky.

Now he was over the approximate center of the pond. He shipped his oars and peered over the side. There was an agitation in the water, and nothing could be seen, although he imagined much.

As he stared over the one side, the boat unexpectedly tipped to the other. Gregory swung round. The boat listed heavily to the left so that the oars rolled over that way. He could see nothing. Yet—he heard something. It was a sound much like a hound slowly panting. And whatever made it was about to capsize the boat.

"What is it?" he said, as all the skin pricked up his back and skull.

The boat lurched, for all the world as if someone invisible were trying to get into it. Frightened, he grasped the oar, and, without thinking, swept it over that side of the rowing boat.

It struck something solid where there was only air.

Dropping the oar in surprise, he put out his hand. It touched something yielding. At the same time, his arm was violently struck.

His actions were then entirely governed by instinct. Thought did not enter the matter. He picked up the oar again and smote the thin air with it. It hit something. There was a splash, and the boat righted itself so suddenly he was almost pitched into the water. Even while it still rocked, he was rowing frantically for the shallows, dragging the boat from the water, and running for the safety of the farmhouse.

Only at the door did he pause. His reason returned, his heart began gradually to stop stammering its fright. He stood looking at the seamed wood of the porch, trying to evaluate what he had seen and what had actually happened. But what had happened?

Forcing himself to go back to the pond, he stood by the boat and looked across the sullen face of the water. It lay undisturbed, except by surface ripples. He looked at the boat. A quantity of water lay in the bottom of it. He thought, all that happened was that I nearly capsized, and I let my idiot fears run away with me. Shaking his head, he pulled the boat back to the barn.

Gregory, as he often did, stayed to eat lunch at the farm, but he saw nothing of the farmer till milking time.

Joseph Grendon was in his late forties, and a few years senior to his wife. He had a gaunt, solemn face and a heavy beard that made him look older than he was. For all his seriousness, he greeted Gregory civilly enough. They stood together in the gathering dusk as the cows swung behind them into their regular stalls. Together they walked into the machine house next door, and Grendon lit the oil burners that started the steam engine into mo-

tion that would turn the generator that would supply the
vital spark.

"I smell the future in here," Gregory said, smiling. By
now he had forgotten the shock of the morning.

"The future will have to get on without me. I shall be
dead by then." The farmer spoke as he walked, putting
each word reliably before the next.

"That is what you always say. You're wrong—the future is rushing upon us."

"You ent far wrong there, Master Gregory, but I won't
have no part of it, I reckon. I'm an old man now. Do
you know what I was reading in one of those London
papers last night? They do say as how before another
half-century is out every house in the country will be
supplied with electrical lighting from one big central
power house in London. This here old machine won't be
no good then, will it?"

"It will be the end of the gas industry, that's for sure.
That will cause much unemployment."

"Well, of course, in remote districts like this here
primitive place, you wouldn't get gas in a dozen centuries.
But electrical lighting is easier to conduct from one place
to another than gas is. Here she come!"

This last exclamation was directed at a flicker of light
in the pilot bulb overhead. They stood there contemplating with satisfaction the wonderful machinery. As steam
pressure rose, the great leather belt turned faster and
faster, and the flicker in the pilot bulb grew stronger.
Although Gregory was used to a home lit by both gas and
electricity, he never felt the excitement of it as he did
here, out in the wilds, where the nearest incandescent
bulb was probably in Norwich, a great part of a day's
journey away.

"Why did you really decide to have this plant built,
Joseph?"

"Like I told you, it's safer than lanterns in the sheds
and the sties and anywhere with dry straw about the
place. My father had a bad fire here when I was a boy
that put the wind up me proper . . . Did I ever tell you
as how Bert Neckland's older brother used to work for
me once, till I got this here equipment in? He was a regular Bible-thumper, he was, and do you know what he told
me? He said as how this here electrical lighting was too

bright and devilish to be God's work, and in consequence he refused to let it shine on him. So I told him, I said, Well, I ent having you going round with an umbrella up all hour of darkness, and I gave him his wages and I tell him to clear off out if that's the way he feels."

"And he did?"

"He ent been back here since."

"Idiot! All things are possible now. The Steam Age was wonderful in its way, or must have seemed so to the people that lived in it, but in this new Electric Age—anything's possible. Do you know what I believe, Joseph? I believe that before so very many years are up, we shall have electrical flying machines. Who knows, we may even be able to make them big enough to fly to the moon! Oh, I tell you, I just cannot wait till the New Century. By then, who knows, all men may be united in brotherhood, and then we shall see some progress."

"I don't know. I shall be united in my grave by then."

"Nonsense, you can live to be a hundred."

Now a pale flickering radiance illuminated the room. By contrast, everything outside looked black. Grendon nodded in satisfaction, made some adjustments to the burners and they went outside.

Free from the bustle of the steam engine, they could hear the noise the cows were making. At milking time, the animals were usually quiet; something had upset them. The farmer ran quickly into the milking shed with Gregory on his heels.

The new light radiating from a bulb hanging above the stalls showed the beasts of restless demeanor and rolling eye. Bert Neckland stood as far away from the door as possible, grasping his stick and letting his mouth hang open.

"What in blazes you staring at, bor?" Grendon asked.

Neckland slowly shut his mouth.

"We had a scare," he said. "Something came in here," he said.

"Did you see what it was?" Gregory asked.

"No, there weren't nothing to see. It was a ghost, that's what it was. It come right in here and touched the cows. It touched me too. It was a ghost."

The farmer snorted. "A tramp more like. You couldn't see because the light wasn't on."

His man shook his head emphatically. "Light weren't that bad. I tell you, whatever it was, it come right up to me and touched me." He stopped and pointed to the edge of the stall. "Look there! See, I weren't telling you no lie, master. It was a ghost, and there's its wet handprint."

They crowded round and examined the worn and chewed timber at the corner of the partition between two stalls. An indefinite patch of moisture darkened the wood. Gregory's thoughts went back to his experience on the pond, and again he felt the prickle of unease along his spine. But the farmer said stoutly "Nonsense, it's a bit of cowslime. Now you get on with the milking, Bert, and let's have no more hossing about, because I want my tea. Where's Cuff?"

Bert looked defiant.

"If you don't believe me, maybe you'll believe the bitch. She saw whatever it was and went for it. It kicked her over, but she ran it out of here."

"I'll see if I can see her," Gregory said.

He ran outside and began calling the bitch. By now it was almost entirely dark. He could see nothing in the wide space of the front yard, and so set off in the other direction, down the path towards the pig sties and the fields, calling Cuff as he went. He paused. Low and savage growls sounded ahead under the elm trees. It was Cuff. He went slowly forward. At this moment, he cursed that electric light meant lack of lanterns and wished too that he had a weapon.

"Who's there?" he called.

The farmer came up by his side. "Let's charge 'em!"

They ran forward. The trunks of the four great elms were clear against the western sky, with water glinting leadenly behind them. The dog became visible. As Gregory saw Cuff, she sailed into the air, whirled round, and flew at the farmer. He flung up his arms and warded off the body. At the same time, Gregory felt a rush of air as if someone unseen had run past him, and a stale muddy smell filled his nostrils. Staggering, he looked behind him. The wan light from the cowsheds spread across the path between the outhouses and the farmhouse. Beyond the light, more distantly, was the silent countryside behind the grain store. Nothing untoward could be seen.

"They killed my old Cuff," said the farmer.

Gregory knelt down beside him to look at the bitch. There was no mark of injury on her, but she was dead, her fine head lying limp.

"She knew there was something there," Gregory said. "She went to attack whatever it was and it got her first. What was it? Whatever in the world was it?"

"They killed my old Cuff," said the farmer again, unhearing. He picked the body up in his arms, turned, and carried it toward the house. Gregory stood where he was, mind and heart equally uneasy.

He jumped violently when a step sounded nearby. It was Bert Neckland.

"What, did that there ghost kill the old bitch?" he asked.

"It killed the bitch certainly, but it was something more terrible than a ghost."

"That's one of them ghosts, bor. I seen plenty in my time. I ent afraid of ghosts, are you?"

"You looked fairly sick in the cowshed a minute ago."

The farmhand put his fists on his hips. He was no more than a couple of years older than Gregory, a stocky young man with a spotty complexion and a snub nose that gave him at once an air of comedy and menace. "Is that so, Master Gregory? Well, you looks pretty funky standing there now."

"I am scared. I don't mind admitting it. But only because we have something here a lot nastier than any spectre."

Neckland came a little closer.

"Then if you are so blooming windy, perhaps you'll be staying away from the farm in future."

"Certainly not." He tried to edge back into the light, but the laborer got in his way.

"If I was you, I should stay away." He emphasized his point by digging an elbow into Gregory's coat. "And just remember that Nancy was interested in me long afore you come along, bor."

"Oh, that's it, is it! I think Nancy can decide for herself in whom she is interested, don't you?"

"I'm *telling* you who she's interested in, see? And mind you don't forget, see?" He emphasized the words with another nudge. Gregory pushed his arm away angrily. Neckland shrugged his shoulders and walked off. As he went, he said, "You're going to get worse than ghosts if you keep hanging 'round here."

Gregory was shaken. The suppressed violence in the man's voice suggested that he had been harboring malice for some time. Unsuspectingly, Gregory had always gone out of his way to be cordial, had regarded the sullenness as mere slow-wittedness and done his socialist best to overcome the barrier between them. He thought of following Neckland and trying to make up with him; but that would look too feeble. Instead, he followed the way the farmer had gone with his dead bitch, and made for the house.

Gregory Rolles was too late back to Cottersall that night to meet his friend Fox. The next night, the weather became exceedingly chilly, and Gabriel Woodcock, the oldest inhabitant, was prophesying snow before the winter was out (a not very venturesome prophecy, to be fulfilled within forty-eight hours, thus impressing most of the inhabitants of the village, for they took pleasure in being impressed and exclaiming and saying "Well, I never!" to each other). The two friends met in The Wayfarer, where the fires were bigger, though the ale was weaker, than in the Three Poachers at the other end of the village.

Seeing to it that nothing dramatic was missed from his account, Gregory related the affairs of the previous day, omitting any reference to Neckland's pugnacity. Fox listened fascinated, neglecting both his pipe and his ale.

"So you see how it is, Bruce," Gregory concluded. "In that deep pond by the mill lurks a vehicle of some sort, the very one we saw in the sky, and in it lives an invisible being of evil intent. You see how I fear for my friends there. Should I tell the police about it, do you think?"

"I'm sure it would not help the Grendons to have old Farrish bumping out there on his penny-farthing," Fox said, referring to the local representative of the law. He took a long draw first on the pipe and then on the glass. "But I'm not sure you have your conclusions quite right, Greg. Understand, I don't doubt the facts, amazing though they are. I mean, we were more or less expecting celestial visitants. The world's recent blossoming with gas and electricity lighting in its cities at night must have been a signal to half the nations of space that we are now civilized down here. But have our visitants done any deliberate harm to anyone?"

"They nearly drowned me and they killed poor Cuff. I don't see what you're getting at. They haven't begun in a very friendly fashion, have they now?"

"Think what the situation must seem like to them. Suppose they come from Mars or the Moon—we know their world must be absolutely different from Earth. They may be terrified. And it can hardly be called an unfriendly act to try to get into your rowing boat. The first unfriendly act was yours, when you struck out with the oar."

Gregory bit his lip. His friend had a point. "I was scared."

"It may have been because they were scared that they killed Cuff. The dog attacked them, after all, didn't she? I feel sorry for these creatures, alone in an unfriendly world."

"You keep saying 'these'! As far as we know, there is only one of them."

"My point is this, Greg. You have completely gone back on your previous enlightened attitude. You are all for killing these poor things instead of trying to speak to them. Remember what you were saying about other worlds being full of socialists? Try thinking of these chaps as invisible socialists and see if that doesn't make them easier to deal with."

Gregory fell to stroking his chin. Inwardly, he acknowledged that Bruce Fox's words made a great impression on him. He had allowed panic to prejudice his judgment; as a result, he had behaved as immoderately as a savage in some remote corner of the Empire confronted by his first steam locomotive.

"I'd better get back to the farm and sort things out as soon as possible," he said. "If these things really do need help, I'll help them."

"That's it. But try not to think of them as 'things.' Think of them as—as—I know, as The Aurigans."

"Aurigans it is. But don't be so smug, Bruce. If you'd been in that boat—"

"I know, old friend, I'd have died of fright." To this monument of tact, Fox added, "Do as you say, go back and sort things out as soon as possible. I'm longing for the

next installment of this mystery. It's quite the jolliest
thing since Sherlock Holmes."

Gregory Rolles went back to the farm. But the sorting out
of which Bruce had spoken took longer than he expected.
This was chiefly because the Aurigans seemed to have
settled quietly into their new home after the initial day's
troubles.

They came forth no more from the pond, as far as he
could discover; at least they caused no more disturbance.
The young graduate particularly regretted this since he
had taken his friend's words much to heart, and wanted
to prove how enlightened and benevolent he was towards
this strange form of life. After some days, he came to believe the Aurigans must have left as unexpectedly as they
arrived. Then a minor incident convinced him otherwise;
and that same night, in his snug room over the baker's
shop, he described it to his correspondent in Worcester
Park, Surrey.

Dear Mr. Wells,
I must apologize for my failure to write earlier,
owing to lack of news concerning the Grendon Farm
affair.
Only today, the Aurigans showed themselves
again!—if indeed "showed" is the right word for invisible creatures.
Nancy Grendon and I were in the orchard feeding
the hens. There is still much snow lying about, and
everywhere is very white. As the poultry came running to Nancy's tub, I saw a disturbance further
down the orchard—merely some snow dropping
from an apple bough, but the movement caught my
eye, and I then saw a *procession* of falling snow
proceed towards us from tree to tree. The grass is
long there, and I soon noted the stalks being thrust
aside by *an unknown agency!* I directed Nancy's attention to the phenomenon. The motion in the grass
stopped only a few yards from us.
Nancy was startled, but I determined to acquit
myself more like a Briton than I had previously. Accordingly I advanced and said, "Who are you? What

do you want? We are your friends if you are friendly."

No answer came. I stepped forward again, and now the grass again fell back, and I could see by the way it was pressed down that the creature must have large feet. By the movement of the grasses, I could see he was running. I cried to him and ran, too. He went round the side of the house, and then over the frozen mud in the farmyard. I could see no further trace of him. But instinct led me forward, past the barn to the pond.

Surely enough, I then saw the cold, muddy water rise and heave, as if engulfing a body that slid quietly in. Shards of broken ice were thrust aside, and by an outward motion, I could see where the strange being went. In a flurry and a small whirlpool, he was gone, and, I have no doubt dived down to the mysterious star vehicle.

These things—people—I know not what to call them—must be aquatic; perhaps they live in the canals of the Red Planet. But imagine, Sir—an invisible mankind! The idea is almost as wonderful and fantastic as something from your novel, *The Time Machine*.

Pray give me your comment, and trust in my sanity and accuracy as a reporter!

Yours in friendship,
GREGORY ROLLES.

What he did not tell was the way Nancy had clung to him after, in the warmth of the parlor, and confessed her fear. And he had scorned the idea that these beings could be hostile, and had seen the admiration in her eyes, and had thought that she was, after all, a dashed pretty girl, and perhaps worth braving the wrath of those two very different people for: Edward Rolles, his father, and Bert Neckland, the farm laborer.

At that point Mrs. Grendon came in, and the two young people moved rapidly apart. Mrs. Grendon went more slowly. The new life within her was large now, and she carried herself accordingly. So as not to distress her, they told her nothing of what they had seen. Nor was there time for discussion, for the farmer and his two men came tramping into the kitchen, kicking off their boots and demanding lunch.

It was at lunch a week later, when Gregory was again at the farm, taking with him an article on electricity as a pretext for his visit, that the subject of the stinking dew was first discussed.

Grubby was the first to mention it in Gregory's hearing. Grubby, with Bert Neckland, formed the whole strength of Joseph Grendon's labor force; but whereas Neckland was considered couth enough to board in the farmhouse (he had a gaunt room in the attic), Grubby was fit only to sleep in a little flint-and-chalk hut well away from the farm building. His "house," as he dignified the miserable hut, stood below the orchard and near the sties, the occupants of which lulled Grubby to sleep with their snorts.

"Reckon we ent ever had a dew like that before, Mr. Grendon," he said, his manner suggesting to Gregory that he had made this observation already this morning; Grubby never ventured to say anything original.

"Heavy as an autumn dew," said the farmer firmly, as if there had been an argument on that point.

Silence fell, broken only by a general munching and, from Grubby, a particular guzzling, as they all made their way through huge platefuls of stewed rabbit and dumplings.

"It weren't no ordinary dew, that I do know," Grubby said after a while.

"It stank of toadstools," Neckland said. "Or rotten pond water."

More munching.

"I have read of freak dews before," Gregory told the company. "And you hear of freak rains, when frogs fall out of the sky. I've even read of hailstones with live frogs and toads embedded in them."

"There's always something beyond belief as you have read of, Master Gregory," Neckland said. "But we happen to be talking about this here dew that fell right on this here farm this here morning. There weren't no frogs in it either."

"Well it's gone now, so I can't see why you're worried about it," Nancy said.

"We ent ever had a dew like that before, Miss Nancy," Grubby said.

"I know I had to wash my washing again," Mrs. Grendon said. "I left it out all night and it stank really foul this morning."

"It may be something to do with the pond," Gregory said. "Some sort of freak of evaporation."

Neckland snorted. From his position at the top of the table, the farmer halted his shoveling operations to point a fork at Gregory.

"You may well be right there. Because I tell you what, that there dew only come down on our land and property. A yard the other side of the gate, the road was dry. Bone dry it was."

"Right you are there, master," Neckland agreed. "And while the West Field was dripping with the stuff, I saw for myself that the bracken over the hedge weren't wet at all. Ah, it's a rum go!"

"Say what you like, we ent ever had a dew like it," Grubby said. He appeared to be summing up the feeling of the company.

Leading off the parlor was a smaller room. Although it shared a massive fireplace with the parlor—for the whole house was built round and supported by this central brick stack—fires were rarely lit in the smaller room. This was the Best Room. Here Joseph Grendon occasionally retired to survey—with some severity and discomfort—his accounts. Otherwise the room was scarcely used.

After his meal, Grendon retired belching into the Best Room, and Gregory followed. This was where the farmer kept his modest store of books, his Carlyles, Ainsworths, Ruskins, and Lyttons, together with the copy of *The Time Machine*, which Gregory had presented to him at Christmas, complete with a socially-inspired inscription. But the room was chiefly notable for the stuffed animals it contained, some encased in glass.

These animals had evidently been assaulted by a blunder in taxidermy, for they stood in poses that would in life have been beyond them, even supposing them to have been equipped with the extra joints and malformations indicated by their post mortemnal shapes. They numbered among them creatures that bore chance resemblances to owls, dogs, foxes, cats, goats, and calves. Only the stuffed

fish carried more than a wan likeness to their living coun-
terparts, and they had felt such an autumn after death
that all their scales had been shed like leaves.

Gregory looked doubtfully at these monsters in which
man's forming hand was more evident than God's. There
were so many of them that some had overflowed into the
parlor; in the Best Room, it was their multitude as well as
their deformity that appalled. All the same, seeing how
gloomily Grendon scowled over his ledger, Gregory said,
thinking to cheer the older man, "You should practice
some more taxidermy, Joseph."

"Ah." Without looking up.

"The hobby would be pleasant for you."

"Ah." Now he did look up. "You're young and you
know only the good side of life. You're ignorant, Master
Gregory, for all your university learning. You don't know
how the qualities get whittled away from a man until by
the time he's my age, there's only persistence left."

"That's not—"

"I shall never do another stuffing job. I ent got time! I
ent really got time for nothing but this here old farm."

"But that's not true! You—"

"I say it is true, and I don't talk idle. I pass the time of
day with you; I might even say I like you; but you don't
mean nothing to me." He looked straight at Gregory as he
spoke and then slowly lowered his eyes with what might
have been sadness. "Neither does Marjorie mean nothing
to me now, though that was different afore we married. I
got this here farm, you see, and I'm the farm and it is
me."

He was stuck for words, and the beady eyes of the specimens ranged about him stared at him unhelpfully.

"Of course it's hard work," Gregory said.

"You don't understand, bor. Nobody do. This here land
is no good. It's barren. Every year, it grows less and less.
It ent got no more life than what these here animals have.
So that means I am barren too—year by year, I got less
substance."

He stood up suddenly, angry perhaps at himself.

"You better go home, Master Gregory."

"Joe, I'm terribly sorry. I wish I could help . . ."

"I know you mean kindly. You go home while the

night's fine." He peered out into the blank yard. "Let's hope we don't get another stinking dewfall tonight."

The strange dew did not fall again. As a topic of conversation, it was limited, and even on the farm, where there was little new to talk about, it was forgotten in a few days. The February passed, being neither much worse nor much better than most Februaries, and ended in heavy rainstorms. March came, letting in a chilly spring over the land. The animals on the farm began to bring forth their young.

They brought them forth in amazing numbers, as if to overturn all the farmer's beliefs in the unproductiveness of his land.

"I never seen anything like it!" Grendon said to Gregory. Nor had Gregory seen the taciturn farmer so excited. He took the young man by the arm and marched him into the barn.

There lay Trix, the nannie goat. Against her flank huddled three little brown and white kids, while a fourth stood nearby, wobbling on its spindly legs.

"Four of 'em! Have you ever heard of a goat throwing off *four* kids? You better write to the papers in London about this, Gregory! But just you come down to the pigsties."

The squealing from the sties was louder than usual. As they marched down the path towards them, Gregory looked up at the great elms, their outlines dusted in green, and thought he detected something sinister in the noises, something hysterical that was perhaps matched by an element in Grendon's own bearing.

The Grendon pigs were mixed breeds, with a preponderance of Large Blacks. They usually gave litters of something like ten piglets. Now there was not a litter without fourteen in it; one enormous black sow had eighteen small pigs jostling about her. The noise was tremendous and, standing looking down on this swarming life, Gregory told himself that he was foolish to imagine anything uncanny in it; he knew so little about farm life.

" 'Course, they ent all going to live," the farmer said. "The old sows ent got enough dugs to feed that brood. But it's a record lot! I reckon you ought to write to that there *Norwich Advertiser* about it."

Grubby lumbered up with two pails of feed, his great round face flushed as if in rapport with all the fecundity about him.

"Never seen so many pigs," he said. "You ought to write to that there newspaper in Norwich about it, bor. There ent never been so many pigs."

Gregory had no chance to talk to Nancy on the subject. She and her mother had driven to town in the trap, for it was market day in Cottersall. After he had eaten with Grendon and the men—Mrs. Grendon had left them a cold lunch—Gregory went by himself to look about the farm, still with a deep and (he told himself) unreasoning sense of disturbance inside him.

A pale sunshine filled the afternoon. It could not penetrate far down into the water of the pond. But as Gregory stood by the horse trough staring at the expanse of water, he saw that it teemed with young tadpoles and frogs. He went closer. What he had regarded as a sheet of rather stagnant water was alive with small swimming things. As he looked, a great beetle surged out of the depths and seized a tadpole. The tadpoles were also providing food for two ducks that, with their young, were swimming by the reeds on the far side of the pond. And how many young did the ducks have? An armada of chicks was there, parading in and out of the rushes.

He walked round behind the barn and the cowsheds, where the ground was marshy, and across the bridge at the back of the machine house. The haystacks stood here, and behind them a wild stretch of hedge. As he went, Gregory watched for birds' nests. In the woodpile was a redstart's nest, in the marsh a meadow pipit's, in the hedge nests of sparrows and blackbirds. All were piled high with eggs— far too many eggs.

For a minute, he stood uncertainly, then began to walk slowly back the way he had come. Nancy stood between two of the haystacks. He started in surprise at seeing her. He called her name, but she stood silent with her back to him.

Puzzled, he went forward and touched her on the shoulder. Her head swung round. He saw her long teeth, the yellow curve of bone that had been her nose—but it was a sheep's head, falling backwards off a stick over which her old cloak had been draped. It lay on the ground by her bonnet, and he stared down at it in dismay, trying to quiet the leap of his heart. And at that moment, Neckland jumped out and caught him by the wrist.

"Ha, that gave thee a scare, my hearty, didn't it? I saw 'ee hanging round here. Why don't you get off out of here and never come back, bor? I warned you before, and I ent going to warn you again, do you hear? You leave Nancy alone, you and your books!"

Gregory wrenched his hand away.

"You did this, did you, you bloody ignorant lout? What do you think you are playing at there? How do you think Nancy or her mother would like it if they saw what you had done? Suppose I showed this to Farmer Grendon? Are you off your head, Neckland?"

"Don't you call me a ignorant lout, or I'll knock off that there block of yours, that I will. I'm a-giving you a good scare, you cheeky tick, and I'm a-warning you to keep away from here."

"I don't want your warnings, and I refuse to heed them. It's up to the Grendons whether or not I come here, not you. You keep to your place and I'll keep to mine. If you try this sort of thing again, we shall come to blows."

Neckland looked less pugnacious than he had a moment ago. He said, cockily enough, "I ent afraid of you."

"Then I may give you cause to be," Gregory said. Turning on his heel, he walked swiftly away—alert at the same time for an attack from the rear. But Neckland slunk away as silently as he had come.

Crossing the yard, Gregory went over to the stable and saddled Daisy. He swung himself up and rode away without bidding good-bye to anyone.

At one point, he looked over his shoulder. The farm crouched low and dark above the desolate land. Sky predominated over everything. The Earth seemed merely a strip of beach before a great tumbled ocean of air and light and space and things ill-defined; and from that ocean had come . . . he did not know, nor did he know how to find out, except by waiting and seeing if the strange vessel from the seas of space had brought evil or blessing.

Riding into Cottersall, he went straight to the market place. He saw the Grendon trap, with Nancy's little pony, Hetty, between the shafts, standing outside the grocer's shop. Mrs. Grendon and Nancy were just coming out.

Jumping to the ground, Gregory led Daisy over to them and bid them good day.

"We are going to call on my friend Mrs. Edwards and her daughters," Mrs. Grendon said.

"I wondered, Mrs. Grendon, if you'd allow me to speak with Nancy privately, just for ten minutes."

Mrs. Grendon was well wrapped against the wind; she made a monumental figure as she looked at her daughter and considered.

"Seeing you talks to her at the farm, I don't see why you shouldn't talk to her here, but I don't want to cause no scandal, Master Gregory, and I'm sure I don't know where you can go to talk private. I mean, folks are more staid in their ways in Norfolk than they used to be in my young days, and I don't want any scandal. Can't it wait till you come to see us at the farm again?"

"If you would be so kind, Mrs. Grendon, I would be very obliged if I might speak privately with her now. My landlady, Mrs. Fenn, has a little downstairs parlor at the back of the shop, and I know she would let us speak there. It would be quite respectable."

"Drat respectable! Let people think what they will, I say." All the same, she stood for some time in meditation. Nancy remained by her mother with her eyes on the ground. Gregory looked at her and seemed to see her anew. Under her blue coat, fur-trimmed, she wore her orange-and-brown-squared gingham dress. She had a bonnet on her head. Her complexion was pure and blemishless, her skin as firm and delicate as a plum, and her dark eyes were hidden under long lashes. Her lips were steady, pale, and clearly defined, with appealing tucks at each corner. He felt almost like a thief, stealing a sight of her beauty while she was not regarding him.

"I'm going on to Mrs. Edwards," Marjorie Grendon declared at last. "I don't care what you two do so long as you behave—but I shall, mind, if you aren't with me in a half-hour, Nancy, do you hear?"

"Yes, mother."

The baker's shop was in the next street. Gregory and Nancy walked there in silence. Gregory shut Daisy in the stable and they went together into the parlor through the back door. At this time of day, Mr. Fenn was resting upstairs and his wife looking after the shop so the little room was empty.

Nancy sat upright in a chair and said, "Well, Gregory, what's all this about? Fancy dragging me off from my mother like that in the middle of town!"

"Nancy, don't be cross. I had to see you."

She pouted. "You come out to the old farm often enough and don't show any particular wish to see me there."

"That's nonsense. I always come to see you—lately in particular. Besides, you're more interested in Bert Neckland, aren't you?"

"Bert Neckland, indeed! Why should I be interested in him? Not that it's any of your business if I am."

"It is my business, Nancy. I love you, Nancy!"

He had not meant to blurt it out in quite that fashion, but now it was out, it was out, and he pressed home his disadvantage by crossing the room, kneeling at her feet, and taking her hands in his.

"I thought you only came out to the farm to see my father."

"It was like that at first, Nancy, but no more."

"You've got interested in farming now, haven't you? That's what you come for now, isn't it?"

"Well, I certainly am interested in the farm, but I want to talk about you. Nancy, darling Nancy, say that you like me just a little. Encourage me somewhat."

"You are a very fine gentleman, Gregory, and I feel very kind towards you, to be sure, but . . ."

"But?"

She gave him the benefit of her downcast eyes again.

"Your station in life is very different from mine, and besides—well, you don't *do* anything."

He was shocked into silence. With the natural egotism of youth, he had not seriously thought that she could have any firm objection to him; but in her words he suddenly saw the truth of his position, at least as it was revealed to her.

"Nancy—I—well, it's true I do not seem to you to be working at present. But I do a lot of reading and studying here, and I write to several important people in the world. And all the time I am coming to a great decision about

what my career will be. I do assure you I am no loafer if
that's what you think."

"No, I don't think that. But Bert says you often spend a
convivial evening in that there Wayfarer."

"Oh, he does, does he? And what business is it of his if
I do—or of yours, come to that? What a damned cheek!"

She stood up. "If you have nothing left to say but a lot
of swearing, I'll be off to join my mother if you don't
mind."

"Oh, by Jove, I'm making a mess of this!" He caught
her wrist. "Listen, my sweet thing. I ask you only this,
that you try and look on me favorably. And also that you
let me say a word about the farm. Some strange things are
happening there, and I seriously don't like to think of you
being there at night. All these young things being born, all
these little pigs—it's uncanny!"

"I don't see what's uncanny no more than my father
does. I know how hard he works, and he's done a good
job rearing his animals, that's all. He's the best farmer
round Cottersall by a long chalk."

"Oh, certainly. He's a wonderful man. But he didn't put
seven or eight eggs into a hedge-sparrow's nest, did he?
He didn't fill the pond with tadpoles and newts till it looks
like a broth, did he? Something strange is happening on
your farm this year, Nancy, and I want to protect you if I
can."

The earnestness with which he spoke, coupled perhaps
with his proximity and the ardent way he pressed her
hand, went a good way toward mollifying Nancy.

"Dear Gregory, you don't know anything about farm
life, I don't reckon, for all your books. But you're very
sweet to be concerned."

"I shall always be concerned about you, Nancy, you
beautiful creature."

"You'll make me blush!"

"Please do, for then you look even lovelier than usual!"
He put an arm around her. When she looked up at him,
he caught her up close to his chest and kissed her fervently.

She gasped and broke away, but not with too great
haste.

"Oh, Gregory! Oh, Gregory! I must go to mother now!"

"Another kiss first! I can't let you go until I get another."

He took it, and stood by the door trembling with excitement as she left. "Come and see us again soon," she whispered.

"With dearest pleasure," he said. But the next visit held more dread than pleasure.

The big cart was standing in the yard full of squealing piglets when Gregory arrived. The farmer and Neckland were bustling about it. The farmer, shrugging into his overcoat, greeted Gregory cheerfully.

"I've a chance to make a good quick profit on these little chaps. Old sows can't feed them, but sucking pig fetches its price in Norwich so Bert and me are going to drive over to Heigham and put them on the train."

"They're grown since I last saw them!"

"Ah, they put on over two pounds a day. Bert, we'd better get a net and spread over this lot, or they'll be diving out. They're that lively!"

The two men made their way over to the barn, clomping through the mud. Mud squelched behind Gregory. He turned.

In the muck between the stables and the cart, footprints appeared, two parallel tracks. They seemed to imprint themselves with no agency but their own. A cold flow of acute supernatural terror overcame Gregory, so that he could not move. The scene seemed to go gray and palsied as he watched the tracks come towards him.

The carthorse neighed uneasily, the prints reached the cart, the cart creaked, as if something has climbed aboard. The piglets squealed with terror. One dived clear over the wooden sides. Then a terrible silence fell.

Gregory still could not move. He heard an unaccountable sucking noise in the cart, but his eyes remained rooted on the muddy tracks. Those impressions were of something other than a man: something with dragging feet that were in outline something like a seal's flippers. Suddenly he found his voice, "Mr. Grendon!" he cried.

Only as the farmer and Bert came running from the barn with the net did Gregory dare look into the cart.

One last piglet, even as he looked, seemed to be deflating rapidly, like a rubber balloon collapsing. It went limp and lay silent among the other little empty bags of pig skin. The cart creaked. Something splashed heavily off across the farmyard in the direction of the pond.

Grendon did not see. He had run to the cart and was staring like Gregory in dismay at the deflated corpses. Neckland stared too, and was the first to find his voice.

"Some sort of disease got 'em all, just like that! Must be one of them there new diseases from the continent of Europe!"

"It's no disease," Gregory said. He could hardly speak, for his mind had just registered the fact that there were no bones left in or amid the deflated pig bodies.

"It's no disease—look, the pig that got away is still alive."

The animal that had jumped from the cart had injured its leg and now lay in the ditch some feet away, panting. The farmer went over to it and lifted it out.

"It escaped the disease by jumping out," Neckland said. "Master, we better go and see how the rest of them be down in the sties."

"Ah, that we had," Grendon said. He handed the pig over to Gregory, his face set. "No good taking one alone to market. I'll get Grubby to unharness the horse. Meanwhile, perhaps you'd be good enough to take this little chap in to Marjorie. At least we can all eat a bit of roast pig for dinner tomorrow."

"Mr. Grendon, this is no disease. Have the veterinarian over from Heigham and let him examine these bodies."

"Don't you tell me how to run my farm, young man. I've got trouble enough."

Despite this rebuff, Gregory could not keep away. He had to see Nancy, and he had to see what occurred at the farm. The morning after the horrible thing happened to the pigs, he received a letter from his most admired correspondent, Mr. H. G. Wells, one paragraph of which read: "At bottom, I think I am neither optimist nor pessimist. I tend to believe both that we stand on the threshold of an epoch of magnificent progress—certainly such an epoch is within our grasp—and that we may have reached the *fin du globe* prophesied by our gloomier *fin de siècle* prophets. I am not at all surprised to hear that such a vast issue may be resolving itself on a remote farm near Cottersall, Norfolk—all unknown to anyone but the two of us. Do not think that I am in other than a state of terror, even when I cannot help exclaiming 'What a lark!' "

Too preoccupied to be as excited over such a letter as he would ordinarily have been, Gregory tucked it away in his jacket pocket and went to saddle up Daisy.

Before lunch, he stole a kiss from Nancy and planted another on her over-heated left cheek as she stood by the vast range in the kitchen. Apart from that, there was little pleasure in the day. Grendon was reassured to find that none of the other piglets had fallen ill of the strange shrinking disease, but he remained alert against the possibility of it striking again. Meanwhile, another miracle had occurred. In the lower pasture, in a tumble-down shed, he had a cow that had given birth to four calves during the night. He did not expect the animal to live, but the calves were well enough and being fed from a bottle by Nancy.

The farmer's face was dull for he had been up all night with the laboring cow, and he sat down thankfully at the head of the table as the roast pig arrived on its platter.

It proved uneatable. In no time, they were all flinging down implements in disgust. The flesh had a bitter taste for which Neckland was the first to account.

"It's diseased!" he growled. "This here animal had the disease all the time. We didn't ought to eat this here meat or we may all be dead ourselves inside of a week!"

They were forced to make a snack on cold salted beef and cheese and pickled onions, none of which Mrs. Grendon could face in her condition. She retreated upstairs in tears at the thought of the failure of her carefully prepared dish, and Nancy ran after her to comfort her.

After the dismal meal, Gregory spoke to Grendon.

"I have decided I must go to Norwich tomorrow for a few days, Mr. Grendon," he said. "You are in trouble here, I believe. Is there anything, any business, I can transact for you in the city? Can I find you a veterinary surgeon there?"

Grendon clapped his shoulder. "I know you mean well, and I thank 'ee for it, but you don't seem to realize that veterinaries cost a load of money and aren't always too helpful when they do come. Just suppose we had some young idiot here who told us all our stock is poisoned and we had to kill it? That would be a right look-out, eh?"

"Just because Gregory Rolles has plenty of money, he thinks everyone has," Neckland sneered.

The farmer turned furiously on him. "Who asked you to open your trap, bor? You keep your trap shut when there's a private conversation going on as don't concern you at all. Why aren't you out cleaning down the cow-shed since you ett all that last loaf?"

When Neckland had gone, Grendon said, "Bert's a good lad, but he don't like you at all. Now you was saying we had trouble here. But a farm is always trouble, Gregory—some years one sort of trouble, some years another. But I ent ever seen such fine growth as this year, and I tell 'ee straight I'm delighted, proper delighted. Some pigs have died, but that ent going to stop me doing my best by all the rest of 'em."

"But they will be unmarketable if they all taste like the one today."

Grendon smote his palm. "You're a real worrier. They may grow out of this bitter taste. And then again, if they don't, people have to buy them before they can taste them, don't they? I'm a poor man, Gregory, and when a bit of fortune comes my way, I can't afford to let it get away. In fact, I tell 'ee this, and even Bert don't know it yet, but tomorrow or the next day, I got Seeley the builder coming over here to put me up some more wood sheds down by Grubby's hut to give the young animals more room."

"Good. Then let me do something for you, Joseph, in return for all your kindness to me. Let me bring a vet back from Norwich at my own expense, just to have a look round, nothing more."

"Blow me if you aren't stubborn as they come. I'm telling you, same as my dad used to say, if I finds any person on my land as I didn't ask here, I'm getting that there gun of mine down and I'm peppering him with buckshot, same as I did with them two old tramps last year. Fair enough, bor?"

"I suppose so."

"Then I must go and see to the cow. And stop worrying about what you don't understand."

After the farmer had gone, Gregory stood for a long

time looking out of the window, waiting for Nancy to come down, worrying over the train of events. But the view was peaceful enough. He was the only person worrying, he reflected. Even the shrewd Mr. H. G. Wells, his correspondent, seemed to take his reports with a pinch of salt—he who of all men in England would sympathetically receive the news of the miraculous when it came to Earth, even if it failed to arrive in the form predicted in his recent novel, *The Wonderful Visit*. Be that as it might, he was going to Norwich and the wise uncle who lived there as soon as he could—as soon, in fact, as he had kissed dear Nancy good-bye.

The wise uncle was indeed sympathetic. He was altogether a gentler man than his brother Edward, Gregory's father. He looked with sympathy at the plan of the farm that Gregory drew, he looked with sympathy at the sketch of the muddy footprint, he listened with sympathy to an account of what happened. And at the end of it all he said, "Ghosts!"

When Gregory tried to argue with him, he said firmly, "My dear boy, I fear the modern marvels of our age have gone to your head. You know of such engineering structures as the cantilever bridge over the Firth of Forth, and you know as we all do of the colossal tower Eiffel has built in Paris—though if it stands ten years, I'll eat my hat. Now, no one will deny these things are marvelous, but they are things that rest on the ground. You're trying to tell me that engineers on this world or some other world might build a machine—a vehicle—that could fly from one heavenly body to another. Well then, *I'm* telling you that no engineer can do such a thing—and I'm not just saying that, but I'm quoting a law about it. There's a law about engineers not being able to sail in some sort of damned Eiffel Tower with engines from Mars to Earth, or the Sun to Earth, or whatever you will—a law to be read in your Bible and echoed in the pages of *The Cornhill*. No, my boy, the modern age has gone to your head, but it's old-fashioned ghosts that have gone to your farm."

So Gregory walked into the city, and inspected the booksellers, and made several purchases, and never doubted for a moment that his uncle, though infinitely sympathetic, and adroit at slipping one a sovereign on parting, was sadly less wise than he had hitherto seemed:

a discovery that seemed to reflect how Gregory had grown up and how times were changing.

But Norwich was a pleasant city and his uncle's house a comfortable house in which to stay, and he lingered there a week where he had meant to spend only three days at the most.

Consequently, conscience stirred in him when he again approached the Grendon farm along the rough road from Cottersall. He was surprised to see how the countryside had altered since he was last this way. New foilage gleamed everywhere, and even the heath looked a happier place. But as he came to the farm, he saw how overgrown it was. Great ragged elder and towering cow parsley had shot up so that at first they hid all the buildings. He fancied the farm had been spirited away until, spurring Daisy on, he saw the black mill emerge from behind a clump of nearby growth. The south meadows were deep in rank grass. Even the elms seemed much shaggier than before and loomed threateningly over the house.

As he clattered over the flat wooden bridge and through the open gate into the yard, Gregory noted huge hairy nettles craning out of the adjoining ditches. Birds fluttered everywhere. Yet the impression he received was one of death rather than life. A great quiet lay over the place, as if it were under a curse that eliminated noise and hope.

He realized this effect was partly because Lardie, the young collie bitch who had taken the place of Cuff, was not running up barking as she generally did with visitors. The yard was deserted. Even the customary fowls had gone. As he led Daisy into the stables, he saw a heavy piebald in the first stall and recognized it as Dr. Crouchorn's. His anxieties took more definite shape.

Since the stable was now full, he led his mare across to the stone trough by the pond and hitched her there before walking over to the house. The front door was open. Great ragged dandelions grew against the porch. The creeper, hitherto somewhat sparse, pressed into the lower windows. A movement in the rank grass caught his eye, and he looked down, drawing back his riding boot. An enormous toad crouched under weed, the head of a still writhing grass snake in its mouth. The toad seemed to eye Gregory fixedly, as if trying to determine whether the man

envied its gluttony. Shuddering in disgust, he hurried into
the house.

Three of Trix's kids, well grown now, strutted about
the parlor, nibbling at the carpet and climbing into the
massive armchairs, staring at a stuffed caricature of a goat
that stood in its glass case by the window. Judging by the
chaos in the room, they had been there some while and
had had a game on the table. But they possessed the room
alone, and a quick glance into the kitchen revealed nobody there either.

Muffled sounds came from upstairs. The stairs curled
round the massive chimneypiece and were shut off from
the lower rooms by a latched door. Gregory had never
been invited upstairs, but he did not hesitate. Throwing
the door open, he started up the dark stairwell and almost
at once ran into a body.

Its softness told him that this was Nancy; she stood in
the dark weeping. Even as he caught her and breathed
her name, she broke from his grasp and ran from him up
the stairs. He could hear the noises more clearly now and
the sound of crying—though at the moment he was not
listening. Nancy ran to a door on the landing nearest to
the top of the stairs, burst into the room beyond, and
closed it. When Gregory tried the latch, he heard the bolt
slide to on the other side.

"Nancy!" he called. "Don't hide from me. What is it?
What's happening?"

She made no answer. As he stood there baffled against
the door, the next door along the passage opened and Dr.
Crouchorn emerged, clutching his little black bag. He was
a tall, somber man with deep lines on his face which inspired such fear in his patients that a remarkable percentage of them did as he bid and recovered. Even here, he
wore the top hat that, simply by remaining constantly in
position, contributed to the doctor's fame in the neighborhood.

"What's the trouble, Dr. Crouchorn?" Gregory asked as
the medical man shut the door behind him and started
down the stairs. "Has the plague struck this house, or
something equally terrible?"

"Plague, young man, plague? No, it is something much
more unnatural than that."

He stared at Gregory unsmilingly, as if promising himself inwardly not to move a muscle again until Gregory asked the obvious.

"What did you call for, doctor?"

"The hour of Mrs. Grendon's confinement struck during the night," he said, still poised on the top step.

A wave of relief swept over Gregory. He had forgotten Nancy's mother! "She's had her baby? Was it a boy?"

The doctor nodded in slow motion. "She bore two boys, young man." He hesitated, and then a muscle in his face twitched and he said in a rush, "She also bore seven daughters. Nine children! And they all . . . they all live. It's impossible. Until I die—"

He could not finish. Tipping his hat, he hurried down the stairs, leaving Gregory to look fixedly at the wallpaper while his mind whirled as if it would convert itself into liquid. Nine children! Nine! It was as if she were no different from an animal in a sty. And the wallpaper pattern took on a diseased and vivid look as if the house itself embodied sickness. The mewling noise from the bedroom seemed also the emblem of something inhuman calling its need.

He stood there in a daze, the sickly infant cries boring into him. From beyond the stone walls that oppressed him, he heard the noise of a horse ridden at hard gallop over the wooden bridge and down the track to Cottersall, dying with distance. From Nancy's room came no sound. Gregory guessed she had hidden herself from him for shame, and at last stirred himself into moving down the dark and curving stairwell. A stable cat scuttled out from under the bottom stair, a dozen baby tabbies in pursuit. The goats still held possession of the room. The fire was but scattered ashes in the hearth and had not been tended since the crisis of the night.

"I bet you're surprised!"

Gregory swung round. From the kitchen came Grubby, clutching a wedge of bread and meat in his fist. He chewed with his mouth open, grinning at Gregory.

"Farmer Grendon be a proper ram!" he exclaimed. "Ent no other man in this country could beget himself nine kids at one go!"

"Where is the farmer?"

"I say there ent no other man in this here county—"

"Yes, I heard what you said. Where is the farmer?"

"Working, I suppose. But I tell 'ee, bor, there ent no other man—"

Leaving Grubby munching and talking, Gregory strode out into the yard. He came on Grendon around the corner of the house. The farmer had a pitchfork full of hay, which he was carrying over his shoulder into the cow-sheds. Gregory stood in his way, but he pushed past.

"I want to speak to you, Joseph."

"There's work to be done. Pity you can't see that."

"I want to speak about your wife."

Grendon made no reply. He worked like a demon, toss-ing the hay down, turning for more. In any case, it was difficult to talk. The cows and calves, closely confined, seemed to set up a perpetual uneasy noise of lowing and un-cow-like grunts. Gregory followed the farmer round to the hayrick, but the man walked like one possessed. His eyes seemed sunk into his head, his mouth was puckered until his lips were invisible. When Gregory laid a hand on his arm, he shook it off. Stabbing up another great load of hay, he swung back towards the sheds so violently that Gregory had to jump out of his way.

Gregory lost his temper. Following Grendon back into the cowshed, he swung the bottom of the two-part door shut, and bolted it on the outside. When Grendon came back, he did not budge.

"Joseph, what's got into you? Why are you suddenly so heartless? Surely your wife needs you by her?"

His eyes had a curious blind look as he turned them at Gregory. He held the pitchfork before him in both hands almost like a weapon as he said, "I been with her all night, bor, while she brought forth her increase."

"But now—"

"She got a nursing woman from Dereham Cottages with her now. I been with her all night. Now I got to see to the farm—things keep growing, you know."

"They're growing too much, Joseph. Stop and think—"

"I've no time for talking." Dropping the pitchfork, he elbowed Gregory out of the way, unbolted the door, and flung it open. Grasping Gregory firmly by the biceps of one arm, he began to propel him along to the vegetable beds down by South Meadows.

The early lettuce were gigantic here. Everything bristled out of the ground. Recklessly, Grendon ran among the lines of new green, pulling up fists full of young radishes, carrots, spring onions, scattering them over his shoulder as fast as he plucked them from the ground.

"See, Gregory—all bigger than you ever seen 'em, and weeks early! The harvest is going to be a bumper. Look at the fields! Look at the orchard!" With wide gesture, he swept a hand towards the lines of trees, buried in the mounds of snow-and-pink of their blossom. "Whatever happens, we got to take advantage of it. It may not happen another year. Why—it's like a fairy story!"

He said no more. Turning, he seemed already to have forgotten Gregory. Eyes down at the ground that had suddenly achieved such abundance, he marched back towards the sheds, from whence now came the sound of Neckland washing out milk churns.

The spring sun was warm on Gregory's back. He told himself that everything looked normal. The farm was flourishing. From beyond the sties came shouts, distantly, and the sounds of men working, where the builder was preparing to erect more sheds. Perhaps, he told himself dully, he was worrying about nothing. Slowly, he walked towards the back of the house. There was nothing he could do here; it was time to return to Cottersall. But first he must see Nancy.

Nancy was in the kitchen. Neckland had brought her in a stoup of fresh milk, and she was supping it wearily from a ladle.

"Oh, Greg, I'm sorry I ran from you. I was so upset." She came to him, still holding the ladle but dangling her arms over his shoulders in a familiar way she had not used before. "Poor mother, I fear her mind is unhinged with—with bearing so many children. She's talking such strange stuff as I never heard before, and I do believe she fancies as she's a child again."

"Is it to be wondered at?" he said, smoothing her hair with his hand. "She'll be better once she's recovered from the shock."

They kissed each other, and after a minute she passed him a ladleful of milk. He drank and then spat it out in disgust.

"Ugh! What's got into the milk? Is Neckland trying to poison you or something? Have you tasted it? It's as bitter as sloes!"

She pulled a puzzled face. "I thought it tasted rather strange, but not unpleasant. Here, let me try again."

"No, it's too horrible. Some Sloan's Liniment must have got mixed in it."

Despite his warning, she put her lips to the metal spoon and sipped, then shook her head. "You're imagining things, Greg. It does taste a bit different, 'tis true, but there's nothing wrong with it."

"Sweetheart, it's horrible. I'm going to get your father to taste it and see what he thinks."

"I wouldn't bother him just now, Greg, if I was you. You know how busy he is, and tired, and attending on mother during the night has put him back in his work. I will mention it to him at dinner—which I must now prepare. Them there goats have made such a muck in here, not to mention that Grubby! You'll stay to take a bite with us, I hope?"

"No, Nancy, I'm off now. I have a letter awaiting me that I must answer; it arrived when I was in Norwich."

She bit her lip and snapped her fingers. "There, how terrible awful you'll think me! I never asked you how you enjoyed yourself in the big city! It must be wonderful to be a man of leisure, never with no work to do nor meals to prepare."

"You still hold that against me! Listen, my lovely Nancy, this letter is from a Dr. Hudson-Ward, an old acquaintance of my father's. He is headmaster of a school in Gloucester, and he wishes me to join the staff there as teacher on most favorable terms. So you see I may not be idle much longer!"

Laughing, she clung to him. "That's wonderful, my darling! What a handsome schoolmaster you will make. But Gloucester—that's over the other side of the country. I suppose we shan't be seeing you again once you get there."

"Nothing's settled yet, Nancy."

"You'll be gone in a week and we shan't never see you again. Once you get to that old school, you will never think of your Nancy no more."

He cupped her face in his hands. "Are you my Nancy? Do you care for me?"

Her eyelashes came over her dark eyes. "Greg, things are so muddled here—I mean—yes, I do care, I dread to think I'd not see you again."

Recalling her saying that, he rode away a quarter of an hour later very content at heart—and entirely neglectful of the dangers to which he left her exposed.

Rain fell lightly as Gregory Rolles made his way that evening to the Wayfarer Inn. His friend Bruce Fox was already there, ensconced in one of the snug seats by the ingle nook.

On this occasion, Fox was more interested in purveying details of his sister's forthcoming wedding than in listening to what Gregory had to tell, and since some of his future brother-in-law's friends soon arrived, and had to buy and be bought libation, the evening became a merry and thoughtless one. And in a short while, the ale having its good effect, Gregory also forgot what he wanted to say and began wholeheartedly to enjoy the company.

Next morning, he awoke with a heavy head and in a dismal state of mind. Mrs. Fenn, clattering round the room and lighting his fire, did not improve matters; he could tell from her demeanor that he had come home late and made a noise on the stairs. But the Mrs. Fenns of this world, he reflected irritably, were born to suffer such indignities, and the more regularly the better. He told himself this thought was not in accord with his socialist principles, but they felt as sluggish as his liver this morning.

The day was too wet for him to go out and take exercise. He sat moodily in a chair by the window, delaying an answer to Dr. Hudson-Ward, the headmaster. Lethargically, he turned to a small leather-bound volume on serpents which he had acquired in Norwich a few days earlier. After a while, a passage caught his particular attention:

Most serpents of the venomous variety, with the exception of the opisthoglyphs, release their victims from their fangs after striking. The victims die in some cases in but a few seconds, while in other cases the onset of moribundity may be delayed by hours or days. The saliva of some serpents contains not only venom but a special digestive virtue. The deadly Coral Snake of Brazil, though attaining no more than a foot in length, has this virtue in abundance. Accordingly, when it bites an animal or a human being, the victim not only dies in profound agony in a matter of seconds, but his interior parts are then dissolved, so that even the bones become no more than jelly. Then may the little serpent suck all of the victim out as a kind of soup or broth from the original wound in its skin, which latter alone remains intact.

For a long while, Gregory sat where he was in the window with the book open in his lap, thinking about the Grendon farm and about Nancy. He reproached himself for having done so little for his friends there, and gradually resolved on a plan of action the next time he rode out; but his visit was to be delayed for some days; the wet weather had set in with more determination than the end of April and the beginning of May generally allowed.

Despite that, he heard news of Grendon on the second day of rain as he took his supper with the Fenns. It was market day. Ladling stew, the baker's wife said, "That there idiot laborer on Joe Grendon's place is going to get himself locked up if he ent careful. Did you hear about him today, Master Gregory?"

"What did he do, Mrs. Fenn?"

"Why, what didn't he do? Delivered the milk round as usual, so I hear, and nobody wouldn't buy none, seeing as it has been off for the past I-don't-know-how-long. So Grubby swore terrible and vowed he had the best milk in town, and took a great sup at the churn to prove it. And then them two Betts boys started throwing stones, and of course that set Grubby off! He caught one of 'em and ducked his head in the milk, and then flung the bucket right smack through his father's nice glass window. Imagine that! So out come old man Betts and his great big missus, and they lambasts old Grubby with beansticks till he drives off cursing and vowing he'll never sell nobody good milk no more!"

The baker laughed. "That would have been a sight worth seeing of! I reckon they all gone mad out at Joe's place. Old Seeley the builder come in yesterday morning, and he reckon Joe's doing better this year than what he ever did, while everyone else round here is having a thin time. According to Seeley, Marjorie Grendon had quins, but you know old Seeley is a bit of a joker. Dr. Crouchorn would have let on if she'd had quins, I reckon."

"Dr. Crouchorn was weeping drunk last night from all accounts."

"So I hear. That ent like him, be it?"

"First time it was ever known, though they do say he liked his bottle when he was a youngster."

Listening to the gossip as it shuttled back and forth between husband and wife, Gregory found little appetite for his stew. Moodily, he returned to his room and tried to concentrate on a letter to the worthy Dr. Hudson-Ward in the county of Gloucestershire. He knew he should take the job, indeed he felt inclined to do so; but first he knew he had to see Nancy safe. The indecision he felt caused him to delay answering the doctor until the next day, when he feebly wrote that he would be glad to accept the post offered at the price offered, but begged to have a week to think about it. When he took the letter down to the post woman in The Three Poachers, the rain was still falling.

One morning, the rains were suddenly vanished, the blue and wide East Anglian skies were back, and Gregory saddled up Daisy and rode out along the miry track he had so often taken. As he arrived at the farm, Grubby and Neckland were at work in the ditch, unblocking it with shovels. He saluted them and rode in. As he was about to put the mare into the stables, he saw Grendon and Nancy standing on the patch of waste ground under the windowless east side of the house. He went slowly to join them, noting as he walked how dry the ground was here, as if no rain had fallen in a fortnight. But this observation was drowned in shock as he saw the nine little crosses Grendon was sticking into nine freshly turned mounds of earth.

Nancy stood weeping. They both looked up as Gregory approached, but Grendon went stubbornly on with his task.

"Oh, Nancy, Joseph, I'm so sorry about this!" Gregory exclaimed. "To think that they've all—but where's the parson? Where's the parson, Joseph? Why are *you* burying them, without a proper service or anything?"

"I told father, but he took no heed!" Nancy exclaimed.

Grendon had reached the last grave. He seized the last crude wooden cross, lifted it above his head, and stabbed

it down into the ground as if he would pierce the heart of
what lay under it. Only then did he straighten and speak.

"We don't need a parson here. I've no time to waste
with parsons. I have work to do if you ent."

"But these are your children, Joseph! What has got into
you?"

"They are part of the farm now, as they always was."
He turned, rolling his shirt sleeves further up his brawny
arms, and strode off in the direction of the ditching activities.

Gregory took Nancy in his arms and looked at her tear-
stained face. "What a time you must have been having
these last few days!"

"I—I thought you'd gone to Gloucester, Greg! Why
didn't you come? Every day I waited for you to come!"

"It was so wet and flooded."

"It's been lovely weather since you were last here.
Look how everything has grown!"

"It poured with rain every single day in Cottersall."

"Well, I never! That explains why there is so much water flowing in the Oast and in the ditches. But we've had
only a few light showers."

"Nancy, tell me, how did these poor little mites die?"

"I'd rather not say if you don't mind."

"Why didn't your father get in Parson Landson? How
could he be so lacking in feeling?"

"Because he didn't want anyone from the outside world
to know. That's why he's sent the builders away again.
You see—oh, I must tell you, my dear—it's mother. She
has gone completely off her head, completely! It was the
evening before last when she took her first turn outside the
back door."

"You don't mean to say she—"

"Ow, Greg, you're hurting my arms! She—she crept upstairs when we weren't noticing and she—she stifled each
of the babies in turn, Greg, under the best goose-
feather pillow."

He could feel the color leaving his cheeks. Solicitously,
she led him to the back of the house. They sat together on
the orchard railings while he digested the words in silence.

"How is your mother now, Nancy?"

"She's silent. Father had to bar her in her room for

safety. Last night she screamed a lot. But this morning she's quiet."

He looked dazedly about him. The appearance of everything was speckled, as if the return of his blood to his head had somehow infected it with a rash. The blossom had gone almost entirely from the fruit trees in the orchard, and already the embryo apples showed signs of swelling. Nearby broad beans bowed under enormous pods. Seeing his glance, Nancy dipped into her apron pocket and produced a bunch of shining, crimson radishes as big as tangerines.

"Have one of these. They're crisp and wet and hot, just as they should be."

Indifferently he accepted and bit the tempting globe. At once he had to spit the portion out. There again was that vile bitter flavor!

"Oh, but they're lovely!" Nancy protested.

"Not even 'rather strange' now—simply 'lovely'? Nancy, don't you see, something uncanny and awful is taking place here. I'm sorry, but I can't see otherwise. You and your father should leave here at once."

"*Leave* here, Greg? Just because you don't like the taste of these lovely radishes? How can we leave here? Where should we go? See this here house? My granddad died here, and his father before him. It's our *place*. We can't just up and off, not even after this bit of trouble. Try another radish."

"For heaven's sake, Nancy, they taste as if the flavor was intended for creatures with a palate completely different from ours . . . Oh . . ." He stared at her. "And perhaps they are. Nancy, I tell you—"

He broke off, sliding from the railing. Neckland had come up from one side, still plastered in mud from his work in the ditch, his collarless shirt flapping open. In his hand, he grasped an ancient and military-looking pistol.

"I'll fire this if you come nearer," he said. "It goes okay, never worry, and it's loaded, Master Gregory. Now you're a-going to listen to me!"

"Bert, put that thing away!" Nancy exclaimed. She moved forward to him, but Gregory pulled her back and stood before her.

"Don't be a bloody idiot, Neckland. Put it away!"

"I'll shoot you, bor, I'll shoot you, I swear, if you mucks

about." His eyes were glaring, and the look on his dark face left no doubt that he meant what he said. "You're going to swear to me that you're going to clear off of this farm on that nag of yours and never come back again."

"I'm going straight to tell my father, Bert," Nancy warned.

The pistol twitched.

"If you move, Nancy, I warn you I'll shoot this fine chap of yours in the leg. Besides, your father don't care about Master Gregory anymore—he's got better things to worry him."

"Like finding out what's happening here?" Gregory said. "Listen, Neckland, we're all in trouble. This farm is being run by a group of nasty little monsters. You can't see them because they're invisible—"

The gun exploded. As he spoke, Nancy had attempted to run off. Without hesitating, Neckland fired down at Gregory's knees. Gregory felt the shot pluck his trouser leg and knew himself unharmed. With the knowledge came rage. He flung himself at Neckland and hit him hard over the heart. Falling back, Neckland dropped the pistol and swung his fist wildly. Gregory struck him again. As he did so, the other grabbed him and they began furiously hitting each other. When Gregory broke free, Neckland grappled with him again. There was more pummeling of ribs.

"Let me go, you swine!" Gregory shouted. He hooked his foot behind Neckland's ankle, and they both rolled over onto the grass. At this point, a sort of flood bank had been raised long ago between the house and the low-lying orchard. Down this the two men rolled, fetching up sharply against the stone wall of the kitchen. Neckland got the worst of it, catching his head on the corner, and lay there stunned. Gregory found himself looking at two feet encased in ludicrous stockings. Slowly, he rose to his feet, and confronted Mrs. Grendon at less than a yard's distance. She was smiling.

He stood there, and gradually straightened his back, looking at her anxiously.

"So there you are, Jackie, my Jackalums," she said. The smile was wider now and less like a smile. "I wanted to talk to you. You are the one who knows about the things that walk on the lines, aren't you?"

"I don't understand, Mrs. Grendon."

"Don't call me that there daft old name, sonnie. You know all about the little grey things that aren't supposed to be there, don't you?"

"Oh, those . . . Suppose I said I did know?"

"The other naughty children will pretend they don't know what I mean, but you know, don't you? You know about the little grey things."

The sweat stood out on his brow. She had moved nearer. She stood close, staring into his eyes, not touching him; but he was acutely conscious that she could touch him at any moment. From the corner of his eye, he saw Neckland stir and crawl away from the house, but there were other things to occupy him.

"These little grey things," he said. "Did you save the nine babies from them?"

"They gray things wanted to kiss them, you see, but I couldn't let them. I was clever. I hid them under the goose-feather pillow and now even *I* can't find them." She began to laugh, making a horrible low whirring sound in her throat.

"They're small and grey and wet, aren't they?" Gregory said sharply. "They've got big feet, webbed like frogs, but they're heavy and short, aren't they, and they have fangs like a snake, haven't they?"

She looked doubtful. Then her eye seemed to catch a movement. She looked fixedly to one side. "Here come one now, the female one," she said.

Gregory turned to look where she did. Nothing was visible. His mouth was dry. "How many are there, Mrs. Grendon?"

Then he saw the short grass stir, flatten, and rise near at hand, and let out a cry of alarm. Wrenching off his riding boot, he swung it in an arc, low above the ground. It struck something concealed in thin air. Almost at once, he received a terrific kick in the thigh and fell backwards. Despite the hurt, fear made him jump up immediately.

Mrs. Grendon was changing. Her mouth collapsed as if it would run off one corner of her face. Her head sagged to one side. Her shoulders fell. A deep crimson blush momentarily suffused her features, then drained, and as it drained she dwindled like a deflated rubber balloon. Gregory sank to his knees, whimpering, buried his face in his palms and pressed his hands to the grass. Darkness overcame him.

His senses must have left him only for a moment. When he pulled himself up again, the almost empty bag of woman's clothes was still settling slowly on the ground.

"Joseph! Joseph!" he yelled. Nancy had fled. In a distracted mixture of panic and fury, he dragged his boot on again and rushed round the house towards the cowsheds.

Neckland stood halfway between barn and mill, rubbing his skull. In his rattled state, the sight of Gregory apparently in full pursuit made him run away.

"Neckland!" Gregory shouted. He ran like mad for the other. Neckland bolted for the mill, jumped inside, tried to pull the door to, lost his nerve, and ran up the wooden stairs. Gregory bellowed after him.

The pursuit took them right up to the top of the mill. Neckland had lost too much wit even to kick over the bolt of the trapdoor. Gregory burst it and climbed out panting. Thoroughly cowed, Neckland backed towards the opening until he was almost out on the little platform above the sails.

"You'll fall out, you idiot," Gregory warned. "Listen, Neckland, you have no reason to fear me. I want no enmity between us. There's a bigger enemy we must fight. Look!"

He came towards the low door and looked down at the dark surface of the pond. Neckland grabbed the overhead pulley for security and said nothing.

"Look down at the pond," Gregory said. "That's where the Aurigans live. My God—Bert, look, there goes one!"

The urgency in his voice made the farmhand look down where he pointed. Together, the two men watched as a depression slid over the black water; an overlapping chain of ripples swung back from it. At approximately the middle of the pond, the depression became a commotion. A small whirlpool formed and died, and the ripples began to settle.

"There's your ghost, Bert," Gregory gasped. "That must have been the one that got poor Mrs. Grendon. Now do you believe?"

"I never heard of a ghost as lived under water," Neckland gasped.

"A ghost never harmed anyone—we've already had a sample of what these terrifying things can do. Come on, Bert, shake hands, understand I bear you no hard feelings. Oh, come on, man! I know how you feel about Nancy, but she must be free to make her own choice in life."

They shook hands and grinned rather foolishly at each other.

"We better go and tell the farmer what we seen," Neckland said. "I reckon that thing done what happened to Lardie last evening."

"Lardie? What's happened to her? I thought I hadn't seen her today."

"Same as happened to the little pigs. I found her just inside the barn. Just her coat was left, that's all. No insides! Like she'd been sucked dry."

"Let's go, Bert."

It took Gregory twenty minutes to summon the council of war on which he had set his mind. The party gathered in the farmhouse in the parlor. By this time, Nancy had somewhat recovered from the shock of her mother's death and sat in an armchair with a shawl about her shoulders. Her father stood nearby with his arms folded, looking impatient, while Bert Neckland lounged by the door. Only Grubby was not present. He had been told to get on with the ditching.

"I'm going to have another attempt to convince you all that you are in very grave danger," Gregory said. "You won't see it for yourselves, so I—"

He paused. There was a dragging noise on the landing upstairs, a board creaked.

"Who the devil's up there?" Grendon growled. He made towards the stairwell.

"Don't go, father!" Nancy screamed, but her father flung open the door and made his way up. Gregory bit his lip. The Aurigans had never ventured into the house before.

In a moment, Grendon returned with a monstrous piglet in his arms.

"Keep the confounded animals out of the house, Nancy," he said, pushing the creature squealing out of the front door.

The interruption made Gregory realize how his nerves

still jangled. He set his back to the sawdust-filled parody
of a goat watching them from its case and spoke quickly.

"The situation is that we're all animals together at present. Do you remember that strange meteor that fell out of
the sky last winter, Joseph? And do you remember that
ill-smelling dew early in the spring. They were not un-
connected, and they are connected with all that's happen-
pening now. That meteor was a space machine of some
sort, I firmly believe, and it brought in it a kind of life
that—that is not so much hostile to terrestrial life as
indifferent to its quality. The creatures from that machine—I call them Aurigans—spread the dew over the
farm. It was a growth accelerator, a manure or fertilizer
that speeds growth in plants and animals."

"So much better for us!" Grendon said.

"But it's not better. The things grow wildly, yes, but the
taste is altered to suit the palates of those things out there.
You've seen what happened. You can't sell anything.
People won't touch your eggs or milk or meat—they
taste too foul."

"But that's a lot of nonsense. We'll sell in Norwich.
Our produce is better than it ever was. We eat it, don't
we?"

"Yes, Joseph, *you* eat it. But anyone who eats at your
table is doomed. Don't you understand—you are all 'fer-
tilized' just as surely as the pigs and chickens. Your place
has been turned into a superfarm, and you are all meat to
the Aurigans."

That set a silence in the room until Nancy said in a small
voice, "You don't believe such a terrible thing."

"I suppose these unseen creatures told you all this?"
Grendon said truculently.

"Judge by the evidence, as I do. Your wife—I must be
brutal, Joseph—your wife was eaten, like the dog and the
pigs. As everything else will be in time. The Aurigans
aren't even cannibals. They aren't like us. They don't care
whether we have souls or intelligences any more than we
really care whether the bullocks have."

"No one's going to eat me," Neckland said, looking de-
cidedly white about the gills.

"How can you stop them? They're invisible, and I think
they can strike like snakes. They're aquatic and I think
they may be only two feet tall. How can you protect your-

self?" He turned to the farmer. "Joseph, the danger is very great and not only to us here. At first, they may have offered us no harm while they got the measure of us—otherwise I'd have died in your rowing boat. Now there's no longer doubt of their hostile intent. I beg you to let me go to Heigham and telephone to the chief of police in Norwich, or at least to the local militia, to get them to come and help us."

The farmer shook his head slowly and pointed a finger at Gregory.

"You soon forgot them talks we had, bor, all about the coming age of socialism and how the powers of the state was going to wither away. Directly we get a bit of trouble, you want to call in the authorities. There's no harm here a few savage dogs like my old Cuff can't handle, and I don't say as I ent going to get a couple of dogs, but you'm a fule if you reckon I'm getting the authorities down here. Fine old socialist you turn out to be!"

"You have no room to talk about that!" Gregory exclaimed. "Why didn't you let Grubby come here? If you were a socialist, you'd treat the men as you treat yourself. Instead, you leave him out in the ditch. I wanted him to hear this discussion."

The farmer leaned threateningly across the table at him.

"Oh, you did, did you? Since when was this your farm? And Grubby can come and go as he likes when it's his, so put that in your pipe and smoke it, bor! Who do you think you are?" He moved closer to Gregory, apparently happy to work off his fears as anger. "You'm trying to scare us all off this here little old bit of ground, ent you? Well, the Grendons ent a scaring sort, see! Now I'll tell you something. See that rifle there on the wall? That be loaded. And if you ent off this farm by midday, that rifle ont be on that wall no more. It'll be here, bor, right here in my two hands, and I'll be letting you have it right where you'll feel it most."

"You can't do that, father," Nancy said. "You know Gregory is a friend of ours."

"For God's sake, Joseph," Gregory said, "see where your enemy lies. Bert, tell Mr. Grendon what we saw on the pond, go on."

Neckland was far from keen to be dragged into this argument. He scratched his head, drew a red-and-white-spotted kerchief from round his neck to wipe his face, and muttered, "We saw a sort of ripple on the water, but I didn't see nothing really, Master Gregory. I mean, it could have been the wind, couldn't it?"

"Now you be warned, Gregory," the farmer repeated. "You be off my land by noon by the sun, and that mare of yours, or I ont answer for it." He marched out into the pale sunshine, and Neckland followed.

Nancy and Gregory stood staring at each other. He took her hands, and they were cold.

"You believe what I was saying, Nancy?"

"Is that why the food did at one point taste bad to us, and then soon tasted well enough again?"

"It can only have been that at that time your systems were not fully adjusted to the poison. Now they are. You're being fed up, Nancy, just like the livestock—I'm sure of it! I fear for you, darling love, I fear so much. What are we to do? Come back to Cottersall with me! Mrs. Fenn has another fine little drawing room upstairs that I'm sure she would rent."

"Now you're talking nonsense, Greg! How can I? What would people say? No, you go away for now and let the tempest of father's wrath abate, and if you could come back tomorrow, you will find he will be milder for sure, because I plan to wait on him tonight and talk to him about you. Why, he's half daft with grief and doesn't know what he says."

"All right, my darling. But stay inside as much as you can. The Aurigans have not come indoors yet, as far as we know, and it may be safer here. And lock all the doors and put the shutters over the windows before you go to bed. And get your father to take that rifle of his upstairs with him."

The evenings were lengthening with confidence towards summer now, and Bruce Fox arrived home before sunset. As he jumped from his bicycle this evening, he found his friend Gregory impatiently awaiting him.

They went indoors together and, while Fox ate a large tea, Gregory told him what had been happening at the farm that day.

"You're in trouble," Fox said. "Look, tomorrow's Sunday. I'll skip church and come out with you. You need help."

"Joseph may shoot me. He'll be certain to if I bring along a stranger. You can help me tonight by telling me where I can purchase a young dog straight away to protect Nancy."

"Nonsense, I'm coming with you. I can't bear hearing all this at second hand anyhow. We'll pick up a pup in any event—the blacksmith has a litter to be rid of. Have you got any plan of action?"

"Plan? No, not really."

"You must have a plan. Grendon doesn't scare too easily, does he?"

"I imagine he's scared well enough. Nancy says he's scared. He just isn't imaginative enough to see what he can do but carry on working as hard as possible."

"Look, I know these farmers. They won't believe anything till you rub their noses in it. What we must do is *show* him an Aurigan."

"Oh, splendid, Bruce. And how do you catch one?"

"You trap one."

"Don't forget they're invisible—hey, Bruce, yes, by Jove, you're right! I've the very idea! Look, we've nothing more to worry about if we can trap one. We can trap the lot, however many there are, and we can kill the little horrors when we have trapped them."

Fox grinned over the top of a chunk of cherry cake. "We're agreed, I suppose, that these Aurigans aren't socialist utopians any longer?"

It helped a great deal, Gregory thought, to be able to visualize roughly what the alien life form looked like. The volume on serpents had been a happy find, for not only did it give an idea of how the Aurigans must be able to digest their prey so rapidly—"a kind of soup or broth"—but presumably it gave a clue to their appearance. To live in a space machine, they would probably be fairly small, and they seemed to be semiaquatic. It all went to make up a picture of a strange being: skin perhaps scaled like a fish, great flipper feet like a frog, barrel-like diminutive stature, and a tiny head with two great fangs in the jaw. There was no doubt that the invisibility cloaked a really ugly-looking dwarf!

As the macabre image passed through his head, Gregory and Bruce Fox were preparing their trap. Fortunately Grendon had offered no resistance to their entering the farm; Nancy had evidently spoken to good effect. And he had suffered another shock. Five fowls had been reduced to little but feathers and skin that morning almost before his eyes, and he was as a result sullen and indifferent to what went on. Now he was out in a distant field, working, and the two young men were allowed to carry out their plans unmolested—though not without an occasional anxious glance at the pond—while a worried Nancy looked on from the farmhouse window.

She had with her a sturdy young mongrel dog of eight months, which Gregory and Bruce had brought along, called Gyp. Grendon had obtained two ferocious hounds from a distant neighbor. These wide-mouthed brutes were secured on long running chains that enabled them to patrol from the horse trough by the pond, down the west side of the house almost to the elms and the bridge leading over to West Field. They barked stridently most of the time and seemed to cause a general unease among the other animals, all of which gave voice restlessly this forenoon.

The dogs would be a difficulty, Nancy had said, for they refused to touch any of the food the farm could provide. It was hoped they would take it when they became hungry enough.

Grendon had planted a great board by the farm gate and on the board had painted a notice telling everyone to keep away.

Armed with pitchforks, the two young men carried flour sacks out from the mill and placed them at strategic positions across the yard as far as the gate. Gregory went to the cowsheds and let out one of the calves there on a length of binder twine under the very teeth of the barking dogs—he only hoped they would prove as hostile to the Aurigans as they seemed to be to human life.

As he was pulling the calf across the yard, Grubby appeared.

"You'd better stay away from us, Grubby. We're trying to trap one of the ghosts."

"Master, if I catch one, I shall strangle him, straight I will."

"A pitchfork is a better weapon. These ghosts are dangerous little beasts at close quarters."

"I'm strong, bor, I tell 'ee! I'd strangle un!"

To prove his point, Grubby rolled his striped and tattered sleeve even further up his arm and exposed to Gregory and Fox his enormous biceps. At the same time, he wagged his great heavy head and lolled his tongue out of his mouth, perhaps to demonstrate some of the effects of strangulation.

"It's a very fine arm," Gregory agreed. "But look, Grubby, we have a better idea. We are going to do this ghost to death with pitchforks; if you want to join in, you'd better get a spare one from the stable."

Grubby looked at him with a sly-shy expression and stroked his throat. "I'd be better at strangling, bor. I've always wanted to strangle someone."

"Why should you want to do that, Grubby?"

The laborer lowered his voice. "I always wanted to see how difficult it would be. I'm strong, you see. I got my strength up as a lad doing some of this here strangling— but never men, you know, just cattle."

Backing away a pace, Gregory said, "This time, Grubby, it's pitchforks for us." To settle the issue, he went into the stables, got a pitchfork, and returned to thrust it into Grubby's hand.

"Let's get on with it," Fox said.

They were all ready to start. Fox and Grubby crouched down in the ditch on either side of the gate, weapons at the ready. Gregory emptied one of the bags of flour over the yard in a patch just before the gate so that anyone leaving the farm would have to walk through it. Then he led the calf towards the pond.

The young animal set up an uneasy mooing, and most of the beasts nearby seemed to answer. The chickens and hens scattered about the yard in the pale sunshine as if demented. Gregory felt the sweat trickle down his back, although his skin was cold with the chemistries of suspense. With a slap on its rump, he forced the calf into the water of the pond. It stood there unhappily until he led it out again and slowly back across the yard, past the mill and the grain store on his right, past Mrs. Grendon's neglected flowerbed on his left, towards the gate where his allies waited. And for all his determination not to do so, he could not stop himself looking backwards at the leaden surface of the pond to see if anything followed him. He led the calf through the gate and stopped. No tracks but his and the calf's showed in the strewn flour.

"Try it again," Fox advised. "Perhaps they are taking a nap down there."

Gregory went through the routine again, and a third and fourth time, on each occasion smoothing the flour after he had been through it. Each time, he saw Nancy watching helplessly from the house. Each time he felt a little more sick with tension.

Yet when it happened, it took him by surprise. He had got the calf to the gate for a fifth time when Fox's shout joined the chorus of animal noises. The pond had shown no special ripple so the Aurigan had come from some dark-purposed prowl of the farm—suddenly its finned footsteps were marking the flour.

Yelling with excitement, Gregory dropped the rope that led the calf and ducked to one side. Seizing up an opened bag of flour by the gatepost, he flung its contents before the advancing figure.

The bomb of flour exploded all over the Aurigan. Now it was revealed in chalky outline. Despite himself, Gregory found himself screaming in terror as the ghastliness was revealed in whirling white. It was especially the size that frightened: this dread thing, remote from human form, was too big for earthly nature—ten feet high, perhaps twelve! Invincible and horribly quick, it came rushing forward with unnumbered arms striking out towards him.

Next morning, Dr. Crouchorn and his silk hat appeared at Gregory's bedside, thanked Mrs. Fenn for some hot water, and dressed Gregory's leg wound.

"You got off lightly, considering," the old man said. "But if you will take a piece of advice from me, Mr. Rolles, you will cease to visit the Grendon farm. It's an evil place and you'll come to no good there."

Gregory nodded. He had told the doctor nothing except that Grendon had run up and shot him in the leg; which was true enough, but that it omitted most of the story.

"When will I be up again, doctor?"

"Oh, young flesh heals soon enough, or undertakers would be rich men and doctors paupers. A few days should see you right as rain. But I'll be visiting you again tomorrow, until when you are to stay flat on your back and keep that leg motionless."

"I understand."

The doctor made a ferocious face. "You understand but will you take heed? I'm warning you, if you take one step on that leg, it will turn purple and fall off." He nodded slowly and emphatically, and the lines on his face deepened to such a great extent that anyone familiar with the eccentricities of his physiognomy would be inclined to estimate that he was smiling.

"I suppose I may write a letter, doctor?"

"I suppose you may, young man."

Directly Dr. Crouchorn had gone, Gregory took pen and paper and addressed some urgent lines to Nancy. They told her that he loved her very much and could not bear to think of her remaining on the farm; that he could not get to see her for a few days because of his leg wound; and that she must immediately come away on Hetty with a bag full of her things and stay at The Wayfarer, where there was a capital room for which he would pay. That if she thought anything of him, she must put the simple plan into action this very day, and send him word round from the inn when she was established there.

With some satisfaction, Gregory read this through twice, signed it and added kisses, and summoned Mrs. Fenn with the aid of a small bell she had provided for that purpose.

He told her that the delivery of the letter was a matter of extreme urgency. He would entrust it to Tommy, the baker's boy, to deliver when his morning round was over, and would give him a shilling for his efforts. Mrs. Fenn was not enthusiastic about this, but with a little flattery was persuaded to speak to Tommy. She left the bedroom clutching both letter and shilling.

At once, Gregory began another letter, this one to Mr. H. G. Wells. It was some while since he had last addressed his correspondent, and so he had to make a somewhat lengthy report; but eventually he came to the events of the previous day.

●

So horrified was I by the sight of the Aurigan (he wrote) that I stood where I was, unable to move, while the flour blew about us. And how can I now convey to you—who are perhaps the most interested person in this vital subject in all the British Isles— what the monster looked like, outlined in white? My impressions were, of course, both brief and indefinite, but the main handicap is that there is nothing on Earth to liken this weird being to!

It appeared, I suppose, most like some horrendous goose, but the neck must be imagined as almost as thick as the body—indeed, it was almost all body, or all neck, whichever way you look at it. And on top of this neck was no head but a terrible array of various sorts of arms, a nest of writhing cilia, antennae, and whips, for all the world as if an octopus were entangled with a Portuguese Man-o'-war as big as itself, with a few shrimp and starfish legs thrown in. Does this sound ludicrous? I can only swear to you that as it bore down on me, perhaps twice my own height or more, I found it something almost too terrifying for human eyes to look on—and yet I did not see it, but merely the flour that adhered to it!

That repulsive sight would have been the last my eyes ever dwelt on had it not been for Grubby, the simple farmhand I have had occasion to mention before.

As I threw the flour, Grubby gave a great cry and rushed forward, dropping the pitchfork. He jumped at the creature as it turned on me. This put out our plan, which was that he and Bruce Fox should pitchfork the creature to death. Instead, he grasped it as high as he possibly could and commenced to squeeze with the full force of his mighty muscles. What a terrifying contest! What a fear-fraught combat!

Collecting his wits, Bruce charged forward and attacked with his pitchfork. It was his battle cry that brought me back from my paralysis into action. I ran and seized Grubby's pitchfork and also charged. That thing had arms for us all! It struck out, and I have no doubt now that several arms held poisoned needle teeth for I saw one come towards me, gaping like a snake's mouth. Need I stress the danger—particularly when you recall that the effect of the flour cloud was only partial, and there were still invisible arms flailing round us!

Our saving was that the Aurigan was cowardly. I saw Bruce jab it hard, and a second later I rammed my pitchfork right through its foot. At once it had had enough. Grubby fell to the ground as it retreated. It moved at amazing speed, back towards the pool. We were in pursuit! And all the beasts of the barnyard uttered their cries to it.

As it launched itself into the water, we both flung our pitchforks at its form. But it swam out strongly and then dived below the surface, leaving only ripples and a scummy trail of flour.

We stood staring at the water for an instant and then with common accord ran back to Grubby. He was dead. He lay face up and was no longer recognizable. The Aurigan must have struck him with its poisoned fangs as soon as he attacked. Grubby's skin was stretched tight and glistened oddly. He had turned a dull crimson. All his internal substance had been transformed to liquid by the rapid-working venoms of the Aurigan; he was like a sort of giant, man-shaped, rotten haggis.

There were wound marks across his neck and throat and what had been his face, and from these wounds his substance drained so that he slowly deflated into his trampled bed of flour and dust. Perhaps the sight of the fabled Medusa's head, that turned men to stone, was no worse than this, for we stood there utterly paralyzed. It was a blast from Farmer Grendon's rifle that brought us back to life.

He had threatened to shoot me. Now seeing us despoiling his flour stocks and apparently about to make off with a calf, he fired at us. We had no choice but to run for it. Grendon was in no explaining mood. Good Nancy came running out to stop him, but Neckland was charging up, too, with the pair of savage dogs growling at the end of their chains.

Bruce and I had ridden up on my Daisy. I had left her saddled. Bringing her out of the stable at a trot, I heaved Bruce up into the saddle and was about to climb on myself when the gun went off again and I felt a burning pain in my leg. Bruce dragged me into the saddle and we were off—I half unconscious.

Here I lie now in bed, and should be about again in a couple of days. Fortunately the shot did not harm any bones.

So you see how the farm is now a place of the damned! Once, I thought it might even become a new Eden, growing the food of the gods for men like gods. Instead—alas! the first meeting between humanity and beings from another world has proved disastrous, and the Eden is become a battleground for a war of worlds. How can our anticipations for the future be anything other than gloomy?

Before I close this over-long account, I must answer a query in your letter and pose another to you, more personal than yours to me.

First, you question if the Aurigans are entirely invisible and say—if I may quote your letter—"Any alteration in the refractive index of the eye lenses would make vision impossible, but without such alteration the eyes would be visible as glassy globules. And for vision it is also necessary that there should be visual purple behind the retina and an opaque cornea. How then do your Aurigans manage for vision?" The answer must be that they do without eyesight as we know it, for I naturally think they maintain a complete invisibility. How they "see" I know not, but whatever sense they use, it is effective. How they communicate I know not—our fellow made not the slightest sound when I speared his foot! —yet it is apparent they must communicate effectively. Perhaps they tried originally to communicate with us through a mysterious sense we do not possess and, on receiving no answer, assumed us to be as dumb as our dumb animals. If so, what a tragedy!

Now to my personal inquiry. I know, sir, that you must grow more busy as you grow more famous; but I feel that what transpires here in this remote corner of East Anglia is of momentous import to the world and the future. Could you not take it upon yourself to pay us a visit here? You would be comfortable at one of our two inns, and the journey here by railway is efficient if tedious—you can easily get a regular wagon from Heigham station here, a distance of only eight miles. You could then view Grendon's farm for yourself, and perhaps one of these interstellar beings too. I feel you are as much amused as concerned by the accounts you receive from the undersigned, but I swear not one detail is exaggerated. Say you can come!

If you need persuasion, reflect on how much delight it will give to:

> 'Your sincere admirer and friend,
> GREGORY ROLLES.'

Reading this long letter through, scratching out two superfluous adjectives, Gregory lay back in some satisfaction. He had the feeling he was still involved in the struggle although temporarily out of action.

But the late afternoon brought him disquieting news. Tommy the baker's boy had gone out as far as the Grendon farm. Then the ugly legends circulating in the village about the place had risen in his mind, and he had stood wondering whether he should go on. An unnatural babble of animal noise came from the farm, mixed with hammering, and when Tommy crept forward and saw the farmer himself looking as black as a puddle and building a great thing like a gibbet in the yard, he had lost his nerve and rushed back the way he came, the letter to Nancy undelivered.

Bruce Fox arrived that evening to see how his friend was, and Gregory tried to persuade him to take the letter. But Fox was successfully able to plead a prior engagement. They talked for a while, mainly running over the horrors of the previous day once more, and then Fox left.

Gregory lay on the bed worrying about Nancy until Mrs. Fenn brought up supper on a tray. At least it was clear now why the Aurigans had not entered the farmhouse; they were far too large to do so. She was safe as long as she kept indoors—as far as anyone on that doomed plot was safe.

He fell asleep early that night. In the early hours of the morning, a nightmare visited him. He was in a strange city where all the buildings were new and the people wore shining clothes. In one square grew a tree. The Gregory in the dream stood in a special relationship to the tree: he fed it. It was his job to push people who were passing by the tree against its surface. The tree was a saliva tree. Down its smooth bark ran quantities of saliva from red lips like leaves up in the boughs. It grew enormous on the people on which it fed. As they were thrown against it, they passed into the substance of the tree. Some of the saliva splashed onto Gregory. But instead of dissolving him, it caused everything he touched to be dissolved. He put his arms about the girl he loved, and as his mouth went towards hers, her skin peeled away from her face.

He woke weeping desperately and fumbling blindly for the ring of the gas mantle.

Dr. Crouchorn came late next morning and told Gregory he should have at least three more days complete rest for the recovery of the muscles of his leg. Gregory lay there in a state of acute dissatisfaction with himself. Recalling the vile dream, he thought how negligent he had been towards Nancy, the girl he loved. His letter to her still lay undelivered by his bedside. After Mrs. Fenn had brought up his dinner, he determined that he must see Nancy for himself. Leaving the food, he pulled himself out of bed and dressed slowly.

The leg was more painful than he had expected, but he got himself downstairs and out to the stable without too much trouble. Daisy seemed pleased to see him. He rubbed her nose and rested his head against her long cheek in sheer pleasure at being with her again.

"This may be the last time you have to undertake this particular journey, my girl," he said.

Saddling her was comparatively easy. Getting into the saddle involved much bodily anguish. But eventually he was comfortable and they turned along the familiar and desolate road to the domain of the Aurigans. His leg was worse than he had bargained for. More than once, he had to get the mare to stop while he let the throbbing subside. He saw he was losing blood plentifully.

As he approached the farm, he observed what the baker's boy had meant by saying Grendon was building a gibbet. A pole had been set up in the middle of the yard. A cable ran to the top of it, and a light was rigged there so that the expanse of the yard could be illuminated by night.

Another change had taken place. A wooden fence had been built behind the horse trough, cutting off the pond from the farm. But at one point, ominously, a section of it had been broken down and splintered and crushed, as if some monstrous thing had walked through the barrier unheeding.

A ferocious dog was chained just inside the gate, barking its head off to the consternation of the poultry. Gregory dare not enter. As he stood pondering the best way to tackle this fresh problem, the door of the farmhouse opened and Nancy peeped out. He called and signaled frantically to her.

Timidly she ran across and let him in, dragging the dog back. Gregory hitched Daisy to the gatepost and kissed her cheek, soothed by the feel of her sturdy body in his arms.

"Where's your father?"

"My dearest, your leg, your poor leg! It's bleeding yet!"

"Never mind my leg. Where's your father?"

"He's down in South Meadow, I think."

"Good! I'm going to speak with him. Nancy, I want you to go indoors and pack some belongings. I'm taking you away with me."

"I can't leave father!"

"You must. I'm going to tell him now." As he limped across the yard, she called fearfully, "He has that there gun of his'n with him all the time—do be careful!"

The two dogs on a running chain followed him all the way down the side of the house, almost choking in their efforts to get at him, their teeth flashing uncomfortably close to his ankles.

Near the elms he saw that several wild birds lay in the grass. One was still fluttering feebly. He could only assume they had worn themselves out trying to feed their immense and hungry broods. Which was what would happen to the farmer in time, he reflected. He noticed Neckland below Grubby's little hut, busy sawing wood; the farmer was not with him. On impulse, Gregory turned into the sties.

It was gloomy there. In the gloom, Grendon worked. He dropped his bucket when he saw Gregory there and came forward threateningly.

"You come back? Why don't you stay away? Can't you see the notice by the gate? I don't want you here no more, bor. I know you mean well, and I intend you no harm, but I'll kill 'ee, understand, kill 'ee if you ever come here again. I've plenty of worries without you to add to them. Now then, get you going!"

Gregory stood his ground.

"Mr. Grendon, are you as mad as your wife was before she died? Do you understand that you may meet Grubby's fate at any moment? Do you realize what you are harboring in your pond?"

"I ent a fule. But suppose them there things do eat everything, humans included? Suppose this is now their farm? They still got to have someone tend it. So I reckon they ent going to harm me. So long as they sees me work hard, they ent going to harm me."

"You're being fattened, do you understand? For all the hard work you do, you must have put on a stone this last month. Doesn't that scare you?"

Something of the farmer's pose broke for a moment. He cast a wild look round. "I ent saying I ent scared. I'm saying I'm doing what I have to do. We don't own our lives. Now do me a favor and get out of here."

Instinctively Gregory's glance had followed Grendon's. For the first time, he saw in the dimness the size of the pigs. Their great broad, black backs were visible over the top of the sties. They were the size of young oxen.

"This is a farm of death," he said.

"Death's always the end of all of us, pig or cow or man alike."

"Right-ho, Mr. Grendon, you can think like that if you like. It's not my way of thinking, nor am I going to see your dependants suffer from your madness. Mr. Grendon, sir, I wish to ask for your daughter's hand in marriage."

For the first three days that she was away from her home, Nancy Grendon lay in her room in The Wayfarer near to death. It seemed as if all ordinary food poisoned her. But gradually under Dr. Crouchorn's ministration—terrified perhaps by the rage she suspected he would vent upon her should she fail to get better—she recovered her strength.

"You look so much better today," Gregory said, clasping her hand. "You'll soon be up and about again, once your system is free of all the evil nourishment of the farm."

"Greg, dearest, promise me you will not go to the farm again. You have no need to go now I'm not there."

He cast his eyes down and said, "Then you don't have to get me to promise, do you?"

"I just want to be sure we neither of us go there again. Father, I feel sure, bears a charmed life. But I . . . I feel now as if I'm waking from a nightmare!"

"Don't think about it! Look, I've brought you some flowers!"

He produced a clay pot overloaded with wallflowers with gigantic blooms and gave it to her.

She smiled and said, "They're so large! Greg, they're, they're from the farm, aren't they? They're unnaturally large."

"I thought you'd like a souvenir of the nicer side of your home."

With all her strength, she hurled the pot across the room. It struck the door and broke. The dark earth scattered over the boards, and the flowers lay broken on the floor.

"You dare bring the curse in here! And, Greg, this means you've been back to the farm, doesn't it, since we come away together?"

He nodded his head, looking defiantly at her. "I had to see what was happening."

"Please don't go there again, Greg, please. It's as if I was now coming to my senses again—but I don't want it to be as if you was losing yours! Supposing those things followed us here to Cottersall, those Aurigans?"

"You know, Nancy, I've wondered several times why they remain on the farm as they do. You would think that once they found they could so easily defeat human beings, they would attack everyone, or send for more of their own kind and try to invade us. Yet they seem perfectly content to remain in that one small space."

She smiled. "I may not be very clever compared with

you, but I tell 'ee the answer to that one. They ent interested in going anywhere. I think there's just two of them,
and they come to our little old world for a holiday in their
space machine, same as we might go to Great Yarmouth
for a couple of days for our honeymoon. Perhaps they're
on their honeymoon."

"On honeymoon! What a ghastly idea!"

"Well, on holiday then. That was father's idea—he
says as there's just two of them, treating Earth as a quiet
place to stay. People like to eat well when they're on holiday, don't they?"

He stared at Nancy aghast.

"But that's horrible! You're trying to make the Aurigans out to be *pleasant!*"

"Of course I ent, you silly ha'p'orth! But I expect they
seem pleasant to each other."

"Well, I prefer to think of them as menaces."

"All the more reason for you to keep away from
them!"

But to be out of sight was not to be out of mind's reach.
Gregory received another letter from Dr. Hudson-Ward, a
kind and encouraging one, but he made no attempt to
answer it. He felt he could not bear to take up any work
that would remove him from the neighborhood, although
the need to work, in view of his matrimonial plans, was
now pressing; the modest allowance his father made him
would not support two in any comfort. Yet he could not
bring his thought to grapple with such practical problems. It was another letter he looked for, and the horrors of the farm that obsessed him. And the next night, he
dreamed of the saliva tree again.

In the evening, he plucked up enough courage to tell
Fox and Nancy about it. They met in the little snug at
the back of The Wayfarer's public bars, a discreet and
private place with red plush on the seats. Nancy was her
usual self again and had been out for a brief walk in the
afternoon sunshine.

"People wanted to give themselves to the saliva tree.
And although I didn't see this for myself, I had the distinct feeling that perhaps they weren't actually killed so
much as changed into something else—something less human maybe. And this time, I saw the tree was made of
metal of some kind and was growing bigger and bigger

by pumps—you could see through the saliva tree to big armatures and pistons, and out of the branches steam was pouring."

Fox laughed, a little unsympathetically. "Sounds to me like the shape of things to come when even plants are grown by machinery. Events are preying on your mind, Greg! Listen, my sister is going to Norwich tomorrow, driving in her uncle's trap. Why don't the two of you go with her? She's going to buy some adornments for her bridal gown, so that should interest you, Nancy. Then you could stay with Greg's uncle for a couple of days. I assure you I will let you know immediately if the Aurigans invade Cottersall, so you won't miss anything."

Nancy seized Gregory's arm. "Can we please, Gregory, can we? I ent been to Norwich for long enough and it's a fine city."

"It would be a good idea," he said doubtfully.

Both of them pressed him until he was forced to yield. He broke up the little party as soon as he decently could, kissed Nancy goodnight, and walked hurriedly back down the street to the baker's. Of one thing he was certain: if he must leave the district even for a short while, he had to see what was happening at the farm before he went.

The farm looked in the summer's dusk as it had never done before. Massive wooden screens nine feet high had been erected and hastily creosoted. They stood about in forlorn fashion, intended to keep the public gaze from the farm, but lending it unmeaning. They stood not only in the yard but at irregular intervals along the boundaries of the land, inappropriately among fruit trees, desolately amid bracken, irrelevantly in swamp. A sound of furious hammering punctuated by the unwearying animal noises indicated that more screens were still being built.

But what lent the place its unearthly look was the lighting. The solitary pole supporting electric light now had five companions: one by the gate, one by the pond, one behind the house, one outside the engine house, one down by the pigsties. Their hideous yellow glare reduced the scene to the sort of unlikely picture that might be found and puzzled over in the eternal midnight of an Egyptian tomb.

Gregory was too wise to try and enter by the gate. He

hitched Daisy to the low branches of a thorn tree and set off over waste land, entering Grendon's property by the South Meadow. As he walked stealthily towards the distant outhouses, he could see how the farmland differed from the territory about it. The corn was already so high it seemed in the dark almost to threaten by its ceaseless whisper of movement. The fruits had ripened fast. In the strawberry beds were great strawberries like pears. The marrows lay on their dunghill like bloated bolsters, gleaming from a distant shaft of light. In the orchard the trees creaked, weighed down by distorted footballs that passed for apples; with a heavy autumnal thud one fell over-ripe to the ground. Everywhere on the farm, there seemed to be slight movement and noise, so much so that Gregory stopped to listen.

A wind was rising. The sails of the old mill shrieked like a gull's cry as they began to turn. In the engine house, the steam engine pumped out its double unfaltering note as it generated power. The dogs still raged, the animals added their uneasy chorus. He recalled the saliva tree; here as in the dream, it was as if agriculture had become industry and the impulses of nature were swallowed by the new god of Science. In the bark of the tree rose the dark steam of novel and unknown forces.

He talked himself into pressing forward again. He moved carefully through the baffling slices of shadow and illumination created by the screens and lights, and arrived near the back door of the farmhouse. A lantern burnt in the kitchen window. As Gregory hesitated, the crunch of broken glass came from within.

Cautiously he edged himself past the window and peered in through the doorway. From the parlor he heard the voice of Grendon. It held a curious muffled tone, as if the man spoke to himself.

"Lie there! You're no use to me. This is a trial of strength. Oh, God, preserve me to let me prove myself! Thou has made my land barren till now—now let me harvest it! I don't know what You're doing. I didn't mean to presume, but this here farm is my life. Curse 'em, curse 'em all! They're all enemies." There was more of it; the man was muttering like one drunk. With a horrid fascination, Gregory was drawn forward till he had crossed the kitchen flags and stood on the verge of the larger room.

He peered round the half open door until he could see
the farmer, standing obscurely in the middle of the room.

A candle stood in the neglected hearth, its flickering
flame glassily reflected in the cases of maladroit animals.
Evidently the house electricity had been cut to give additional power to the new lights outside.

Grendon's back was to Gregory. One gaunt and un-
shaven cheek was lit by candlelight. His back seemed a
little bent by the weight of what he imagined his duties,
yet looking at that leather-clad back now, Gregory experienced a sort of reverence for the independence of the
man, and for the mystery that lay under his plainness.
He watched as Grendon moved out through the front
door, leaving it hanging wide, and passed into the yard,
still muttering to himself. He walked round the side of the
house and was hidden from view as the sound of his tread
was lost amid the renewed barking of dogs.

The tumult did not drown a groan from near at hand.
Peering into the shadows, Gregory saw a body lying
under the table. It rolled over, crunching broken glass as
it did so, and exclaimed in a dazed way. Without being
able to see clearly, Gregory knew it was Neckland. He
climbed over to the man and propped his head up, kicking away a stuffed fish as he did so.

"Don't kill me, bor! I only want to get away from here.
I only want to get away."

"Bert? It's Greg here. Bert, are you badly hurt?"

He could see some wounds. The fellow's shirt had been
practically torn from his back, and the flesh on his side
and back was cut from where he had rolled in the glass.
More serious was a great weal over one shoulder, changing to a deeper color as Gregory looked at it. A brawl
had taken place. Under the table lay another fish, its
mouth gaping as if it still died, and the pseudo-goat, one
button eye of which had rolled out of its socket. The cases
from which they had come lay shattered by the wall.

Wiping his face and speaking in a more rational voice,
Neckland said, "Gregory? I thought as you was down
Cottersall? What you doing here? He'll kill you proper if
he finds you here!"

"What happened to you, Bert? Can you get up?"

The laborer was again in possession of his faculties. He
grabbed Gregory's forearm and said imploringly. "Keep

your voice down, for Christ's sake, or he'll hear us and come back and settle my hash for once for all! He's gone clean off his head, says as these pond things are having a holiday here. He nearly knocked my head off my shoulder with that stick of his! Lucky I got a thick head!"

"What was the quarrel about?"

"I tell you straight, bor, I have got the wind up proper about this here farm. They things as live in the pond will eat me and suck me up like they done Grubby if I stay here anymore. So I run off when Joe Grendon weren't looking, and I come in here to gather up my traps and my bits and leave here at once. This whole place is evil, a bed of evil, and it ought to be destroyed. Hell can't be worse than this here farm!"

"So he caught you in here, did he?"

"I saw him rush in and I flung that there fish at him, and the goat. But he had me! Now I'm getting out, and I'd advise you to do the same. You must be daft, come back here like you did!"

As he spoke, he pulled himself to his feet and stood, keeping his balance with Gregory's aid. Grunting, he made his way over the staircase.

"Bert," Gregory said, "supposing we rush Grendon and lay him out. We can then get him in the cart and all leave together."

Neckland turned to stare at him, his face hidden in shadows, nursing his shoulder with one hand.

"You try it!" he said, and then he turned and went steadily up the stairs.

Gregory stood where he was, keeping one eye on the window. He had come to the farm without any clear notion in his head, but now that the idea had been formulated, he saw that it was up to him to try and remove Grendon from his farm. He felt obliged to do it, for although he had lost his former regard for Grendon, a sort of fascination for the man held him, and he was incapable of leaving any human being, however perverse, to face alone the alien horrors of the farm. It occurred to him that he might get help from the distant houses, Dereham Cottages, if only the farmer were rendered in one way or another unable to pepper the intruders with shot.

The machine house possessed only one high window,

and that was barred. It was built of brick and had a stout
door which could be barred and locked from outside. Perhaps it would be possible to lure Grendon into there; outside aid could then be obtained.

Not without apprehension, Gregory went to the open
door and peered out into the confused dark. He stared
anxiously at the ground for sight of a footstep more sinister than the farmer's, but there was no indication that the
Aurigans were active. He stepped into the yard.

He had not gone two yards before a woman's screams
rang out. The sound seemed to clamp an icy grip about
Gregory's ribs, and into his mind came a picture of poor
mad Mrs. Grendon. Then he recognized the voice in its
few shouted words as Nancy's. Even before the sound cut
off, he began to pelt down the dark side of the house as
fast as he could run.

Only later did he realize how he seemed to be running against a great army of animal cries. Loudest was
the babel of the pigs; every swine seemed to have some
message deep and nervous and indecipherable to deliver
to an unknown source; and it was to the sties that Gregory
ran, plunging past the giant screens under the high and
sickly light.

The noise in the sties was deafening. Every animal
was attacking its pen with its sharp hooves. One light
swung over the middle pen. With its help, Gregory saw
immediately how terrible was the change that had come
over the farm since his last visit. The sows had swollen
enormously and their great ears clattered against their
cheeks like boards. Their hirsute backs curved almost to
the rafters of their prison.

Grendon was at the far entrance. In his arms he held
the unconscious form of his daughter. A sack of pig feed
lay scattered by his feet. He had one pen gate half open
and was trying to thrust his way in against the flank of a
pig whose mighty shoulder came almost level with his.
He turned and stared at Gregory with a face whose
blankness was more terrifying than any expression of
rage.

There was another presence in the place. A pen gate
near to Gregory swung open. The two sows wedged in
the narrow sty gave out a terrible falsetto squealing,
clearly scenting the presence of an unappeasable hunger.

They kicked out blindly, and all the other animals plunged with a sympathetic fear. Struggle was useless. An Aurigan was there; the figure of Death itself, with its unwearying scythe and unaltering smile of bone, was as easily avoided as this poisoned and unseen presence. A rosy flush spread over the back of one of the sows. Almost at once, her great bulk began to collapse; in a moment, her substance had been ingested.

Gregory did not stay to watch the sickening action. He was running forward, for the farmer was again on the move. And now it was clear what he was going to do. He pushed into the end sty and dropped his daughter down into the metal food trough. At once, the sows turned with smacking jaws to deal with this new fodder. His hands free, Grendon moved to a bracket set in the wall. There lay his gun.

Now the uproar in the sties had reached its loudest. The sow whose companion had been so rapidly ingested broke free and burst into the central aisle. For a moment she stood—mercifully, for otherwise Gregory would have been trampled—as if dazed by the possibility of liberty. The place shook and the other swine fought to get to her. Brick crumbled, pen gates buckled. Gregory jumped aside as the second pig lumbered free, and next moment the place was full of grotesque fighting bodies, fighting their way to liberty.

He had reached Grendon, but the stampede caught them even as they confronted each other. A hoof stabbed down on Grendon's instep. Groaning, he bent forward and was at once swept underfoot by his creature. Gregory barely had time to vault into the nearest pen before they thundered by. Nancy was trying pitifully to climb out of the trough as the two beasts to which she had been offered fought to kick their way free. With a ferocious strength—without reason—almost without consciousness—Gregory hauled her up, jumped until he swung up on one of the overhead beams, wrapped a leg round the beam, hung down till he grasped Nancy, pulled her up with him.

They were safe, but the safety was not permanent. Through the din and dust, they could see that the gigantic beasts were wedged tightly in both entrances. In the middle was a sort of battlefield where the animals fought to reach the opposite end of the building; they were gradually tearing each other to pieces but the sties too were threatened with demolition.

"The Aurigan is here somewhere," Gregory shouted. "We aren't safe from it by any means."

"You were foolish to come here, Greg," Nancy said. "I found you had gone, and I had to follow you. But Father—I don't think he even recognized me!"

At least, Gregory thought, she had not seen her father trampled underfoot. Involuntarily glancing in that direction, he saw the shotgun that Grendon had never managed to reach still lying across a bracket on the wall. By crawling along a transverse beam, he could reach it easily. Bidding Nancy sit where she was, he wriggled along the beam, only a foot or two above the heaving backs of the swine. At least the gun should afford them some protection: the Aurigan, despite all its ghastly differences from humanity, would hardly be immune to lead.

As he grasped the old-fashioned weapon and pulled it up, Gregory was suddenly filled with an intense desire to kill one of the invisible monsters. In that instant, he recalled an earlier hope he had had of them: that they might be superior beings, beings of wisdom and enlightened power, coming from a better society where higher moral codes directed the activities of its citizens. He had thought that only to such a civilization would the divine gift of traveling through interplanetary space be granted. But perhaps the opposite held true: perhaps such a great objective could be gained only by species ruthless enough to disregard more humane ends. As soon as he thought it, his mind was overpowered with a vast diseased vision of the universe, where such races as dealt in love and kindness and intellect cowered forever on their little globes, while all about them went the slayers of the universe, sailing where they would to satisfy their cruelties and their endless appetites.

He heaved his way back to Nancy above the bloody porcine fray.

She pointed mutely. At the far end the entrance had crumbled away, and the sows were bursting forth into the night. But one sow fell and turned crimson as it fell, sogging over the floor like a shapeless bag. Another, passing the same spot, suffered the same fate.

Was the Aurigan moved by anger? Had the pigs, in
their blind charging, injured it? Gregory raised the gun
and aimed. As he did so, he saw a faint hallucinatory
column in the air; enough dirt and mud and blood had
been thrown up to spot the Aurigan and render him
partly visible. Gregory fired.

The recoil nearly knocked him off his perch. He shut
his eyes, dazed by the noise, and was dimly aware of
Nancy clinging to him, shouting, "Oh, you marvelous
man, you marvelous man! You hit that old bor right
smack on target!"

He opened his eyes and peered through the smoke and
dust. The shade that represented the Aurigan was totter-
ing. It fell. It fell among the distorted shapes of the two
sows it had killed, and corrupt fluids splattered over the
paving. Then it rose again. They saw its progress to the
broken door, and then it had gone.

For a minute they sat there, staring at each other, triumph and speculation mingling on both their faces.
Apart from one badly injured beast, the building was
clear of pigs now. Gregory climbed to the floor and
helped Nancy down beside him. They skirted the loath-
some masses as best they could and staggered into the
fresh air.

Up beyond the orchard, strange lights showed in the
rear windows of the farmhouse.

"It's on fire! Oh, Greg, our poor home is afire! Quick,
we must gather what we can! All father's lovely cases—"

He held her fiercely, bent so that he spoke straight into
her face. "Bert Neckland did this! He did it! He told me
the place ought to be destroyed and that's what he did."

"Let's go then—"

"No, no, Nancy, we must let it burn! Listen! There's a
wounded Aurigan loose here somewhere. We didn't kill
him. If those things feel rage, anger, spite, they'll be set
to kill us now—don't forget there's more than one of'em!
We aren't going that way if we want to live. Daisy's just
across the meadow here, and she'll bear us both safe
home."

"Greg, dearest, this is my home!" she cried in her despair.

The flames were leaping higher. The kitchen window
broke in a shower of glass. He was running with her in

the opposite direction, shouting wildly, "I'm your home now! I'm your home now!"

Now she was running with him, no longer protesting, and they plunged together through the high rank grass.

When they gained the track and the restive mare, they paused to take breath and look back.

The house was well ablaze now. Clearly nothing could save it. Sparks had carried to the windmill, and one of the sails was ablaze. About the scene, the electric lights shone spectral and pale on the tops of their poles. An occasional running figure of a gigantic animal dived about its own purposes. Suddenly, there was a flash as of lightning and all the electric lights went out. One of the stampeding animals had knocked down a pole; crashing into the pond, it short-circuited the system.

"Let's get away," Gregory said, and he helped Nancy onto the mare. As he climbed up behind her, a roaring sound developed, grew in volume and altered in pitch. Abruptly it died again. A thick cloud of steam billowed above the pond. From it rose the space machine, rising rising, rising, suddenly a sight to take the heart in awe. It moved up into the soft night sky, was lost for a moment, began to glow dully, was seen to be already tremendously far away.

Desperately Gregory looked for it, but it had gone, already beyond the frail confines of the terrestrial atmosphere. An awful desolation settled on him, the more awful for being irrational, and then he thought and cried his thought aloud, "Perhaps they were only holiday-makers here! Perhaps they enjoyed themselves here and will tell their friends of this little globe! Perhaps Earth has a future only as a resort for millions of the Aurigan kind!"

The church clock was striking midnight as they passed the first cottages of Cottersall.

"We'll go direct to the inn," Gregory said. "I can't well disturb Mrs. Fenn at this late hour, but your landlord will fetch us food and hot water and see that your cuts are bandaged."

"I'm right as rain, love, but I'd be glad of your company."

"I warn you, you shall have too much of it from now on!"

The door of the inn was locked, but a light burned inside, and in a moment the landlord himself opened to them, all eager to hear a bit of gossip he could pass on to his customers.

"So happens as there's a gentleman up in Number Three wishes to speak with you in the morning," he told Gregory. "Very nice gentleman came on the night train, only got in here an hour past, off the wagon."

Gregory made a wry face.

"My father, no doubt."

"Oh, no sir. His name is a Mr. Wills or Wells—his signature was a mite difficult to make out."

"Wells! Mr. Wells! So he's come!" He caught Nancy's hands, shaking them in his excitement. "Nancy, one of the greatest men in England is here! There's no one more profitable for such a tale as ours. I'm going up to speak with him right away."

Kissing her lightly on the cheek, he hurried up the stairs and knocked on the door of Number Three.

HE WHO SHAPES

by Roger Zelazny

I

Lovely as it was, with the blood and all, Render could sense that it was about to end.

Therefore, each microsecond would be better off as a minute, he decided—and perhaps the temperature should be increased . . . Somewhere, just at the periphery of everything, the darkness halted its constriction.

Something, like a crescendo of subliminal thunders, was arrested at one raging note. That note was a distillate of shame and pain and fear.

The Forum was stifling.

Caesar cowered outside the frantic circle. His forearm covered his eyes but it could not stop the seeing, not this time.

The senators had no faces and their garments were spattered with blood. All their voices were like the cries of birds. With an inhuman frenzy they plunged their daggers into the fallen figure.

All, that is, but Render.

The pool of blood in which he stood continued to widen. His arm seemed to be rising and falling with a mechanical regularity, and his throat might have been shaping bird-cries, but he was simultaneously apart from and a part of the scene.

For he was Render, the Shaper.

Crouched, anguished, and envious, Caesar wailed his protests.

"You have slain him! You have murdered Marcus Antonius—a blameless, useless fellow!"

Render turned to him, and the dagger in his hand was quite enormous and quite gory.

"Aye," said he.

The blade moved from side to side. Caesar, fascinated by the sharpened steel, swayed to the same rhythm.

"Why?" he cried. "Why?"

"Because," answered Render, "he was a far nobler Roman than yourself."

"You lie! It is not so!"

Render shrugged and returned to the stabbing.

"It is not true!" screamed Caesar. "Not true!"

Render turned to him again and waved the dagger. Puppetlike, Caesar mimicked the pendulum of the blade.

"Not true?" smiled Render. "And who are you to question an assassination such as this? You are no one! You detract from the dignity of this occasion! Begone!"

Jerkily, the pink-faced man rose to his feet, his hair half-wispy, half-wetplastered, a disarray of cotton. He turned, moved away; and as he walked, he looked back over his shoulder.

He had moved far from the circle of assassins, but the scene did not diminish in size. It retained an electric clarity. It made him feel even further removed, ever more alone and apart.

Render rounded a previously unnoticed corner, and stood before him a blind beggar.

Caesar grasped the front of his garment.

"Have you an ill omen for me this day?"

"Beware!" jeered Render.

"Yes! Yes!" cried Caesar. " 'Beware!' That is good! Beware what?"

"The ides—"

"Yes? The ides—?"

"—of Octember."

He released the garment.

"What is that you say? What is Octember?"

"A month."

"You lie! There is no month of Octember!"

"And that is the date noble Caesar need fear—the non-existent time, the never-to-be-calendared occasion."

Render vanished around another sudden corner.

"Wait! Come back!"

Render laughed, and the Forum laughed with him. The bird-cries became a chorus of inhuman jeers.

"You mock me!" wept Caesar.

The Forum was an oven, and the perspiration formed like a glassy mask over Caesar's narrow forehead, sharp nose, chinless jaw.

"I want to be assassinated, too!" he sobbed. "It isn't fair!"

And Render tore the Forum and the senators and the grinning corpse of Antony to pieces and stuffed them into a black sack—with the unseen movement of a single finger—and last of all went Caesar.

Charles Render sat before the ninety white buttons and the two red ones, not really looking at any of them. His right arm moved in its soundless sling, across the lap-level surface of the console—pushing some of the buttons, skipping over others, moving on, retracing its path to press the next in the order of the Recall Series.

Sensations throttled, emotions reduced to nothing, Representative Erikson knew the oblivion of the womb.

There was a soft click.

Render's hand had glided to the end of the bottom row of buttons. An act of conscious intent—will, if you like—was required to push the red button.

Render freed his arm and lifted off his crown of Medusa-hair leads and microminiature circuitry. He slid from behind his desk-couch and raised the hood. He walked to the window and transpared it, fingering forth a cigarette.

One minute in the ro-womb, he decided. *No more. This is a crucial one . . . Hope it doesn't snow till later—those clouds look mean . . .*

It was smooth yellow trellises and high towers, glassy and gray, all smouldering into evening under a shale-colored sky; the city was squared volcanic islands, glowing in the end-of-day light, rumbling deep down under the earth; it was fat, incessant rivers of traffic, rushing.

Render turned away from the window and approached the great egg that lay beside his desk, smooth and glittering. It threw back a reflection that smashed all aquilinity from his nose, turned his eyes to gray saucers, transformed his hair into a light-streaked skyline; his reddish necktie became the wide tongue of a ghoul.

He smiled, reached across the desk. He pressed the second red button.

With a sigh, the egg lost its dazzling opacity and a horizontal crack appeared about its middle. Through the now-transparent shell, Render could see Erikson grimacing, squeezing his eyes tight, fighting against a return to consciousness and the thing it would contain. The upper half of the egg rose vertical to the base, exposing him, knobby and pink on half-shell. When his eyes opened, he did not look at Render. He rose to his feet and began dressing. Render used this time to check the ro-womb.

He leaned back across his desk and pressed the buttons: temperature control, full range, *check;* exotic sounds —he raised the earphone—*check,* on bells, on buzzes, on violin notes and whistles, on squeals and moans, on traffic noises and the sound of surf; *check,* on the feedback circuit—holding the patient's own voice, trapped earlier in analysis; *check,* on the sound blanket, the moisture spray, the odor banks; *check,* on the couch agitator and the colored lights, the taste stimulants. . . .

Render closed the egg and shut off its power. He pushed the unit into the closet, palmed shut the door. The tapes had registered a valid sequence.

"Sit down," he directed Erikson.

The man did so, fidgeting with his collar.

"You have full recall," said Render, "so there is no need for me to summarize what occurred. Nothing can be hidden from me. I was there."

Erikson nodded.

"The significance of the episode should be apparent to you."

Erikson nodded again, finally finding his voice. "But was it valid?" he asked. "I mean, you constructed the dream and you controlled it, all the way. I didn't really *dream* it—in the way I would normally dream. Your ability to make things happen stacks the deck for whatever you're going to say—doesn't it?"

Render shook his head slowly, flicked an ash into the southern hemisphere of his globe-made-ashtray, and met Erikson's eyes.

"It is true that I supplied the format and modified the forms. You, however, filled them with an emotional significance, promoted them to the status of symbols corresponding to your problem. If the dream was not a valid analogue, it would not have provoked the reactions it did. It would have been devoid of the anxiety-patterns which were registered on the tapes.

"You have been in analysis for many months now," he continued, "and everything I have learned thus far serves to convince me that your fears of assassination are without any basis in fact."

Erikson glared.

"Then why the hell do I have them?"

"Because," said Render, "you would like very much to be the subject of an assassination."

Erikson smiled then, his composure beginning to return.

"I assure you, doctor, I have never contemplated suicide, nor have I any desire to stop living."

He produced a cigar and applied a flame to it. His hand shook.

"When you came to me this summer," said Render, "you stated that you were in fear of an attempt on your life. You were quite vague as to why anyone should want to kill you—"

"My position! You can't be a Representative as long as I have and make no enemies!"

"Yet," replied Render, "it appears that you have managed it. When you permitted me to discuss this with your detectives, I was informed that they could unearth nothing to indicate that your fears might have any real foundation. Nothing."

"They haven't looked far enough—or in the right places. They'll turn up something."

"I'm afraid not."

"Why?"

"Because, I repeat, your feelings are without any objective basis. Be honest with me. Have you any information whatsoever indicating that someone hates you enough to want to kill you?"

"I receive many threatening letters . . ."

"As do all Representatives—and all of those directed to you during the past year have been investigated and found to be the work of cranks. Can you offer me *one* piece of evidence to substantiate your claims?"

Erikson studied the tip of his cigar.

"I came to you on the advice of a colleague," he said, "came to you to have you poke around inside my mind to find me something of that sort, to give my detectives something to work with. Someone I've injured severely perhaps—or some damaging piece of legislation I've dealt with . . ."

"—And I found nothing," said Render, "nothing, that is, but the cause of your discontent. Now, of course, you are afraid to hear it, and you are attempting to divert me from explaining my diagnosis—"

"I am not!"

"Then listen. You can comment afterwards if you want, but you've poked and dawdled around here for months, unwilling to accept what I present to you in a dozen different forms. Now I am going to tell you outright what it is, and you can do what you want about it."

"Fine."

"First," he said, "you would like very much to have an enemy or enemies—"

"Ridiculous!"

"—because it is the only alternative to having friends—"

"I have lots of friends!"

"—because nobody wants to be completely ignored, to be an object for whom no one has really strong feelings. Hatred and love are the ultimate forms of human regard. Lacking one and unable to achieve it, you sought the other. You wanted it so badly that you succeeded in convincing yourself it existed. But there is always a psychic pricetag on these things. Answering a genuine emotional need with a body of desire-surrogates does not produce real satisfaction but anxiety, discomfort—because in these matters the psyche should be an open system. You did not seek outside yourself for human regard. You were closed off. You created that which you needed from the stuff of your own being. You are a man very much in need of strong relationships with other people."

"Manure!"

"Take it or leave it," said Render. "I suggest you take it."

"I've been paying you for half a year to help find out who wants to kill me. Now you sit there and tell me I made the whole thing up to satisfy a desire to have some-one hate me."

"Hate you, or love you. That's right."

"It's absurd! I meet so many people that I carry a pocket recorder and a lapel-camera, just so I can recall them all . . ."

"Meeting quantities of people is hardly what I was speaking of. Tell me, *did* that dream sequence have a strong meaning for you?"

Erikson was silent for several tickings of the huge wallclock.

"Yes," he finally conceded, "it did. But your interpre-tation of the matter is still absurd. Granting, though just for the sake of argument, that what you say is correct—what would I do to get out of this bind?"

Render leaned back in his chair.

"Rechannel the energies that went into producing the thing. Meet some people as yourself, Joe Erikson, rather than Representative Erikson. Take up something you can do with other people—something non-political, and per-haps somewhat competitive—and make some real friends or enemies, preferably the former. I've encouraged you to do this all along."

"Then tell me something else."

"Gladly."

"Assuming you *are* right, why is it that I am neither liked nor hated and never have been? I have a responsi-ble position in the Legislature. I meet people all the time. Why am I so neutral a . . . thing?"

Highly familiar now with Erikson's career, Render had to push aside his true thoughts on the matter as they were of no operational value. He wanted to cite him Dante's observations concerning the trimmers—those souls who, denied heaven for their lack of virtue, were also denied entrance to hell for a lack of significant vices—in short, the ones who trimmed their sails to move them with every wind of the times, who lacked direction, who were not really concerned toward which ports they were pushed. Such was Erikson's long and colorless career of migrant loyalties, of political reversals.

Render said:

"More and more people find themselves in such circumstances these days. It is due largely to the increasing complexity of society and the depersonalization of the individual into a sociometric unit. Even the act of cathecting toward other persons has grown more forced as a result. There are so many of us these days."

Erikson nodded, and Render smiled inwardly.

Sometimes the gruff line, and then the lecture . . .

"I've got the feeling you could be right," said Erikson. "Sometimes I *do* feel like what you just described—a unit, something depersonalized . . ."

Render glanced at the clock.

"What you choose to do about it from here is, of course, your own decision to make. I think you'd be wasting your time to remain in analysis any longer. We are now both aware of the cause of your complaint. I can't take you by the hand and show you how to lead your life. I can indicate, I can commiserate—but no more deep probing. Make an appointment as soon as you feel a need to discuss your activities and relate them to my diagnosis."

"I will," nodded Erikson, "and—damn that dream! It got to me. You can make them seem as vivid as waking life—more vivid . . . It may be a long while before I can forget it."

"I hope so."

"Okay, doctor." He rose to his feet, extended a hand. "I'll probably be back in a couple weeks. I'll give this socializing a fair try." He grinned at the word he normally frowned upon. "In fact I'll start now. May I buy you a drink around the corner, downstairs?"

Render met the moist palm which seemed as weary of the performance as a lead actor in too successful a play. He felt almost sorry as he said, "Thank you, but I have an engagement."

Render helped him on with his coat then, handed him his hat, saw him to the door.

"Well, good night."

"Good night."

As the door closed soundlessly behind him, Render re-crossed the dark Astrakhan to his mahogany fortress and flipped his cigarette into the southern hemisphere. He leaned back in his chair, hands behind his head, eyes closed.

"Of course it was more real than life," he informed no one in particular. "I shaped it."

Smiling, he reviewed the dream sequence step by step, wishing some of his former instructors could have witnessed it. It had been well-constructed and powerfully executed, as well as being precisely appropriate for the case at hand. But then, he was Render, the Shaper—one of the two hundred or so special analysts whose own psychic makeup permitted them to enter into neurotic patterns without carrying away more than an esthetic gratification from the mimesis of aberrance—a Sane Hatter.

Render stirred his recollections. He had been analyzed himself, analyzed and passed upon as a granite-willed, ultra-stable outsider—tough enough to weather the basilisk gaze of a fixation, walk unscathed amidst the chimarae of perversions, force dark Mother Medusa to close her eyes before the caduceus of his art. His own analysis had not been difficult. Nine years before (it seemed much longer) he had suffered a willing injection of novocain into the most painful area of his spirit. It was after the auto wreck, after the death of Ruth and of Miranda their daughter that he had begun to feel detached. Perhaps he did not want to recover certain empathies, perhaps his own world was now based upon a certain rigidity of feeling. If this was true, he was wise enough in the ways of the mind to realize it, and perhaps he had decided that such a world had its own compensations.

His son Peter was now ten years old. He was attending a school of quality, and he penned his father a letter every week. The letters were becoming progressively literate, showing signs of a precociousness of which Render could not but approve. He would take the boy with him to Europe in the summer.

As for Jill—Jill DeVille (what a luscious, ridiculous name! He loved her for it)—she was growing, if anything, more interesting to him. (He wondered if this was an indication of early middle age.) He was vastly taken by her unmusical nasal voice, her sudden interest in architecture, her concern with the unremovable mole on the right side of her otherwise well-designed nose. He should really call her immediately and go in search of a new restaurant. For some reason though, he did not feel like it.

It had been several weeks since he had visited his club, The Partridge and Scalpel, and he felt a strong desire to eat from an oaken table, alone, in the split-level dining room with the three fireplaces, beneath the artificial torches and the boars' heads like gin ads. So he pushed his perforated membership card into the phone-slot on his desk, and there were two buzzes behind the voice-screen.

"Hello, Partridge and Scalpel," said the voice. "May I help you?"

"Charles Render," he said. "I'd like a table in about half an hour."

"How many will there be?"

"Just me."

"Very good, sir. Half an hour then. That's 'Render'? *R-e-n-d-e-r?*"

"Right."

"Thank you."

He broke the connection, rose from his desk. Outside the day had vanished.

The monoliths and the towers gave forth their own light now. A soft snow, like sugar, was sifting down through the shadows and transforming itself into beads on the windowpane.

Render shrugged into his overcoat, turned off the lights, locked the inner office. There was a note on Mrs. Hedges's blotter.

Miss DeVille called, it said.

He crumpled the note and tossed it into the waste-chute. He would call her tomorrow and say he had been working until late on his lecture.

He switched off the final light, clapped his hat onto his head, and passed through the outer door, locking it as he went. The drop took him to the sub-subcellar where his auto was parked.

It was chilly in the sub-sub, and his footsteps seemed loud on the concrete as he passed among the parked vehicles. Beneath the glare of the naked lights, his S–7

Spinner was a sleek gray cocoon from which it seemed turbulent wings might at any moment emerge. The double row of antennae, which fanned forward from the slope of its hood, added to this feeling. Render thumbed open the door.

He touched the ignition and there was the sound of a lone bee awakening in a great hive. The door swung soundlessly shut as he raised the steering wheel and locked it into place. He spun up the spiral ramp and came to a rolling stop before the big overhead.

As the door rattled upward, he lighted his destination screen and turned the knob that shifted the broadcast map. Left to right, top to bottom, section by section, he shifted it until he located the portion of Carnegie Avenue he desired. He punched out its coordinates and lowered the wheel. The car switched over to monitor and moved out onto the highway marginal. Render lit a cigarette.

Pushing his seat back into the centerspace, he left all the windows transparent. It was pleasant to half-recline and watch the oncoming cars drift past him like swarms of fireflies. He pushed his hat back on his head and stared upward.

He could remember a time when he had loved snow, when it had reminded him of novels by Thomas Mann and music by Scandinavian composers. In his mind now, though, there was another element from which it could never be wholly dissociated. He could visualize so clearly the eddies of milk-white coldness that swirled about his old manual-steer auto, flowing into its fire-charred interior to rewhiten that which had been blackened; so clearly, as though he had walked toward it across a chalky lakebottom—it, the sunken wreck, and he, the diver—unable to open his mouth to speak for fear of drowning; and he knew whenever he looked upon falling snow that somewhere skulls were whitening. But nine years had washed away much of the pain, and he also knew that the night was lovely.

He was sped along the wide, wide roads, shot across high bridges, their surfaces slick and gleaming beneath his lights, was woven through frantic cloverleafs, and plunged into a tunnel whose dimly glowing walls blurred by him like a mirage. Finally he switched the windows to opaque and closed his eyes.

He could not remember whether he had dozed for a moment or not, which meant he probably had. He felt the car slowing, and he moved the seat forward and turned on the windows again. Almost simultaneously, the cut-off buzzer sounded. He raised the steering wheel and pulled into the parking dome, stepped out onto the ramp and left the car to the parking unit, receiving his ticket from that box-headed robot, which took its solemn revenge on mankind by sticking forth a cardboard tongue at everyone it served.

As always, the noises were as subdued as the lighting. The place seemed to absorb sound and convert it into warmth, to lull the tongue with aromas strong enough to be tasted, to hypnotize the ear with the vivid crackle of the triple hearths.

Render was pleased to see that his favorite table, in the corner off to the right of the smaller fireplace, had been held for him. He knew the menu from memory, but he studied it with zeal as he sipped a Manhattan and worked up an order to match his appetite. Shaping sessions always left him ravenously hungry.

"Dr. Render . . . ?"

"Yes?" He looked up.

"Dr. Shallot would like to speak with you," said the waiter.

"I don't know anyone named Shallot," he said. "Are you sure he doesn't want Bender? He's a surgeon from Metro who sometimes eats here . . ."

The waiter shook his head.

"No sir—'Render.' See here?" He extended a three-by-five card on which Render's full name was typed in capital letters. "Dr. Shallot has dined here nearly every night for the past two weeks," he explained, "and on each occasion has asked to be notified if you came in."

"Hmm?" mused Render. "That's odd. Why didn't he just call me at my office?"

The waiter smiled and make a vague gesture.

"Well, tell him to come on over," he said, gulping his Manhattan, "and bring me another of these."

"Unfortunately, Shallot is blind," explained the waiter. "It would be easier if you—"

"All right, sure." Render stood up, relinquishing his

favorite table with a strong premonition that he would not be returning to it that evening.

"Lead on."

They threaded their way among the diners, heading up to the next level. A familiar face said "hello" from a table set back against the wall, and Render nodded a greeting to a former seminar pupil whose name was Jurgens or Jirkans or something like that.

He moved on into the smaller dining room wherein only two tables were occupied. No, three. There was one set in the corner at the far end of the darkened bar, partly masked by an ancient suit of armor. The waiter was heading him in that direction.

They stopped before the table, and Render stared down into the darkened glasses that had tilted upward as they approached. Dr. Shallot was a woman, somewhere in the vicinity of her early thirties. Her low bronze bangs did not fully conceal the spot of silver that she wore on her forehead like a caste-mark. Render inhaled, and her head jerked slightly as the tip of his cigarette flared. She appeared to be staring straight up into his eyes. It was an uncomfortable feeling, even knowing that all she could distinguish of him was that which her minute photo-electric cell transmitted to her visual cortex over the hair-fine wire implants attached to that oscillator-convertor: in short, the glow of his cigarette.

"Dr. Shallot, this is Dr. Render," the waiter was saying.

"Good evening," said Render.

"Good evening," she said. "My name is Eileen, and I've wanted very badly to meet you." He thought he detected a slight quaver in her voice. "Will you join me for dinner?"

"My pleasure," he acknowledged, and the waiter drew out the chair.

Render sat down, noting that the woman across from him already had a drink. He reminded the waiter of his second Manhattan.

"Have you ordered yet?" he inquired.

"No."

". . . And two menus—" he started to say, then bit his tongue.

"Only one," she smiled.

"Make it none," he amended and recited the menu.

They ordered. Then:

"Do you always do that?"

"What?"

"Carry menus in your head."

"Only a few," he said, "for awkward occasions. What was it you wanted to see—talk to me about?"

"You're a neuroparticipant therapist," she stated, "a Shaper."

"And you are.—?"

"—a resident in psychiatry at State Psych. I have a year remaining."

"You knew Sam Riscomb then."

"Yes, he helped me get my appointment. He was my adviser."

"He was a very good friend of mine. We studied together at Menninger."

She nodded.

"I'd often heard him speak of you—that's one of the reasons I wanted to meet you. He's responsible for encouraging me to go ahead with my plans, despite my handicap."

Render stared at her. She was wearing a dark green dress which appeared to be made of velvet. About three inches to the left of the bodice was a pin which might have been gold. It displayed a red stone which could have been a ruby around which the outline of a goblet was cast. Or was it really two profiles that were outlined, staring through the stone at one another? It seemed vaguely familiar to him, but he could not place it at the moment. It glittered expensively in the dim light.

Render accepted his drink from the waiter.

"I want to become a neuroparticipant therapist," she told him.

And if she had possessed vision, Render would have thought she was staring at him, hoping for some response in his expression. He could not quite calculate what she wanted him to say.

"I commend your choice," he said, "and I respect your ambition." He tried to put his smile into his voice. "It is not an easy thing, of course, not all of the requirements being academic ones."

"I know," she said. "But then, I have been blind since birth and it was not an easy thing to come this far."

"Since birth?" he repeated. "I thought you might have lost your sight recently. You did your undergrad work then and went on through med school without eyes . . . That's—rather impressive."

"Thank you," she said, "but it isn't. Not really. I heard about the first neuroparticipants—Bartelmetz and the rest—when I was a child, and I decided then that I wanted to be one. My life ever since has been governed by that desire."

"What did you do in the labs?" he inquired. "Not being able to see a specimen, look through a microscope . . . ? Or all that reading?"

"I hired people to read my assignments to me. I taped everything. The school understood that I wanted to go into psychiatry, and they permitted a special arrangement for labs. I've been guided through the dissection of cadavers by lab assistants, and I've had everything described to me. I can tell things by touch . . . and I have a memory like yours with the menu," she smiled. "The quality of psychoparticipation phenomena can only be gauged by the therapist himself, at that moment outside of time and space as we normally know it, when he stands in the midst of a world erected from the stuff of another man's dreams, recognizes there the non-Euclidian architecture of aberrance, and then takes his patient by the hand and tours the landscape . . . if he can lead him back to the common earth, then his judgments were sound, his actions valid."

"From *Why No Psychometrics in This Place,*" reflected Render.

"—by Charles Render, M.D."

"Our dinner is already moving in this direction," he noted, picking up his drink as the speed-cooked meal was pushed toward them in the kitchen-buoy.

"That's one of the reasons I wanted to meet you," she continued, raising her glass as the dishes rattled before her. "I want you to help me become a Shaper."

Her shaded eyes, as vacant as a statue's, sought him again.

"Yours is a completely unique situation," he commented. "There has never been a congenitally blind neuroparticipant—for obvious reasons. I'd have to consider all the aspects of the situation before I could advise you. Let's eat now, though. I'm starved."

"All right. But my blindness does not mean that I have never seen."

He did not ask her what she meant by that because prime ribs were standing in front of him now and there was a bottle of Chambertin at his elbow. He did pause long enough to notice, though, as she raised her left hand from beneath the table, that she wore no rings.

"I wonder if it's still snowing," he commented as they drank their coffee. "It was coming down pretty hard when I pulled into the dome."

"I hope so," she said, "even though it diffuses the light and I can't 'see' anything at all through it. I like to feel it falling about me and blowing against my face."

"How do you get about?"

"My dog, Sigmund—I gave him the night off," she smiled. "—he can guide me anywhere. He's a mutie Shepherd."

"Oh?" Render grew curious. "Can he talk much?"

She nodded.

"That operation wasn't as successful on him as on some of them, though. He has a vocabulary of about four hundred words, but I think it causes him pain to speak. He's quite intelligent. You'll have to meet him sometime."

Render began speculating immediately. He had spoken with such animals at recent medical conferences and had been startled by their combination of reasoning ability and their devotion to their handlers. Much chromosome tinkering, followed by delicate embryo-surgery, was required to give a dog a brain capacity greater than a chimpanzee's. Several followup operations were necessary to produce vocal abilities. Most such experiments ended in failure, and the dozen or so puppies a year on which they succeeded were valued in the neighborhood of a hundred-thousand dollars each. He realized then, as he lit a cigarette and held the light for a moment, that the stone in Miss Shallot's medallion was a genuine ruby. He began to suspect that her admission to a medical school might, in addition to her academic record, have

been based upon a sizeable endowment to the college of
her choice. Perhaps he was being unfair, though, he
chided himself.

"Yes," he said, "we might do a paper on canine neuroses. Does he ever refer to his father as 'that son of a
female Shepherd'?"

"He never met his father," she said quite soberly. "He
was raised apart from other dogs. His attitude could
hardly be typical. I don't think you'll ever learn the
functional psychology of the dog from a mutie."

"I imagine you're right," he dismissed it. "More coffee?"

"No, thanks."

Deciding it was time to continue the discussion, he
said, "So you want to be a Shaper . . ."

"Yes."

"I hate to be the one to destroy anybody's high ambitions," he told her. "Like poison, I hate it. Unless they
have no foundation at all in reality. Then I can be ruthless. So—honestly, frankly, and in all sincerity, I do not
see how it could ever be managed. Perhaps you're a fine
psychiatrist—but in my opinion, it is a physical and mental impossibility for you ever to become a neuroparticipant. As for my reasons—"

"Wait," she said. "Not here, please. Humor me. I'm
tired of this stuffy place—take me somewhere else to talk.
I think I might be able to convince you there *is* a way."

"Why not?" he shrugged. "I have plenty time. Sure—
you call it. Where?"

"Blindspin?"

He suppressed an unwilling chuckle at the expression,
but she laughed aloud.

"Fine," he said, "but I'm still thirsty."

A bottle of champagne was tallied, and he signed the
check despite her protests. It arrived in a colorful "Drink
While You Drive" basket, and they stood then, and she
was tall, but he was taller.

Blindspin.

A single name for a multitude of practices centered
about the auto-driven auto. Flashing across the country
in the sure hands of an invisible chauffeur, windows all
opaque, night dark, sky high, tires assailing the road be-

low like four phantom buzzsaws—and starting from scratch and ending in the same place, and never knowing where you are going or where you have been—it is possible, for a moment, to kindle some feeling of individuality in the coldest brainpan, to produce a momentary awareness of self by virtue of an apartness from all but a sense of motion. This is because movement through darkness is the ultimate abstraction of life itself—at least that's what one of the Vital Comedians said, and everybody in the place laughed.

Actually now, the phenomenon known as blindspin first became prevalent (as might be suspected) among certain younger members of the community when monitored highways deprived them of the means to exercise their automobiles in some of the more individualistic ways which had come to be frowned upon by the National Traffic Control Authority. Something had to be done.

It was.

The first, disastrous reaction involved the simple engineering feat of disconnecting the broadcast control unit after one had entered onto a monitored highway. This resulted in the car's vanishing from the ken of the monitor and passing back into the control of its occupants. Jealous as a deity, a monitor will not tolerate that which denies its programmed omniscience; it will thunder and lightning in the Highway Control Station nearest the point of last contact, sending winged seraphs in search of that which has slipped from sight.

Often, however, this was too late in happening for the roads are many and well-paved. Escape from detection was, at first, relatively easy to achieve.

Other vehicles, though, necessarily behave as if a rebel has no actual existence. Its presence cannot be allowed for.

Boxed-in, on a heavily traveled section of roadway, the offender is subject to immediate annihilation in the event of any overall speedup or shift in traffic pattern that involves movement through his theoretically vacant position. This, in the early days of monitor-controls, caused a rapid series of collisions. Monitoring devices later became far more sophisticated, and mechanized cutoffs reduced the collision incidence subsequent to such an action. The quality of the pulpefactions and contusions which did occur, however, remained unaltered.

The next reaction was based on a thing which had been overlooked because it was obvious. The monitors took people where they wanted to go only because people told them they wanted to go there. A person pressing a random series of coordinates without reference to any map would either be left with a stalled automobile and a "RECHECK YOUR COORDINATES" light, or would suddenly be whisked away in any direction. The latter possesses a certain romantic appeal in that it offers speed, unexpected sights, and free hands. Also it is perfectly legal; and it is possible to navigate all over two continents in this manner if one is possessed of sufficient wherewithal and gluteal stamina.

As is the case in all such matters, the practice diffused upwards through the age brackets. School teachers who only drove on Sundays fell into disrepute as selling points for used autos. Such is the way a world ends, said the entertainer.

End or no, the car designed to move on monitored highways is a mobile efficiency unit, complete with latrine, cupboard, refrigerator compartment, and gaming table. It also sleeps two with ease and four with some crowding. On occasion, three can be a real crowd.

Render drove out of the dome and into the marginal aisle. He halted the car.

"Want to jab some coordinates?" he asked.

"You do it. My fingers know too many."

Render punched random buttons. The Spinner moved onto the highway. Render asked speed of the vehicle then, and it moved into the high-acceleration lane.

The Spinner's lights burnt holes in the darkness. The city backed away fast; it was a smouldering bonfire on both sides of the road, stirred by sudden gusts of wind, hidden by white swirlings, obscured by the steady fall of gray ash. Render knew his speed was only about sixty percent of what it would have been on a clear, dry night.

He did not blank the windows, but leaned back and stared out through them. Eileen "looked" ahead into what light there was. Neither of them said anything for ten or fifteen minutes.

The city shrank to sub-city as they sped on. After a time, short sections of open road began to appear.

"Tell me what it looks like outside," she said.

"Why didn't you ask me to describe your dinner or the suit of armor beside our table?"

"Because I tasted one and felt the other. This is different."

"There is snow falling outside. Take it away and what you have left is black."

"What else?"

"There is slush on the road. When it starts to freeze, traffic will drop to a crawl unless we outrun this storm. The slush looks like an old, dark syrup just starting to get sugary on top."

"Anything else?"

"That's it, lady."

"Is it snowing harder or less hard than when we left the club?"

"Harder, I should say."

"Would you pour me a drink?" she asked him.

"Certainly."

They turned their seats inward, and Render raised the table. He fetched two glasses from the cupboard.

"Your health," said Render after he had poured.

"Here's looking at you."

Render downed his drink. She sipped hers. He waited for her next comment. He knew that two cannot play at the Socratic game, and he expected more questions before she said what she wanted to say.

She said: "What is the most beautiful thing you have ever seen?"

Yes, he decided, he had guessed correctly.

He replied without hesitation: "The sinking of Atlantis."

"I was serious."

"So was I."

"Would you care to elaborate?"

"I sank Atlantis," he said, "personally.

"It was about three years ago. And God! it was lovely! It was all ivory towers and golden minarets and silver balconies. There were bridges of opal and crimson pennants and a milk-white river flowing between lemon-colored banks. There were jade steeples, and trees as old as the world tickling the bellies of clouds, and ships in the great sea-harbor of Xanadu as delicately constructed as musical instruments, all swaying with the tides. The twelve princes of the realm held court in the dozen-pillared Colliseum of the Zodiac to listen to a Greek tenor sax play at sunset.

"The Greek, of course, was a patient of mine—para-noiac. The etiology of the thing is rather complicated, but that's what I wandered into inside his mind. I gave him free rein for a while, and in the end I had to split Atlantis in half and sink it full fathom five. He's playing again, and you've doubtless heard his sounds if you like such sounds at all. He's good. I still see him periodically, but he is no longer the last descendant of the greatest minstrel of Atlantis. He's just a fine, late twentieth-century saxman.

"Sometimes though, as I look back on the apocalypse I worked within his vision of grandeur, I experience a fleeting sense of lost beauty—because for a single moment his abnormally intense feelings were my feelings, and he felt that his dream was the most beautiful thing in the world."

He refilled their glasses.

"That wasn't exactly what I meant," she said.

"I know."

"I meant something real."

"It was more real than real, I assure you."

"I don't doubt it, but . . ."

"—But I destroyed the foundation you were laying for your argument. Okay, I apologize. I'll hand it back to you. Here's something that could be real:

"We are moving along the edge of a great bowl of sand," he said. "Into it, the snow is gently drifting. In the spring the snow will melt, the waters will run down into the earth or be evaporated away by the heat of the sun. Then only the sand will remain. Nothing grows in the sand, except for an occasional cactus. Nothing lives here but snakes, a few birds, insects, burrowing things, and a wandering coyote or two. In the afternoon these things will look for shade. Any place where there's an old fence post or a rock or a skull or a cactus to block out the sun, there you will witness life cowering before the elements.

But the colors are beyond belief, and the elements are more lovely, almost, than the things they destroy."

"There is no such place near here," she said.

"If I say it, then there is. Isn't there? I've seen it."

"Yes . . . You're right."

"And it doesn't matter if it's a painting by a woman named O'Keeffe or something right outside our window, does it? If I've seen it?"

"I acknowledge the truth of the diagnosis," she said. "Do you want to speak it for me?"

"No, go ahead."

He refilled the small glasses once more.

"The damage is in my eyes," she told him, "not my brain."

He lit her cigarette.

"I can see with other eyes if I can enter other brains."

He lit his own cigarette.

"Neuroparticipation is based upon the fact that two nervous systems can share the same impulses, the same fantasies . . ."

"*Controlled* fantasies."

"I could perform therapy and at the same time experience genuine visual impressions."

"No," said Render.

"You don't know what it's like to be cut off from a whole area of stimuli! To know that a Mongoloid idiot can experience something you can never know—and that he cannot appreciate it because, like you, he was condemned before birth in a court of biological hapstance in a place where there is no justice—only fortuity, pure and simple."

"The universe did not invent justice. Man did. Unfortunately man must reside in the universe."

"I'm not asking the universe to help me—I'm asking you."

"I'm sorry," said Render.

"Why won't you help me?"

"At this moment you are demonstrating my main reason."

"Which is . . . ?"

"Emotion. This thing means far too much to you. When the therapist is in-phase with a patient he is narco-electrically removed from most of his own bodily sensations. This is necessary—because his mind must be completely absorbed by the task at hand. It is also necessary that his emotions undergo a similar suspension. This, of course, is impossible in the one sense that a person always emotes to some degree. But the therapist's emotions are sublimated into a generalized feeling of exhilaration—or, as in my own case, into an artistic reverie. With you, however, the 'seeing' would be too much. You would be in constant danger of losing control of the dream."

"I disagree with you."

"Of course you do. But the fact remains that you would be dealing, and dealing constantly, with the abnormal. The power of a neurosis is unimaginable to ninety-nine point etcetera percent of the population because we can never adequately judge the intensity of our own, let alone those of others, when we only see them from the outside. That is why no neuroparticipant will ever undertake to treat a full-blown psychotic. The few pioneers in that area are all themselves in therapy today. It would be like diving into a maelstrom. If the therapist loses the upper hand in an intense session, he becomes the Shaped rather than the Shaper. The synapses respond like a fission reaction when nervous impulses are artificially augmented. The transference effect is almost instantaneous.

"I did an awful lot of skiing five years ago. This is because I was a claustrophobe. I had to run, and it took me six months to beat the thing—all because of one tiny lapse that occurred in a measureless fraction of an instant. I had to refer the patient to another therapist. And this was only a minor repercussion—If you were to go ga-ga over the scenery, girl, you could wind up in a rest home for life."

She finished her drink, and Render refilled the glass. The road was open and clear. The darkness eased more and more of itself between the falling flakes. The Spinner picked up speed.

"All right," she admitted, "maybe you're right. Still, though, I think you can help me."

"How?" he asked.

"Accustom me to seeing so that the images will lose their novelty, the emotions wear off. Accept me as a patient and rid me of my sight-anxiety. Then what you have said so far will cease to apply. I will be able to undertake the training then and give my full attention to therapy. I'll be able to sublimate the sight-pleasure into something else."

Render wondered.

Perhaps it could be done. It would be a difficult undertaking, though.

It might also make therapeutic history.

No one was really qualified to try it because no one had ever tried it before.

But Eileen Shallot was a rarity—no, a unique item—for it was likely she was the only person in the world who combined the necessary technical background with the unique problem.

He drained his glass, refilled it, refilled hers.

He was still considering the problem as the "RE-COOR-DINATE" light came on and the car pulled into a cutoff and stood there. He switched off the buzzer and sat there for a long while, thinking.

It was not often that other persons heard him acknowledge his feelings regarding his skill. His colleagues considered him modest. Offhand, though, it might be noted that he was aware that the day a better neuroparticipant began practicing would be the day that a troubled Homo sapiens was to be treated by something but immeasurably less than angels.

Two drinks remained. Then he tossed the emptied bottle into the backbin.

"You know something?" he finally said.

"What?"

"It might be worth a try."

He swiveled about then and leaned forward to re-coordinate, but she was there first. As he pressed the buttons and the S–7 swung around, she kissed him. Below her dark glasses her cheeks were moist.

II

The suicide bothered him more than it should have, and Mrs. Lambert had called the day before to cancel her appointment. So Render decided to spend the morning being pensive. Accordingly he entered the office wearing a cigar and a frown.

"Did you see . . . ?" asked Mrs. Hedges.

"Yes." He pitched his coat onto the table that stood in the far corner of the room. He crossed to the window, stared down. "Yes," he repeated, "I was driving by with my windows clear. They were still cleaning up when I passed."

"Did you know him?"

"I don't even know the name yet. How could I?"

"Priss Tully just called me—she's a receptionist for that engineering outfit up on the eighty-sixth. She says it was James Irizarry, an ad designer who had offices down the hall from them. That's a long way to fall. He must have been unconscious when he hit, huh? He bounced off the building. If you open the window and lean out you can see—off to the left there—where . . ."

"Never mind, Bennie. Your friend have any idea why he did it?"

"Not really. His secretary came running up the hall, screaming. Seems she went in his office to see him about some drawings, just as he was getting up over the sill. There was a note on his board. 'I've had everything I wanted,' it said. 'Why wait around?' Sort of funny, huh? I don't mean *funny* . . ."

"Yeah. Know anything about his personal affairs?"

"Married. Coupla kids. Good professional rep. Lots of business. Sober as anybody. He could afford an office in this building."

"Good Lord!" Render turned. "Have you got a case file there or something?"

"You know," she shrugged her thick shoulders, "I've got friends all over this hive. We always talk when things go slow. Prissy's my sister-in-law anyhow—"

"You mean that if I dived through this window right now, my current biography would make the rounds in the next five minutes?"

"Probably," she twisted her bright lips into a smile, "give or take a couple. But don't do it today, huh? You know, it would be kind of anticlimactic, and it wouldn't get the same coverage as a solus.

"Anyhow," she continued, "you're a mind-mixer. You wouldn't do it."

"You're betting against statistics," he observed. "The

medical profession, along with attorneys, manages about three times as many as most other work areas."

"Hey!" She looked worried. "Go 'way from my window!

"I'd have to go to work for Dr. Hanson then," she added "and he's a slob."

He moved to her desk.

"I never know when to take you seriously," she decided.

"I appreciate your concern," he nodded, "indeed I do. As a matter of fact, I have never been statistic-prone—I should have repercussed out of the neuropy game four years ago."

"You'd be a headline, though," she mused. "All those reporters asking me about you . . . Hey, why do they do it, huh?"

"Who?"

"Anybody."

"How should I know, Bennie? I'm only a humble psyche-stirrer. If I could pinpoint a general underlying cause—and then maybe figure a way to anticipate the thing—why, it might even be better than my jumping, for newscopy. But I can't do it because there is no single, simple reason—I don't think."

"Oh."

"About thirty-five years ago it was the ninth leading cause of death in the United States. Now it's number six for north and South America. I think it's seventh in Europe."

"And nobody will ever really know why Irizarry jumped?"

Render swung a chair backwards and seated himself. He knocked an ash into her petite and gleaming tray. She emptied it into the waste-chute hastily and coughed a significant cough.

"Oh, one can always speculate," he said, "and one in my profession will. The first thing to consider would be the personality traits which might predispose a man to periods of depression. People who keep their emotions under rigid control, people who are conscientious and rather compulsively concerned with small matters . . ." He knocked another fleck of ash into her tray and watched as she reached out to dump it, then quickly drew her hand back again. He grinned an evil grin. "In short," he finished, "some of the characteristics of people in professions which require individual, rather than group performance—medicine, law, the arts."

She regarded him speculatively.

"Don't worry, though," he chuckled, "I'm pleased as hell with life."

"You're kind of down in the mouth this morning."

"Pete called me. He broke his ankle yesterday in gym class. They ought to supervise those things more closely. I'm thinking of changing his school."

"Again?"

"Maybe, I'll see. The headmaster is going to call me this afternoon. I don't like to keep shuffling him, but I do want him to finish school in one piece."

"A kid can't grow up without an accident or two. It's ... statistics."

"Statistics aren't the same thing as destiny, Bennie. Everybody makes his own."

"Statistics or destiny?"

"Both, I guess."

"I think that if something's going to happen, it's going to happen."

"I don't. I happen to think that the human will, backed by a sane mind, can exercise some measure of control over events. If I didn't think so, I wouldn't be in the racket I'm in."

"The world's a machine—you know—cause, effect. Statistics do imply the prob—"

"The human mind is not a machine, and I do not know cause and effect. Nobody does."

"You have a degree in chemistry, as I recall. You're a scientist, Doc."

"So I'm a Trotskyite deviationist," he smiled stretching, "and you were once a ballet teacher." He got to his feet and picked up his coat.

"By the way, Miss Deville called, left a message. She said: 'How about St. Moritz?' "

"Too ritzy," he decided aloud. "It's going to be Davos."

Because the suicide bothered him more than it should have, Render closed the door to his office and turned off the windows and turned on the phonograph. He put on the desk light only.

How has the quality of human life been changed, he wrote, *since the beginnings of the industrial revolution?*

He picked up the paper and reread the sentence. It was the topic he had been asked to discuss that coming Saturday. As was typical in such cases, he did not know what to say because he had too much to say and only an hour to say it in.

He got up and began to pace the office, now filled with Beethoven's Eighth Symphony.

"The power to hurt," he said, snapping on a lapel microphone and activating his recorder, "has evolved in a direct relationship to technological advancement." His imaginary audience grew quiet. He smiled. "Man's potential for working simple mayhem has been multiplied by mass-production; his capacity for injuring the psyche through personal contacts has expanded in an exact ratio to improved communication facilities. But these are all matters of common knowledge and are not the things I wish to consider tonight. Rather, I should like to discuss what I choose to call autopsychomimeses—the self-generated anxiety complexes which on first scrutiny appear quite similar to classic patterns, but which actually represent radical dispersions of psychic energy. They are peculiar to our times . . ."

He paused to dispose of his cigar and formulate his next words.

"Autopsychomimesis," he thought aloud, "a self-perpetuated imitation complex—almost an attention-getting affair. A jazzman, for example, who acted hopped-up half the time, even though he had never used an addictive narcotic and only dimly remembered any-one who had, because all the stimulants and tranquilizers of today are quite benign. Like Quixote, he aspired after a legend when his music alone should have been sufficient outlet for his tensions.

"Or my Korean War Orphan, alive today by virtue of the Red Cross and UNICEF and foster parents whom he never met. He wanted a family so badly that he made one up. And what then? He hated his imaginary father and he loved his imaginary mother quite dearly, for he was a highly intelligent boy and he too longed after the half-true complexes of tradition. Why?

"Today everyone is sophisticated enough to understand the time-honored patterns of psychic disturbance. Today many of the reasons for those disturbances have been removed—not as radically as my now-adult war orphan's, but with as remarkable an effect. We are living in a neurotic past. Again, why? Because our present times are geared to physical health, security, and well-being. We have abolished hunger, though the backwoods orphan would still rather receive a package of food concentrates from a human being who cares for him than to obtain a warm meal from an automat unit in the middle of the jungle.

"Physical welfare is now every man's right, in excess. The reaction to this has occurred in the area of mental health. Thanks to technology, the reasons for many of the old social problems have passed, and along with them went many of the reasons for psychic distress. But between the black of yesterday and the white of tomorrow is the great gray of today, filled with nostalgia and fear of the future, which cannot be expressed on a purely material plane, and which is now being represented by a willful seeking after historical anxiety-modes . . ."

The phone-box buzzed briefly. Render did not hear it over the Eighth.

"We are afraid of what we do not know," he continued, "and tomorrow is a very great unknown. My own specialized area of psychiatry did not even exist thirty years ago. Science is capable of advancing itself so rapidly now that there is a genuine public uneasiness—I might say 'distress'—as to the logical outcome: the total mechanization of everything in the world . . ."

He passed near the desk as the phone buzzed again. He switched off his microphone and softened the Eighth.

"Hello?"

"Moritz," she said.

"Davos," he replied firmly.

"Charlie, you are most exasperating!"

"Jill, dear, so are you."

"Shall we discuss it tonight?"

"There is nothing to discuss!"

"You'll pick me up at five, though?"

He hesitated, then:

"Yes, at five. How come the screen is blank?"

"I've had my hair fixed. I'm going to surprise you again."

He suppressed an idiot chuckle, said, "Pleasantly, I hope. Okay, see you then," waited for her "good-bye," and broke the connection.

He transpared the windows, turned off the light on his desk, and looked outside.

Gray again overhead, and many slow flakes of snow —wandering, not being blown about much—moving downwards and then losing themselves in the tumult. . . .

He also saw, when he opened the window and leaned out, the place off to the left where Irizarry had left his next-to-last mark on the world.

He closed the window and listened to the rest of the symphony. It had been a week since he had gone blind-spinning with Eileen. Her appointment was for one o'clock.

He remembered her fingertips brushing over his face, like leaves, or the bodies of insects, learning his appearance in the ancient manner of the blind. The memory was not altogether pleasant. He wondered why.

Far below a patch of hosed pavement was blank once again; under a thin, fresh shroud of white, it was slippery as glass. A building custodian hurried outside and spread salt on it before someone slipped and hurt himself.

Sigmund was the myth of Fenris come alive. After Render had instructed Mrs. Hedges, "Show them in," the door had begun to open, was suddenly pushed wider, and a pair of smoky-yellow eyes stared in at him. The eyes were set in a strangely misshapen dog-skull.

Sigmund's was not a low canine brow, slanting up slightly from the muzzle; it was a high, shaggy cranium, making the eyes appear even more deep-set than they actually were. Render shivered slightly at the size and aspect of that head. The muties he had seen had all been puppies. Sigmund was full grown, and his gray-black fur had a tendency to bristle, which made him appear somewhat larger than a normal specimen of the breed.

He stared in at Render in a very undoglike way and

made a growling noise, which sounded too much like, "Hello, doctor," to have been an accident.

Render nodded and stood.

"Hello, Sigmund," he said. "Come in."

The dog turned his head, sniffing the air of the room— as though deciding whether or not to trust his ward within its confines. Then he returned his stare to Render, dipped his head in an affirmative, and shouldered the door open. Perhaps the entire encounter had taken only one disconcerting second.

Eileen followed him, holding lightly to the double-leashed harness. The dog padded soundlessly across the thick rug—head low, as though he were stalking something. His eyes never left Render's.

"So this is Sigmund . . . ? How are you, Eileen?"

"Fine. Yes, he wanted very badly to come along, and *I* wanted you to meet him."

Render led her to a chair and seated her. She unsnapped the double guide from the dog's harness and placed it on the floor. Sigmund sat down beside it and continued to stare at Render.

"How is everything at State Psych?"

"Same as always. May I bum a cigarette, doctor? I forgot mine."

He placed it between her fingers, furnished a light. She was wearing a dark blue suit and her glasses were flame blue. The silver spot on her forehead reflected the glow of his lighter; she continued to stare at that point in space after he had withdrawn his hand. Her shoulder-length hair appeared a trifle lighter than it had seemed on the night they met; today it was like a fresh-minted copper coin.

Render seated himself on the corner of his desk, drawing up his world-ashtray with his toe.

"You told me before that being blind did not mean that you had never seen. I didn't ask you to explain it then. But I'd like to ask you now."

"I had a neuroparticipation session with Dr. Riscomb," she told him, "before he had his accident. He wanted to accommodate my mind to visual impressions. Unfortunately there was never a second session."

"I see. What did you do in that session?"

She crossed her ankles, and Render noted they were well-turned.

"Colors, mostly. The experience was quite overwhelming."

"How well do you remember them? How long ago was it?"

"About six months ago—and I shall never forget them. I have even dreamt in color patterns since then."

"How often?"

"Several times a week."

"What sort of associations do they carry?"

"Nothing special. They just come into my mind along with other stimuli now—in a pretty haphazard way."

"How?"

"Well, for instance, when you ask me a question it's a sort of yellowish-orangish pattern that I 'see.' Your greeting was a kind of silvery thing. Now that you're just sitting there listening to me, saying nothing, I associate you with a deep, almost violet, blue."

Sigmund shifted his gaze to the desk and stared at the side panel.

Can he hear the recorder spinning inside? wondered Render. *And if he can, can he guess what it is and what it's doing?*

If so, the dog would doubtless tell Eileen—not that she was unaware of what was now an accepted practice —and she might not like being reminded that he considered her case as therapy, rather than a mere mechanical adaptation process. If he thought it would do any good (he smiled inwardly at the notion), he would talk to the dog in private about it.

Inwardly he shrugged.

"I'll construct a rather elementary fantasy world then," he said finally, "and introduce you to some basic forms today."

She smiled; and Render looked down at the myth who crouched by her side, its tongue a piece of beefsteak hanging over a picket fence.

Is he smiling, too?

"Thank you," she said.

Sigmund wagged his tail.

"Well then," Render disposed of his cigarette near Madagascar, "I'll fetch out the 'egg' now and test it. In

the meantime," he pressed an unobtrusive button, "perhaps some music would prove relaxing."

She started to reply, but a Wagnerian overture snuffed
out the words. Render jammed the button again, and
there was a moment of silence during which he said,
"Heh-heh. Thought Respighi was next."

It took two more pushes for him to locate some Roman
pines.

"You could have left him on," she observed. "I'm quite
fond of Wagner."

"No thanks," he said, opening the closet, "I'd keep
stepping in all those piles of leitmotifs."

The great egg drifted out into the office, soundless as
a cloud. Render heard a soft growl behind as he drew it
toward the desk. He turned quickly.

Like the shadow of a bird, Sigmund had gotten to his
feet, crossed the room, and was already circling the machine and sniffing at it—tail taut, ears flat, teeth bared.

"Easy, Sig," said Render. "It's an Omnichannel Neu-
ral T & R Unit. It won't bite or anything like that. It's
just a machine, like a car, or a teevee, or a dishwasher.
That's what we're going to use today to show Eileen what
some things look like."

"Don't like it," rumbled the dog.

"Why?"

Sigmund had no reply so he stalked back to Eileen
and laid his head in her lap.

"Don't like it," he repeated, looking up at her.

"Why?"

"No words," he decided. "We go home now?"

"No," she answered him. "You're going to curl up in
the corner and take a nap, and I'm going to curl up in
that machine and do the same thing—sort of."

"No good," he said, tail drooping.

"Go on now," she pushed him, "lie down and behave
yourself."

He acquiesced, but he whined when Render blanked
the windows and touched the button that transformed
his desk into the operator's seat.

He whined once more when the egg, connected now to
an outlet, broke in the middle and the top slid back and
up, revealing the interior.

Render seated himself. His chair became a contour

couch and moved in halfway beneath the console. He sat upright, and it moved back again, becoming a chair. He touched a part of the desk and half the ceiling disengaged itself, reshaped itself, and lowered to hover overhead like a huge bell. He stood and moved around to the side of the ro-womb. Respighi spoke of pines and such, and Render disengaged an earphone from beneath the egg and leaned back across his desk. Blocking one ear with his shoulder and pressing the microphone to the other, he played upon the buttons with his free hand. Leagues of surf drowned the tone poem; miles of traffic overrode it; a great clanging bell sent fracture lines running through it; and the feedback said: ". . . Now that you are just sitting there listening to me, saying nothing, I associate you with a deep, almost violet, blue . . ."

He switched to the face mask and monitored, *one*—cinnamon, *two*—leaf mold, *three*—deep reptilian musk . . . and down through thirst, and the tastes of honey and vinegar and salt, and back on up through lilacs and wet concrete, a before-the-storm whiff of ozone, and all the basic olfactory and gustatory cues for morning, afternoon, and evening in the town.

The couch floated normally in its pool of mercury, magnetically stabilized by the walls of the egg. He set the tapes.

The ro-womb was in perfect condition.

"Okay," said Render, turning, "everything checks."

She was just placing her glasses atop her folded garments. She had undressed while Render was testing the machine. He was perturbed by her narrow waist, her large, dark-pointed breasts, her long legs. She was too well-formed for a woman of her height, he decided.

He realized, though, as he stared at her that his main annoyance was, of course, the fact that she was his patient.

"Ready here," she said, and he moved to her side.

He took her elbow and guided her to the machine. Her fingers explored its interior. As he helped her enter the unit, he saw that her eyes were a vivid sea-green. Of this, too, he disapproved.

"Comfortable?"

"Yes."

"Okay then, we're set. I'm going to close it now. Sweet dreams."

The upper shell dropped slowly. Closed, it grew opaque, then dazzling. Render was staring down at his own distorted reflection.

He moved back in the direction of his desk.

Sigmund was on his feet, blocking the way.

Render reached down to pat his head, but the dog jerked it aside.

"Take me, with," he growled.

"I'm afraid that can't be done, old fellow," said Render. "Besides, we're not really going anywhere. We'll just be dozing, right here, in this room."

The dog did not seem mollified.

"Why?"

Render sighed. An argument with a dog was about the most ludicrous thing he could imagine when sober.

"Sig," he said, "I'm trying to help her learn what things look like. You doubtless do a fine job guiding her around in this world which she cannot see—but she needs to know what it looks like now, and I'm going to show her."

"Then she, will not, need me."

"Of course she will." Render almost laughed. The pathetic thing was here bound so closely to the absurd thing he could not help it. "I can't restore her sight," he explained. "I'm just going to transfer her some sight-abstractions—sort of lend her my eyes for a short time. Savvy?"

"No," said the dog. "Take mine."

Render turned off the music.

The whole mutie-master relationship might be worth six volumes, he decided, *in German.*

He pointed to the far corner.

"Lie down, over there, like Eileen told you. This isn't going to take long, and when it's all over, you're going to leave the same way you came—you leading. Okay?"

Sigmund did not answer, but he turned and moved off to the corner, tail drooping again.

Render seated himself and lowered the hood, the operator's modified version of the ro-womb. He was alone before the ninety white buttons and the two red ones. The world ended in the blackness beyond the console. He loosened his necktie and unbuttoned his collar.

He removed the helmet from its receptacle and checked its leads. Donning it then, he swung the half-mask up over his lower face and dropped the darksheet down to meet with it. He rested his right arm in the sling, and with a single tapping gesture, he eliminated his patient's consciousness.

A Shaper does not press white buttons consciously. He wills conditions. Then deeply implanted muscular reflexes exert an almost imperceptible pressure against the sensitive arm-sling, which glides into the proper position and encourages an extended finger to move forward. A button is pressed. The sling moves on.

Render felt a tingling at the base of his skull; he smelled fresh-cut grass.

Suddenly he was moving up the great gray alley between the worlds.

After what seemed a long time, Render felt that he was footed on a strange Earth. He could see nothing; it was only a sense of presence that informed him he had arrived. It was the darkest of all the dark nights he had ever known.

He willed that the darkness disperse. Nothing happened.

A part of his mind came awake again, a part he had not realized was sleeping; he recalled whose world he had entered.

He listened for her presence. He heard fear and anticipation.

He willed color. First, red. . . .

He felt a correspondence. Then there was an echo.

Everything became red; he inhabited the center of an infinite ruby.

Orange. Yellow. . . .

He was caught in a piece of amber.

Green now, and he added the exhalations of a sultry sea. Blue, and the coolness of evening.

He stretched his mind then, producing all the colors at once. They came in great swirling plumes.

Then he tore them apart and forced a form upon them.

An incandescent rainbow arced across the black sky.

He fought for browns and grays below him. Selfluminescent, they appeared—in shimmering, shifting patches.

Somewhere, a sense of awe. There was no trace of hysteria, though, so he continued with the Shaping.

He managed a horizon, and the blackness drained away beyond it. The sky grew faintly blue, and he ventured a herd of dark clouds. There was resistance to his efforts at creating distance and depth so he reinforced the tableau with a very faint sound of surf. A transference from an auditory concept of distance came on slowly then as he pushed the clouds about. Quickly, he threw up a high forest to offset a rising wave of acrophobia.

The panic vanished.

Render focused his attention on tall trees—oaks and pines, poplars and sycamores. He hurled them about like spears in ragged arrays of greens and browns and yellows, unrolled a thick mat of morning-moist grass, dropped a series of gray boulders and greenish logs at irregular intervals, and tangled and twined the branches overhead, casting a uniform shade throughout the glen.

The effect was staggering. It seemed as if the entire world was shaken with a sob, then silent.

Through the stillness he felt her presence. He had decided it would be best to lay the groundwork quickly, to set up a tangible headquarters, to prepare a field for operations. He could backtrack later, he could repair and amend the results of the trauma in the sessions yet to come; but this much, at least, was necessary for a beginning.

With a start he realized that the silence was not a withdrawal. Eileen had made herself imminent in the trees and the grass, the stones and the bushes; she was personalizing their forms, relating them to tactile sensations, sounds, temperatures, aromas.

With a soft breeze, he stirred the branches of the trees. Just beyond the bounds of seeing, he worked out the splashing sounds of a brook.

There was a feeling of joy. He shared it.

She was bearing it extremely well so he decided to extend the scope of the exercise. He let his mind wander among the trees, experiencing a momentary doubling of vision, during which time he saw an enormous hand rising in an aluminum carriage toward a circle of white.

He was beside the brook now, and he was seeking her, carefully.

He drifted with the water. He had not yet taken on a form. The splashes became a gurgling as he pushed the brook through shallow places and over rocks. At his insistence, the waters became more articulate.

"Where are you?" asked the brook.

Here! Here!

Here!

. . . and here! replied the trees, the bushes, the stones, the grass.

"Choose one," said the brook as it widened, rounded a mass of rock, then bent its way down a slope, heading toward a blue pool.

I cannot was the answer from the wind.

"You must." The brook widened and poured itself into the pool, swirled about the surface, then stilled itself and reflected branches and dark clouds. "Now!"

Very well, echoed the wood, *in a moment.*

The mist rose above the lake and drifted to the bank of the pool.

"Now," tinkled the mist.

Here, then . . .

She had chosen a small willow. It swayed in the wind; it trailed its branches in the water.

"Eileen Shallot," he read, "regard the lake."

The breezes shifted; the willow bent.

It was not difficult for him to recall her face, her body. The tree spun as though rootless. Eileen stood in the midst of a quiet explosion of leaves; she stared, frightened, into the deep blue mirror of Render's mind, the lake.

She covered her face with her hands, but it could not stop the seeing.

"Behold yourself," said Render.

She lowered her hands and peered downwards. Then she turned in every direction slowly; she studied herself. Finally:

"I feel I am quite lovely," she said. "Do I feel so because you want me to, or is it true?"

She looked all about as she spoke, seeing the Shaper.

"It is true," said Render from everywhere.

"Thank you."

There was a swirl of white, and she was wearing a belted garment of damask. The light in the distance brightened almost imperceptibly. A faint touch of pink began at the base of the lowest cloudbank.

"What is happening there?" she asked, facing that direction.

"I am going to show you a sunrise," said Render, "and I shall probably botch it a bit—but then, it's my first professional sunrise under these circumstances."

"Where are *you?*" she asked.

"Everywhere," he replied.

"Please take on a form so that I can see you."

"All right."

"Your natural form."

He willed that he be beside her on the bank, and he was.

Startled by a metallic flash, he looked downward. The world receded for an instant, then grew stable once again. He laughed, and the laugh froze as he thought of something.

He was wearing the suit of armor that had stood beside their table in the Partridge and Scalpel on the night they met.

She reached out and touched it.

"The suit of armor by our table," she acknowledged, running her fingertips over the plates and the junctures. "I associated it with you that night."

". . . And you stuffed me into it just now," he commented. "You're a strong-willed woman."

The armor vanished, and he was wearing his gray-brown suit and loose-knit, bloodclot necktie and a professional expression.

"Behold the real me," he smiled faintly. "Now, to the sunset. I'm going to use all the colors. Watch!"

They seated themselves on the green park bench which had appeared behind them, and Render pointed in the direction he had decided upon as east.

Slowly the sun worked through its morning attitudes. For the first time in this particular world, it shone down like a god, and reflected off the lake, and broke the clouds, and set the landscape to smouldering beneath the mist that arose from the moist wood.

Watching, watching intently, staring directly into the

ascending bonfire, Eileen did not move for a long while, nor speak. Render could sense her fascination.

She was staring at the source of all light; it reflected back from the gleaming coin on her brow, like a single drop of blood.

Render said, "That is the sun, and those are clouds," and he clapped his hands and the clouds covered the sun, and there was a soft rumble overhead, "and that is thunder," he finished.

The rain fell then, shattering the lake and tickling their faces, making sharp striking sounds on the leaves, then soft tapping sounds, dripping down from the branches overhead, soaking their garments and plastering their hair, running down their necks and falling into their eyes, turning patches of brown earth to mud.

A splash of lightning covered the sky, and a second later there was another peal of thunder.

". . . And this is a summer storm," he lectured. "You see how the rain affects the foliage, and ourselves. What you just saw in the sky before the thunderclap was lightning."

". . . Too much," she said. "Let up on it for a moment, please."

The rain stopped instantly, and the sun broke through the clouds.

"I have the damnedest desire for a cigarette," she said, "but I left mine in another world."

As she said it, one appeared already lighted between her fingers.

"It's going to taste rather flat," said Render strangely.

He watched her for a moment, then:

"I didn't give you that cigarette," he noted. "You picked it from my mind."

The smoke laddered and spiraled upward, was swept away.

". . . Which means that for the second time today I have underestimated the pull of that vacuum in your mind—in the place where sight ought to be. You are assimilating these new impressions very rapidly. You're even going to the extent of groping after new ones. Be careful. Try to contain that impulse."

"It's like a hunger," she said.

"Perhaps we had best conclude this session now."

Their clothing was dry again. A bird began to sing.

"No, wait! Please! I'll be careful. I want to see more things."

"There is always the next visit," said Render. "But I suppose we can manage one more. Is there something you want very badly to see?"

"Yes. Winter. Snow."

"Okay," smiled the Shaper, "then wrap yourself in that furpiece . . ."

The afternoon slipped by rapidly after the departure of his patient. Render was in a good mood. He felt emptied and filled again. He had come through the first trial without suffering any repercussions. He decided that he was going to succeed. His satisfaction was greater than his fear. It was with a sense of exhilaration that he returned to working on his speech.

". . . And what is the power to hurt?" he inquired of the microphone.

"We live by pleasure and we live by pain," he answered himself. "Either can frustrate and either can encourage. But while pleasure and pain are rooted in biology, they are conditioned by society: thus are values to be derived. Because of the enormous masses of humanity, hectically changing positions in space every day throughout the cities of the world, there has come into necessary being a series of totally inhuman controls upon these movements. Every day they nibble their way into new areas––driving our cars, flying our planes, interviewing us, diagnosing our diseases––and I cannot even venture a moral judgment upon these intrusions. They have become necessary. Ultimately, they may prove salutary.

"The point I wish to make, however, is that we are often unaware of our own values. We cannot honestly tell what a thing means to us until it is removed from our life-situation. If an object of value ceases to exist, then the psychic energies which were bound up in it are released. We seek after new objects of value in which to invest this––mana, if you like, or libido, if you don't. And no one thing that has vanished during the past three or four or five decades was, in itself, massively significant; and no new thing that came into being during that time is massively malicious toward the people it has replaced or the people it in some manner controls. A society, though, is made up of many things, and when these things are changed too rapidly the results are unpredictable. An intense study of mental illness is often quite revealing as to the nature of the stresses in the society where the illness was made. If anxiety-patterns fall into special groups and classes, then something of the discontent of society can be learned from them. Carl Jung pointed out that when consciousness is repeatedly frustrated in a quest for values, it will turn its search to the unconscious; failing there, it will proceed to quarry its way into the hypothetical collective unconscious. He noted, in the postwar analyses of ex-Nazis, that the longer they searched for something to erect from the ruins of their lives—having lived through a period of classical iconoclasm and then seen their new ideals topple as well—the longer they searched, the further back they seemed to reach into the collective unconscious of their people. Their dreams themselves came to take on patterns out of the Teutonic mythos.

"This, in a much less dramatic sense, is happening today. There are historical periods when the group tendency for the mind to turn in upon itself, to turn back, is greater than at other times. We are living in such a period of Quixotism, in the original sense of the term. This is because the power to hurt in our time is the power to ignore, to baffle—and it is no longer the exclusive property of human beings—"

A buzz interrupted him then. He switched off the recorder, touched the phone-box.

"Charles Render speaking," he told it.

"This is Paul Charter," lisped the box. "I am headmaster at Dilling."

"Yes?"

The picture cleared. Render saw a man whose eyes were set close together beneath a high forehead. The forehead was heavily creased; the mouth twitched as it spoke.

"Well, I want to apologize again for what happened. It was a faulty piece of equipment that caused—"

"Can't you afford proper facilities? Your fees are high enough."

"It was a *new* piece of equipment. It was a factory defect—"

"Wasn't there anybody in charge of the class?"

"Yes, but—"

"Why didn't he inspect the equipment? Why wasn't he on hand to prevent the fall?"

"He *was* on hand, but it happened too fast for him to do anything. As for inspecting the equipment for factory defects, that isn't his job. Look, I'm very sorry. I'm quite fond of your boy. I can assure you nothing like this will ever happen again."

"You're right, there. But that's because I'm picking him up tomorrow morning and enrolling him in a school that exercises proper safety precautions."

Render ended the conversation with a flick of his finger.

After several minutes had passed, he stood and crossed the room to his small wall safe, which was partly masked, though not concealed, by a shelf of books. It took only a moment for him to open it and withdraw a jewel box containing a cheap necklace and a framed photograph of a man resembling himself, though somewhat younger, and a woman whose upswept hair was dark and whose chin was small, and two youngsters between them—the girl holding the baby in her arms and forcing her bright, bored smile on ahead. Render always stared for only a few seconds on such occasions, fondling the necklace, and then he shut the box and locked it away again for many months.

Whump! Whump! went the bass. *Tchg-tchg-tchga-tchg,* the gourds.

The gelatins splayed reds, greens, blues, and god-awful yellows about the amazing metal dancers.

HUMAN? asked the marquee.

ROBOTS? (immediately below).

COME SEE FOR YOURSELF! (across the bottom cryptically).

So they did.

Render and Jill were sitting at a microscopic table, thankfully set back against a wall, beneath charcoal caricatures of personalities largely unknown (there being so many personalities among the subcultures of a city of

fourteen-million people). Nose crinkled with pleasure,
Jill stared at the present focal point of this particular
subculture, occasionally raising her shoulders to ear
level to add emphasis to a silent laugh or a small squeal
because the performers were just *too* human—the way
the ebon robot ran his fingers along the silver robot's
forearm as they parted and passed. . . .

Render alternated his attention between Jill and the
dancers and a wicked-looking decoction that resembled
nothing so much as a small bucket of whiskey sours
strewn with seaweed (through which the Kraken might
at any moment arise to drag some hapless ship down to
its doom).

"Charlie, I think they're really people!"

Render disentangled his gaze from her hair and
bouncing earrings.

He studied the dancers down on the floor somewhat
below the table area surrounded by music.

There *could* be humans within those metal shells. If
so, their dance was a thing of extreme skill. Though the
manufacture of sufficiently light alloys was no problem,
it would be some trick for a dancer to cavort so freely—
and for so long a period of time, and with such effortless-
seeming ease—within a head-to-toe suit of armor without
so much as a grate or a click or a clank.

Soundless. . . .

They glided like two gulls; the larger, the color of polished anthracite, and the other, like a moonbeam falling
through a window upon a silk-wrapped manikin.

Even when they touched, there was no sound—or if
there was, it was wholly masked by the rhythms of the
band.

Whump-whump! Tchga-tchg!

Render took another drink.

Slowly, it turned into an apache-dance. Render checked
his watch. Too long for normal entertainers, he decided.
They must be robots. As he looked up again, the black
robot hurled the silver robot perhaps ten feet and turned
his back on her.

There was no sound of striking metal.

Wonder what a setup like that costs? he mused.

"Charlie! There was no sound! How do they do that?"

"Really?" asked Render.

The gelatins were yellow again, then red, then blue, then green.

"You'd think it would damage their mechanisms, wouldn't you?"

The white robot crawled back, and the other swiveled his wrist around and around, a lighted cigarette between the fingers. There was laughter as he pressed it mechanically to his lipless, faceless face. The silver robot confronted him. He turned away again, dropped the cigarette, ground it out slowly, soundlessly, then suddenly turned back to his partner. Would he throw her again? No. . . .

Slowly then, like the great-legged birds of the East, they recommenced their movement, slowly and with many turnings away.

Something deep within Render was amused, but he was too far gone to ask it what was funny. So he went looking for the Kraken in the bottom of the glass instead.

Jill was clutching his biceps then, drawing his attention back to the floor.

As the spotlight tortured the spectrum, the black robot raised the silver one high above his head, slowly, slowly, and then commenced spinning with her in that position— arms outstretched, back arched, legs scissored—very slowly at first. Then faster.

Suddenly they were whirling with an unbelievable speed, and the gelatins rotated faster and faster.

Render shook his head to clear it.

They were mving so rapidly that they *had* to fall— human or robot. But they didn't. They were a mandala. They were a gray-form uniformity. Render looked down.

Then slowing, and slower, slower. Stopped.

The music stopped.

Blackness followed. Applause filled it.

When the lights came on again, the two robots were standing statuelike, facing the audience. Very, very slowly, they bowed.

The applause increased.

Then they turned and were gone.

Then the music came on, and the light was clear again. A babble of voices arose. Render slew the Kraken.

"What d'you think of that?" she asked him.

Render made his face serious and said, "Am I a man dreaming I am a robot, or a robot dreaming I am a man?" He grinned, then added, "I don't know."

She punched his shoulder gaily at that, and he observed that she was drunk.

"I am not," she protested. "Not much anyhow. Not as much as you."

"Still, I think you ought to see a doctor about it. Like me. Like now. Let's get out of here and go for a drive."

"Not yet, Charlie. I want to see them once more, huh? Please?"

"If I have another drink, I won't be able to see that far."

"Then order a cup of coffee."

"Yaagh!"

"Then order a beer."

"I'll suffer without."

There were people on the dance floor now, but Render's feet felt like lead.

He lit a cigarette.

"So you had a dog talk to you today?"

"Yes. Something very disconcerting about that . . ."

"Was she pretty?"

"It was a boy dog. And boy, was he ugly!"

"Silly. I mean his mistress."

"You know I never discuss cases, Jill."

"You told me about her being blind and about the dog. All I want to know is if she's pretty."

"Well . . . yes and no." He bumped her under the table and gestured vaguely. "Well, you know . . ."

"Same thing all the way around," she told the waiter who had appeared suddenly out of an adjacent pool of darkness, nodded, and vanished as abruptly.

"There go my good intentions," sighed Render. "See how you like being examined by a drunken sot, that's all I can say."

"You'll sober up fast, you always do. Hippocratics and all that."

He sniffed, glanced at his watch.

"I have to be in Connecticut tomorrow. Pulling Pete out of that damned school . . ."

She sighed, already tired of the subject.

"I think you worry too much about him. Any kid can

bust an ankle. It's a part of growing up. I broke my wrist
when I was seven. It was an accident. It's not the school's
fault those things sometimes happen."

"Like hell," said Render, accepting his dark drink
from the dark tray the dark man carried. "If they can't
do a good job, I'll find someone who can."

She shrugged.

"You're the boss. All I know is what I read in the papers.

"—And you're still set on Davos, even though you
know you meet a better class of people at St. Moritz?"
she added.

"We're going there to ski, remember? I like the runs
better at Davos."

"I can't score any tonight, can I?"

He squeezed her hand.

"You always score with me, honey."

And they drank their drinks and smoked their cigarettes and held their hands until the people left the dance
floor and filed back to their microscopic tables, and the
gelatins spun round and round, tinting clouds of smoke
from hell to sunrise and back again, and the bass went
whump

Tchga-tchga!

"Oh, Charlie! Here they come again!"

The sky was clear as crystal. The roads were clean. The
snow had stopped.

Jill's breathing was the breathing of a sleeper. The S–7
arced across the bridges of the city. If Render sat very
still, he could convince himself that only his body was
drunk; but whenever he moved his head, the universe
began to dance about him. As it did so, he imagined himself within a dream and Shaper of it all.

For one instant this was true. He turned the big clock
in the sky backward, smiling as he dozed. Another instant
and he was awake again, and unsmiling.

The universe had taken revenge for his presumption.
For one reknown moment with the helplessness which
he had loved beyond helping, it had charged him the
price of the lake-bottom vision once again; and as he had
moved once more toward the wreck at the bottom of the
world—like a swimmer, as unable to speak—he heard

from somewhere high over the Earth, and filtered down to him through the waters above the Earth, the howl of the Fenris Wolf as it prepared to devour the moon; and as this occurred, he knew that the sound was as like to the trump of a judgment as the lady by his side was unlike the moon. Every bit. In all ways. And he was afraid.

III

". . . The plain, the direct, and the blunt. This is Winchester Cathedral," said the guidebook. "With its floor-to-ceiling shafts, like so many huge tree trunks, it achieves a ruthless control over its spaces: the ceilings are flat; each bay, separated by those shafts, is itself a thing of certainty and stability. It seems, indeed, to reflect something of the spirit of William the Conqueror. Its disdain of mere elaboration and its passionate dedication to the love of another world would make it seem, too, an appropriate setting for some tale out of Mallory . . ."

"Observe the scalloped capitals," said the guide. "In their primitive fluting, they anticipated what was later to become a common motif . . ."

"Faugh!" said Render—softly though because he was in a group inside a church.

"Shh!" said Jill (Fotlock—that was her real last name) DeVille.

But Render was impressed as well as distressed.

Hating Jill's hobby, though, had become so much of a reflex with him that he would sooner have taken his rest seated beneath an oriental device that dripped water on his head than to admit he occasionally enjoyed walking through the arcades and the galleries, the passages and the tunnels, and getting all out of breath climbing up the high, twisty stairways of towers.

So he ran his eyes over everything, burnt everything down by shutting them, then built the place up again out of the still smouldering ashes of memory, all so that at a later date he would be able to repeat the performance, offering the vision to his one patient who could see only in this manner. This building he disliked less than most. Yes, he would take it back to her.

The camera in his mind photographing the surroundings, Render walked with the others, overcoat over his arm, his fingers anxious to reach after a cigarette. He kept busy, ignoring his guide, realizing this to be the nadir of all forms of human protest. As he walked through Winchester, he thought of his last two sessions with Eileen Shallot. He recalled his almost unwilling Adam-attitude as he had named all the animals passing before them, led of course by the *one* she had wanted to see, colored fearsome by his own unease. He had felt pleasantly bucolic after boning up on an old Botany text and then proceeding to Shape and name the flowers of the fields.

So far they had stayed out of the cities, far away from the machines. Her emotions were still too powerful at the sight of the simple, carefully introduced objects to risk plunging her into so complicated and chaotic a wilderness yet; he would build her city slowly.

Something passed rapidly, high above the cathedral, uttering a sonic boom. Render took Jill's hand in his for a moment and smiled as she looked up at him. Knowing she verged upon beauty, Jill normally took great pains to achieve it. But today her hair was simply drawn back and knotted behind her head, and her lips and eyes were pale; and her exposed ears were tiny and white and somewhat pointed.

"Observe the scalloped capitals," he whispered. "In their primitive fluting, they anticipated what was later to become a common motif."

"Faugh!" said she.

"Shh!" said a sunburnt little woman nearby, whose face seemed to crack and fall back together again as she pursed and unpursed her lips.

Later as they strolled back toward their hotel, Render said, "Okay on Winchester?"

"Okay on Winchester."

"Happy?"

"Happy."

"Good, then we can leave this afternoon."

"All right."

"For Switzerland . . ."

She stopped and toyed with a button on his coat.

"Couldn't we just spend a day or two looking at some old chateaux first? After all, they're just across the Chan-

nel, and you could be sampling all the local wines while
I looked . . ."

"Okay," he said.

She looked up, a trifle surprised.

"What? No argument?" she smiled. "Where is your
fighting spirit? To let me push you around like this . . . ?"

She took his arm then, and they walked on as he said,
"Yesterday, while we were galloping about in the innards
of that old castle, I heard a weak moan, and then a voice
cried out, 'For the love of God, Montresor!' I think it
was my fighting spirit because I'm certain it was my
voice. I've given up *der geist der stets verneint. Pax
vobiscum!* Let us be gone to France. *Alors!*"

"Dear Rendy, it'll only be another day or two . . ."

"Amen," he said, "though my skis that were waxed are
already waning."

So they did that, and on the morn of the third day
when she spoke to him of castles in Spain, he reflected
aloud that while psychologists drink and only grow angry, psychiatrists have been known to drink, grow angry and break things. Construing this as a veiled threat
aimed at the Wedgewoods she had collected, she acquiesced to his desire to go skiing.

Free! Render almost screamed it.

His heart was pounding inside his head. He leaned
hard. He cut to the left. The wind strapped at his face; a
shower of ice crystals, like bullets of emery, fired by him,
scraped against his cheek—

He was moving. Aye—the world had ended at Weiss-
flujoch, and Dorftali led down and away from his portal.

His feet were two gleaming rivers which raced across
the stark, curving plains; they could not be frozen in
their course. Downward. He flowed. Away from all the
rooms of the world. Away from the stifling lack of intensity, from the day's hundred spoon-fed welfares,
from the killing pace of the forced amusements that
hacked at the Hydra, leisure; away.

And as he fled down the run he felt a strong desire to
look back over his shoulder, as though to see whether
the world he had left behind and above had set one
fearsome embodiment of itself, like a shadow, to trail
along after him, hunt him down, and to drag him back to

a warm and well-lit coffin in the sky, there to be laid to rest with a spike of aluminum driven through his will and a garland of alternating currents smothering his spirit.

"I hate you," he breathed between clenched teeth, and the wind carried the words back; and he laughed then for he always analyzed his emotions as a matter of reflex; and he added, "Exit Orestes, mad, pursued by the Furies . . ."

After a time the slope leveled out, and he reached the bottom of the run and had to stop.

He smoked one cigarette then and rode back up to the top so that he could come down it again for nontherapeutic reasons.

That night he sat before a fire in the big lodge, feeling its warmth soaking into his tired muscles. Jill massaged his shoulders as he played Rorschach with the flames, and he came upon a blazing goblet which was snatched away from him in the same instant by the sound of his name being spoken somewhere across the Hall of the Nine Hearths.

"Charles Render!" said the voice (only it sounded more like "Sharlz Runder"), and his head instantly jerked in that direction, but his eyes danced with too many afterimages for him to isolate the source of the calling.

"Maurice?" he queried after a moment, "Bartelmetz?"

"Aye," came the reply, and then Render saw the familiar grizzled visage, set neckless and balding above the red and blue shag sweater that was stretched mercilessly about the wine-keg rotundity of the man who now picked his way in their direction, deftly avoiding the strewn crutches and the stacked skis and the people who, like Jill and Render, disdained sitting in chairs.

Render stood, stretching, and shook hands as he came upon them.

"You've put on more weight," Render observed. "That's unhealthy."

"Nonsense, it's all muscle. How have you been, and what are you up to these days?" He looked down at Jill, and she smiled back at him.

"This is Miss DeVille," said Render.

"Jill," she acknowledged.

He bowed slightly, finally releasing Render's aching hand.

". . . And this is Professor Maurice Bartelmetz of Vienna," finished Render, "a benighted disciple of all forms of dialectical pessimism and a very distinguished pioneer in neuroparticipation—although you'd never guess it to look at him. I had the good fortune to be his pupil for over a year."

Bartelmetz nodded and agreed with him, taking in the Schnapsflasche Render brought forth from a small plastic bag and accepting the collapsible cup which he filled to the brim.

"Ah, you are a good doctor still," he sighed. "You have diagnosed the case in an instant and you make the proper prescription. *Nozdrovia!*"

"Seven years in a gulp," Render acknowledged, refilling their glasses.

"Then we shall make time more malleable by sipping it."

They seated themselves on the floor, and the fire roared up through the great brick chimney as the logs burnt themselves back to branches, to twigs, to thin sticks, ring by yearly ring.

Render replenished the fire.

"I read your last book," said Bartelmetz finally, casually, "about four years ago."

Render reckoned that to be correct.

"Are you doing any research work these days?"

Render poked lazily at the fire.

"Yes," he answered, "sort of."

He glanced at Jill, who was dozing with her cheek against the arm of the huge leather chair that held his emergency bag, the planes of her face all crimson and flickering shadow.

"I've hit upon a rather unusual subject and started with a piece of jobbery I eventually intend to write about."

"Unusual? In what way?"

"Blind from birth for one thing."

"You're using the ONT&R?"

"Yes. She's going to be a Shaper."

"Verfluchter! Are you aware of the possible repercussions?"

"Of course."

"You've heard of unlucky Pierre?"

"No."

"Good, then it was successfully hushed. Pierre was a philosophy student at the University of Paris, and he was doing a dissertation on the evolution of consciousness. This past summer he decided it would be necessary for him to explore the mind of an ape, for purposes of comparing a moins-nausee mind with his own, I suppose. At any rate, he obtained illegal access to an ONT&R and to the mind of our hairy cousin. It was never ascertained how far along he got in exposing the animal to the stimuli-bank, but it is to be assumed that such items as would not be immediately trans-subjective between man and ape—traffic sounds and *so weiter*—were what frightened the creature. Pierre is still residing in a padded cell, and all his responses are those of a frightened ape.

"So, while he did not complete his own dissertation," he finished, "he may provide significant material for someone else's."

Render shook his head.

"Quite a story," he said softly, "but I have nothing that dramatic to contend with. I've found an exceedingly stable individual—a psychiatrist, in fact—one who's already spent time in ordinary analysis. She wants to go into neuroparticipation, but the fear of a sight-trauma was what was keeping her out. I've been gradually exposing her to a full range of visual phenomena. When I've finished, she should be completely accommodated to sight so that she can give her full attention to therapy and not be blinded by vision, so to speak. We've already had four sessions."

"And?"

". . . And it's working fine."

"You are certain about it?"

"Yes, as certain as anyone can be in these matters."

"Mm-hmm," said Bartelmetz. "Tell me, do you find her excessively strong-willed? By that I mean, say, perhaps an obsessive-compulsive pattern concerning anything to which she's been introduced so far?"

"No."

"Has she ever succeeded in taking over control of the fantasy?"

"No!"

"You lie," he said simply.

Render found a cigarette. After lighting it, he smiled.

"Old father, old artificer," he conceded, "age has not withered your perceptiveness. I may trick me, but never you. Yes, as a matter of fact, she *is* very difficult to keep under control. She is not satisfied just to see. She wants to Shape things for herself already. It's quite understandable—both to her and to me—but conscious apprehension and emotional acceptance never do seem to get together on things. She has become dominant on several occasions, but I've succeeded in resuming control almost immediately. After all, I *am* master of the bank."

"Hmm," mused Bartelmetz. "Are you familiar with a Buddhist text, *Shankara's Catechism?*"

"I'm afraid not."

"Then I lecture you on it now. It posits—obviously not for theraputic purposes—a true ego and a false ego. The true ego is that part of man which is immortal and shall proceed on to nirvana: the soul, if you like. Very good. Well, the false ego, on the other hand, is the normal mind, bound round with the illusions—the consciousness of you and I and everyone we have ever known professionally. Good?—Good. Now, the stuff this false ego is made up of they call skandhas. These include the feelings, the perceptions, the aptitudes, consciousness itself, and even the physical form. Very unscientific. Yes. Now they are not the same thing as neuroses, or one of Mister Ibsen's life-lies, or an hallucination—no, even though they are all wrong, being parts of a false thing to begin with. Each of the five skandhas is a part of the eccentricity that we call identity—then on top come the neuroses and all the other messes which follow after and keep us in business. Okay? Okay. I give you this lecture because I need a dramatic term for what I will say, because I wish to say something dramatic. View the skandhas as lying at the bottom of the pond; the neuroses, they are ripples on the top of the water; the 'true ego,' if there is one, is buried deep beneath the sand at the bottom. So. The ripples fill up the, the, *zwischenwelt*—between the object and the subject. The skandhas are a part of the subject, basic, unique, the stuff of his being. So far, you are with me?"

"With many reservations."

"Good. Now I have defined my term somewhat, I will use it. You are fooling around with skandhas, not simple neuroses. You are attempting to adjust this woman's overall conception of herself and of the world. You are using the ONT&R to do it. It is the same thing as fooling with a psychotic or an ape. All may seem to go well, but—at any moment it is possible you may do something, show her some sight or some way of seeing which will break in upon her selfhood, break a skandha—and pouf! —it will be like breaking through the bottom of the pond. A whirlpool will result, pulling you—where? I do not want you for a patient, young man, young artificer, so I counsel you not to proceed with this experiment. The ONT&R should not be used in such a manner."

Render flipped his cigarette into the fire and counted on his fingers:

"One," he said, "You are making a mystical mountain out of a pebble. All I am doing is adjusting her consciousness to accept an additional area of perception. Much of it is simple transference work from the other senses. Two, her emotions were quite intense initially because it *did* involve a trauma—but we've passed that stage already. Now it is only a novelty to her. Soon it will be a commonplace. Three, Eileen is a psychiatrist herself; she is educated in these matters and deeply aware of the delicate nature of what we are doing. Four, her sense of identity and her desires, or her skandhas, or whatever you want to call them, are as firm as the Rock of Gibraltar. Do you realize the intense application required for a blind person to obtain the education she has obtained? It took a will of ten-point steel and the emotional control of an ascetic as well—"

"—And if something that strong should break in a timeless moment of anxiety," smiled Bartelmetz sadly, "may the shades of Sigmund Freud and Carl Jung walk by your side in the valley of darkness."

"—And five," he added suddenly, staring into Render's eyes. "Five," he ticked it off on one finger. "Is she pretty?"

Render looked back into the fire.

"Very clever," sighed Bartelmetz, "I cannot tell whether you are blushing or not, with the rosy glow of the flames upon your face. I fear that you are, though, which would mean that you are aware that you yourself could be the source of the inciting stimulus. I shall burn a candle tonight before a portrait of Adler and pray that he give you the strength to compete successfully in your duel with your patient."

Render looked at Jill, who was still sleeping. He reached out and brushed a lock of her hair back into place.

"Still," said Bartelmetz, "if you do proceed and all goes well, I shall look forward with great interest to the reading of your work. Did I ever tell you that I have treated several Buddhists and never found a 'true ego'?"

Both men laughed.

Like me but not like me, that one on a leash, smelling of fear, small, gray, and unseeing. Rrowl and he'll choke on his collar. His head is empty as the oven till she pushes the button and it makes dinner. Make talk and they never understand, but they are like me. One day I will kill one—why? . . . Turn here.

"Three steps. Up. Glass doors. Handle to right."

Why? Ahead, drop-shaft. Gardens under, down. Smells nice there. Grass, wetdirt, trees and cleanair. I see. Birds are recorded though. I see all. I.

"Drop-shaft. Four steps."

Down. Yes. Want to make loud noises in throat, feel silly. Clean, smooth, many of trees. God . . . She likes sitting on bench chewing leaves, smelling smooth air. Can't see them like me. Maybe now, some. . . ? No.

Can't Bad Sigmund me on grass, trees, here. Must hold it. Pity. Best place . . .

"Watch for steps."

Ahead. To right, to left, to right, to left, trees and grass now. Sigmund sees. Walking . . . Doctor with machine gives her his eyes. *Rrowl* and he will not choke. No fear-smell.

Dig deep hole in ground, bury eyes. God is blind. Sigmund to see. Her eyes now filled, and he is afraid of teeth. Will make her to see and take her high up in the sky to

see, away. Leave me here, leave Sigmund with none to
see, alone. I will dig a deep hole in the ground . . .

It was after ten in the morning when Jill awoke. She did
not have to turn her head to know that Render was already gone. He never slept late. She rubbed her eyes,
stretched, turned onto her side, and raised herself on her
elbow. She squinted at the clock on the bedside table, simultaneously reaching for a cigarette and her lighter.

As she inhaled, she realized there was no ashtray.
Doubtless Render had moved it to the dresser because he
did not approve of smoking in bed. With a sigh that ended
in a snort, she slid out of the bed and drew on her wrap
before the ash grew too long.

She hated getting up, but once she did she would permit
the day to begin and continue on without lapse through its
orderly progression of events.

"Damn him," she smiled. She had wanted her breakfast
in bed, but it was too late now.

Between thoughts as to what she would wear, she observed an alien pair of skis standing in the corner. A sheet
of paper was impaled on one. She approached it.

"Join me?" asked the scrawl.

She shook her head in an emphatic negative and felt
somewhat sad. She had been on skis twice in her life, and
she was afraid of them. She felt that she should really try
again after his being a reasonably good sport about the
chateaux, but she could not even bear the memory of the
unseemly downward rushing—which on two occasions,
had promptly deposited her in a snowbank—without
wincing and feeling once again the vertigo that had seized
her during the attempts.

So she showered and dressed and went downstairs for
breakfast.

All nine fires were already roaring as she passed the big
hall and looked inside. Some red-faced skiers were holding their hands up before the blaze of the central hearth.
It was not crowded though. The racks held only a few
pairs of dripping boots, bright caps hung on pegs, moist
skis stood upright in their place beside the door. A few
people were seated in the chairs set further back toward
the center of the hall, reading papers, smoking, or talking

quietly. She saw no one she knew so she moved on toward the dining room.

As she passed the registration desk, the old man who worked there called out her name. She approached him and smiled.

"Letter," he explained, turning to a rack. "Here it is," he announced, handing it to her. "Looks important."

It had been forwarded three times, she noted. It was a bulky brown envelope, and the return address was that of her attorney.

"Thank you."

She moved off to a seat beside the big window that looked out upon a snow garden, a skating rink, and a distant winding trail dotted with figures carrying skis over their shoulders. She squinted against the brightness as she tore open the envelope.

Yes, it was final. Her attorney's note was accompanied by a copy of the divorce decree. She had only recently decided to end her legal relationship to Mister Fotlock, whose name she had stopped using five years earlier, when they had separated. Now that she had the thing, she wasn't sure exactly what she was going to do with it. It would be a hell of a surprise for dear Rendy, though, she decided. She would have to find a reasonably innocent way of getting the information to him. She withdrew her compact and practiced a "Well?" expression. Well, there would be time for that later, she mused. Not too much later, though . . . Her thirtieth birthday, like a huge black cloud, filled an April but four months distant. Well . . . She touched her quizzical lips with color, dusted more powder over her mole, and locked the expression within her compact for future use.

In the dining room she saw Dr. Bartelmetz seated before an enormous mound of scrambled eggs, great chains of dark sausages, several heaps of yellow toast, and a half-emptied flask of orange juice. A pot of coffee steamed on the warmer at his elbow. He leaned slightly forward as he ate, wielding his fork like a windmill blade.

"Good morning," she said.

He looked up.

"Miss DeVille—Jill . . . Good morning." He nodded at the chair across from him. "Join me, please."

She did so, and when the waiter approached, she nodded and said, "I'll have the same thing, only about ninety percent less."

She turned back to Bartelmetz.

"Have you seen Charles today?"

"Alas, I have not," he gestured, open-handed, "and I wanted to continue our discussion while his mind was still in the early stages of wakefulness and somewhat malleable. Unfortunately," he took a sip of coffee, "he who sleeps well enters the day somewhere in the middle of its second act."

"Myself, I usually come in around intermission and ask someone for a synopsis," she explained. "So why not continue the discussion with me? I'm always malleable, and my skandhas are in good shape."

Their eyes met, and he took a bite of toast.

"Aye," he said at length, "I had guessed as much. Well, good. What do you know of Render's work?"

She adjusted herself in the chair.

"Mmm. He being a special specialist in a highly specialized area, I find it difficult to appreciate the few things he does say about it. I'd like to be able to look inside other people's minds sometimes—to see what they're thinking about *me,* of course—but I don't think I could stand staying there very long. Especially," she gave a mock shudder, "the mind of somebody with—problems. I'm afraid I'd be too sympathetic or too frightened or something. Then, according to what I've read—pow!— like sympathetic magic, it would be my problem.

"Charles never has problems though," she continued, "at least, none that he speaks to me about. Lately I've been wondering, though. That blind girl and her talking dog seem to be too much with him."

"Talking dog?"

"Yes, her seeing-eye dog is one of those surgical mutants."

"How interesting . . . Have you ever met her?"

"Never."

"So," he mused.

"Sometimes a therapist encounters a patient whose problems are so akin to his own that the sessions become extremely mordant," he noted. "It has always been the case with me when I treat a fellow psychiatrist. Perhaps

Charles sees in this situation a parallel to something which has been troubling him personally. I did not administer his personal analysis. I do not know all the ways of his mind, even though he was a pupil of mine for a long while. He was always self-contained, somewhat reticent; he could be quite authoritative on occasion, however. —What are some of the other things that occupy his attention these days?"

"His son Peter is a constant concern. He's changed the boy's school five times in five years."

Her breakfast arrived. She adjusted her napkin and drew her chair closer to the table.

"—and he has been reading case histories of suicides recently, and talking about them, and talking about them, and talking about them."

"To what end?"

She shrugged and began eating.

"He never mentioned why," she said, looking up again. "Maybe he's writing something . . ."

Bartelmetz finished his eggs and poured more coffee.

"Are you afraid of this patient of his?" he inquired.

"No . . . Yes," she responded, "I am."

"Why?"

"I am afraid of sympathetic magic," she said, flushing slightly.

"Many things could fall under that heading."

"Many indeed," she acknowledged. And after a moment, "We are united in our concern for his welfare and in agreement as to what represents the threat. So may I ask you a favor?"

"You may."

"Talk to him again," she said. "Persuade him to drop the case."

He folded his napkin.

"I intended to do that after dinner," he stated, "because I believe in the ritualistic value of rescue-motions. They shall be made."

*   *   *

Dear Father-Image,

Yes, the school is fine, my ankle is getting that way, and my classmates are a congenial lot. No, I am not short on cash, undernourished, or having difficulty fitting into the new curriculum. Okay?

The building I will not describe, as you have already seen the macabre thing. The grounds I cannot describe, as they are presently residing beneath cold white sheets. Brrr! I trust yourself to be enjoying the arts wint'rish. I do not share your enthusiasm for summer's opposite, except within picture frames or as an emblem on ice cream bars.

The ankle inhibits my mobility, and my roommate has gone home for the weekend—both of which are really blessings (saith Pangloss), for I now have the opportunity to catch up on some reading. I will do so forthwith.

Prodigally,
Peter

*   *   *

Render reached down to pat the huge head. It accepted the gesture stoically, then turned its gaze up to the Austrian whom Render had asked for a light, as if to say, "Must I endure this indignity?" The man laughed at the expression, snapping shut the engraved lighter on which Render noted the middle initial to be a small v.

"Thank you," he said. And to the dog: "What is your name?"

"Bismark," it growled.

Render smiled.

"You remind me of another of your kind," he told the dog. "One Sigmund, by name, a companion and guide to a blind friend of mine, in America."

"My Bismark is a hunter," said the young man. "There is no quarry that can outthink him, neither the deer nor the big cats."

The dog's ears pricked forward, and he stared up at Render with proud, blazing eyes.

"We have hunted in Africa and the northern and southwestern parts of America. Central America, too. He never loses the trail. He never gives up. He is a beautiful brute, and his teeth could have been made in Solingen."

"You are indeed fortunate to have such a hunting companion."

"I hunt," growled the dog. "I follow . . . Sometimes, I have, the kill . . ."

"You would not know of the one called Sigmund then, or the woman he guides—Miss Eileen Shallot?" asked Render.

The man shook his head.

"No, Bismark came to me from Massachusetts, but I was never to the Center personally. I am not acquainted with other mutie handlers."

"I see. Well, thank you for the light. Good afternoon."

"Good afternoon."

"Good, after, noon . . ."

Render strolled on up the narrow street, hands in his pockets. He had excused himself and not said where he was going. This was because he had had no destination in mind. Bartelmetz's second essay at counseling had almost led him to say things he would later regret. It was easier to take a walk than to continue the conversation.

On a sudden impulse he entered a small shop and bought a cuckoo clock which had caught his eye. He felt certain that Bartelmetz would accept the gift in the proper spirit. He smiled and walked on. And what was that letter to Jill which the desk clerk had made a special trip to their table to deliver at dinnertime? he wondered. It had been forwarded three times, and its return address was that of a law firm. Jill had not even opened it but had smiled, overtipped the old man, and tucked it into her purse. He would have to hint subtly as to its contents. She would be sure to tell him out of pity.

The icy pillars of the sky suddenly seemed to sway before him as a cold wind leapt down out of the north. Render hunched his shoulders and drew his head further below his collar. Clutching the cuckoo clock, he hurried back up the street.

That night the serpent that holds its tail in its mouth belched, the Fenris Wolf made a pass at the moon, the little clock said "cuckoo," and tomorrow came on like Manolete's last bull, shaking the gate of horn with the bellowed promise to tread a river of lions to sand.

Render promised himself he would lay off the gooey fondue.

•

Later, much later, when they skipped through the skies in a kite-shaped cruiser, Render looked down upon the darkened Earth, dreaming its cities full of stars, looked up at the sky where they were all reflected, looked about him at the tape-screens watching all the people who blinked into them, and at the coffee, tea, and mixed drinks dispensers who sent their fluids forth to explore the insides of the people they required to push their buttons, then looked across at Jill whom the old buildings had compelled to walk among their walls—because he knew she felt he should be looking at her then—felt his seat's demand that he convert it into a couch, did so, and slept.

IV

Her office was full of flowers, and she liked exotic perfumes. Sometimes she burned incense.

She liked soaking in overheated pools, walking through falling snow, listening to too much music, played perhaps too loudly, drinking five or six varieties of liqueurs (usually reeking of anise, sometimes touched with wormwood) every evening. Her hands were soft and lightly freckled. Her fingers were long and tapered. She wore no rings.

Her fingers traced and retraced the floral swellings on the side of her chair as she spoke into the recording unit.

". . . Patient's chief complaints on admission were nervousness, insomnia, stomach pains, and a period of depression. Patient has had a record of previous admissions for short periods of time. He had been in this hospital in 1995 for a manic depressive psychosis, depressed type, and he returned here again, 2–3–96. He was in another hospital, 9–20–97. Physical examination revealed a BP of 170/100. He was normally developed and well-nourished on the date of examination, 12–11–98. On this date patient complained of chronic backache, and there was noted some moderate symptoms of alcohol withdrawal. Physical examination further revealed no pathology except that the patient's tendon reflexes were exaggerated but equal. These symptoms were the result of alcohol withdrawal. Upon admission he was shown to be not psychotic, neither delusional nor hallucinated. He was well-oriented as to place, time, and person. His psychological condition was evaluated, and he was found to be somewhat grandiose and expansive and more than a little hostile. He was considered a potential trouble maker. Because of his experience as a cook, he was assigned to work in the kitchen. His general condition then showed definite improvement. He is less tense and is cooperative. Diagnosis: Manic depressive reaction (external precipitating stress unknown). The degree of psychiatric impairment is mild. He is considered competent. To be continued on therapy and hospitalization."

She turned off the recorder then and laughed. The sound frightened her. Laughter is a social phenomenon and she was alone. She played back the recording then, chewing on the corner of her handkerchief while the soft, clipped words were returned to her. She ceased to hear them after the first dozen or so.

When the recorder stopped talking, she turned it off. She was alone. She was very alone. She was so damned alone that the little pool of brightness which occurred when she stroked her forehead and faced the window—that little pool of brightness suddenly became the most important thing in the world. She wanted it to be an ocean of light. Or else she wanted to grow so small herself that the effect would be the same: she wanted to drown in it.

It had been three weeks yesterday. . . .

Too long, she decided, *I should have waited. No! Impossible! But what if he goes as Riscomb went? No! He won't. He would not. Nothing can hurt him. Never. He is all strength and armor. But, but we should have waited till next month to start. Three weeks . . . Sight withdrawal—that's what it is. Are the memories fading? Are they weaker? What does a tree look like? Or a cloud? I can't remember! What is red? What is green? God! It's hysteria! I'm watching and I can't stop it! Take a pill! A pill!*

Her shoulders began to shake. She did not take a pill, though, but bit down harder on the handkerchief until her sharp teeth tore through its fabric.

"Beware," she recited a personal beatitude, "those who hunger and thirst after justice, for we *will* be satisfied.

"And beware the meek," she continued, "for we shall attempt to inherit the Earth.

"And beware . . ."

There was a brief buzz from the phone-box. She put

away her handkerchief, composed her face, turned the
unit on.

"Hello . . . ?"

"Eileen, I'm back. How've you been?"

"Good, quite well in fact. How was your vacation?"

"Oh, I can't complain. I had it coming for a long time. I
guess I deserve it. Listen, I brought some things back to
show you—like Winchester Cathedral. You want to come
in this week? I can make it any evening."

*Tonight No. I want it too badly. It will set me back if
he sees . . .*

"How about tomorrow night?" she asked. "Or the one
after?"

"Tomorrow will be fine," he said. "Meet you at the P &
S, around seven?"

"Yes, that would be pleasant. Same table?"

"Why not? I'll reserve it."

"All right. I'll see you then."

"Good-bye."

The connection was broken.

Suddenly, then, at that moment, colors swirled again
through her head; and she saw trees—oaks and pines,
poplars and sycamores—great, and green and brown and
iron-colored; and she saw wads of fleecy clouds, dipped in
paint pots, swabbing a pastel sky; and a burning sun, and
a small willow tree, and a lake of a deep, almost violet,
blue. She folded her torn handkerchief and put it away.

She pushed a button beside her desk and music filled
the office: Scriabin. Then she pushed another button and
replayed the tape she had dictated, half-listening to each.

Pierre sniffed suspiciously at the food. The attendant
moved away from the tray and stepped out into the hall,
locking the door behind him. The enormous salad waited
on the floor. Pierre approached cautiously, snatched a
handful of lettuce, gulped it.

He was afraid.

*If only the steel would stop crashing, and crashing
against steel, somewhere in that dark night . . . If only . . .*

Sigmund rose to his feet, yawned, stretched. His hind legs
trailed out behind him for a moment, then he snapped to
attention and shook himself. She would be coming home

soon. Wagging his tail slowly, he glanced up at the human-level clock with the raised numerals, verified his feelings, then crossed the apartment to the TV. He rose onto his hind legs, rested one paw against the table, and used the other to turn on the set.

It was nearly time for the weather report, and the roads would be icy.

"I have driven through countywide graveyards," wrote Render, "vast forests of stone that spread further every day.

"Why does man so zealously guard his dead? Is it because this is the monumentally democratic way of immortalization, the ultimate affirmation of the power to hurt —that is to say, life—and the desire that it continue on forever? Unamuno has suggested that this is the case. If it is, then a greater percentage of the population actively sought immortality last year than ever before in history . . ."

Tch-tchg, tchg
"Do you think they're really people?"
"Naw, they're too good."

The evening was star glint and soda over ice. Render wound the S–7 into the cold sub-subcellar, found his parking place, nosed into it.

There was a damp chill that emerged from the concrete to gnaw like rats' teeth at their flesh. Render guided her toward the lift, their breath preceding them in dissolving clouds.

"A bit of a chill in the air," he noted.

She nodded, biting her lip.

Inside the lift, he sighed, unwound his scarf, lit a cigarette.

"Give me one, please," she requested, smelling the tobacco.

He did.

They rose slowly, and Render leaned against the wall, puffing a mixture of smoke and crystallized moisture.

"I met another mutie shep," he recalled, "in Switzerland. Big as Sigmund. A hunter, though, and as Prussian as they come," he grinned.

"Sigmund likes to hunt, too," she observed. "Twice every year we go up to the North Woods and I turn him loose. He's gone for days at a time, and he's always quite happy when he returns. Never says what he's done, but he's never hungry. Back when I got him, I guessed that he would need vacations from humanity to stay stable. I think I was right."

The lift stopped, the door opened, and they walked out into the hall, Render guiding her again.

Inside his office, he poked at the thermostat and warm air sighed through the room. He hung their coats in the inner office and brought the great egg out from its nest behind the wall. He connected it to an outlet and moved to convert his desk into a control panel.

"How long do you think it will take?" she asked, running her fingertips over the smooth, cold curves of the egg. "The whole thing, I mean. The entire adaptation to seeing."

He wondered.

"I have no idea," he said, "no idea whatsoever yet. We got off to a good start, but there's still a lot of work to be done. I think I'll be able to make a good guess in another three months."

She nodded wistfully, moved to his desk, explored the controls with fingerstrokes like ten feathers.

"Careful you don't push any of those."

"I won't. How long do you think it will take me to learn to operate one?"

"Three months to learn it. Six, to actually become proficient enough to use it on anyone and an additional six under close supervision before you can be trusted on your own. About a year altogether."

"Uh-huh." She chose a chair.

Render touched the seasons to life, and the phases of day and night, the breath of the country, the city, the elements that raced naked through the skies, and all the dozens of dancing cues he used to build worlds. He smashed the clock of time and tasted the seven or so ages of man.

"Okay," he turned, "everything is ready."

It came quickly, and with a minimum of suggestion on Render's part. One moment there was grayness. Then a dead-white fog. Then it broke itself apart, as though a quick wind had arisen, although he neither heard nor felt a wind.

He stood beside the willow tree beside the lake, and she stood half-hidden among the branches and the lattices of shadow. The sun was slanting its way into evening.

"We have come back," she said, stepping out, leaves in her hair. "For a time I was afraid it had never happened, but I see it all again, and I remember now."

"Good," he said. "Behold yourself." And she looked into the lake.

"I have not changed," she said. "I haven't changed . . ."

"No."

"But you have," she continued, looking up at him. "You are taller, and there is something different . . ."

"No," he answered.

"I am mistaken," she said quickly, "I don't understand everything I see yet.

"I will, though."

"Of course."

"What are we going to do?"

"Watch," he instructed her.

Along a flat, no-colored river of road she just then noticed beyond the trees came the car. It came from the farthest quarter of the sky, skipping over the mountains, buzzing down the hills, circling through the glades, and splashing them with the colors of its voice—the gray and the silver of synchronized potency—and the lake shivered from its sounds, and the car stopped a hundred feet away, masked by the shrubberies; and it waited. It was the S–7.

"Come with me," he said, taking her hand. "We're going for a ride."

They walked among the trees and rounded the final cluster of bushes. She touched the sleek cocoon, its antennae, its tires, its windows, and the windows transpared as she did so. She stared through them at the inside of the car, and she nodded.

"It is your Spinner."

"Yes." He held the door for her. "Get in. We'll return to the club. The time is now. The memories are fresh, and they should be reasonably pleasant, or neutral."

"Pleasant," she said, getting in.

He closed the door, then circled the car and entered. She watched as he punched imaginary coordinates. The car leapt ahead, and he kept a steady stream of trees flowing by them. He could feel the rising tension so he did not vary the scenery. She swiveled her seat and studied the interior of the car.

"Yes," she finally said, "I can perceive what everything is."

She stared out the window again. She looked at the rushing trees. Render stared out and looked upon rushing anxiety-patterns. He opaqued the windows.

"Good," she said, "thank you. Suddenly it was too much to see—all of it, moving past like a . . ."

"Of course," said Render, maintaining the sensations of forward motion. I'd anticipated that. You're getting tougher, though."

After a moment, "Relax," he said, "relax now," and somewhere a button was pushed, and she relaxed, and they drove on, and on and on, and finally the car began to slow, and Render said. "Just for one nice, slow glimpse now, look out your window."

She did.

He drew upon every stimulus in the bank which could promote sensations of pleasure and relaxation, and he dropped the city around the car, and the windows became transparent, and she looked out upon the profiles of towers and a block of monolithic apartments, and then she saw three rapid cafeterias, an entertainment palace, a drugstore, a medical center of yellow brick with an aluminum caduceus set above its archway, and a glassed-in high school, now emptied of its pupils, a fifty-pump gas station, another drugstore, and many more cars, parked or roaring by them, and people, people moving in and out of the doorways and walking before the buildings and getting into the cars and getting out of the cars; and it was summer, and the light of late afternoon filtered down upon the colors of the city and the colors of the garments the people wore as they moved along the boulevard, as they loafed upon the terraces, as they crossed the balconies, leaned on balustrades and windowsills, emerged from a corner kiosk, entered one, stood talking to one another; a woman walking a poodle rounded a corner; rockets went to and fro in the high sky.

The world fell apart then, and Render caught the pieces.

He maintained an absolute blackness, blanketing every sensation but that of their movement forward.

After a time a dim light occurred, and they were still seated in the Spinner, windows blanked again, and the air as they breathed it became a soothing unguent.

"Lord," she said, "the world is so filled. Did I really see all of that?"

"I wasn't going to do that tonight, but you wanted me to. You seemed ready."

"Yes," she said, and the windows became transparent again. She turned away quickly.

"It's gone," he said. "I only wanted to give you a glimpse."

She looked, and it was dark outside now, and they were crossing over a high bridge. They were moving slowly. There was no other traffic. Below them were the Flats where an occasional smelter flared like a tiny, drowsing volcano, spitting showers of orange sparks skyward; and there were many stars—they glistened on the breathing water that went beneath the bridge; they silhouetted by pinprick the skyline that hovered dimly below its surface. The slanting struts of the bridge marched steadily by.

"You have done it," she said, "and I thank you." Then: "Who are you, really?" (He must have wanted her to ask that.)

"I am Render," he laughed. And they wound their way through a dark, now-vacant city, coming at last to their club and entering the great parking dome.

Inside he scrutinized all her feelings, ready to banish the world at a moment's notice. He did not feel he would have to, though.

They left the car, moved ahead. They passed into the club, which he had decided would not be crowded tonight. They were shown to their table at the foot of the bar in the small room with the suit of armor, and they sat down and ordered the same meal over again.

"No," he said, looking down, "it belongs over there."

The suit of armor appeared once again beside the table, and he was once again inside his gray suit and black tie and silver tie clasp shaped like a tree limb.

They laughed.

"I'm just not the type to wear a tin suit, so I wish you'd stop seeing me that way."

"I'm sorry," she smiled. "I don't know how I did that, or why."

"I do, and I decline the nomination. Also, I caution you once again. You are conscious of the fact that this is all an illusion. I had to do it that way for you to get the full benefit of the thing. For most of my patients, though, it is the real item while they are experiencing it. It makes a counter-trauma or a symbolic sequence even more powerful. You are aware of the parameters of the game, however, and whether you want it or not, this gives you a different sort of control over it than I normally have to deal with. Please be careful."

"I'm sorry. I didn't mean to."

"I know. Here comes the meal we just had."

"Ugh! It looks dreadful! Did we eat all that stuff?"

"Yes," he chuckled. "That's a knife, that's a fork, that's a spoon. That's roast beef, and those are mashed potatoes, those are peas, that's butter . . ."

"Goodness I don't feel so well."

". . . And those are the salads, and those are the salad dressings. This is a brook trout—mmm! These are French fried potatoes. This is a bottle of wine. Hmm—let's see—Romanee-Conti since I'm not paying for it—and a bottle of Yquem for the trou—Hey!"

The room was wavering.

He bared the table, he banished the restaurant. They were back in the glade. Through the transparent fabric of the world, he watched a hand moving along a panel. Buttons were being pushed. The world grew substantial again. Their emptied table was set beside the lake now, and it was still nighttime and summer, and the tablecloth was very white under the glow of the giant moon that hung overhead.

"That was stupid of me," he said. "Awfully stupid. I should have introduced them one at a time. The actual sight of basic oral stimuli can be very distressing to a person seeing them for the first time. I got so wrapped up in the Shaping that I forgot the patient, which is just dandy! I apologize."

"I'm okay now. Really I am."

He summoned a cool breeze from the lake.

". . . And that is the moon," he added lamely.

She nodded, and she was wearing a tiny moon in the center of her forehead; it glowed like the one above them, and her hair and dress were all of silver.

The bottle of Romanee-Conti stood on the table, and two glasses.

"Where did that come from?"

She shrugged. He poured out a glassful.

"It may taste kind of flat," he said.

"It doesn't. Here." She passed it to him.

As he sipped it, he realized it had a taste—a *fruite* such as might be quashed from the grapes grown in the Isles of the Blest, a smooth, muscular *charnu*, and a *capiteux* centrifuged from the fumes of a field of burning poppies. With a start he knew that his hand must be traversing the route of the perceptions, symphonizing the sensual cues of a transference and a counter-transference which had come upon him all unawares, there beside the lake.

"So it does," he noted, "and now it is time we returned."

"So soon? I haven't seen the cathedral yet . . ."

"So soon."

He willed the world to end, and it did.

"It is cold out there," she said as she dressed, "and dark."

"I know. I'll mix us something to drink while I clear the unit."

"Fine."

He glanced at the tapes and shook his head. He crossed to his bar cabinet.

"It's not exactly Romanee-Conti," he observed, reaching for a bottle.

"So what? I don't mind."

Neither did he at that moment. So he cleared the unit, they drank their drinks, and he helped her into her coat, and they left.

As they rode, the lift down to the sub-sub he willed the world to end again, but it didn't.

Dad,

I hobbled from school to taxi and taxi to spaceport for the local Air Force Exhibit—Outward, it was called. (Okay, I exaggerated the hobble. It got me extra attention, though.) The whole bit was aimed at seducing young manhood into a five-year hitch, as I saw it. But it worked. I wanna join up. I wanna go Out There. Think they'll take me when I'm old enuff? I mean take me Out—not some crummy desk job. Think so?

I do.

There was this dam lite colonel ('scuse the French) who saw this kid lurching around and pressing his nose 'gainst the big windowpanes, and he decided to give him the subliminal sell. Great! He pushed me through the gallery and showed me all the pitchers of AF triumphs, from Moonbase to Marsport. He lectured me on the Great Traditions of the Service and marched me into a flic room where the Corps had good clean fun on tape, wrestling one another in null-G "where it's all skill and no brawn," and making tinted water sculpture-work way in the middle of the air and doing dismounted drill on the skin of a cruiser. Oh, joy!

Seriously, though, I'd like to be there when they hit the Outer Five—and On Out. Not because of the bogus balonus in the throwaways, and suchlike crud, but because I think someone of sensibility should be along to chronicle the thing in the proper way. You know, raw frontier observer. Francis Parkman, Mary Austin, like that. So I decided I'm going.

The AF boy with the chicken stuff on his shoulders wasn't in the least way patronizing, gods be praised. We stood on the balcony and watched ships lift off, and he told me to go forth and study real hard and I might be riding them some day. I did not bother to tell him that I'm hardly intellectually deficient and that I'll have my B.A. before I'm old enough to do anything with it, even join his Corps. I just watched the ships lift off and said, "Ten years from now I'll be looking down, not up." Then he told me how hard his own training had been so I did not ask howcum he got stuck with a lousy dirtside assignment like this one. Glad I didn't, now I think on it. He looked more like one of their ads than one of their real people. Hope I never look like an ad.

Thank you for the monies and the warm sox and Mozart's String Quintets, which I'm hearing right now. I wanna put in my bid for Luna instead of Europe next summer. Maybe. . . ? Possibly. . . ? Contingently. . . ? Huh? If I can smash that new test you're designing for me. . . ? Anyhow, please think about it.

Your son,
Pete

"Hello. State Psychiatric Institute."

"I'd like to make an appointment for an examination."

"Just a moment. I'll connect you with the Appointment Desk."

"Hello. Appointment Desk."

"I'd like to make an appointment for an examination."

"Just a moment . . . What sort of examination."

"I want to see Dr. Shallot, Eileen Shallot. As soon as possible."

"Just a moment. I'll have to check her schedule . . . Could you make it at two o'clock next Tuesday?"

"That would be just fine."

"What is the name, please?"

"DeVille. Jill DeVille."

"All right, Miss DeVille. That's two o'clock, Tuesday."

"Thank you."

The man walked beside the highway. Cars passed along the highway. The cars in the high-acceleration lane blurred by.

Traffic was light.

It was 10:30 in the morning and cold.

The man's fur-lined collar was turned up, his hands were in his pockets, and he leaned into the wind. Beyond the fence, the road was clean and dry.

The morning sun was buried in clouds. In the dirty light, the man could see the tree a quarter-mile ahead.

His pace did not change. His eyes did not leave the tree. The small stones clicked and crunched beneath his shoes.

When he reached the tree, he took off his jacket and folded it neatly.

He placed it upon the ground and climbed the tree.

As he moved out onto the limb, which extended over the fence, he looked to see that no traffic was approaching. Then he seized the branch with both hands, lowered himself, hung a moment, and dropped onto the highway.

It was a hundred yards wide, the eastbound half of the highway.

He glanced west, saw there was still no traffic coming his way, then began to walk toward the center island. He knew he would never reach it. At this time of day the cars were moving at approximately one-hundred-sixty miles an hour in the high-acceleration lane. He walked on.

A car passed behind him. He did not look back. If the windows were opaqued, as was usually the case, then the occupants were unaware he had crossed their path. They would hear of it later and examine the front end of their vehicle for possible sign of such an encounter.

A car passed in front of him. Its windows were clear. A glimpse of two faces, their mouths made into O's, was presented to him, then torn from his sight. His own face remained without expression. His pace did not change. Two more cars rushed by, windows darkened. He had crossed perhaps twenty yards of highway.

Twenty-five. . . .

Something in the wind or beneath his feet told him it was coming. He did not look.

Something in the corner of his eye assured him it was coming. His gait did not alter.

Cecil Green had the windows transpared because he liked it that way. His left hand was inside her blouse, and her skirt was piled up on her lap, and his right hand was resting on the lever which would lower the seats. Then she pulled away, making a noise down inside her throat.

His head snapped to the left.

He saw the walking man.

He saw the profile, which never turned to face him fully. He saw that the man's gait did not alter.

Then he did not see the man.

There was a slight jar, and the windshield began cleaning itself. Cecil Green raced on.

He opaqued the windows.

"How. . . ?" he asked after she was in his arms again and sobbing.

"The monitor didn't pick him up . . ."

"He must not have touched the fence . . ."

"He must have been out of his mind!"

"Still, he could have picked an easier way."

It could have been any face . . . Mine?
Frightened, Cecil lowered the seats.

Charles Render was writing the "Necropolis" chapter for
The Missing Link is Man, which was to be his first
book in over four years. Since his return he had set aside
every Tuesday and Thursday afternoon to work on it, iso-
lating himself in his office, filling pages with a chaotic
longhand.

"There are many varieties of death, as opposed to dying . . ." he was writing just as the intercom buzzed
briefly, then long, then again briefly.

"Yes?" he asked it, pushing down on the switch.

"You have a visitor," and there was a short intake of
breath between "a" and "visitor."

He slipped a small aerosol into his side pocket, then
rose and crossed the office.

He opened the door and looked out.

"Doctor . . . Help . . ."

Render took three steps, then dropped to one knee.

"What's the matter?"

"Come she is . . . sick," he growled.

"Sick? How? What's wrong?"

"Don't know. You come."

Render stared into the unhuman eyes.

"What kind of sick?" he insisted.

"Don't know," repeated the dog. "Won't talk. Sits. I . . .
feel, she is sick."

"How did you get here?"

"Drove. Know the co, or, din, ates . . . Left car, outside."

"I'll call her right now." Render turned.

"No good. Won't answer."

He was right.

Render returned to his inner office for his coat and
medkit. He glanced out the window and saw where her
car was parked, far below, just inside the entrance to the
marginal, where the monitor had released it into manual
control. If no one assumed that control, a car was automatically parked in neutral. The other vehicles were
passed around it.

So simple even a dog can drive one, he reflected. *Better
get downstairs before a cruiser comes along. It's probably*

reported itself stopped there already. Maybe not, though.
Might still have a few minutes grace.

He glanced at the huge clock.

"Okay, Sig," he called out. "Let's go."

They took the lift to the ground floor, left by way of the front entrance, and hurried to the car.

Its engine was still idling.

Render opened the passenger door and Sigmund leapt in. He squeezed by him into the driver's seat then, but the dog was already pushing the primary coordinates and the address tabs with his paw.

Looks like I'm in the wrong seat.

He lit a cigarette as the car swept ahead into a U-underpass. It emerged on the opposite marginal, sat poised a moment, then joined the traffic flow. The dog directed the car into the high-acceleration lane.

"Oh," said the dog, "oh."

Render felt like patting his head at that moment, but he looked at him, saw that his teeth were bared, and decided against it.

"When did she start acting peculiar?" he asked.

"Came home from work. Did not eat. Would not answer me, when I talked. Just sits."

"Has she ever been like this before?"

"No."

What could have precipitated it? But maybe she just had a bad day. After all, he's only a dog—sort of. No. He'd know. But what, then?

"How was she yesterday—and when she left home this morning?"

"Like always."

Render tried calling her again. There was still no answer.

"You, did, it," said the dog.

"What do you mean?"

"Eyes. Seeing. You. Machine. Bad."

"No," said Render, and his hand rested on the unit of stun-spray in his pocket.

"Yes," said the dog, turning to him again. "You will, make her well. . . ?"

"Of course," said Render.

Sigmund stared ahead again.

Render felt physically exhilarated and mentally sluggish.

He sought the confusion factor. He had had these feelings about the case since that first session. There was something very unsettling about Eileen Shallot: a combination of high intelligence and helplessness, of determination and vulnerability, of sensitivity and bitterness.

Do I find that especially attractive? No. It's just the counter-transference, damn it!

"You smell afraid," said the dog.

"Then color me afraid," said Render, "and turn the page."

They slowed for a series of turns, picked up speed again, slowed again, picked up speed again. Finally they were traveling along a narrow section of roadway through a semiresidential area of town. The car turned up a side street, proceeded about half a mile farther, clicked softly beneath its dashboard, and turned into the parking lot behind a high brick apartment building. The click must have been a special servomech which took over from the point where the monitor released it because the car crawled across the lot, headed into its transparent parking stall, then stopped. Render turned off the ignition.

Sigmund had already opened the door on his side. Render followed him into the building, and they rode the elevator to the fiftieth floor. The dog dashed on ahead up the hallway, pressed his nose against a plate set low in a doorframe, and waited. After a moment, the door swung several inches inward. He pushed it open with his shoulder and entered. Render followed, closing the door behind him.

The apartment was large, its walls pretty much unadorned, its color combinations unnerving. A great library of tapes filled one corner; a monstrous combination-broadcaster stood beside it. There was a wide bowlegged table set in front of the window, and a low couch along the right-hand wall; there was a closed door beside the couch; an archway to the left apparently led to other rooms. Eileen sat in an overstuffed chair in the far corner by the window. Sigmund stood beside the chair.

Render crossed the room and extracted a cigarette from his case. Snapping open his lighter, he held the flame until her head turned in that direction.

"Cigarette?" he asked.

"Charles?"

"Right."

"Yes, thank you. I will."

She held out her hand, accepted the cigarette, put it to her lips.

"Thanks. What are you doing here?"

"Social call. I happened to be in the neighborhood."

"I didn't hear a buzz, or a knock."

"You must have been dozing. Sig let me in."

"Yes, I must have." She stretched. "What time is it?"

"It's close to four-thirty."

"I've been home over two hours then . . . Must have been very tired . . ."

"How do you feel now?"

"Fine," she declared. "Care for a cup of coffee?"

"Don't mind if I do."

"A steak to go with it?"

"No thanks."

"Bacardi in the coffee?"

"Sounds good."

"Excuse me then. It'll only take a moment."

She went through the door beside the sofa, and Render caught a glimpse of a large, shiny, automatic kitchen.

"Well?" he whispered to the dog.

Sigmund shook his head.

"Not same."

Render shook his head.

He deposited his coat on the sofa, folding it carefully about the medkit. He sat beside it and thought.

Did I throw too big a chunk of seeing at once? Is she suffering from depressive side-effects—say, memory repressions, nervous fatigue? Did I upset her sensory adaptation syndrome somehow? Why have I been proceeding so rapidly anyway? There's no real hurry. Am I so damned eager to write the thing up?—Or am I doing it because she wants me to? Could she be that strong, consciously or unconsciously? Or am I that vulnerable—somehow?

She called him to the kitchen to carry out the tray. He set it on the table and seated himself across from her.

"Good coffee," he said, burning his lips on the cup.

"Smart machine," she stated, facing his voice.

Sigmund stretched out on the carpet next to the table,

lowered his head between his forepaws, sighed, and closed his eyes.

"I've been wondering," said Render, "whether or not there were any after-effects to that last session—like increased synesthesiac experiences, or dreams involving forms, or hallucinations or . . ."

"Yes," she said flatly, "dreams."

"What kind?"

"That last session. I've dreamt it over and over."

"Beginning to end?"

"No, there's no special order to the events. We're riding through the city or over the bridge, or sitting at the table, or walking toward the car—just flashes like that. Vivid ones."

"What sort of feelings accompany these—flashes?"

"I don't know. They're all mixed up."

"What are your feelings now as you recall them."

"The same, all mixed up."

"Are you afraid?"

"N-no. I don't think so."

"Do you want to take a vacation from the thing? Do you feel we've been proceeding too rapidly?"

"No. That's not it at all. It's—well, it's like learning to swim. When you finally learn how, why then you swim and you swim and you swim until you're all exhausted. Then you just lie there gasping in air and remembering what it was like, while your friends all hover and chew you out for overexerting yourself—and it's a good feeling, even though you do take a chill and there's pins and needles inside all your muscles. At least, that's the way I do things. I felt that way after the first session and after this last one. First times are always very special times . . . The pins and the needles are gone, though, and I've caught my breath again. Lord, I don't want to stop now! I feel fine."

"Do you usually take a nap in the afternoon?"

The ten red fingernails moved across the tabletop as she stretched.

". . . Tired," she smiled, swallowing a yawn. "Half the staff's on vacation or sick leave, and I've been beating my brains out all week. I was about ready to fall on my face when I left work. I feel all right now that I've rested, though."

She picked up her coffee cup with both hands, took a large swallow.

"Uh-huh," he said. "Good. I was a bit worried about you. I'm glad to see there was no reason."

She laughed.

"Worried? You've read Dr. Riscomb's notes on my analysis—and on the ONT&R trial—and you think I'm the sort to worry about? Ha! I have an operationally beneficent neurosis concerning my adequacy as a human being. It focuses my energies, co-ordinates my efforts toward achievement. It enhances my sense of identity . . ."

"You do have one hell of a memory," he noted. "That's almost verbatim."

"Of course."

"You had Sigmund worried today, too."

"Sig? How?"

The dog stirred uneasily, opened one eye.

"Yes," he growled, glaring up at Render. "He needs a ride, home."

"Have you been driving the car again?"

"Yes."

"After I told you not to?"

"Yes."

"Why?"

"I was a, fraid. You would, not, answer me, when I talked."

"I was *very* tired—and if you ever take the car again. I'm going to have the door fixed so you can't come and go as you please."

"Sorry."

"There's nothing wrong with me."

"I, see."

"You are *never* to do it again."

"Sorry." His eye never left Render; it was like a burning lens.

Render looked away.

"Don't be too hard on the poor fellow," he said. "After all, he thought you were ill and he went for the doctor. Supposing he'd been right? You'd owe him thanks, not a scolding."

Unmollified, Sigmund glared a moment longer and closed his eye.

"He has to be told when he does wrong," she finished.

"I suppose," he said, drinking his coffee. "No harm done anyhow. Since I'm here, let's talk shop. I'm writing something and I'd like an opinion."

"Great. Give me a footnote?"

"Two or three. In your opinion, do the general underlying motivations that lead to suicide differ in different periods of history or in different cultures?"

"My well-considered opinion is no, they don't," she said. "Frustrations can lead to depressions or frenzies; and if these are severe enough, they can lead to self-destruction. You ask me about motivations and I think they stay pretty much the same. I feel this is a cross-cultural, cross-temporal aspect of the human condition. I don't think it could be changed without changing the basic nature of man."

"Okay. Check. Now, what of the inciting element?" he asked. "Let man be a constant, his environment is still a variable. If he is placed in an overprotective life-situation, do you feel it would take more or less to depress him—or stimulate him to frenzy—than it would take in a not so protective environment?"

"Hmm. Being case-oriented, I'd say it would depend on the man. But I see what you're driving at: a mass predisposition to jump out windows at the drop of a hat—the window even opening itself for you because you asked it to—the revolt of the bored masses. I don't like the notion. I hope it's wrong."

"So do I, but I was thinking of symbolic suicides, too—functional disorders that occur for pretty flimsy reasons."

"Aha! Your lecture last month: autopsychomimesis. I have the tape. Well-told, but I can't agree."

"Neither can I now. I'm rewriting that whole section, 'Thanatos in Cloudcuckooland,' I'm calling it. It's really the death-instinct moved nearer the surface."

"If I get you a scalpel and a cadaver, will you cut out the death-instinct and let me touch it?"

"Couldn't," he put the grin into his voice, "it would be all used up in a cadaver. Find me a volunteer, though, and he'll prove my case by volunteering."

"Your logic is unassailable," she smiled. "Get us some more coffee, okay?"

Render went to the kitchen, spiked and filled the cups,

drank a glass of water, returned to the living room. Eileen had not moved; neither had Sigmund.

"What do you do when you're not busy being a Shaper?" she asked him.

"The same things most people do—eat, drink, sleep, talk, visit friends and non-friends, visit places, read . . ."

"Are you a forgiving man?"

"Sometimes. Why?"

"Then forgive me. I argued with a woman today, a woman named DeVille."

"What about?"

"You—and she accused me of such things it were better my mother had not born me. Are you going to marry her?"

"No, marriage is like alchemy. It served an important purpose once, but I hardly feel it's here to stay."

"Good."

"What did you say to her?"

"I gave her a clinic referral card that said, 'Diagnosis: Bitch. Prescription: Drug therapy and a tight gag.' "

"Oh," said Render, showing interest.

"She tore it up and threw it in my face."

"I wonder why?"

She shrugged, smiled, made a gridwork on the table-cloth.

" 'Fathers and elders, I ponder,' " sighed Render, " 'what is hell?' "

" 'I maintain it is the suffering of being unable to love,' " she finished. "Was Dostoevsky right?"

"I doubt it. I'd put him into group therapy, myself. That'd be *real* hell for him—with all those people acting like his characters and enjoying it so."

Render put down his cup, pushed his chair away from the table.

"I suppose you must be going now?"

"I really should," said Render.

"And I can't interest you in food?"

"No."

She stood.

"Okay, I'll get my coat."

"I could drive back myself and just set the car to return."

"No! I'm frightened by the notion of empty cars driving around the city. I'd feel the thing was haunted for the next two-and-a-half weeks.

"Besides," she said, passing through the archway, "you promised me Winchester Cathedral."

"You want to do it today?"

"If you can be persuaded."

As Render stood deciding, Sigmund rose to his feet. He stood directly before him and stared upward into his eyes. He opened his mouth and closed it several times, but no sounds emerged. Then he turned away and left the room.

"No," Eileen's voice came back, "you will stay here until I return."

Render picked up his coat and put it on, stuffing the medkit into the far pocket.

As they walked up the hall toward the elevator, Render thought he heard a very faint and very distant howling sound.

In this place, of all places, Render knew he was the master of all things.

He was at home on those alien worlds, without time, those worlds where flowers copulate and the stars do battle in the heavens, falling at last to the ground, bleeding like so many spilt and shattered chalices, and the seas part to reveal stairways leading down, and arms emerge from caverns, waving torches that flame like liquid faces —a midwinter night's nightmare, summer go a-begging, Render knew—for he had visited those worlds on a professional basis for the better part of a decade. With the crooking of a finger, he could isolate the sorcerers, bring them to trial for treason against the realm—aye, and he could execute them, could appoint their successors.

Fortunately this trip was only a courtesy call. . . .

He moved forward through the glade, seeking her.

He could feel her awakening presence all about him.

He pushed through the branches, stood beside the lake. It was cold, blue, and bottomless, the lake reflecting that slender willow which had become the station of her arrival.

"Eileen!"

The willow swayed toward him, swayed away.

"Eileen! Come forth!"

Leaves fell, floated upon the lake, disturbed its mirror-like placidity, distorted the reflections.

"Eileen?"

All the leaves yellowed at once then, dropped down into the water. The tree ceased its swaying. There was a strange sound in the darkening sky, like the humming of high wires on a cold day.

Suddenly there was a double file of moons passing through the heavens.

Render selected one, reached up, and pressed it. The others vanished as he did so, and the world brightened; the humming went out of the air.

He circled the lake to gain a subjective respite from the rejection-action and his counter to it. He moved up along an aisle of pines toward the place where he wanted the cathedral to occur. Birds sang now in the trees. The wind came softly by him. He felt her presence quite strongly.

"Here, Eileen. Here."

She walked beside him then, green silk, hair of bronze, eyes of molten emerald; she wore an emerald in her forehead. She walked in green slippers over the pine needles, saying: "What happened?"

"You were afraid."

"Why?"

"Perhaps you fear the cathedral. Are you a witch?" he smiled.

"Yes, but it's my day off."

He laughed, and he took her arm, and they rounded an island of foliage, and there was the cathedral reconstructed on a grassy rise, pushing its way above them and above the trees, climbing into the middle air, breathing out organ notes, reflecting a stray ray of sunlight from a plane of glass.

"Hold tight to the world," he said. "Here comes the guided tour."

They moved forward and entered.

" '. . . With its floor-to-ceiling shafts, like so many huge tree trunks, it achieves a ruthless control over its spaces,' " he said. "—Got that from the guidebook. This is the north transept . . ."

" 'Greensleeves,' " she said, "the organ is playing 'Greensleeves.' "

"So it is. You can't blame me for that though. Observe the scalloped capitals—"

"I want to go nearer the music."

"Very well. This way then."

Render felt that something was wrong. He could not put his finger on it.

Everything retained its solidity. . . .

Something passed rapidly then, high above the cathedral, uttering a sonic boom. Render smiled at that, remembering now; it was like a slip of the tongue: for a moment he had confused Eileen with Jill—yes, that was what had happened.

Why, then. . . .

A burst of white was the altar. He had never seen it before, anywhere. All the walls were dark and cold about them. Candles flickered in corners and high niches. The organ chorded thunder under invisible hands.

Render knew that something was wrong.

He turned to Eileen Shallot, whose hat was a green cone towering up into the darkness, trailing wisps of green veiling. Her throat was in shadow, but. . . .

"That necklace—Where?"

"I don't know," she smiled.

The goblet she held radiated a rosy light. It was reflected from her emerald. It washed him like a draft of cool air.

"Drink?" she asked.

"Stand still," he ordered.

He willed the walls to fall down. They swam in shadow.

"Stand still!" he repeated urgently. "Don't do anything. Try not even to think."

"—Fall down!" he cried. And the walls were blasted in all directions, and the roof was flung over the top of the world, and they stood amid ruins lighted by a single taper. The night was black as pitch.

"Why did you do that?" she asked, still holding the goblet out toward him.

"Don't think. Don't think anything," he said. "Relax. You are very tired. As that candle flickers and wanes so does your consciousness. You can barely keep awake. You can hardly stay on your feet. Your eyes are closing. There is nothing to see here anyway."

He willed the candle to go out. It continued to burn.

"I'm not tired. Please have a drink."

He heard organ music through the night. A different tune, one he did not recognize at first.

"I need your cooperation."

"All right. Anything."

"Look! The moon!" he pointed.

She looked upward and the moon appeared from behind an inky cloud.

". . . And another, and another."

Moons, like strung pearls, proceeded across the blackness.

"The last one will be red," he stated.

It was.

He reached out then with his right index finger, slid his arm sideways along his field of vision, then tried to touch the red moon.

His arm ached, it burned. He could not move it.

"Wake up!" he screamed.

The red moon vanished, and the white ones.

"Please take a drink."

He dashed the goblet from her hand and turned away. When he turned back, she was still holding it before him.

"A drink?"

He turned and fled into the night.

It was like running through a waist-high snowdrift. It was wrong. He was compounding the error by running —he was minimizing his strength, maximizing hers. It was sapping his energies, draining him.

He stood still in the midst of the blackness.

"The world around me moves," he said. "I am its center."

"Please have a drink," she said, and he was standing in the glade beside their table set beside the lake. The lake was black, and the moon was silver and high and out of his reach. A single candle flickered on the table, making her hair as silver as her dress. She wore the moon on her brow. A bottle of Romanee-Conti stood on the white cloth beside a wide-brimmed wine glass. It was filled to overflowing, that glass, and rosy beads clung to its lip. He was very thirsty, and she was lovelier than anyone he had ever seen before, and her necklace sparkled, and the breeze came cool off the lake, and there was something—something he should remember. . . .

He took a step toward her, and his armor clinked lightly as he moved. He reached toward the glass and his right arm stiffened with pain and fell back to his side.

"You are wounded!"

Slowly, he turned his head. The blood flowed from the open wound in his biceps and ran down his arm and dripped from his fingertips. His armor had been breached. He forced himself to look away.

"Drink this, love. It will heal you."

She stood.

"I will hold the glass."

He stared at her as she raised it to his lips.

"Who am I?" he asked.

She did not answer him, but something replied—within a splashing of waters out over the lake:

"You are Render, the Shaper."

"Yes, I remember," he said; and turning his mind to the one lie which might break the entire illusion, he forced his mouth to say, "Eileen Shallot, I hate you."

The world shuddered and swam about him, was shaken as by a huge sob.

"Charles!" she screamed, and the blackness swept over them.

"Wake up! Wake up!" he cried, and his right arm burned and ached and bled in the darkness.

He stood alone in the midst of a white plain. It was silent, it was endless. It sloped away toward the edges of the world. It gave off its own light, and the sky was no sky but was nothing overhead. Nothing. He was alone. His own voice echoed back to him from the end of the world: ". . . hate you," it said, ". . . hate you."

He dropped to his knees. He was Render.

He wanted to cry.

A red moon appeared above the plain, casting a ghastly light over the entire expanse. There was a wall of mountains to the left of him, another to his right.

He raised his right arm. He helped it with his left hand. He clutched his wrist, extended his index finger. He reached for the moon.

Then there came a howl from high in the mountains, a great wailing cry—half-human, all challenge, all loneliness, and all remorse. He saw it then, treading upon the mountains, its tail brushing the snow from their highest peaks, the ultimate loup-garou of the North—Fenris, son of Loki—raging at the heavens.

It leapt into the air. It swallowed the moon.

It landed near him, and its great eyes blazed yellow. It stalked him on soundless pads across the cold white fields that lay between the mountains; and he backed away from it, up hills and down slopes, over crevasses and rifts, through valleys, past stalagmites and pinnacles—under the edges of glaciers, beside frozen river beds, and always downwards—until its hot breath bathed him and its laughing mouth was opened above him.

He turned then, and his feet became two gleaming rivers carrying him away.

The world jumped backwards. He glided over the slopes. Downward. Speeding—

Away. . . .

He looked back over his shoulder.

In the distance the gray shape loped after him.

He felt that it could narrow the gap if it chose. He had to move faster.

The world reeled about him. Snow began to fall.

He raced on.

Ahead, a blur, a broken outline.

He tore through the veils of snow, which now seemed to be falling upward from off the ground—like strings of bubbles.

He approached the shattered form.

Like a swimmer, he approached—unable to open his mouth to speak for fear of drowning—of drowning and not knowing, of never knowing.

He could not check his forward motion; he was swept tidelike toward the wreck. He came to a stop at last before it.

Some things never change. They are things that have long ceased to exist as objects and stand solely as never-to-be-calendared occasions outside that sequence of elements called Time.

Render stood there and did not care if Fenris leapt upon his back and ate his brains. He had covered his eyes, but he could not stop the seeing. Not this time. He did not care about anything. Most of himself lay dead at his feet.

There was a howl. A gray shape swept past him.

The baleful eyes and bloody muzzle rooted within the wrecked car, champing through the steel, the glass, groping inside for. . . .

"No! Brute! Chewer of corpses!" he cried. "The dead are sacred! *My* dead are sacred!"

He had a scalpel in his hand then, and he slashed expertly at the tendons, the bunches of muscle on the straining shoulders, the soft belly, the ropes of the arteries.

Weeping, he dismembered the monster, limb by limb, and it bled and it bled, fouling the vehicle and the remains within it with its infernal animal juices, dripping and running until the whole plain was reddened and writhing about him.

Render fell across the pulverized hood, and it was soft and warm and dry. He wept upon it.

"Don't cry," she said.

He was hanging onto her shoulder then, holding her tightly, there beside the black lake beneath the moon that was Wedgewood. A single candle flickered upon their table. She held the glass to his lips.

"Please drink it."

"Yes, give it to me!"

He gulped the wine that was all softness and lightness. It burned within him. He felt his strength returning.

"I am . . ."

"—Render, the Shaper," splashed the lake.

"No!"

He turned and ran again, looking for the wreck. He had to go back, to return. . . .

"You can't."

"I can!" he cried. "I can, if I try . . ."

Yellow flames coiled through the thick air. Yellow serpents. They coiled, glowing, about his ankles. Then through the murk, two-headed and towering, approached his Adversary.

Small stones rattled past him. An overpowering odor cork-screwed up his nose and into his head.

"Shaper!" came the bellow from one head.

"You have returned for the reckoning!" called the other.

Render stared, remembering.

"No reckoning, Thaumiel," he said. "I beat you and I chained you for—Rothman, yes, it was Rothman—the cabalist." He traced a pentagram in the air. "Return to Qliphoth. I banish you."

"This place be Qliphoth."

". . . By Khamael, the angel of blood, by the hosts of Seraphim, in the Name of Elohim Gebor, I bid you vanish!"

"Not this time," laughed both heads.

It advanced.

Render backed slowly away, his feet bound by the yellow serpents. He could feel the chasm opening behind him. The world was a jigsaw puzzle coming apart. He could see the pieces separating.

"Vanish!"

The giant roared out its double-laugh.

Render stumbled.

"This way, love!"

She stood within a small cave to his right.

He shook his head and backed toward the chasm.

Thaumiel reached out toward him.

Render toppled back over the edge.

"Charles!" she screamed, and the world shook itself apart with her wailing.

"Then Vernichtung," he answered as he fell. "I join you in darkness."

Everything came to an end.

"I want to see Dr. Charles Render."

"I'm sorry, that is impossible."

"But I skip-jetted all the way here just to thank him. I'm a new man! He changed my life!"

"I'm sorry, Mr. Erikson. When you called this morning, I told you it was impossible."

"Sir, I'm Representative Erikson—and Render once did me a great service."

"Then you can do him one now. Go home."

"You can't talk to me that way!"

"I just did. Please leave. Maybe next year sometime . . ."

"But a few words can do wonders . . ."

"Save them!"

"I-I'm sorry . . ."

Lovely as it was, pinked over with the morning—the slop-
ping, steaming bowl of the sea—he knew that it *had* to
end. Therefore. . . .

He descended the high tower stairway, and he entered
the courtyard. He crossed to the bower of roses, and he
looked down upon the pallet set in its midst.

"Good morrow, m'lord," he said.

"To you the same," said the knight, his blood mingling
with the earth, the flowers, the grasses, flowing from his
wound, sparkling over his armor, dripping from his fingertips.

"Naught hath healed?"

The knight shook his head.

"I empty. I wait."

"Your waiting is near ended."

"What mean you?" He sat upright.

"The ship. It approacheth harbor."

The knight stood. He leaned his back against a mossy
tree trunk. He stared at the huge, bearded servitor who
continued to speak, words harsh with barbaric accents:

"It cometh like a dark swan before the wind—returning."

"Dark, say you? Dark?"

"The sails be black, Lord Tristram."

"You lie!"

"Do you wish to see? To see for yourself?—Look then!"
He gestured.

The earth quaked, the wall toppled. The dust swirled
and settled. From where they stood they could see the ship
moving into the harbor on the wings of the night.

"No! You lied!—See! They are white!"

The dawn danced upon the waters. The shadows fled
from the ship's sails.

"No, you fool! Black! They *must* be!"

"White! White!—Isolde! You have kept faith! You have
returned!"

He began running toward the harbor.

"Come back!—Your wound!—You are ill!—Stop . . ."

The sails were white beneath a sun that was a red button, which the servitor reached quickly to touch.

Night fell.

1966

THE SECRET PLACE

by Richard McKenna

This morning my son asked me what I did in the war. He's fifteen, and I don't know why he never asked me before. I don't know why I never anticipated the question.

He was just leaving for camp, and I was able to put him off by saying I did government work. He'll be two weeks at camp. As long as the counselors keep pressure on him, he'll do well enough at group activities. The moment they relax it, he'll be off studying an ant colony or reading one of his books. He's on astronomy now. The moment he comes home, he'll ask me again just what I did in the war, and I'll have to tell him.

But I don't understand just what I did in the war. Sometimes I think my group fought a death fight with a local myth and only Colonel Lewis realized it. I don't know who won. All I know is that war demands of some men risks more obscure and ignoble than death in battle. I know it did of me.

It began in 1931, when a local boy was found dead in the desert near Barker, Oregon. He had with him a sack of gold ore and one thumb-sized crystal of uranium oxide. The crystal ended as a curiosity in a Salt Lake City assay office until, in 1942, it became of strangely great importance. Army agents traced its probable origin to a hundred-square-mile area near Barker. Dr. Lewis was called to duty as a reserve colonel and ordered to find the vein. But the whole area was overlain by thousands of feet of Miocene lava flows, and of course it was geological insanity to look there for a pegmatite vein. The area had no drainage pattern and had never been glaciated. Dr. Lewis protested that the crystal could have gotten there only by prior human agency.

It did him no good. He was told he's not to reason why. People very high up would not be placated until much money and scientific effort had been spent in a search. The army sent him young geology graduates, including me, and demanded progress reports. For the sake of morale, in a kind of frustrated desperation, Dr. Lewis decided to make the project a model textbook exercise in mapping the number and thickness of the basalt beds over the search area all the way down to the prevolcanic Miocene surface. That would at least be a useful addition to Columbia Plateau lithology. It would also be proof positive that no uranium ore existed there, so it was not really cheating.

That Oregon countryside was a dreary place. The search area was flat, featureless country with black lava outcropping everywhere through scanty gray soil in which sagebrush grew hardly knee high. It was hot and dry in summer, and dismal with thin snow in winter. Winds howled across it at all seasons. Barker was about a hundred wooden houses on dusty streets and some hay farms along a canal. All the young people were away at war or war jobs, and the old people seemed to resent us. There were twenty of us, apart from the contract drill crews who lived in their own trailer camps, and we were gown against town, in a way. We slept and ate at Colthorpe House, a block down the street from our headquarters. We had our own "gown" table there, and we might as well have been men from Mars.

I enjoyed it just the same. Dr. Lewis treated us like students, with lectures and quizzes and assigned reading. He was a fine teacher and a brilliant scientist, and we loved him. He gave us all a turn at each phase of the work. I started on surface mapping and then worked with the drill crews, who were taking cores through the basalt and into the granite thousands of feet beneath. Then I worked on taking gravimetric and seismic readings. We had fine team spirit, and we all knew we were getting priceless training in field geophysics. I decided privately that after the war I would take my doctorate in geophysics. Under Dr. Lewis, of course.

In early summer of 1944, the field phase ended. The contract drillers left. We packed tons of well logs and many boxes of gravimetric data sheets and seismic tapes for a move to Dr. Lewis's Midwestern university. There we would get more months of valuable training while we worked our data into a set of structure contour maps. We were all excited and talked a lot about being with girls again and going to parties. Then the army said part of the staff had to continue the field search. For technical compliance, Dr. Lewis decided to leave one man, and he chose me.

It hit me hard. It was like being flunked out unfairly. I thought he was heartlessly brusque about it.

"Take a jeep run through the area with a Geiger once a day," he said. "Then sit in the office and answer the phone."

"What if the army calls when I'm away?" I asked sullenly.

"Hire a secretary," he said. "You've an allowance for that."

So off they went and left me with the title of field chief and only myself to boss. I felt betrayed to the hostile town. I decided I hated Colonel Lewis and wished I could get revenge. A few days later, old Dave Gentry told me how.

He was a lean, leathery old man with a white mustache, and I sat next to him in my new place at the "town" table. Those were grim meals. I heard remarks about healthy young men skulking out of uniform and wasting tax money. One night I slammed my fork into my half-emptied plate and stood up.

"The army sent me here and the army keeps me here," I told the dozen old men and women at the table. "I'd like to go overseas and cut Japanese throats for you kind hearts and gentle people, I really would! Why don't you all write your congressman?"

I stamped outside and stood at one end of the veranda, boiling. Old Dave followed me out.

"Hold your horses, son," he said. "They hate the government, not you. But government's like the weather, and you're a man they can get aholt of."

"With their teeth," I said bitterly.

"They got reasons," Dave said. "Lost mines ain't supposed to be found the way you people are going at it. Besides that, the Crazy Kid mine belongs to us here in Barker."

He was past seventy, and he looked after horses in the local feedyard. He wore a shabby, open vest over faded suspenders and gray flannel shirts, and nobody would ever have looked for wisdom in that old man. But it was there.

"This is big, new, lonesome country, and it's hard on people," he said. "Every town's got a story about a lost mine or a lost gold cache. Only kids go looking for it. It's enough for most folks just to know it's there. It helps 'em to stand the country."

"I see," I said. Something stirred in the back of my mind.

"Barker never got its lost mine until thirteen years ago," Dave said. "Folks just naturally can't stand to see you people find it this way, by main force and so soon after."

"We know there isn't any mine," I said. "We're just proving it isn't there."

"If you could prove that, it'd be worse yet," he said. "Only you can't. We all saw and handled that ore. It was quartz, just rotten with gold in wires and flakes. The boy went on foot from his house to get it. The lode's got to be right close by out there."

He waved toward our search area. The air above it was luminous with twilight, and I felt a curious surge of interest. Colonel Lewis had always discouraged us from speculating on that story. If one of us brought it up, I was usually the one who led the hooting and we all suggested he go over the search area with a dowsing rod. It was an article of faith with us that the vein did not exist. But now I was all alone and my own field boss.

We each put up one foot on the veranda rail and rested our arms on our knees. Dave bit off a chew of tobacco and told me about Owen Price.

"He was always a crazy kid, and I guess he read every book in town," Dave said. "He had a curious heart, that boy."

I'm no folklorist, but even I could see how myth elements were already creeping into the story. For one thing, Dave insisted the boy's shirt was torn off and he had lacerations on his back.

"Like a cougar clawed him," Dave said. "Only they ain't never been cougars in that desert. We backtracked that boy till his trail crossed itself so many times it was no use, but we never found one cougar track."

I could discount that stuff, of course, but still the story gripped me. Maybe it was Dave's slow, sure voice; perhaps the queer twilight; possibly my own wounded pride. I thought of how great lava upwellings sometimes tear loose and carry along huge masses of the country rock. Maybe such an erratic mass lay out there, perhaps only a few hundred feet across and so missed by our drill cores, but rotten with uranium. If I could find it, I would make a fool of Colonel Lewis. I would discredit the whole science of geology. I, Duard Campbell, the despised and rejected one, could do that. The front of my mind shouted that it was nonsense, but something far back in my mind began composing a devastating letter to Colonel Lewis and comfort flowed into me.

"There's some say the boy's youngest sister could tell where he found it if she wanted," Dave said. "She used to go into that desert with him a lot. She took on pretty wild when it happened and then was struck dumb, but I hear she talks again now." He shook his head. "Poor little Helen. She promised to be a pretty girl."

"Where does she live?" I asked.

"With her mother in Salem," Dave said. "She went to business school, and I hear she works for a lawyer there."

Mrs. Price was a flinty old woman who seemed to control her daughter absolutely. She agreed Helen would be my secretary as soon as I told her the salary. I got Helen's security clearance with one phone call; she had already been investigated as part of tracing that uranium crystal. Mrs. Price arranged for Helen to stay with a family she knew in Barker, to protect her reputation. It was in no danger. I meant to make love to her, if I had to, to charm her out of her secret, if she had one, but I would not harm her. I knew perfectly well that I was only playing a game called "The Revenge of Duard Campbell." I knew I would not find any uranium.

Helen was a plain little girl, and she was made of frightened ice. She wore low-heeled shoes and cotton stockings and plain dresses with white cuffs and collars. Her one good feature was her flawless fair skin against which her peaked, black Welsh eyebrows and smoky blue eyes gave her an elfin look at times. She liked to sit neatly tucked into herself, feet together, elbows in, eyes cast down, voice hardly audible, as smoothly self-contained as an egg. The desk I gave her faced mine, and she sat like that across from me and did the busy work I gave her, and I could not get through to her at all.

I tried joking, and I tried polite little gifts and attentions, and I tried being sad and needing sympathy. She listened and worked and stayed as far away as the moon. It was only after two weeks and by pure accident that I found the key to her.

I was trying the sympathy gambit. I said it was not so bad, being exiled from friends and family, but what I could not stand was the dreary sameness of that search area. Every spot was like every other spot, and there was no single, recognizable *place* in the whole expanse. It sparked something in her, and she roused up at me.

"It's full of just wonderful places," she said.

"Come out with me in the jeep and show me one," I challenged.

She was reluctant, but I hustled her along regardless. I guided the jeep between outcrops, jouncing and lurching. I had our map photographed on my mind, and I knew where we were every minute, but only by map coordinates. The desert had our marks on it: well sites, seismic blast holes, wooden stakes, cans, bottles and papers blowing in that everlasting wind, and it was all dismally the same anyway.

"Tell me when we pass a 'place' and I'll stop," I said.

"It's all places," she said. "Right here's a place."

I stopped the jeep and looked at her in surprise. Her voice was strong and throaty. She opened her eyes wide and smiled; I had never seen her look like that.

"What's special, that makes it a place?" I asked.

She did not answer. She got out and walked a few steps. Her whole posture was changed. She almost danced along. I followed and touched her shoulder.

"Tell me what's special," I said.

She faced around and stared right past me. She had a new grace and vitality, and she was a very pretty girl.

"It's where all the dogs are," she said.

"Dogs?"

I looked around at the scrubby sagebrush and thin soil

and ugly black rock and back at Helen. Something was wrong.

"Big, stupid dogs that go in herds and eat grass," she said. She kept turning and gazing. "Big cats chase the dogs and eat them. The dogs scream and scream. Can't you hear them?"

"That's crazy!" I said. "What's the matter with you?"

I might as well have slugged her. She crumpled instantly back into herself, and I could hardly hear her answer.

"I'm sorry. My brother and I used to play out fairy tales here. All this was a kind of fairyland to us." Tears formed in her eyes. "I haven't been here since . . . I forgot myself. I'm sorry."

I had to swear I needed to dictate "field notes" to force Helen into that desert again. She sat stiffly with pad and pencil in the jeep while I put on my act with the Geiger and rattled off jargon. Her lips were pale and compressed, and I could see her fighting against the spell the desert had for her, and I could see her slowly losing.

She finally broke down into that strange mood, and I took good care not to break it. It was weird but wonderful, and I got a lot of data. I made her go out for "field notes" every morning and each time it was easier to break her down. Back in the office she always froze again, and I marveled at how two such different persons could inhabit the same body. I called her two phases "Office Helen" and "Desert Helen."

I often talked with old Dave on the veranda after dinner. One night he cautioned me.

"Folks here think Helen ain't been right in the head since her brother died," he said. "They're worrying about you and her."

"I feel like a big brother to her," I said. "I'd never hurt her, Dave. If we find the lode, I'll stake the best claim for her."

He shook his head. I wished I could explain to him how it was only a harmless game I was playing and no one would ever find gold out there. Yet, as a game, it fascinated me.

Desert Helen charmed me when, helplessly, she had to uncover her secret life. She was a little girl in a woman's body. Her voice became strong and breathless with excitement, and she touched me with the same wonder that turned her own face vivid and elfin. She ran laughing through the black rocks and scrubby sagebrush, and momentarily she made them beautiful. She would pull me along by the hand, and sometimes we ran as much as a mile away from the jeep. She treated me as if I were a blind or foolish child.

"No, no, Duard, that's a cliff!" she would say, pulling me back.

She would go first so I could find the stepping stones across streams. I played up. She pointed out woods and streams and cliffs and castles. There were shaggy horses with claws, golden birds, camels, witches, elephants, and many other creatures. I pretended to see them all, and it made her trust me. She talked and acted out the fairy tales she had once played with Owen. Sometimes he was enchanted and sometimes she, and the one had to dare the evil magic of a witch or giant to rescue the other. Sometimes I was Duard and other times I almost thought I was Owen.

Helen and I crept into sleeping castles, and we hid with pounding hearts while the giant grumbled in search of us and we fled, hand in hand, before his wrath.

Well, I had her now. I played Helen's game but I never lost sight of my own. Every night I sketched in on my map whatever I had learned that day of the fairyland topography. Its geomorphology was remarkably consistent.

When we played, I often hinted about the giant's treasure. Helen never denied it existed, but she seemed troubled and evasive about it. She would put her finger to her lips and look at me with solemn, round eyes.

"You only take the things nobody cares about," she would say. "If you take the gold or jewels, it brings you terrible bad luck."

"I got a charm against bad luck, and I'll let you have it, too," I said once. "It's the biggest, strongest charm in the whole world."

"No. It all turns into trash. It turns into goat beans and dead snakes and things," she said crossly. "Owen told me. It's a rule, in fairyland."

Another time we talked about it as we sat in a gloomy

ravine near a waterfall. We had to keep our voices low or we would wake up the giant. The waterfall was really the giant snoring, and it was also the wind that blew forever across that desert.

"Doesn't Owen ever take anything?" I asked.

I had learned by then that I must always speak of Owen in the present tense.

"Sometimes he has to," she said. "Once right here the witch had me enchanted into an ugly toad. Owen put a flower on my head and that made me be Helen again."

"A really truly flower? That you could take home with you?"

"A red and yellow flower bigger than my two hands," she said. "I tried to take it home, but all the petals came off."

"Does Owen ever take anything home?"

"Rocks, sometimes," she said. "We keep them in a secret nest in the shed. We think they might be magic eggs."

I stood up. "Come and show me."

She shook her head vigorously and drew back. "I don't want to go home," she said. "Not ever."

She squirmed and pouted, but I pulled her to her feet.

"Please, Helen, for me," I said. "Just for one little minute."

I pulled her back to the jeep, and we drove to the old Price place. I had never seen her look at it when we passed it, and she did not look now. She was freezing fast back into Office Helen. But she led me around the sagging old house with its broken windows and into a tumbledown shed. She scratched away some straw in one corner, and there were the rocks. I did not realize how excited I was until disappointment hit me like a blow in the stomach.

They were worthless waterworn pebbles of quartz and rosy granite. The only thing special about them was that they could never have originated on that basalt desert.

After a few weeks we dropped the pretense of field notes and simply went into the desert to play. I had Helen's fairyland almost completely mapped. It seemed to be a recent fault block mountain with a river parallel to its base and a gently sloping plain across the river. The scarp face was wooded and cut by deep ravines, and it had castles perched on its truncated spurs. I kept checking Helen on it and never found her inconsistent. Several times when she was in doubt, I was able to tell her where she was, and that let me even more deeply into her secret life. One morning I discovered just how deeply.

She was sitting on a log in the forest and plaiting a little basket out of fern fronds. I stood beside her. She looked up at me and smiled.

"What shall we play today, Owen?" she asked.

I had not expected that, and I was proud of how quickly I rose to it. I capered and bounded away and then back to her and crouched at her feet.

"Little sister, little sister, I'm enchanted," I said. "Only you in all the world can uncharm me."

"I'll uncharm you," she said in that little girl voice. "What are you, brother?"

"A big, black dog," I said. "A wicked giant named Lewis Rawbones keeps me chained up behind his castle while he takes all the other dogs out hunting."

She smoothed her gray skirt over her knees. Her mouth drooped.

"You're lonesome, and you howl all day, and you howl all night," she said. "Poor doggie."

I threw back my head and howled.

"He's a terrible, wicked giant, and he's got all kinds of terrible magic," I said. "You mustn't be afraid, little sister. As soon as you uncharm me, I'll be a handsome prince and I'll cut off his head."

"I'm not afraid." Her eyes sparkled. "I'm not afraid of fire or snakes or pins or needles or anything."

"I'll take you away to my kingdom and we'll live happily ever afterward. You'll be the most beautiful queen in the world, and everybody will love you."

I wagged my tail and laid my head on her knees. She stroked my silky head and pulled my long black ears.

"Everybody will love me." She was very serious now. "Will magic water uncharm you, poor old doggie?"

"You have to touch my forehead with a piece of the giant's treasure," I said. "That's the only onliest way to uncharm me."

I felt her shrink away from me. She stood up, her face suddenly crumpled with grief and anger.

"You're not Owen, you're just a man! Owen's enchanted

and I'm enchanted, too, and nobody will ever uncharm
us!"

She ran away from me, and she was already Office
Helen by the time she reached the jeep.

After that day she refused flatly to go into the desert
with me. It looked as if my game was played out. But I
gambled that Desert Helen could still hear me, underneath somewhere, and I tried a new strategy. The office
was an upstairs room over the old dance hall, and I suppose in frontier days skirmishing had gone on there between men and women. I doubt anything went on as
strange as my new game with Helen.

I always had paced and talked while Helen worked.
Now I began mixing common-sense talk with fairyland
talk, and I kept coming back to the wicked giant, Lewis
Rawbones. Office Helen tried not to pay attention, but
now and then I caught Desert Helen peeping at me out of
her eyes. I spoke of my blighted career as a geologist
and how it would be restored to me if I found the lode. I
mused on how I would live and work in exotic places
and how I would need a wife to keep house for me and
help with my paper work. It disturbed Office Helen. She
made typing mistakes and dropped things. I kept it up for
days, trying for just the right mixture of fact and fantasy,
and it was hard on Office Helen.

One night old Dave warned me again.

"Helen's looking peaked, and there's talk around. Miz
Fowler says Helen don't sleep, and she cries at night, and
she won't tell Miz Fowler what's wrong. You don't happen
to know what's bothering her, do you?"

"I only talk business stuff to her," I said. "Maybe she's
homesick. I'll ask her if she wants a vacation." I did not
like the way Dave looked at me. "I haven't hurt her. I
don't mean her any harm, Dave," I said.

"People get killed for what they do, not for what they
mean," he said. "Son, there's men in this here town would
kill you quick as a coyote if you hurt Helen Price."

I worked on Helen all the next day, and in the afternoon I hit just the right note and I broke her defenses. I
was not prepared for the way it worked out. I had just
said, "All life is a kind of playing. If you think about it
right, everything we do is a game." She poised her pencil

and looked straight at me as she had never done in that office, and I felt my heart speed up.

"You taught me how to play, Helen. I was so serious that I didn't know how to play."

"Owen taught me to play. He had magic. My sisters couldn't play anything but dolls and rich husbands, and I hated them."

Her eyes opened wide, and her lips trembled, and she was almost Desert Helen right there in the office.

"There's magic and enchantment in regular life if you look at it right," I said. "Don't you think so, Helen?"

"I know it!" she said. She turned pale and dropped her pencil. "Owen was enchanted into having a wife and three daughters, and he was just a boy. But he was the only man we had, and all of them but me hated him because we were so poor." She began to tremble, and her voice went flat. "He couldn't stand it. He took the treasure, and it killed him." Tears ran down her cheeks. "I tried to think he was only enchanted into play-dead, and if I didn't speak or laugh for seven years, I'd uncharm him."

She dropped her head on her hands. I was alarmed. I came over and put my hand on her shoulder.

"I did speak." Her shoulders heaved with sobs. "They made me speak, and now Owen won't ever come back."

I bent and put my arm across her shoulders.

"Don't cry, Helen. He'll come back," I said. "There are other magics to bring him back."

I hardly knew what I was saying. I was afraid of what I had done, and I wanted to comfort her. She jumped up and threw off my arm.

"I can't stand it! I'm going home!"

She ran out into the hall and down the stairs, and from the window I saw her run down the street, still crying. All of a sudden my game seemed cruel and stupid to me, and right that moment I stopped it. I tore up my map of fairyland and my letters to Colonel Lewis, and I wondered how in the world I could ever have done all that.

After dinner that night old Dave motioned me out to one end of the veranda. His face looked carved out of wood.

"I don't know what happened in your office today, and

for your sake I better not find out. But you send Helen
back to her mother on the morning stage, you hear me?"

"All right, if she wants to go," I said. "I can't just fire
her."

"I'm speaking for the boys. You better put her on that
morning stage, or we'll be around to talk to you."

"All right, I will, Dave."

I wanted to tell him how the game was stopped now
and how I wanted a chance to make things up with Helen,
but I thought I had better not. Dave's voice was flat and
savage with contempt, and old as he was, he frightened
me.

Helen did not come to work in the morning. At nine
o'clock I went out myself for the mail. I brought a large
mailing tube and some letters back to the office. The first
letter I opened was from Dr. Lewis, and almost like magic
it solved all my problems.

On the basis of his preliminary structure contour
maps, Dr. Lewis had gotten permission to close out the
field phase. Copies of the maps were in the mailing tube
for my information. I was to hold an inventory and be
ready to turn everything over to an army quartermaster
team coming in a few days. There was still a great mass
of data to be worked up in refining the maps. I was to
join the group again, and I would have a chance at the
lab work after all.

I felt pretty good. I paced and whistled and snapped
my fingers. Iwished Helen would come, to help on the
inventory. Then I opened the tube and looked idly at the
maps. There were a lot of them, featureless bed after bed
of basalt, like layers of a cake ten miles across. But when
I came to the bottom map, of the prevolcanic Miocene
landscape, the hair on my neck stood up.

*I had made that map myself. It was Helen's fairyland.
The topography was point by point the same.*

I clenched my fists and stopped breathing. Then it hit
me a second time, and the skin crawled up my back.

*The game was real. I couldn't end it. All the time the
game had been playing me. It was still playing me.*

I ran out and down the street and overtook old Dave
hurrying toward the feedyard. He had a holstered gun on
each hip.

"Dave, I've got to find Helen," I said.

"Somebody seen her hiking into the desert just at daylight," he said. "I'm on my way for a horse." He did not slow his stride. "You better get out there in your stinkwagon. If you don't find her before we do, you better just keep on going, son."

I ran back and got the jeep and roared it out across the scrubby sagebrush. I hit rocks, and I do not know why I did not break something. I knew where to go and feared what I would find there. I knew I loved Helen Price more than my own life, and I knew I had driven her to her death.

I saw her far off running and dodging. I headed the jeep to intercept her and I shouted, but she neither saw me nor heard me. I stopped and jumped out and ran after her, and the world darkened. Helen was all I could see, and I could not catch up with her.

"Wait for me, little sister!" I screamed after her. "I love you, Helen! Wait for me!"

She stopped and crouched, and I almost ran over her. I knelt and put my arms around her, and then it was on us.

They say in an earthquake, when the direction of up and down tilts and wobbles, people feel a fear that drives them mad if they cannot forget it afterward. This was worse. Up and down and here and there and now and then all rushed together. The wind roared through the rock beneath us, and the air thickened crushingly above our heads. I know we clung to each other, and we were there for each other while nothing else was, and that is all I know until we were in the jeep and I was guiding it back toward town as headlong as I had come.

Then the world had shape again under a bright sun. I saw a knot of horsemen on the horizon. They were heading for where Owen had been found. That boy had run a long way, alone and hurt and burdened.

I got Helen up to the office. She sat at her desk with her head down on her hands, and she quivered violently. I kept my arm around her.

"It was only a storm inside our two heads, Helen," I said over and over. "Something black blew away out of us. The game is finished, and we're free, and I love you."

Over and over I said that, for my sake as well as hers. I meant and believed it. I said she was my wife and we would marry and go a thousand miles away from that desert to raise our children. She quieted to a trembling, but she would not speak. Then I heard hoofbeats and the creak of leather in the street below, and then I heard slow footsteps on the stairs.

Old Dave stood in the doorway. His two guns looked as natural on him as hands and feet. He looked at Helen, bowed over the desk, and then at me, standing beside her.

"Come on down, son. The boys want to talk to you," he said.

I followed him into the hall and stopped.

"She isn't hurt," I said. "The lode is really out there, Dave, but nobody is ever going to find it."

"Tell that to the boys."

"We're closing out the project in a few more days," I said. "I'm going to marry Helen and take her away with me."

"Come down or we'll drag you down!" he said harshly. "We'll send Helen back to her mother."

I was afraid. I did not know what to do.

"No, you won't send me back to my mother!"

It was Helen beside me in the hall. She was Desert Helen, but grown up and wonderful. She was pale, pretty, aware, and sure of herself.

"I'm going with Duard," she said. "Nobody in the world is ever going to send me around like a package again."

Dave rubbed his jaw and squinted his eyes at her.

"I love her, Dave," I said. "I'll take care of her all my life."

I put my left arm around her, and she nestled against me. The tautness went out of old Dave, and he smiled. He kept his eyes on Helen.

"Little Helen Price," he said wonderingly. "Who ever would've thought it?" He reached out and shook us both gently. "Bless you youngsters," he said and blinked his eyes. "I'll tell the boys it's all right."

He turned and went slowly down the stairs. Helen and

I looked at each other, and I think she saw a new face, too.

That was sixteen years ago. I am a professor myself now, graying a bit at the temples. I am as positivistic a scientist as you will find anywhere in the Mississippi drainage basin. When I tell a seminar student, "That assertion is operationally meaningless," I can make it sound downright obscene. The students blush and hate me, but it is for their own good. Science is the only safe game, and it's safe only if it is kept pure. I work hard at that, I have yet to meet the student I can not handle.

My son is another matter. We named him Owen Lewis, and he has Helen's eyes and hair and complexion. He learned to read on the modern sane and sterile children's books. We haven't a fairy tale in the house—but I have a science library. And Owen makes fairy tales out of science. He is taking the measure of space and time now, with Jeans and Eddington. He cannot possibly understand a tenth of what he reads, in the way I understand it. But he understands all of it in some other way privately his own.

Not long ago he said to me, "You know, Dad, it isn't only space that's expanding. Time's expanding too, and that's what makes us keep getting farther away from when we used to be."

And I have to tell him just what I did in the war. I know I found manhood and a wife. The how and why of it I think and hope I am incapable of fully understanding. But Owen has, through Helen, that strangely curious heart. I'm afraid. I'm afraid he will understand.

CALL HIM LORD

by Gordon R. Dickson

> *He called and commanded me*
> *—Therefore, I knew him;*
> *But later on, failed me; and*
> *—Therefore, I slew him!*
>
> —"Song of the Shield Bearer"

The sun could not fail in rising over the Kentucky hills, nor could Kyle Arnam in waking. There would be eleven hours and forty minutes of daylight. Kyle rose, dressed, and went out to saddle the gray gelding and the white stallion. He rode the stallion until the first fury was out of the arched and snowy neck; and then led both horses around to tether them outside the kitchen door. Then he went in to breakfast.

The message that had come a week before was beside his plate of bacon and eggs. Teena, his wife, was standing at the breadboard with her back to him. He sat down and began eating, rereading the letter as he ate.

". . . The Prince will be traveling incognito under one of his family titles, as Count Sirii North; and should not be addressed as 'Majesty.' *You will call him 'Lord'* . . ."

"Why does it have to be you?" Teena asked.

He looked up and saw how she stood with her back to him.

"Teena—" he said, sadly.

"Why?"

"My ancestors were bodyguards to his—back in the

232

wars of conquest against the aliens. I've told you that," he said. "My forefathers saved the lives of his, many times when there was no warning—a Rak spaceship would suddenly appear out of nowhere to lock on, even to a flagship. And even an Emperor found himself fighting for his life, hand to hand."

"The aliens are all dead now, and the Emperor's got a hundred other worlds! Why can't his son take his Grand Tour on them? Why does he have to come here to Earth —and you?"

"There's only one Earth."

"And only one you, I suppose?"

He sighed internally and gave up. He had been raised by his father and his uncle after his mother died, and in an argument with Teena he always felt helpless. He got up from the table and went to her, putting his hands on her and gently trying to turn her about. But she resisted.

He sighed inside himself again and turned away to the weapons cabinet. He took out a loaded slug pistol, fitted it into the stubby holster it matched, and clipped the holster to his belt at the left of the buckle, where the hang of his leather jacket would hide it. Then he selected a dark-handled knife with a six-inch blade and bent over to slip it into the sheath inside his boot top. He dropped the cuff of his trouser leg back over the boot top and stood up.

"He's got no right to be here," said Teena fiercely to the breadboard. "Tourists are supposed to be kept to the museum areas and the tourist lodges."

"He's not a tourist. You know that," answered Kyle patiently. "He's the Emperor's oldest son and his great-grandmother was from Earth. His wife will be, too. Every fourth generation the Imperial line has to marry back into Earth stock. That's the law—still." He put on his leather jacket, sealing it closed only at the bottom to hide the slug-gun holster, half turned to the door—then paused.

"Teena?" he asked.

She did not answer.

"Teena!" he repeated. He stepped to her, put his hands on her shoulders, and tried to turn her to face him. Again she resisted, but this time he was having none of it.

He was not a big man, being of middle height, round-faced, with sloping and unremarkable-looking, if thick, shoulders. But his strength was not ordinary. He could bring the white stallion to its knees with one fist wound in its mane—and no other man had ever been able to do that. He turned her easily to look at him.

"Now listen to me—" he began. But before he could finish, all the stiffness went out of her, and she clung to him, trembling.

"He'll get you into trouble—I know he will!" she choked, muffledly into his chest. "Kyle, don't go! There's no law making you go!"

He stroked the soft hair of her head, his throat stiff and dry. There was nothing he could say to her. What she was asking was impossible. Ever since the sun had first risen on men and women together, wives had clung to their husbands at times like this, begging for what could not be. And always the men had held them, as Kyle was holding her now—as if understanding could somehow be pressed from one body into the other—and saying nothing because there was nothing that could be said.

So Kyle held her for a few moments longer, and then reached behind him to unlock her intertwined fingers at his back and loosen her arms around him. Then, he went. Looking back through the kitchen window as he rode off on the stallion, leading the gray horse, he saw her standing just where he had left her. Not even crying, but standing with her arms hanging down, her head down, not moving.

He rode away through the forest of the Kentucky hillside. It took him more than two hours to reach the lodge. As he rode down the valleyside toward it, he saw a tall, bearded man, wearing the robes they wore on some of the Younger Worlds, standing at the gateway to the interior courtyard of the rustic, wooded lodge.

When he got close, he saw that the beard was graying and the man was biting his lips. Above a straight, thin nose, the eyes were bloodshot and circled beneath as if from worry or lack of sleep.

"He's in the courtyard," said the gray-bearded man as Kyle rode up. "I'm Montlaven, his tutor. He's ready to go." The darkened eyes looked almost pleadingly up at Kyle.

"Stand clear of the stallion's head," said Kyle. "And take me in to him."

"Not that horse, for him—" said Montlaven, looking distrustfully at the stallion as he backed away.

"No," said Kyle. "He'll ride the gelding."

"He'll want the white."

"He can't ride the white," said Kyle. "Even if I let him, he couldn't ride this stallion. I'm the only one who can ride him. Take me in."

The tutor turned and led the way into the grassy courtyard, surrounding a swimming pool and looked down upon, on three sides, by the windows of the lodge. In a lounging chair by the pool sat a tall young man in his late teens with a mane of blond hair, a pair of stuffed saddlebags on the grass beside him. He stood up as Kyle and the tutor came toward him.

"Majesty," said the tutor as they stopped, "this is Kyle Arnam, your bodyguard for the three days here."

"Good morning, Bodyguard . . . Kyle, I mean." The Prince smiled mischievously. "Light, then. And I'll mount."

"You ride the gelding, Lord," said Kyle.

The Prince stared at him, tilted back his handsome head and laughed.

"I can ride, man!" he said. "I ride well."

"Not this horse, Lord," said Kyle, dispassionately. "No one rides this horse but me."

The eyes flashed wide, the laugh faded—then returned.

"What can I do?" The wide shoulders shrugged. "I give in—always I give in. Well, almost always." He grinned up at Kyle, his lips thinned but frank. "All right."

He turned to the gelding and with a sudden leap was in the saddle. The gelding snorted and plunged at the shock, then steadied as the young man's long fingers tightened expertly on the reins and the fingers of the other hand patted a gray neck. The Prince raised his eyebrows, looking over at Kyle, but Kyle sat stolidly.

"I take it you're armed, good Kyle?" the Prince said slyly. "You'll protect me against the natives if they run wild?"

"Your life is in my hands, Lord," said Kyle. He unsealed the leather jacket at the bottom and let it fall open to show the slug pistol in its holster for a moment. Then he resealed the jacket again at the bottom.

"Will—" The tutor put his hand on the young man's

knee. "Don't be reckless, boy. This is Earth and the people here don't have rank and custom like we do. Think before you—"

"Oh, cut it out, Monty!" snapped the Prince. "I'll be just as incognito, just as humble, as archaic and independent as the rest of them. You think I've no memory! Anyway, it's only for three days or so until my Imperial father joins me. Now let me go!"

He jerked away, turned to lean forward in the saddle, and abruptly put the gelding into a bolt for the gate. He disappeared through it, and Kyle drew hard on the stallion's reins as the big white horse danced and tried to follow.

"Give me his saddlebags," said Kyle.

The tutor bent and passed them up. Kyle made them fast on top of his own across the stallion's withers. Looking down, he saw there were tears in the bearded man's eyes.

"He's a fine boy. You'll see. You'll know he is!" Montlaven's face, upturned, was mutely pleading.

"I know he comes from a fine family," said Kyle slowly. "I'll do my best for him." And he rode off out of the gateway after the gelding.

When he came out of the gate, the Prince was nowhere in sight. But it was simple enough for Kyle to follow, by dinted brown earth and crushed grass, the marks of the gelding's path. This brought him at last through some pines to a grassy open slope where the Prince sat looking skyward through a single-lens box.

When Kyle came up, the Prince lowered the instrument and, without a word, passed it over. Kyle put it to his eye and looked skyward. There was the whir of the tracking unit and one of Earth's three orbiting power stations swam into the field of vision of the lens.

"Give it back," said the Prince.

"I couldn't get a look at it earlier," went on the young man as Kyle handed the lens to him. "And I wanted to. It's a rather expensive present, you know—it and the other two like it—from our Imperial treasury. Just to keep your planet from drifting into another ice age. And what do we get for it?"

"Earth, Lord," answered Kyle. "As it was before men went out to the stars."

"Oh, the museum areas could be maintained with one station and a half-million caretakers," said the Prince. "It's the other two stations and you billion or so free-loaders I'm talking about. I'll have to look into it when I'm Emperor. Shall we ride?"

"If you wish, Lord." Kyle picked up the reins of the stallion, and the two horses with their riders moved off across the slope.

". . . And one more thing," said the Prince as they entered the farther belt of pine trees. "I don't want you to be misled—I'm really very fond of old Monty back there. It's just that I wasn't really planning to come here at all—*Look at me, Bodyguard!*"

Kyle turned to see the blue eyes that ran in the Imperial family, blazing at him. Then, unexpectedly, they softened. The Prince laughed.

"You don't scare easily, do you, Bodyguard . . . Kyle, I mean?" he said. "I think I like you after all. But look at me when I talk."

"Yes, Lord."

"That's my good Kyle. Now I was explaining to you that I'd never actually planned to come here on my Grand Tour at all. I didn't see any point in visiting this dusty old museum world of yours with people still trying to live like they lived in the Dark Ages. But—my Imperial father talked me into it."

"Your father, Lord?" asked Kyle.

"Yes, he bribed me, you might say," said the Prince thoughtfully. "He was supposed to meet me here for these three days. Now, he's messaged there's been a slight delay—but that doesn't matter. The point is, he belongs to the school of old men who still think your Earth is something precious and vital. Now, I happen to like and admire my father, Kyle. You approve of that?"

"Yes, Lord."

"I thought you would. Yes, he's the one man in the human race I look up to. And to please him, I'm making this Earth trip. And to please him—only to please *him*, Kyle—I'm going to be an easy Prince for you to conduct around to your natural wonders and watering spots and whatever. Now, you understand me—and how this trip is going to go. Don't you?" He stared at Kyle.

"I understand," said Kyle.

"That's fine," said the Prince, smiling once more. "So now you can start telling me all about these trees and birds and animals so that I can memorize their names and please my father when he shows up. What are those little birds I've been seeing under the trees—brown on top and whitish underneath? Like that one—there!"

"That's a Veery, Lord," said Kyle. "A bird of the deep woods and silent places. Listen—" He reached out a hand to the gelding's bridle and brought both horses to a halt. In the sudden silence, off to their right they could hear a silver bird-voice, rising and falling in a descending series of crescendos and diminuendos that softened at last into silence. For a moment after the song was ended, the Prince sat staring at Kyle, then seemed to shake himself back to life.

"Interesting," he said. He lifted the reins Kyle had let go, and the horses moved forward again. "Tell me more."

For more than three hours, as the sun rose toward noon, they rode through the wooded hills with Kyle identifying bird and animal, insect, tree, and rock. And for three hours the Prince listened—his attention flashing and momentary, but intense. But when the sun was overhead that intensity flagged.

"That's enough," he said. "Aren't we going to stop for lunch? Kyle, aren't there any towns around here?"

"Yes, Lord," said Kyle. "We've passed several."

"Several?" The Prince stared at him. "Why haven't we come into one before now? Where are you taking me?"

"Nowhere, Lord," said Kyle. "You lead the way. I only follow."

"I?" said the Prince. For the first time he seemed to become aware that he had been keeping the gelding's head always in advance of the stallion. "Of course. But now it's time to eat."

"Yes, Lord," said Kyle. "This way."

He turned the stallion's head down the slope of the hill they were crossing, and the Prince turned the gelding after him.

"And now listen," said the Prince as he caught up. "Tell me I've got it all right." And to Kyle's astonishment, he began to repeat, almost word for word, everything that Kyle had said. "Is it all there? Everything you told me?"

"Perfectly, Lord," said Kyle. The Prince looked slyly at him.

"Could you do that, Kyle?"

"Yes," said Kyle. "But these are things I've known all my life."

"You see?" The Prince smiled. "That's the difference between us, good Kyle. You spend your life learning something—I spend a few hours and I know as much about it as you do."

"Not as much, Lord," said Kyle, slowly.

The Prince blinked at him, then jerked his hand dismissingly and half-angrily, as if he were throwing something aside.

"What little else there is probably doesn't count," he said.

They rode down the slope and through a winding valley and came out at a small village. As they rode clear of the surrounding trees, a sound of music came to their ears.

"What's that?" The Prince stood up in his stirrups. "Why, there's dancing going on, over there."

"A beer garden, Lord. And it's Saturday—a holiday here."

"Good. We'll go there to eat."

They rode around to the beer garden and found tables back away from the dance floor. A pretty, young waitress came and they ordered, the Prince smiling sunnily at her until she smiled back—then hurried off as if in mild confusion. The Prince ate hungrily when the food came and drank a stein and a half of brown beer, while Kyle ate more lightly and drank coffee.

"That's better," said the Prince, sitting back at last. "I had an appetite . . . Look there, Kyle! Look, there are five, six . . . seven drifter platforms parked over there. Then you don't all ride horses?"

"No," said Kyle. "It's as each man wishes."

"But if you have drifter platforms, why not other civilized things?"

"Some things fit, some don't, Lord," answered Kyle. The Prince laughed.

"You mean you try to make civilization fit this old-fashioned life of yours, here?" he said. "Isn't that the wrong way around——" He broke off. "What's that they're

playing now? I like that. I'll bet I could do that dance."
He stood up. "In fact, I think I will."

He paused, looking down at Kyle.

"Aren't you going to warn me against it?" he asked.

"No, Lord," said Kyle. "What you do is your own affair."

The young man turned away abruptly. The waitress
who had served them was passing, only a few tables
away. The Prince went after her and caught up with her
by the dance floor railing. Kyle could see the girl protesting—but the Prince hung over her, looking down from his
tall height, smiling. Shortly, she had taken off her apron
and was out on the dance floor with him, showing him the
steps of the dance. It was a polka.

The Prince learned with fantastic quickness. Soon, he
was swinging the waitress around with the rest of the
dancers, his foot stamping on the turns, his white teeth
gleaming. Finally the number ended, and the members
of the band put down their instruments and began to
leave the stand.

The Prince, with the girl trying to hold him back,
walked over to the band leader. Kyle got up quickly
from his table and started toward the floor.

The band leader was shaking his head. He turned
abruptly and slowly walked away. The Prince started after
him, but the girl took hold of his arm, saying something
urgent to him.

He brushed her aside, and she stumbled a little. A
busboy among the tables on the far side of the dance
floor, not much older than the Prince and nearly as tall,
put down his tray and vaulted the railing onto the polished hardwood. He came up behind the Prince and took
hold of his arm, swinging him around.

". . . Can't do that here." Kyle heard him say, as Kyle
came up. The Prince struck out like a panther—like a
trained boxer—with three quick lefts in succession into
the face of the busboy, the Prince's shoulder bobbing, the
weight of his body in behind each blow.

The busboy went down. Kyle, reaching the Prince,
herded him away through a side gap in the railing. The
young man's face was white with rage. People were
swarming onto the dance floor.

"Who was that? What's his name?" demanded the Prince between his teeth. "He put his hand on me! Did you see that? *He put his hand on me!*"

"You knocked him out," said Kyle. "What more do you want?"

"He manhandled me—*me!*" snapped the Prince. "I want to find out who he is!" He caught hold of the bar to which the horses were tied, refusing to be pushed farther. "He'll learn to lay hands on a future Emperor!"

"No one will tell you his name," said Kyle. And the cold note in his voice finally seemed to reach through to the Prince and sober him. He stared at Kyle.

"Including you?" he demanded at last.

"Including me, Lord," said Kyle.

The Prince stared a moment longer, then swung away. He turned, jerked loose the reins of the gelding, and swung into the saddle. He rode off. Kyle mounted and followed.

They rode in silence into the forest. After a while, the Prince spoke without turning his head.

"And you call yourself a bodyguard," he said, finally.

"Your life is in my hands, Lord," said Kyle. The Prince turned a grim face to look at him.

"Only my life?" said the Prince. "As long as they don't kill me, they can do what they want? Is that what you mean?"

Kyle met his gaze steadily.

"Pretty much so, Lord," he said.

The Prince spoke with an ugly note in his voice.

"I don't think I like you, after all, Kyle," he said. "I don't think I like you at all."

"I'm not here with you to be liked, Lord," said Kyle.

"Perhaps not," said the Prince thickly. "But I know *your* name!"

They rode on in continued silence for perhaps another half hour. But then gradually the angry hunch went out of the young man's shoulders and the tightness out of his jaw. After a while he began to sing to himself, a song in a language Kyle did not know; and as he sang, his cheerfulness seemed to return. Shortly, he spoke to Kyle, as if there had never been anything but pleasant moments between them.

Mammoth Cave was close, and the Prince asked to

visit it. They went there and spent some time going through the cave. After that they rode their horses up along the left bank of the Green River. The Prince seemed to have forgotten all about the incident at the beer garden and seemed to be out to charm everyone they met. As the sun was at last westering toward the dinner hour, they came finally to a small hamlet back from the river with a roadside inn mirrored in an artificial lake beside it, and guarded by oak and pine trees behind.

"This looks good," said the Prince. "We'll stay overnight here, Kyle."

"If you wish, Lord," said Kyle.

They halted, and Kyle took the horses around to the stable, then entered the inn to find the Prince already in the small bar off the dining room, drinking beer and charming the waitress. This waitress was younger than the one at the beer garden had been; a little girl with soft, loose hair and round, brown eyes that showed their delight in the attention of the tall, good-looking, young man.

"Yes," said the Prince to Kyle, looking out of the corners of the Imperial blue eyes at him, after the waitress had gone to get Kyle his coffee, "this is the very place."

"The very place?" said Kyle.

"For me to get to know the people better—what did you think, good Kyle?" said the Prince and laughed at him. "I'll observe the people here and you can explain them—won't that be good?"

Kyle gazed at him, thoughtfully.

"I'll tell you whatever I can, Lord," he said.

They drank—the Prince his beer, and Kyle his coffee —and went in a little later to the dining room for dinner. The Prince, as he had promised at the bar, was full of questions about what he saw—and what he did not see.

". . . But why go on living in the past, all of you here?" he asked Kyle. "A museum world is one thing. But a museum people—" he broke off to smile and speak to the little, soft-haired waitress, who had somehow been diverted from the bar to wait upon their dining-room table.

"Not a museum people, Lord," said Kyle. "A living

people. The only way to keep a race and a culture preserved is to keep it alive. So we go on in our own way,
here on Earth, as a living example for the Younger
Worlds to check themselves against."

"Fascinating . . ." murmured the Prince; but his eyes
had wandered off to follow the waitress, who was glowing
and looking back at him from across the now-busy dining room.

"Not fascinating. Necessary, Lord," said Kyle. But he
did not believe the younger man had heard him.

After dinner, they moved back to the bar. And the
Prince, after questioning Kyle a little longer, moved up
to continue his researches among the other people standing
at the bar. Kyle watched for a little while. Then, feeling
it was safe to do so, slipped out to have another look at
the horses and to ask the innkeeper to arrange a saddle
lunch put up for them the next day.

When he returned, the Prince was not to be seen.

Kyle sat down at a table to wait, but the Prince did
not return. A cold, hard knot of uneasiness began to
grow below Kyle's breastbone. A sudden pang of alarm
sent him swiftly back out to check the horses. But they
were cropping peacefully in their stalls. The stallion
whickered, low-voiced, as Kyle looked in on him, and
turned his white head to look back at Kyle.

"Easy, boy," said Kyle and returned to the inn to find
the innkeeper.

But the innkeeper had no idea where the Prince might
have gone.

". . . If the horses aren't taken, he's not far," the innkeeper said. "There's no trouble he can get into around
here. Maybe he went for a walk in the woods. I'll leave
word for the night staff to keep an eye out for him when
he comes in. Where'll you be?"

"In the bar until it closes—then my room," said Kyle.

He went back to the bar to wait and took a booth near
an open window. Time went by and gradually the number of other customers began to dwindle. Above the
ranked bottles, the bar clock showed nearly midnight.
Suddenly, through the window Kyle heard a distant
scream of equine fury from the stables.

He got up and went out quickly. In the darkness outside, he ran to the stables and burst in. There in the fee-

ble illumination of the stable's night lighting, he saw the Prince, pale-faced, clumsily saddling the gelding in the center aisle between the stalls. The door to the stallion's stall was open. The Prince looked away as Kyle came in.

Kyle took three swift steps to the open door and looked in. The stallion was still tied, but his ears were back, his eyes rolling, and a saddle lay tumbled and dropped on the stable floor beside him.

"Saddle up," said the Prince thickly from the aisle. "We're leaving." Kyle turned to look at him.

"We've got rooms at the inn here," he said.

"Never mind. We're riding. I need to clear my head." The young man got the gelding's cinch tight, dropped the stirrups, and swung heavily up into the saddle. Without waiting for Kyle, he rode out of the stable into the night.

"So, boy . . ." said Kyle soothingly to the stallion. Hastily he untied the big white horse, saddled him, and set out after the Prince. In the darkness there was no way of ground-tracking the gelding; but he leaned forward and blew into the ear of the stallion. The surprised horse neighed in protest, and the whinny of the gelding came back from the darkness of the slope up ahead and over to Kyle's right. He rode in that direction.

He caught the Prince on the crown of the hill. The young man was walking the gelding, reins loose, and singing under his breath—the same song in an unknown language he had sung earlier. But, now as he saw Kyle, he grinned loosely and began to sing with more emphasis. For the first time Kyle caught the overtones of something mocking and lusty about the incomprehensible words. Understanding broke suddenly in him.

"The girl!" he said. "The little waitress. Where is she?"

The grin vanished from the Prince's face, then came slowly back again. The grin laughed at Kyle.

"Why, where d'you think?" The words slurred on the Prince's tongue and Kyle, riding close, smelled the beer heavy on the young man's breath. "In her room, sleeping and happy. Honored . . . though she doesn't know it . . . by an Emperor's son. And expecting to find me there in the morning. But I won't be. Will we, good Kyle?"

"Why did you do it, Lord?" asked Kyle quietly.

"Why?" The Prince peered at him, a little drunkenly

in the moonlight. "Kyle, my father has four sons. I've got three younger brothers. But I'm the one who's going to be Emperor, and Emperors don't answer questions."

Kyle said nothing. The Prince peered at him. They rode on together for several minutes in silence.

"All right, I'll tell you why," said the Prince more loudly after a while as if the pause had been only momentary. "It's because you're not *my* bodyguard, Kyle. You see, I've seen through you. I know whose bodyguard you are. You're *theirs!*"

Kyle's jaw tightened. But the darkness hid his reaction.

"All right—" The Prince gestured loosely, disturbing his balance in the saddle. "That's all right. Have it your way. I don't mind. So, we'll play points. There was that lout at the beer garden who put his hands on me. But no one would tell me his name, you said. All right, you managed to bodyguard him. One point for you. But you didn't manage to bodyguard the girl at the inn back there. One point for me. Who's going to win, good Kyle?"

Kyle took a deep breath.

"Lord," he said, "some day it'll be your duty to marry a woman from Earth—"

The Prince interrupted him with a laugh, and this time there was an ugly note in it.

"You flatter yourselves," he said. His voice thickened. "That's the trouble with you—all you Earth people—you flatter yourselves."

They rode on in silence. Kyle said nothing more, but kept the head of the stallion close to the shoulder of the gelding, watching the young man closely. For a little while the Prince seemed to doze. His head sank on his chest, and he let the gelding wander. Then after a while, his head began to come up again, his automatic horseman's fingers tightened on the reins, and he lifted his head to stare around in the moonlight.

"I want a drink," he said. His voice was no longer thick, but it was flat and uncheerful. "Take me where we can get some beer, Kyle."

Kyle took a deep breath.

"Yes, Lord," he said.

He turned the stallion's head to the right, and the gelding followed. They went up over a hill and down to the edge of a lake. The dark water sparkled in the moonlight, and the farther shore was lost in the night. Lights shone through the trees around the curve of the shore.

"There, Lord," said Kyle. "It's a fishing resort, with a bar."

They rode around the shore to it. It was a low, casual building, angled to face the shore; a dock ran out from it to which fishing boats were tethered, bobbing slightly on the black water. Light gleamed through the windows as they hitched their horses and went to the door.

The barroom they stepped into was wide and bare. A long bar faced them with several planked fish on the wall behind it. Below the fish were three bartenders—the one in the center, middle-aged and wearing an air of authority with his apron. The other two were young and muscular. The customers, mostly men, scattered at the square tables and standing at the bar, wore rough working clothes or equally casual vacationers' garb.

The Prince sat down at a table back from the bar, and Kyle sat down with him. When the waitress came, they ordered beer and coffee, and the Prince half-emptied his stein the moment it was brought to him. As soon as it was completely empty, he signaled the waitress again.

"Another," he said. This time he smiled at the waitress when she brought his stein back. But she was a woman in her thirties, pleased but not overwhelmed by his attention. She smiled lightly back and moved off to return to the bar where she had been talking to two men her own age, one fairly tall, the other shorter, bullet-headed, and fleshy.

The Prince drank. As he put his stein down, he seemed to become aware of Kyle and turned to look at him.

"I suppose," said the Prince, "you think I'm drunk?"

"Not yet," said Kyle.

"No," said the Prince, "That's right. Not yet. But perhaps I'm going to be. And if I decide I am, who's going to stop me?"

"No one, Lord."

"That's right," the young man said, "that's right." He drank deliberately from his stein until it was empty and then signaled the waitress for another. A spot of color was beginning to show over each of his high cheekbones. "When you're on a miserable little world with miserable little people . . . hello, Bright Eyes!" he interrupted himself as the waitress brought his beer. She laughed and went back to her friends. ". . . You have to amuse yourself any way you can," he wound up.

He laughed to himself.

"When I think how my father, and Monty—everybody —used to talk this planet up to me—" he glanced aside at Kyle. "Do you know at one time I was actually scared —well, not scared exactly, nothing scares me . . . say *concerned*—about maybe having to come here, some day?" He laughed again. "Concerned that I wouldn't measure up to you Earth people! Kyle, have you ever been to any of the Younger Worlds?"

"No," said Kyle.

"I thought not. Let me tell you, good Kyle, the worst of the people there are bigger and better-looking and smarter and everything than anyone I've seen here. And I, Kyle, I—the Emperor-to-be—am better than any of them. So, guess how all you here look to me?" He stared at Kyle, waiting. "Well, answer me, good Kyle. Tell me the truth. That's an order."

"It's not up to you to judge, Lord," said Kyle.

"Not—? Not up to me?" The blue eyes blazed. *"I'm* going to be Emperor!"

"It's not up to any one man, Lord," said Kyle. "Emperor or not. An Emperor's needed as the symbol that can hold a hundred worlds together. But the real need of the race is to survive. It took nearly a million years to evolve a survival-type intelligence here on Earth. And out on the newer worlds people are bound to change. If something gets lost out there, some necessary element lost out of the race, there needs to be a pool of original genetic material here to replace it."

The Prince's lips grew wide in a savage grin.

"Oh, good, Kyle—good!" he said. "Very good. Only I've heard all that before. Only I don't believe it. You see—I've seen you people now. And you don't outclass us, out on the Younger Worlds. *We* outclass *you*. We've gone on and got better while you stayed still. And you know it."

The young man laughed softly, almost in Kyle's face.

"All you've been afraid of, is that we'd find out. And I

have." He laughed again. "I've had a look at you; and now I know. I'm bigger, better, and braver than any man in this room—and you know why? Not just because I'm the son of the Emperor, but because it's born in me! Body, brains, and everything else! I can do what I want here, and no one on this planet is good enough to stop me. Watch."

He stood up, suddenly.

"Now, I want that waitress to get drunk with me," he said. "And this time I'm telling you in advance. Are you going to try and stop me?"

Kyle looked up at him. Their eyes met.

"No, Lord," he said. "It's not my job to stop you."

The Prince laughed.

"I thought so," he said. He swung away and walked between the tables toward the bar and the waitress, still in conversation with the two men. The Prince came up to the bar on the far side of the waitress and ordered a new stein of beer from the middle-aged bartender. When it was given to him, he took it, turned around, and rested his elbows on the bar, leaning back against it. He spoke to the waitress, interrupting the taller of the two men.

"I've been wanting to talk to you," Kyle heard him say.

The waitress, a little surprised, looked around at him. She smiled, recognizing him—a little flattered by the directness of his approach, a little appreciative of his clean good looks, a little tolerant of his youth.

"*You* don't mind, do you?" said the Prince, looking past her to the bigger of the two men, the one who had just been talking. The other stared back, and their eyes met without shifting for several seconds. Abruptly, angrily, the man shrugged and turned about with his back hunched against them.

"You see?" said the Prince, smiling back at the waitress. "He knows I'm the one you ought to be talking to, instead of—"

"All right, sonny. Just a minute."

It was the shorter, bullet-headed man, interrupting. The Prince turned to look down at him with a fleeting expression of surprise. But the bullet-headed man was already turning to his taller friend and putting a hand on his arm.

"Come on back, Ben," the shorter man was saying. "The kid's a little drunk, is all." He turned back to the Prince. "You shove off now," he said. "Clara's with us."

The Prince stared at him blankly. The stare was so fixed that the shorter man had started to turn away, back to his friend and the waitress, when the Prince seemed to wake.

"Just a minute—" he said in his turn.

He reached out a hand to one of the fleshy shoulders below the bullet head. The man turned back, knocking the hand calmly away. Then, just as calmly, he picked up the Prince's full stein of beer from the bar and threw it in the young man's face.

"Get lost," he said unexcitedly.

The Prince stood for a second with the beer dripping from his face. Then, without even stopping to wipe his eyes clear he threw the beautifully trained left hand he had demonstrated at the beer garden.

But the shorter man, as Kyle had known from the first moment of seeing him, was not like the busboy the Prince had decisioned so neatly. This man was thirty pounds heavier, fifteen years more experienced, and by build and nature a natural bar fighter. He had not stood there waiting to be hit, but had already ducked and gone forward to throw his thick arms around the Prince's body. The young man's punch bounced harmlessly off the round head, and both bodies hit the floor, rolling in among the chair and table legs.

Kyle was already more than halfway to the bar, and the three bartenders were already leaping the wooden hurdle that walled them off. The taller friend of the bullet-headed man, hovering over the two bodies, his eyes glittering, had his boot drawn back ready to drive the point of it into the Prince's kidneys. Kyle's forearm took him economically like a bar of iron across the tanned throat.

He stumbled backwards, choking. Kyle stood still, hands open and down, glancing at the middle-aged bartender.

"All right," said the bartender. "But don't do anything more." He turned to the two younger bartenders. "All right. Haul him off!"

The pair of younger, aproned men bent down and

came up with the bullet-headed man expertly hand-locked between them. The man made one surging effort to break loose and then stood still.

"Let me at him," he said.

"Not in here," said the older bartender. "Take it outside."

Between the tables, the Prince staggered unsteadily to his feet. His face was streaming blood from a cut on his forehead, but what could be seen of it was white as a drowning man's. His eyes went to Kyle, standing beside him, and he opened his mouth—but what came out sounded like something between a sob and a curse.

"All right," said the middle-aged bartender again. "Outside, both of you. Settle it out there."

The men in the room had packed around the little space by the bar. The Prince looked about and for the first time seemed to see the human wall hemming him in. His gaze wobbled to meet Kyle's.

"Outside . . . ?" he said chokingly.

"You aren't staying in here," said the older bartender, answering for Kyle. "I saw it. You started the whole thing. Now settle it any way you want—but you're both going outside. Now. Get moving!"

He pushed at the Prince, but the Prince resisted, clutching at Kyle's leather jacket with one hand.

"Kyle—"

"I'm sorry, Lord," said Kyle. "I can't help. It's your fight."

"Let's get out of here," said the bullet-headed man.

The Prince stared around at them as if they were some strange set of beings he had never known to exist before.

"No . . ." he said.

He let go of Kyle's jacket. Unexpectedly his hand darted in towards Kyle's belly holster and came out holding the slug pistol.

"Stand back!" he said, his voice high-toned. "Don't try to touch me!"

His voice broke on the last words. There was a strange sound, half-grunt, half-moan, from the crowd; and it swayed back from him. Manager, bartenders, watchers —all but Kyle and the bullet-headed man drew back.

"You dirty slob . . ." said the bullet-headed man distinctly. "I knew you didn't have the guts."

"Shut up!" The Prince's voice was high and cracking. "Shut up! Don't any of you try to come after me!"

He began backing away toward the front door of the bar. The room watched in silence, even Kyle standing still. As he backed, the Prince's back straightened. He hefted the gun in his hand. When he reached the door, he paused to wipe the blood from his eyes with his left sleeve, and his smeared face looked with a first touch of regained arrogance at them.

"Swine!" he said.

He opened the door and backed out, closing it behind him. Kyle took one step that put him facing the bullet-headed man. Their eyes met, and he could see the other recognizing the fighter in him as he had earlier recognized it in the bullet-headed man.

"Don't come after us," said Kyle.

The bullet-headed man did not answer. But no answer was needed. He stood still.

Kyle turned, ran to the door, stood on one side of it, and flicked it open. Nothing happened; and he slipped through, dodging to his right at once, out of the line of any shot aimed at the opening door.

But no shot came. For a moment he was blind in the night darkness, then his eyes began to adjust. He went by sight, feel, and memory toward the hitching rack. By the time he got there, he was beginning to see.

The Prince was untying the gelding and getting ready to mount.

"Lord," said Kyle.

The Prince let go of the saddle for a moment and turned to look over his shoulder at him.

"Get away from me," said the Prince thickly.

"Lord," said Kyle, low-voiced and pleading, "you lost your head in there. Anyone might do that. But don't make it worse now. Give me back the gun, Lord."

"Give you the gun?"

The young man stared at him—and then he laughed.

"Give *you* the gun?" he said again. "So you can let someone beat me up some more? So you can not-guard me with it?"

"Lord," said Kyle, "please. For your own sake—give me back the gun."

"Get out of here," said the Prince thickly, turning back to mount the gelding. "Clear out before I put a slug in you."

Kyle drew a slow, sad breath. He stepped forward and tapped the Prince on the shoulder.

"Turn around, Lord," he said.

"I warned you—" shouted the Prince, turning.

He came around as Kyle stooped, and the slug pistol flashed in his hand from the light of the bar windows. Kyle, bent over, was lifting the cuff of his trouser leg and closing his fingers on the hilt of the knife in his boot sheath. He moved simply, skillfully, and with a speed nearly double that of the young man, striking up into the chest before him until the hand holding the knife jarred against the cloth covering flesh and bone.

It was a sudden, hard-driven, swiftly merciful blow. The blade struck upwards between the ribs, lying open to an underhanded thrust, plunging deep into the heart. The Prince grunted with the impact, driving the air from his lungs; and he was dead as Kyle caught his slumping body in leather-jacketed arms.

Kyle lifted the tall body across the saddle of the gelding and tied it there. He hunted on the dark ground for the fallen pistol and returned it to his holster. Then he mounted the stallion and, leading the gelding with its burden, started the long ride back.

Dawn was graying the sky when at last he topped the hill overlooking the lodge where he had picked up the Prince almost twenty-four hours before. He rode down towards the courtyard gate.

A tall figure, indistinct in the predawn light, was waiting inside the courtyard as Kyle came through the gate; and it came running to meet him as he rode toward it. It was the tutor, Montlaven, and he was weeping as he ran to the gelding and began to fumble at the cords that tied the body in place.

"I'm sorry . . ." Kyle heard himself saying; and was dully shocked by the deadness and remoteness of his voice. "There was no choice. You can read it all in my report tomorrow morning—"

He broke off. Another, even taller figure had appeared in the doorway of the lodge giving on the courtyard. As Kyle turned towards it, this second figure descended the few steps to the grass and came to him.

"Lord—" said Kyle. He looked down into features like those of the Prince, but older, under graying hair. This man did not weep like the tutor, but his face was set like iron.

"What happened, Kyle?" he said.

"Lord," said Kyle, "you'll have my report in the morning . . ."

"I want to know," said the tall man. Kyle's throat was dry and stiff. He swallowed, but swallowing did not ease it.

"Lord," he said, "you have three other sons. One of them will make an Emperor to hold the worlds together."

"What did he do? Whom did he hurt? Tell me!" The tall man's voice cracked almost as his son's voice had cracked in the bar.

"Nothing. No one," said Kyle stiff-throated. "He hit a boy not much older than himself. He drank too much. He may have got a girl in trouble. It was nothing he did to anyone else. It was only a fault against himself." He swallowed. "Wait until tomorrow, Lord, and read my report."

"No!" The tall man caught at Kyle's saddle horn with a grip that checked even the white stallion from moving. "Your family and mine have been tied together by this for three-hundred years. What was the flaw in my son to make him fail his test back here on Earth? *I want to know!"*

Kyle's throat ached and was dry as ashes.

"Lord," he answered, "he was a coward."

The hand dropped from his saddle horn as if struck down by a sudden strengthlessness. And the Emperor of a hundred worlds fell back like a beggar, spurned in the dust.

Kyle lifted his reins and rode out of the gate into the forest away on the hillside. The dawn was breaking.

THE LAST CASTLE

by Jack Vance

I

1.

Toward the end of a stormy summer afternoon, with the sun finally breaking out under ragged black rain-clouds, Castle Janeil was overwhelmed and its population destroyed. Until almost the last moment factions among the castle clans contended as to how Destiny properly should be met. The gentlemen of most prestige and account elected to ignore the entire undignified circumstance and went about their normal pursuits, with neither more nor less punctilio than usual. A few cadets, desperate to the point of hysteria, took up weapons and prepared to resist the final assault. Still others, perhaps a quarter of the total population, waited passively, ready—almost happy—to expiate the sins of the human race. In the end, death came uniformly to all, and all extracted as much satisfaction from their dying as this essentially graceless process could afford. The proud sat turning the pages of their beautiful books, discussing the qualities of a century-old essence, or fondling a favorite Phane, and died without deigning to heed the fact. The hotheads raced up the muddy slope which, outraging all normal rationality, loomed above the parapets of Janeil. Most were buried under sliding rubble, but a few gained the ridge to gun, hack and stab, until they themselves were shot, crushed by the half-alive power-wagons, hacked or stabbed. The contrite waited in the classic posture of expiation—on their knees, heads bowed—and perished, so they believed, by a process in which the Meks were symbols and human sin the reality. In the end all were dead: gentlemen, ladies, Phanes in the pavilions; Peasants in the stables. Of all those who had inhabited Janeil, only the Birds survived, creatures awkward, gauche and raucous, oblivious to pride and faith, more concerned with the wholeness of their hides than the dignity of their castle. As the Meks swarmed down over the parapets, the Birds departed their cotes and, screaming strident insults, flapped east toward Hagedorn, now the last castle of Earth.

2.

Four months before, the Meks had appeared in the park before Janeil, fresh from the Sea Island massacre. Climbing to the turrets and balconies, sauntering the Sunset Promenade, from ramparts and parapets, the gentlemen and ladies of Janeil, some two thousand in all, looked down at the brown-gold warriors. Their mood was complex—amused indifference, flippant disdain, and a substratum of doubt and foreboding; all the product of three basic circumstances—their own exquisitely subtle civilization, the security provided by Janeil's walls, and the fact that they could conceive no recourse, no means for altering circumstances.

The Janeil Meks had long since departed to join the revolt; there remained only Phanes, Peasants and Birds from which to fashion what would have been the travesty of a punitive force. At the moment there seemed no need for such a force. Janeil was deemed impregnable. The walls, two hundred feet tall, were black rock-melt contained in the meshes of a silver-blue steel alloy. Solar cells provided energy for all the needs of the castle, and in the event of emergency, food could be synthesized from carbon dioxide and water vapor, as well as syrup for Phanes, Peasants and Birds. Such a need was not envisaged. Janeil was self-sufficient and secure, though inconveniences might arise when machinery broke down and there were no Meks to repair it. The situation then was disturbing but hardly desperate. During the day the gentlemen so inclined brought forth energy-guns and sport-rifles and killed as many Meks as the extreme range allowed.

After dark the Meks brought forward power-wagons and earth-movers, and began to raise a dike around Janeil. The folk of the castle watched without comprehension until the dike reached a height of fifty feet and dirt began to spill down against the walls. Then the dire purpose of the Meks became apparent, and insouciance gave way to dismal foreboding. All the gentlemen of Janeil were erudite in at least one realm of knowledge; certain were mathematical theoreticians, while others had made a profound study of the physical sciences. Some of these, with a detail of Peasants to perform the sheerly physical exertion, attempted to restore the energy-cannon to functioning condition. Unluckily, the cannon had not been maintained in good order. Various components were obviously corroded or damaged. Conceivably these components might have been replaced from the Mek shops on the second sublevel, but none of the group had any knowledge of the Mek nomenclature or warehousing system. Warrick Madency Arban (Arban of the Madency family in the Warrick clan) suggested that a work-force of Peasants search the warehouse, but in view of the limited mental capacity of the Peasants, nothing was done and the whole plan to restore the energy-cannon came to naught.

The gentlefolk of Janeil watched in fascination as the dirt piled higher and higher around them, in a circular mound like a crater. Summer neared its end, and on one stormy day dirt and rubble rose above the parapets, and began to spill over into the courts and piazzas: Janeil must soon be buried and all within suffocated. It was then that a group of impulsive young cadets, with more élan than dignity, took up weapons and charged up the slope. The Meks dumped dirt and stone upon them, but a handful gained the ridge where they fought in a kind of dreadful exaltation.

Fifteen minutes the fight raged and the earth became sodden with rain and blood. For one glorious moment the cadets swept the ridge clear, and had not most of their fellows been lost under the rubble, anything might have occurred. But the Meks regrouped and thrust forward. Ten men were left, then six, then four, then one, then none.

The Meks marched down the slope, swarmed over the battlements, and with somber intensity killed all within. Janeil, for seven hundred years the abode of gallant gentlemen, and gracious ladies, had become a lifeless hulk.

3.

The Mek, standing as if a specimen in a museum case, was a manlike creature, native, in his original version, to a planet of Etamin. His tough rusty-bronze hide glistened metallically as if oiled or waxed; the spines thrusting back from scalp and neck shone like gold, and indeed were coated with a conductive copper-chrome film. His sense organs were gathered in clusters at the site of a man's ears; his visage—it was often a shock, walking the lower corridors, to come suddenly upon a Mek—was corrugated muscle, not dissimilar to the look of an uncovered human brain. His maw, a vertical irregular cleft at the base of this "face," was an obsolete organ by reason of the syrup sac which had been introduced under the skin of the shoulders; the digestive organs, originally used to extract nutrition from decayed swamp vegetation and coelenterates, had atrophied. The Mek typically wore no garment except possibly a work-apron or a tool-belt, and in the sunlight his rust-bronze skin made a handsome display. This was the Mek solitary, a creature intrinsically as effective as man—perhaps more by virtue of his superb brain which also functioned as a radio transceiver. Working in the mass, by the teeming thousands, he seemed less admirable, less competent: a hybrid of subman and cockroach.

Certain savants, notably Morninglight's D. R. Jardine and Salonson of Tuang, considered the Mek bland and phlegmatic, but the profound Claghorn of Castle Hagedorn asserted otherwise. The emotions of the Mek, said Claghorn, were different from human emotions, and only vaguely comprehensible to man. After diligent research Claghorn isolated over a dozen Mek emotions.

In spite of such research, the Mek revolt came as an utter surprise, no less to Claghorn, D. R. Jardine and Salonson than to anyone else. Why? asked everyone. How could a group so long submissive have contrived so murderous a plot?

The most reasonable conjecture was also the simplest: the Mek resented servitude and hated the Earthmen who had removed him from his natural environment. Those who argued against this theory claimed that it projected human emotions and attitudes into a nonhuman organism, that the Mek had every reason to feel gratitude toward the gentlemen who had liberated him from the conditions of Etamin Nine. To this, the first group would inquire, "Who projects human attitudes now?" And the retort of their opponents was often, "Since no one knows for certain, one projection is no more absurd than another."

II

1.

Castle Hagedorn occupied the crest of a black diorite crag overlooking a wide valley to the south. Larger, more majestic than Janeil, Hagedorn was protected by walls a mile in circumference, and three hundred feet tall. The parapets stood a full nine hundred feet above the valley, with towers, turrets and observation aeries rising even higher. Two sides of the crag, at east and west, dropped sheer to the valley. The north and south slopes, a trifle less steep, were terraced and planted with vines, artichokes, pears and pomegranates. An avenue rising from the valley circled the crag and passed through a portal into the central plaza. Opposite stood the great Rotunda, with at either side the tall Houses of the twenty-eight families.

The original castle, constructed immediately after the return of men to Earth, stood on the site now occupied by the plaza. The tenth Hagedorn, assembling an enormous force of Peasants and Meks, had built the new walls, after which he demolished the old castle. The twenty-eight Houses dated from this time, five hundred years before.

Below the plaza were three service levels: the stables and garages at the bottom, next the Mek shops and Mek living quarters, then the various storerooms, warehouses and special shops—bakery, brewery, lapidary, arsenal, repository and the like.

The clans of Hagedorn, their colors and associated families:

CLANS	COLORS	FAMILIES
Xanten	yellow; black piping	Haude, Quay, Idelsea, Esledune, Salonson, Roseth.
Beaudry	dark blue; white piping	Onwane, Zadig, Prine, Fer, Sesune.
Overwhele	gray, green; red rosettes	Claghorn, Abreu, Woss, Hinken, Zumbeld.
Aure	brown, black	Zadhause, Fotergil, Marune, Baudune, Godalming, Lesmanic.
Isseth	purple, dark red	Mazeth, Floy, Luder-Hepman, Uegus, Kerrithew, Bethune.

The first gentleman of the castle, elected for life, is known as "Hagedorn."

The clan chief, selected by the family elders, bears the name of his clan, thus: "Xanten," "Beaudry," "Overwhele," "Aure," "Isseth"—both clans and clan chiefs.

The family elder, selected by household heads, bears the name of his family. Thus "Idelsea," "Zadhause," "Bethune," and "Claghorn," are both families and family elders.

The remaining gentlemen and ladies bear first the clan, then the family, then the personal name. Thus: Aure Zadhause Ludwick, abbreviated to A.Z. Ludwick, and Beaudry Fer Dariane, abbreviated to B.F. Dariane.

The current Hagedorn, twenty-sixth of the line, was a
Claghorn of the Overwheles. His selection had occasioned
general surprise, because O.C. Charle, as he had been before his elevation, was a gentleman of no remarkable
presence. His elegance, flair and erudition were only ordinary; he had never been notable for any significant
originality of thought. His physical proportions were good;
his face was square and bony, with a short straight nose,
a benign brow and narrow gray eyes. His expression, normally a trifle abstracted—his detractors used the word
"vacant"—by a simple lowering of the eyelids, a downward twitch of the coarse blond eyebrows at once became stubborn and surly, a fact of which O.C. Charle, or
Hagedorn, was unaware.

The office, while exerting little or no formal authority,
exerted a pervasive influence, and the style of the gentleman who was Hagedorn affected everyone. For this reason
the selection of Hagedorn was a matter of no small importance, subject to hundreds of considerations, and it was
the rare candidate who failed to have some old solecism
or gaucherie discussed with embarrassing candor. While
the candidate might never take overt umbrage, friend-
ships were inevitably sundered, rancors augmented, repu-
tations blasted. O.C. Charle's elevation represented a
compromise between two factions among the Overwheles,
to which clan the privilege of selection had fallen.

The gentlemen between whom O.C. Charle represented
a compromise were both highly respected, but distinguished by basically different attitudes toward existence.
The first was the talented Garr of the Zumbeld family. He
exemplified the traditional virtues of Castle Hagedorn:
he was a notable connoisseur of essences, and he dressed
with absolute savoir, with never so much as a pleat nor a
twist of the characteristic Overwhele rosette awry. He
combined insouciance and flair with dignity; his repartee
coruscated with brilliant allusions and turns of phrase;
when aroused his wit was utterly mordant. He could quote
every literary work of consequence; he performed expertly upon the nine-stringed lute, and was thus in constant demand at the Viewing of Antique Tabards. He was
an antiquarian of unchallenged erudition and knew the
locale of every major city of Old Earth, and could dis-
course for hours upon the history of the ancient times. His

military expertise was unparalleled at Hagedorn, and challenged only by D.K. Magdah of Castle Delora and perhaps Brusham of Tuang. Faults? Flaws? Few could be cited: over-punctilio which might be construed as wasp-ishness; an intrepid pertinacity which could be considered ruthlessness. O.Z. Garr could never be dismissed as insipid or indecisive, and his personal courage was beyond dispute. Two years before, a stray band of Nomads had ventured into Lucerne Valley, slaughtering Peasants, stealing cattle and going so far as to fire an arrow into the chest of an Isseth cadet. O.Z. Garr instantly assembled a punitive company of Meks, loaded them aboard a dozen power-wagons, and set forth in pursuit of the Nomads, finally overtaking them near Drene River, by the ruins of Worster Cathedral. The Nomads were unexpectedly strong, unexpectedly crafty, and were not content to turn tail and flee. During the fighting, O.Z. Garr displayed the most exemplary demeanor, directing the attack from the seat of his power-wagon, a pair of Meks standing by with shields to ward away arrows. The conflict ended in a rout of the Nomads; they left twenty-seven lean, black-cloaked corpses strewn on the field, while only twenty Meks lost their lives.

O.Z. Garr's opponent in the election was Claghorn, elder of the Claghorn family. As with O.Z. Garr, the exquisite discriminations of Hagedorn society came to Claghorn as easily as swimming to a fish. He was no less erudite than O.Z. Garr, though hardly so versatile, his principle field of study being the Meks, their physiology, linguistic modes, and social patterns. Claghorn's conversation was more profound, but less entertaining and not so trenchant as that of O.Z. Garr; he seldom employed the extravagant tropes and allusions which characterized Garr's discussions, preferring a style of speech which was unadorned. Claghorn kept no Phanes; O.Z. Garr's four matched Gossamer Dainties were marvels of delight, and at the Viewing of Antique Tabards Garr's presentations were seldom outshone. The important contrast between the two men lay in their philosophic outlook. O.Z. Garr, a traditionalist, a fervent exemplar of his society, subscribed to its tenets without reservation. He was beset by neither doubt nor guilt; he felt no desire to alter the conditions which afforded more than two thousand gentlemen and

ladies lives of great richness. Claghorn, while by no means
an Expiationist, was known to feel dissatisfaction with the
general tenor of life at Castle Hagedorn, and argued so
plausibly that many folk refused to listen to him, on the
grounds that they became uncomfortable. But an indefinable malaise ran deep, and Claghorn had many influential
supporters.

When the time came for ballots to be cast, neither O.Z.
Garr nor Claghorn could muster sufficient support. The
office finally was conferred upon a gentleman who never
in his most optimistic reckonings had expected it—a gentleman of decorum and dignity but no great depth; without flippancy, but likewise without vivacity; affable but
disinclined to force an issue to a disagreeable conclusion:
O.C. Charle, the new Hagedorn.

Six months later, during the dark hours before dawn,
the Hagedorn Meks evacuated their quarters and departed,
taking with them power-wagons, tools, weapons and electrical equipment. The act had clearly been long in the
planning, for simultaneously the Meks at each of the eight
other castles made a similar departure.

The initial reaction at Castle Hagedorn, as elsewhere,
was incredulity, then shocked anger, then—when the implications of the act were pondered—a sense of foreboding and calamity.

The new Hagedorn, the clan chiefs and certain other
notables appointed by Hagedorn met in the formal council
chamber to consider the matter. They sat around a great
table covered with red velvet: Hagedorn at the head;
Xanten and Isseth at his left; Overwhele, Aure and
Beaudry at his right; then the others, including O.Z. Garr,
I.K. Linus, A.G. Bernal, a mathematical theoretician of
great ability, and B.F. Wyas, an equally sagacious antiquarian who had identified the sites of many ancient cities
—Palmyra, Lübeck, Eridu, Zanesville, Burton-on-Trent
and Massilia, among others. Certain family elders filled
out the council: Marune and Baudune of Aure; Quay,
Roseth and Idelsea of Xanten; Uegus of Isseth, Claghorn
of Overwhele.

All sat silent for a period of ten minutes, arranging
their minds and performing the silent act of psychic ac-
commodations known as "intression."

At last Hagedorn spoke. "The castle is suddenly bereft

of its Meks. Needless to say, this is an inconvenient condition, to be adjusted as swiftly as possible. Here, I am sure, we find ourselves of one mind."

He looked around the table. All thrust forward carved ivory tablets to signify assent—all save Claghorn, who however did not stand it on end to signify dissent.

Isseth, a stern white-haired gentleman magnificently handsome in spite of his seventy years, spoke in a grim voice. "I see no point in cogitation or delay. What we must do is clear. Admittedly the Peasants are poor material from which to recruit an armed force. Nonetheless, we must assemble them, equip them with sandals, smocks and weapons so that they do not discredit us, and put them under good leadership: O.Z. Garr or Xanten. Birds can locate the vagrants, whereupon we will track them down, order the Peasants to give them a good drubbing, and herd them home on the double."

Xanten, thirty-five years old—extraordinarily young to be a clan chief—and a notorious firebrand, shook his head. "The idea is appealing but impractical. Peasants simply could not stand up to the Meks, no matter how we trained them."

The statement was manifestly accurate. The Peasants, small andromorphs originally of Spica Ten, were not so much timid as incapable of performing a vicious act.

A dour silence held the table. O.Z. Garr finally spoke. "The dogs have stolen our power-wagons, otherwise I'd be tempted to ride out and chivy the rascals home with a whip." *

* This, only an approximate translation, fails to capture the pungency of the language. Several words have no contemporary equivalents. "Skirkling" as in "to send skirkling," denotes a frantic pell-mell flight in all directions, accompanied by a vibration or twinkling or jerking motion. To "volith" is to toy idly with a matter, the implication being that the person involved is of such Jovian potency that all difficulties dwindle to contemptible triviality. "Raudlebogs" are the semi-intelligent beings of Etamin Four, who were brought to Earth, trained first as gardeners, then construction workers, then sent home in disgrace because of certain repulsive habits they refused to forego.

The statement of O.Z. Garr, therefore, becomes something like this: "Were power-wagons at hand, I'd volith riding forth with a whip to send the raudlebogs skirkling home."

"A matter of perplexity," said Hagedorn, "is syrup. Naturally they carried away what they could. When this is exhausted—what then? Will they starve? Impossible for them to return to their original diet. What was it? Swamp mud? Eh, Claghorn, you're the expert in these matters. Can the Meks return to a diet of mud?"

"No," said Claghorn. "The organs of the adult are atrophied. If a cub were started on the diet, he'd probably survive."

"Just as I assumed." Hagedorn scowled portentously down at his clasped hands to conceal his total lack of any constructive proposal.

A gentleman in the dark blue of the Beaudrys appeared in the doorway; he poised himself, held high his right arm and bowed so that the fingers swept the floor.

Hagedorn rose to his feet. "Come forward, B.F. Robarth; what is your news?" For this was the significance of the newcomer's genuflection.

"The news is a message broadcast from Halcyon. The Meks have attacked; they have fired the structure and are slaughtering all. The radio went dead one minute ago."

All swung around, some jumped to their feet. "Slaughter?" croaked Claghorn.

"I am certain that by now Halcyon is no more."

Claghorn sat staring with eyes unfocused. The others discussed the dire news in voices heavy with horror.

Hagedorn once more brought the council back to order. "This is clearly an extreme situation—the gravest, perhaps, of our entire history. I am frank to state that I can suggest no decisive counteract."

Overwhele inquired, "What of the other castles? Are they secure?"

Hagedorn turned to B.F. Robarth. "Will you be good enough to make general radio contact with all other castles, and inquire as to their condition?"

Xanten said, "Others are as vulnerable as Halcyon: Sea Island and Delora, in particular, and Maraval as well."

Claghorn emerged from his reverie. "The gentlemen and ladies of these places, in my opinion, should consider taking refuge at Janeil or here, until the uprising is quelled."

Others around the table looked at him in surprise and

puzzlement. O.Z. Garr inquired in the silkiest of voices: "You envision the gentlefolk of these castles scampering to refuge at the cock-a-hoop swaggering of the lower orders?"

"Indeed, should they wish to survive," responded Claghorn politely. A gentleman of late middle age, Claghorn was stocky and strong, with black-gray hair, magnificent green eyes, and a manner which suggested great internal force under stern control. "Flight by definition entails a certain diminution of dignity," he went on to say. "If O.Z. Garr can propound an elegant manner of taking to one's heels, I will be glad to learn it, and everyone else should likewise heed, because in the days to come the capability may be of comfort to all."

Hagedorn interposed before O.Z. Garr could reply. "Let us keep to the issues. I confess I cannot see to the end of all this. The Meks have demonstrated themselves to be murderers; how can we take them back into our service? But if we don't—well, to say the least, conditions will be austere until we can locate and train a new force of technicians. We must consider along these lines."

"The spaceships!" exclaimed Xanten. "We must see to them at once!"

"What's this?" inquired Beaudry, a gentleman of rock-hard face. "How do you mean, 'see to them'?"

"They must be protected from damage! What else? They are our link to the Home Worlds. The maintenance Meks probably have not deserted the hangars, since if they propose to exterminate us, they will want to deny us the spaceships."

"Perhaps you care to march with a levy of Peasants to take the hangars under firm control?" suggested O.Z. Garr in a somewhat supercilious voice. A long history of rivalry and mutual detestation existed between himself and Xanten.

"It may be our only hope," said Xanten. "Still—how does one fight with a levy of Peasants? Better that I fly to the hangars and reconnoiter. Meanwhile, perhaps you, and others with military expertise, will take in hand the recruitment and training of a Peasant militia."

"In this regard," stated O.Z. Garr, "I await the outcome of our current deliberations. If it develops that there lies the optimum course, I naturally will apply my competences to the fullest degree. If your own capabilities are best fulfilled by spying out the activities of the Meks, I hope that you will be largehearted enough to do the same."

The two gentlemen glared at each other. A year previously their enmity had almost culminated in a duel. Xanten, a gentleman tall, clean-limbed and nervously active, was gifted with great natural flair, but likewise evinced a disposition too easy for absolute elegance. The traditionalists considered him "sthross," indicating a manner flawed by an almost imperceptible slackness and lack of punctilio: not the best possible choice for clan chief.

Xanten's response to O.Z. Garr was blandly polite. "I shall be glad to take this task upon myself. Since haste is of the essence I will risk the accusation of precipitousness and leave at once. Hopefully I return to report tomorrow." He rose, performed a ceremonious bow to Hagedorn, another all-inclusive salute to the council and departed.

He crossed to Esledune House, where he maintained an apartment on the thirteenth level: four rooms furnished in the style known as Fifth Dynasty, after an epoch in the history of the Altair Home Planets, from which the human race had returned to Earth. His current consort, Araminta, a lady of the Onwane family, was absent on affairs of her own, which suited Xanten well enough. After plying him with questions she would have discredited his simple explanation, preferring to suspect an assignation at his country place. Truth to tell, he had become bored with Araminta and had reason to believe that she felt similarly—or perhaps his exalted rank had provided her less opportunity to preside at glittering social functions than she had expected. They had bred no children. Araminta's daughter by a previous connection had been tallied to her. Her second child must then be tallied to Xanten, preventing him from siring another child.*

---

* The population of Castle Hagedorn was fixed; each gentleman and each lady was permitted a single child. If by chance another were born the parent must either find someone who had not yet sired to sponsor it, or dispose of it another way. The usual procedure was to give the child into the care of the Expiationists.

Xanten doffed his yellow council vestments, and, assisted by a young Peasant buck, donned dark yellow hunting-breeches with black trim, a black jacket, black boots. He drew a cap of soft black leather over his head, and slung a pouch over his shoulder, into which he loaded weapons: a coiled blade, an energy-gun.

Leaving the apartment, he summoned the lift and descended to the first-level armory, where normally a Mek clerk would have served him. Now Xanten, to his vast disgust, was forced to take himself behind the counter, and rummage here and there. The Meks had removed most of the sport-rifles, all the pellet ejectors and heavy energy-guns; an ominous circumstance, thought Xanten. At last he found a steel slingwhip, spare power slugs for his gun, a brace of fire grenades and a high-powered monocular.

He returned to the lift and rode to the top level, ruefully considering the long climb when eventually the mechanism broke down, with no Meks at hand to make repairs. He thought of the apoplectic furies of rigid traditionalists such as Beaudry and chuckled: eventful days lay ahead!

Stopping at the top level, he crossed to the parapets and proceeded around to the radio room. Customarily three Mek specialists connected into the apparatus by wires clipped to their quills sat typing messages as they arrived; now B.F. Robarth stood before the mechanism, uncertainly twisting the dials, his mouth wry with deprecation and distaste for the job.

"Any further news?" Xanten asked.

B.F. Robarth gave him a sour grin. "The folk at the other end seem no more familiar with this cursed tangle than I. I hear occasional voices. I believe that the Meks are attacking Castle Delora."

Claghorn had entered the room behind Xanten. "Did I hear you correctly? Delora Castle is gone?"

"Not gone yet, Claghorn. But as good as gone. The Delora walls are little better than a picturesque crumble."

"Sickening situation!" muttered Xanten. "How can sentient creatures perform such evil? After all these centuries, how little we actually know of them!" As he spoke he recognized the tactlessness of his remark; Claghorn had devoted much time to a study of the Meks.

"The act itself is not astounding," said Claghorn shortly. "It has occurred a thousand times in human history."

Mildly surprised that Claghorn should use human history in reference to a case involving the suborders, Xanten asked, "You were never aware of this vicious aspect to the Mek nature?"

"No. Never. Never indeed."

Claghorn seemed unduly sensitive, thought Xanten. Understandable, all in all. Claghorn's basic doctrine as set forth during the Hagedorn selection was by no means simple, and Xanten neither understood it nor completely endorsed what he conceived to be its goals; but it was plain that the revolt of the Meks had cut the ground out from under Claghorn's feet. Probably to the somewhat bitter satisfaction of O.Z. Garr, who must feel vindicated in his traditionalist doctrines.

Claghorn said tersely, "The life we've been leading couldn't last forever. It's a wonder it lasted as long as it did."

"Perhaps so," said Xanten in a soothing voice. "Well, no matter. All things change. Who knows? The Peasants may be planning to poison our food. . . . I must go." He bowed to Claghorn, who returned him a crisp nod, and to B.F. Robarth, then departed the room.

He climbed the spiral staircase—almost a ladder—to the cotes, where the Birds lived in an invincible disorder, occupying themselves with gambling, quarrels and a version of chess, with rules incomprehensible to every gentleman who had tried to understand it.

Castle Hagedorn maintained a hundred Birds, tended by a gang of long-suffering Peasants, whom the Birds held in vast disesteem. The Birds were garish, garrulous creatures, pigmented red, yellow or blue, with long necks, jerking inquisitive heads and an inherent irreverence which no amount of discipline or tutelage could overcome. Spying Xanten, they emitted a chorus of rude jeers: "Somebody wants a ride! Heavy thing!" "Why don't the self-anointed two-footers grow wings for themselves?" "My friend, never trust a Bird! We'll sky you, then fling you down on your fundament!"

"Quiet!" called Xanten. "I need six fast silent Birds

for an important mission. Are any capable of such a task?"

"Are any capable, he asks!" *"A ros ros ros!* When none of us have flown for a week!" "Silence? We'll give you silence, yellow and black!"

"Come then. You. You. You of the wise eye. You there. You with the cocked shoulder. You with the green pompon. To the basket."

The Birds designated, jeering, grumbling, reviling the Peasants, allowed their syrup sacs to be filled, then flapped to the wicker seat where Xanten waited. "To the space depot at Vincenne," he told them. "Fly high and silently. Enemies are abroad. We must learn what harm if any has been done to the spaceships."

"To the depot, then!" Each Bird seized a length of rope tied to an overhead framework; the chair was yanked up with a jerk calculated to rattle Xanten's teeth, and off they flew, laughing, cursing each other for not supporting more of the load, but eventually all accommodating themselves to the task and flying with a coordinated flapping of the thirty-six sets of wings. To Xanten's relief, their garrulity lessened; silently they flew south, at a speed of fifty or sixty miles per hour.

The afternoon was already waning. The ancient countryside, scene to so many comings and goings, so much triumph and so much disaster, was laced with long black shadows. Looking down, Xanten reflected that though the human stock was native to this soil, and though his immediate ancestors had maintained their holdings for seven hundred years, Earth still seemed an alien world. The reason of course was by no means mysterious or rooted in paradox. After the Six-Star War, Earth had lain fallow for three thousand years, unpopulated save for a handful of anguished wretches who somehow had survived the cataclysm and who had become semibarbaric Nomads. Then seven hundred years ago certain rich lords of Altair, motivated to some extent by political disaffection, but no less by caprice, had decided to return to Earth. Such was the origin of the nine great strongholds, the resident gentlefolk and the staffs of specialized andromorphs. . . . Xanten flew over an area where an antiquarian had directed excavations, revealing a plaza flagged with white stone, a broken obelisk, a tumbled statue. . . .

The sight, by some trick of association, stimulated Xanten's mind to an astonishing vision, so simple and yet so grand that he looked around, in all directions, with new eyes. The vision was Earth repopulated with men, the land cultivated, Nomads driven back into the wilderness.

At the moment the image was farfetched. And Xanten, watching the soft contours of Old Earth slide below, pondered the Mek revolt which had altered his life with such startling abruptness.

Claghorn had long insisted that no human condition endured forever, with the corollary that the more complicated such a condition, the greater its susceptibility to change. In which case the seven-hundred-year continuity of Castle Hagedorn—as artificial, extravagant and intricate as life could be—became an astonishing circumstance in itself. Claghorn had pushed his thesis further. Since change was inevitable, he argued that the gentlefolk should soften the impact by anticipating and controlling the changes—a doctrine which had been attacked with great fervor. The traditionalists labeled all of Claghorn's ideas demonstrable fallacy, and cited the very stability of castle life as proof of its viability. Xanten had inclined first one way, then the other, emotionally involved with neither cause. If anything, the fact of O.Z. Garr's traditionalism had nudged him toward Claghorn's views, and now it seemed as if events had vindicated Claghorn. Change had come, with an impact of the maximum harshness and violence.

There were still questions to be answered, of course. Why had the Meks chosen this particular time to revolt? Conditions had not altered appreciably for five hundred years, and the Meks had never previously hinted dissatisfaction. In fact they had revealed nothing of their feelings, though no one had ever troubled to ask them—save Claghorn.

The Birds were veering east to avoid the Ballarat Mountains, to the west of which were the ruins of a great city, never satisfactorily identified. Below lay the Lucerne Valley, at one time a fertile farmland. If one looked with great concentration, the outline of the various holdings could sometimes be distinguished. Ahead, the spaceship hangars were visible, where Mek technicians maintained four spaceships, jointly the property of Hagehorn, Janeil,

Tuang, Morninglight and Maraval, though, for a variety of reasons, the ships were never used.

The sun was setting. Orange light twinkled and flickered on the metal walls. Xanten called instructions up to the Birds: "Circle down. Alight behind that line of trees, but fly low so that none will see."

Down on stiff wings curved the Birds, six ungainly necks stretched toward the ground. Xanten was ready for the impact; the Birds never seemed able to alight easily when they carried a gentleman. When the cargo was something in which they felt a personal concern, dandelion fluff would never have been disturbed by the jar.

Xanten expertly kept his balance, instead of tumbling and rolling in the manner preferred by the Birds. "You all have syrup," he told them. "Rest; make no noise; do not quarrel. By tomorrow's sunset, if I am not here, return to Castle Hagedorn and say that Xanten was killed."

"Never fear!" cried the Birds. "We will wait forever!" "At any rate till tomorrow's sunset!" "If danger threatens, if you are pressed—*a ros ros ros!* Call for the Birds." *"A ros!* We are ferocious when aroused!"

"I wish it were true," said Xanten. "The Birds are arrant cowards; this is well-known. Still, I value the sentiment. Remember my instructions, and quiet above all! I do not wish to be set upon and stabbed because of your clamor."

The Birds made indignant sounds. "Injustice, injustice! We are quiet as the dew!"

"Good." Xanten hurriedly moved away lest they should bellow new advice or reassurances after him.

Passing through the forest, he came to an open meadow at the far edge of which, perhaps a hundred yards distant, was the rear of the first hangar. He stopped to consider. Several factors were involved. First: the maintenance Meks, with the metal structure shielding them from radio contact, might still be unaware of the revolt. Hardly likely, he decided, in view of the otherwise careful planning. Second: the Meks, in continuous communication with their fellows, acted as a collective organism. The aggregate functions more competently than its parts, and the individual was not prone to initiative. Hence, vigilance was likely to be extreme. Third: if they expected anyone to attempt a discreet approach, they would necessarily scrutinize most closely the route which he proposed to take.

Xanten decided to wait in the shadows another ten minutes, until the setting sun shining over his shoulder should most effectively blind any who might watch.

Ten minutes passed. The hangars, burnished by the dying sunlight, bulked long, tall, completely quiet. In the intervening meadow long golden grass waved and rippled in a cool breeze. . . . Xanten took a deep breath, hefted his pouch, arranged his weapons and strode forth. It did not occur to him to crawl through the grass.

He reached the back of the nearest hangar without challenge. Pressing his ear to the metal he heard nothing. He walked to the corner, looked down the side: no sign of life. Xanten shrugged. Very well, then—to the door.

He walked beside the hangar, the setting sun casting a long black shadow ahead of him. He came to a door opening into the hangar administrative office. Since there was nothing to be gained by trepidation, Xanten thrust the door aside and entered.

The offices were empty. The desks, where centuries before underlings had sat, calculating invoices and bills of lading, were bare, polished free of dust. The computers and information banks, black enamel, glass, white and red switches, looked as if they had been installed only the day before.

Xanten crossed to a glass pane overlooking the hangar floor, shadowed under the bulk of the ship.

He saw no Meks. But on the floor of the hangar, arranged in neat rows and heaps, were elements and assemblies of the ship's control mechanism. Service panels gaped wide into the hull to show where the devices had been detached.

Xanten stepped from the office out into the hangar. The spaceship had been disabled, put out of commission. Xanten looked along the neat rows of parts. Certain savants of various castles were expert in the theory of space-time transfer; S.X. Rosenbox of Maraval had even derived a set of equations which, if translated into machinery, eliminated the troublesome Hamus effect. But not one gentleman, even were he so oblivious to personal honor as to touch a hand to a tool, would know how to replace, connect and tune the mechanisms heaped upon the hangar floor.

The malicious work had been done—when? Impossible to say.

Xanten returned to the office, stepped back out into the twilight, and walked to the next hangar. Again no Meks; again the spaceship had been gutted of its control mechanism. Xanten proceeded to the third hangar, where conditions were the same.

At the fourth hangar he discerned the faint sounds of activity. Stepping into the office, looking through the glass wall into the hangar, he found Meks working with their usual economy of motion, in a near-silence which was uncanny.

Xanten, already uncomfortable from skulking through the forest, became enraged by the cool destruction of his property. He strode forth into the hangar. Slapping his thigh to attract attention, he called in a harsh voice, "Return the components to place! How dare you vermin act in such a manner!"

The Meks turned about their black countenances to study him through black-headed lens-clusters at each side of their heads.

"What!" bellowed Xanten. "You hesitate?" He brought forth his steel whip, usually more of a symbolic adjunct than a punitive instrument, and slashed it against the ground. "Obey! This ridiculous revolt is at its end!"

The Meks still hesitated, and events wavered in the balance. None made a sound, though messages were passing among them, appraising the circumstances, establishing a consensus. Xanten could allow them no such leisure. He marched forward, wielding the whip, striking at the only area where the Meks felt pain: the ropy face. "To your duties," he roared. "A fine maintenance crew are you! A destruction crew is more like it!"

The Meks made the soft blowing sound which might mean anything. They fell back, and now Xanten noted one standing at the head of the companionway leading into the ship: a Mek larger than any he had seen before, and one in some fashion different. This Mek was aiming a pellet gun at his head. With an unhurried flourish, Xanten whipped away a Mek who had leaped forward with a knife, and without deigning to aim, fired at and destroyed the Mek who stood on the companionway, even as the slug sang past his head.

The other Meks were nevertheless committed to an attack. All surged forward. Lounging disdainfully against the hull, Xanten shot them as they came, moving his head once to avoid a chunk of metal, again reaching to catch a throw-knife and hurl it into the face of him who had thrown it.

The Meks drew back, and Xanten guessed that they had agreed on a new tactic: either to withdraw for weapons, or perhaps to confine him within the hangar. In any event no more could be accomplished here. He made play with the whip and cleared an avenue to the office. With tools, metal bars and forgings striking the glass behind him, he sauntered through the office and out into the night.

The full moon was rising: a great yellow globe casting a smoky saffron glow, like an antique lamp. Mek eyes were not well adapted for night-seeing, and Xanten waited by the door. Presently Meks began to pour forth, and Xanten hacked at their necks as they came.

The Meks drew back inside the hangar. Wiping his blade, Xanten strode off the way he had come, looking neither right nor left. He stopped short. The night was young. Something tickled his mind: the recollection of the Mek who had fired the pellet gun. He had been larger, possibly a darker bronze, but, more significantly, he had displayed an indefinable poise, almost authority —though such a word, when used in connection with the Meks, was anomalous. On the other hand, someone must have planned the revolt, or at least originated the concept. It might be worthwhile to extend the reconnaissance, though his primary information had been secured.

Xanten turned back and crossed the landing area to the barracks and garages. Once more, frowning in discomfort, he felt the need for discretion. What times these were! when a gentleman must skulk to avoid such as the Meks! He stole up behind the garages where a half dozen power-wagons* lay dozing.

_____
* Power-wagons, like the Meks, originally swamp-creatures from Etamin Nine, were great rectangular slabs of muscle, slung into a rectangular frame and protected from sunlight, insects and rodents by a synthetic pelt. Syrup sacs communicated

Xanten looked them over. All were of the same sort, a metal frame with four wheels, an earth-moving blade at the front. Nearby must be the syrup stock. Xanten presently found a bin containing a number of canisters. He loaded a dozen on a nearby wagon, slashed the rest with his knife, so that the syrup gushed across the ground. The Meks used a somewhat different formulation; their syrup would be stocked at a different locale, presumably inside the barracks.

Xanten mounted a power-wagon, twisted the *awake* key, tapped the *go* button and pulled a lever which set the wheels into reverse motion. The power-wagon lurched back. Xanten halted it, turned it so that it faced the barracks. He did likewise with three others, then set them all into motion, one after the other. They trundled forward; the blades cut open the metal wall of the barracks, the roof sagged. The power-wagons continued, pushing the length of the interior, crushing all in their way.

Xanten nodded in profound satisfaction and returned to the power-wagon he had reserved for his own use. Mounting to the seat, he waited. No Meks issued from the barracks. Apparently they were deserted, with the entire crew busy at the hangars. Still, hopefully, the syrup stocks had been destroyed, and many might perish by starvation.

From the direction of the hangars came a single Mek, evidently attracted by the sounds of destruction. Xanten crouched on the seat, and as it passed, coiled his whip around the stocky neck. He heaved; the Mek spun to the ground.

Xanten leaped down, seized its pellet gun. Here was another of the larger Meks, and now Xanten saw it to be without a syrup sac, a Mek in the original state. Astounding! How did the creature survive? Suddenly there were many new questions to be asked—hopefully a few to be answered. Standing on the creature's head, Xanten hacked away the long antenna quills which protruded from the

with their digestive apparatus, wires led to motor nodes in the rudimentary brain. The muscles were clamped to rocker arms which actuated rotors and drive-wheels. The power-wagons, economical, long-lived and docile, were principally used for heavy cartage, earth-moving, heavy tillage and other arduous jobs.

back of the Mek's scalp. It was now insulated, alone, on its own resources—a situation to reduce the most stalwart Mek to apathy.

"Up!" ordered Xanten. "Into the back of the wagon!" He cracked the whip for emphasis.

The Mek at first seemed disposed to defy him, but after a blow or two obeyed. Xanten climbed into the seat and started the power-wagon, directed it to the north. The Birds would be unable to carry both himself and the Mek —or in any event they would cry and complain so raucously that they might as well be believed at first. They might or might not wait until the specified hour of tomorrow's sunset; as likely as not they would sleep the night in a tree, awake in a surly mood and return at once to Castle Hagedorn.

All through the night the power-wagon trundled, with Xanten on the seat and his captive huddled in the rear.

III

1.

The gentlefolk of the castles, for all their assurance, disliked to wander the countryside by night, by reason of what some derided as superstitious fear. Others cited travelers benighted beside moldering ruins and their subsequent visions: the eldritch music they had heard, or the whimper of moonmirkins, or the far horns of spectral huntsmen. Others had seen pale lavender and green lights, and wraiths which ran with long strides through the forest; and Hode Abbey, now a dank tumble, was notorious for the White Hag and the alarming toll she exacted.

A hundred such cases were known, and while the hardheaded scoffed, none needlessly traveled the countryside by night. Indeed, if ghosts truly haunt the scenes of tragedy and heartbreak, then the landscape of Old Earth must be home to ghosts and specters beyond all numbering— especially that region across which Xanten rolled in the power-wagon, where every rock, every meadow, every vale and swale was crusted thick with human experience.

The moon rose high; the wagon trundled north along an ancient road, the cracked concrete slabs shining pale in the moonlight. Twice Xanten saw flickering orange lights off to the side, and once, standing in the shade of a cypress tree, he thought he saw a tall quiet shape, silently watching him pass. The captive Mek sat plotting mischief, Xanten well knew. Without its quills it must feel depersonified, bewildered, but Xanten told himself that it would not do to doze.

The road led through a town, certain structures of which still stood. Not even the Nomads took refuge in these old towns, fearing either miasma or perhaps the redolence of grief.

The moon reached the zenith. The landscape spread away in a hundred tones of silver, black and gray. Looking about, Xanten thought that for all the notable pleasures of civilized life, there was yet something to be said for the spaciousness and simplicity of Nomadland. The Mek made a stealthy movement. Xanten did not so much as turn his head. He cracked his whip in the air. The Mek became quiet.

All through the night the power-wagon rolled along the old road, with the moon sinking into the west. The eastern horizon glowed green and lemon-yellow, and presently, as the pallid moon disappeared, the sun rose over the distant line of mountains. At this moment, off to the right, Xanten spied a drift of smoke.

He halted the wagon. Standing up on the seat, he craned his neck to spy a Nomad encampment about a quarter-mile distant. He could distinguish three or four dozen tents of various sizes and a dozen dilapidated power-wagons. On the hetman's tall tent he thought he saw a black ideogram that he recognized. If so, this would be the tribe which not long before had trespassed on the Hagedorn domain, and which O.Z. Garr had repulsed.

Xanten settled himself upon the seat, composed his garments, set the power-wagon in motion and guided it toward the camp.

A hundred black-cloaked men, tall and lean as ferrets, watched his approach. A dozen sprang forward, and whipping arrows to bows, aimed them at his heart. Xanten turned them a glance of supercilious inquiry, drove the wagon up to the hetman's tent, halted. He rose to his feet. "Hetman," he called. "Are you awake?"

The hetman parted the canvas which closed off his tent,

peered out and after a moment came forth. Like the others he wore a garment of limp black cloth, swathing head and body alike. His face thrust through a square opening: narrow blue eyes, a grotesquely long nose, a chin long, skewed and sharp.

Xanten gave him a curt nod. "Observe this." He jerked his thumb toward the Mek in the back of the wagon. The hetman flicked aside his eyes, studied the Mek a tenth-second and returned to a scrutiny of Xanten. "His kind have revolted against the gentlemen," said Xanten. "In fact they massacre all the men of Earth. Hence, we of Castle Hagedorn make this offer to the Nomads. Come to Castle Hagedorn. We will feed, clothe and arm you. We will train you to discipline and the arts of formal warfare. We will provide the most expert leadership within our power. We will then annihilate the Meks, expunge them from Earth. After the campaign, we will train you to technical skills, and you may pursue profitable and interesting careers in the service of the castles."

The hetman made no reply for a moment. Then his weathered face split into a ferocious grin. He spoke in a voice which Xanten found surprisingly well modulated. "So your beasts have finally risen up to rend you! A pity they forbore so long! Well, it is all one to us. You are both alien folk and sooner or later your bones must bleach together."

Xanten pretended incomprehension. "If I understand you aright, you assert that in the face of alien assault, all men must fight a common battle; and then, after the victory, cooperate still to their mutual advantage. Am I correct?"

The hetman's grin never wavered. "You are not men. Only we of Earth soil and Earth water are men. You and your weird slaves are strangers together. We wish you success in your mutual slaughter."

"Well, then," declared Xanten, "I heard you aright after all: Appeals to your loyalty are ineffectual, so much is clear. What of self-interest, then? The Meks, failing to expunge the gentlefolk of the castles, will turn upon the Nomads and kill them as if they were so many ants."

"If they attack us, we will war on them," said the hetman. "Otherwise let them do as they will."

Xanten glanced thoughtfully at the sky. "We might be

willing, even now, to accept a contingent of Nomads into the service of Castle Hagedorn, this to form a cadre from which a larger, more versatile group may be formed."

Fom the side, another Nomad called in an offensively jeering voice, "You will sew a sac on our backs where you can pour your syrup, hey?"

Xanten replied in an even voice, "The syrup is highly nutritious and supplies all bodily needs."

"Why, then, do you not consume it yourself?"

Xanten disdained reply.

The hetman spoke. "If you wish to supply us weapons, we will take them, and use them against whomever threatens us. But do not expect us to defend you. If you fear for your lives, desert your castles and become Nomads."

"Fear for our lives?" exclaimed Xanten. "What nonsense! Never! Castle Hagedorn is impregnable, as is Janeil, and most of the other castles as well."

The hetman shook his head. "Any time we choose we could take Hagedorn, and kill all you popinjays in your sleep."

"What!" cried Xanten in outrage. "Are you serious?"

"Certainly. On a black night we would send a man aloft on a great kite and drop him down on the parapets. He would lower a line, haul up ladders and in fifteen minutes the castle is taken."

Xanten pulled at his chin. "Ingenious, but impractical. The Birds would detect such a kite. Or the wind would fail at a critical moment. . . . All this is beside the point. The Meks fly no kites. They plan to make a display against Janeil and Hagedorn, then, in their frustration, go forth and hunt Nomads."

The hetman moved back a step. "What then? We have survived similar attempts by the men of Hagedorn. Cowards all. Hand to hand, with equal weapons, we would make you eat the dirt like the dogs you are."

Xanten raised his eyebrows in elegant disdain. "I fear that you forget yourself. You address a clan chief of Castle Hagedorn. Only fatigue and boredom restrain me from punishing you with this whip."

"Bah!" said the hetman. He crooked a finger to one of his archers. "Spit this insolent lordling."

The archer discharged his arrow, but Xanten, who had been expecting some such act, fired his energy-gun, destroying arrow, bow and the archer's hands. He said, "I see I must teach you common respect for your betters; so it means the whip after all." Seizing the hetman by the scalp, he coiled the whip smartly once, twice, thrice around the narrow shoulders. "Let this suffice. I cannot compel you to fight, but at least I can demand decent respect." He leaped to the ground, and seizing the hetman, pitched him into the back of the wagon alongside the Mek. Then, backing the power-wagon around, he departed the camp without so much as a glance over his shoulder, the thwart of the seat protecting his back from arrows.

The hetman scrambled erect, drew his dagger. Xanten turned his head slightly. "Take care! Or I will tie you to the wagon and you shall run behind in the dust."

The hetman hesitated, made a spitting sound between his teeth, drew back. He looked down at his blade, turned it over and sheathed it with a grunt. "Where do you take me?"

Xanten halted the wagon. "No farther. I merely wished to leave your camp with dignity, without dodging and ducking a hail of arrows. You may alight. I take it you still refuse to bring your men into the service of Castle Hagedorn?"

The hetman once more made the spitting sound between his teeth. "When the Meks have destroyed the castles, we shall destroy the Meks, and Earth will be cleared of star-things."

"You are a gang of intractable savages. Very well, alight, return to your encampment. Reflect well before you again show disrespect to a Castle Hagedorn clan chief."

"Bah," muttered the hetman. Leaping down from the wagon, he stalked back down the track toward his camp.

2.

About noon Xanten came to Far Valley, at the edge of the Hagedorn lands. Nearby was a village of Expiationists: malcontents and neurasthenics in the opinion of castle gentlefolk, and a curious group by any standards. A few had held enviable rank; certain others were savants of recognized erudition; but others yet were persons of neither dignity nor reputation, subscribing to the most bizarre and extreme of philosophies. All now performed toil no different from that relegated to the Peasants, and all seemed to take a perverse satisfaction in what—by castle standards—was filth, poverty and degradation.

As might be expected, their creed was by no means homogeneous. Some might better have been described as "nonconformists" or disassociationists"; another group were "passive expiationists"; and others still, a minority, argued for a dynamic program.

Between castle and village was little intercourse. Occasionally the Expiationists bartered fruit or polished wood for tools, nails, medicaments; or the gentlefolk might make up a party to watch the Expiationists at their dancing and singing. Xanten had visited the village on many such occasions and had been attracted by the artless charm and informality of the folk at their play. Now, passing near the village, Xanten turned aside to follow a lane which wound between tall blackberry hedges and out upon a little common where goats and cattle grazed. Xanten halted the wagon in the shade and saw that the syrup sac was full. He looked back at his captive. "What of you? If you need syrup, pour yourself full. But no, you have no sac. What, then, do you feed upon? Mud? Unsavory fare. I fear none here is rank enough for your taste. Ingest syrup or munch grass, as you will; only do not stray overfar from the wagon, for I watch with an intent eye."

The Mek, sitting hunched in a corner, gave no signal that it comprehended, nor did it move to take advantage of Xanten's offer.

Xanten went to a watering trough and, holding his hands under the trickle which issued from a lead pipe, rinsed his face, then drank a swallow or two from his cupped hand.

Turning, he found that a dozen folk of the village had approached. One he knew well, a man who might have become Godalming, or even Aure, had he not become infected with expiationism.

Xanten performed a polite salute. "A.G. Philidor: it is I, Xanten."

"Xanten, of course. But here I am A.G. Philidor no longer, merely Philidor."

Xanten bowed. "My apologies; I have neglected the full rigor of your informality."

"Spare me your wit," said Philidor. "Why do you bring us a shorn Mek? For adoption, perhaps?" This last alluded to the gentlefolk practice of bringing over-tally babies to the village.

"Now who flaunts his wit? But you have not heard the news?"

"News arrives here last of all. The Nomads are better informed."

"Prepare yourself for surprise. The Meks have revolted against the castles. Halcyon and Delora are demolished, and all killed; perhaps others by this time."

Philidor shook his head. "I am not surprised."

"Well, then, are you not concerned?"

Philidor considered. "To this extent. Our own plans, never very feasible, become more farfetched than ever."

"It appears to me," said Xanten, "that you face grave and immediate danger. The Meks surely intend to wipe out every vestige of humanity. You will not escape."

Philidor shrugged. "Conceivably the danger exists. . . . We will take counsel and decide what to do."

"I can put forward a proposal which you may find attractive," said Xanten. "Our first concern, of course, is to suppress the revolt. There are at least a dozen Expiationist communities, with an aggregate population of two or three thousand—perhaps more. I propose that we recruit and train a corps of highly disciplined troops, supplied from the Castle Hagedorn armory, led by Hagedorn's most expert military theoreticians."

Philidor stared at him incredulously. "You expect us, the Expiationists, to become your soldiers?"

"Why not?" asked Xanten ingenuously. "Your life is at stake no less than ours."

"No one dies more than once."

Xanten in his turn evinced shock. "What? Can this be a former gentleman of Hagedorn speaking? Is this the face a man of pride and courage turns to danger? Is this the lesson of history? Of course not! I need not instruct you in this; you are as knowledgeable as I."

Philidor nodded. "I know that the history of man is not his technical triumphs, his kills, his victories. It is a composite, a mosaic of a trillion pieces, the account of each man's accommodation with his conscience. This is the true history of the race."

Xanten made an airy gesture. "A.G. Philidor, you over-simplify grievously. Do you consider me obtuse? There are many kinds of history. They interact. You emphasize morality. But the ultimate basis of morality is survival. What promotes survival is good; what induces mortifaction is bad."

"Well spoken!" declared Philidor. "But let me propound a parable. May a nation of a million beings destroy a creature who otherwise will infect all with a fatal disease? Yes, you will say. Once more: ten starving beasts hunt you, that they may eat. Will you kill them to save your life? Yes, you will say again, though here you destroy more than you save. Once more: a man inhabits a hut in a lonely valley. A hundred spaceships descend from the sky, and attempt to destroy him. May he destroy these ships in self-defense, even though he is one and they are a hundred thousand? Perhaps you say yes. What, then, if a whole world, a whole race of beings, pits itself against this single man? May he kill all? What if the attackers are as human as himself? What if he were the creature of the first instance, who otherwise will infect a world with disease? You see, there is no area where a simple touchstone avails. We have searched and found none. Hence, at the risk of sinning against Survival, we—I, at least; I can only speak for myself—have chosen a morality which at least allows me calm. I kill—nothing. I destroy—nothing."

"Bah," said Xanten contemptuously. "If a Mek platoon entered this valley and began to kill your children, you would not defend them?"

Philidor compressed his lips, turned away. Another man spoke. "Philidor has defined morality. But who is absolutely moral? Philidor, or I, or you, might desert his morality in such a case."

Philidor said, "Look about you. Is there anyone here you recognize?"

Xanten scanned the group. Nearby stood a girl of extraordinary beauty. She wore a white smock and in the dark hair curling to her shoulders she wore a red flower. Xanten nodded. "I see the maiden O.Z. Garr wished to introduce into his ménage at the castle."

"Exactly," said Philidor. "Do you recall the circumstances?"

"Very well indeed," said Xanten. "There was vigorous objection from the Council of Notables—if for no other reason than the threat to our laws of population control. O.Z. Garr attempted to sidestep the law in this fashion. 'I keep Phanes,' he said. 'At times I maintain as many as six, or even eight, and no one utters a word of protest. I will call this girl Phane and keep her among the rest.' I and others protested. There was almost a duel over this matter. O.Z. Garr was forced to relinquish the girl. She was given into my custody and I conveyed her to Far Valley."

Philidor nodded. "All this is correct. Well—we attempted to dissuade Garr. He refused to be dissuaded, and threatened us with his hunting force of perhaps thirty Meks. We stood aside. Are we moral? Are we strong or weak?"

"Sometimes it is better," said Xanten, "to ignore morality. Even though O.Z. Garr is a gentleman and you are but Expiationists. . . . Likewise in the case of the Meks. They are destroying the castles, and all the men of Earth. If morality means supine acceptance, then morality must be abandoned!"

Philidor gave a sour chuckle. "What a remarkable situation. The Meks are here, likewise Peasants and Birds and Phanes, all altered, transported and enslaved for human pleasure. Indeed, it is this fact that occasions our guilt, for which we must expiate, and now you want us to compound this guilt!"

"It is a mistake to brood overmuch about the past," said Xanten. "Still, if you wish to preserve your option to brood, I suggest that you fight Meks now, or at the very least take refuge in the castle."

"Not I," said Philidor. "Perhaps others may choose to do so."

"You will wait to be killed?"

"No. I and no doubt others will take refuge in the remote mountains."

Xanten clambered back aboard the power-wagon. "If you change your mind, come to Castle Hagedorn."

He departed.

The road continued along the valley, wound up a hillside, crossed a ridge. Far ahead, silhouetted against the sky, stood Castle Hagedorn.

IV

1.

Xanten reported to the council.

"The spaceships cannot be used. The Meks have rendered them inoperative. Any plan to solicit assistance from the Home Worlds is pointless."

"This is sorry news," said Hagedorn with a grimace. "Well, then, so much for that."

Xanten continued. "Returning by power-wagon I encountered a tribe of Nomads. I summoned the hetman and explained to him the advantages of serving Castle Hagedorn. The Nomads, I fear, lack both grace and docility. The hetman gave so surly a response that I departed in disgust.

"At Far Valley I visited the Expiationist village, and made a similar proposal, but with no great success. They are as idealistic as the Nomads are churlish. Both are of a fugitive tendency. The Expiationists spoke of taking refuge in the mountains. The Nomads presumably will retreat into the steppes."

Beaudry snorted. "How will flight help them? Perhaps they gain a few years—but eventually the Meks will find every last one of them; such is their methodicity."

"In the meantime," O.Z. Garr declared peevishly, "we might have organized them into an efficient combat corps, to the benefit of all. Well, then let them perish; we are secure."

"Secure, yes," said Hagedorn gloomily. "But what when the power fails? When the lifts break down? When air circulation cuts off so that we either stifle or freeze? What then?"

O.Z. Garr gave his head a grim shake. "We must steel ourselves to undignified expedients, with as good grace as possible. But the machinery of the castle is sound, and I expect small deterioration or failure for conceivably five or ten years. By that time anything may occur."

Claghorn, who had been leaning indolently back in his seat, spoke at last. "This essentially is a passive program. Like the defection of the Nomads and Expiationists, it looks very little beyond the immediate moment."

O.Z. Garr spoke in a voice carefully polite. "Claghorn is well aware that I yield to none in courteous candor, as well as optimism and directness: in short, the reverse of passivity. But I refuse to dignify a stupid little inconvenience by extending it serious attention. How can he label this procedure passivity? Does the worthy and honorable head of the Claghorns have a proposal which more effectively maintains our status, our standards, our self-respect?"

Claghorn nodded slowly, with a faint half-smile which O.Z. Garr found odiously complacent. "There is a simple and effective method by which the Meks might be defeated."

"Well, then!" cried Hagedorn. "Why hesitate? Let us hear it!"

Claghorn looked around the red velvet-covered table, considering the faces of all: the dispassionate Xanten; Beaudry, burly, rigid, face muscles clenched in an habitual expression unpleasantly like a sneer; old Isseth, as handsome, erect and vital as the most dashing cadet; Hagedorn, troubled, glum, his inward perplexity all too evident; the elegant Garr; Overwhele, thinking savagely of the inconveniences of the future; Aure, toying with his ivory tablet, either bored, morose or defeated; the others displaying various aspects of doubt, foreboding, hauteur, dark resentment, impatience; and in the case of Floy, a quiet smile—or as Isseth later characterized it, an imbecilic smirk—intended to convey his total disassociation from the entire irksome matter.

Claghorn took stock of the faces, and shook his head. "I will not at the moment broach this plan, as I fear it is unworkable. But I must point out that under no circumstances can Castle Hagedorn be as before, even should we survive the Mek attack."

"Bah!" exclaimed Beaudry. "We lose dignity, we become ridiculous, by even so much as discussing the beasts."

Xanten stirred himself. "A distasteful subject, but remember! Halcyon is destroyed, and Delora, and who knows what others? Let us not thrust our heads in the

sand! The Meks will not waft away merely because we
ignore them."

"In any event," said O.Z. Garr. "Janeil is secure and
we are secure. The other folk, unless they are already
slaughtered, might do well to visit us during the inconvenience, if they can justify the humiliation of flight to themselves. I myself believe that the Meks will soon come to
heel, anxious to return to their posts."

Hagedorn shook his head gloomily. "I find this hard to
believe. But very well, then, we shall adjourn."

2.

The radio communication system was the first of the
castle's vast array of electrical and mechanical devices to
break down. The failure occurred so soon and so decisively
that certain of the theoreticians, notably I. K. Harde and
Uegus, postulated sabotage by the departing Meks.
Others remarked that the system had never been absolutely dependable, that the Meks themselves had been
forced to tinker continuously with the circuits, that the
failure was simply a result of faulty engineering. I. K.
Harde and Uegus inspected the unwieldy apparatus, but
the cause of failure was not obvious. After a half-hour of
consultation they agreed that any attempt to restore the
system would necessitate complete redesign and reengi-
neering, with consequent construction of testing and cali-
bration devices, and the fabrication of a complete new
family of components. "This is manifestly impossible,"
stated Uegus in his report to the council. "Even the simplest useful system would require several technician-years.
There is not even one single technician to hand. We must
therefore await the availability of trained and willing
labor."

"In retrospect," stated Isseth, the oldest of the clan
chiefs, "it is clear that in many ways we have been less
than provident. No matter that the men of the Home
Worlds are vulgarians! Men of shrewder calculation than
our own would have maintained interworld connection."

"Lack of shrewdness and providence were not the deter-
ring factors," stated Claghorn. "Communication was discouraged simply because the early lords were unwilling that

Earth should be overrun with Home-World parvenus. It is as simple as that."

Isseth grunted, and started to make a rejoinder, but Hagedorn said hastily, "Unluckily, as Xanten tells us, the spaceships have been rendered useless, and while certain of our number have a profound knowledge of the theoretical considerations, again who is there to perform the toil? Even were the hangars and spaceships themselves under our control."

O.Z. Garr declared, "Give me six platoons of Peasants and six power-wagons equipped with high-energy cannon, and I'll regain the hangars; no difficulties there!"

Beaudry said, "Well, here's a start, at least. I'll assist in the training of the Peasants, and though I know nothing of cannon operation, rely on me for any advice I can give."

Hagedorn looked around the group, frowned, pulled at his chin. "There are difficulties to this program. First, we have at hand only the single power-wagon in which Xanten returned from his reconnaissance. Then, what of our energy-cannons? Has anyone inspected them? The Meks were entrusted with maintenance, but it is possible, even likely, that they wrought mischief here as well. O.Z. Garr, you are reckoned an expert military theoretician; what can you tell us in this regard?"

"I have made no inspection to date," stated O.Z. Garr. "Today the Display of Antique Tabards will occupy us all until the Hour of Sundown Appraisal*." He looked at his watch. "Perhaps now is as good a time as any to adjourn, until I am able to provide detailed information in regard to the cannons."

Hagedorn nodded his heavy head. "The time indeed grows late. Your Phanes appear today?"

"Only two," replied O.Z. Garr. "The Lazule and the Eleventh Mystery. I can find nothing suitable for the Gossamer Delights nor my little Blue Fay, and the Gloriana

---

* Display of Antique Tabards; Hour of Sundown Appraisal: the literal sense of the first term was yet relevant; that of the second had become lost and the phrase was a mere formalism, connoting that hour of late afternoon when visits were exchanged, and wines, liqueurs and essences tasted: in short, a time of relaxation and small talk before the more formal convivialities of dining.

still requires tutelage. Today B. Z. Maxelwane's Variflors should repay the most attention."

"Yes," said Hagedorn. "I have heard other remarks to this effect. Very well, then, until tomorrow. Eh, Claghorn, you have something to say?"

"Yes, indeed," Claghorn said mildly. "We have all too little time at our disposal. Best we make the most of it. I seriously doubt the efficacy of Peasant troops; to pit Peasants against Meks is like sending rabbits against wolves. What we need, rather than rabbits, are panthers."

"Ah, yes," Hagedorn said vaguely. "Yes, indeed."

"Where, then, are panthers to be found?" Claghorn looked inquiringly around the table. "Can no one suggest a source? A pity. Well, then, if panthers fail to appear, I suppose rabbits must do. Let us go about the business of converting rabbits into panthers, and instantly. I suggest that we postpone all fetes and spectacles until the shape of our future is more certain."

Hagedorn raised his eyebrows, opened his mouth to speak, closed it again. He looked intently at Claghorn to ascertain whether or not he joked. Then he looked dubiously around the table.

Beaudry gave a rather brassy laugh. "It seems that erudite Claghorn cries panic."

O.Z. Garr stated: "Surely, in all dignity, we cannot allow the impertinence of our servants to cause us such eye-rolling alarm. I am embarrassed even to bring the matter forward."

"I am not embarrassed," said Claghorn, with the full-faced complacence which so exasperated O.Z. Garr. "I see no reason why you should be. Our lives are threatened, in which case a trifle of embarrassment, or anything else, becomes of secondary importance."

O.Z. Garr rose to his feet, performed a brusque salute in Claghorn's direction, of such a nature as to constitute a calculated affront. Claghorn, rising, performed a similar salute, so grave and overly complicated as to invest Garr's insult with burlesque overtones. Xanten, who detested O.Z. Garr, laughed aloud.

O.Z. Garr hesitated, then, sensing that under the circumstances taking the matter further would be regarded as poor form, strode from the chamber.

3.

'The Viewing of Antique Tabards, an annual pageant of Phanes wearing sumptuous garments, took place in the Great Rotunda to the north of the central plaza. Possibly half of the gentlemen, but less than a quarter of the ladies, kept Phanes. These were creatures native to the caverns of Albireo Seven's moon: a docile race, both playful and affectionate, which after several thousand years of selective breeding had become sylphs of piquant beauty. Clad in a delicate gauze which issued from pores behind their ears, along their upper arms and down their backs, they were the most inoffensive of creatures, anxious always to please, innocently vain. Most gentlemen regarded them with affection, but rumors sometimes told of ladies drenching an especially hated Phane in tincture of ammonia, which matted her pelt and destroyed her gauze forever.

A gentleman besotted by a Phane was considered a figure of fun. The Phane though so carefully bred as to seem a delicate girl, if used sexually became crumpled and haggard, with gauzes drooping and discolored, and everyone would know that such and such a gentleman had misused his Phane. In this regard, at least, the women of the castles might exert their superiority, and did so by conducting themselves with such extravagant provocation that the Phanes in contrast seemed the most ingenuous and fragile of nature sprites. Their life-span was perhaps thirty years, during the last ten of which, after they had lost their beauty, they encased themselves in mantles of gray gauze and performed menial tasks in boudoirs, kitchens, pantries, nurseries and dressing rooms.

The Viewing of Antique Tabards was an occasion more for the viewing of Phanes than the tabards, though these, woven of Phane-gauze, were of great intrinsic beauty in themselves.

The Phane owners sat in a lower tier, tense with hope and pride, exulting when one made an especially splendid display, plunging into black depths when the ritual postures were performed with other than grace and elegance. During each display, highly formal music was plucked from a lute by a gentleman from a clan different to that of the Phane owner, the owner never playing the lute to the performance of his own Phane. The display was never overtly a competition and no formal acclamation was allowed, but all watching made up their minds as to which was the most entrancing and graceful of the Phanes, and the repute of the owner was thereby exalted.

The current Viewing was delayed almost half an hour by reason of the defection of the Meks, and certain hasty improvisations had been necessary. But the gentlefolk of Castle Hagedorn were in no mood to be critical and took no heed of the occasional lapses as a dozen young Peasant bucks struggled to perform unfamiliar tasks. The Phanes were as entrancing as ever, bending, twisting, swaying to plangent chords of the lute, fluttering their fingers as if feeling for raindrops, crouching suddenly and gliding, then springing upright as straight as wands, finally bowing and skipping from the platform.

Halfway through the program a Peasant sidled awkwardly into the Rotunda, and mumbled in an urgent manner to the cadet who came to inquire his business. The cadet at once made his way to Hagedorn's polished jet booth. Hagedorn listened, nodded, spoke a few terse words and settled calmly back in his seat as if the message had been of no consequence, and the gentlefolk of the audience were reassured.

The entertainment proceeded. O.Z. Garr's delectable pair made a fine show, but it was generally felt that Lirlin, a young Phane belonging to Isseth Floy Gazuneth, for the first time at a formal showing, made the most captivating display.

The Phanes appeared for a last time, moving all together through a half-improvised minuet, then performing a final half gay, half regretful salute, departed the Rotunda. For a few moments more the gentlemen and ladies would remain in their booths, sipping essences, discussing the display, arranging affairs and assignations. Hagedorn sat frowning, twisting his hands. Suddenly he rose to his feet. The Rotunda instantly became silent.

"I dislike intruding an unhappy note at so pleasant an occasion," said Hagedorn. "But the news has just been given to me, and it is fitting that all should know. Janeil Castle is under attack. The Meks are there in great force, with hundreds of power-wagons. They have circled the castle with a dike which prevents any effective use of the Janeil energy-cannon.

"There is no immediate danger to Janeil, and it is difficult to comprehend what the Meks hope to achieve, the Janeil walls being all of two hundred feet high.

"The news, nevertheless, is somber, and it means that eventually we must expect a similar investment—though it is even more difficult to comprehend how Meks could hope to inconvenience us. Our water derives from four wells sunk deep into the earth. We have great stocks of food. Our energy is derived from the sun. If necessary, we could condense water and synthesize food from the air—at least I have been so assured by our great biochemical theoretician, X. B. Ladisname. Still—this is the news. Make of it what you will. Tomorrow the Council of Notables will meet."

V

1.

"Well, then," said Hagedorn to the council, "for once let us dispense with formality. O.Z. Garr: what of our cannon?"

O.Z. Garr, wearing the magnificent gray and green uniform of the Overwhele Dragoons, carefully placed his morion on the table, so that the panache stood erect. "Of twelve cannon, four appear to be functioning correctly. Four have been sabotaged by excision of the power-leads. Four have been sabotaged by some means undetectable to careful investigation. I have commandeered a half dozen Peasants who demonstrate a modicum of mechanical ability, and have instructed them in detail. They are currently engaged in splicing the leads. This is the extent of my current information in regard to the cannon."

"Moderately good news," said Hagedorn. "What of the proposed corps of armed Peasants?"

"The project is under way. A. F. Mull and I. A. Berzelius are now inspecting Peasants with a view to recruitment and training. I can make no sanguine projection as to the military effectiveness of such a corps, even if trained and led by such as A. F. Mull, I. A. Berzelius and myself. The Peasants are a mild, ineffectual race, admirably suited to the grubbing of weeds, but with no stomach whatever for fighting."

Hagedorn glanced around the council. "Are there any other suggestions?"

Beaudry spoke in a harsh, angry voice. "Had the villains but left us our power-wagons, we might have mounted the cannon aboard—the Peasants are equal to this, at least. Then we could roll to Janeil and blast the dogs from the rear."

"These Meks seem utter fiends!" declared Aure. "What conceivably do they have in mind? Why, after all these centuries, must they suddenly go mad?"

"We all ask ourselves the same question," said Hagedorn. "Xanten, you returned from reconnaissance with a captive. Have you attempted to question him?"

"No," said Xanten. "Truth to tell, I haven't thought of him since."

"Why not attempt to question him? Perhaps he can provide a clue or two."

Xanten nodded assent. "I can try. Candidly, I expect to learn nothing."

"Claghorn, you are the Mek expert," said Beaudry. "Would you have thought the creatures capable of so intricate a plot? What do they hope to gain? Our castles?"

"They are certainly capable of precise and meticulous planning," said Claghorn. "Their ruthlessness surprises me —more, possibly, than it should. I have never known them to covet our material possessions, and they show no tendency toward what we consider the concomitants of civilization: fine discriminations of sensation and the like. I have often speculated—I won't dignify the conceit with the status of a theory—that the structural logic of a brain is of rather more consequence than we reckon with. Our own brains are remarkable for their utter lack of rational structure. Considering the haphazard manner in which our thoughts are formed, registered, indexed and recalled, any single rational act becomes a miracle. Perhaps we are incapable of rationality; perhaps all thought is a set of impulses generated by one emotion, monitored by another, ratified by a third. In contrast, the Mek brain is a marvel of what seems to be careful engineering. It is roughly cubical and consists of microscopic cells interconnected by organic fibrils, each a monofilament molecule of negligible electrical resistance. Within each cell is a film of silica, a fluid of variable conductivity and dielectric properties, a cusp of a complex mixture of metallic oxides. The brain is capable of storing great quantities of information in an orderly pattern. No fact is lost, unless it is purposely forgotten, a capacity which the Meks possess. The brain also functions as a radio transceiver, possibly as a radar transmitter and detector, though this again is speculation.

"Where the Mek brain falls short is in its lack of emotional color. One Mek is precisely like another, without any personality differentiation perceptible to us. This, clearly, is a function of their communicative system: unthinkable for a unique personality to develop under these conditions. They served us efficiently and—so we thought—loyally, because they felt nothing about their condition, neither pride in achievement, nor resentment, nor shame. Nothing whatever. They neither loved us nor hated us, nor do they now. It is hard for us to conceive this emotional vacuum, when each of us feels something about everything. We live in a welter of emotions. They are as devoid of emotion as an ice cube. They were fed, housed and maintained in a manner they found satisfactory. Why did they revolt? I have speculated at length, but the single reason which I can formulate seems so grotesque and unreasonable that I refuse to take it seriously. If this after all is the correct explanation. . . ." His voice drifted away.

"Well?" demanded O.Z. Garr peremptorily. "What, then?"

"Then—it is all the same. They are committed to the destruction of the human race. My speculation alters nothing."

Hagedorn turned to Xanten. "All this should assist you in your inquiries."

"I was about to suggest that Claghorn assist me, if he is so inclined," said Xanten.

"As you like," said Claghorn, "though in my opinion the information, no matter what, is irrelevant. Our single concern should be a means to repel them and to save our lives."

"And—except the force of 'panthers' you mentioned at our previous session—you can conceive of no subtle weapon?" asked Hagedorn wistfully. "A device to set up electrical resonances in their brains, or something similar?"

"Not feasible," said Claghorn. "Certain organs in the creatures' brains function as overload switches. Though it is true that during this time they might not be able to communicate." After a moment's reflection he added thoughtfully, "Who knows? A. G. Bernal and Uegus are theoreticians with a profound knowledge of such projections. Perhaps they might construct such a device, or several, against a possible need."

Hagedorn nodded dubiously, and looked toward Uegus. "Is this possible?"

Uegus frowned. " 'Construct'? I can certainly design such an instrument. But the components—where? Scattered through the storerooms helter-skelter, some functioning, others not. To achieve anything meaningful I must become no better than an apprentice, a Mek." He became incensed, and his voice hardened. "I find it hard to believe that I should be forced to point out this fact. Do you hold me and my talents, then, of such small worth?"

Hagedorn hastened to reassure him. "Of course not! I for one would never think of impugning your dignity."

"Never!" agreed Claghorn. "Nevertheless, during this present emergency, we will find indignities imposed upon us by events, unless now we impose them upon ourselves."

"Very well," said Uegus, a humorless smile trembling at his lips. "You shall come with me to the storeroom. I will point out the components to be brought forth and assembled; you shall perform the toil. What do you say to that?"

"I say yes, gladly, if it will be of real utility. However, I can hardly perform the labor for a dozen different theoreticians. Will any others serve besides myself?"

No one responded. Silence was absolute, as if every gentleman present held his breath.

Hagedorn started to speak, but Claghorn interrupted. "Pardon, Hagedorn, but here, finally, we are stuck upon a basic principle, and it must be settled now."

Hagedorn looked desperately around the council. "Has anyone relevant comment?"

"Claghorn must do as his innate nature compels," declared O.Z. Garr in the silkiest of voices. "I cannot dictate to him. As for myself, I can never demean my status as a gentleman of Hagedorn. This creed is as natural to me as drawing breath; if ever it is compromised I become a travesty of a gentleman, a grotesque mask of myself. This is Castle Hagedorn, and we represent the culmination of human civilization. Any compromise therefore becomes degradation; any expedient diminution of our standards becomes dishonor. I have heard the word 'emergency' used. What a deplorable sentiment! To dignify the ratlike snappings and gnashings of such as the Meks with the word 'emergency' is to my mind unworthy of a gentleman of Hagedorn!"

A murmur of approval went around the council table.

Claghorn leaned far back in his seat, chin on his chest, as if in relaxation. His clear blue eyes went from face to face, then returned to O.Z. Garr whom he studied with dispassionate interest. "Obviously you direct your words to me," he said, "and I appreciate their malice. But this is a small matter." He looked away from O.Z. Garr, to stare up at the massive diamond and emerald chandelier. "More important is the fact that the council as a whole, in spite of my earnest persuasion, seems to endorse your viewpoint. I can urge, expostulate, insinuate no longer, and I will not leave Castle Hagedorn. I find the atmosphere stifling. I trust that you survive the attack of the Meks, though I doubt that you will. They are a clever, resourceful race, untroubled by qualms or preconceptions, and we have long underestimated their quality."

Claghorn rose from his seat, inserted the ivory tablet into its socket. "I bid you all farewell."

Hagedorn hastily jumped to his feet and held forth his arms imploringly. "Do not depart in anger, Claghorn! Reconsider! We need your wisdom, your expertise!"

"Assuredly you do," said Claghorn. "But even more, you need to act upon the advice I have already extended. Until then, we have no common ground, and any further interchange is futile and tiresome." He made a brief, all-inclusive salute and departed the chamber.

Hagedorn slowly resumed his seat. The others made uneasy motions, coughed, looked up at the chandelier, studied their ivory tablets. O. Z. Garr muttered something to B. F. Wyas who sat beside him, who nodded solemnly. Hagedorn spoke in a subdued voice. "We will miss the presence of Claghorn, his penetrating if unorthodox insights. . . . We have accomplished little. Uegus, perhaps you will give thought to the projector under discussion. Xanten, you were to question the captive Mek. O. Z. Garr, you undoubtedly will see to the repair of the energy-cannon. . . . Aside from these small matters, it appears that we have evolved no general plan of action, to help either ourselves or Janeil."

Marune spoke. "What of the other castles? Are they still extant? We have had no news. I suggest that we send Birds to each castle, to learn their condition."

Hagedorn nodded. "Yes, this is a wise motion. Perhaps you will see to this, Marune?"

"I will do so."

"Good. We will now adjourn."

2.

The Birds dispatched by Marune of Aure, one by one returned. Their reports were similar:

"Sea Island is deserted. Marble columns are tumbling along the beach. Pearl Dome is collapsed. Corpses float in the Water Garden."

"Maraval reeks of death. Gentlemen, Peasants, Phanes —all dead. Alas! Even the Birds have departed!"

"Delora: *a ros ros ros!* A dismal scene! No sign of life!"

"Alume is desolate. The great wooden door is smashed. The Green Flame is extinguished."

"There is nothing at Halcyon. The Peasants were driven into a pit."

"Tuang: silence."

"Morninglight: death."

VI

1.

Three days later, Xanten constrained six Birds to a lift-chair, directed them first on a wide sweep around the castle, then south to Far Valley.

The Birds aired their usual complaints, then bounded down the deck in great ungainly hops which threatened to throw Xanten immediately to the pavement. At last gaining the air, they flew up in a spiral; Castle Hagedorn became an intricate miniature far below, each House marked by its unique cluster of turrets and aeries, its own eccentric roof line, its long streaming pennon.

The Birds performed the prescribed circle, skimming the crags and spires of North Ridge; then, setting wings aslant the upstream, they coasted away toward Far Valley.

Over the pleasant Hagedorn domain flew the Birds and Xanten: over orchards, fields, vineyards, Peasant villages. They crossed Lake Maude with its pavilions and docks, the meadows beyond where the Hagedorn cattle and sheep grazed, and presently came to Far Valley, at the limit of Hagedorn lands.

Xanten indicated where he wished to alight; the Birds, who would have preferred a site closer to the village where they could have watched all that transpired, grumbled and cried out in wrath and set Xanten down so roughly that had he not been alert the shock would have pitched him head over heels.

Xanten alighted without elegance but at least remained on his feet. "Await me here!" he ordered. "Do not stray; attempt no flamboyant tricks among the lift-straps. When I return I wish to see six quiet Birds, in neat formation, lift-straps untwisted and untangled. No bickering, mind you! No loud caterwauling, to attract unfavorable comment! Let all be as I have ordered!"

The Birds sulked, stamped their feet, ducked aside their necks, made insulting comments just under the level of Xanten's hearing. Xanten, turning them a final glare of admonition, walked down the lane which led to the village.

The vines were heavy with ripe blackberries and a number of the girls of the village filled baskets. Among them was the girl O. Z. Garr had thought to preempt for his personal use. As Xanten passed, he halted and performed a courteous salute. "We have met before, if my recollection is correct."

The girl smiled, a half rueful, half whimsical smile. "Your recollection serves you well. We met at Hagedorn, where I was taken a captive. And later, when you conveyed me here, after dark, though I could not see your face." She extended her basket. "Are you hungry. Will you eat?"

Xanten took several berries. In the course of the conversation he learned that the girl's name was Glys Meadowsweet, that her parents were not known to her, but were presumably gentlefolk of Castle Hagedorn who had exceeded their birth tally. Xanten examined her even more carefully than before, but could see resemblance to none of the Hagedorn families. "You might derive from Castle Delora. If there is any family resemblance I can detect, it is to the Cosanzas of Delora—a family noted for the beauty of its ladies."

"You are not married?" she asked artlessly.

"No," said Xanten, and indeed he had dissolved his relationship with Araminta only the day before. "What of you?"

She shook her head. "I would never be gathering blackberries otherwise; it is work reserved for maidens. . . . Why do you come to Far Valley?"

"For two reasons. The first to see you." Xanten heard himself say this with surprise. But it was true, he realized with another small shock of surprise. "I have never spoken with you properly and I have always wondered if you were as charming and gay as you are beautiful."

The girl shrugged and Xanten could not be sure whether she was pleased or not, compliments from gentlemen sometimes setting the stage for a sorry aftermath. "Well, no matter. I came also to speak to Claghorn."

"He is yonder," she said in a voice toneless, even cool, and pointed. "He occupies that cottage." She returned to her blackberry picking. Xanten bowed and proceeded to the cottage the girl had indicated.

Claghorn, wearing loose knee-length breeches of gray homespun, worked with an ax chopping faggots into stove-lengths. At the sight of Xanten he halted his toil, leaned on the ax and mopped his forehead. "Ah, Xanten, I am pleased to see you. How are the folk of Castle Hagedorn?"

"As before. There is little to report, even had I come to bring you news."

"Indeed, indeed?" Claghorn leaned on the ax handle surveying Xanten with a bright blue gaze.

"At our last meeting," went on Xanten, "I agreed to

question the captive Mek. After doing so I am distressed that you were not at hand to assist, so that you might have resolved certain ambiguities in the responses."

"Speak on," said Claghorn. "Perhaps I shall be able to do so now."

"After the council meeting I descended immediately to the storeroom where the Mek was confined. It lacked nutriment; I gave it syrup and a pail of water, which it sipped sparingly, then evinced a desire for minced clams. I summoned kitchen help and sent them for this commodity and the Mek ingested several pints. As I have indicated, it was an unusual Mek, standing as tall as myself and lacking a syrup sac. I conveyed it to a different chamber, a storeroom for brown plush furniture, and ordered it to a seat.

"I looked at the Mek and it looked at me. The quills which I removed were growing back; probably it could at last receive from Meks elsewhere. It seemed a superior beast, showing neither obsequiousness nor respect, and answered my questions without hesitation.

"First I remarked: 'The gentlefolk of the castles are astounded by the revolt of the Meks. We had assumed that your life was satisfactory. Were we wrong?'

" 'Evidently.' I am sure that this was the word signaled, though never had I suspected the Meks of dryness or wit of any sort.

" 'Very well, then,' I said. 'In what manner?'

" 'Surely it is obvious,' he said. 'We no longer wished to toil at your behest. We wished to conduct our lives by our own traditional standards."

"The response surprised me. I was unaware that the Meks possessed standards of any kind, much less traditional standards."

Claghorn nodded. "I have been similarly surprised by the scope of the Mek mentality."

"I reproached the Mek: 'Why kill? Why destroy our lives in order to augment your own?' As soon as I had put the question I realized that it had been unhappily phrased. The Mek, I believe, realized the same; however, in reply he signaled something very rapidly which I believe was: 'We knew we must act with decisiveness. Your own protocol made this necessary. We might have returned to Etamin Nine, but we prefer this world Earth, and will make it our own, with our own great slipways, tubs and basking ramps.'

"This seemed clear enough, but I sensed an adumbration extending yet beyond. I said, 'Comprehensible. But why kill, why destroy? You might have taken yourself to a different region. We could not have molested you.'

" 'Infeasible, by your own thinking. A world is too small for two competing races. You intended to send us back to dismal Etamin Nine.'

" 'Ridiculous!' I said. 'Fantasy, absurdity. Do you take me for a mooncalf?'

" 'No,' the creature insisted. 'Two of Castle Hagedorn's notables were seeking the highest post. One assured us that, if elected, this would become his life's aim.'

" 'A grotesque misunderstanding,' I told him. 'One man, a lunatic, cannot speak for all men!'

" 'No? One Mek speaks for all Meks. We think with one mind. Are not mèn of a like sort?'

" 'Each thinks for himself. The lunatic who assured you this tomfoolery is an evil man. But at least matters are clear. We do not propose to send you to Etamin Nine. Will you withdraw from Janeil, take yourselves to a far land and leave us in peace?'

" 'No,' he said. 'Affairs have proceeded too far. We will now destroy all men. The truth of the statement is clear: one world is too small for two races.'

" 'Unluckily, then, I must kill you,' I told him. 'Such acts are not to my liking, but, with opportunity, you would kill as many gentlemen as possible.' At this the creature sprang upon me and I killed it with an easier mind than had it sat staring.

"Now you know all. It seems that either you or O. Z. Garr stimulated the cataclysm. O. Z. Garr? Unlikely. Impossible. Hence, you, Claghorn, you! have this weight upon your soul!"

Claghorn frowned down at the ax. "Weight, yes. Guilt, no. Ingenuousness, yes; wickedness, no."

Xanten stood back. "Claghorn, your coolness astounds me! Before, when rancorous folk like O. Z. Garr conceived you a lunatic—"

"Peace, Xanten!" exclaimed Claghorn. "This extravagant breast-beating becomes maladroit. What have I done wrong? My fault is that I tried too much. Failure is tragic, but a phthisic face hanging over the cup of the future is worse. I meant to become Hagedorn, I would have sent the slaves home. I failed, the slaves revolted. So do not speak another word. I am bored with the subject. You cannot imagine how your bulging eyes and your concave spine oppress me."

"Bored you may be," cried Xanten. "You decry my eyes, my spine—but what of the thousands dead?"

"How long would they live in any event? Lives as cheap as fish in the sea. I suggest that you put by your reproaches and devote a similar energy to saving yourself. Do you realize that a means exists? You stare at me blankly. I assure you that what I say is true, but you will never learn the means from me."

"Claghorn," said Xanten, "I flew to this spot intending to blow your arrogant head from your body—" Claghorn, no longer heeding, had returned to his wood-chopping.

"Claghorn!" cried Xanten. "Attend me!"

"Xanten, take your outcries elsewhere, if you please. Remonstrate with your Birds."

Xanten swung on his heel and marched back down the lane. The girls picking berries looked at him questioningly and moved aside. Xanten halted to look up and down the lane. Glys Meadowsweet was nowhere to be seen. In a new fury he continued. He stopped short. On a fallen tree a hundred feet from the Birds sat Glys Meadowsweet, examining a blade of grass as if it had been an astonishing artifact of the past. The Birds, for a marvel, had actually obeyed him and waited in a fair semblance of order.

Xanten looked up toward the heavens, kicked at the turf. He drew a deep breath and approached Glys Meadowsweet. He noted that she had tucked a flower into her long loose hair.

After a second or two she looked up and searched his face. "Why are you so angry?"

Xanten slapped his thigh, then seated himself beside her. " 'Angry'? No. I am out of my mind with frustration. Claghorn is as obstreperous as a sharp rock. He knows how Castle Hagedorn can be saved but he will not divulge his secret."

Glys Meadowsweet laughed—an easy, merry sound, like nothing Xanten had ever heard at Castle Hagedorn. " 'Secret'? When even I know it?"

"It must be a secret," said Xanten. "He will not tell me."

"Listen. If you fear the Birds will hear, I will whisper." She spoke a few words into his ear.

Perhaps the sweet breath befuddled Xanten's mind. But the explicit essence of the revelation failed to strike home into his consciousness. He made a sound of sour amusement. "No secret there. Only what the prehistoric Scythians termed *bathos*. Dishonor to the gentlemen! Do we dance with the Peasants? Do we serve the Birds essences and discuss with them the sheen of our Phanes?"

" 'Dishonor,' then?" She jumped to her feet. "Then it is also dishonor for you to talk to me, to sit here with me, to make ridiculous suggestions—"

"I made no suggestions!" protested Xanten. "I sit here in all decorum—"

"Too much decorum, too much honor!" With a display of passion which astounded Xanten, Glys Meadowsweet tore the flower from her hair and hurled it to the ground. "There! Hence!"

"No," said Xanten in sudden humility. He bent, picked up the flower, kissed it, replaced it in her hair. "I am not over-honorable. I will try my best." He put his arms on her shoulders, but she held him away.

"Tell me," she inquired with a very mature severity, "do you own any of those peculiar insect-women?"

"I? Phanes? I own no Phanes."

With this, Glys Meadowsweet relaxed and allowed Xanten to embrace her, while the Birds clucked, guffawed and made vulgar scratching sounds with their wings.

VII

1.

The summer waxed warm. On June 30 Janeil and Hagedorn celebrated the Fete of Flowers, even though the dike was rising high around Janeil. Shortly after, Xanten flew six select Birds into Castle Janeil by night, and proposed to the council that the population be evacuated by Bird-lift—as many as possible, as many who wished to leave. The council listened with stony faces and without comment passed on to a consideration of other affairs.

Xanten returned to Castle Hagedorn. Using the most careful methods, speaking only to trusted comrades, Xanten enlisted thirty or forty cadets and gentlemen to his persuasion, though inevitably he could not keep the doctrinal thesis of his program secret.

The first reaction of the traditionalists was mockery and charges of poltroonery. At Xanten's insistence, challenges were neither issued nor accepted by his hot-blooded associates.

On the evening of September 9 Castle Janeil fell. The news was brought to Castle Hagedorn by excited Birds who told the grim tale again and again in voices ever more hysterical.

Hagedorn, now gaunt and weary, automatically called a council meeting; it took note of the gloomy circumstances. "We, then, are the last castle! The Meks cannot conceivably do us harm; they can build dikes around our castle walls for twenty years and only work themselves to distraction. We are secure; but it is a strange and portentous thought to realize that at last, here at Castle Hagedorn, live the last gentlemen of the race!"

Xanten spoke in a voice strained with earnest conviction. "Twenty years—fifty years—what difference to the Meks? Once they surround us, once they deploy, we are trapped. Do you comprehend that now is our last opportunity to escape the great cage that Castle Hagedorn is to become?"

" 'Escape,' Xanten? What a word! For shame!" hooted O. Z. Garr. "Take your wretched band, escape! To steppe or swamp or tundra! Go as you like, with your poltroons, but be good enough to give over these incessant alarms!"

"Garr, I have found conviction since I became a 'poltroon.' Survival is good morality. I have this from the mouth of a noted savant."

"Bah! Such as whom?"

"A.G. Philidor, if you must be informed of every detail."

O.Z. Garr clapped his hand to his forehead. "Do you refer to Philidor, the Expiationist? He is of the most extreme stripe, an Expiationist to out-expiate all the rest! Xanten, be sensible, if you please!"

"There are years ahead for all of us," said Xanten in a wooden voice, "if we free ourselves from the castle."

"But the castle is our life!" declared Hagedorn. "In essence, Xanten, what would we be without the castle? Wild animals? Nomads?"

"We would be alive."

O.Z. Garr gave a snort of disgust and turned away to inspect a wall hanging.

Hagedorn shook his head in doubt and perplexity. Beaudry threw his hands up into the air. "Xanten, you have the effect of unnerving us all. You come in here and inflict this dreadful sense of urgency—but why? In Castle Hagedorn we are as safe as in our mothers' arms. What do we gain by throwing aside all—honor, dignity, comfort, civilized niceties—for no other reason than to slink through the wilderness?"

"Janeil was safe," said Xanten. "Today where is Janeil? Death, mildewed cloth, sour wine. What we gain by *slinking* is the assurance of survival. And I plan much more than simple *slinking*."

"I can conceive of a hundred occasions when death is better than life!" snapped Isseth. "Must I die in dishonor and disgrace? Why may my last years not be passed in dignity?"

Into the room came B.F. Robarth. "Councilmen, the Meks approach Castle Hagedorn."

Hagedorn cast a wild look around the chamber. "Is there a consensus? What must we do?"

Xanten threw up his hands. "Everyone must do as he thinks best! I argue no more: I am done, Hagedorn. Will you adjourn the council so that we may be about our affairs? I to my *slinking?*"

"Council is adjourned," said Hagedorn, and all went to stand on the ramparts.

Up the avenue into the castle trooped Peasants from the surrounding countryside, packets slung over their shoulders. Across the valley, at the edge of Bartholomew Forest, was a clot of power-wagons and an amorphous brown-gold mass: Meks.

Aure pointed west. "Look—there they come, up the Long Swale." He turned, peered east. "And look, there at Bambridge: Meks!"

By common consent, all swung about to scan North

Ridge. O.Z. Garr pointed to a quiet line of brown-gold shapes. "There they wait, the vermin! They have penned us in! Well, then, let them wait!" He swung away, rode the lift down to the plaza, and crossed swiftly to Zumbeld House, where he worked the rest of the afternoon with his Gloriana, of whom he expected great things.

2.

The following day the Meks formalized the investment. Around Castle Hagedorn a great circle of Mek activity made itself apparent: sheds, warehouses, barracks. Within this periphery, just beyond the range of the energy-cannon, power-wagons thrust up mounds of dirt.

During the night these mounds lengthened toward the castle, similarly the night after. At last the purpose of the mounds became clear: they were a protective cover above passages or tunnels leading toward the crag on which Castle Hagedorn rested.

The following day several of the mounds reached the base of the crag. Presently a succession of power-wagons loaded with rubble began to flow from the far end. They issued, dumped their loads and once again entered the tunnels.

Eight of these aboveground tunnels had been established. From each trundled endless loads of dirt and rock, gnawed from the crag on which Castle Hagedorn sat. To the gentlefolk who crowded the parapets the meaning of the work at last became clear.

"They make no attempt to bury us," said Hagedorn. "They merely mine out the crag from below us!"

On the sixth day of the siege, a great segment of the hillside shuddered, slumped and a tall pinnacle of rock reaching almost up to the base of the walls collapsed.

"If this continues," muttered Beaudry, "our time will be less than that of Janeil."

"Come, then," called O.Z. Garr, suddenly active. "Let us try our energy-cannon. We'll blast open their wretched tunnels, and then what will the rascals do?" He went to the nearest emplacement and shouted down for Peasants to remove the tarpaulin.

Xanten, who happened to be standing nearby, said, "Allow me to assist you." He jerked away the tarpaulin. "Shoot now, if you will."

O.Z. Garr stared at him uncomprehendingly, then leaped forward and swiveled the great projector about so that it aimed at a mound. He pulled the switch; the air crackled in front of the ringed snout, rippled, flickered with purple sparks. The target area steamed, became black, then dark red, then slumped into an incandescent crater. But the underlying earth, twenty feet in thickness, afforded too much insulation; the molten puddle became white-hot but failed to spread or deepen. The energy-cannon gave a sudden chatter, as electricity short-circuited through corroded insulation. The cannon went dead. O.Z. Garr inspected the mechanism in anger and disappointment; then, with a gesture of repugnance, he turned away. The cannons were clearly of limited effectiveness.

Two hours later, on the east side of the crag, another great sheet of rock collapsed, and just before sunset a similar mass sheered from the western face, where the wall of the castle rose almost in an uninterrupted line from the cliff below.

At midnight Xanten and those of his persuasion, with their children and consorts, departed Castle Hagedorn. Six teams of Birds shuttled from the flight deck to a meadow near Far Valley, and long before dawn had transported the entire group. There were none to bid them farewell.

3.

A week later another section of the east cliff fell away, taking a length of rock-melt buttress with it. At the tunnel mouths the piles of excavated rubble had become alarmingly large.

The terraced south face of the crag was the least disturbed, the most spectacular damage having occurred to east and west. Suddenly, a month after the initial assault, a great section of the terrace slumped forward, leaving an irregular crevasse which interrupted the avenue and hurled down the statues of former notables emplaced at intervals along the avenue's balustrade.

Hagedorn called a council meeting. "Circumstances," he said in a wan attempt at facetiousness, "have not bettered themselves. Our most pessimistic expectations have been exceeded: a dismal situation. I confess that I do not relish the prospect of toppling to my death among all my smashed belongings."

Aure made a desperate gesture. "A similar thought haunts me! Death—what of that? All must die! But when I think of my precious belongings, I become sick. My books trampled! my fragile vases smashed! my tabards ripped! my rugs buried! my Phanes strangled! my heirloom chandeliers flung aside! These are my nightmares."

"Your possessions are no less precious than any others," said Beaudry shortly. "Still, they have no life of their own; when we are gone, who cares what happens to them?"

Marune winced. "A year ago I put down eighteen dozen flasks of prime essence; twelve dozen Green Rain; three each of Balthazar and Faidor. Think of these, if you would contemplate tragedy!"

"Had we only known!" groaned Aure. "I would have—I would have. . . ." His voice trailed away.

O.Z. Garr stamped his foot in impatience. "Let us avoid lamentation at all costs! We had a choice, remember? Xanten beseeched us to flee; now he and his like go skulking and foraging through the north mountains with the Expiationists. We chose to remain, for better or worse and unluckily the worse is occurring. We must accept the fact like gentlemen."

To this the council gave melancholy assent. Hagedorn brought forth a flask of priceless Rhadamanth, and poured with a prodigality which previously would have been unthinkable. "Since we have no future—to our glorious past!"

That night disturbances were noted here and there around the ring of Mek investment: flames at four separate points, a faint sound of hoarse shouting. On the following day it seemed that the tempo of activity had lessened a trifle.

During the afternoon, however, a vast segment of the east cliff fell away. A moment later, as if after majestic deliberation, the tall east wall split off and toppled, leaving the backs of six great Houses exposed to the open sky.

An hour after sunset a team of Birds settled to the flight-deck. Xanten jumped from the seat. He ran down the circular staircase to the ramparts and came down to the plaza by Hagedorn's palace.

Hagedorn, summoned by a kinsman, came forth to stare at Xanten in surprise. "What do you do here? We expected you to be safely north with the Expiationists!"

"The Expiationists are not safely north," said Xanten. "They have joined the rest of us. We are fighting."

Hagedorn's jaw dropped. "Fighting? The gentlemen are fighting Meks?"

"As vigorously as possible."

Hagedorn shook his head in wonder. "The Expiationists too? I understood that they had planned to flee north."

"Some have done so, including A.G. Philidor. There are factions among the Expiationists just as here. Most are not ten miles distant. The same with the Nomads. Some have taken their power-wagons and fled. The rest kill Meks with fanatic fervor. Last night you saw our work. We fired four storage warehouses, destroyed syrup tanks, killed a hundred or more Meks, as well as a dozen power-wagons. We suffered losses, which hurt us because there are few of us and many Meks. This is why I am here. We need more men. Come fight beside us!"

Hagedorn turned, motioning to the great central plaza. "I will call forth the folk from their Houses. Talk to everyone."

4.

The Birds, complaining bitterly at the unprecedented toil, worked all night, transporting the gentlemen who, sobered by the imminent destruction of Castle Hagedorn, were now willing to abandon all scruples and fight for their lives. The staunch traditionalists still refused to compromise their honor, but Xanten gave them cheerful assurance: "Remain here, then, prowling the castle like so many furtive rats. Take what comfort you can in the fact that you are being protected; the future holds little else for you."

And many who heard him stalked away in disgust.

Xanten turned to Hagedorn. "What of you? Do you come or do you stay?"

Hagedorn heaved a deep sigh, almost a groan. "Castle Hagedorn is at an end. No matter what the eventuality. I come with you."

5.

The situation had suddenly altered. The Meks, established in a loose ring around Castle Hagedorn, had calculated upon no resistance from the countryside and little from the castle. They had established their barracks and syrup depots with thought only for convenience and none for defense; raiding parties, consequently, were able to approach, inflict damage and withdraw before sustaining serious losses of their own. Those Meks posted along North Ridge were harassed almost continuously, and finally were driven down with many losses. The circle around Castle Hagedorn became a cusp; then two days later, after the destruction of five more syrup depots, the Meks drew back even farther. Throwing up earthworks before the two tunnels leading under the south face of the crag, they established a more or less tenable defensive position, but now instead of beleaguering, they became the beleaguered, even though power-wagons of broken rock still issued from the crag.

Within the area thus defended, the Meks concentrated their remaining syrup stocks, tools, weapons, ammunition. The area outside the earthworks was floodlit after dark and guarded by Meks armed with pellet guns, making any frontal assault impractical.

For a day the raiders kept to the shelter of the surrounding orchards, appraising the new situation. Then a new tactic was attempted. Six light carriages were improvised and loaded with bladders of a light inflammable oil, with a fire genade attached. To each of these carriages ten birds were harnessed, and at midnight sent aloft, with a man for each carriage. Flying high, the Birds then glided down through the darkness over the Mek position, where the fire bombs were dropped. The area instantly seethed with flame. The syrup depot burned; the power-wagons, awakened by the flames, rolled frantically back and forth, crushing Meks and stores, colliding with each other, adding vastly to the terror of the fire. The Meks who survived took shelter in the tunnels. Certain of the floodlights were extinguished, and taking advantage of the confusion, the men attacked the earthworks. After a short, bitter battle, the men killed all the sentinels and took up positions commanding the mouths of the tunnels, which now contained all that remained of the Mek army. It seemed as if the Mek uprising had been put down.

VIII

1.

The flames died. The human warriors—three hundred men from the castle, two hundred Expiationists and about three hundred Nomads—gathered about the tunnel mouth and, during the balance of the night, considered methods to deal with the immured Meks. At sunrise, those men of Castle Hagedorn, whose children and consorts were yet inside, went to bring them forth. With them, upon their return, came a group of castle gentlemen: among them Beaudry, O.Z. Garr, Isseth and Aure. They greeted their onetime peers, Hagedorn, Xanten, Claghorn and others, crisply, but with a certain austere detachment which recognized that loss of prestige incurred by those who fought Meks as if they were equals.

"Now what is to happen?" Beaudry inquired of Hagedorn. "The Meks are trapped but you can't bring them forth. Not impossibly they have syrup stored within for the power-wagons; they may well survive for months."

O.Z. Garr, assessing the situation from the standpoint of a military theoretician, came forward with a plan of action. "Fetch down the cannon—or have your underlings do so—and mount them on power-wagons. When the vermin are sufficiently weak, roll the cannon in and wipe out all but a labor force for the castle: we formerly worked four hundred, and this should suffice."

"Hal!" exclaimed Xanten. "It gives me great pleasure to inform you that this will never be. If any Meks survive they will repair the spaceships and instruct us in their maintenance and we will then transport them and Peasants back to their native worlds."

"How, then, do you expect us to maintain our lives?" demanded Garr coldly.

"You have the syrup generator. Fit yourselves with sacs and drink syrup."

Garr tilted back his head, stared coldly down his nose.

"This is your voice, yours alone, and your insolent opinion. Others are to be heard from. Hagedorn—you were once a gentleman. Is this also your philosophy, that civilization should wither?"

"It need not wither," said Hagedorn, "provided that all of us—you as well as we—toil for it. There can be no more slaves. I have become convinced of this."

O.Z. Garr turned on his heel, swept back up the avenue into the castle, followed by the most traditional-minded of his comrades. A few moved aside and talked among themselves in low tones, with one or two black looks for Xanten and Hagedorn.

From the ramparts of the castle came a sudden outcry: "The Meks! They are taking the castle! They swarm up the lower passages! Attack, save us!"

The men below stared up in consternation. Even as they looked, the castle portals swung shut.

"How is this possible?" demanded Hagedorn. "I swear all entered the tunnels!"

"It is only too clear," said Xanten bitterly. "While they undermined, they drove a tunnel up to the lower levels!"

Hagedorn started forward as if he would charge up the crag alone, then halted. "We must drive them out. Unthinkable that they pillage our castle!"

"Unfortunately," said Claghorn, "the walls bar us as effectively as they did the Meks."

"We can send up a force by Bird-car! Once we consolidate, we can hunt them down, exterminate them."

Claghorn shook his head. "They can wait on the ramparts and flight deck and shoot down the Birds as they approach. Even if we secured a foothold there would be great bloodshed: one of us killed for every one of them. And they still outnumber us three or four to one."

Hagedorn groaned. "The thought of them reveling among my possessions, strutting about in my clothes, swilling my essences—it sickens me!"

"Listen!" said Claghorn. From on high they heard the hoarse yells of men, the crackle of energy-cannon. "Some of them, at least, hold out on the ramparts!"

Xanten went to a nearby group of Birds who were for once awed and subdued by events. "Lift me up above the castle, out of range of the pellets, but where I can see what the Meks do!"

"Care, take care!" croaked one of the Birds. "Ill things occur at the castle."

"Never mind; convey me up, above the ramparts!"

The Birds lifted him, swung in a great circle around the crag and above the castle, sufficiently distant to be safe from the Mek pellet guns. Beside those cannon which yet operated stood thirty men and women. Between the great Houses, the Rotunda and the palace, everywhere the cannon could not be brought to bear, swarmed Meks. The plaza was littered with corpses: gentlemen, ladies and their children—all those who had elected to remain at Castle Hagedorn.

At one of the cannon stood O.Z. Garr. Spying Xanten he gave a shout of hysterical rage, swung up the cannon, fired a bolt. The Birds, screaming, tried to swerve aside, but the bolt smashed two. Birds, car, Xanten fell in a great tangle. By some miracle, the four yet alive caught their balance and a hundred feet from the ground, with a frenzied groaning effort, they slowed their fall, steadied, hovered an instant, sank to the ground. Xanten staggered free of the tangle. Men came running. "Are you safe?" called Claghorn.

"Safe, yes. Frightened as well." Xanten took a deep breath and went to sit on an outcrop of rock.

"What's happening up there?" asked Claghorn.

"All dead," said Xanten, "all but a score. Garr has gone mad. He fired on me."

"Look! Meks on the ramparts!" cried A.L. Morgan.

"There!" cried someone else. "Men! They jump! . . . No, they are flung!"

Some were men, some were Meks whom they had dragged with them; with awful slowness they toppled to their deaths. No more fell. Castle Hagedorn was in the hands of the Meks.

Xanten considered the complex silhouette, at once so familiar and so strange. "They can't hope to hold out. We need only destroy the sun-cells, and they can synthesize no syrup."

"Let us do it now," said Claghorn, "before they think of this and man the cannon! Birds!"

He went off to give the orders, and forty Birds, each clutching two rocks the size of a man's head, flapped up, circled the castle and presently returned to report the sun-cells destroyed.

Xanten said, "All that remains is to seal the tunnel entrances against a sudden eruption, which might catch us off guard—then patience."

"What of the Peasants in the stables—and the Phanes?" asked Hagedorn in a forlorn voice.

Xanten gave his head a slow shake. "He who was not an Expiationist before must become one now."

Claghorn muttered, "They can survive two months—no more."

But two months passed, and three months, and four months: then one morning the great portals opened and a haggard Mek stumbled forth. He signaled: "Men: we starve. We have maintained your treasures. Give us our lives or we destroy all before we die."

Claghorn responded: "These are our terms. We give you your lives. You must clean the castle, remove and bury the corpses. You must repair the spaceships and teach us all you know regarding them. We will then transport you to Etamin Nine."

2.

Five years later Xanten and Glys Meadowsweet, with their two children, had reason to travel north from their home near Sande River. They took occasion to visit Castle Hagedorn, where now lived only two or three dozen folk, among them Hagedorn.

He had aged, so it seemed to Xanten, His hair was white; his face, once bluff and hearty, had become thin, almost waxen. Xanten could not determine his mood.

They stood in the shade of a walnut tree, with castle and crag looming above them. "This is now a great museum," said Hagedorn. "I am curator, and this will be the function of all the Hagedorns who come after me, for there is incalculable treasure to guard and maintain. Already the feeling of antiquity has come to the castle. The Houses are alive with ghosts. I see them often, especially on the nights of the fetes. . . . Ah, those were the times, were they not, Xanten?"

"Yes, indeed," said Xanten. He touched the heads of his two children. "Still, I have no wish to return to them.

We are men now, on our own world, as we never were before."

Hagedorn gave a somewhat regretful assent. He looked up at the vast structure, as if now were the first occasion he had laid eyes on it. "The folk of the future—what will they think of Castle Hagedorn? Its treasures, its books, its tabards?"

"They will come, they will marvel," said Xanten. "Almost as I do today."

"There is much at which to marvel. Will you come within, Xanten? There are still flasks of noble essence laid by."

"Thank you, no," said Xanten. "There is too much to stir old memories. We will go our way, and I think immediately."

Hagedorn nodded sadly. "I understand very well. I myself am often given to reverie these days. Well then, good-bye, and journey home with pleasure."

"We will do so, Hagedorn. Thank you and good-bye."

1967

AYE, AND GOMORRAH . . .

by Samuel R. Delany

And came down in Paris:

Where we raced along the Rue de Médicis with Bo and Lou and Muse inside the fence, Kelly and me outside, making faces through the bars, making noise, making the Luxembourg Gardens roar at two in the morning. Then climbed out and down to the square in front of St. Sulpice where Bo tried to knock me into the fountain.

At which point Kelly noticed what was going on around us, got an ashcan cover, and ran into the pissoir, banging the walls. Five guys scooted out; even a big pissoir only holds four.

A very blond young man put his hand on my arm and smiled. "Don't you think, Spacer, that you . . . people should leave?"

I looked at his hand on my blue uniform. *Est-ce que tu es un frelk?*

His eyebrows rose, then he shook his head. "Une *frelk,*" he corrected. "No. I am not. Sadly for me. You look as though you may once have been a man. But now . . ." He smiled. "You have nothing for me now. The police." He nodded across the street where I noticed the gendarmerie for the first time. "They don't bother us. You are strangers, though . . ."

But Muse was already yelling, "Hey, come on! Let's get out of here, huh?" And left. And went up again.

And came down in Houston:

"God damn!" Muse said. "Gemini Flight Control—you

mean this is where it all started? Let's get *out* of here,
please!"

So took a bus out through Pasadena, then the monoline
to Galveston, and were going to take it down the Gulf, but
Lou found a couple with a pickup truck—

"Glad to give you a ride, Spacers. You people up there
on them planets and things, doing all that good work for
the government."

—who were going south, them and the baby, so we
rode in the back for two hundred and fifty miles of sun
and wind.

"You think they're frelks?" Lou asked, elbowing me. "I
bet they're frelks. They're just waiting for us to give 'em
the come-on."

"Cut it out. They're a nice, stupid pair of country kids."

"That don't mean they ain't frelks!"

"You don't trust anybody, do you?"

"No."

And finally a bus again that rattled us through Browns-
ville and across the border into Matamoros where we staggered down the steps into the dust and the scorched
evening with a lot of Mexicans and chickens and Texas
Gulf shrimp fishermen—who smelled worst—and *we*
shouted the loudest. Forty-three whores—I counted—had
turned out for the shrimp fishermen, and by the time we
had broken two of the windows in the bus station, they
were all laughing. The shrimp fishermen said they
wouldn't buy us no food but would get us drunk if we
wanted 'cause that was the custom with shrimp fishermen.
But we yelled, broke another window; then while I was
lying on my back on the telegraph office steps, singing, a
woman with dark lips bent over and put her hands on my
cheeks. "You are very sweet." Her rough hair fell forward. "But the men, they are standing around and watching *you*. And that is taking up *time*. Sadly, their time is
our *money*. Spacer, do you not think you . . . people
should leave?"

I grabbed her wrist. "*¡Usted!*" I whispered. "*¿Usted es
una frelka?*"

"*Frelko en español.*" She smiled and patted the sunburst
that hung from my belt buckle. "Sorry. But you have
nothing that . . . would be useful to me. It is too bad for

you look like you were once a woman, no? And I like women, too . . ."

I rolled off the porch.

"Is this a drag or is this a drag!" Muse was shouting. "Come *on!* Let's *go!*"

We managed to get back to Houston before dawn, somehow. And went up.

And came down in Istanbul:

That morning it rained in Istanbul.

At the commissary we drank our tea from pear-shaped glasses, looking out across the Bosphorus. The Princes Islands lay like trash heaps before the prickly city.

"Who knows their way in this town?" Kelly asked.

"Aren't we going around together?" Muse demanded. "I thought we were going around together."

"They held up my check at the purser's office," Kelly explained. "I'm flat broke. I think the purser's got it in for me." and shrugged. "Don't want to, but I'm going to have to hunt up a rich frelk and come on friendly," went back to the tea; *then* noticed how heavy the silence had become. "Aw, come *on,* now! You gape at me like that and I'll bust every bone in that carefully-conditioned-from-puberty body of yours. Hey, you!" meaning me. "Don't give me that holier-than-thou gawk like you never went with no frelk!"

It was starting.

"I'm not gawking," I said and got quietly mad.

The longing, the old longing.

Bo laughed to break tensions. "Say, last time I was in Istanbul—about a year before I joined up with this platoon—I remember we were coming out of Taksim Square down Istiqlal. Just past all the cheap movies we found a little passage lined with flowers. Ahead of us were two other spacers. It's a market in there, and farther down they got fish and then a courtyard with oranges and candy and sea urchins and cabbage. But flowers in front. Anyway, we noticed something funny about the spacers. It wasn't their uniforms: they were perfect. The haircuts: fine. It wasn't till we heard them talking—they were a man and woman dressed up like spacers, trying *to pick up frelks!* Imagine, queer for frelks!"

"Yeah," Lou said. "I seen that before. There were a lot of them in Rio."

"We beat hell out of them two," Bo concluded. 'We got them in a side street and went to *town!*"

Muse's tea glass clicked on the counter. "From Taksim down Istiqlal till you get to the flowers? Now why didn't you say that's where the frelks were, huh?" A smile on Kelly's face would have made that okay. There was no smile.

"Hell," Lou said, "nobody ever had to tell me where to look. I go out in the street and frelks smell me coming. I can spot 'em halfway along Piccadilly. Don't they have nothing but tea in this place? Where can you get a drink?"

Bo grinned. "Moslem country, remember? But down at the end of the Flower Passage, there're a lot of little bars with green doors and marble counters where you can get a liter of beer for about fifteen cents in lira. And there're all these stands selling deep-fat-fried bugs and pig's gut sandwiches—"

"You ever notice how frelks can put it away? I mean liquor, not . . . pig's guts."

And launched off into a lot of appeasing stories. We ended with the one about the frelk some spacer tried to roll who announced: "There are two things I go for. One is spacers; the other is a good fight . . ."

But they only allay. They cure nothing. Even Muse knew we would spend the day apart now.

The rain had stopped so we took the ferry up the Golden Horn. Kelly straight off asked for Taksim Square and Istiqlal and was directed to a dolmush, which we discovered was a taxicab, only it just goes one place and picks up lots and lots of people on the way. And it's cheap.

Lou headed off over Ataturk Bridge to see the sights of New City. Bo decided to find out what the Dolma Boche really was; and when Muse discovered you could go to Asia for fifteen cents—one lira and fifty krush—well, Muse decided to go to Asia.

I turned through the confusion of traffic at the head of the bridge and up past the gray, dripping walls of Old City, beneath the trolley wires. There are times when yelling and helling won't fill the lack. There are times when you must walk by yourself because it hurts so much to be alone.

I walked up a lot of little streets with wet donkeys and

wet camels and women in veils; and down a lot of big streets with buses and trash baskets and men in business suits.

Some people stare at spacers; some people don't. Some people stare or don't stare in a way a spacer gets to recognize within a week after coming out of training school at sixteen. I was walking in the park when I caught her watching. She saw me see and looked away.

I ambled down the wet asphalt. She was standing under the arch of a small, empty mosque shell. As I passed, she walked out into the courtyard among the cannons.

"Excuse me."

I stopped.

"Do you know whether or not this is the shrine of St. Irene?" Her English was charmingly accented. "I've left my guidebook home."

"Sorry. I'm a tourist, too."

"Oh." She smiled. "I am Greek. I thought you might be Turkish because you are so dark."

"American red Indian." I nodded. Her turn to curtsy.

"I see. I have just started at the university here in Istanbul. Your uniform, it tells me that you are . . ."—and in the pause, all speculations resolved—"a spacer."

I was uncomfortable. "Yeah." I put my hands in my pockets, moved my feet around on the soles of my boots, licked my third from the rear left molar—did all the things you do when you're uncomfortable. *You're so exciting when you look like that,* a frelk told me once. "Yeah, I am." I said it too sharply, too loudly, and she jumped a little.

So now she knew I knew she knew I knew, and I wondered how we would play out the Proust bit.

"I'm Turkish," she said. "I'm not Greek. I'm not just starting. I'm a graduate in art history here at the university. These little lies one makes for strangers to protect one's ego . . . why? Sometimes I think my ego is very small."

That's one strategy.

"How far away do you live?" I asked. "And what's the going rate in Turkish lira?" That's another.

"I can't pay you." She pulled her raincoat around her hips. She was very pretty. "I would like to." She shrugged and smiled. "But I am . . . a poor student. Not a rich one.

If you want to turn around and walk away, there will be no hard feelings. I shall be sad though."

I stayed on the path. I thought she'd suggest a price after a little while. She didn't.

And *that's* another.

I was asking myself. *What do you want the damn money for anyway?* when a breeze upset water from one of the park's great cypresses.

"I think the whole business is sad." She wiped drops from her face. There had been a break in her voice, and for a moment I looked too closely at the water streaks. "I think it's sad that they have to alter you to make you a spacer. If they hadn't, then *we* . . . If spacers had never been, then we could not be . . . the way we are. Did you start out male or female?"

Another shower. I was looking at the ground and droplets went down my collar.

"Male," I said. "It doesn't matter."

"How old are you? Twenty-three, twenty-four?"

"Twenty-three," I lied. It's reflex. I'm twenty-five, but the younger they think you are, the more they pay you. But I didn't *want* her *damn* money—

"I guessed right, then." She nodded. "Most of us are experts on spacers. Do you find that? I suppose we have to be." She looked at me with wide black eyes. At the end of the stare, she blinked rapidly. "You would have been a fine man. But now you are a spacer, building water-conservation units on Mars, programing mining computers on Ganymede, servicing communication relay towers on the moon. The alteration . . ." Frelks are the only people I've ever heard say "the alteration" with so much fascination and regret. "You'd think they'd have found some other solution. They could have found another way than neutering you, turning you into creatures not even androgynous; things that are—"

I put my hand on her shoulder, and she stopped like I'd hit her. She looked to see if anyone was near. Lightly, so lightly then, she raised her hand to mine.

I pulled my hand away. "That are what?"

"They could have found another way." Both hands in her pockets now.

"They could have. Yes. Up beyond the ionosphere, there's too much radiation for those precious gonads to work right anywhere you might want to do something that would keep you there over twenty-four hours, like the moon, or Mars, or the satellites of Jupiter—"

"They could have made protective shields. They could have done more research into biological adjustment—"

"Population Explosion time," I said. "No, they were hunting for any excuse to cut down kids back then—especially deformed ones."

"Ah yes." She nodded. "We're still fighting our way up from the neo-puritan reaction to the sex freedom of the twentieth century."

"It was a fine solution." I grinned and hung my hand over my crotch. "I'm happy with it." I've never known why that's so much more obscene when a spacer does it.

"Stop it," she snapped, moving away.

"What's the matter?"

"Stop it," she repeated. "Don't do that! You're a child."

"But they choose us from children whose sexual responses are hopelessly retarded at puberty."

"And your childish, violent substitutes for love? I suppose that's one of the things that's attractive. Yes, I know you're a child."

"Yeah? What about frelks?"

She thought a while. "I think they are the sexually retarded ones they miss. Perhaps it was the right solution. You really don't regret you have no sex?"

"We've got you," I said.

"Yes." She looked down. I glanced to see the expression she was hiding. It was a smile. "You have your glorious, soaring life, *and* you have us." Her face came up. She glowed. "You spin in the sky, the world spins under you, and you step from land to land, while we . . ." She turned her head right, left, and her black hair curled and uncurled on the shoulder of her coat. "We have our dull, circled lives, bound in gravity, *worshipping* you!"

She looked back at me. "Perverted, yes? In love with a bunch of corpses in free fall!" She suddenly hunched her shoulders. "I don't like having a free-fall-sexual-displacement complex."

"That always sounded like too much to say."

She looked away. "I don't like being a frelk. Better?"

"I wouldn't like it either. Be something else."

"You don't choose your perversions. *You* have no perversions at all. You're free of the whole business. I love you for that, spacer. My love starts with the fear of love. Isn't that beautiful? A pervert substitutes something unattainable for 'normal' love: the homosexual, a mirror, the fetishist, a shoe, or a watch, or a girdle. Those with free-fall-sexual-dis—"

"Frelks."

"Frelks substitute"—she looked at me sharply again—"loose, swinging meat."

"That doesn't offend me."

"I wanted it to."

"Why?"

"You don't have desires. You wouldn't understand."

"Go on."

"I want you because you can't want me. That's the pleasure. If someone really had a sexual reaction to . . . us, we'd be scared away. I wonder how many people there were before there were you, waiting for your creation. We're necrophiles. I'm sure grave robbing has fallen off since you started going up. But you don't understand . . ." She paused. "If you did, then I wouldn't be scuffing leaves now and trying to think from whom I could borrow sixty lira." She stepped over the knuckles of a root that had cracked the pavement. "And that, incidentally, is the going rate in Istanbul."

I calculated. "Things still get cheaper as you go east."

"You know," and she let her raincoat fall open, "you're different from the others. You at least *want* to know—"

I said, "If I spat on you for every time you'd said that to a spacer, you'd drown."

"Go back to the moon, loose meat." She closed her eyes. "Swing on up to Mars. There are satellites around Jupiter where you might do some good. Go up and come down in some other city."

"Where do you live?"

"You want to come with me?"

"Give me something," I said. "Give me *some*thing—it doesn't have to be worth sixty lira. Give me something that you like, anything of yours that means something to you."

"No!"

"Why not?"

"Because I—"

"—don't want to give up part of that ego. None of you frelks do!"

"You really don't understand I just don't want to buy you?"

"You have nothing to buy me with."

"You are a child," she said. "I love you."

We reached the gate of the park. She stopped, and we stood time enough for a breeze to rise and die in the grass. "I . . ." she offered tentatively, pointing without taking her hand from her coat pocket. "I live right down there."

"All right," I said. "Let's go."

A gas main had once exploded along this street, she explained to me, a gushing road of fire as far as the docks, overhot and overquick. It had been put out within minutes, no building had fallen, but the charred facias glittered. "This is sort of an artist and student quarter." We crossed the cobbles. "Yuri Pasha, number fourteen. In case you're ever in Istanbul again." Her door was covered with black scales, the gutter was thick with garbage.

"A lot of artists and professional people are frelks," I said, trying to be inane.

"So are lots of other people." She walked inside and held the door. "We're just more flamboyant about it."

On the landing there was a portrait of Ataturk. Her room was on the second floor. "Just a moment while I get my key—"

Marsscapes! Moonscapes! On her easel was a six-foot canvas showing the sunrise flaring on a crater's rim! There were copies of the original Observer pictures of the moon pinned to the wall, and pictures of every smooth-faced general in the International Spacer Corps.

On one corner of her desk was a pile of those photo magazines about spacers that you can find in most kiosks all over the world: I've seriously heard people say they were printed for adventurous-minded high school children. They've never seen the Danish ones. She had a few of those, too. There was a shelf of art books, art history texts. Above them were six feet of cheap paper-covered space operas: *Sin on Space Station #12, Rocket, Rake, Savage Orbit.*

"Arrack?" she asked. "Ouzo, or pernod? You've got

your choice. But I may pour them all from the same bottle." She set out glasses on the desk, then opened a waist-high cabinet that turned out to be an icebox. She stood up with a tray of lovelies: fruit puddings, Turkish delight, braised meats.

"What's this?"

"Dolmades. Grape leaves filled with rice and pignolias."

"Say it again?"

"Dolmades. Comes from the same Turkish word as 'dolmush.' They both mean 'stuffed.'" She put the tray beside the glasses. "Sit down."

I sat on the studio-couch-that-becomes-bed. Under the brocade I felt the deep, fluid resilience of a glycogel mattress. They've got the idea that it approximates the feeling of free fall. "Comfortable? Would you excuse me for a moment? I have some friends down the hall. I want to see them for a moment." She winked. "They like spacers."

"Are you going to take up a collection for me?" I asked. "Or do you want them to line up outside the door and wait their turn?"

She sucked a breath. "Actually I was going to suggest both." Suddenly she shook her head. "Oh, what do you want!"

"What will you give me? I want something," I said. "That's why I came. I'm lonely. Maybe I want to find out how far it goes. I don't know yet."

"It goes as far as you will. Me? I study, I read, paint, talk with my friends"—she came over to the bed, sat down on the floor—"go to the theater, look at spacers who pass me on the street, till one looks back; I am lonely, too." She put her head on my knee. "I want something. But," and after a minute neither of us had moved, "you are not the one who will give it to me."

"You're not going to pay me for it," I countered. "You're not, are you?"

On my knee her head shook. After a while she said, all breath and no voice. "Don't you think you . . . should leave?"

"Okay," I said and stood up.

She sat back on the hem of her coat. She hadn't taken it off yet.

I went to the door.

"Incidentally." She folded her hands in her lap. "There is a place in New City you might find what you're looking for, called the Flower Passage—"

I turned toward her, angry. "The frelk hangout? Look, I don't *need* money! I said *any*thing would do! I don't want—"

She had begun to shake her head, laughing quietly. Now she lay her cheek on the wrinkled place where I had sat. "Do you persist in misunderstanding? You said you were lonely. It is a spacer hangout. When you leave, I am going to visit my friends and talk about . . . ah, yes, the beautiful one that got away. I thought you might find . . . perhaps someone you knew."

With anger, it ended.

"Oh," I said. "Oh, it's a spacer hangout. Yeah. Well, thanks."

And went out. And found the Flower Passage, and Kelly and Lou and Bo and Muse. Kelly was buying beer so we all got drunk, and ate fried fish and fried clams and fried sausage, and Kelly was waving the money around, saying, "You should have seen him! The changes I put that frelk through, you should have *seen* him! Eighty lira is the going rate here, and he gave me a hundred and fifty!" and drank more beer.

And went up.

GONNA ROLL THE BONES

by Fritz Leiber

Suddenly Joe Slattermill knew for sure he'd have to get out quick or else blow his top and knock out with the shrapnel of his skull the props and patches holding up his decaying home, that was like a house of big wooden and plaster and wallpaper cards except for the huge fireplace and ovens and chimney across the kitchen from him.

Those were stone-solid enough, though. The fireplace was chin-high, at least twice that long, and filled from end to end with roaring flames. Above were the square doors of the ovens in a row—his Wife baked for part of their living. Above the ovens was the wall-long mantelpiece, too high for his Mother to reach or Mr. Guts to jump any more, set with all sorts of ancestral curios, but any of them that weren't stone or glass or china had been so dried and darkened by decades of heat that they looked like nothing but shrunken human heads and black golf balls. At one end were clustered his Wife's square gin bottles. Above the mantelpiece hung one old chromo, so high and so darkened by soot and grease that you couldn't tell whether the swirls and fat cigar shape were a whaleback steamer plowing through a hurricane or a spaceship plunging through a storm of light-driven dust motes.

As soon as Joe curled his toes inside his boots, his Mother knew what he was up to. "Going bumming," she mumbled with conviction. "Pants pockets full of cartwheels of house money, too, to spend on sin." And she went back to munching the long shreds she stripped fumblingly with her right hand off the turkey carcass set close to the terrible heat, her left hand ready to fend off Mr. Guts, who stared at her yellow-eyed, gaunt-flanked, with long mangy tail a-twitch. In her dirty dress, streaky as the turkey's sides, Joe's Mother looked like a bent brown bag and her fingers were lumpy twigs.

Joe's Wife knew as soon or sooner, for she smiled thin-eyed at him over her shoulder from where she towered at the centermost oven. Before she closed its door, Joe glimpsed that she was baking two long, flat, narrow, fluted loaves and one high, round-domed one. She was thin as death and disease in her violet wrapper. Without looking, she reached out a yard-long, skinny arm for the nearest gin bottle and downed a warm slug and smiled again. And without word spoken, Joe knew she'd said, "You're going out and gamble and get drunk and lay a floozy and come home and beat me and go to jail for it," and he had a flash of the last time he'd been in the dark gritty cell and she'd come by moonlight, which showed the green and yellow lumps on her narrow skull where he'd hit her, to whisper to him through the tiny window in back and slip him a half-pint through the bars.

And Joe knew for certain that this time it would be that bad and worse, but just the same he heaved up himself and his heavy, muffledly clanking pockets and shuffled straight to the door, muttering, "Guess I'll roll the bones, up the pike a stretch and back," swinging his bent, knobby-elbowed arms like paddlewheels to make a little joke about his words.

When he'd stepped outside, he held the door open a hand's breadth behind him for several seconds. When he finally closed it, a feeling of deep misery struck him. Earlier years, Mr. Guts would have come streaking along to seek fights and females on the roofs and fences, but now the big tom was content to stay home and hiss by the fire and snatch for turkey and dodge a broom, quarreling and comforting with two housebound women. Nothing had followed Joe to the door but his Mother's chomping and her gasping breaths and the clink of the gin bottle going back on the mantel and the creaking of the floor boards under his feet.

The night was up-side-down deep among the frosty stars. A few of them seemed to move, like the white-hot jets of spaceships. Down below it looked as if the whole town

of Ironmine had blown or buttoned out the light and gone
to sleep, leaving the streets and spaces to the equally unseen breezes and ghosts. But Joe was still in the hemisphere of the musty dry odor of the worm-eaten carpentry
behind him, and as he felt and heard the dry grass of the
lawn brush his calves, it occurred to him that something
deep down inside him had for years been planning things
so that he and the house and his Wife and Mother and
Mr. Guts would all come to an end together. Why the
kitchen heat hadn't touched off the tindery place ages ago
was a physical miracle.

Hunching his shoulders, Joe stepped out, not up the
pike but down the dirt road that led past Cypress Hollow
Cemetery to Night Town.

The breezes were gentle but unusually restless and
variable tonight, like leprechaun squalls. Beyond the
drunken, whitewashed cemetery fence dim in the starlight, they rustled the scraggly trees of Cypress Hollow
and made it seem they were stroking their beards of Span-
ish moss. Joe sensed that the ghosts were just as restless
as the breezes, uncertain where and whom to haunt, or
whether to take the night off, drifting together in sorrowfully lecherous companionship. While among the trees,
the red-green vampire lights pulsed faintly and irregu-
larly, like sick fireflies or a plague-stricken space fleet.
The feeling of deep misery stuck with Joe and deepened,
and he was tempted to turn aside and curl up in any convenient tomb or around some half-toppled head board
and cheat his Wife and the other three behind him out of
a shared doom. He thought: Gonna roll the bones, gonna
roll 'em up and go to sleep. But while he was deciding, he
got past the sagged-open gate and the rest of the delirious
fence and Shantyville, too.

At first Night Town seemed dead as the rest of Ironmine, but then he noticed a faint glow, sick as the vampire lights but more feverish, and with it a jumping music,
tiny at first as a jazz for jitterbugging ants. He stepped
along the springy sidewalk, wistfully remembering the
days when the spring was all in his own legs and he'd
bound into a fight like a bobcat or a Martian sand-spider.
God, it had been years now since he had fought a real
fight, or felt *the power*. Gradually the midget music got
raucous as a bunnyhug for grizzly bears and loud as a

polka for elephants, while the glow became a riot of gas flares and flambeaux and corpse-blue mercury tubes and jiggling pink neon ones that all jeered at the stars where the spaceships roved. Next thing, he was facing a three-story false front flaring everywhere like a devil's rainbow with a pale blue topping of St. Elmo's fire. There were wide, swinging doors in the center of it, spilling light above and below. Above the doorway, golden calcium light scrawled over and over again with wild curlicues and flourishes, "The Boneyard," while a fiendish red kept printing out, "Gambling."

So the new place they'd all been talking about for so long had opened at last! For the first time that night, Joe Slattermill felt a stirring of real life in him and the faintest caress of excitement.

Gonna roll the bones, he thought.

He dusted off his blue-green work clothes with big, careless swipes and slapped his pockets to hear the clank. Then he threw back his shoulders and grinned his lips sneeringly and pushed through the swinging door as if giving a foe the straight-armed heel of his palm.

Inside, The Boneyard seemed to cover the area of a township, and the bar looked as long as the railroad tracks. Round pools of light on the green poker tables alternated with hourglass shapes of exciting gloom, through which drink girls and change girls moved like white-legged witches. By the jazz-stand in the distance, belly dancers made *their* white, hourglass shapes. The gamblers were thick and hunched down as mushrooms, all bald from agonizing over the fall of a card or a die or the dive of an ivory ball, while the Scarlet Women were like fields of poinsettia.

The calls of the croupiers and the slaps of dealt cards were as softly yet fatefully staccato as the rustle and beat of the jazz drums. Every tight-locked atom of the place was controlledly jumping. Even the dust motes jigged tensely in the cones of light.

Joe's excitement climbed, and he felt sift through him, like a breeze that heralds a gale, the faintest breath of a confidence which he knew could become a tornado. All thoughts of his house and Wife and Mother dropped out of his mind, while Mr. Guts remained only as a crazy young tom walking stiff-legged around the rim of his consciousness. Joe's own leg muscles twitched in sympathy, and he felt them grow supplely strong.

He coolly and searchingly looked the place over, his hand going out like it didn't belong to him to separate a drink from a passing, gently bobbing tray. Finally his gaze settled on what he judged to be the Number One Crap Table. All the Big Mushrooms seemed to be there, bald as the rest but standing tall as toadstools. Then through a gap in them, Joe saw on the other side of the table a figure still taller, but dressed in a long dark coat with collar turned up and a dark slouch hat pulled low so that only a triangle of white face showed. A suspicion and a hope rose in Joe, and he headed straight for the gap in the Big Mushrooms.

As he got nearer, the white-legged and shiny-topped drifters eddying out of his way, his suspicion received confirmation after confirmation, and his hope budded and swelled. Back from one end of the table was the fattest man he'd ever seen, with a long cigar and a silver vest and a gold tie clasp at least eight inches wide that just said in thick script, "Mr. Bones." Back a little from the other end was the nakedest change girl yet and the only one he'd seen whose tray, slung from her bare shoulders and indenting her belly just below her breasts, was stacked with gold in gleaming little towers and with jet-black chips. While the dice-girl, skinnier and taller and longer armed than his Wife even, didn't seem to be wearing much but a pair of long white gloves. She was all right if you went for the type that isn't much more than pale skin over bones with breasts like china doorknobs.

Beside each gambler was a high, round table for his chips. The one by the gap was empty. Snapping his fingers at the nearest silver change girl, Joe traded all his greasy dollars for an equal number of pale chips and tweaked her left nipple for luck. She playfully snapped her teeth toward his fingers.

Not hurrying but not wasting any time, he advanced and carelessly dropped his modest stacks on the empty table and took his place in the gap. He noted that the second Big Mushroom on his right had the dice. His heart but no other part of him gave an extra jump. Then he steadily lifted his eyes and looked straight across the table. The coat was a shimmering, elegant pillar of black

satin with jet buttons, the upturned collar of fine, dull
plush, black as the darkest cellar, as was the slouch hat
with down-turned brim and for band only a thin braid of
black horsehair. The arms of the coat were long, lesser
satin pillars, ending in slim, long-fingered hands that
moved swiftly when they did, but held each position of
rest with a statue's poise.

Joe still couldn't see much of the face except for smooth
lower forehead with never a bead or trickle of sweat—
the eyebrows were like straight snippets of the hat's braid
—and gaunt, aristocratic cheeks and narrow but somewhat flat nose. The complexion of the face wasn't as white
as Joe had first judged. There was a faint touch of brown
in it, like ivory that's just begun to age, or Venusian soap-
stone. Another glance at the hands confirmed this.

Behind the man in black was a knot of just about the
flashiest and nastiest customers, male or female, Joe had
ever seen. He knew from one look that each bedia-
monded, pomaded bully had a belly gun beneath the flap
of his flowered vest and a blackjack in his hip pocket, and
each snake-eyed sporting girl a stiletto in her garter and a
pearl-handled, silver-plated derringer under the sequined
silk in the hollow between her jutting breasts.

Yet at the same time Joe knew they were just trim-
mings. It was the man in black, their master, who was
the deadly one, the kind of man you know at a glance
you couldn't touch and live. If without asking you merely
laid a finger on his sleeve, no matter how lightly and respectfully, an ivory hand would move faster than thought
and you'd be stabbed or shot. Or maybe just the touch
would kill you, as if every black article of his clothing
were charged from his ivory skin outward with a high-
voltage, high-amperage ivory electricity. Joe looked at the
shadowed face again and decided he wouldn't care to try
it.

For it was the eyes that were the most impressive feature. All great gamblers have dark-shadowed, deep-set
eyes. But this one's eyes were sunk so deep you couldn't
even be sure you were getting a gleam of them. They
were inscrutability incarnate. They were unfathomable.
They were like black holes.

But all this didn't disappoint Joe one bit, though it did
terrify him considerably. On the contrary, it made him ex-

ult. His first suspicion was completely confirmed, and his hope spread into full flower.

This must be one of those really big gamblers who hit Ironmine only once a decade at most, come from the Big City on one of the river boats that ranged the watery dark like luxurious comets, spouting long thick tails of sparks from their sequoia-tall stacks with top foliage of curvy-snipped sheet iron. Or like silver space-liners with dozens of jewel-flamed jets, their portholes a-twinkle like ranks of marshaled asteroids.

For that matter, maybe some of those really big gamblers actually came from other planets where the night-time pace was hotter and the sporting life a delirium of risk and delight.

Yes, this was the kind of man Joe had always yearned to pit his skill against. He felt *the power* begin to tingle in his rock-still fingers, just a little.

Joe lowered his gaze to the crap table. It was almost as wide as a man is tall, at least twice as long, unusually deep, and lined with black, not green, felt so that it looked like a giant's coffin. There was something familiar about its shape, which he couldn't place. Its bottom, though not its sides or ends, had a twinkling iridescence, as if it had been lightly sprinkled with very tiny diamonds. As Joe lowered his gaze all the way and looked directly down, his eyes barely over the table, he got the crazy notion that it went down all the way through the world, so that the diamonds were the stars on the other side, visible despite the sunlight there, just as Joe was always able to see the stars by day up the shaft of the mine he worked in, and so that if a cleaned-out gambler, dizzy with defeat, toppled forward into it, he'd fall forever, toward the bottommost bottom, be it Hell or some black galaxy. Joe's thoughts swirled, and he felt the cold, hard-fingered clutch of fear at his crotch. Someone was crooning beside him, "Come on, Big Dick."

Then the dice, which had meanwhile passed to the Big Mushroom immediately on his right, came to rest near the table's center, contradicting and wiping out Joe's vision. But instantly there was another oddity to absorb him. The ivory dice were large and unusually round-cornered with dark red spots that gleamed like real rubies, but the spots were arranged in such a way that each

face looked like a miniature skull. For instance, the seven
thrown just now, by which the Big Mushroom to his right
had lost his point, which had been ten, consisted of a
two with the spots evenly spaced toward one side, like
eyes, instead of toward opposite corners, and of a five
with the same red eye-spots but also a central red nose
and two spots close together below that to make teeth.

The long, skinny, white-gloved arm of the dice-girl
snaked out like an albino cobra and scooped up the dice
and whisked them onto the rim of the table right in front
of Joe. He inhaled silently, picked up a single chip from
his table, and started to lay it beside the dice, then realized that wasn't the way things were done here, and put
it back. He would have liked to examine the chip more
closely, though. It was curiously lightweight and pale tan,
about the color of cream with a shot of coffee in it, and it
had embossed on its surface a symbol he could feel,
though not see. He didn't know what the symbol was, that
would have taken more feeling. Yet its touch had been
very good, setting the power tingling full-blast in his
shooting hand.

Joe looked casually yet swiftly at the faces around the
table, not missing the Big Gambler across from him, and
said quietly, "Roll a penny," meaning of course one pale
chip, or a dollar.

There was a hiss of indignation from all the Big Mushrooms, and the moonface of big-bellied Mr. Bones grew
purple as he started forward to summon his bouncers.

The Big Gambler raised a black-satined forearm and
sculptured hand, palm down. Instantly Mr. Bones froze
and the hissing stopped faster than that of a meteor prick
in self-sealing space steel. Then in a whispery, cultured
voice, without the faintest hint of derision, the man in
black said, "Get on him, gamblers."

Here, Joe thought, was a final confirmation of his suspicion, had it been needed. The really great gamblers
were always perfect gentlemen and generous to the poor.

With only the tiny, respectful hint of a guffaw, one of
the Big Mushrooms called to Joe, "You're faded."

Joe picked up the ruby-featured dice.

Now ever since he had first caught two eggs on one
plate, won all the marbles in Ironmine, and juggled six
alphabet blocks so they finally fell in a row on the rug

spelling "Mother," Joe Slattermill had been almost incredibly deft at precision throwing. In the mine he could carom a rock off a wall of ore to crack a rat's skull fifty feet away in the dark, and he sometimes amused himself by tossing little fragments of rock back into the holes from which they had fallen so that they stuck there, perfectly fitted in, for at least a second. Sometimes, by fast tossing, he could fit seven or eight fragments into the hole from which they had fallen, like putting together a puzzle block. If he could ever have got into space, Joe would undoubtedly have been able to pilot six Moonskimmers at once and do figure eights through Saturn's rings blindfold.

Now the only real difference between precision-tossing rocks or alphabet blocks and dice is that you have to bounce the latter off the end wall of a crap table, and that just made it a more interesting test of skill for Joe.

Rattling the dice now, he felt the power in his fingers and palm as never before.

He made a swift, low roll so that the bones ended up exactly in front of the white-gloved dice-girl. His natural seven was made up, as he'd intended, of a four and a three. In red-spot features they were like the five, except that both had only one tooth and the three no nose. Sort of baby-faced skulls. He had won a penny—that is, a dollar.

"Roll two cents," said Joe Slattermill.

This time, for variety, he made his natural with an eleven. The six was like the five, except it had three teeth, the best-looking skull of the lot.

"Roll a nickel less one."

Two big Mushrooms divided that bet with a covert smirk at each other.

Now Joe rolled a three and an ace. His point was four. The ace, with its single spot off center toward a side, still somehow looked like a skull—maybe of a Lilliputian Cyclops.

He took a while making his point, once absentmindedly rolling three successive tens the hard way. He wanted to watch the dice-girl scoop up the cubes. Each time it seemed to him that her snake-swift fingers went under the dice while they were still flat on the felt. Finally he decided it couldn't be an illusion. Although the dice couldn't penetrate the felt, her white-gloved fingers somehow could, dipping in a flash through the black, diamond-sparkling material as if it weren't there.

Right away the thought of a crap-table-size hole through the earth came back to Joe. This would mean that the dice were rolling and lying on a perfectly transparent flat surface, impenetrable for them but nothing else. Or maybe it was only the dice-girl's hands that could penetrate the surface, which would turn into a mere fantasy Joe's earlier vision of a cleaned-out gambler taking the Big Dive down that dreadful shaft, which made the deepest mine a mere pin dent.

Joe decided he had to know which was true. Unless absolutely unavoidable, he didn't want to take the chance of being troubled by vertigo at some crucial stage of the game.

He made a few more meaningless throws, from time to time crooning for realism, "Come on, Little Joe." Finally he settled on his plan. When he did at last make his point —the hard way, with two twos—he caromed the dice off the far corner so that they landed exactly in front of him. Then, after a minimum pause for his throw to be seen by the table, he shot his left hand down under the cubes, just a flicker ahead of the dice-girl's strike, and snatched them up.

Wow! Joe had never had a harder time in his life making his face and manner conceal what his body felt, not even when the wasp had stung him on the neck just as he had been for the first time putting his hand under the skirt of his prudish, fickle, demanding Wife-to-be. His fingers and the back of his hand were in as much agony as if he'd stuck them into a blast furnace. No wonder the dice-girl wore white gloves. They must be asbestos. And a good thing he hadn't used his shooting hand, he thought as he ruefully watched the blisters rise.

He remembered he'd been taught in school what Twenty-Mile Mine also demonstrated: that the earth was fearfully hot under its crust. The crap-table-size hole must pipe up that heat, so that any gambler taking the Big Dive would fry before he'd fallen a furlong and come out less than a cinder in China.

As if his blistered hand weren't bad enough, the Big Mushrooms were all hissing at him again and Mr. Bones had purpled once more and was opening his melon-size mouth to shout for his bouncers.

Once again a lift of the Big Gambler's hand saved Joe. The whispery, gentle voice called, "Tell him, Mr. Bones."

The latter roared toward Joe, "No gambler may pick up the dice he or any other gambler has shot. Only my dice-girl may do that. Rule of the house!"

Joe snapped Mr. Bones the barest nod. He said coolly, "Rolling a dime less two," and when that still peewee bet was covered, he shot Phoebe for his point and then fooled around for quite a while, throwing anything but a five or a seven, until the throbbing in his left hand should fade and all his nerves feel rock-solid again. There had never been the slightest alteration in the power in his right hand; he felt that strong as ever, or stronger.

Midway of this interlude, the Big Gambler bowed slightly but respectfully toward Joe, hooding those unfathomable eye sockets, before turning around to take a long black cigarette from his prettiest and evilest-looking sporting girl. Courtesy in the smallest matters, Joe thought, another mark of the master devotee of games of chance. The Big Gambler sure had himself a flash crew all right, though in idly looking them over again as he rolled, Joe noted one bummer toward the back who didn't fit in—a raggedy-elegant chap with the elf-locked hair and staring eyes and TB-spotted cheeks of a poet.

As he watched the smoke trickling up from under the black slouch hat, he decided that either the lights across the table had dimmed or else the Big Gambler's complexion was yet a shade darker than he'd thought at first. Or it might even be—wild fantasy—that the Big Gambler's skin was slowly darkening tonight, like a meerschaum pipe being smoked a mile a second. That was almost funny to think of—there was enough heat in this place, all right, to darken meerschaum, as Joe knew from sad experience, but so far as he was aware it was all under the table.

None of Joe's thoughts, either familiar or admiring, about the Big Gambler decreased in the slightest degree his certainty of the supreme menace of the man in black and his conviction that it would be death to touch him. And if any doubts had stirred in Joe's mind, they would have been squelched by the chilling incident which next occurred.

The Big Gambler had just taken into his arms his prettiest-evilest sporting girl and was running an aristocratic hand across her haunch with perfect gentility when the poet chap, green-eyed from jealousy and lovesickness, came leaping forward like a wildcat and aimed a long gleaming dagger at the black satin back.

Joe couldn't see how the blow could miss, but without taking his genteel right hand off the sporting girl's plush rear end, the Big Gambler shot out his left arm like a steel spring straightening. Joe couldn't tell whether he stabbed the poet chap in the throat, or judo-chopped him there, or gave him the Martian double-finger, or just touched him, but anyhow the fellow stopped as dead as if he'd been shot by a silent elephant gun or an invisible ray pistol, and he slammed down on the floor. A couple of darkies came running up to drag off the body and nobody paid the least attention, such episodes apparently being taken for granted at The Boneyard.

It gave Joe quite a turn, and he almost shot Phoebe before he intended to.

But by now the waves of pain had stopped running up his left arm, and his nerves were like metal-wrapped, new guitar strings, so three rolls later he shot a five, making his point, and set in to clean out the table.

He rolled nine successive naturals, seven sevens and two elevens, pyramiding his first wager of a single chip to a stake of over four thousand dollars. None of the Big Mushrooms had dropped out yet, but some of them were beginning to look worried and a couple were sweating. The Big Gambler still hadn't covered any part of Joe's bets, but he seemed to be following the play with interest from the cavernous depths of his eye sockets.

Then Joe got a devilish thought. Nobody could beat him tonight, he knew, but if he held onto the dice until the table was cleaned out, he'd never get a chance to see the Big Gambler exercise *his* skill, and he was truly curious about that. Besides, he thought, he ought to return courtesy for courtesy and have a crack at being a gentleman himself.

"Pulling out forty-one dollars less a nickel," he announced. "Rolling a penny."

This time there wasn't any hissing, and Mr. Bones's moonface didn't cloud over. But Joe was conscious that the Big Gambler was staring at him disappointedly, or sorrowfully, or maybe just speculatively.

Joe immediately crapped out by throwing boxcars, rather pleased to see the two best-looking tiny skulls grinning ruby-toothed side by side, and the dice passed to the Big Mushroom on his left.

"Knew when his streak was over," he heard another Big Mushroom mutter with grudging admiration.

The play worked rather rapidly around the table, nobody getting very hot and the stakes never more than medium high. "Shoot a fin." "Rolling a sawbuck." "An Andrew Jackson." "Rolling thirty bucks." Now and then Joe covered part of a bet, winning more than he lost. He had over seven thousand dollars, real money, before the bones got around to the Big Gambler.

That one held the dice for a long moment on his statue-steady palm while he looked at them reflectively, though not the hint of a furrow appeared in his almost brownish forehead down which never a bead of sweat trickled. He murmured. "Rolling a double sawbuck," and when he had been faded, he closed his fingers, lightly rattled the cubes—the sound was like big seeds inside a small gourd only half dry—and negligently cast the dice toward the end of the table.

It was a throw like none Joe had ever seen before at any crap table. The dice traveled flat through the air without turning over, struck the exact juncture of the table's end and bottom, and stopped there dead, showing a natural seven.

Joe was distinctly disappointed. On one of his own throws, he was used to calculating something like, "Launch three-up, five north, two and a half rolls in the air, hit on the six-five-three corner, three-quarter roll and a one-quarter side-twist right, hit end on the one-two edge, one-half reverse role and three-quarter side-twist left, land on five face, roll over twice, come up two," and that would be for just one of the dice, and a really commonplace throw, without extra bounces.

By comparison, the technique of the Big Gambler had been ridiculously, abysmally, horrifyingly simple. Joe could have duplicated it with the greatest ease, of course.

It was no more than an elementary form of his old pastime of throwing fallen rocks back into their holes. But Joe had never once thought of pulling such a babyish trick at the crap table. It would make the whole thing too easy and destroy the beauty of the game.

Another reason Joe had never used the trick was that he'd never dreamed he'd be able to get away with it. By all the rules he'd ever heard of, it was a most questionable throw. There was the possibility that one or the other die hadn't completely reached the end of the table or lay a wee bit cocked against the end. Besides, he reminded himself, weren't both dice supposed to rebound off the end, if only for a fraction of an inch?

However, as far as Joe's very sharp eyes could see, both dice lay perfectly flat and sprang up against the end wall. Moreover, everyone else at the table seemed to accept the throw, the dice-girl had scooped up the cubes, and the Big Mushrooms who had faded the man in black were paying off. As far as the rebound business went, well, The Boneyard appeared to put a slightly different interpretation on the rule, and Joe believed in never questioning House Rules except in dire extremity—both his Mother and Wife had long since taught him it was the least troublesome way.

Besides, there hadn't been any of his own money riding on that roll.

In a voice like wind through Cypress Hollow or on Mars, the Big Gambler announced, "Roll a century." It was the biggest bet yet tonight, ten thousand dollars, and the way the Big Gambler said it made it seem something more than that. A hush fell on The Boneyard, they put the mutes on the jazz horns, the croupiers' calls became more confidential, the cards fell softlier, even the roulette balls seemed to be trying to make less noise as they rattled into their cells. The crowd around the Number One Crap Table quietly thickened. The Big Gambler's flash boys and girls formed a double semicircle around him, ensuring him lots of elbow room.

That century bet, Joe realized, was thirty bucks more than his own entire pile. Three or four of the Big Mushrooms had to signal each other before they'd agreed how to fade it.

The Big Gambler shot another natural seven with exactly the same flat, stop-dead throw.

He bet another century and did it again.

And again.

And again.

Joe was getting mighty concerned and pretty indignant, too. It seemed unjust that the Big Gambler should be winning such huge bets with such machinelike, utterly unromantic rolls. Why, you couldn't even call them rolls, the dice never turned over an iota, in the air or after. It was the sort of thing you'd expect from a robot, and a very dully programed robot at that. Joe hadn't risked any of his own chips fading the Big Gambler, of course, but if things went on like this he'd have to. Two of the Big Mushrooms had already retired sweatingly from the table, confessing defeat, and no one had taken their places. Pretty soon there'd be a bet the remaining Big Mushrooms couldn't entirely cover between them, and then he'd have to risk some of his own chips or else pull out of the game himself—and he couldn't do that, not with the power surging in his right hand like chained lightning.

Joe waited and waited for someone else to question one of the Big Gambler's shots, but no one did. He realized that, despite his efforts to look imperturbable, his face was slowly reddening.

With a little lift of his left hand, the Big Gambler stopped the dice-girl as she was about to snatch at the cubes. The eyes that were like black wells directed themselves at Joe, who forced himself to look back into them steadily. He still couldn't catch the faintest gleam in them. All at once he felt the lightest touch-on-neck of a dreadful suspicion.

With the utmost civility and amiability, the Big Gambler whispered, "I believe that the fine shooter across from me has doubts about the validity of my last throw, though he is too much of a gentleman to voice them. Lottie, the card test."

The wraith-tall, ivory dice-girl plucked a playing card from below the table, and with a venomous flash of her little white teeth spun it low across the table through the air at Joe. He caught the whirling pasteboard and examined it briefly. It was the thinnest, stiffest, flattest, shiniest playing card Joe had ever handled. It was also the Joker, if that meant anything. He spun it back lazily into her hand, and she slid it very gently, letting it descend by its own weight, down the end wall against which the two dice lay. It came to rest in the tiny hollow their rounded edges made against the black felt. She deftly moved it about without force, demonstrating that there was no space between either of the cubes and the table's end at any point.

"Satisfied?" the Big Gambler asked. Rather against his will, Joe nodded. The Big Gambler bowed to him. The dice-girl smirked her short, thin lips and drew herself up, flaunting her white-china-doorknob breasts at Joe.

Casually, almost with an air of boredom, the Big Gambler returned to his routine of shooting a century and making a natural seven. The Big Mushrooms wilted fast and one by one tottered away from the table. A particularly pink-faced Toadstool was brought extra cash by a gasping runner, but it was no help, he only lost the additional centuries. While the stacks of pale and black chips beside the Big Gambler grew skyscraper-tall.

Joe got more and more furious and frightened. He watched like a hawk or spy satellite the dice nesting against the end wall, but never could spot justification for calling for another card test, or nerve himself to question the House Rules at this late date. It was maddening, in fact insanitizing, to know that if only he could get the cubes once more he could shoot circles around that black pillar of sporting aristocracy. He damned himself a googolplex of ways for the idiotic, conceited, suicidal impulse that had led him to let go of the bones when he'd had them.

To make matters worse, the Big Gambler had taken to gazing steadily at Joe with those eyes like coal mines. Now he made three rolls running without even glancing at the dice or the end wall, as far as Joe could tell. Why, he was getting as bad as Joe's Wife or Mother—watching, watching, watching Joe.

But the constant staring of those eyes that were not eyes was mostly throwing a terrific scare into him. Supernatural terror added itself to his certainty of the deadliness of the Big Gambler. Just who, Joe kept asking himself, had he got into a game with tonight? There was curiosity and there was dread—a dreadful curiosity as strong as his desire to get the bones and win. His hair rose, and he was all over goose bumps, though the power was still pulsing in his hand like a braked locomotive or a rocket wanting to lift from the pad.

At the same time the Big Gambler stayed just that—a black satin-coated, slouch-hatted elegance, suave, courtly, lethal. In fact, almost the worst thing about the spot Joe found himself in was that after admiring the Big Gambler's perfect sportsmanship all night, he must now be disenchanted by his machinelike throwing and try to catch him out on any technicality he could.

The remorseless mowing down of the Big Mushrooms went on. The empty spaces outnumbered the Toadstools. Soon there were only three left.

The Boneyard had grown still as Cypress Hollow or the Moon. The jazz had stopped and the gay laughter and the shuffle of feet and the squeak of goosed girls and the clink of drinks and coins. Everybody seemed to be gathered around the Number One Crap Table, rank on silent rank.

Joe was racked by watchfulness, sense of injustice, self-contempt, wild hopes, curiosity, and dread. Especially the last two.

The complexion of the Big Gambler, as much as you could see of it, continued to darken. For one wild moment Joe found himself wondering if he'd got into a game with a nigger, maybe a witchcraft-drenched Voodoo Man whose white make-up was wearing off.

Pretty soon there came a century wager which the two remaining Big Mushrooms couldn't fade between them. Joe had to make up a sawbuck from his miserably tiny pile or get out of the game. After a moment's agonizing hesitation, he did the former.

And lost his ten.

The two Big Mushrooms reeled back into the hushed crowd.

Pit-black eyes bored into Joe. A whisper: "Rolling your pile."

Joe felt well up in him the shameful impulse to confess himself licked and run home. At least his six-thousand dollars would make a bit with his Wife and Ma.

But he just couldn't bear to think of the crowd's laughter or the thought of living with himself knowing that he'd had a final chance, however slim, to challenge the Big Gambler and passed it up.

He nodded.

The Big Gambler shot. Joe leaned out over and down the table, forgetting his vertigo, as he followed the throw with eagle or space-telescope eyes.

"Satisfied?"

Joe knew he ought to say, "Yes," and slink off with head held as high as he could manage. It was the gentlemanly thing to do. But then he reminded himself that he wasn't a gentleman, but just a dirty, working-stiff miner with a talent for precision hurling.

He also knew that it was probably very dangerous for him to say anything but "Yes," surrounded as he was by enemies and strangers. But then he asked himself what right had he, a miserable, mortal, homebound failure, to worry about danger.

Besides, one of the ruby-grinning dice looked just the tiniest hair out of line with the other.

It was the biggest effort yet of Joe's life, but he swallowed and managed to say, "No. Lottie, the card test."

The dice-girl fairly snarled and reared up and back as if she were going to spit in his eyes, and Joe had a feeling her spit was cobra venom. But the Big Gambler lifted a finger at her in reproof, and she skimmed the card at Joe, yet so low and viciously that it disappeared under the black felt for an instant before flying up into Joe's hand.

It was hot to the touch and singed a pale brown all over, though otherwise unimpaired. Joe gulped and spun it back high.

Sneering poisoned daggers at him, Lottie let it glide down the end wall . . . and after a moment's hesitation, it slithered behind the die Joe had suspected.

A bow and then the whisper: "You have sharp eyes, sir. Undoubtedly that die failed to reach the wall. My sincerest apologies and . . . your dice, sir."

Seeing the cubes sitting on the black rim in front of him almost gave Joe apoplexy. All the feelings racking him, including his curiosity, rose to an almost unbelievable pitch of intensity, and when he'd said, "Rolling my pile," and the Big Gambler had replied, "You're faded," he yielded to an uncontrollable impulse and cast the two dice straight at the Big Gambler's ungleaming, midnight eyes.

They went right through into the Big Gambler's skull

and bounced around inside there, rattling like big seeds in a big gourd not quite yet dry.

Throwing out a hand, palm back, to either side to indicate that none of his boys or girls or anyone else must make a reprisal on Joe, the Big Gambler dryly gargled the two cubical bones, then spat them out so that they landed in the center of the table, the one die flat, the other leaning against it.

"Cocked dice, sir," he whispered as graciously as if no indignity whatever had been done him. "Roll again."

Joe shook the dice reflectively, getting over the shock. After a little bit he decided that though he could now guess the Big Gambler's real name, he'd still give him a run for his money.

A little corner of Joe's mind wondered how a live skeleton hung together. Did the bones still have gristle and thews, were they wired, was it done with force-fields, or was each bone a calcium magnet clinging to the next?— this tying in somehow with the generation of the deadly ivory electricity.

In the great hush of The Boneyard, someone cleared his throat, a Scarlet Woman tittered hysterically, a coin fell from the nakedest change girl's tray with a golden clink and rolled musically across the floor.

"Silence," the Big Gambler commanded and in a movement almost too fast to follow whipped a hand inside the bosom of his coat and out to the crap table's rim in front of him. A short-barreled, silver revolver lay softly gleaming there. "Next creature, from the humblest nigger night-girl to you, Mr. Bones, who utters a sound while my worthy opponent rolls, gets a bullet in the head."

Joe gave him a courtly bow back, it felt funny, and then decided to start his run with a natural seven made up of an ace and a six. He rolled and this time the Big Gambler, judging from the movements of his skull, closely followed the course of the cubes with his eyes that weren't there.

The dice landed, rolled over, and lay still. Incredulously, Joe realized that for the first time in his crapshooting life he'd made a mistake. Or else there was a power in the Big Gambler's gaze greater than that in his own right hand. The six cube had come down okay, but the ace had taken an extra half-roll and come down six, too.

"End of the game," Mr. Bones boomed sepulchrally.

The Big Gambler raised a brown skeletal hand. "Not necessarily," he whispered. His black eyepits aimed themselves at Joe like the mouths of siege guns. "Joe Slattermill, you still have something of value to wager, if you wish. Your life."

At that a giggling and a hysterical tittering and a guffawing and a braying and shrieking burst uncontrollably out of the whole Boneyard. Mr. Bones summed up the sentiments when he bellowed over the rest of the racket, "Now what use or value is there in the life of a bummer like Joe Slattermill? Not two cents, ordinary money."

The Big Gambler laid a hand on the revolver gleaming before him, and all the laughter died.

"I have a use for it," the Big Gambler whispered. "Joe Slattermill, on my part I will venture all my winnings of tonight, and throw in the world and everything in it for a side bet. You will wager your life, and on the side your soul. You to roll the dice. What's your pleasure?"

Joe Slattermill quailed, but then the drama of the situation took hold of him. He thought it over and realized he certainly wasn't going to give up being stage center in a spectacle like this to go home broke to his Wife and Mother and decaying house and the dispirited Mr. Guts. Maybe, he told himself encouragingly, there wasn't a power in the Big Gambler's gaze, maybe Joe had just made his one and only crap-shooting error. Besides, he was more inclined to accept Mr. Bones's assessment of the value of his life than the Big Gambler's.

"It's a bet," he said.

"Lottie, give him the dice."

Joe concentrated his mind as never before, the power tingled triumphantly in his hand, and he made his throw.

The dice never hit the felt. They went swooping down, then up, in a crazy curve far out over the end of the table, and then came streaking back like tiny red-glinting meteors toward the face of the Big Gambler, where they suddenly nested and hung in his black eye sockets, each with the single red gleam of an ace showing.

Snake eyes.

The whisper, as those red-glinting dice-eyes stared

mockingly at him: "Joe Slattermill, you've crapped out."

Using thumb and middle finger—or bone rather—of either hand, the Big Gambler removed the dice from his eye sockets and dropped them in Lottie's white-gloved hand.

"Yes, you've crapped out, Joe Slattermill," he went on tranquilly. "And now you can shoot yourself"— he touched the silver gun—"or cut your throat"—he whipped a gold-handled bowie knife out of his coat and laid it beside the revolver—"or poison yourself"—the two weapons were joined by a small black bottle with white skull and crossbones on it—"or Miss Flossie here can kiss you to death." He drew forward beside him his prettiest, evilest-looking sporting girl. She preened herself and flounced her short, violet skirt and gave Joe a provocative, hungry look, lifting her carmine upper lip to show her long white canines.

"Or else," the Big Gambler added, nodding significantly toward the black-bottomed crap table, "you can take the Big Dive."

Joe said evenly, "I'll take the Big Dive."

He put his right foot on his empty chip table, his left on the black rim, fell forward . . . and suddenly kicking off from the rim, launched himself in a tiger spring straight across the crap table at the Big Gambler's throat, solacing himself with the thought that certainly the poet chap hadn't seemed to suffer long.

As he flashed across the exact center of the table, he got an instant photograph of what really lay below, but his brain had no time to develop that snapshot, for the next instant he was plowing into the Big Gambler.

Stiffened brown palm edge caught him in the temple with a lightninglike judo chop . . . and the brown fingers or bones flew all apart like puff paste. Joe's left hand went through the Big Gambler's chest as if there were nothing there but black satin coat, while his right hand, straight-armedly clawing at the slouch-hatted skull, crunched it to pieces. Next instant Joe was sprawled on the floor with some black clothes and brown fragments.

He was on his feet in a flash and snatching at the Big Gambler's tall stacks. He had time for one left-handed grab. He couldn't see any gold or silver or any black chips, so he stuffed his left pants pocket with a handful of the pale chips and ran.

Then the whole population of The Boneyard was on him and after him. Teeth, knives, and brass knuckles flashed. He was punched, clawed, kicked, tripped, and stamped on with spike heels. A gold-plated trumpet with a bloodshot-eyed black face behind it bopped him on the head. He got a white flash of the golden dice-girl and made a grab for her, but she got away. Someone tried to mash a lighted cigar in his eye. Lottie, writhing and flailing like a white boa constrictor, almost got a simultaneous strangle hold and scissors on him. From a squat, wide-mouth bottle, Flossie, snarling like a feline fiend, threw what smelt like acid past his face. Mr. Bones peppered shots around him from the silver revolver. He was stabbed at, gouged, rabbit-punched, scragmauled, slugged, kneed, bitten, bearhugged, butted, beaten and had his toes trampled.

But somehow none of the blows or grabs had much real force. It was like fighting ghosts. In the end it turned out that the whole population of The Boneyard, working together, had just a little more strength than Joe. He felt himself being lifted by a multitude of hands and pitched out through the swinging doors so that he thudded down on his rear end on the board sidewalk. Even that didn't hurt much. It was more like a kick of encouragement.

He took a deep breath and felt himself over and worked his bones. He didn't seem to have suffered any serious damage. He stood up and looked around. The Boneyard was dark and silent as the grave, or the planet Pluto, or all the rest of Ironmine. As his eyes got accustomed to the starlight and occasional roving spaceship-gleam, he saw a padlocked, sheet-iron door where the swinging ones had been.

He found he was chewing on something crusty that he'd somehow carried in his right hand all the way through the final fracas. Mighty tasty, like the bread his Wife baked for best customers. At that instant his brain developed the photograph it had taken when he had glanced down as he flashed across the center of the crap table. It was a thin wall of flames moving sideways across the table and just beyond the flames the faces of his Wife, Mother, and Mr. Guts, all looking very surprised. He realized that what he was chewing was a fragment of the Big Gambler's skull, and he remembered the shape of the three loaves his Wife had started to bake when he left the house. And he understood the magic shed made to let him get a little ways away and feel half a man, and then come diving home with his fingers burned.

He spat out what was in his mouth and pegged the rest of the bit of giant-popover skull across the street.

He fished in his left pocket. Most of the pale poker chips had been mashed in the fight, but he found a whole one and explored its surface with his fingertips. The symbol embossed on it was a cross. He lifted it to his lips and took a bite. It tasted delicate but delicious. He ate it and felt his strength revive. He patted his bulging left pocket. At least he'd start out well-provisioned.

Then he turned and headed straight for home, but he took the long way, around the world.

BEHOLD THE MAN

by Michael Moorcock

He has no material power as the god-emperors had; he has only a following of desert people and fishermen. They tell him he is a god; he believes them. The followers of Alexander said: "He is unconquerable, therefore he is a god." The followers of this man do not think at all; he was their act of spontaneous creation. Now he leads them, this madman called Jesus of Nazareth.

And he spoke, saying unto them: Yeah verily I *was* Karl Glogauer and now I am Jesus the Messiah, the Christ.

And it was so.

I

The time machine was a sphere full of milky fluid in which the traveler floated, enclosed in a rubber suit, breathing through a mask attached to a hose leading to the wall of the machine. The sphere cracked as it landed, and the fluid spilled into the dust and was soaked up. Instinctively Glogauer curled himself into a ball as the level of the liquid fell and he sank to the yielding plastic of the sphere's inner lining. The instruments, cryptographic, unconventional, were still and silent. The sphere shifted and rolled as the last of the liquid dripped from the gash in its side.

Momentarily, Glogauer's eyes opened and closed, then his mouth stretched in a kind of yawn, and his tongue fluttered, and he uttered a groan that turned into a ululation.

He heard himself. The Voice of Tongues, he thought. The language of the unconscious. But he could not guess what he was saying.

His body became numb, and he shivered. His passage through time had not been easy and even the thick fluid had not wholly protected him, though it had doubtless saved his life. Some ribs were certainly broken. Painfully, he straightened his arms and legs and began to crawl over the slippery plastic towards the crack in the machine. He could see harsh sunlight, a sky like shimmering steel. He pulled himself halfway through the crack, closing his eyes as the full strength of the sunlight struck them. He lost consciousness.

Christmas term, 1949. He was nine years old, born two years after his father had reached England from Austria.

The other children were screaming with laughter in the gravel of the playground. The game had begun earnestly enough, and somewhat nervously Karl had joined in in the same spirit. Now he was crying.

"Let me *down!* Please, Mervyn, stop it!"

They had tied him with his arms spreadeagled against the wire-netting of the playground fence. It bulged outwards under his weight, and one of the posts threatened to come loose. Mervyn Williams, the boy who had proposed the game, began to shake the post so that Karl was swung heavily back and forth on the netting.

"Stop it!"

He saw that his cries only encouraged them, and he clenched his teeth, becoming silent.

He slumped, pretending unconsciousness; the school ties they had used as bonds cut into his wrists. He heard the children's voices drop.

"Is he all right?" Molly Turner was whispering.

"He's only kidding," Williams replied uncertainly.

He felt them untying him, their fingers fumbling with the knots. Deliberately he sagged, then fell to his knees, grazing them on the gravel, and dropped face down to the ground.

Distantly, for he was half-convinced by his own deception, he heard their worried voices.

Williams shook him.

"Wake up, Karl. Stop mucking about."

He stayed where he was, losing his sense of time until he heard Mr. Matson's voice over the general babble.

"What on earth were you doing, Williams?"

"It was a play, sir, about Jesus. Karl was being Jesus. We tied him to the fence. It was his idea, sir. It was only a game, sir."

Karl's body was stiff, but he managed to stay still, breathing shallowly.

"He's not a strong boy like you, Williams. You should have known better."

"I'm sorry, sir. I'm really sorry." Williams sounded as if he were crying.

Karl felt himself lifted; felt the triumph. . . .

He was being carried along. His head and side were so painful that he felt sick. He had had no chance to discover where exactly the time machine had brought him, but turning his head now, he could see by the way the man on his right was dressed that he was at least in the Middle East.

He had meant to land in the year 29 A.D. in the wilderness beyond Jerusalem, near Bethlehem. Were they taking him to Jerusalem now?

He was on a stretcher that was apparently made of animal skins; this indicated that he was probably in the past, at any rate. Two men were carrying the stretcher on their shoulders. Others walked on both sides. There was a smell of sweat and animal fat and a musty smell he could not identify. They were walking towards a line of hills in the distance.

He winced as the stretcher lurched and the pain in his side increased. For the second time he passed out.

He woke up briefly, hearing voices. They were speaking what was evidently some form of Aramaic. It was night, perhaps, for it seemed very dark. They were no longer moving. There was straw beneath him. He was relieved. He slept.

> *In those days came John the Baptist preaching in the wilderness of Judaea, And saying, Repent ye: for the kingdom of heaven is at hand. For this is he that was spoken of by the prophet Esaias, saying,*

> *The voice of one crying in the wilderness, Prepare*
> *ye the way of the Lord, make his paths straight. And*
> *the same John had his raiment of camel's hair, and*
> *a leathern girdle about his loins; and his meat*
> *was locusts and wild honey. Then went out to him*
> *Jerusalem, and all Judaea, and all the region round*
> *about Jordan, And were baptized of him in Jordan,*
> *confessing their sins.*
>
> (Matthew 3:1–6)

They were washing him. He felt the cold water running over his naked body. They had managed to strip off his protective suit. There were now thick layers of cloth against his ribs on the right, and bands of leather bound them to him.

He felt very weak now, and hot, but there was less pain.

He was in a building—or perhaps a cave; it was too gloomy to tell—lying on a heap of straw that was saturated by the water. Above him, two men continued to sluice water down on him from their earthenware pots. They were stern-faced, heavily-bearded men in cotton robes.

He wondered if he could form a sentence they might understand. His knowledge of written Aramaic was good, but he was not sure of certain pronunciations.

He cleared his throat. "Where—be—this—place?"

They frowned, shaking their heads and lowering their water jars.

"I—seek—a—Nazarene—Jesus. . . ."

"Nazarene. Jesus." One of the men repeated the words, but they did not seem to mean anything to him. He shrugged.

The other, however, only repeated the word Nazarene, speaking it slowly as if it had some special significance for him. He muttered a few words to the other man and went towards the entrance of the room.

Karl Glogauer continued to try to say something the remaining man would understand.

"What—year—doth—the Roman Emperor—sit—in Rome?"

It was a confusing question to ask, he realized. He knew Christ had been crucified in the fifteenth year of Tiberius' reign, and that was why he had asked the question. He tried to phrase it better.

"How many—year—doth Tiberius rule?"

"Tiberius?" The man frowned.

Glogauer's ear was adjusting to the accent now, and he tried to simulate it better. "Tiberius. The emperor of the Romans. How many years has he ruled?"

"How many?" The man shook his head. "I know not."

At least Glogauer had managed to make himself understood.

"Where is this place?" he asked.

"It is the wilderness beyond Machaerus," the man replied. "Know you not that?"

Machaerus lay to the southeast of Jerusalem on the other side of the Dead Sea. There was no doubt that he was in the past and that the period was sometime in the reign of Tiberius for the man had recognized the name easily enough.

His companion was now returning, bringing with him a huge fellow with heavily muscled, hairy arms and a great barrel chest. He carried a big staff in one hand. He was dressed in animal skins and was well over six feet tall. His black, curly hair was long, and he had a black, bushy beard that covered the upper half of his chest. He moved like an animal, and his large, piercing brown eyes looked reflectively at Glogauer.

When he spoke, it was in a deep voice, but too rapidly for Glogauer to follow. It was Glogauer's turn to shake his head.

The big man squatted down beside him. "Who art thou?"

Glogauer paused. He had not planned to be found in this way. He had intended to disguise himself as a traveler from Syria, hoping that the local accents would be different enough to explain his own unfamiliarity with the language. He decided that it was best to stick to this story and hope for the best.

"I am from the north," he said.

"Not from Egypt?" the big man asked. It was as if he had expected Glogauer to be from there. Glogauer decided that if this was what the big man thought, he might just as well agree to it.

"I came out of Egypt two years since," he said.

The big man nodded, apparently satisfied. "So you are a magus from Egypt. That is what we thought. And your name is Jesus, and you are the Nazarene."

"I *seek* Jesus, the Nazarene," Glogauer said.

"Then what is your name?" The man seemed disappointed.

Glogauer could not give his own name. It would sound too strange to them. On impulse, he gave his father's first name. "Emmanuel," he said.

The man nodded, again satisfied. "Emmanuel."

Glogauer realized belatedly that the choice of name had been an unfortunate one in the circumstances, for Emmanuel meant in Hebrew "God with us" and doubtless had a mystic significance for his questioner.

"And what is your name?" he asked.

The man straightened up, looking broodingly down on Glogauer. "You do not know me? You have not heard of John, called the Baptist?"

Glogauer tried to hide his surprise, but evidently John the Baptist saw that his name was familiar. He nodded his shaggy head. "You do know of me, I see. Well, magus, now I must decide, eh?"

"What must you decide?" Glogauer asked nervously.

"If you be the friend of the prophecies or the false one we have been warned against by Adonai. The Romans would deliver me into the hands of mine enemies, the children of Herod."

"Why is that?"

"You must know why, for I speak against the Romans who enslave Judaea, and I speak against the unlawful things that Herod does, and I prophesy the time when all those who are not righteous shall be destroyed and Adonai's kingdom will be restored on Earth as the old prophets said it would be. I say to the people, 'Be ready for that day when ye shall take up the sword to do Adonai's will.' The unrighteous know that they will perish on this day, and they would destroy me."

Despite the intensity of his words, John's tone was matter of fact. There was no hint of insanity or fanaticism in his face or bearing. He sounded most of all like an Anglican vicar reading a sermon whose meaning for him had lost its edge.

The essence of what he said, Karl Glogauer realized, was that he was arousing the people to throw out the Romans and their puppet Herod and establish a more "righteous" regime. The attributing of this plan to "Adonai" (one of the spoken names of Jahweh and meaning The Lord) seemed, as many scholars had guessed in the twentieth century, a means of giving the plan extra weight. In a world where politics and religion, even in the west, were inextricably bound together, it was necessary to ascribe a supernatural origin to the plan.

Indeed, Glogauer thought, it was more than likely that John believed his idea had been inspired by God, for the Greeks on the other side of the Mediterranean had not yet stopped arguing about the origins of inspiration—whether it originated in a man's head or was placed there by the gods. That John accepted him as an Egyptian magician of some kind did not surprise Glogauer particularly, either. The circumstances of his arrival must have seemed extraordinarily miraculous and at the same time accept- able, particularly to a sect like the Essenes who practiced self-mortification and starvation and must be quite used to seeing visions in this hot wilderness. There was no doubt now that these people were the neurotic Essenes, whose ritual washing—baptism—and self-deprivation, coupled with the almost paranoiac mysticism that led them to invent secret languages and the like, was a sure indication of their mentally unbalanced condition. All this occurred to Glogauer the psychiatrist manqué, but Glogauer the man was torn between the poles of extreme rationalism and the desire to be convinced by the mysti- cism itself.

"I must meditate," John said, turning toward the cave entrance. "I must pray. You will remain here until guid- ance is sent to me."

He left the cave, striding rapidly away.

Glogauer sank back on the wet straw. He was without doubt in a limestone cave, and the atmosphere in the cave was surprisingly humid. It must be very hot outside. He felt drowsy.

II

Five years in the past. Nearly two thousand in the future. Lying in the hot, sweaty bed with Monica. Once again, another attempt to make normal love had metamor- phosed into the performance of minor aberrations, which seemed to satisfy her better than anything else.

Their real courtship and fulfillment was yet to come. As usual, it would be verbal. As usual, it would find its climax in argumentative anger.

"I suppose you're going to tell me you're not satisfied again." She accepted the lighted cigarette he handed to her in the darkness.

"I'm all right," he said.

There was silence for a while as they smoked.

Eventually, and in spite of knowing what the result would be if he did so, he found himself talking.

"It's ironic, isn't it?" he began.

He waited for her reply. She would delay for a little while yet.

"What is?" she said at last.

"All this. You spend all day trying to help sexual neurotics to become normal. You spend your nights doing what they do."

"Not to the same extent. You know it's all a matter of degree."

"So you say."

He turned his head and looked at her face in the starlight from the window. She was a gaunt-featured redhead with the calm, professional seducer's voice of the psychiatric social worker that she was. It was a voice that was soft, reasonable, and insincere. Only occasionally, when she became particularly agitated, did her voice begin to indicate her real character. Her features never seemed to be in repose, even when she slept. Her eyes were forever wary, her movements rarely spontaneous. Every inch of her was protected, which was probably why she got so little pleasure from ordinary lovemaking.

"You just can't let yourself go, can you?" he said.

"Oh, shut up, Karl. Have a look at yourself if you're looking for a neurotic mess."

Both were amateur psychiatrists—she a psychiatric social worker, he merely a reader, a dabbler, though he had done a year's study some time ago when he had planned to become a psychiatrist. They used the terminology of psychiatry freely. They felt happier if they could name something.

He rolled away from her, groping for the ashtray on the bedside table, catching a glance of himself in the dressing table mirror. He was a sallow, intense, moody Jewish bookseller with a head full of images and unresolved obsessions, a body full of emotions. He always lost these arguments with Monica. Verbally she was the dominant one. This kind of exchange often seemed to him more perverse than their lovemaking, where usually at least his role was masculine. Essentially, he realized, he was passive, masochistic, indecisive. Even his anger, which came frequently, was impotent. Monica was ten years older than he was, ten years more bitter. As an individual, of course, she had far more dynamism than he had; but as a psychiatric social worker she had had just as many failures. She plugged on, becoming increasingly cynical on the surface but still, perhaps, hoping for a few spectacular successes with patients. They tried to do too much, that was the trouble, he thought. The priests in the confessional supplied a panacea; the psychiatrists tried to cure, and most of the time they failed. But at least they tried, he thought, and then wondered if that was, after all, a virtue.

"I did look at myself," he said.

Was she sleeping? He turned. Her wary eyes were still open, looking out of the window.

"I did look at myself," he repeated. "The way Jung did. 'How can I help those persons if I am myself a fugitive and perhaps also suffer from the *morbus sacer* of a neurosis?' That's what Jung asked himself . . ."

"That old sensationalist. That old rationalizer of his own mysticism. No wonder you never became a psychiatrist."

"I wouldn't have been any good. It was nothing to do with Jung. . ."

"Don't take it out on me. . ."

"You've told me yourself that you feel the same—you think it's useless. . ."

"After a hard week's work, I might say that. Give me another fag."

He opened the packet on the bedside table and put two cigarettes in his mouth, lighting them and handing one to her.

Almost abstractedly, he noticed that the tension was increasing. The argument was, as ever, pointless. But it was not the argument that was the important thing; it was simply the expression of the essential relationship.

He wondered if that was in any way important, either.

"You're not telling the truth." He realized that there was no stopping now that the ritual was in full swing.

"I'm telling the practical truth. I've no compulsion to give up my work. I've no wish to be a failure. . ."

"Failure? You're more melodramatic than I am."

"You're too earnest, Karl. You want to get out of yourself a bit."

He sneered. "If I were you, I'd give up my work, Monica. You're no more suited for it than I was."

She shrugged. "You're a petty bastard."

"I'm not jealous of you if that's what you think. You'll never understand what I'm looking for."

Her laugh was artificial, brittle. "Modern man in search of a soul, eh? Modern man in search of a crutch, I'd say. And you can take that any way you like."

"We're destroying the myths that make the world go round."

"Now you say 'And what are we putting in their place?' You're stale and stupid, Karl. You've never looked rationally at anything—including yourself."

"What of it? You say the myth is unimportant."

"The reality that creates it is important."

"Jung knew that the myth can also create the reality."

He stretched his legs. In doing so, he touched hers and he recoiled. He scratched his head. She still lay there smoking, but she was smiling now.

"Come on," she said. "Let's have some stuff about Christ."

He said nothing. She handed him the stub of her cigarette, and he put it in the ashtray. He looked at his watch. It was two o'clock in the morning.

"Why do we do it?" he said.

"Because we must." She put her hand to the back of his head and pulled it towards her breast. "What else can we do?"

We Protestants must sooner or later face this question: Are we to understand the "imitation of Christ" in the sense that we should copy his life and, if I may use the expression, ape his stigmata; or in the deeper sense that we are to live our own proper lives as truly as he lived his in all its implications? It is no easy matter to live a life that is modeled on Christ's, but it is unspeakably harder to live one's own life as truly as Christ lived his. Anyone who did this would . . . be misjudged, derided, tortured, and crucified. . . . A neurosis is a dissociation of personality.

(JUNG, Modern Man in Search of a Soul)

For a month, John the Baptist was away and Glogauer lived with the Essenes, finding it surprisingly easy as his ribs mended to join in their daily life. The Essenes' township consisted of a mixture of single-story houses, built of limestone and clay brick, and the caves that were to be found on both sides of the shallow valley. The Essenes shared their goods in common, and this particular sect had wives, though many Essenes led completely monastic lives. The Essenes were also pacifists, refusing to own or to make weapons—yet this sect plainly tolerated the warlike Baptist. Perhaps their hatred of the Romans overcame their principles. Perhaps they were not sure of John's entire intention. Whatever the reason for their toleration, there was little doubt that John the Baptist was virtually their leader.

The life of the Essenes consisted of ritual bathing three times a day, of prayer, and of work. The work was not difficult. Sometimes Glogauer guided a plough pulled by two other members of the sect; sometimes he looked after the goats that were allowed to graze on the hillsides. It was a peaceful, ordered life, and even the unhealthy aspects were so much a matter of routine that Glogauer hardly noticed them for anything else after a while.

Tending the goats, he would lie on a hilltop, looking out over the wilderness, which was not a desert, but rocky scrubland sufficient to feed animals like goats or sheep. The scrubland was broken by low-lying bushes and a few small trees growing along the banks of the river that doubtless ran into the Dead Sea. It was uneven ground. In outline, it had the appearance of a stormy lake, frozen and turned yellow and brown. Beyond the Dead Sea lay Jerusalem. Obviously Christ had not entered the city for the last time yet. John the Baptist would have to die before that happened.

The Essenes' way of life was comfortable enough for all its simplicity. They had given him a goatskin loincloth and a staff and, except for the fact that he was watched by day and night, he appeared to be accepted as a kind of lay member of the sect.

Sometimes they questioned him casually about his chariot—the time machine they intended soon to bring in from the desert—and he told them that it had borne him from Egypt to Syria and then to here. They accepted the miracle calmly. As he had suspected, they were used to miracles.

The Essenes had seen stranger things than his time machine. They had seen men walk on water and angels descend to and from heaven; they had heard the voice of God and His archangels as well as the tempting voice of Satan and his minions. They wrote all these things down in their vellum scrolls. They were merely a record of the supernatural as their other scrolls were records of their daily lives and of the news that traveling members of their sect brought to them.

They lived constantly in the presence of God and spoke to God and were answered by God when they had sufficiently mortified their flesh and starved themselves and chanted their prayers beneath the blazing sun of Judaea.

Karl Glogauer grew his hair long and let his beard come unchecked. He mortified his flesh and starved himself and chanted his prayers beneath the sun, as they did. But he rarely heard God and only once thought he saw an archangel with wings of fire.

In spite of his willingness to experience the Essenes' hallucinations, Glogauer was disappointed, but he was surprised that he felt so well considering all the self-inflicted hardships he had to undergo, and he also felt relaxed in the company of these men and women who were undoubtedly insane. Perhaps it was because their insanity was not so very different from his own that after a while he stopped wondering about it.

John the Baptist returned one evening, striding over the hills followed by twenty or so of his closest disciples. Glogauer saw him as he prepared to drive the goats into their cave for the night. He waited for John to get closer.

The Baptist's face was grim, but his expression softened as he saw Glogauer. He smiled and grasped him by the upper arm in the Roman fashion.

"Well, Emmanuel, you are our friend, as I thought you were. Sent by Adonai to help us accomplish His will. You shall baptize me on the morrow, to show all the people that He is with us."

Glogauer was tired. He had eaten very little and had spent most of the day in the sun, tending the goats. He yawned, finding it hard to reply. However, he was relieved. John had plainly been in Jerusalem, trying to discover if the Romans had sent him as a spy. John now seemed reassured and trusted him.

He was worried, however, by the Baptist's faith in his powers.

"John," he began. "I'm no seer . . ."

The Baptist's face clouded for a moment, then he laughed awkwardly. "Say nothing. Eat with me tonight. I have wild honey and locusts."

Glogauer had not yet eaten this food, which was the staple of travelers who did not carry provisions but lived off the food they could find on the journey. Some regarded it as a delicacy.

He tried it later, as he sat in John's house. There were only two rooms in the house. One was for eating in, the other for sleeping in. The honey and locusts was too sweet for his taste, but it was a welcome change from barley or goat meat.

He sat cross-legged, opposite John the Baptist, who ate with relish. Night had fallen. From outside came low murmurs and the moans and cries of those at prayer.

Glogauer dipped another locust into the bowl of honey that rested between them. "Do you plan to lead the people of Judaea in revolt against the Romans?" he asked.

The Baptist seemed disturbed by the direct question. It was the first of its nature that Glogauer had put to him.

"If it be Adonai's will," he said, not looking up as he leant towards the bowl of honey.

"The Romans know this?"

"I do not know, Emmanuel, but Herod the incestuous has doubtless told them I speak against the unrighteous."

"Yet the Romans do not arrest you."

"Pilate dare not—not since the petition was sent to the Emperor Tiberius."

"Petition?"

"Aye, the one that Herod and the Pharisees signed when Pilate the procurator did place votive shields in the palace at Jerusalem and seek to violate the Temple. Tiberius rebuked Pilate and since then, though he still hates the Jews, the procurator is more careful in his treatment of us."

"Tell me, John, do you know how long Tiberius has ruled in Rome?" He had not had the chance to ask that question again until now.

"Fourteen years."

It was 28 A.D.—something less than a year before the crucifixion would take place, and his time machine was smashed.

Now John the Baptist planned armed rebellion against the occupying Romans, but, if the Gospels were to be believed, would soon be decapitated by Herod. Certainly no large-scale rebellion had taken place at this time. Even those who claimed that the entry of Jesus and his disciples into Jerusalem and the invasion of the Temple were plainly the actions of armed rebels had found no records to suggest that John had led a similar revolt.

Glogauer had come to like the Baptist very much. The man was plainly a hardened revolutionary who had been planning revolt against the Romans for years and had slowly been building up enough followers to make the attempt successful. He reminded Glogauer strongly of the resistance leaders of the Second World War. He had a similar toughness and understanding of the realities of his position. He knew that he would only have one chance to smash the cohorts garrisoned in the country. If the revolt became protracted, Rome would have ample time to send more troops to Jerusalem.

"When do you think Adonai intends to destroy the unrighteous through your agency?" Glogauer said tactfully.

John glanced at him with some amusement. He smiled. "The Passover is a time when the people are restless and resent the strangers most," he said.

"When is the next Passover?"

"Not for many months."

"How can I help you?"

"You are a magus."

"I can work no miracles."

John wiped the honey from his beard. "I cannot believe that, Emmanuel. The manner of your coming was miraculous. The Essenes did not know if you were a devil or a messenger from Adonai."

"I am neither."

"Why do you confuse me, Emmanuel? I know that you are Adonai's messenger. You are the sign that the Essenes sought. The time is almost ready. The kingdom of heaven shall soon be established on earth. Come with me. Tell the people that you speak with Adonai's voice. Work mighty miracles."

"Your power is waning, is that it?" Glogauer looked sharply at John. "You need me to renew your rebels' hopes?"

"You speak like a Roman, with such lack of subtlety." John got up angrily. Evidently, like the Essenes he lived with, he preferred less direct conversation. There was a practical reason for this, Glogauer realized, in that John and his men feared betrayal all the time. Even the Essenes' records were partially written in cipher, with one innocent-looking word or phrase meaning something else entirely.

"I am sorry, John. But tell me if I am right." Glogauer spoke softly.

"Are you not a magus, coming in that chariot from nowhere?" The Baptist waved his hands and shrugged his shoulders. "My men saw you! They saw the shining thing take shape in air, crack, and let you enter out of it. Is that not magical? The clothing you wore—was that earth raiment? The talismans within the chariot—did they not speak of powerful magic? The prophet said that a magus would come from Egypt and be called Emmanuel. So it is written in the Book of Micah! Are none of these things true?"

"Most of them. But there are explanations—" He broke off, unable to think of the nearest word to "rational." "I am an ordinary man, like you. I have no power to work miracles! I am just a man!"

John glowered. "You mean you refuse to help us?"

"I'm grateful to you and the Essenes. You saved my life almost certainly. If I can repay that . . ."

John nodded his head deliberately. "You can repay it, Emmanuel."

"How?"

"Be the great magus I need. Let me present you to all those who become impatient and would turn away from Adonai's will. Let me tell them the manner of your coming to us. Then you can say that all is Adonai's will and that they must prepare to accomplish it."

John stared at him intensely.

"Will you, Emmanuel?"

"For your sake, John. And in turn, will you send men to bring my chariot here as soon as possible? I wish to see if it may be mended."

"I will."

Glogauer felt exhilarated. He began to laugh. The Baptist looked at him with slight bewilderment. Then he began to join him.

Glogauer laughed on. History would not mention it, but he, with John the Baptist, would prepare the way for Christ.

Christ was not born yet. Perhaps Glogauer knew it, one year before the crucifixion.

And the Word was made flesh, and dwelt among us (and we beheld his glory, the glory as of the only begotten of the Father), full of grace and truth. John bare witness of him, and cried, saying, This was he of whom I spake, He that cometh after me is preferred before me; for he was before me.

(John 1:14–15)

Even when he had first met Monica, they had had long arguments. His father had not then died and left him the money to buy the Occult Bookshop in Great Russell Street opposite the British Museum. He was doing all sorts of temporary work, and his spirits were very low. At that time Monica had seemed a great help, a great guide through the mental darkness engulfing him. They had both lived close to Holland Park and went there for walks almost every Sunday of the summer of 1962. At twenty-two, he was already obsessed with Jung's strange brand of Christian mysticism. She, who despised Jung, had soon begun to denigrate all his ideas. She never really convinced him. But, after a while, she had succeeded in confusing him. It would be another six months before they went to bed together.

It was uncomfortably hot.

They sat in the shade of the cafeteria, watching a distant cricket match. Nearer to them, two girls and a boy sat on the grass, drinking orange squash from plastic cups. One of the girls had a guitar across her lap, and she set the cup down and began to play, singing a folk song in a high, gentle voice. Glogauer tried to listen to the words. As a student, he had always liked traditional folk music.

"Christianity is dead." Monica sipped her tea. "Religion is dying. God was killed in 1945."

"There may yet be a resurrection," he said.

"Let us hope not. Religion was the creation of fear. Knowledge destroys fear. Without fear, religion can't survive."

"You think there's no fear about these days?"

"Not the same kind, Karl."

"Haven't you ever considered the *idea* of Christ?" he asked her, changing his tack. "What that means to Christians?"

"The idea of the tractor means as much to a Marxist," she replied.

"But what came first? The idea or the actuality of Christ?"

She shrugged. "The actuality, if it matters. Jesus was a Jewish troublemaker organizing a revolt against the Romans. He was crucified for his pains. That's all we know and all we need to know."

"A great religion couldn't have begun so simply."

"When people need one, they'll make a great religion out of the most unlikely beginnings."

"That's my point, Monica." He gesticulated at her, and she drew away slightly. "The *idea* preceded the *actuality* of Christ."

"Oh, Karl, don't go on. The actuality of *Jesus* preceded the idea of *Christ*."

A couple walked past, glancing at them as they argued.

Monica noticed them and fell silent. She got up and he rose as well, but she shook her head. "I'm going home, Karl. You stay here. I'll see you in a few days."

He watched her walk down the wide path towards the park gates.

The next day when he got home from work, he found a letter. She must have written it after she had left him and posted it the same day.

Dear Karl,

Conversation doesn't seem to have much effect on you, you know. It's as if you listen to the tone of the voice, the rhythm of the words without ever hearing what is trying to be communicated. You're a bit like a sensitive animal who can't understand what's being said to it, but can tell if the person talking is pleased or angry and so on. That's why I'm writing to you—to try to get my idea across. You respond too emotionally when we're together.

You make the mistake of considering Christianity as something that developed over the course of a few years, from the death of Jesus to the time the Gospels were written. But Christianity wasn't new. Only the name was new. Christianity was merely a stage in the meeting, cross-fertilization metamorphosis of Western logic and Eastern mysticism. Look how the religion itself changed over the centuries, re-interpreting itself to meet changing times. Christianity is just a new name for the conglomeration of old myths and philosophies. All the Gospels do is retell the sun myth and garble some of the ideas from the Greeks and Romans. Even in the second century, Jewish scholars were showing it up for the mishmash it was! They pointed out the strong similarities between the various sun myths and the Christ myth. The miracles didn't happen—they were invented later, borrowed from here and there.

Remember the old Victorians who used to say that Plato was really a Christian because he anticipated Christian thought? Christian thought! Christianity was a vehicle for ideas in circulation for centuries before Christ. Was Marcus Aurelius a Christian? He was writing in the direct tradition of

*Western philosophy. That's why Christianity caught
on in Europe and not in the East! You should have
been a theologian with your bias, not a psychiatrist.
The same goes for your friend Jung.*

*Try to clear your head of all this morbid non-
sense and you'll be a lot better at your job.*

Yours,
Monica.

He screwed the letter up and threw it away. Later
that evening he was tempted to look at it again, but he
resisted the temptation.

III

John stood up to his waist in the river. Most of the
Essenes stood on the banks watching him. Glogauer
looked down at him.

"I cannot, John. It is not for me to do it."

The Baptist muttered, "You must."

Glogauer shivered as he lowered himself into the river
beside the Baptist. He felt light-headed. He stood there
trembling, unable to move.

His foot slipped on the rocks of the river and John
reached out and gripped his arm, steadying him.

In the clear sky, the sun was at zenith, beating down
on his unprotected head.

"Emmanuel!" John cried suddenly. "The spirit of
Adonai is within you!"

Glogauer still found it hard to speak. He shook his
head slightly. It was aching, and he could hardly see.
Today he was having his first migraine attack since he
had come here. He wanted to vomit. John's voice sounded
distant.

He swayed in the water.

As he began to fall toward the Baptist, the whole
scene around him shimmered. He felt John catch him
and heard himself say desperately: "John, baptize *me!*"
And then there was water in his mouth and throat and
he was coughing.

John's voice was crying something. Whatever the words
were, they drew a response from the people on both

banks. The roaring in his ears increased, its quality changing. He thrashed in the water, then felt himself lifted to his feet.

The Essenes were swaying in unison, every face lifted upwards towards the glaring sun.

Glogauer began to vomit into the water, stumbling as John's hands gripped his arms painfully and guided him up the bank.

A peculiar, rhythmic humming came from the mouths of the Essenes as they swayed; it rose as they swayed to one side, fell as they swayed to the other.

Glogauer covered his ears as John released him. He was still retching, but it was dry now, and worse than before.

He began to stagger away, barely keeping his balance, running, with his ears still covered; running over the rocky scrubland; running as the sun throbbed in the sky and its heat pounded at his head; running away.

> *But John forbade him, saying, I have need to be baptized of thee, and comest thou to me? And Jesus answering said unto him, Suffer it to be so now: for thus it becometh us to fulfill all righteousness. Then he suffered him. And Jesus, when he was baptized, went up straightway out of the water: and, lo, the heavens were opened unto him, and he saw the Spirit of God descending like a dove, and lighting upon him: And lo a voice from heaven, saying, This is my beloved Son, in whom I am well pleased.*
>
> (Matthew 3:14–17)

He had been fifteen, doing well at the grammar school. He had read in the newspapers about the Teddy Boy gangs that roamed South London, but the odd youth he had seen in pseudo-Edwardian clothes had seemed harmless and stupid enough.

He had gone to the pictures in Brixton Hill and decided to walk home to Streatham because he had spent most of the bus money on an ice cream. They came out of the cinema at the same time. He hardly noticed them as they followed him down the hill.

Then, quite suddenly, they had surrounded him. Pale,

mean-faced boys, most of them a year or two older
than he was. He realized that he knew two of them
vaguely. They were at the big council school in the same
street as the grammar school. They used the same football ground.

"Hello," he said weakly.

"Hello, son," said the oldest Teddy Boy. He was chewing gum, standing with one knee bent, grinning at him.
"Where you going, then?"

"Home."

"Heouwm," said the biggest one, imitating his accent.
"What are you going to do when you get there?"

"Go to bed." Karl tried to get through the ring, but
they wouldn't let him. They pressed him back into a shop
doorway. Beyond them, cars droned by on the main
road. The street was brightly lit with street lamps and
neon from the shops. Several people passed, but none of
them stopped. Karl began to feel panic.

"Got no homework to do, son?" said the boy next to
the leader. He was redheaded and freckled and his eyes
were a hard gray.

"Want to fight one of us?" another boy asked. It was
one of the boys he knew.

"No. I don't fight. Let me go."

"You scared, son?" said the leader, grinning. Ostenta-
tiously, he pulled a streamer of gum from his mouth and
then replaced it. He began chewing again.

"No. Why would I want to fight you?"

"You reckon you're better than us, is that it, son?"

"No." He was beginning to tremble. Tears were coming
into his eyes. " 'Course not."

" 'Course not, son."

He moved forward again, but they pushed him back
into the doorway.

"You're the bloke with the kraut name, ain't you?"
said the other boy he knew. "Glow-worm or somethink."

"Glogauer. Let me go."

"Won't your mummy like it if you're back late?"

"More a yid name than a kraut name."

"You a yid, son?"

"He looks like a yid."

"You a yid, son?"

"You a Jewish boy, son?"

"You a yid, son?"

"Shut up!" Karl screamed. He pushed into them. One of them punched him in the stomach. He grunted with pain. Another pushed him, and he staggered.

People were still hurrying by on the pavement. They glanced at the group as they went past. One man stopped, but his wife pulled him on. "Just some kids larking about," she said.

"Get his trousers down," one of the boys suggested with a laugh. "That'll prove it."

Karl pushed through them, and this time they didn't resist. He began to run down the hill.

"Give him a start," he heard one of the boys say.

He ran on.

They began to follow him, laughing.

They did not catch up with him by the time he turned into the avenue where he lived. He reached the house and ran along the dark passage beside it. He opened the back door. His stepmother was in the kitchen.

"What's the matter with you?" she said.

She was a tall, thin woman, nervous and hysterical. Her dark hair was untidy.

He went past her into the breakfast-room.

"What's the matter, Karl?" she called. Her voice was high-pitched.

"Nothing," he said.

He didn't want a scene.

It was cold when he woke up. The false dawn was gray, and he could see nothing but barren country in all directions. He could not remember a great deal about the previous day, except that he had run a long way.

Dew had gathered on his loincloth. He wet his lips and rubbed the skin over his face. As he always did after a migraine attack, he felt weak and completely drained. Looking down at his naked body, he noticed how skinny he had become. Life with the Essenes had caused that, of course.

He wondered why he had panicked so much when John had asked him to baptize him. Was it simply honesty —something in him which resisted deceiving the Essenes into thinking he was a prophet of some kind? It was hard to know.

He wrapped the goatskin about his hips and tied it tightly just above his left thigh. He supposed he had better try to get back to the camp and find John and apologize, see if he could make amends.

The time machine was there now, too. They had dragged it there, using only rawhide ropes.

If a good blacksmith could be found, or some other metalworker, there was just a chance that it could be repaired. The journey back would be dangerous.

He wondered if he ought to go back right away, or try to shift to a time nearer to the actual crucifixion. He had not gone back specifically to witness the crucifixion, but to get the mood of Jersualem during the Feast of the Passover, when Jesus was supposed to have entered the city. Monica had thought Jesus had stormed the city with an armed band. She had said that all the evidence pointed to that. All the evidence of one sort did point to it, but he could not accept the evidence. There was more to it, he was sure. If only he could meet Jesus. John had apparently never heard of him, though he had told Glogauer that there was a prophecy that the Messiah would be a Nazarene. There were many prophecies, and many of them conflicted.

He began to walk back in the general direction of the Essene camp. He could not have come so far. He would soon recognize the hills where they had their caves.

Soon it was very hot and the ground more barren. The air wavered before his eyes. The feeling of exhaustion with which he had awakened increased. His mouth was dry, and his legs were weak. He was hungry and there was nothing to eat. There was no sign of the range of hills where the Essenes had their camp.

There was one hill about two miles away to the south. He decided to make for it. From there he would probably be able to get his bearings, perhaps even see a township where they would give him food.

The sandy soil turned to floating dust around him as his feet disturbed it. A few primitive shrubs clung to the ground and jutting rocks tripped him.

He was bleeding and bruised by the time he began, painfully, to clamber up the hillside.

The journey to the summit (which was much farther away than he had originally judged) was difficult. He would slide on the loose stones of the hillside, falling on his face, bracing his torn hands and feet to stop himself from sliding down to the bottom, clinging to tufts of grass and lichen that grew here and there, embracing larger projections of rock when he could, resting frequently, his mind and body both numb with pain and weariness.

He sweated beneath the sun. The dust stuck to the moisture on his half-naked body, caking him from head to foot. The goatskin was in shreds.

The barren world reeled around him, sky somehow merging with land, yellow rock with white clouds. Nothing seemed still.

He reached the summit and lay there gasping. Everything had become unreal.

He heard Monica's voice, thought he glanced at her for a moment from the corner of his eye.

Don't be melodramatic, Karl. . .

She had said that many times. His own voice replied now.

I'm born out of my time, Monica. This age of reason has no place for me. It will kill me in the end.

Her voice replied.

Guilt and fear and your own masochism. You could be a brilliant psychiatrist, but you've given in to all your own neuroses so completely. . .

"Shut up!"

He rolled over on his back. The sun blazed down on his tattered body.

"Shut up!"

The whole Christian syndrome, Karl. You'll become a Catholic convert next I shouldn't doubt. Where's your strength of mind?

"Shut up! Go away, Monica."

Fear shapes your thoughts. You're not searching for a soul or even a meaning for life. You're searching for comforts.

"Leave me alone, Monica!"

His grimy hands covered his ears. His hair and beard were matted with dust. Blood had congealed on the minor wounds that were now on every part of his body. Above, the sun seemed to pound in unison with his heartbeats.

You're going downhill, Karl, don't you realize that?

Downhill. Pull yourself together. You're not entirely incapable of rational thought. . .

"Oh, Monica! Shut up!"

His voice was harsh and cracked. A few ravens circled the sky above him now. He heard them calling back at him in a voice not unlike his own.

God died in 1945. . .

"It isn't 1945—it's 28 A.D. God is alive!"

How you can bother to wonder about an obvious syncretistic religion like Christianity—Rabbinic Judaism, Stoic ethics, Greek mystery cults, Oriental ritual. . .

"It doesn't matter!"

Not to you in your present state of mind. . .

"I need God!"

That's what it boils down to, doesn't it? Okay, Karl, carve your own crutches. Just think what you could have been if you'd have come to terms with yourself. . .

Glogauer pulled his ruined body to its feet and stood on the summit of the hill and screamed.

The ravens were startled. They wheeled in the sky and flew away.

The sky was darkening now.

> *Then was Jesus led up of the Spirit into the wilderness to be tempted of the devil. And when he had fasted forty days and forty nights, he was afterward anhungered.*
>
> (Matthew 4: 1–2)

IV

The madman came stumbling into the town. His feet stirred the dust and made it dance and dogs barked around him as he walked mechanically, his head turned upwards to face the sun, his arms limp at his sides, his lips moving.

To the townspeople, the words they heard were in no familiar language; yet they were uttered with such intensity and conviction that God himself might be using this emaciated, naked creature as his spokesman.

They wondered where the madman had come from.

The white town consisted primarily of double- and

single-storied houses of stone and clay-brick, built around a market place that was fronted by an ancient, simple synagogue outside which old men sat and talked, dressed in dark robes. The town was prosperous and clean, thriving on Roman commerce. Only one or two beggars were in the streets and these were well-fed. The streets followed the rise and fall of the hillside on which they were built. They were winding streets, shady and peaceful: country streets. There was a smell of newly cut timber everywhere in the air, and the sound of carpentry for the town was chiefly famous for its skilled carpenters. It lay on the edge of the Plain of Jezreel, close to the trade route between Damascus and Egypt, and wagons were always leaving it, laden with the work of the town's craftsmen. The town was called Nazareth.

The madman had found it by asking every traveler he saw where it was. He had passed through other towns— Philadelphia, Gerasa, Pella, and Scythopolis, following the Roman roads—asking the same question in his outlandish accent: "Where lies Nazareth?"

Some had given him food on the way. Some had asked for his blessing, and he had laid hands on them, speaking in that strange tongue. Some had pelted him with stones and driven him away.

He had crossed the Jordan by the Roman viaduct and continued northwards towards Nazareth.

There had been no difficulty in finding the town, but it had been difficult for him to force himself towards it. He had lost a great deal of blood and had eaten very little on the journey. He would walk until he collapsed and lie there until he could go on, or, as had happened increasingly, until someone found him and had given him a little sour wine or bread to revive him.

Once some Roman legionaries had stopped and with brusque kindness asked him if he had any relatives they could take him to. They had addressed him in pidgin-Aramaic and had been surprised when he replied in a strangely accented Latin that was purer than the language they spoke themselves.

They asked him if he was a Rabbi or a scholar. He told them he was neither. The officer of the legionaries had offered him some dried meat and wine. The men were part of a patrol that passed this way once a month.

They were stocky, brown-faced men with hard, clean-shaven faces. They were dressed in stained leather kilts and breastplates and sandals, and had iron helmets on their heads, scabbarded short swords at their hips. Even as they stood around him in the evening sunlight, they did not seem relaxed. The officer, softer-voiced than his men but otherwise much like them save that he wore a metal breastplate and a long cloak, asked the madman what his name was.

For a moment the madman had paused, his mouth opening and closing, as if he could not remember what he was called.

"Karl," he said at length, doubtfully. It was more a suggestion than a statement.

"Sounds almost like a Roman name," said one of the legionaries.

"Are you a citizen?" the officer asked.

But the madman's mind was wandering evidently. He looked away from them, muttering to himself.

All at once, he looked back at them and said: "Nazareth?"

"That way." The officer pointed down the road that cut between the hills. "Are you a Jew?"

This seemed to startle the madman. He sprang to his feet and tried to push through the soldiers. They let him through, laughing. He was a harmless madman.

They watched him run down the road.

"One of their prophets, perhaps," said the officer, walking towards his horse. The country was full of them. Every other man you met claimed to be spreading the message of their god. They didn't make much trouble and religion seemed to keep their minds off rebellion. *We should be grateful,* thought the officer.

His men were still laughing.

They began to march down the road in the opposite direction to the one the madman had taken.

Now the madman was in Nazareth, and the townspeople looked at him with curiosity and more than a little suspicion as he staggered into the market square. He could be a wandering prophet or he could be possessed by devils. It was often hard to tell. The rabbis would know.

As he passed the knots of people standing by the merchants' stalls, they fell silent until he had gone by. Women pulled their heavy woolen shawls about their well-fed bodies, and men tucked in their cotton robes so that he would not touch them. Normally their instinct would have been to have taxed him with his business in the town, but there was an intensity about his gaze, a quickness and vitality about his face, in spite of his emaciated appearance, that made them treat him with some respect and they kept their distance.

When he reached the center of the market place, he stopped and looked around him. He seemed slow to notice the people. He blinked and licked his lips.

A woman passed, eyeing him warily. He spoke to her, his voice soft, the words carefully formed. "Is this Nazareth?"

"It is." She nodded and increased her pace.

A man was crossing the square. He was dressed in a woolen robe of red and brown stripes. There was a red skull cap on his curly, black hair. His face was plump and cheerful. The madman walked across the man's path and stopped him. "I seek a carpenter."

"There are many carpenters in Nazareth. The town is famous for its carpenters. I am a carpenter myself. Can I help you?" The man's voice was good-humored, patronizing.

"Do you know a carpenter called Joseph? A descendant of David. He has a wife called Mary and several children. One is named Jesus."

The cheerful man screwed his face into a mock frown and scratched the back of his neck. "I know more than one Joseph. There is one poor fellow in yonder street." He pointed. "He has a wife called Mary. Try there. You should soon find him. Look for a man who never laughs."

The madman looked in the direction in which the man pointed. As soon as he saw the street, he seemed to forget everything else and strode towards it.

In the narrow street he entered the smell of cut timber was even stronger. He walked ankle-deep in woodshavings. From every building came the thud of hammers, the scrape of saws. There were planks of all sizes resting against the pale, shaded walls of the houses and there was hardly room to pass between them. Many of the carpenters had their benches just outside their doors. They were carving bowls, operating simple lathes, shaping wood into everything imaginable. They looked up as the madman entered the street and approached one old carpenter in a leather apron who sat at his bench carving a figurine. The man had gray hair and seemed short-sighted. He peered up at the madman.

"What do you want?"

"I seek a carpenter called Joseph. He has a wife—Mary."

The old man gestured with his hand that held the half-completed figurine. "Two houses along on the other side of the street."

The house the madman came to had very few planks leaning against it, and the quality of the timber seemed poorer than the other wood he had seen. The bench near the entrance was warped on one side, and the man who sat hunched over it, repairing a stool, seemed misshapen also. He straightened up as the madman touched his shoulder. His face was lined and pouched with misery. His eyes were tired and his thin beard had premature streaks of gray. He coughed slightly, perhaps in surprise at being disturbed.

"Are you Joseph?" asked the madman.

"I've no money."

"I want nothing—just to ask a few questions."

"I'm Joseph. Why do you want to know?"

"Have you a son?"

"Several, and daughters, too."

"Your wife is called Mary? You are of David's line."

The man waved his hand impatiently. "Yes, for what good either have done me. . ."

"I wish to meet one of your sons. Jesus. Can you tell me where he is?"

"That good-for-nothing. What has he done now?"

"Where is he?"

Joseph's eyes became more calculating as he stared at the madman. "Are you a seer of some kind? Have you come to cure my son?"

"I am a prophet of sorts. I can foretell the future."

Joseph got up with a sigh: "You can see him. Come."

He led the madman through the gateway into the
cramped courtyard of the house. It was crowded with
pieces of wood, broken furniture, and implements, rotting sacks of shavings. They entered the darkened house.
In the first room—evidently a kitchen—a woman stood
by a large clay stove. She was tall and bulging with fat.
Her long, black hair was unbound and greasy, falling
over large, lustrous eyes that still had the heat of sensual-
ity. She looked the madman over.

"There's no food for beggars," she grunted. "He eats
enough as it is." She gestured with a wooden spoon at a
small figure sitting in the shadow of a corner. The figure
shifted as she spoke.

"He seeks our Jesus," said Joseph to the woman. "Perhaps he comes to ease our burden."

The woman gave the madman a sidelong look and
shrugged. She licked her red lips with a fat tongue.
"Jesus!"

The figure in the corner stood up.

"That's him," said the woman with a certain satisfaction.

The madman frowned, shaking his head rapidly. "No."

The figure was misshapen. It had a pronounced
hunched back and a cast in its left eye. The face was
vacant and foolish. There was a little spittle on the lips.
It giggled as its name was repeated. It took a crooked
step forward. "Jesus," it said. The word was slurred and
thick. "Jesus."

"That's all he can say." The woman sneered. "He's
always been like that."

"God's judgment," said Joseph bitterly.

"What is wrong with him?" There was a pathetic, desperate note in the madman's voice.

"He's always been like that." The woman turned back
to the stove. "You can have him if you want him. Addled
inside and outside. I was carrying him when my parents
married me off to that half-man. . . ."

"You shameless—" Joseph stopped as his wife glared
at him. He turned to the madman. "What's your business
with our son?"

"I wished to talk to him. I . . ."

"He's no oracle—no seer—we used to think he might
be. There are still people in Nazareth who come to him

to cure them or tell their fortunes, but he only giggles at them and speaks his name over and over again. . ."

"Are—you sure—there is not—something about him —you have not noticed?"

"Sure!" Mary snorted sardonically. "We need money badly enough. If he had any magical powers, we'd know."

Jesus giggled again and limped away into another room.

"It is impossible," the madman murmured. Could history itself have changed? Could he be in some other dimension of time where Christ had never been?

Joseph appeared to notice the look of agony in the madman's eyes.

"What is it?" he said. "What do you see? You said you foretold the future. Tell us how we will fare?"

"Not *now*," said the prophet, turning away. "Not *now*."

He ran from the house and down the street with its smell of planed oak, cedar, and cypress. He ran back to the market place and stopped, looking wildly about him. He saw the synagogue directly ahead of him. He began to walk towards it.

The man he had spoken to earlier was still in the market place, buying cooking pots to give to his daughter as a wedding gift. He nodded towards the strange man as he entered the synagogue. "He's a relative of Joseph the carpenter," he told the man beside him. "A prophet, I shouldn't wonder."

The madman, the prophet, Karl Glogauer, the time-traveler, the neurotic psychiatrist manqué, the searcher for meaning, the masochist, the man with a death-wish and the messiah-complex, the anachronism, made his way into the synagogue gasping for breath. He had seen the man he had sought. He had seen Jesus, the son of Joseph and Mary. He had seen a man he recognized without any doubt as a congenital imbecile.

"All men have a messiah-complex, Karl," Monica had said.

The memories were less complete now. His sense of time and identity was becoming confused.

"There were dozens of messiahs in Galilee at the time.

That Jesus should have been the one to carry the myth and the philosophy was a coincidence of history. . .”

“There must have been more to it than that, Monica.”

Every Tuesday in the room above the Occult Bookshop, the Jungian discussion group would meet for purposes of group analysis and therapy. Glogauer had not organized the group, but he had willingly lent his premises to it and had joined it eagerly. It was a great relief to talk with like-minded people once a week. One of his reasons for buying the Occult Bookshop was so that he would meet interesting people like those who attended the Jungian discussion group.

An obsession with Jung brought them together, but everyone had special obsessions of his own. Mrs. Rita Blen charted the courses of flying saucers, though it was not clear if she believed in them or not. Hugh Joyce believed that all Jungian archetypes derived from the original race of Atlantides who had perished millennia before. Alan Cheddar, the youngest of the group, was interested in Indian mysticism, and Sandra Peterson, the organizer, was a great witchcraft specialist. James Headington was interested in time. He was the group’s pride; he was Sir James Headington, war-time inventor, very rich and with all sorts of decorations for his contribution to the Allied victory. He had had the reputation of being a great improviser during the war, but after it he had become something of an embarrassment to the War Office. He was a crank, they thought, and what was worse, he aired his crankiness in public.

Every so often, Sir James would tell the other members of the group about his time machine. They humored him. Most of them were liable to exaggerate their own experiences connected with their different interests.

One Tuesday evening, after everyone else had left, Headington told Glogauer that his machine was ready.

“I can’t believe it,” Glogauer said truthfully.

“You’re the first person I’ve told.”

“Why me?”

“I don’t know. I like you—and the shop.”

“You haven’t told the government.”

Headington had chuckled. “Why should I? Not until I’ve tested it fully anyway. Serves them right for putting me out to pasture.”

"You don't know it works?"

"I'm sure it does. Would you like to see it?"

"A time machine." Glogauer smiled weakly.

"Come and see it."

"Why me?"

"I thought you might be interested. I know you don't hold with the orthodox view of science. . ."

Glogauer felt sorry for him.

"Come and see," said Headington.

He went down to Banbury the next day. The same day he left 1976 and arrived in 28 A.D.

The synagogue was cool and quiet with a subtle scent of incense. The rabbis guided him into the courtyard. They, like the townspeople, did not know what to make of him, but they were sure it was not a devil that possessed him. It was their custom to give shelter to the roaming prophets who were now everywhere in Galilee, though this one was stranger than the rest. His face was immobile, and his body was stiff, and there were tears running down his dirty cheeks. They had never seen such agony in a man's eyes before.

"Science can say how, but it never asks why," he had told Monica. "It can't answer."

"Who wants to know?" she'd replied.

"I do."

"Well, you'll never find out, will you?"

"Sit down, my son," said the rabbi. "What do you wish to ask of us?"

"Where is Christ?" he said. "Where is Christ?"

They did not understand the language.

"Is it Greek?" asked one, but another shook his head.

Kyrios: The Lord.

Adonai: The Lord.

Where was the Lord?

He frowned, looking vaguely about him.

"I must rest," he said in their language.

"Where are you from?"

He could not think what to answer.

"Where are you from?" a rabbi repeated.

"Ha-Olam Hab-bah . . ." he murmured at length.

They looked at one another. *"Ha-Olam Hab-bah,"* they said.

Ha-Olam Hab-bah; Ha-Olam Haz-zeh: The world to come and the world that is.

"Do you bring us a message?" said one of the rabbis. They were used to prophets, certainly, but none like this one. "A message?"

"I do not know," said the prophet hoarsely. "I must rest. I am hungry."

"Come. We will give you food and a place to sleep."

He could only eat a little of the rich food, and the bed with its straw-stuffed mattress was too soft for him. He was not used to it.

He slept badly, shouting as he dreamed, and, outside the room, the rabbis listened but could understand little of what he said.

Karl Glogauer stayed in the synagogue for several weeks. He would spend most of his time reading in the library, searching through the long scrolls for some answer to his dilemma. The words of the Testaments, in many cases capable of a dozen interpretations, only confused him further. There was nothing to grasp, nothing to tell him what had gone wrong.

The rabbis kept their distance for the most part. They had accepted him as a holy man. They were proud to have him in their synagogue. They were sure that he was one of the special chosen of God and they waited patiently for him to speak to them.

But the prophet said little, muttering only to himself in snatches of their own language and snatches of the incomprehensible language he often used, even when he addressed them directly.

In Nazareth, the townsfolk talked of little else but the mysterious prophet in the synagogue, but the rabbis would not answer their questions. They would tell the people to go about their business, that there were things they were not yet meant to know. In this way, as priests had always done, they avoided questions they could not answer while at the same time appearing to have much more knowledge than they actually possessed.

Then one sabbath, he appeared in the public part of

the synagogue and took his place with the others who
had come to worship.

The man who was reading from the scroll on his left
stumbled over the words, glancing at the prophet from
the corner of his eye.

The prophet sat and listened, his expression remote.

The Chief Rabbi looked uncertainly at him, then
signed that the scroll should be passed to the prophet.
This was done hesitantly by a boy who placed the scroll
into the prophet's hands.

The prophet looked at the words for a long time and
then began to read. The prophet read without compre-
hending at first what he read. It was the book of Esaias.

> *The Spirit of the Lord is upon me, because he*
> *hath anointed me to preach the gospel to the poor;*
> *he hath sent me to heal the broken-hearted, to*
> *preach deliverance to the captives, and recovering*
> *of sight to the blind, to set at liberty them that are*
> *bruised, to preach the acceptable year of the Lord.*
> *And he closed the book, and gave it again to the*
> *minister, and sat down. And the eyes of all of them*
> *that were in the synagogue were fastened on him.*
>   (Luke 4: 18–20)

V

They followed him now, as he walked away from Nazareth towards the Lake of Galilee. He was dressed in the
white linen robe they had given him, and though they
thought he led them, they, in fact, drove him before them.

"He is our messiah," they said to those who inquired.
And there were already rumors of miracles.

When he saw the sick, he pitied them and tried to do
what he could because they expected something of him.
Many he could do nothing for, but others, obviously in
psychosomatic conditions, he could help. They believed
in his power more strongly than they believed in their
sickness. So he cured them.

When he came to Capernaum, some fifty people followed him into the streets of the city. It was already
known that he was in some way associated with John the

Baptist, who enjoyed huge prestige in Galilee and had been declared a true prophet by many Pharisees. Yet this man had a power greater, in some ways, than John's. He was not the orator that the Baptist was, but he had worked miracles.

Capernaum was a sprawling town beside the crystal lake of Galilee, its houses separated by large market gardens. Fishing boats were moored at the white quayside, as well as trading ships that plied the lakeside towns. Though the green hills came down from all sides to the lake, Capernaum itself was built on flat ground, sheltered by the hills. It was a quiet town and, like most others in Galilee, had a large population of gentiles. Greek, Roman, and Egyptian traders walked its streets and many had made permanent homes there. There was a prosperous middle-class of merchants, artisans, and ship-owners, as well as doctors, lawyers, and scholars, for Capernaum was on the borders of the provinces of Galilee, Trachonitis, and Syria and though a comparatively small town, was a useful junction for trade and travel.

The strange, mad prophet in his swirling linen robes, followed by the heterogeneous crowd that was primarily composed of poor folk but also could be seen to contain men of some distinction, swept into Capernaum. The news spread that this man really could foretell the future, that he had already predicted the arrest of John by Herod Antipas and soon after Herod had imprisoned the Baptist of Peraea. He did not make the predictions in general terms, using vague words the way other prophets did. He spoke of things that were to happen in the near future, and he spoke of them in detail.

None knew his name. He was simply the prophet from Nazareth, or the Nazarene. Some said he was a relative, perhaps the son, of a carpenter in Nazareth, but this could be because the written words for "son of a carpenter" and "magus" were almost the same, and the confusion had come about in that way. There was even a very faint rumor that his name was Jesus. The name had been used once or twice, but when they asked him if that was, indeed, his name, he denied it or else, in his abstracted way, refused to answer at all.

His actual preaching tended to lack the fire of John's.

This man spoke gently, rather vaguely, and smiled often. He spoke of God in a strange way, too, and he appeared to be connected, as John was, with the Essenes for he preached against the accumulation of personal wealth and spoke of mankind as a brotherhood, as they did.

But it was the miracles that they watched for as he was guided to the graceful synagogue of Capernaum. No prophet before him had healed the sick and seemed to understand the troubles that people rarely spoke of. It was his sympathy that they responded to, rather than the words he spoke.

For the first time in his life, Karl Glogauer had forgotten about Karl Glogauer. For the first time in his life, he was doing what he had always sought to do as a psychiatrist.

But it was not his life. He was bringing a myth to life —a generation before that myth would be born. He was completing a certain kind of psychic circuit. He was not changing history, but he was giving history more substance.

He could not bear to think that Jesus had been nothing more than a myth. It was in his power to make Jesus a physical reality rather than the creation of a process of mythogenesis.

So he spoke in the synagogues and he spoke of a gentler God than most of them had heard of, and where he could remember them, he told them parables.

And gradually the need to justify what he was doing faded, and his sense of identity grew increasingly more tenuous and was replaced by a different sense of identity where he gave greater and greater substance to the rôle he had chosen. It was an archetypal rôle. It was a rôle to appeal to a disciple of Jung. It was a rôle that went beyond a mere imitation. It was a rôle that he must now play out to the very last grand detail. Karl Glogauer had discovered the reality he had been seeking.

> And in the synagogue there was a man, which had a spirit of an unclean devil, and cried out with a loud voice, saying, Let us alone; what have we to do with thee, thou Jesus of Nazareth? art thou come to destroy us? I know thee who thou art; the Holy One of God. And Jesus rebuked him, saying,

Hold thy peace, and come out of him. And when the devil had thrown him in the midst, he came out of him, and hurt him not. And they were all amazed, and spoke among themselves, saying, What a word is this! for with authority and power he commandeth the unclean spirits, and they come out. And the fame of him went out into every place of the country round about.

(Luke 4: 33–37)

"Mass hallucination. Miracles, flying saucers, ghosts, it's all the same," Monica had said.

"Very likely," he had replied. "But *why* did they see them?"

"Because they wanted to."

"Why did they want to?"

"Because they were afraid."

"You think that's all there is to it?"

"Isn't it enough?"

When he left Capernaum for the first time, many more people accompanied him. It had become impractical to stay in the town for the business of the town had been brought almost to a standstill by the crowds that sought to see him work his simple miracles.

He spoke to them in the spaces beyond the towns. He talked with intelligent, literate men who appeared to have something in common with him. Some of them were the owners of fishing fleets—Simon, James, and John among them. Another was a doctor, another a civil servant who had first heard him speak in Capernaum.

"There must be twelve," he said to them one day. "There must be a zodiac."

He was not careful in what he said. Many of his ideas were strange. Many of the things he talked about were unfamiliar to them. Some Pharisees thought he blasphemed.

One day he met a man he recognized as an Essene from the colony near Machaerus.

"John would speak with you," said the Essene.

"Is John not dead yet?" he asked the man.

"He is confined at Peraea. I would think Herod is too

frightened to kill him. He lets John walk about within the walls and gardens of the palace, lets him speak with his men, but John fears that Herod will find the courage soon to have him stoned or decapitated. He needs your help."

"How can I help him? He is to die. There is no hope for him."

The Essene looked uncomprehendingly into the mad eyes of the prophet.

"But, master, there is no one else who can help him."

"I have done all that he wished me to do," said the prophet. "I have healed the sick and preached to the poor."

"I did not know he wished this. Now he needs help, master. You could save his life."

The prophet had drawn the Essene away from the crowd.

"His life cannot be saved."

"But if it is not the unrighteous will prosper and the Kingdom of Heaven will not be restored."

"His life cannot be saved."

"Is it God's will?"

"If I am God, then it is God's will."

Hopelessly, the Essene turned and began to walk away from the crowd.

John the Baptist would have to die. Glogauer had no wish to change history, only to strengthen it.

He moved on, with his following, through Galilee. He had selected his twelve educated men, and the rest who followed him were still primarily poor people. To them he offered their only hope of fortune. Many were those who had been ready to follow John against the Romans, but now John was imprisoned. Perhaps this man would lead them in revolt, to loot the riches of Jerusalem and Jericho and Caesarea. Tired and hungry, their eyes glazed by the burning sun, they followed the man in the white robe. They needed to hope, and they found reasons for their hope. They saw him work greater miracles.

Once he preached to them from a boat, as was often his custom, and as he walked back to the shore through the shallows, it seemed to them that he walked over the water.

All through Galilee in the autumn, they wandered, hearing from everyone the news of John's beheading. Despair at the Baptist's death turned to renewed hope in this new prophet who had known him.

In Caesarea they were driven from the city by Roman guards used to the wildmen with their prophecies who roamed the country.

They were banned from other cities as the prophet's fame grew. Not only the Roman authorities, but the Jewish ones as well seemed unwilling to tolerate the new prophet as they had tolerated John. The political climate was changing.

It became hard to find food. They lived on what they could find, hungering like starved animals.

He taught them how to pretend to eat and take their minds off their hunger.

Karl Glogauer, witch-doctor, psychiatrist, hypnotist, messiah.

Sometimes his conviction in his chosen rôle wavered, and those that followed him would be disturbed when he contradicted himself. Often, now, they called him the name they had heard, Jesus the Nazarene. Most of the time he did not stop them from using the name, but at others he became angry and cried a peculiar, guttural name.

"Karl Glogauer! Karl Glogauer!"

And they said, Behold, he speaks with the voice of Adonai.

"Call me not by that name!" he would shout, and they would become disturbed and leave him by himself until his anger had subsided.

When the weather changed and the winter came, they went back to Capernaum, which had become a stronghold of his followers.

In Capernaum he waited the winter through, making prophecies.

Many of these prophecies concerned himself and the fate of those that followed him.

Then charged he his disciples that they should tell no man that he was Jesus the Christ. From that time forth began Jesus to shew unto his disciples,

> *how that he must go unto Jerusalem, and suffer
> many things of the elders and chief priests and
> scribes, and be killed, and be raised again the third
> day.*
>
> (Matthew 16: 20–21)

They were watching television at her flat. Monica was
eating an apple. It was between six and seven on a warm
Sunday evening. Monica gestured at the screen with her
half-eaten apple.

"Look at that nonsense," she said. "You can't honestly
tell me it means anything to you."

The program was a religious one about a pop-opera in
a Hampstead Church. The opera told the story of the
crucifixion.

"Pop-groups in the pulpit," she said. "What a come-
down."

He didn't reply. The program seemed obscene to him
in an obscure way. He couldn't argue with her.

"God's corpse is really beginning to rot now," she
jeered. "Whew! The stink!"

"Turn it off, then," he said quietly.

"What't the pop-group called? The Maggots?"

"Very funny. I'll turn it off, shall I?"

"No, I want to watch. It's funny."

"Oh, turn it off!"

"Imitation of Christ!" she snorted. "It's a bloody caricature."

A Negro singer, who was playing Christ and singing
flat to a banal accompaniment, began to drone out lifeless lyrics about the brotherhood of man.

"If he sounded like that, no wonder they nailed him
up," said Monica.

He reached forward and switched the picture off.

"I was enjoying it." She spoke with mock disappointment. "It was a lovely swan-song."

Later, she said with a trace of affection that worried
him, "You old fogey. What a pity. You could have been
John Wesley or Calvin or someone. You can't be a messiah these days, not in your terms. There's nobody to
listen."

VI

The prophet was living in the house of a man called Simon, though the prophet preferred to call him Peter. Simon was grateful to the prophet because he had cured his wife of a complaint which she had suffered from for some time. It had been a mysterious complaint, but the prophet had cured her almost effortlessly.

There were a great many strangers in Capernaum at that time, many of them coming to see the prophet. Simon warned the prophet that some were known agents of the Romans or the Pharisees. The Pharisees had not, on the whole, been antipathetic towards the prophet, though they distrusted the talk of miracles that they heard. However, the whole political atmosphere was disturbed and the Roman occupation troops, from Pilate, through his officers, down to the troops, were tense, expecting an outbreak but unable to see any tangible signs that one was coming.

Pilate himself hoped for trouble on a large scale. It would prove to Tiberius that the emperor had been too lenient with the Jews over the matter of the votive shields. Pilate would be vindicated, and his power over the Jews increased. At present he was on bad terms with all the Tetrarchs of the provinces—particularly the unstable Herod Antipas who had seemed at one time his only supporter. Aside from the political situation, his own domestic situation was upset in that his neurotic wife was having her nightmares again and was demanding far more attention from him than he could afford to give her.

There might be a possibility, he thought, of provoking an incident, but he would have to be careful that Tiberius never learned of it. This new prophet might provide a focus, but so far the man had done nothing against the laws of either the Jews or the Romans. There was no law that forbade a man to claim he was a messiah, as some said this one had done, and he was hardly inciting the people to revolt—rather the contrary.

Looking through the window of his chamber, with a view of the minarets and spires of Jerusalem, Pilate considered the information his spies had brought him.

Soon after the festival that the Romans called

Saturnalia, the prophet and his followers left Capernaum again and began to travel through the country.

There were fewer miracles now that the hot weather had passed, but his prophecies were eagerly asked. He warned them of all the mistakes that would be made in the future, and of all the crimes that would be committed in his name.

Through Galilee he wandered, and through Samaria, following the good Roman roads towards Jerusalem.

The time of the Passover was coming close now.

In Jerusalem, the Roman officials discussed the coming festival. It was always a time of the worst disturbances. There had been riots before during the Feast of the Passover, and doubtless there would be trouble of some kind this year, too.

Pilate spoke to the Pharisees, asking for their cooperation. The Pharisees said they would do what they could, but they could not help it if the people acted foolishly.

Scowling, Pilate dismissed them.

His agents brought him reports from all over the territory. Some of the reports mentioned the new prophet, but said that he was harmless.

Pilate thought privately that he might be harmless now, but if he reached Jerusalem during the Passover, he might not be so harmless.

Two weeks before the Feast of the Passover, the prophet reached the town of Bethany near Jerusalem. Some of his Galilean followers had friends in Bethany and these friends were more than willing to shelter the man they had heard of from other pilgrims on their way to Jerusalem and the Great Temple.

The reason they had come to Bethany was that the prophet had become disturbed at the number of the people following him.

"There are too many," he had said to Simon. "Too many, Peter."

Glogauer's face was haggard now. His eyes were set deeper into their sockets, and he said little.

Sometimes he would look around him vaguely, as if unsure where he was.

News came to the house in Bethany that Roman agents had been making inquiries about him. It did not seem to disturb him. On the contrary, he nodded thoughtfully, as if satisfied.

Once he walked with two of his followers across country to look at Jerusalem. The bright yellow walls of the city looked splendid in the afternoon light. The towers and tall buildings, many of them decorated in mosaic reds, blues, and yellows, could be seen from several miles away.

The prophet turned back towards Bethany.

"When shall we go into Jerusalem?" one of his followers asked him.

"Not yet," said Glogauer. His shoulders were hunched and he grasped his chest with his arms and hands as if cold.

Two days before the Feast of the Passover in Jerusalem, the prophet took his men towards the Mount of Olives and a suburb of Jerusalem that was built on its side and called Bethphage.

"Get me a donkey," he told them. "A colt. I must fulfill the prophecy now."

"Then all will know you are the Messiah," said Andrew.

"Yes."

Glogauer sighed. He felt afraid again, but this time it was not physical fear. It was the fear of an actor who was about to make his final, most dramatic scene and who was not sure he could do it well.

There was cold sweat on Glogauer's upper lip. He wiped it off.

In the poor light he peered at the men around him. He was still uncertain of some of their names. He was not interested in their names, particularly, only in their number. There were ten here. The other two were looking for the donkey.

They stood on the grassy slope of the Mount of Olives, looking towards Jerusalem and the great Temple which lay below. There was a light, warm breeze blowing.

"Judas?" said Glogauer inquiringly.

There was one called Judas.

"Yes, master," he said. He was tall and good looking with curly red hair and neurotic intelligent eyes. Glogauer believed he was an epileptic.

Glogauer looked thoughtfully at Judas Iscariot. "I will

want you to help me later," he said, "when we have entered Jerusalem."

"How, master?"

"You must take a message to the Romans."

"The Romans?" Iscariot looked troubled. "Why?"

"It must be the Romans. It can't be the Jews—they would use a stake or an axe. I'll tell you more when the time comes."

The sky was dark now, and the stars were out over the Mount of Olives. It had become cold. Glogauer shivered.

> *Rejoice greatly, O daughter of Zion,*
> *Shout, O daughter of Jerusalem:*
> *Behold, thy King cometh unto thee!*
> *He is just and having salvation;*
> *Lowly and riding upon an ass,*
> *And upon a colt, the foal of an ass.*
>   (Zechariah 9:9)

"Osha'na! Osha'na! Osha'na!"

As Glogauer rode the donkey into the city, his followers ran ahead, throwing down palm branches. On both sides of the street were crowds, forewarned by the followers of his coming.

Now the new prophet could be seen to be fulfilling the prophecies of the ancient prophets, and many believed that he had come to lead them against the Romans. Even now, possibly, he was on his way to Pilate's house to confront the procurator.

"Osha'na! Osha'na!"

Glogauer looked around distractedly. The back of the donkey, though softened by the coats of his followers, was uncomfortable. He swayed and clung to the beast's mane. He heard the words, but could not make them out clearly.

"Osha'na! Osha'na!"

It sounded like "hosanna" at first, before he realized that they were shouting the Aramaic for "Free us."

"Free us! Free us!"

John had planned to rise in arms against the Romans this Passover. Many had expected to take part in the rebellion.

They believed that he was taking John's place as a rebel leader.

"No," he muttered at them as he looked around at their expectant faces. "No, I am the messiah. I cannot free you. I can't. . ."

They did not hear him above their own shouts.

Karl Glogauer entered Christ. Christ entered Jerusalem. The story was approaching its climax.

"Osha'na!"

It was not in the story. He could not help them.

> *Verily, verily, I say unto you, that one of you shall betray me. Then the disciples looked on one another, doubting of whom he spake. Now there was leaning on Jesus' bosom one of his disciples, whom Jesus loved. Simon Peter therefore beckoned to him, that he should ask who it should be of whom he spake. He then lying on Jesus' breast saith unto him, Lord, who is it? Jesus answered, He it is, to whom I shall give a sop, when I have dipped it. And when he had dipped the sop, he gave it to Judas Iscariot, the son of Simon. And after the sop Satan entered into him. Then said Jesus unto him, That thou doest, do quickly.*

(John 13:21–27)

Judas Iscariot frowned with some uncertainty as he left the room and went out into the crowded street, making his way towards the governor's palace. Doubtless he was to perform a part in a plan to deceive the Romans and have the people rise up in Jesus' defense, but he thought the scheme foolhardy. The mood amongst the jostling men, women, and children in the streets was tense. Many more Roman soldiers than usual patrolled the city.

Pilate was a stout man. His face was self-indulgent, and his eyes were hard and shallow. He looked disdainfully at the Jew.

"We do not pay informers whose information is proved to be false," he warned.

"I do not seek money, lord," said Judas, feigning the

ingratiating manner that the Romans seemed to expect of the Jews. "I am a loyal subject of the Emperor."

"Who is this rebel?"

"Jesus of Nazareth, lord. He entered the city today . . ."

"I know. I saw him. But I heard he preached of peace and obeying the law."

"To deceive you, lord."

Pilate frowned. It was likely. It smacked of the kind of deceit he had grown to anticipate in these soft-spoken people.

"Have you proof?"

"I am one of his lieutenants, lord. I will testify to his guilt."

Pilate pursed his heavy lips. He could not afford to offend the Pharisees at this moment. They had given him enough trouble. Caiaphas, in particular, would be quick to cry "injustice" if he arrested the man.

"He claims to be the rightful king of the Jews, the descendant of David," said Judas, repeating what his master had told him to say.

"Does he?" Pilate looked thoughtfully out of the window.

"As for the Pharisees, lord . . ."

"What of them?"

"The Pharisees distrust him. They would see him dead. He speaks against them."

Pilate nodded. His eyes were hooded as he considered this information. The Pharisees might hate the madman, but they would be quick to make political capital out of his arrest.

"The Pharisees want him arrested," Judas continued. "The people flock to listen to the prophet, and today many of them rioted in the Temple in his name."

"Is this true?"

"It is true, lord." It was true. Some half-a-dozen people had attacked the money-changers in the Temple and tried to rob them. When they had been arrested, they had said they had been carrying out the will of the Nazarene.

"I cannot make the arrest," Pilate said musingly. The situation in Jerusalem was already dangerous, but if they were to arrest this "king," they might find that they precipitated a revolt. Tiberius would blame him, not the

Jews. The Pharisees must be won over. They must make the arrest. "Wait here," he said to Judas. "I will send a message to Caiaphas."

> *And they came to a place which was named Geth-semane: and he saith to his disciples, Sit ye here, while I shall pray. And he taketh with him Peter and James and John, and began to be sore amazed, and to be very heavy; And saith unto them, My soul is exceeding sorrowful unto death: tarry ye here, and watch.*
>
> (Mark 14:32–34)

Glogauer could see the mob approaching now. For the first time since Nazareth he felt physically weak and exhausted. They were going to kill him. He had to die; he accepted that, but he was afraid of the pain that was to come. He sat down on the ground of the hillside, watching the torches as they came closer.

> *"The ideal of martyrdom only ever existed in the minds of a few ascetics,"* Monica had said. *"Otherwise it was morbid masochism, an easy way to forgo ordinary responsibility, a method of keeping repressed people under control. . ."*
>
> *"It isn't as simple as that. . ."*
>
> *"It is, Karl."*

He could show Monica now. His regret was that she was unlikely ever to know. He had meant to write everything down and put it into the time machine and hope that it would be recovered. It was strange. He was not a religious man in the usual sense. He was an agnostic. It was not conviction that had led him to defend religion against Monica's cynical contempt for it; it was rather *lack* of conviction in the ideal in which she had set her own faith, the ideal of science as a solver of all problems. He could not share her faith, and there was nothing else but religion, though he could not believe in the kind of God of Christianity. The God seen as a mystical force of the mysteries of Christianity and other great religions had not been personal enough for him. His rational mind had told him that God did not exist in any personal form. His unconscious had told him that faith in science was not enough.

"Science is basically opposed to religion," Monica had once said harshly. *"No matter how many Jesuits get together and rationalize their views of science, the fact remains that religion cannot accept the fundamental attitudes of science, and it is implicit to science to attack the fundamental principles of religion. The only area in which there is no difference and need be no war is in the ultimate assumption. One may or may not assume there is a supernatural being called God. But as soon as one begins to defend one's assumption, there must be strife."*

"You're talking about organized religion. . ."

"I'm talking about religion as opposed to a belief. Who needs the ritual of religion when we have the far superior ritual of science to replace it? Religion is a reasonable substitute for knowledge. But there is no longer any need for substitutes, Karl. Science offers a sounder basis on which to formulate systems of thought and ethics. We don't need the carrot of heaven and the big stick of hell anymore when science can show the consequences of actions and men can judge easily for themselves whether those actions are right or wrong."

"I can't accept it."

"That's because you're sick. I'm sick, too, but at least I can see the promise of health."

"I can only see the threat of death. . ."

As they had agreed, Judas kissed him on the cheek and the mixed force of Temple guards and Roman soldiers surrounded him.

To the Romans he said, with some difficulty, "I am the King of the Jews." To the Pharisees' servants he said: "I am the messiah who has come to destroy your masters." Now he was committed, and the final ritual was to begin.

VII

It was an untidy trial, an arbitrary mixture of Roman and Jewish law which did not altogether satisfy anyone. The object was accomplished after several conferences between Pontius Pilate and Caiaphas and three attempts to bend and merge their separate legal systems in order to fit the expediencies of the situation. Both needed a scapegoat for their different purposes, and so at last the result was achieved and the madman convicted, on the one hand of rebellion against Rome and on the other of heresy.

A peculiar feature of the trial was that the witnesses were all followers of the man and yet had seemed eager to see him convicted.

The Pharisees agreed that the Roman method of execution would fit the time and the situation best in this case and it was decided to crucify him. The man had prestige, however, so that it would be necessary to use some of the tried Roman methods of humiliation in order to make him into a pathetic and ludicrous figure in the eyes of the pilgrims. Pilate assured the Pharisees that he would see to it, but he made sure that they signed documents that gave their approval to his actions.

And the soldiers led him away into the hall, called Praetorium; and they call together the whole band. And they clothed him with purple, and platted a crown of thorns, and put it about his head, And began to salute him, Hail, King of the Jews! And they smote him on the head with a reed, and did spit upon him, and bowing their knees worshipped him. And when they had mocked him, they took off the purple from him, and put his own clothes on him, and led him out to crucify him.

(Mark 15:16–20)

His brain was clouded now, by pain and by the ritual of humiliation; by his having completely given himself up to his rôle.

He was too weak to bear the heavy wooden cross and he walked behind it as it was dragged towards Golgotha by a Cyrenian whom the Romans had press-ganged for the purpose.

As he staggered through the crowded, silent streets, watched by those who had thought he would lead them against the Roman overlords, his eyes filled with tears so that his sight was blurred and he occasionally staggered off the road and was nudged back onto it by one of the Roman guards.

"You are too emotional, Karl. Why don't you use that brain of yours and pull yourself together? . . ."

He remembered the words, but it was difficult to remember who had said them or who Karl was.

The road that led up the side of the hill was stony and he slipped sometimes, remembering another hill he had climbed long ago. It seemed to him that he had been a child, but the memory merged with others and it was impossible to tell.

He was breathing heavily and with some difficulty. The pain of the thorns in his head was barely felt, but his whole body seemed to throb in unison with his heartbeat. It was like a drum.

It was evening. The sun was setting. He fell on his face, cutting his head on a sharp stone, just as he reached the top of the hill. He fainted.

And they bring him unto the place of Golgotha, which is, being interpreted, The place of a skull. And they gave him to drink wine mingled with myrrh: but he received it not.

(Mark 15:22–23)

He knocked the cup aside. The soldier shrugged and reached out for one of his arms. Another soldier already held the other arm.

As he recovered consciousness, Glogauer began to tremble violently. He felt the pain intensely as the ropes bit into the flesh of his wrists and ankles. He struggled.

He felt something cold placed against his palm. Although it only covered a small area in the center of his hand, it seemed very heavy. He heard a sound that also was in rhythm with his heartbeats. He turned his head to look at the hand.

The large iron peg was being driven into his hand by a soldier swinging a mallet as he lay on the cross which was at this moment horizontal on the ground. He watched, wondering why there was no pain. The soldier swung the mallet higher as the peg met the resistance of the wood. Twice he missed the peg and struck Glogauer's fingers.

Glogauer looked to the other side and saw that the second soldier was also hammering in a peg. Evidently he missed the peg a great many times because the fingers of the hand were bloody and crushed.

The first soldier finished hammering in his peg and

turned his attention to the feet. Glogauer felt the iron slide through his flesh, heard it hammered home.

Using a pulley, they began to haul the cross into a vertical position. Glogauer noticed that he was alone. There were no others being crucified that day.

He got a clear view of the lights of Jerusalem below him. There was still a little light in the sky but not much. Soon it would be completely dark. There was a small crowd looking on. One of the women reminded him of Monica. He called to her.

"Monica?"

But his voice was cracked, and the word was a whisper. The woman did not look up.

He felt his body dragging at the nails which supported it. He thought he felt a twinge of pain in his left hand. He seemed to be bleeding very heavily.

It was odd, he reflected, that it should be him hanging here. He supposed that it was the event he had originally come to witness. There was little doubt, really. Everything had gone perfectly.

The pain in his left hand increased.

He glanced down at the Roman guards who were playing dice at the foot of his cross. They seemed absorbed in their game. He could not see the markings of the dice from this distance.

He sighed. The movement of his chest seemed to throw extra strain on his hands. The pain was quite bad now. He winced and tried somehow to ease himself back against the wood.

The pain began to spread through his body. He gritted his teeth. It was dreadful. He gasped and shouted. He writhed.

There was no longer any light in the sky. Heavy clouds obscured stars and moon.

From below came whispered voices.

"Let me down," he called. "Oh, please let me down!"

The pain filled him. He slumped forward, but nobody released him.

A little while later he raised his head. The movement caused a return of the agony and again he began to writhe on the cross.

"Let me down. Please. Please stop it!"

Every part of his flesh, every muscle and tendon and

bone of him was filled with an almost impossible degree
of pain.

He knew he would not survive until the next day as he
had thought he might. He had not realized the extent of
his pain.

> *And at the ninth hour Jesus cried with a loud*
> *voice, saying, Eloi, Eloi, lama sabachthani? which is,*
> *being interpreted, My God, my God, why hast thou*
> *forsaken me?*
>
> **(Mark 15:34)**

Glogauer coughed. It was a dry, barely heard sound.
The soldiers below the cross heard it because the night
was now so quiet.

"It's funny," one said. "Yesterday they were worshipping him. Today they seemed to want us to kill him—
even the ones who were closest to him."

"I'll be glad when we get out of this country," said another.

He heard Monica's voice again. *"It's weakness and*
fear, Karl, that's driven you to this. Martyrdom is a con-
ceit. Can't you see that?"

Weakness and fear.

He coughed once more and the pain returned, but it
was duller now.

Just before he died, he began to talk again, muttering
the words until his breath was gone. "It's a lie. It's a lie.
It's a lie."

Later, after his body was stolen by the servants of some
doctors who believed it to have special properties, there
were rumors that he had not died. But the corpse was already rotting in the doctors' dissecting rooms and would
soon be destroyed.

1968

THE PLANNERS

by Kate Wilhelm

Rae stopped before the one-way glass, stooped, and peered at the gibbon infant in the cage. Darin watched her bitterly. She straightened after a moment, hands in smock pockets, face innocent of any expression what-so-goddam-ever, and continued to saunter toward him through the aisle between the cages.

"You still think it is cruel, and worthless?"

"Do you, Dr. Darin?"

"Why do you always do that? Answer my question with one of your own?"

"Does it infuriate you?"

He shrugged and turned away. His lab coat was on the chair where he had tossed it. He pulled it on over his sky-blue sport shirt.

"How is the Driscoll boy?" Rae asked.

He stiffened, then relaxed again. Still not facing her, he said, "Same as last week, last year. Same as he'll be until he dies."

The hall door opened, and a very large, very homely face appeared. Stu Evers looked past Darin, down the aisle. "You alone? I thought I heard voices."

"Talking to myself," Darin said. "The committee ready yet?"

"Just about. Dr. Jacobsen is stalling with his nose-throat spray routine, as usual." He hesitated a moment, glancing again down the row of cages, then at Darin. "Wouldn't you think a guy allergic to monkeys would find some other line of research?"

406

Darin looked, but Rae was gone. What had it been this time: the Driscoll boy, the trend of the project itself? He wondered if she had a life of her own when she was away. "I'll be out at the compound," he said. He passed Stu in the doorway and headed toward the livid greenery of Florida forests.

The cacophony hit him at the door. There were four-hundred-sixty-nine monkeys on the thirty-six acres of wooded ground the research department was using. Each monkey was screeching, howling, singing, cursing, or otherwise making its presence known. Darin grunted and headed toward the compound. The Happiest Monkeys in the World, a newspaper article had called them. Singing Monkeys, a subhead announced. MONKEYS GIVEN SMART-NESS PILLS, the most enterprising paper had proclaimed. *Cruelty Charged,* added another in subdued, sorrowful tones.

The compound was three acres of carefully planned and maintained wilderness, completely enclosed with thirty-foot-high, smooth plastic walls. A transparent dome covered the area. There were one-way windows at intervals along the wall. A small group stood before one of the windows: the committee.

Darin stopped and gazed over the interior of the compound through one of the windows. He saw Heloise and Skitter contentedly picking nonexistent fleas from one another. Adam was munching on a banana; Homer was lying on his back idly touching his feet to his nose. A couple of the chimps were at the water fountain, not drinking, merely pressing the pedal and watching the fountain, now and then immersing a head or hand in the bowl of cold water. Dr. Jacobsen appeared and Darin joined the group.

"Good morning, Mrs. Bellbottom," Darin said politely. "Did you know your skirt has fallen off?" He turned from her to Major Dormouse. "Ah, Major, and how many of the enemy have you swatted to death today with your pretty little yellow rag?" He smiled pleasantly at a pimply young man with a camera. "Major, you've brought a professional peeping tom. More stories in the paper, with pictures this time?" The pimply young man shifted his position, fidgeted with the camera. The major was fiery; Mrs. Bellbottom was on her knees peering under a bush, looking for her skirt. Darin blinked. None of them had on any clothing. He turned toward the window. The chimps were drawing up a table, laden with tea things, silver, china, tiny finger sandwiches. The chimps were all wearing flowered shirts and dresses. Hortense had on a ridiculous flop-brimmed sun hat of pale green straw. Darin leaned against the fence to control his laughter.

"Soluble ribonucleic acid," Dr. Johnson was saying when Darin recovered, "sRNA for short. So from the gross beginnings when entire worms were trained and fed to other worms that seemed to benefit from the original training, we have come to these more refined methods. We now extract the sRNA molecule from the trained animals and feed it, the sRNA molecules in solution, to untrained specimens and observe the results."

The young man was snapping pictures as Jacobsen talked. Mrs. Whoosis was making notes, her mouth a lipless line, the sun hat tinging her skin with green. The sun on her patterned red and yellow dress made it appear to jiggle, giving her fleshy hips a constant rippling motion. Darin watched, fascinated. She was about sixty.

". . . my colleague, who proposed this line of experimentation, Dr. Darin," Jacobsen said finally, and Darin bowed slightly. He wondered what Jacobsen had said about him, decided to wait for any questions before he said anything.

"Dr. Darin, is it true that you also extract this substance from people?"

"Every time you scratch yourself, you lose this substance," Darin said. "Every time you lose a drop of blood, you lose it. It is in every cell of your body. Sometimes we take a sample of human blood for study, yes."

"And inject it into those animals?"

"Sometimes we do that," Darin said. He waited for the next, the inevitable question, wondering how he would answer it. Jacobsen had briefed them on what to answer, but he couldn't remember what Jacobsen had said. The question didn't come. Mrs. Whoosis stepped forward, staring at the window.

Darin turned his attention to her; she averted her eyes, quickly fixed her stare again on the chimps in the compound. "Yes, Mrs., uh . . . Madam?" Darin prompted her. She didn't look at him.

"Why? What is the purpose of all this?" she asked. Her voice sounded strangled. The pimpled young man was inching toward the next window.

"Well," Darin said, "our theory is simple. We believe that learning ability can be improved drastically in nearly every species. The learning curve is the normal, expected bell-shaped curve, with a few at one end who have the ability to learn quite rapidly, with the majority in the center who learn at an average rate, and a few at the other end who learn quite slowly. With our experiments we are able to increase the ability of those in the broad middle, as well as those in the deficient end of the curve so that their learning abilities match those of the fastest learners of any given group . . ."

No one was listening to him. It didn't matter. They would be given the press release he had prepared for them, written in simple language, no polysyllables, no complicated sentences. They were all watching the chimps through the windows. He said, "So we gabbled the gazooka three times wretchedly until the spirit of camping fired the girls." One of the committee members glanced at him. "Whether intravenously or orally, it seems to be equally effective," Darin said, and the perspiring man turned again to the window. "Injections every morning . . . rejections, planned diet, planned parenthood, planned plans planning plans." Jacobsen eyed him suspiciously. Darin stopped talking and lighted a cigarette. The woman with the unquiet hips turned from the window, her face very red. "I've seen enough," she said. "This sun is too hot out here. May we see the inside laboratories now?"

Darin turned them over to Stu Evers inside the building. He walked back slowly to the compound. There was a grin on his lips when he spotted Adam on the far side, swaggering triumphantly, paying no attention to Hortense who was rocking back and forth on her haunches, looking very dazed. Darin saluted Adam, then, whistling, returned to his office. Mrs. Driscoll was due with Sonny at 1 P.M.

Sonny Driscoll was fourteen. He was five feet nine inches, weighed one hundred sixty pounds. His male nurse was six feet two inches and weighed two hundred twenty-seven pounds. Sonny had broken his mother's arm when he was twelve; he had broken his father's arm and

leg when he was thirteen. So far the male nurse was intact. Every morning Mrs. Driscoll lovingly washed and
dressed her baby, fed him, walked him in the yard, spoke
happily to him of plans for the coming months, or sang
nursery songs to him. He never seemed to see her. The
male nurse, Johnny, was never farther than three feet
from his charge when he was on duty.

Mrs. Driscoll refused to think of the day when she
would have to turn her child over to an institution. Instead she placed her faith and hope in Darin.

They arrived at two-fifteen, earlier than he had expected them, later than they had promised to be there.

"The kid kept taking his clothes off," Johnny said mo-
rosely. The kid was taking them off again in the office.
Johnny started toward him, but Darin shook his head. It
didn't matter. Darin got his blood sample from one of the
muscular arms, shot the injection into the other one.
Sonny didn't seem to notice what he was doing. He never
seemed to notice. Sonny refused to be tested. They got
him to the chair and table, but he sat staring at nothing,
ignoring the blocks, the bright balls, the crayons, the
candy. Nothing Darin did or said had any discernible effect. Finally the time was up. Mrs. Driscoll and Johnny
got him dressed once more and left. Mrs. Driscoll thanked
Darin for helping her boy.

Stu and Darin held class from four to five daily. Kelly
O'Grady had the monkeys tagged and ready for them
when they showed up at the schoolroom. Kelly was very
tall, very slender and red-haired. Stu shivered if she accidentally brushed him in passing; Darin hoped one day
Stu would pull an Adam on her. She sat primly on her
high stool with her notebook on her knee, unaware of the
change that came over Stu during school hours or, if
aware, uncaring. Darin wondered if she was really a
Barbie doll fully programmed to perform laboratory duties and nothing else.

He thought of the Finishing School for Barbies where
long-legged, high-breasted, stomachless girls went to get
shaved clean, get their toenails painted pink, their nipples
removed, and all body openings sewn shut, except for
their mouths, which curved in perpetual smiles and led
nowhere.

The class consisted of six black spider-monkeys who

had not been fed yet. They had to do six tasks in order:
1) pull a rope; 2) cross the cage and get a stick that was
released by the rope; 3) pull the rope again; 4) get the
second stick that would fit into the first; 5) join the sticks
together; 6) using the lengthened stick, pull a bunch of
bananas close enough to the bars of the cage to reach
them and take them inside where they could eat them.
At five the monkeys were returned to Kelly, who wheeled
them away one by one back to the stockroom. None of
them had performed all the tasks, although two had gone
through part of them before the time ran out.

Waiting for the last of the monkeys to be taken back to
its quarters, Stu asked, "What did you do to that bunch of
idiots this morning? By the time I got them, they all acted
dazed."

Darin told him about Adam's performance; they were
both laughing when Kelly returned. Stu's laugh turned to
something that sounded almost like a sob. Darin wanted
to tell him about the school Kelly must have attended,
thought better of it, and walked away instead.

His drive home was through the darkening forests of
interior Florida for sixteen miles on a narrow straight
road.

"Of course, I don't mind living here," Lea had said
once, nine years ago when the Florida appointment had
come through. And she didn't mind. The house was
air-conditioned; the family car, Lea's car, was air-
conditioned; the backyard had a swimming pool big
enough to float the Queen Mary. A frightened, large-eyed
Florida girl did the housework, and Lea gained weight
and painted sporadically, wrote sporadically—poetry—
and entertained faculty wives regularly. Darin suspected
that sometimes she entertained faculty husbands also.

"Oh, Professor Dimples, one hour this evening? That
will be fifteen dollars, you know." He jotted down the appointment and turned to Lea. "Just two more today and
you will have your car payment. How about that!" She
twined slinky arms about his neck, pressing tight high
breasts hard against him. She had to tilt her head slightly
for his kiss. "Then your turn, darling. For free." He tried
to kiss her; something stopped his tongue, and he realized
that the smile was on the outside only, that the opening
didn't really exist at all.

He parked next to an MG, not Lea's, and went inside the house where the martinis were always snapping cold. "Darling, you remember Greta, don't you? She is going to give me lessons twice a week. Isn't that exciting?"

"But you already graduated." Darin murmured. Greta was not tall and not long-legged. She was a little bit of a thing. He thought probably he did remember her from somewhere or other, vaguely. Her hand was cool in his.

"Greta has moved in; she is going to lecture on modern art for the spring semester. I asked her for private lessons and she said yes."

"Greta Farrel," Darin said, still holding her small hand. They moved away from Lea and wandered through the open windows to the patio where the scent of orange blossoms was heavy in the air.

"Greta thinks it must be heavenly to be married to a psychologist." Lea's voice followed them. "Where are you two?"

"What makes you say a thing like that?" Darin asked.

"Oh, when I think of how you must understand a woman, know her moods and the reasons for them. You must know just what to do and when, and when to do something else . . . Yes, just like that."

His hands on her body were hot, her skin cool. Lea's petulant voice drew closer. He held Greta in his arms and stepped into the pool where they sank to the bottom, still together. She hadn't gone to the Barbie school. His hands learned her body; then his body learned hers. After they made love, Greta drew back from him regretfully.

"I do have to go now. You are a lucky man, Dr. Darin. No doubts about yourself, complete understanding of what makes you tick."

He lay back on the leather couch staring at the ceiling. "It's always that way, Doctor. Fantasies, dreams, illusions. I know it is because this investigation is hanging over us right now, but even when things are going relatively well, I still go off on a tangent like that for no real reason." He stopped talking.

In his chair Darin stirred slightly, his fingers drumming softly on the arm, his gaze on the clock whose hands were stuck. He said, "Before this recent pressure, did you have such intense fantasies?"

"I don't think so," Darin said thoughtfully, trying to remember.

The other didn't give him time. He asked, "And can you break out of them now when you have to, or want to?"

"Oh, sure," Darin said.

Laughing, he got out of his car, patted the MG, and walked into his house. He could hear voices from the living room, and he remembered that on Thursdays Lea really did have her painting lesson.

Dr. Lacey left five minutes after Darin arrived. Lacey said vague things about Lea's great promise and untapped talent, and Darin nodded sober agreement. If she had talent, it certainly was untapped so far. He didn't say so.

Lea was wearing a hostess suit, flowing sheer panels of pale blue net over a skin-tight leotard that was midnight blue. Darin wondered if she realized that she had gained weight in the past few years. He thought so.

"Oh, that man is getting impossible," she said when the MG blasted away from their house. "Two years now, and he still doesn't want to put my things on show."

Looking at her, Darin wondered how much more her things could be on show.

"Don't dawdle too long with your martini," she said. "We're due at the Ritters' at seven for clams."

The telephone rang for him while he was showering. It was Stu Evers. Darin stood dripping water while he listened.

"Have you seen the evening paper yet? That broad made the statement that conditions are extreme at the station, that our animals are made to suffer unnecessarily."

Darin groaned softly. Stu went on, "She is bringing her entire women's group out tomorrow to show proof of her claims. She's a bigwig in the SPCA, or something."

Darin began to laugh then. Mrs. Whoosis had her face pressed against one of the windows, other fat women in flowered dresses had their faces against the rest. None of them breathed or moved. Inside the compound Adam laid Hortense, then moved on to Esmeralda, to Hilda. . . .

"Goddamn it, Darin, it isn't funny!" Stu said.

"But it is. It is."

Clams at the Ritters' were delicious. Clams, hammers, buckets of butter, a mountainous salad, beer, and finally

coffee liberally laced with brandy. Darin felt cheerful and
contented when the evening was over. Ritter was in Med.
Eng. Lit. but he didn't talk about it, which was merciful.
He was sympathetic about the stink with the SPCA. He
thought scientists had no imagination. Darin agreed with
him, and soon he and Lea were on their way home.

"I am so glad that you didn't decide to stay late," Lea
said, passing over the yellow line with a blast of the horn.
"There is a movie on tonight that I am dying to see."

She talked, but he didn't listen, training of twelve years
drawing out an occasional grunt at what must have been
appropriate times. "Ritter is such a bore," she said. They
were nearly home. "As if you had anything to do with
that incredible statement in tonight's paper."

"What statement?"

"Didn't you even read the article? For heaven's sake,
why not? Everyone will be talking about it . . ." She
sighed theatrically. "Someone quoted a reliable source
who said that within the foreseeable future, simply by de-
veloping the leads you now have, you will be able to produce monkeys that are as smart as normal human beings."
She laughed, a brittle meaningless sound.

"I'll read the article when we get home," he said. She
didn't ask about the statement, didn't care if it was true or
false, if he had made it or not. He read the article while
she settled down before the television. Then he went for a
swim. The water was warm, the breeze cool on his skin.
Mosquitoes found him as soon as he got out of the pool,
so he sat behind the screening of the verandah. The blu-
ish light from the living room went off after a time, and
there was only the dark night. Lea didn't call him when
she went to bed. He knew she went very softly, closing
the door with care so that the click of the latch wouldn't
disturb him if he was dozing on the verandah.

He knew why he didn't break it off. Pity. The most
corrosive emotion endogenous to man. She was the product of the doll school that taught that the trip down the
aisle was the end, the fulfillment of a maiden's dreams;
shocked and horrified to learn that it was another beginning, some of them never recovered. Lea never had.
Never would. At sixty she would purse her lips at the
sexual display of uncivilized animals, whether human or
not, and she would be disgusted and help formulate laws

to ban such activities. Long ago he had hoped a child would be the answer, but the school did something to them on the inside, too. They didn't conceive, or if conception took place, they didn't carry the fruit, and if they carried it, the birth was of a stillborn thing. The ones that did live were usually the ones to be pitied more than those who fought and were defeated *in utero.*

A bat swooped low over the quiet pool and was gone again against the black of the azaleas. Soon the moon would appear, and the chimps would stir restlessly for a while, then return to deep untroubled slumber. The chimps slept companionably close to one another without thought of sex. Only the nocturnal creatures, and the human creatures, performed coitus in the dark. He wondered if Adam remembered his human captors. The colony in the compound had been started almost twenty years ago, and since then none of the chimps had seen a human being. When it was necessary to enter the grounds, the chimps were fed narcotics in the evening to insure against their waking. Props were changed then, new obstacles added to the old conquered ones. Now and then a chimp was removed for study, usually ending up in dissection. But not Adam. He was father of the world. Darin grinned in the darkness.

Adam took his bride aside from the other beasts and knew that she was lovely. She was his own true bride, created for him, intelligence to match his own burning intelligence. Together they scaled the smooth walls and glimpsed the great world that lay beyond their garden. Together they found the opening that led to the world that was to be theirs, and they left behind them the lesser beings. And the god searched for them and finding them not, cursed them and sealed the opening so that none of the others could follow. So it was that Adam and his bride became the first man and woman and from them flowed the progeny that was to inhabit the entire world. And one day Adam said, for shame woman, seest thou that thou art naked? And the woman answered, so are you, big boy, so are you. So they covered their nakedness with leaves from the trees, and thereafter they performed their sexual act in the dark of night so that man could not look on his woman, nor she on him. And they were thus cleansed of shame. Forever and ever. Amen. Hallelujah.

Darin shivered. He had drowsed after all, and the night wind had grown chill. He went to bed. Lea drew away from him in her sleep. She felt hot to his touch. He turned to his left side, his back to her, and he slept.

"There is potential x," Darin said to Lea the next morning at breakfast. "We don't know where x is actually. It represents the highest intellectual achievement possible for the monkeys, for example. We test each new batch of monkeys that we get and sort them—x–1, x–2, x–3, suppose, and then we breed for more x–1s. Also we feed the other two groups the sRNA that we extract from the original x–1s. Eventually we get a monkey that is higher than our original x–1, and we reclassify right down the line and start over, using his sRNA to bring the others up to his level. We make constant checks to be sure we aren't allowing inferior strains to mingle with our highest achievers, and we keep control groups that are given the same training, the same food, the same sorting process, but no sRNA. We test them against each other."

Lea was watching his face with some interest as he talked. He thought he had got through, until she said, "Did you realize that your hair is almost solid white at the temples? All at once it is turning white."

Carefully he put his cup back on the saucer. He smiled at her and got up. "See you tonight," he said.

They also had two separate compounds of chimps that had started out identically. Neither had received any training whatever through the years they had been kept isolated from each other and from man. Adam's group had been fed sRNA daily from the most intelligent chimps they had found. The control group had been fed none. The control-group chimps had yet to master the intricacies of the fountain with its ice-cold water; they used the small stream that flowed through the compound. The control group had yet to learn that fruit on the high, fragile branches could be had if one used the telescoping sticks to knock them down. The control group huddled without protection or under the scant cover of palm trees when it rained and the dome was opened. Adam long ago had led his group in the construction of a rude but functional hut where they gathered when it rained.

Darin saw the women's committee filing past the compound when he parked his car. He went straight to the console in his office, flicked on a switch and manipulated buttons and dials, leading the group through the paths, opening one, closing another to them, until he led them to the newest of the compounds, where he opened the gate and let them inside. Quickly he closed the gate again and watched their frantic efforts to get out. Later he turned the chimps loose on them, and his grin grew broader as he watched the new-men ravage the old women. Some of the offspring were black and hairy, others pink and hairless, some intermediate. They grew rapidly, lined up with arms extended to receive their daily doses, stood before a machine that tested them instantaneously, and were sorted. Some of them went into a disintegration room, others out into the world.

A car horn blasted in his ears. He switched off his ignition, and he got out as Stu Evers parked next to his car. "I see the old bats got here," Stu said. He walked toward the lab with Darin. "How's the Driscoll kid coming along?"

"Negative," Darin said. Stu knew they had tried using human sRNA on the boy and failed consistently. It was too big a step for his body to cope with. "So far he has shown total intolerance to A–127. Throws it off almost instantly."

Stuart was sympathetic and noncommittal. No one else had any faith whatever in Darin's own experiment. A–127 might be too great a step upward, Darin thought. The *Ateles* spider monkey from Brazil was too bright.

He called Kelly from his office and asked about the newly arrived spider monkeys they had tested the day before. Blood had been processed; a sample was available. He looked over his notes and chose one that had shown interest in the tasks without finishing any of them. Kelly promised him the prepared syringe by 1 P.M.

What no one connected with the project could any longer doubt was that those simians, and the men who had been injected with sRNA from the Driscoll boy, had actually had their learning capacities inhibited, some of them apparently permanently.

Darin didn't want to think about Mrs. Driscoll's reaction if ever she learned how they had been using her boy. Rae sat at the corner of his desk and drawled insolently, "I might tell her myself, Dr. Darin. I'll say, Sorry, Ma'am,

.

you'll have to keep your idiot out of here; you're damaging the brains of our monkeys with his polluted blood. Okay, Darin?"

"My God, what are you doing back again?"

"Testing," she said. "That's all, just testing."

Stu called him to observe the latest challenge to Adam's group, to take place in forty minutes. Darin had forgotten that he was to be present. During the night a tree had been felled in each compound, its trunk crossing the small stream, damming it. At eleven the water fountains were to be turned off for the rest of the day. The tree had been felled at the far end of the compound, close to the wall where the stream entered, so that the trickle of water that flowed past the hut was cut off. Already the group not taking sRNA was showing signs of thirst. Adam's group was unaware of the interrupted flow.

Darin met Stu and they walked together to the far side where they would have a good view of the entire compound. The women had left by then. "It was too quiet for them this morning," Stu said. "Adam was making his rounds; he squatted on the felled tree for nearly an hour before he left it and went back to the others."

They could see the spreading pool of water. It was muddy, uninviting looking. At eleven-ten it was generally known within the compound that the water supply had failed. Some of the old chimps tried the fountain; Adam tried it several times. He hit it with a stick and tried it again. Then he sat on his haunches and stared at it. One of the young chimps whimpered pitiably. He wasn't thirsty yet, merely puzzled and perhaps frightened. Adam scowled at him. The chimp cowered behind Hortense, who bared her fangs at Adam. He waved menacingly at her, and she began picking fleas from her offspring. When he whimpered again, she cuffed him. The young chimp looked from her to Adam, stuck his forefinger in his mouth and ambled away. Adam continued to stare at the useless fountain. An hour passed. At last Adam rose and wandered nonchalantly toward the drying stream. Here and there a shrinking pool of muddy water steamed in the sun. The other chimps followed Adam. He followed the stream through the compound toward the wall that was its source. When he came to the pool, he squatted again. One of the young chimps circled the pool cautiously, reached down, and touched the dirty water, drew back, reached for it again, and then drank. Several of the others drank also. Adam continued to squat. At twelve-forty Adam moved again. Grunting and gesturing to several younger males, he approached the treetrunk. With much noise and meaningless gestures, they shifted the trunk. They strained, shifted it again. The water was released and poured over the heaving chimps. Two of them dropped the trunk and ran. Adam and the other two held. The two returned.

They were still working when Darin had to leave, to keep his appointment with Mrs. Driscoll and Sonny. They arrived at one-ten. Kelly had left the syringe with the new formula in Darin's small refrigerator. He injected Sonny, took his sample, and started the tests. Sometimes Sonny cooperated to the extent of lifting one of the articles from the table and throwing it. Today he cleaned the table within ten minutes. Darin put a piece of candy in his hand; Sonny threw it from him. Patiently Darin put another piece in the boy's hand. He managed to keep the eighth piece in the clenched hand long enough to guide the hand to Sonny's mouth. When it was gone, Sonny opened his mouth for more. His hands lay idly on the table. He didn't seem to relate the hands to the candy with the pleasant taste. Darin tried to guide a second to his mouth, but Sonny refused to hold a piece a second time.

When the hour was over and Sonny was showing definite signs of fatigue, Mrs. Driscoll clutched Darin's hands in hers. Tears stood in her eyes. "You actually got him to feed himself a little bit," she said brokenly. "God bless you, Dr. Darin. God bless you!" She kissed his hand and turned away as the tears started to spill down her cheeks.

Kelly was waiting for him when the group left. She collected the new sample of blood to be processed. "Did you hear about the excitement down at the compound? Adam's building a dam of his own."

Darin stared at her for a moment. The breakthrough? He ran back to the compound. The near side this time was where the windows were being used. It seemed that the entire staff was there, watching silently. He saw Stu and edged in by him. The stream twisted and curved through the compound less than ten inches deep, not over two feet anywhere. At one spot stones lay under it;

elsewhere the bottom was of hard-packed sand. Adam
and his crew were piling up stones at the one suitable
place for their dam, very near their hut. The dam they
were building was two feet thick. It was less than five feet
from the wall, fifteen feet from where Darin and Stu
shared the window. When the dam was completed, Adam
looked along the wall. Darin thought the chimp's eyes
paused momentarily on his own. Later he heard that
nearly every other person watching felt the same momentary pause as those black, intelligent eyes sought out and
held other intelligence.

". . . next thunderstorm. Adam and the flood . . ."

". . . eventually seeds instead of food . . ."

". . . his brain. Convolutions as complex as any man's."

Darin walked away from them, snatches of future plans
in his ears. There was a memo on his desk. Jacobsen was
turning over the SPCA investigatory committee to him. He
was to meet with the university representatives, the local
SPCA group, and the legal representatives of all concerned on Monday next at 10 A.M. He wrote out his daily
report on Sonny Driscoll. Sonny had been on too good behavior for too long. Would this last injection give him just
the spark of determination he needed to go on a rampage?
Darin had alerted Johnny, the bodyguard, whoops, male
nurse, for just such a possibility, but he knew Johnny
didn't think there was any danger from the kid. He hoped
Sonny wouldn't kill Johnny, then turn on his mother and
father. He'd probably rape his mother if that much goal-
directedness ever flowed through him. And the three men
who had volunteered for the injections from Sonny's
blood? He didn't want to think of them at all, therefore
couldn't get them out of his mind as he sat at his desk staring at nothing. Three convicts. That's all, just convicts
hoping to get a parole for helping science along. He
laughed abruptly. They weren't planning anything now.
Not that trio. Not planning for a thing. Sitting, waiting for
something to happen, not thinking about what it might be,
or when, or how they would be affected. Not thinking.
Period.

"But you can always console yourself that your motives
were pure, that it was all for Science, can't you, Dr.
Darin?" Rae asked mockingly.

He looked at her. "Go to hell," he said.

It was late when he turned off his light. Kelly met him in the corridor that led to the main entrance. "Hard day, Dr. Darin?"

He nodded. Her hand lingered momentarily on his arm. "Good·night," she said, turning in to her own office. He stared at the door for a long time before he let himself out and started toward his car. Lea would be furious with him for not calling. Probably she wouldn't speak at all until nearly bedtime when she would explode into tears and accusations. He could see the time when her tears and accusations would strike home, when Kelly's body would still be a tangible memory, her words lingering in his ears. And he would lie to Lea, not because he would care actually if she knew, but because it would be expected. She wouldn't know how to cope with the truth. It would entangle her to the point where she would have to try an abortive suicide, a screaming-for-attention attempt that would ultimately tie him in tear-soaked knots that would never be loosened. No, he would lie, and she would know he was lying, and they would get by. He started the car, aimed down the long sixteen miles that lay before him. He wondered where Kelly lived. What it would do to Stu when he realized. What it would do to his job if Kelly should get nasty, eventually. He shrugged. Barbie dolls never got nasty. It wasn't built in.

Lea met him at the door, dressed only in a sheer gown, her hair loose and unsprayed. Her body flowed into his so that he didn't need Kelly at all. And he was best man when Stu and Kelly were married. He called to Rae, "Would that satisfy you?" but she didn't answer. Maybe she was gone for good this time. He parked the car outside his darkened house and leaned his head on the steering wheel for a moment before getting out. If not gone for good, at least for a long time. He hoped she would stay away for a long time.

MOTHER TO THE WORLD

by Richard Wilson

His name was Martin Rolfe. She called him Mr. Ralph.

She was Cecelia Beamer, called Siss.

He was a vigorous, intelligent, lean and wiry forty-two, a shade under six feet tall. His hair, black, was thinning but still covered all of his head; and all his teeth were his own. His health was excellent. He'd never had a cavity or an operation, and he fervently hoped he never would.

She was a slender, strong young woman of twenty-eight, five feet four. Her eyes, nose, and mouth were regular and well-spaced, but the combination fell short of beauty. She wore her hair, which was dark blond, not quite brown, straight back and long in two pigtails which she braided daily, after a ritualistic hundred brushings. Her figure was better than average for her age and therefore good, but she did nothing to emphasize it. Her disposition was cheerful when she was with someone; when alone her tendency was to work hard at the job at hand, giving it her serious attention. Whatever she was doing was the most important thing in the world to her just then and she had a compulsion to do it absolutely right. She was indefatigable but she liked, almost demanded, to be praised for what she did well.

Her amusements were simple ones. She liked to talk to people but most people quickly became bored with what she had to say—she was inclined to be repetitive. Fortunately for her, she also liked to talk to animals, birds included.

She was a retarded person with the mentality of an

eight-year-old.

Eight can be a delightful age. Rolfe remembered his son at eight—bright, inquiring, beginning to emerge from childhood but not so fast as to lose any of his innocent charm; a refreshing, uninhibited conversationalist with an original viewpoint on life. The boy had been a challenge to him and a constant delight. He held on to that memory, drawing sustenance from it, for her.

Young Rolfe was dead now, along with his mother and three billion other people.

Rolfe and Siss were the only ones left in all the world.

It was M.R. that had done it, he told her. Massive Retaliation; from the Other Side.

When American bombs rained down from long-range jets and rocket carriers, nobody'd known the Chinese had what they had. Nobody'd suspected it of that relatively backward country which the United States had believed it was softening up, in a brushfire war, for enforced diplomacy.

Rolfe hadn't been aware of any speculation that Peking's scientists were concentrating their research not on weapons but on biochemistry. Germ warfare, sure. There'd been propaganda from both sides about that, but nothing had been hinted about a biological agent, as it must have been, that could break down human cells and release the water.

"M.R.," he told her. "Better than nerve gas or the neutron bomb." Like those, it left the buildings and equipment intact. Unlike them, it didn't leave any messy corpses—only the bones, which crumbled and blew away. Except the bone dust trapped inside the pathetic mounds of clothing that lay everywhere in the city.

"Are they coming over now that they beat us?"

"I'm sure they intended to. But there can't be any of them left. They outsmarted themselves, I guess. The wind must have blown it right back at them. I don't really know what happened, Siss. All I know is that everybody's gone now, except you and me."

"But the animals—"

Rolfe had found it best in trying to explain something to Siss to keep it simple, especially when he didn't under-

424   *Richard Wilson*

stand it himself. Just as he had learned long ago that if he
didn't know how to pronounce a word he should say it
loud and confidently.

So all he told Siss was that the bad people had got hold
of a terrible weapon called M.R.—she'd heard of that—
and used it on the good people and that nearly everybody
had died. Not the animals, though, and damned if he
knew why.

"Animals don't sin," Siss told him.

"That's as good an explanation as any I can think of,"
he said. She was silent for a while. Then she said: "Your
name—initials—are M.R., aren't they?"

He'd never considered it before, but she was right. Martin Rolfe—Massive Retaliation. I hope she doesn't blame
everything on me, he thought. But then she spoke again.
"M.R. That's short for Mister. What I call you. Your
name that I have for you. Mister Ralph."

"Tell me again how we were saved, Mr. Ralph."

She used the expression in an almost evangelical sense,
making him uncomfortable. Rolfe was a practical man, a
realist and freethinker.

"You know as well as I do, Siss," he said. "It's because
Professor Cantwell was doing government research and
because he was having a party. You certainly remember;
Cantwell was your boss."

"I know that. But you tell it so good, and I like to hear
it."

"All right. Bill Cantwell was an old friend of mine
from the army, and when I came to New York, I gave
him a call at the university. It was the first time I'd talked
to him in years; I had no idea he'd married again and had
set up housekeeping in Manhattan."

"And had a working girl named Siss," she put in.

"The very same," he agreed. Siss never referred to herself as a maid, which was what she had been. "And so
when I asked Bill if he could put me up, I thought it
would be in his old bachelor apartment. He said sure,
just like that, and I didn't find out till I got there, late in
the evening, that he had a new wife and was having a
houseparty and had invited two couples from out of town
to stay over."

"I gave my room to Mr. and Mrs. Glenn from Columbus," Siss said.

"And the Torquemadas, of Seville, had the regular guest room." Whoever they were; he didn't remember names the way she did. "So that left two displaced persons, you and me."

"Except for the Nassers."

The Nassers, as she pronounced it, were the two self-contained rooms in the Cantwell basement. The NASAs, or the Nasas, was what Cantwell called them because the National Aeronautics and Space Administration had given him a contract to study the behavior of human beings in a closed system.

Actually the money had gone to Columbia University, where Cantwell was a professor of mechanical and aerospace engineering.

"A sealed-off environment," Rolfe said. "But because Columbia didn't have the space just at that time, and because the work was vital, NASA gave Cantwell permission to build the rooms in his own home. They were—still are—in his basement, and that's where you and I slept that fateful night when the world ended."

"I still don't understand."

"We were completely sealed off in there," Rolfe said. "We weren't breathing Earth air, and we weren't connected in any way to the rest of the world. We might as well have been out in space or on the moon. So when it happened to everybody else—to Professor and Mrs. Cantwell, and to the Glenns and the Torquemadas and to the Nassers in Egypt and the Joneses in Jones Beach and all the people at Columbia, and in Washington and Moscow and Pretoria and London and Peoria and Medicine Hat and La Jolla and all those places all over—it didn't happen to us. That's because Professor Cantwell was a smart man and his closed systems worked."

"And we were saved."

"That's one way of looking at it."

"What's the other way?"

"We were doomed."

From his notebooks:

Siss asked why I'm so sure there's nobody but us left in the whole world. A fair question. Of course

I'm not absolutely positively cross-my-heart-and-hope-to-die, swear-on-a-Bible convinced that there isn't a poor live slob hidden away in some remote corner. Other people besides Bill must have been working with closed systems; certainly any country with a space program would be, and maybe some of *their* nassers were inhabited, too. I hadn't heard that any astronauts or cosmonauts were in orbit that day, but if they were and got down safely, I guess they could be alive somewhere.

But I've listened to the rest of the world on some of the finest radio equipment ever put together and there hasn't been a peep out of it. I've listened and signaled and listened and signaled and listened. Nothing. Nil. Short wave, long wave, AM, FM, UHF, marine band, everywhere. Naught. Not a thing. Lots of automatic signals from unmanned satellites, of course, and the quasars are still being heard from, but nothing human.

I've sent out messages on every piece of equipment connected to Con Ed's EE net. RCA, American Cable & Radio, the Bell System, Western Union, The Associated Press, UPI, Reuters' world news network, *The New York Times*'s multifarious teletypes, even the Hilton Hotels' international reservations system. Nothing. By this time I'd become fairly expert at communications, and I'd found the Pentagon network at AT&T. Silent. Ditto the hot line to the Kremlin. I read the monitor teletype and saw the final message from Washington to Moscow. Strictly routine. No hint that anything was amiss anywhere. Just as it must have been at the Army message center at Pearl Harbor on another Sunday morning a generation ago.

This is for posterity, these facts. My evidence is circumstantial. But to Siss I say: "There's nobody left but us. I know. You'll have to take my word for it that the rest of the world is as empty as New York."

Nobody here but us chickens, boss. Us poor flightless birds. One middle-aged rooster and one sad little hen, somewhat deficient in the upper story. What do you want us to do, boss? What's the next step in the great cosmic scheme? Tell us: where do we go from here?

But don't tell me; tell Siss. I don't expect an answer; she does. She's the one who went into the first church she found open that Sunday morning (some of them were locked, you know) and said all the prayers she knew, and asked for mercy for her relatives, and her friends, and her employers, and for me, and for all the dead people who had been alive only yesterday, and finally for herself; and then she asked why. She was in there for an hour and when she came out, I don't think she'd had an answer.

Nobody here but us chickens, boss. What do you want us to do now, fricassee ourselves?

Late on the morning of doomsday they had taken a walk down Broadway, starting from Cantwell's house near the Columbia campus.

There were a number of laughs to be had from cars in comical positions, if anybody was in a laughing mood. Some were standing obediently behind white lines at intersections, and obviously their drivers had been overtaken during a red light. With its driver gone, each such car had simply stood there, its engine dutifully using up all the gas in its tank and then coughing to a stop. Others had nosed gently into shop windows, or less gently into other cars or trucks. One truck loaded with New Jersey eggs had overturned, and its cargo was dripping in a yellowy white puddle. Rolfe, his nose twitching as if in anticipation of a warm day next week, made a mental note never to return to that particular spot.

Several times he found a car that had been run up upon from behind by another. It was as if, knowing they would never again be manufactured, they were trying copulation.

While Siss was in church Rolfe found a car that had not idled away all its gas and he made a dry run through the streets. He discovered that he could navigate pretty well around the stalled or wrecked cars, though occasionally he had to drive up on the sidewalk or make a three-block detour to get back to Broadway.

Then he and Siss, subdued after church, went downtown.

"Whose car is this, Mr. Ralph?" she asked him.

"My car, Siss. Would you like one, too?"

"I can't drive."

"I'll teach you. It may come in handy."

"I was the only one in church," she said. It hadn't got through to her yet, he thought; not completely.

"Who were you expecting?" he asked kindly.

"God, maybe."

She was gazing straight ahead, clutching her purse in her lap. She had the expression of a person who had been let down.

At 72nd Street a beer truck had demolished the box office of the Trans-Lux movie house and foamy liquid was still trickling out of it, across the sidewalk and along the gutter and into a sewer. Rolfe stopped the car and got out. An aluminum barrel had been punctured. The beer leaking from it was cool. He leaned over and let it run into his mouth for a while.

The Trans-Lux had been having a Fellini festival; the picture was *8½*. On impulse he went inside and came back to the car with the reels of film in a black tin box. He remembered the way the movie had opened, with all the cars stalled in traffic. Like Broadway, except that the Italian cars had people in them. He put the box in the rear of the car and said, "We'll go to the movies sometime." Siss looked at him blankly.

At Columbus Circle a Broadway bus had locked horns with a big van carrying furniture from North Carolina. At 50th Street a Mustang had nosed gently into the front of a steak house, as if someone had led it to a hitching post.

He made an illegal left turn at 42nd Street, noting what was playing at the Rialto: two naughty, daring, sexy, nudie pix, incdluding a rerun of *My Bare Lady*. He didn't stop for that one.

At the old Newsweek Building, east of Broadway, an Impala had butted into the ground-floor liquor store. The plate glass lay smashed but the bottles in the window were intact. He made a mental note. Across the street, one flight up, was the Keppel Folding Boat Company, which had long intrigued him. Soon it might be useful to unfold one and sail off to a better place. He marked it in his mind.

Bookstores, 42nd Street style. Dirty books and magazines. Girly books. Deviant, flagellant, homosexual, lesbian, sadistic books. Pornographic classics restored to the common man—*Memoirs of a Woman of Pleasure. The Kama Sutra,* quaint but lasciviously advertised. Books of nudes for the serious artist (no retoucher's airbrush here, men!).

Nudie pix in packets, wrapped in pliofilm, at a buck and a half the set. Large girls in successive states of undress. How big can a breast be before it disgusts? What is the optimum bosom size? A-cup? D-cup? It would depend on the number to be fed, wouldn't it? And how hungry they were? Or was that criterion passé?

He looked over at Siss, who wasn't looking at him or the bookstores or the dirty-movie houses but straight ahead. She had a nice figure. About a C.

But it was never the body alone; it was the mind that went with it and the voice with which it spoke.

"What are you thinking, Siss?" he asked.

"Nothing," she said. It was probably true. "What are *you* thinking?"

Riposte. How could he tell her?

He improvised. They were passing Bryant Park. "Pigeons in the park," he said. "I'm thinking of the pigeons. Hungrier than yesterday because nobody's buying peanuts for them, bringing slices of bread from home; there's no bread lady buying bagfuls for them at Horn & Hardart's day-old bakery shop."

"It's a sad time, isn't it, Mr. Ralph?"

"Yes, Siss; a sad time."

They got to First Avenue and the UN. There wasn't anybody there, either.

Notes for a History of the World was what he wrote on page one of his notebook.

On page two he had alternate titles, some facetious:

The True History of the Martin Rolfe Family on the Planet Earth; or *Two for Tomorrow.*

Recollections of a World Well Lost.

How the Population Crisis Was Solved.

What Next? or, If *You* Don't Do It, Marty, Who the Hell Will?

From his notebooks:

Thank God for movies. We'd be outen our minds by now if I hadn't taught myself to be a projectionist.

Radio City Music Hall apparently's only movie on Con Ed's EE list. Bit roomy for Siss and me but getting used to it. Sometimes she sits way down front, I in mezzanine, and we shout to each other when Gregory Peck does heroic things.

Collected first runs to add to *8½* from all major Manhattan houses—Capitol, Criterion, Cinema I & II, State, etc.—so we have good backlog. Also, if Siss likes, we run it again right away or next night. I don't mind. Then there are the 42nd St. houses and the art houses and the nabes & Mod. Museum film library. Shouldn't run out for a long time.

Days are for exploring and shopping. I go armed because of the animals. Siss stays home at hotel.

(*Why* are there animals? Find out. *Where* find out; how?)

The dogs in packs are worst. So far they haven't attacked, and a shot fired in the air scares them off. So far.

Later they left the city. It had been too great a strain to live a life half primitive, half luxurious. The contrast was too much. And the rats were getting bolder. The rats and the dogs.

They had lived there at first for the convenience. He picked a hotel on Park Avenue. He put Siss in a single room and took a suite down the hall for himself.

He guessed correctly that there'd be huge refrigerators and freezers stocked with food enough for years.

The hotel, with its world-famous name, was one of the places the Consolidated Edison Company had boasted was on its Emergency Electricity net, along with City Hall, the Empire State Building, the tunnels and bridges, Governors Island and other key installations. The EE net, worked out for Civil Defense (what had ever become of Civil Defense?), guaranteed uninterrupted electricity to selected customers through the use of deep, underground grids and conduits, despite flood, fire, pestilence, or war.

A promotional piece claimed that only total annihilation could knock out the system.

There was a hint of the way it worked in a slogan that Con Ed considered using before the government censors decided it would have given too much away: ". . . as long as the Hudson flows."

Whatever the secret, he and Siss had electricity, from which so many blessings flowed, for as long as they stayed in the city.

From his notebooks:

I've renamed our hotel The Living End. Siss calls it our house, or maybe Our House.

I won't let her go out by herself, but she has the run of the hotel. She won't use the self-service elevators. Doesn't trust them. Don't blame her. She cooks in the hotel kitchen and carries our meals up two flights on a tray.

Garbage disposal no problem. There's an incinerator that must work by electricity. So far it's taken everything I've dumped down it. I can't feel any heat, but it doesn't stink.

We're getting some outdoor stinks, though. Animal excrement that nobody cleans up (I'd be doing nothing else if I started). Uncollected garbage. Rotting food in supermarkets and other places without EE.

There are certain streets I avoid now. Whole sections, when the wind is wrong.

Bad night at the Living End. Had a nightmare.

I dreamed that Siss and I, home from the Music Hall (Cary Grant and Audrey Hepburn in something from the sixties), were having a fight. I don't know about what, but we were shouting, and I was calling her unforgivable names, and she was saying she was going to climb up to the 20th floor and jump, when the phone rang . . .

I woke up, seeming to hear the echo of the last ring. The phone was there on the floor under the night table.

I didn't dare pick it up.

•

It must have happened just before dawn when Manhattan was as deserted as it ever got.

I took a chance on the EE and went up in the elevators to the top of the Empire State Bldg. First time I'd ever been up—also the last, probably. What a sight. Plenty of cars, cabs, trucks, buses rammed into each other & sides of bldgs but lots more just came to natural (!) stop in midstreet or near curb. Very feasible to drive around and out of town, tho probably not thru tunnels. GW Bridge shd be okay with its 8 lanes. Have to get out of town one day anyhow, so best explore in advance.

Planes. No sign that any crashed but bet lots did somewhere. Everything looks orderly at NY airports.

Fires. Few black spots—signs of recent fires. Nothing major.

Harbor & rivers. Some ships, lots of boats drifting around loose. No sign of collisions; nothing big capsized.

Animals. Dog packs here and there. Sound of their barking rises high. *Nasty* sound. Birds, all kinds.

Air very dry.

Down in the street again, Rolfe began to think about the animals other than the dogs that ran in packs. How long would it be until the bigger ones—the wolves and bears and mountain lions—found their way into the city? He decided to visit Abercrombie & Fitch and arm himself with something heavier than the pistol he carried. Big-bore stuff, whatever they called it.

Rolfe was admiring an elephant gun in the fantastic store (Hemingway had shopped here, and probably Martin and Osa Johnson and Frank Buck and others from the lost past) when he remembered another sound he'd heard from the top of the Empire State Building. It had puzzled him, but now he could identify it. It had been the trumpeting of an elephant. An elephant in Manhattan? The circus wasn't in town—He knew then, but for the moment he pushed aside the thought and its implications.

After he had picked out the guns, and a wicked gas-operated underwater javelin for good measure, he outfitted himself in safari clothes. Khaki shorts and high socks, a big-pocketed bush jacket, a sun helmet. Hurrah for Captain Spalding! He looked a true Marxman, he thought, humming the song Groucho had sung and admiring himself in a full-length mirror.

He took a cartridge belt and boxes of shells and first-aid and water-purification kits and a trapper's knife and a light-weight trail ax and a compass and binoculars and snowshoes and deerskin gloves and a tough pair of boots. He staggered out onto Madison Avenue and dumped everything into the back of the cream-colored Lincoln convertible he was driving that day.

The trumpeting of the elephant had come from the Central Park Zoo, of course. He drove in from Fifth Avenue and parked near the restaurant opposite the sea lions' pool. He could see three of them lying quietly on a stone ledge, just above the water, watching him. He wondered when they'd last been fed.

First, though, he went to the administration building and let himself in with lock-picking tools. He had become adept at the burglary trade. He found a set of what seemed to be master keys and tried them first at the aviary. They worked.

The names of the birds, on the faded wooden plaques, were as colorful as their plumage. There were a Papuan lory, a sulphur-crested cockatoo, the chiffchaff and kookaburra bird, laughing jackass and motmot, chachalaca, drongo and poor old puffin. He opened their cages and watched their tentative, gaudy passage to freedom.

A pelican waddled out comically, suspicion in its round eyes. He ducked a hawk and cowered from a swift, fierce eagle. An owl lingered, blinking, until he shooed it toward the doors. He left to the last two brooding vultures, hesitating to free creatures so vile. But there was a role for scavengers, too. He opened their cage and ran, to get outdoors before they did.

After the cacophony of the aviary, he was surprised at the silence as he neared the monkey house. The big chimps were nothing to fool around with. But the monkey house was empty. The signs were there and the smell remained, but the apes, big and small, were not. Could they have freed themselves? But all the cages were locked.

Puzzled, he went on to the smaller mammals, freeing the harmless ones, the raccoons, the mongooses, the deflowered skunks, the weasels, and prairie dogs—even the spiny porcupine, which looked over its shoulder at him as it shuffled toward the doors.

He freed the foxes, too, and they bounded off as if to complete an interrupted mission. "Go get the rats," Rolfe yelled after them.

He marked the location of the big cats. He'd come back to them with his guns.

Last of all he freed the lone elephant, scarcely grown, whose trumpet call had summoned him. The elephant— an unofficial sign said it was a female, Geraldine—followed him at a distance almost to the car, then broke into a clumsy trot and drank from the sea lions' pool.

As Rolfe was returning to the cages with the guns, he knew why there weren't any monkeys. The big and little apes were hominids, like man. Their evolutionary climb had doomed them, too.

He killed the beasts of prey. It was an awful business. He was not a good shot even at close range, and the executions took many bullets. A sinuous, snarling black panther took six before he was sure. The caged beasts, refusing to stand still for the mercy killings, made it hot, bloody, stinking work. He guessed it was necessary.

Finally he was done. Quivering and sweating, he returned to the car. The sea lions honked and swam across to his side of the pool. He could see now that there were three babies and two adults.

What was he to do with them? He couldn't bring himself to a final butchery. And what was he to do about all the other captive animals—in the Bronx Zoo uptown, in zoos all over the world? He couldn't be a one-man Animal Rescue League.

Rolfe had a momentary fantasy in which he enticed the sea lions into the car (four in the back, one in the front) and drove them to the East River where they flopped into the water and swam toward the sea, honking with gratitude.

But he knew that in his present state of exhaustion he couldn't lift even the babies, and there was no way for them to get out of their enclosure unaided. Maybe he could come back with a truck and plank and fish to tempt them with. He left the problem, and that of the Bronx and

Prospect Parks Zoos and the Aquarium (not to get too far afield) and started the car.

Geraldine looked after him. He would have liked a little trumpet of farewell, but she had found some long grass and was eating.

As he drove back to the Living End through the wider streets, weaving carefully around the stalled cars, his mind was full of the other trapped beasts great and small, starving and soon to go mad from thirst, as if in punishment for having outlived man.

Only then did the other thought crash into his consciousness—what of the millions of pets trapped in the houses of their vanished owners? Dogs and cats, unable to open the refrigerators or the cans in the pantries. Some would have the craft to tear open packages of dried food and would learn to drink from leaking faucets or from toilet bowls. But at best they could prolong their miserable existence for only a few more days.

What was he to do about the pets? What could he do? Run around the city freeing them? Where would he start? Should he free all those on the north sides of odd-numbered streets? Or those on the ground floors of houses in named streets beginning with consonants? What were the rules? How did you play God?

He resolved not to talk to Siss about it. He wouldn't have her breaking her heart over a billion doomed animals; she had enough to mourn.

From his notebooks:

What should I call today? Rolfeday? Sissuary the 13th? Year Zero?

Shd hav kept track but don't really know how many days it's been since I walked out of Bill's storage vault and found myself ½ the human pop. of the whole furshlugginer world.

Asked Siss. *She* remembers. It has been exactly 11 days since the holocaust. She accounted for every one of them. Moren I cld do: they started to run together for me after the first three.

OK, so it's Sissuary the 11th, Year One, Anno Rolfe. *Some*body's got to keep a record.

How many days in Sissuary? We'll see. Got to name the second month before closing out the first.

It was difficult for him to look back and remember exactly when he had first realized with certainty that this was the woman with whom he was fated to spend the rest of his life, when it had dawned on him that this moron was to be his bosom companion, that he had to take care of her, provide for her, *talk* to her (and *listen* to her), answer her stupid questions, *sleep* with her!

The realization must have come about the time he began to experience his stomach aches. They weren't pains; they were more like a gnawing at the vitals of his well-being, a pincers movement by the enemy that was trapping him where he didn't want to be, with someone he didn't want to be with, a leaden weight that was smothering his freedom.

Some of her traits nearly drove him out of his mind. He was oversensitive, he supposed, but he had to wince and tried to close his ears every time she converted a sneeze into a clearly enunciated "Ah *choo!*" and waited for him to bless her.

Worse because more frequent was her way of grunting audibly when she was picking up something or pushing something or moving something around. This was to let him know that she was hard at work, for him. After a while he forced himself to praise her while she was at it—her diligence, her strength, her unselfishness—and she stopped making so much noise. He hated himself for being a hypocrite and felt sure she would see through him, but she never did, and in the end his exaggerated praise became a way of life. It stood him in good stead later when he had to tell her white lies about the degree of his affection for her and the great esteem in which he held her.

From his notebooks:

Asked Siss if she'd ever read a book and she said oh yes the Good Book. Parts of it. It used to comfort her a lot more in the old days, apparently. She's read two books all the way thru—Uncle Wiggily and Japanese Fairy Tales, and parts of a Tarzan book. She sometimes used to look at the paper—read the comics, the horoscope, picture captions, the TV listings. Lord save us from ever having to hold a literary conversation.

To be fair I've tried to remember the last 10 books

I read before doom. Probably be a pretty stupid list
if I was following my usual random reading pattern
—off on an Erle Stanley Gardner or James Bond
kick and reading everything available all at once.

Aside from his obligation to humanity to sire a new
race, what was there for him to do? Rolfe considered the
possibilities, dividing them into two groups: necessities
(duties or obligations) and pastimes (including frivoli-
ties).

Under necessities he put:

Keep a journal for posterity, if any. He was already
doing that.

Give Siss the equivalent of a grammar school education;
more if she could take it.

Try to elevate her taste for the sake of the unborn children she would one day influence.

Keep his family fed and sheltered. Would it be necessary to clothe them, except for warmth in the winter? Nu-
dity might be more practical, as well as healthier.

Then he jotted down on a separate piece of paper "Obligation to self paramount" and looked at it. He felt that
he had to come first, with his duty to Siss a little lower (on
the paper and in his estimation) because he was smarter
than she was and therefore more worth saving.

Then he had another look and amended it. Siss was
more worth saving because she was a woman and able to
reproduce her kind.

But not without his help, of course.

Finally he put himself and Siss together at the top of
the list. No good saving one without the other.

Pastimes. Take up a sport to keep fit. What one-man
sports were there? Woodchopping? Fat chance. Too blister prone, he. Hiking? Maybe he and Siss should hike
around the world to make absolutely positively sure there
was nobody else. Or around the eastern United States,
anyhow. Or just up and down the Hudson River Valley?
Somehow walking didn't seem to be his sport, either.

He might take up cooking. Men had always been the
best chefs and now ingenuity would be needed to make
nourishing and palatable meals from what was available
to them. They couldn't depend on canned and preserved
food forever. Okay, he'd be a cook. Of course that was a

sport that tended to put pounds on, not take them off. He'd better find an antidote, like swimming or handball.

How about collecting? What—money? Diamonds? Great art? Neither money nor diamonds obviously; neither had any intrinsic value in a World of Two—and then art was best left where it was, as well-protected as anything in the poor old world. If he wanted Siss to see a Rembrandt or an Andrew Wyeth, he'd take her to it.

From his notebooks:

Collecting old-fashioned windup phonographs against the day when no elec. Also old-fashioned 78 records. Got to keep so many things I can't reproduce.

Music. Good; Siss likes. She enjoys Tchaikowsky, Wagner and Beethoven (what wildness must stir within her poor head sometimes!). She'll sit still for Bach. I can't complain.

We're both crazy about Cole Porter, she for the music, I for the words, those great words, so much more ironic now than he had ever meant them to be. "It's All Right With Me," for instance.

We've found a place. We—Is that the first time I've used the word?

It's far enough away from the city to be really country; beyond the stink and the reminders of dead glory; yet close enough so I can get in for supplies if I need them. I've stored up enough good gassed-up cars so that travel is no problem, but I think I'll try to stay here as much as I can. I used to be a fair woodsman. Let's see how much I remember.

It's peaceful here. My stomach ache is better, all of a sudden.

He insisted on thinking of her as a person who had come into his custody and for whom he was responsible. For a long time all he felt toward her was pity; no desire. And for that reason he also pitied himself.

Because she was what she was, it would be unthinkable for her to touch him in any but the most innocent of ways, as she would one of her animal friends.

And when she called him anything but Mr. Ralph, using a word like honey, he was not flattered because he had heard her apply it also to a squirrel, a bluejay, and a field mouse.

"Mr. Ralph, can I ask you a favor? Would you mind if you took me for a ride?"

It wasn't that she particularly wanted to go anywhere; apparently her enjoyment lay in sharing the front seat with him; he noticed that she sat very close to him, in almost the exact center of the seat and did not, as he had speculated she might, sit at the far right, next to the window.

For her ride she chose an ornate costume which included a hat, a silk scarf, dark glasses, jacket, blouse and skirt, stockings and half-heel shoes.

She picked the costume at what she called the Monkey Ward store while he shopped down the block for a fairly clean convertible with sound tires and a fair amount of gas in the tank.

They rode out past the quarry. Long ago he had stored away the fact that Quarry Road was the highway probably least littered with debris.

There was one bad place where he had to get off into a field to skirt what looked like a 50-car chain-reaction smashup. Otherwise, it was good driving all the way to the lake.

He parked near the old boat-launching site and automatically scanned the watery horizon for any sign of sail or smoke. He had never entirely abandoned hopes of finding other people.

He had brought from the liquor store (catty-corner from Monkey Ward's) a fifth of a high-priced Scotch, and as they sat looking out over the lake, he carefully opened it, preserving the tinfoil for her.

Then he ceremoniously offered her a drink. She declined, as he knew she would, saying:

"Not now, thanks. Maybe some other time." Apparently a piece of etiquette she'd learned was that it was bad manners to refuse anything outright—especially something to eat or drink.

Rolfe said: "I'll have one, though, if you don't mind." And she replied in what must have been a half-remembered witticism, "Take two, they're small."

He took two in succession, neither small.

The lake was serene, the sun was warm but not hot, a breeze blew from the east, and the bugs were infrequent.

"Doesn't it bother you that there's nobody else?" he asked her. "Don't you get *lonesome?*"

But she said: "I'm always lonesome. I was. Now, I'm less lonesome than I was. Thanks to you, Mr. Ralph."

Now what could he say to that? So he sat there, touched but scowling out at the horizon, and then he reached for the very old Scotch (the world had still lived when it was bottled) and took a very big swallow. Only later did he think to offer her one.

"Some other time maybe," she said. "Not right now."

There came a day when her last brassiere lost its hooks, and she obtained his dispensation to stop wearing it. And another when her blouses lost their buttons and refused to stay closed by the mere tucking of their tails into her skirts, and he told her it didn't matter in the least; until finally her last rags fell from her.

She said to him: "You're my Mr. Ralph, honey, and it's not wrong to be this way with you, is it, Mr. Ralph?"

This touched him so that he took her naked, innocent body in his arms and kissed the top of her clean, sweet head, and he said:

"You're my big little girl, and you couldn't do anything wrong if you tried."

And only then, for the first time, he felt a desire for this waif—this innocent in whom the seeds of the whole human race were locked.

She gave him a quick daring kiss on the cheek and ran off, saying: "It's time I started supper now. My gosh, we have to get you fed."

He remembered with shame a pathetic scene early in their life together. They had gone to Monkey Ward's and dressed from the skin out in brand-new evening clothes. He'd had to help her cancel some tasteless combinations, but at last she stood before him like an angel. Or, as he'd said: "Damned if you don't look like a Madison Avenue model."

"You shouldn't swear, Mr. Ralph," she'd said. "But thanks anyhow."

"And you shouldn't talk. You're welcome. Look, we're going to play a game. We're going to a fancy night club.

We're going to make believe you're a mute—that you can't talk. No matter what, you must not say a word. Not a word."

"All right, Mr. Ralph."

"Starting right now, damn it! I'm sorry. I mean starting right now. All you can do is nod or smile. You can touch me if you want to. But you can't talk at all. That's part of the game. Do you understand?"

She started to say yes, then caught herself and nodded.

The silent nod from this beautifully gowned woman immediately made her ten times more attractive. Pleased with himself and with her, he gave her his arm and bowed her into the front seat of the Bentley he had searched out for their evening.

The night club had once been a major one with a resident big-name band. Changing fashion had turned it into a discotheque, so that it had a juke box. He fed it a handful of coins to pay his way into a night of illusion. But the tables were bare and therefore wrong. He found a linen closet and set them with tablecloths and silverware, glasses, candlesticks.

The illusion grew. He found a switch that set in motion a set of colored lights that played on multifaceted colored globes which hung from the ceiling. Another switch set them spinning slowly.

"What do you do in your spare time?" he asked her, knowing she wouldn't reply, but wanting to see how she would react.

She shrugged, smiled a little, and shook her head in what he tried to imagine was an attitude that said she had so little spare time that it was negligible.

She was carrying out her part of the bargain. She did it extremely well. She listened without a word to his conversation, looking into his eyes as he pretended they were two among hundreds of elegant diners. He reconstructed talk from pre-holocaust nights out. He pretended she was a girl he had once been engaged to and told her extravagant things. She looked back at him and smiled, as if mockingly, as the old girl would have done. He pretended it was a later time, with the engagement in ruins and him solacing himself with the wife of his best friend, with the best friend's knowledge and consent, and the girl across from him gave him silent looks of profound sympathy.

He pretended he had hired a call girl and spoke foully to her. She smiled bravely, her lips quivering, saying nothing.

Angered by the illusion which he had created and which mocked him, he drank too much and continued to abuse her—for herself, now; for doing as he had asked, for remaining silent.

The juke box was playing "Begin the Beguine" and ghostly dancers danced inside the circle of tables, under the soft colored lights. He saw them and cursed them for their nonexistence. He got up, knocking his chair over backwards, and shouted at her.

"Speak!" he said. "I release you from your muteness."

She shook her head, no longer smiling.

"Speak! you misbegotten halfwit! You monstrous birdbrained imposter! You scullery maid in a Schiaparelli gown. Speak, you—mental case."

But still she said nothing; merely looked at him with those deep eyes that seemed to understand and forgive.

Only at the very end of their evening out, when he had drunk himself into a stupor and stared across the room over her right shoulder, as if transfixed by his misery, did she speak. And then she said only:

"We better go home, Mr. Ralph, honey."

Then with a strength greater than his, she half-carried him to the car and drove him home and put him to bed. It was a good thing he'd taught her to drive.

He woke up contrite, half remembering that he'd behaved unforgivably.

But she forgave him, as perhaps no one else ever would have, using these words:

"I forgive you, Mr. Ralph. You knewd not what you dood."

He was delighted. "Do not what I would," he said. "Had I but dood what I could, who knew what would have been dood?"

"I don't think that's very nice, Mr. Ralph. I said I forgive you. You're supposed to say thank you and say you're sorry, even if you're not sorry."

He was still laughing at her, even after the realization that he had a hangover.

"Okay. I'm sorry even if I'm not sorry, and it's very

good of you to forgive me for my insufferable behavior, even if nobody asked you to."

"Thank you for saying that, Mr. Ralph. Now I'll fix you a hangover remedy."

"Where did you learn to concoct a hangover remedy, for God's sake?"

"I was a working girl once for a poor man who got intoxicated and his wife. I learned it there."

She gave him no magic potion but an ordinary tomatoey thing laced with pepper and Worcestershire sauce. He drank it down but stubbornly declined to feel better for a full hour. By then he had persuaded Siss he needed a cold beer, and she'd brought him one—disapproving but proud of her ingenuity in having produced it, since they kept no store of alcoholic beverages. She must have made an ingenious search to find a cold beer; he was suddenly proud of her.

But, remembering his performance of the night before, he hated himself.

From the holding of hands to the kiss is not so far a thing as from the not holding of hands to the holding.

One thinks of the innocence of holding hands (children do it; men shake hands), but it is a vast journey from a platonic handclaps, over which there is no lingering, to the clasp which is so intense and telegraphic (accompanied, as it may be, by ardent gazing) that it would be a great surprise if the kiss to which it soon led were rebuffed.

And a kiss may lead anywhere. This he knew. He wondered how much she knew, or felt or surmised.

Dared he take her hand to help her across a stream or a rocky place? So far he had taken her arm, holding her firmly just above the elbow as if she were an elderly woman and he a large Boy Scout. He had no wish yet for anything more intimate.

It was a hesitant, tentative beginning to their romance.

"Do you mind my touching you?" he asked. Lately he had found that it gave him pleasure to touch her hair or trace the outline of her ear, or run his finger along her breastbone. Nothing carnal.

"No; I enjoy it."

And so they married. He arranged a ceremony, not only for her sense of propriety but to satisfy his demand for a kind of stability amid chaos.

He made it as elaborate as possible. He found a big flat rock to be the altar. He picked flowers and garlanded them into a headpiece for her. Let her head be covered, though her body was not.

She surprised him with a piece of writing. Crudely written in pencil on a sheet from a lined pad, it said:

> "To my Mr. Ralph—
> "This is our day to mary to-gether. My day and your day. I feel real good about it even if nobody else cant come. I'll try and make you a good wife with all my heart.
> "I know you do the same thing for me because you are kind and good dear Mr. Ralph.
> > "Your friend and wife
> > "Cecelia Beamer"

It was the first time he knew what Siss was the nickname for.

Never before a sentimental man, Martin took his wife, Cecelia Beamer Rolfe, in his arms and kissed her with tenderness and affection.

He put her wedding-letter, as he thought of it, away in his desk, where it would be safe.

He wanted to consummate the marriage outdoors. It was a perfect June day, the sun warm, the grass soft, a breeze gentle. Lord knew they could not have asked for greater privacy than that of their own planet. But he felt Siss would have been, if not shocked, embarrassed unless four walls surrounded them.

Therefore he took her indoors where she removed her flowery hat and put it in water, in a bowl.

Then she turned to him and said: "Tell me what to do, Mr. Ralph. I don't know what to do for you."

"For us, child," he said. "What we do—whatever we do from now on—is for us. Together."

"I like you saying that. Tell me what I should do."

"You don't have to do anything except be loved and love back in whatever way you feel. Anything you feel and do is right because you're my wife and I'm your husband."

"Would it be wrong for me to want you to hold me—here?" she asked. Eyes cast down, she touched her breasts. "I feel as if I'm bursting, I'm so full of love for my Mr. Ralph. I never thought—back then, that—"

He had to stop her talking and kissed her.

For a ring he had made a circlet of grass. When it broke apart or fell to pieces, he made her another. In a way, he thought sometimes, it was like renewing the vows.

Once, years later, when he was looking for a pencil, he found in the back of her drawer a collection of hundreds of wisps or strands of dried grass. She had saved each of the worn-out rings, obviously. She had kept them in a cheaply manufactured container of plastic masquerading as leather, which said in gaudy lettering "My Jewel Box." These were her gems, her only treasure.

He sometimes asked Siss suddenly, intently: "Are you my friend?" And she would reply: "Yes, I am. Didn't you think so?" And he would be ashamed, but also gratified, and his heart would swell because she had said more than just Yes.

A woman is a race apart, a friend had told him once. "But," Rolfe added to himself, "this is ridiculous." He and Siss could not have been more unlike mentally.

Well, of course. That could have been true even if he'd had the whole world to choose from. Suppose she had been a selfish, empty-headed teenager; how long could he have stood someone like that? Or she could have been a crone, a hag—work-worn, fat, diseased, crippled. You're a pretty lucky guy, Martin Rolfe, Mr. Ralph, sir!

Sexually they were complementary, for instance. But was that enough? Except for little bits of time, no. But those are very important little bits of time, aren't they, Marty? Precious even. Each a potential conception, a possible person.

But aside from that, no; it was not enough.

But because her entire existence was one of trying to please him, she learned eventually to make acceptable verbal responses, and their mating became more satisfactory to him. His stomach ached less frequently.

By trial and error and by diligence, as she learned any

task, she learned to speak to him in bed with an approximation of high intelligence, murmuring words of sympathy, approval, surprise, delight, playfulness, even shock at appropriate times. She learned to modulate her laughter, once coarse and raucous. She learned that a few words, sincerely but carefully expressed, did more for their mutual happiness than a babble, or an ungrammatical gush.

Her physical responses, as of a slave to a beloved master, had always been gratifying to him, except for her one unbreakable habit—her tendency to say "Oh, praise God!" whenever she achieved orgasm, or whenever she thought he had.

Once she had asked him to tell her about his life.

"What about it?" he had asked.

"All about it," she'd said.

"That would be a lot to tell."

"As much as you want to, then, Mr. Ralph."

Without a word of introduction, he would start: "I was sixteen when I first kissed a girl. Awfully old . . ."

He'd always thought it shameful that he'd been unkissed so long and had never confessed it before. It was years later before Siss got up the courage to say: "Mr. Ralph, you told me once you didn't get a kiss till you were sixteen and that's too bad, but do you know how old I was?"

And he had said, No, he didn't, and she'd said:

"Twenty-eight, Mr. Ralph: that's how old. So don't you feel so bad."

And he'd asked her, though he was practically certain, "You mean I was the first one ever to kiss you?"

"The first man, except my father, yes, sir, Mr. Ralph. And do you know what? I'm awfully glad it was you that was the first, and that now nobody else ever will. I'm glad of that."

And so he had to postpone his confession. He had been on the point of telling Siss about his previous marriage—how he had chosen his wife from those available for matrimony among the fairly large number of women he had known.

What a fantastically wide choice he had had! The irony of now with no choice at all made him marvel to think that he could have picked from among millions, had he known doom was to come and that he and his mate, if she too were saved, would be parents to the entire human race. With what care he would have searched, what exacting tests he would have applied, to screen the mass of womanhood for a fitting mate for the last man!

But because he had expected all life to continue, he had chosen from an extremely small sample. Nevertheless he had chosen well.

Later he would tell Siss; not now. He would not hurt her at this time with talk about what, by hindsight, had been a perfect marriage; nor did he feel like hurting himself by contrasting a happy past marriage to an intelligent woman with what he had now.

Now he would tell Siss about another time in his adult past, a sad interlude during which he and his perfect wife had separated and he was living alone.

How foolish to have had that quarrel with his dead perfect wife, he thought. How senseless to have lost all the time that they might have had together.

Yet he had achieved a certain peace in his solitude. And their marriage had been stronger when he returned to her.

"I'm going to tell you about a time when I was living all alone in a little trailer in the woods," he told Siss.

He had been a free-lance editor in those days, doctoring doddering magazines, doing articles for his editor friends, and reading for a publishing house, and so was able to avoid the frenzied daily commute. He used the mails and phone and got into the city a couple of times a month.

He enjoyed an occasional dinner or cocktail party in his exurb; but he valued his privacy enough to decline many invitations and to withdraw to his trailer.

Rolfe himself never entertained. His truck-back trailer home was unsuited for anything but the shortest of visits. He'd have the mailman in for a drink of bourbon on Christmas Eve, or chat with the man who came around to collect for the volunteer ambulance corps, or play ten-second-move chess with the route man who delivered the only food Rolfe ate at home—eggs and the butter he fried them in.

The truck-back home normally sat in the middle of Rolfe's eighteen acres—far enough out of town so that there were woods to surround him and a dammed-up stream in which to swim, but close enough for an electric power line to be run in.

If Rolfe's choice of this way to live during his separation was an eccentricity, then he was eccentric. One other thing about him was a little odd. He had nailed a sign to a tree at the beginning of the track that led off the county road to his place. It said:

PRIVATE ROAD
MINED

The police came around after he put up the sign, which he'd burned into the end of an egg crate with an electric pen. The policemen, a lieutenant and a sergeant, left their car at the county road and walked carefully along the edge of Rolfe's track to the pickup truck in the clearing near the dammed-up stream. A pheasant moved without haste into some undergrowth as they came up to the door over the tailgate.

Rolfe invited them in, making room for them to sit down by lifting a manuscript off the one easy chair and motioning the sergeant to the camp chair in front of the typewriter on the bracket that folded down from the wall. Rolfe sat on the single bunk along the driver's side, having first got Cokes out of the tiny refrigerator. He knew better than to offer liquor to policemen on duty. They chatted for a while before the lieutenant said, "About your sign, Mr. Rolfe; we've had some complaints."

"Call me Martin. Complaints? I like my privacy, that's all."

"My name's Sol," the lieutenant said, "and this is Eric." They shook hands all round again, now that the first-name basis had been established, and Sol said, "About the road being mined. Sure it's private property, and nobody respects the principle of that more than I do, but somebody might get hurt. Somebody who couldn't read, maybe, or who wandered in after dark—not really meaning to trespass, you know."

"Sure," Rolfe said. "I can understand that."

"Besides," the sergeant—Eric—said, "anybody with war surplus ammunition was supposed to have turned it in years ago. It's the law."

"I don't know what you mean," Rolfe said. "I haven't booby-trapped the road. I wouldn't hurt a rabbit, much less a human being. Why, I'm so soft-hearted I don't even fish the stream."

Sol said: "I get it. You just put up the sign to keep people away—like 'Beware of the Dog,' even if you don't have a dog."

"And there really aren't any bouncing Bettys out there then?" Eric said. "I'm relieved. Believe me, we walked mighty easy along the edge."

Martin Rolfe grinned. "Gentlemen, I think I begin to understand. And it's all my fault because I'm such a poor speller. What I was trying to do was to call attention to the fact that it isn't a public road or a hiking trail or a place for young vandals to go if they have a hankering to break windows or set fires in out-of-the-way places. I believe there've been a few such incidents around town."

"Too many," Sol said. "But I still don't know what you mean about being a poor speller."

"What I intended to say on the sign, I guess, was 'Mind you, this is a private road.' It's a kind of New England expression."

"I've heard it," Eric said. "They have signs like that in London, where my wife's from—she was a war bride, you know, Lieutenant—that say 'Mind the step.' "

"That's m-i-n-d, not m-i-n-e-d," Sol said.

"Is that right?" Rolfe asked with a grin. "I told you I wasn't much of a speller. I'd better change the sign then, hadn't I?"

Instead of replying directly, Sol asked, "Ever have trouble with kids back in here?"

"Kids and grown-ups both," Rolfe said. "Different kinds of trouble. Kids broke a window one night. I was asleep and got a shower of broken glass all over my face. Another time a big brave man with a gun shot the hell out of a mother partridge and her brood and left them flopping around. He wasn't even planning to eat them. Did you ever put a living thing out of its misery with your bare hands, Sol? That same day I put up the sign. The partridges and I haven't been bothered since."

Sol got up and let himself out into the clearing. "I had to kill a doe once that some mighty hunter put a hole into but didn't think worth following into the brush." Eric

went out with Martin Rolfe behind him, and all three
walked along the middle of the track to the county road.
Birds chirped at them, and a leisurely rabbit hopped
way.

At the blacktopped road Martin Rolfe went to his sign.
He took a pencil out of his shirt pocket and scratched a
vertical line through the *E* in *mined*. Then he joined the
N and *D* with a proofreader's mark.

The sergeant said, "I don't know that that's too highly
visible. Besides, a couple of rains'll wash it off."

"Oh, come on, Eric," the lieutenant said, getting into
the car. "It's as plain as day."

"Thanks, Lieutenant," Martin said, going over to the
police car to say goodbye. "I never could spell worth a
damn."

"Oh, yeah?" Eric said. "I'll bet you can outspell both
of us any day." He was looking back at the sign as he got
into the car and he tripped, so that he had to grab for the
door to steady himself.

"Mind the step," Martin said.

It was achingly poignant for him to leaf through the
pages of a copy of the *New York Times Magazine* he'd
saved.

How lovable and childlike seemed the people doing the
weird things fashion advertising demanded of them!
How earnest were the statements made in the articles
and the letter pages. For example, there was the ironic,
the heartbreakingly laughable article about the population
explosion—about the insupportable hundreds of millions
there soon would be in India, or the six billion there'd be
on Earth in just a few more years.

Would that there were only as many people as had
read that particular Sunday issue of the *Times*. A million
and a half? World enough. Or even if there existed on
Earth only the few hundred people it had taken to
write, edit, and print that particular issue of the *New
York Times Magazine*. Even if there were only *one* other
than Siss and himself. One man to play chess with, or to
philosophize with.

He thrust away from him the thought that the third
person on Earth might be another woman. It was too dangerous, too explosive a thought. Would he betray Siss for

a normal woman? Certainly he would never abandon her, but betrayal was certain—she would be so easy to fool. What form, other than an intellectual one, would it take? Would he take the new woman blatantly as his mate with a facile explanation to Siss? Would the new one try to banish Siss (he'd never stand for that—would he?), or decree a demeaning role for her in a reorganized household—something he might rationalize himself into accepting? (He could hear the new one saying: "You want our children—Earth's only children—to be intelligent, don't you? You don't want the new world peopled with feeble-minded brats, do you?")

His thoughts went back to the possible consequences if a third person were male. Suppose the man were not a chess player? Suppose he were a mere brute with brutish instincts? Would Martin have to share Siss with him, Eskimo style? Even if he could bring himself (or Siss) to accept such an arrangement, how long could it continue without an explosion?

No—as long as he was fantasizing, it would be simpler to dream up two other people, a man and a woman who had already arranged their own lives, who had made the adjustment.

Still—how long could two couples—and only two—live side by side without something boiling over? Wife-swapping was too prevalent an institution in the bad old days, when there were all kinds of other entertainment, not to be a daily temptation in an all-but-depopulated world.

No—it would be best to have no third or fourth person —not unless there could be an infinity of others besides. . . .

Ah, but he was so *lonely!*

"I'm going to the city," he told Siss.

They had done without the city for a long time. They had made do with the things they had, or could make; they'd let their clothing drop away and hadn't replaced it; they'd grown their own food, made their country house the center of their universe. But now he wanted to go back.

She must have seen something in his eyes. "Let me go for you," she said. "Just tell me what you want."

Sometimes she chose such an ironic way of saying things that he fleetingly suspected her of having not only intelligence but wit.

"Just tell you what I want! As if—" He stopped. As if he could tell her. As if he knew.

He knew only that he had to get away for a little while. He wanted to be alone, with his own memories of a populated Earth.

He also wanted a drink.

Long ago he had made it a rule never to have liquor in the house. It would be too great a temptation to have it handy. He could see himself degenerating into a drunken bum. With an unlimited supply close at hand, a devoted woman to do all the work that needed to be done, he could easily slip into an animalistic role—become a creature with a whiskey-sodden, atrophied brain.

A fitting father and mother to the world such a pair would be!

And so he had made his rule: drink all you want when you have to—in the city—but never bring it home.

And so he had told Siss: "I don't know what I want exactly. I just want to go to the city."

And she had said: "All right, Mr. Ralph, if you have to."

There was her perception again, if that's what it was. "If you have to," she'd said, though he'd talked of want, not need.

"I do," he said. "But I'll come back. Is there anything I can bring you?" She looked around the kitchen and began to say something, then stopped and said instead: "Nothing we really need. You just go, Mr. Ralph, and take as long as you have to. It'll give me a chance to go do that berry-picking I been wanting to."

She was so sweet that he almost decided not to go. But then he kissed her—very thankful, just then, that she was his Siss and not some too-bright shrew of a problem wife —and went. He drove in, naked in a Cadillac.

He had rolled the swivel chair out of the store onto the sidewalk and was sitting in it in the afternoon sunshine. Beside him on the pavement were half a dozen bottles, each uncapped. He was talking to himself.

"As the afternoon sun, blood-red through the haze of

the remnants of a once overpopulated world, imperceptibly glides to its bed, one of the two known survivors becomes quietly plastered." He had a drink on that, then went on:

"What thoughts pass through the mind of this pitiful creature, this naked relic of a man left to eke out the rest of his days on a ruined planet?

"Does he ever recall the glory that once was his and that of his fellows? Or is he so sunk in misery—in the mere scratching of a bare existence from an arid soil—that he has forgotten the heights to which his kind once had risen? Subject pauses in thought and reaches for bottle. Drinks deeply from bottle, but not so deeply as to induce drunken sickenness. Aim of subject is quiet plasterization, happy drunkdom, a nonceness of Nirvana with harm to none and bitterness never. Sicken drunkenness?

"A respite of reverie, perhaps, as subject casts mind back to happy past. Mr. Martin Rolfe in Happier Days."

He picked up his *New York Times Magazine* and leafed through it. It was almost as good as having another drink. There they were—they couldn't have been more than 17—leaping in their panty girdles to show the freedom of action and the elasticity of the crotch. He remembered once having heard a newsman, waiting in the rain for the arrival of a president, say: "Being a reporter is essentially an undignified occupation." So had been being a model, obviously.

Things of the past . . . He thought: "A title for my memoirs—*Things of the Past*." He took up the *Times* again and turned to an ad of a debonair young man in a revolving door holding a copy of the *Wall Street Journal*. "I dreamt I was trapped in a revolving door in my Arcticweave tropical worsted," Rolfe said, summing up the situation. He looked like the 28-year-old Larchmont-type; five years out of college with a Master's, two kids, wife beginning to drink a little bit too much. "If he's trapped there long enough, he may read the paper right through to the shipping pages and ship out to the islands."

Rolfe looked pityingly at the trapped Larchmont-type armed against his predicament only with his Arcticweave suit, his *Wall Street Journal*, and, presumably, a wallet full of wife-and-baby pictures, credit cards, and a commutation ticket issued by a railroad company petitioning to suspend passenger service.

"You poor bastard," Rolfe said.

Of course he was saying it to himself, too. He said it all the way home: "You poor bastard. You poor bastard."

Siss was waiting for him in the cool garden. Gently she led him indoors. She said, with only the slightest hint of reproach (he could stand that much—he deserved more): "You been drinking too much again, Mr. Ralph. You know it's bad for you."

"You're right, Siss. Absolutely right."

"You got to take care of yourself. I try to, but you got to try, too."

Tenderly she put him to bed. He knew then, among other times, how much he needed her, and he struggled to say something nice to her before he dropped off to sleep. Finally he said: "You know, Siss, you're nicer than all those crazy leaping girls in the York Times." That's what she called it, the York Times. "You got a lot more sense, too, than they look as if they had."

From his notebooks:

Got drunk saft. Downtown. Dangerous. Not fair to Siss. Liable get et up by dogs while stinko. Bad show.

Can't bring bottle home, tho. Too great a temptation to get sozzled daily and twice on Sunday.

Why is Sunday worse than other days? I tried to rename it, but Siss insisted we keep it. She also demanded it come every seven days, just like in good old days. Had to give in. So much for calendar reform.

He sought other ways of escaping. He hiked and climbed and explored.

Once he found a spot on the brow of a hill from which one (that is, he) could see for miles but from which no work of man was visible except the top of a silo at the top of a similar hill across a wide valley.

Having found the spot, he cleared wild strawberry plants from beneath a young maple tree, leaving the ferns and the cushiony moss, and lay down to rest. It had been a strenuous climb, and hot, and now the insects were upon him. But though the flies buzzed, they did not often land, and the mosquitoes were torpid and easily slapped. After a while—it was almost noon (as if the hour mattered)—he had a couple of swallows from the flask he carried in his rucksack and ate some cheese. He thought of the flask as his iron rations.

As he rummaged in the rucksack, he found a roll of plastic tape he'd brought along to help him blaze a trail. He hadn't needed it; instead he'd marked his way by cutting branches with a long-handled pruning tool.

But as he lay in the solitude he had sought out and found (how odd to seek solitude in an empty world!), under one of a myriad of trees, where the only sounds were of buzzing insects, chirping birds, the soughing of trees in a soft wind, he knew what to do with the plastic tape. He printed something on a little square of paper, small but legible, and, with the tape, attached it to the lowest bough of his young maple. Now he lay under it, savoring what he had done.

The little sign said: THIS TREE RESERVED.

One June night it rained in great, warm, wind-driven sheets. He had not experienced such a storm since a visit a decade earlier to the tropics.

The pleasure he took in the soaking, bath-temperature rain was enhanced by the danger from the lightning. It stabbed down from the sky as if seeking him out, destroying and burning only yards away, as if it would be a great cosmic joke to strike that one spot on the surface of the Earth and kill the last man.

He defied it, prancing wildly, then halting deliberately as if transfixed when it flashed, posing with outthrust or upthrust arms, yelling, defying the thing or Being that had sent the storm, loosing his pent-up frustrations, his disappointments and hates in the elemental power of the storm.

He had trapped the beast in a pit, unfairly. It had nearly exhausted itself in attempts to leap the sheer walls. At least he hadn't lined the bottom with spikes.

Rolfe could have killed it from above, poisoned it, let it starve. Instead he jumped into the pit armed with two knives, to risk mauling and death.

He realized his folly instantly. The creature was far from

helpless. Its claws were sharp, though its movements were clumsy in the cramped pit-bottom, and its fetid breath was as much a weapon as its fangs.

Only by the sheerest of luck, he felt, did he avoid the claws and fangs long enough to plunge first one knife then the other into the beast's heart.

As its death struggles subsided he lay there, his face buried in the back of its neck, hugging the thing he'd killed, a sadness coming over him as he felt the fading heartbeat.

Later he skinned the beast. He and Siss ate the meat and slept under the pelt. But first he had buried the head in tribute to a worthy antagonist, a kind of salute to another male.

And unto them was born a son.

Siss seemed to know just what to do, by instinct. Clumsily he helped. He cut the umbilical with a boiled pair of scissors. Made a knot. Washed the red little thing.

Eventually Siss lay quiet, dry, serene, holding her swaddled child. He sat on the floor next to the bed and looked and looked at the mother and child. A holy picture, he thought. He sat for hours, staring, wondering. She looked back at him, silent, wondering.

The new human being slept serene.

It could not have been more perfect.

His son. His boy. His and hers but, he felt it fair enough to say, mostly his.

His son Adam. What else had there been to name him? Adam. Trite but noble. He had considered calling him Ralph, but only briefly. It would be too comical to have his mother go around introducing him to their near circle of friends—relatives all, come to think of it—as Ralph Ralph.

There'd be no need for introductions for many years, of course, in a closed society such as theirs. The years did pass.

There was his son, tall for his age, straight, brown, good with his hands. . . .

But bright? Intelligent? How was a father to know? A prejudiced parent sees only the good, ignores what he doesn't want to accept, can be oblivious to faults obvious to anyone else.

He talked to him and got gratifying responses. But wouldn't almost any response be gratifying to a parent? Parents are easily satisfied. Especially fathers of sons.

Had he conditioned himself to the point where he would be satisfied if his son showed more than animal intelligence? The conditioning encompassed an agony of watching as his son grew—watching for signs of mental retardation, of idiocy, of dullness, of torpor.

And then they had a daughter.

From his notebooks:

My son. Brown as a penny. Naked as a jaybird. Slender, muscled, handsome, active, good with his hands.

Bright? Seems so. Obviously too soon to really tell.

Five years old and just made his first kill. Wild dog attacking our goat. Got him in the right eye with a .30–30 at————yards (measure and fill in).

Strong and brave and skilled and good looking.

Let's hope intelligent, too.

Please, God.

My daughter. My precious, my beauty. What a delight you are, with your serene smile and your loving way of wrapping your arms around my leg and looking up at Old Daddy. You're your mother's child, aren't you? So good, so quiet. But you're quick on your feet and your reflexes (I've tested them) are sound. I think we're all right.

The Diary of Siss

(Siss was not very faithful about her diary. The printed word was not her medium. Although her intentions were obviously good, there are fewer than a dozen entries in all, and they are reproduced below. She did not date them. The handwriting in the last entry is slightly better than that of the first, but maybe only because she was using a sharper pencil. A more revealing diary probably would be found in her heart, if that could be read, or in her children.)

Mr. Ralph told me write things down when they

big & inportant I will start now. Today Mr. Ralph married me.

Very happy today. Learning to please my husband.

Very very happy. Today moved to our country house I like it better than the big city.

Today I had a baby, a boy.

My word for today is contentment. I have to spell it and tell what it means. Mr. Ralph says I need an eddukaton, he will eddukate me.

My word for today is education. Mr. Ralph seen what I wrote in my dairy yestdy.

I have 2 words for today diary & yesterday. Also saw not seen.

Today I had a baby, a girl. Ralph said now everything is going to be alright.

And presumably it was. Having doubled the population, the human race seemed to be on a firm footing. There was love in the world; a growing, proud family, and a new self-assurance in Siss—note that he was Ralph now, not Mr. Ralph. We may be sure, though, that the strict if loving father gave her two words for tomorrow: all right. A father, a mother, a son, a daughter. A little learning, a lot of love.

In the summer of his eighth year Adam and his father were in the woods back of the pasture, in the little clearing at the side of the stream that ran pure and sparkling before it broadened into the shallow muddy pond the livestock used. Martin and the boy were eating lunch after a morning of woodcutting and conversation.

Adam, naked like his father, had asked: "Am I going to grow some more hair, like you?"

And Martin said: "Sure, when you get bigger. When you begin to be a man."

And Adam had compared his smooth skin with his father's hard, muscled, hairy body and said: "Mom's got hair in that place, too, but she's different."

So Martin explained, sweating even though he was sitting still now, and his son took it all in, nodding, just as if it were no more important than knowing why the cow had her calf. It was obvious that until now Adam had not connected the function of the bull with the dropping of the calf. Martin explained, in human terms.

"That's pretty neat," Adam said. "When do I get to do it?"

Martin tried to keep his voice matter-of-fact. How do you instruct your son in incest?

The explanation was completed finally, and it was Martin's turn to ask a question. "Think carefully about this, son. If you could save the life of one person—your mother or me but not the other—which would you save?"

Adam answered without hesitation. "I'd save Mother, of course."

Martin looked hard at his strong, handsome son and asked the second part of the question. "Why?"

Adam said: "I didn't mean to hurt your feelings, Dad. I'd save both of you if I could—"

"I know you would. You've been a crack shot since you were five. But there might be only one chance. Your answer is the only possible one, but I have to know why you gave it."

The boy frowned as he struggled to reason out the reply he had made instinctively. "Because—if necessary— she and I could—" Then it came out in a rush: "Because she could be the mother to the world and I could be the father."

Martin shuddered as if a long chill had just passed. It was all right. He embraced his fine, strong, *intelligent* son and wept.

After a little while Siss appeared, walking the path beside the stream, naked as the two of them but different, as Adam had said, and riding the naked baby on her hip.

"Thought we'd join the menfolks for lunch," she said. "I picked some berries for dessert." She carried the blackberries in a mesh bag and some had been bruised, staining the tanned skin a delicate blue just below her slim waist.

Martin said: "You sure make a good-looking picture, you two. Come here and give me a kiss."

The baby kissed him first, then toddled off to smooch up for Adam, who gave her a dutiful peck.

Their father held open his arms and Siss sat beside him, putting the berries aside. She rested her head on his shoulder, serene. Martin folded her to him and kissed her eyes and cheeks and hair and neck and finally her lips, there in the sunshine, by the side of the pure stream, in the presence of all the world.

"Do you think—" she started to say, but Martin said "Hush now. It's all right. Everything's all right, Siss darling." She sighed and relaxed against him. He had never called her darling before. He kissed her again for a long time, and she gradually lay back on the soft ground and raised one knee and bent the other to accommodate her husband.

The baby lost interest and went to wade in the stream, but Adam watched, his elbow on his knee, and once he said, "Don't crush the blackberries," and reached out to get them. He ate a handful slowly.

Then he heard his mother gasp, "Oh, praise God!" and after a moment both his parents became still. And after a little while longer he looked to see that the baby was okay and then went to the interwined, gently breathing bodies, which were more beautiful than anything he had ever seen.

Adam knelt beside them and kissed his father's neck and his mother's lips. Siss opened her arms and enfolded her son, too.

And Adam asked, with his face against his mother's cheek, which was wet and warm, "Is this what love is?"

And his mother answered, "Yes, honey," and his father said, in a muffled kind of way, "It's everything there is, son."

Adam reached out for the berries and put one in his mother's mouth and one in his father's and one in his. Then he got up to give one to the baby.

DRAGONRIDER

by Anne McCaffrey

> The Finger points
> At an Eye blood-red
> Alert the Weyrs
> To sear the Thread.

"YOU STILL doubt, R'gul?" F'lar asked, appearing slightly amused by the older bronze rider's perversity.

R'gul, his handsome features stubbornly set, made no reply to the Weyrleader's taunt. He ground his teeth together as if he could grind away F'lar's authority over him.

"There have been no Threads in Pern's skies for over four hundred Turns. There are no more!"

"There is always that possibility," F'lar conceded amiably. There was not, however, the slightest trace of tolerance in his amber eyes. Nor the slightest hint of compromise in his manner.

He was more like F'lon, his sire, R'gul decided, than a son had any right to be. Always so sure of himself, always slightly contemptuous of what others did and thought. Arrogant, that's what F'lar was. Impertinent, too, and underhanded in the matter of that young Weyrwoman. Why, R'gul had trained her up to be one of the finest Weyrwomen in many Turns. Before he'd finished her instruction, she'd known all the Teaching Ballads and Sagas letter-perfect. And then the silly child had turned to F'lar. Didn't have sense enough to appreciate the merits of an older, more experienced man. Undoubtedly she felt a first obligation to F'lar for discovering her on Search.

"You do, however," F'lar was saying, "admit that when the sun hits the Finger Rock at the moment of dawn, winter solstice has been reached?"

"Any fool knows that's what the Finger Rock is for," R'gul grunted.

"Then why don't you, you old fool, admit that the Eye Rock was placed on Star Stone to bracket the Red Star when it's about to make a Pass?" burst out K'net.

R'gul flushed, half-starting out of his chair, ready to take the young sprout to task for such insolence.

"K'net!" F'lar's voice cracked authoritatively. "Do you really like flying the Igen patrol so much you want another few weeks at it?"

K'net hurriedly seated himself, flushing at the reprimand and the threat.

"There is, you know, R'gul, incontrovertible evidence to support my conclusions," F'lar went on with deceptive mildness. " 'The Finger points/At an Eye blood-red . . .' "

"Don't quote me verses I taught you as a weyrling," R'gul exclaimed heatedly.

"Then have faith in what you taught," F'lar snapped back, his amber eyes flashing dangerously.

R'gul, stunned by the unexpected forcefulness, sank back into his chair.

"You cannot deny, R'gul," F'lar continued quietly, "that no less than half an hour ago the sun balanced on the Finger's tip at dawn and the Red Star was squarely framed by the Eye Rock."

The other dragonriders, bronze as well as brown, murmured and nodded their agreement to that phenomenon. There was also an undercurrent of resentment for R'gul's continual contest of F'lar's policies as the new Weyrleader. Even old S'lel, once R'gul's avowed supporter, was following the majority.

"There have been no Threads in four hundred Turns. There are no Threads," R'gul muttered.

"Then, my fellow dragonman," F'lar said cheerfully, "all you have taught is falsehood. The dragons are, as the Lords of the Holds wish to believe, parasites on the economy of Pern, anachronisms. And so are we.

"Therefore, far be it from me to hold you here against

the dictates of your conscience. You have my permission to leave the Weyr and take up residence where you will."

Someone laughed.

R'gul was too stunned by F'lar's ultimatum to take offense at the ridicule. Leave the Weyr? Was the man mad? Where would he go? The Weyr had been his life. He had been bred up to it for generations. All his male ancestors had been dragonriders. Not all bronze, true, but a decent percentage. His own dam's sire had been a Weyrleader just as he, R'gul, had been until F'lar's Mnementh had flown the new queen.

But dragonmen never left the Weyr. Well, they did if they were negligent enough to lose their dragons, like that Lytol fellow at Ruath Hold. And how could he leave the Weyr *with* a dragon?

What did F'lar want of him? Was it not enough that he was Weyrleader now in R'gul's stead? Wasn't F'lar's pride sufficiently swollen by having bluffed the Lords of Pern into disbanding their army when they were all set to coerce the Weyr and dragonmen? Must F'lar dominate *every* dragonman, body and will, too? He stared a long moment, incredulous.

"I do not believe we are parasites," F'lar said, breaking the silence with a soft, persuasive voice. "Nor anachronistic. There have been long Intervals before. The Red Star does not always pass close enough to drop Threads on Pern. Which is why our ingenious ancestors thought to position the Eye Rock and the Finger Rock as they did . . . to confirm *when* a Pass will be made. And another thing"—his face turned grave—"there have been other times when dragonkind has all but died out . . . and Pern with it because of skeptics like you." F'lar smiled and relaxed indolently in his chair. "I prefer not to be recorded as a skeptic. How shall we record you, R'gul?"

The Council Room was tense. R'gul was aware of someone breathing harshly and realized it was himself. He looked at the adamant face of the young Weyrleader and knew that the threat was not empty. He would either concede to F'lar's authority completely, though concession rankled deeply, or leave the Weyr.

And where could he go, unless to one of the other Weyrs, deserted for hundreds of Turns? And—R'gul's thoughts were savage—wasn't that indication enough of the cessation of Threads? Five empty Weyrs? No, by the Egg of Faranth, he would practice some of F'lar's own brand of deceit and bide his time. When all Pern turned on the arrogant fool, he, R'gul, would be there to salvage something from the ruins.

"A dragonman stays in his Weyr," R'gul said with what dignity he could muster.

"And accepts the policies of the current Weyrleader?" The tone of F'lar's voice made it less of a question and more of an order.

So as not to perjure himself, R'gul gave a curt nod of his head. F'lar continued to stare at him, and R'gul wondered if the man could read his thoughts as his dragon might. He managed to return the gaze calmly. His turn would come. He'd wait.

Apparently accepting the capitulation, F'lar stood up and crisply delegated patrol assignments for the day.

"T'bor, you're weather-watch. Keep an eye on those tithing trains as you do. Have you the morning's report?"

"Weather is fair at dawning . . . all across Telgar and Keroon . . . if all too cold," T'bor said with a wry grin. "Tithing trains have good hard roads, though, so they ought to be here soon." His eyes twinkled with anticipation of the feasting that would follow the supplies' arrival —a mood shared by all to judge by the expressions around the table.

F'lar nodded. "S'lan and D'nol, you are to continue an adroit Search for likely boys. They should be striplings, if possible, but do not pass over anyone suspected of talent. It's all well and good to present for Impression boys reared up in the Weyr traditions." F'lar gave a one-sided smile. "But there are not enough in the Lower Caverns. We, too, have been behind in begetting. Anyway, dragons reach full growth faster than their riders. We must have more young *men* to Impress when Ramoth hatches. Take the southern holds, Ista, Nerat, Fort, and South Boll where maturity comes earlier. You can use the guise of inspecting Holds for greenery to talk to the boys. And take along firestone and run a few flaming passes on those heights that haven't been scoured in—oh —dragon's years. A flaming beast impresses the young and arouses envy."

F'lar deliberately looked at R'gul to see the ex-Weyrleader's reaction to the order. R'gul had been dead set against going outside the Weyr for more candidates. In the first place, R'gul had argued that there were eighteen youngsters in the Lower Caverns, some quite young to be sure, but R'gul would not admit that Ramoth would lay more than the dozen Nemorth had always dropped. In the second place, R'gul persisted in wanting to avoid any action that might antagonize the Lords.

R'gul made no overt protest, and F'lar went on.

"K'net, back to the mines. I want the dispositions of each fire-stone dump checked and quantities available. R'gul, continue drilling recognition points with the weyrlings. They must be positive about their references. If they're used as messengers and suppliers, they may be sent out quickly and with no time to ask questions.

"F'nor, T'sum"—F'lar turned to his own brown riders —"you're clean-up squad today." He allowed himself a grin at their dismay. "Try Ista Weyr. Clear the Hatching Cavern and enough weyrs for a double wing. And, F'nor, don't leave a single Record behind. They're worth preserving.

"That will be all, dragonmen. Good flying." And with that, F'lar rose and strode from the Council Room up to the queen's weyr.

Ramoth still slept, her hide gleaming with health, its color deepening to a shape of gold closer to bronze, indicating her pregnancy. As he passed her, the tip of her long tail twitched slightly.

All the dragons were restless these days, F'lar reflected. Yet when he asked Mnementh, the bronze dragon could give no reason. He woke, he went back to sleep. That was all. F'lar couldn't ask a leading question for that would defeat his purpose. He had to remain discontented with the vague fact that the restlessness was some kind of instinctive reaction.

Lessa was not in the sleeping room, nor was she still bathing. F'lar snorted. That girl was going to scrub her hide off with this constant bathing. She'd had to live grimy to protect herself in Ruath Hold, but bathing twice a day? He was beginning to wonder if this might be a subtle Lessa-variety insult to him personally. F'lar sighed. That girl. Would she never turn to him of her own accord? Would he ever touch that elusive inner core of

Lessa? She had more warmth for his half brother, F'nor, and for K'net, the youngest of the bronze riders, than she had for F'lar who shared her bed.

He pulled the curtain back into place, irritated. Where had she gone to today when, for the first time in weeks, he had been able to get all the wings out of the Weyr just so he could teach her to fly *between?*

Ramoth would soon be too egg-heavy for such activity. He had promised the Weyrwoman, and he meant to keep that promise. She had taken to wearing the wher-hide riding gear as a flagrant reminder of his unfulfilled pledge. From certain remarks she had dropped, he knew she would not wait much longer for his aid. That she would try it on her own didn't suit him at all.

He crossed the queen's weyr again and peered down the passage that led to the Records Room. She was often to be found there, poring over the musty skins. And that was one more matter that needed urgent consideration. Those Records were deteriorating past legibility. Curiously enough, earlier ones were still in good condition and readable. Another technique forgotten.

That girl! He brushed his thick forelock of hair back from his brow in a gesture habitual to him when he was annoyed or worried. The passage was dark, which meant she could not be below in the Records Room.

"Mnementh," he called silently to his bronze dragon, sunning on the ledge outside the queen's weyr. "What is that girl doing?"

Lessa, the dragon replied, stressing the Weyrwoman's name with pointed courtesy, *is talking to Manora. She's dressed for riding,* he added after a slight pause.

F'lar thanked the bronze sarcastically and strode down the passage to the entrance. As he turned the last bend, he all but ran Lessa down.

You hadn't asked me where *she was,* Mnementh plaintively answered F'lar's blistering reprimand.

Lessa rocked back on her heels from the force of their encounter. She glared up at him, her lips thin with displeasure, her eyes flashing.

"Why didn't I have the opportunity of seeing the Red Star through the Eye Rock?" she demanded in a hard, angry voice.

F'lar pulled at his hair. Lessa at her most difficult would complete the list of this morning's trials.

"Too many to accommodate on the Peak as it was," he muttered, determined not to let her irritate him today. "And you already believe."

"I'd've liked to see it," she snapped and pushed past him toward the weyr. "If only in my capacity as Weyrwoman and Recorder."

He caught her arm and felt her body tense. He set his teeth, wishing, as he had a hundred times since Ramoth rose in her first mating flight, that Lessa had not been virgin, too. He had not thought to control his dragon-incited emotions, and Lessa's first sexual experience had been violent. It had surprised him to be first, considering that her adolescent years had been spent drudging for lascivious warders and soldier-types. Evidently no one had bothered to penetrate the curtain of rags and the coat of filth she had carefully maintained as a disguise. He had been a considerate and gentle bedmate ever since, but, unless Ramoth and Mnementh were involved, he might as well call it rape.

Yet he knew someday, somehow, he would coax her into responding wholeheartedly to his lovemaking. He had a certain pride in his skill, and he was in a position to persevere.

Now he took a deep breath and released her arm slowly.

"How fortunate you're wearing riding gear. As soon as the wings have cleared out and Ramoth wakes, I shall teach you to fly *between*."

The gleam of excitement in her eyes was evident even in the dimly lit passageway. He heard her inhale sharply.

"Can't put it off too much longer or Ramoth'll be in no shape to fly at all," he continued amiably.

"You mean it?" Her voice was low and breathless, its usual acid edge missing. "You will teach us today?" He wished he could see her face clearly.

Once or twice he had caught an unguarded expression on her face, loving and tender. He would give much to have that look turned on him. However, he admitted wryly to himself, he ought to be glad that melting regard was directed only at Ramoth and not at another human.

"Yes, my dear Weyrwoman, I mean it. I will teach

you to fly *between* today. If only," and he bowed to her
with a flourish, "to keep you from trying it yourself."

Her low chuckle informed him his taunt was well
aimed.

"Right now, however," he said, indicating for her to
lead the way back to the weyr, "I could do with some
food. We were up before the kitchen."

They had entered the well-lighted weyr, so he did not
miss the trenchant look she shot him over his shoulder.
She would not so easily forgive being left out of the group
at the Star Stone this morning, certainly not with the
bribe of flying *between*.

How different this inner room was now that Lessa was
Weyrwoman, F'lar mused as Lessa called down the service shaft for food. During Jora's incompetent tenure as
Weyrwoman, the sleeping quarters had been crowded
with junk, unwashed apparel, uncleared dishes. The state
of the Weyr and the reduced number of dragons were as
much Jora's fault as R'gul's, for she had indirectly encouraged sloth, negligence, and gluttony.

If he, F'lar, had been just a few years older when
F'lon, his father, had died . . . Jora had been disgusting,
but when dragons rose in mating flight, the condition of
your partner counted for nothing.

Lessa took a tray of bread and cheese and mugs of
the stimulating *klah* from the platform. She served him
deftly.

"You'd not eaten either?" he asked.

She shook her head vigorously, the braid into which
she had plaited her thick, fine dark hair bobbing across
her shoulders. The hairdressing was too severe for her
narrow face, but it did not, if that was her intention, disguise her femininity or the curious beauty of her delicate
features. Again F'lar wondered that such a slight body
contained so much shrewd intelligence and resourceful
. . . cunning—yes, that was the word, cunning. F'lar did
not make the mistake, as others had, of underestimating
her abilities.

"Manora called me to witness the birth of Kylara's
child."

F'lar maintained an expression of polite interest. He
knew perfectly well that Lessa suspected the child was
his, and it could have been, he admitted privately, but he

doubted it. Kylara had been one of the ten candidates from the same Search three years ago that had discovered Lessa. Like others who survived Impression, Kylara had found certain aspects of Weyr life exactly suited to her temperament. She had gone from one rider's weyr to another's. She had even seduced F'lar—not at all against his will, to be sure. Now that he was Weyrleader, he found it wiser to ignore her efforts to continue the relationship. T'bor had taken her in hand and had had his hands full until he retired her to the Lower Caverns, well advanced in pregnancy.

Aside from having the amorous tendencies of a green dragon, Kylara was quick and ambitious. She would make a strong Weyrwoman, so F'lar had charged Manora and Lessa with the job of planting the notion in Kylara's mind. In the capacity of Weyrwoman . . . of another Weyr . . . her intense drives would be used to Pern's advantage. She had not learned the severe lessons of restraint and patience that Lessa had, and she didn't have Lessa's devious mind. Fortunately she was in considerable awe of Lessa, and F'lar suspected that Lessa was subtly influencing this attitude. In Kylara's case, F'lar preferred not to object to Lessa's meddling.

"A fine son," Lessa was saying.

F'lar sipped his *klah*. She was not going to get him to admit any responsibility.

After a long pause Lessa added, "She has named him T'kil."

F'lar suppressed a grin at Lessa's failure to get a rise from him.

"Discreet of her."

"Oh?"

"Yes," F'lar replied blandly. "T'lar might be confusing if she took the second half of her name as is customary. 'T'kil,' however, still indicates sire as well as dam."

"While I was waiting for Council to end," Lessa said after clearing her throat, "Manora and I checked the supply cavern. The tithing trains, which the Holds have been so gracious as to send us"—her voice was sharp—"are due within the week. There will shortly be bread fit to eat," she added, wrinkling her nose at the crumbling gray pastry she was attempting to spread with cheese.

"A nice change," F'lar agreed.

She paused.

"The Red Star performed its scheduled antic?"

He nodded.

"And R'gul's doubts have been wiped away in the enlightening red glow?"

"Not at all." F'lar grinned back at her, ignoring her sarcasm. "Not at all, but he will not be so vocal in his criticism."

She swallowed quickly so she could speak. "You'd do well to cut out his criticism," she said ruthlessly, gesturing with her knife as if plunging it into a man's heart. "He is never going to accept your authority with good grace."

"We need every bronze rider . . . there are only seven, you know," he reminded her pointedly. "R'gul's a good wingleader. He'll settle down when the Threads fall. He needs proof to lay his doubts aside."

"And the Red Star in the Eye Rock is not proof?" Lessa's expressive eyes were wide.

F'lar was privately of Lessa's opinion—that it might be wiser to remove R'gul's stubborn contentiousness. But he could not sacrifice a wingleader, needing every dragon and rider as badly as he did.

"I don't trust him," she added darkly. She sipped at her hot drink, her gray eyes dark over the rim of her mug. As if, F'lar mused, she didn't trust him either.

And she didn't, past a certain point. She had made that plain, and in honesty, he couldn't blame her. She did recognize that every action F'lar took was toward one end . . . the safety and preservation of dragonkind and weyrfolk and consequently the safety and preservation of Pern. To effect that end, he needed her full cooperation. When Weyr business or dragonlore were discussed, she suspended the antipathy he knew she felt for him. In conferences she supported him wholeheartedly and persuasively, but always he suspected the double edge to her comments and saw a speculative, suspicious look in her eyes. He needed not only her tolerance but her empathy.

"Tell me," she said after a long silence, "did the sun touch the Finger Rock before the Red Star was bracketed in the Eye Rock or after?"

"Matter of fact, I'm not sure, as I did not see it my-

self . . . the concurrence lasts only a few moments . . .
but the two are supposed to be simultaneous."

She frowned at him sourly. "Whom did you waste it
on? R'gul?" She was provoked, her angry eyes looked
everywhere but at him.

"I am Weyrleader," he informed her curtly. She was
unreasonable.

She awarded him one long, hard look before she bent
to finish her meal. She ate very little, quickly and neatly.
Compared to Jora, she didn't eat enough in the course of
an entire day to nourish a sick child. But then, there was
no point in ever comparing Lessa to Jora.

He finished his own breakfast, absently piling the
mugs together on the empty tray. She rose silently and
removed the dishes.

"As soon as the Weyr is free, we'll go," he told her.

"So you said." She nodded toward the sleeping queen,
visible through the open arch. "We still must wait upon
Ramoth."

"Isn't she rousing? Her tail's been twitching for an
hour."

"She always does that about this time of day."

F'lar leaned across the table, his brows drawn together
thoughtfully as he watched the golden-forked tip of the
queen's tail jerk spasmodically from side to side.

"Mnementh, too. And always at dawn and early morning. As if somehow they associate that time of day with
trouble . . ."

"Or the Red Star's rising?" Lessa interjected.

Some subtle difference in her tone caused F'lar to
glance quickly at her. It wasn't anger now over having
missed the morning's phenomenon. Her eyes were fixed
on nothing; her face, smooth at first, was soon wrinkled
with a vaguely anxious frown as tiny lines formed between her arching, well-defined brows.

"Dawn . . . that's when all warnings come," she murmured.

"What kind of warning?" he asked with quiet encouragement.

"There was that morning . . . a few days before . . .
before you and Fax descended on Ruath Hold. Something woke me . . . a feeling, like a very heavy pressure
. . . the sensation of some terrible danger threatening."

She was silent. "The Red Star was just rising." The fingers of her left hand opened and closed. She gave a convulsive shudder. Her eyes refocused on him.

"You and Fax did come out of the northeast from Crom," she said sharply, ignoring the fact, F'lar noticed, that the Red Star also rises north of true east.

"Indeed we did," he grinned at her, remembering that morning vividly. "Although," he added, gesturing around the great cavern to emphasize, "I prefer to believe I served you well that day . . . You remember it with displeasure?"

The look she gave him was coldly inscrutable.

"Danger comes in many guises."

"I agree," he replied amiably, determined not to rise to her bait. "Had any other rude awakenings?" he inquired conversationally.

The absolute stillness in the room brought his attention back to her. Her face had drained of all color.

"The day Fax invaded Ruath Hold." Her voice was a barely articulated whisper. Her eyes were wide and staring. Her hands clenched the edge of the table. She said nothing for such a long interval that F'lar became concerned. This was an unexpectedly violent reaction to a casual question.

"Tell me," he suggested softly.

She spoke in unemotional, impersonal tones, as if she were reciting a Traditional Ballad or something that had happened to an entirely different person.

"I was a child. Just eleven. I woke at dawn . . ." Her voice trailed off. Her eyes remained focused on nothing, staring at a scene that had happened long ago.

F'lar was stirred by an irresistible desire to comfort her. It struck him forcibly, even as he was stirred by this unusual compassion, that he had never thought that, Lessa, of all people, would be troubled by so old a terror.

Mnementh sharply informed his rider that Lessa was obviously bothered a good deal. Enough so that her mental anguish was rousing Ramoth from sleep. In less accusing tones Mnementh informed F'lar that R'gul had finally taken off with his weyrling pupils. His dragon Hath, however, was in a fine state of disorientation due to R'gul's state of mind. Must F'lar unsettle everyone in the Weyr . . .

"Oh, be quiet," F'lar retorted under his breath.

"Why?" Lessa demanded in her normal voice.

"I didn't mean you, my dear Weyrwoman," he assured her, smiling pleasantly as if the entranced interlude had never occurred. "Mnementh is full of advice these days."

"Like rider, like dragon," she replied tartly.

Ramoth yawned mightily. Lessa was instantly on her feet, running to her dragon's side, her slight figure dwarfed by the six-foot dragon head.

A tender, adoring expression flooded her face as she gazed into Ramoth's gleaming opalescent eyes. F'lar clenched his teeth, envious, by the Egg, of a rider's affection for her dragon.

In his mind he heard Mnementh's dragon equivalent of laughter.

"She's hungry," Lessa informed F'lar, an echo of her love for Ramoth lingering in the soft line of her mouth, in the kindness of her gray eyes.

"She's always hungry," he observed and followed them out of the weyr.

Mnementh hovered courteously just beyond the ledge until Lessa and Ramoth had taken off. They glided down the Weyr Bowl, over the misty bathing lake, toward the feeding ground at the opposite end of the long oval that comprised the floor of Benden Weyr. The straited, precipitous walls were pierced with the black mouths of single weyr entrances, deserted at this time of day by the few dragons who might otherwise doze on their ledges in the wintry sun.

As F'lar vaulted to Mnementh's smooth bronze neck, he hoped that Ramoth's clutch would be spectacular, erasing the ignominy of the paltry dozen Nemorth had laid in each of her last few clutches.

He had no serious doubts of the improvement after Ramoth's remarkable mating flight with his Mnementh. The bronze dragon smugly echoed his rider's certainty, and both looked on the queen possessively as she curved her wings to land. She was twice Nemorth's size, for one thing; her wings were half-a-wing again longer than Mnementh's, who was the biggest of the seven male bronzes. F'lar looked to Ramoth to repopulate the five empty Weyrs, even as he looked to himself and Lessa to rejuvenate the pride and faith of dragonriders and of Pern itself. He only hoped time enough remained to him to do what was necessary. The Red Star had been bracketed by the Eye Rock. The Threads would soon be falling. Somewhere, in one of the other Weyrs' Records, must be the information he needed to ascertain *when,* exactly, Threads would fall.

Mnementh landed. F'lar jumped down from the curving neck to stand beside Lessa. The three watched as Ramoth, a buck grasped in each of her forefeet, rose to a feeding ledge.

"Will her appetite never taper off?" Lessa asked with affectionate dismay.

As a dragonet, Ramoth had been eating to grow. Her full stature attained, she was of course now eating for her young, and she applied herself conscientiously.

F'lar chuckled and squatted, hunter fashion. He picked up shale-flakes, skating them across the flat dry ground, counting the dust puffs boyishly.

"The time will come when she won't eat everything in sight," he assured Lessa. "But she's young . . ."

". . . and needs her strength," Lessa interrupted, her voice a fair imitation of R'gul's pedantic tones.

F'lar looked up at her, squinting against the wintry sun that slanted down at them.

"She's a finely grown beast, especially compared to Nemorth." He gave a contemptuous snort. "In fact, there *is* no comparison. However, look here," he ordered peremptorily.

He tapped the smoothed sand in front of him, and she saw that his apparently idle gestures had been to a purpose. With a sliver of stone, he drew a design in quick strokes.

"In order to fly a dragon *between,* he has to know where to go. And so do you." He grinned at the astonished and infuriated look of comprehension on her face.

"Ah, but there are certain consequences to an ill-considered jump. Badly visualized reference points often result in staying *between.*" His voice dropped ominously. Her face cleared of its resentment. "So there are certain reference or recognition points arbitrarily taught all weyrlings. "That,"—he pointed first to his facsimile and then to the actual Star Stone with its Finger and Eye

Rock companions on Benden Peak—"is the first recognition point a weyrling learns. When I take you aloft, you will reach an altitude just above the Star Stone, near enough for you to be able to see the hole in the Eye Rock clearly. Fix that picture sharply in your mind's eye, relay it to Ramoth. That will always get you home."

"Understood. But how do I learn recognition points of places I've never seen?"

He grinned up at her. "You're drilled in them. First by your instructor," and he pointed the sliver at his chest, "and then by going there, having directed your dragon to get the visualization from her instructor," and he indicated Mnementh. The bronze dragon lowered his wedge-shaped head until one eye was focused on his rider and his mate's rider. He made a pleased noise deep in his chest.

Lessa laughed up at the gleaming eye and with unexpected affection, patted the soft nose.

F'lar cleared his throat in surprise. He had been aware that Mnementh showed an unusual affection for the Weyrwoman, but he had had no idea Lessa was fond of the bronze. Perversely, he was irritated.

"However," he said, and his voice sounded unnatural to himself, "we take the young riders constantly to and from the main reference points all across Pern, to all the Holds so that they have eyewitness impressions on which to rely. As a rider becomes adept in picking out landmarks, he gets additional references from other riders. Therefore, to go *between,* there is actually only one requirement: a clear picture of where you want to go. *And* a dragon!" He grinned at her. "Also you should always plan to arrive above your reference point in clear air."

Lessa frowned.

"It is better to arrive in open air"—F'lar waved a hand above his head—"rather than underground," and he slapped his open hand onto the dirt. A puff of dust rose warningly.

"But the wings took off within the Bowl itself the day the Lords of the Hold arrived," Lessa reminded him.

F'lar chuckled at her uptake. "True, but only the most seasoned riders. Once we came across a dragon and a rider entombed together in solid rock. They . . . were . . . very young." His eyes were bleak.

"I take the point," she assured him gravely. "That's her fifth," she added, pointing toward Ramoth, who was carrying her latest kill up to the bloody ledge.

"She'll work them off today, I assure you," F'lar remarked. He rose, brushing off his knees with sharp slaps of his riding gloves. "Test her temper."

Lessa did so with a silent, *Had enough?* She grimaced at Ramoth's indignant rejection of the thought.

The queen went swooping down for a huge fowl, rising in a flurry of gray, brown, and white feathers.

"She's not as hungry as she's making you think, the deceitful creature," F'lar chuckled and saw that Lessa had reached the same conclusion. Her eyes were snapping with vexation.

"When you've finished the bird, Ramoth, do let us learn how to fly *between*," Lessa said aloud for F'lar's benefit, "before our good Weyrleader changes his mind."

Ramoth looked up from her gorging, turned her head toward the two riders at the edge of the feeding ground. Her eyes gleamed. She bent her head again to her kill, but Lessa could sense the dragon would obey.

It was cold aloft. Lessa was glad of the fur lining in her riding gear and the warmth of the great golden neck which she bestrode. She decided not to think of the absolute cold of *between* which she had experienced only once. She glanced below on her right where bronze Mnementh hovered, and she caught his amused thought.

F'lar tells me to tell Ramoth to tell you to fix the alignment of the Star Stone firmly in your mind as a homing. Then, Mnementh went on amiably, *we shall fly down to the lake. You will return from* between *to this exact point. Do you understand?*

Lessa found herself grinning foolishly with anticipation and nodded vigorously. How much time was saved because she could speak directly to the dragons! Ramoth made a disgruntled noise deep in her throat. Lessa patted her reassuringly.

"Have you got the picture in your mind, dear one?" she asked, and Ramoth again rumbled, less annoyed because she was catching Lessa's excitement.

Mnementh stroked the cold air with his wings, greenish brown in the sunlight and curved down gracefully toward the lake on the plateau below Benden Weyr. His flight line took him very low over the rim of the Weyr. From Lessa's angle, it looked like a collision course. Ramoth followed closely in his wake. Lessa caught her breath at the sight of the jagged boulders just below Ramoth's wing tips.

It was exhilarating, Lessa crowed to herself, doubly stimulated by the elation that flowed back to her from Ramoth.

Mnementh halted above the farthest shore of the lake, and there, too, Ramoth came to hover.

Mnementh flashed the thought to Lessa that she was to place the picture of where she wished to go firmly in her mind and direct Ramoth to get there.

Lessa complied. The next instant the awesome, bone-penetrating cold of black *between* enveloped them. Before either she or Ramoth were aware of more than that biting touch of cold and impregnable darkness, they were above the Star Stone.

Lessa let out a cry of pure triumph.

It is extremely simple. Ramoth seemed disappointed. Mnementh reappeared beside and slightly below them.

You are to return by the same route to the Lake, he ordered, and before the thought had finished, Ramoth took off.

Mnementh was beside them above the lake, fuming with his own and F'lar's anger. *You did not visualize before transferring. Don't think a first successful trip makes you perfect. You have no conception of the dangers inherent in* between. Never *fail to picture your arrival point again.*

Lessa glanced down at F'lar. Even two wingspans apart, she could see the vivid anger on his face, almost feel the fury flashing from his eyes. And laced through the wrath, a terrible sinking fearfulness for her safety that was a more effective reprimand than his wrath. Lessa's safety, she wondered bitterly, or Ramoth's?

You are to follow us, Mnementh was saying in a calmer tone, *rehearsing in your mind the two reference points you have already learned. We shall jump to and from them this morning, gradually learning other points around Benden.*

They did. Flying as far away as Benden Hold itself, nestled against the foothills above Benden Valley, the

Weyr Peak a far point against the noonday sky, Lessa did not neglect to visualize a clearly detailed impression each time.

This was as marvelously exciting as she had hoped it would be, Lessa confided to Ramoth. Ramoth replied: yes, it was certainly preferable to the time-consuming methods others have to use, but she didn't think it was exciting at all to jump *between* from Benden Weyr to Benden Hold and back to Benden Weyr again. It was dull.

They had met with Mnementh above the Star Stone again. The bronze dragon sent Lessa the message that this was a very satisfying initial session. They would practice some distant jumping tomorrow.

Tomorrow, thought Lessa glumly, some emergency will occur or our hard-working Weyrleader will decide today's session constitutes keeping his promise and that will be that.

There was one jump she could make *between,* from anywhere on Pern, and not miss her mark.

She visualized Ruatha for Ramoth as seen from the heights above the Hold . . . to satisfy that requirement. To be scrupulously clear, Lessa projected the pattern of the firepits. Before Fax invaded and she had had to manipulate its decline, Ruatha had been such a lovely, prosperous valley. She told Ramoth to jump *between.*

The cold was intense and seemed to last for many heartbeats. Just as Lessa began to fear that she had somehow lost them *between,* they exploded into the air above the Hold. Elation filled her. That for F'lar and his excessive caution! With Ramoth she could jump anywhere! For there was the distinctive pattern of Ruatha's fire-guttered heights. It was just before dawn, the Breast Pass between Crom and Ruatha, black cones against the lightening gray sky. Fleetingly she noticed the absence of the Red Star that now blazed in the dawn sky. And fleetingly she noticed a difference in the air. Chill, yes, but not wintry . . . the air held that moist coolness of early spring.

Startled, she glanced downward, wondering if she could have, for all her assurance, erred in some fashion. But no, this was Ruath Hold. The Tower, the inner Court, the aspect of the broad avenue leading down to the crafthold were just as they should be. Wisps of smoke from distant chimneys indicated people were making ready for the day.

Ramoth caught the tenor of her insecurity and began to press for an explanation.

This is Ruatha, Lessa replied stoutly. *It can be no other. Circle the heights. See, there are the firepit lines I gave you. . . .*

Lessa gasped, the coldness in her stomach freezing her muscles.

Below her in the slowly lifting predawn gloom, she saw the figures of many men toiling over the breast of the cliff from the hills beyond Ruatha, men moving with quiet stealth like criminals.

She ordered Ramoth to keep as still as possible in the air so as not to direct their attention upward. The dragon was curious but obedient.

Who would be attacking Ruatha? It seemed incredible. Lytol was, after all, a former dragonman and had savagely repelled one attack already. Could there possibly be a thought of aggression among the Holds now that F'lar was Weyrleader? And what Hold Lord would be foolish enough to mount a territorial war in the winter?

No, not winter. The air was definitely springlike.

The men crept on, over the firepits to the edge of the heights. Suddenly Lessa realized they were lowering rope ladders over the face of the cliff down toward the open shutters of the Inner Hold.

Wildly she clutched at Ramoth's neck, certain of what she saw.

This was the invader Fax, now dead nearly three Turns—Fax and his men as they began their attack on Ruatha nearly thirteen Turns ago.

Yes, there was the Tower guard, his face a white blot turned toward the Cliff itself, watching. He had been paid his bribe to stand silent this morning.

But the watch-wher, trained to give alarm for any intrusion—why was it not trumpeting its warning? Why was it silent?

Because, Ramoth informed her rider with calm logic, *it senses your presence as well as mine, so how could the Hold be in danger?*

No, No! Lessa moaned. *What can I do now? How can I wake them? Where is the girl I was? I was asleep, and then I woke. I remember, I dashed from my room. I was so scared. I went down the steps and nearly fell. I knew I had to get to the watch-wher's kennel. . . . I knew. . . .*

Lessa clutched as Ramoth's neck for support as past acts and mysteries became devastatingly clear.

She herself had warned herself, just as it was her presence on the queen dragon that had kept the watch-wher from giving alarm. For as she watched, stunned and speechless, she saw the small, gray-robed figure that could only be herself as a youngster, burst from the Hold Hall door, race uncertainly down the cold stone steps into the Court, and disappear into the watch-wher's stinking den. Faintly she heard it crying in piteous confusion.

Just as Lessa-the-girl reached that doubtful sanctuary, Fax's invaders swooped into the open window embrasures and began the slaughter of her sleeping family.

"Back—back to the Star Stone!" Lessa cried. In her wide and staring eyes she held the image of the guiding rocks like a rudder for her sanity as well as Ramoth's direction.

The intense cold acted as a restorative. And then they were above the quiet, peaceful wintry Weyr as if they had never paradoxically visited Ruatha.

F'lar and Mnementh were nowhere to be seen.

Ramoth, however, was unshaken by the experience. She had only gone where she had been told to go and had not quite understood that going where she had been told to go had shocked Lessa. She suggested to her rider that Mnementh had probably followed them to Ruatha so if Lessa would give her the *proper* references, she'd take her there. Ramoth's sensible attitude was comforting.

Lessa carefully drew for Ramoth not the child's memory of a long-vanished, idyllic Ruatha but her more recent recollection of the Hold, gray, sullen, at dawning, with a Red Star pulsing on the horizon.

And there they were again, hovering over the valley, the Hold below them on the right. The grasses grew untended on the heights, clogging firepit and brickwork; the scene showed all the deterioration she had encouraged in her effort to thwart Fax of any profit from conquering Ruath Hold.

But, as she watched, vaguely disturbed, she saw a figure emerge from the kitchen, saw the watch-wher creep from its lair and follow the raggedly dressed figure as far across the Court as the chain permitted. She saw the figure ascend the Tower, gaze first eastward, then northeastward. This was still not Ruatha of today and now! Lessa's mind reeled, disoriented. This time she had come back to visit herself of three Turns ago, to see the filthy drudge plotting revenge on Fax.

She felt the absolute cold of *between* as Ramoth snatched them back, emerging once more above the Star Stone. Lessa was shuddering, her eyes frantically taking in the reassuring sight of the Weyr Bowl, hoping she had not somehow shifted backward in time yet again. Mnementh suddenly erupted into the air a few lengths below and beyond Ramoth. Lessa greeted him with a cry of intense relief.

Back to your weyr! There was no disguising the white fury in Mnementh's tone. Lessa was too unnerved to respond in any way other than instant compliance. Ramoth glided swiftly to their ledge, quickly clearing the perch for Mnementh to land.

The rage on F'lar's face as he leaped from Mnementh and advanced on Lessa brought her wits back abruptly. She made no move to evade him as he grabbed her shoulders and shook her violently.

"How dare you risk yourself and Ramoth? Why must you defy me at every opportunity? Do you realize what would happen to all Pern if we lost Ramoth? Where did you go?" He was spitting with anger, punctuating each question that tumbled from his lips by giving her a head-wrenching shake.

"Ruatha," she managed to say, trying to keep herself erect. She reached out to catch at his arms, but he shook her again.

"Ruatha? We were there. You weren't. Where did you go?"

"Ruatha!" Lessa cried louder, clutching at him distractedly because he kept jerking her off balance. She couldn't organize her thoughts with him jolting her around.

She was at Ruatha, Mnementh said firmly.

We were there twice, Ramoth added.

As the dragons' calmer words penetrated F'lar's fury, he stopped shaking Lessa. She hung limply in his grasp, her hands weakly plucking at his arms, her eyes closed, her face gray. He picked her up and strode rapidly into the queen's weyr, the dragons following. He placed her upon the couch, wrapping her tightly in the fur cover. He called down the service shaft for the duty cook to send up hot *klah.*

"All right, what happened?" he demanded.

She didn't look at him, but he got a glimpse of her haunted eyes. She blinked constantly as if she longed to erase what she had just seen.

Finally she got herself somewhat under control and said in a low, tired voice. "I did go to Ruatha. Only . . . I went *back* to Ruatha."

"Back to Ruatha?" F'lar repeated the words stupidly; the significance momentarily eluded him.

It certainly does, Mnementh agreed and flashed to F'lar's mind the two scenes he had picked out of Ramoth's memory.

Staggered by the import of the visualization, F'lar found himself slowly sinking to the edge of the bed.

"You went *between* times?"

She nodded slowly. The terror was beginning to leave her eyes.

"Between times," F'lar murmured. "I wonder . . ."

His mind raced through the possibilities. It might well tip the scales of survival in the Weyr's favor. He couldn't think exactly how to use this extraordinary ability, but there *must* be an advantage in it for dragonfolk.

The service shaft rumbled. He took the pitcher from the platform and poured two mugs.

Lessa's hands were shaking so much that she couldn't get hers to her lips. He steadied it for her, wondering if going *between* times would regularly cause this kind of shock. If so, it wouldn't be any advantage at all. If she'd had enough of a scare this day, she might not be so contemptuous of his orders the next time; which would be to his benefit.

Outside in the weyr, Mnementh snorted his opinion on that. F'lar ignored him.

Lessa was trembling violently now. He put an arm around her, pressing the fur against her slender body. He held the mug to her lips, forcing her to drink. He could feel the tremors ease off. She took long, slow, deep breaths between swallows, equally determined to get herself under control. The moment he felt her stiffen under his arm, he released her. He wondered if Lessa had ever had someone to turn to. Certainly not after Fax invaded her family Hold. She had been only eleven, a child. Had hate and revenge been the only emotions the growing girl had practiced?

She lowered the mug, cradling it in her hands carefully as if it had assumed some undefinable importance to her.

"Now. Tell me," he ordered evenly.

She took a long deep breath and began to speak, her hands tightening around the mug. Her inner turmoil had not lessened; it was merely under control now.

"Ramoth and I were bored with the weyrling exercises," she admitted candidly.

Grimly F'lar recognized that while the adventure might have taught her to be more circumspect, it had not scared her into obedience. He doubted that anything would.

"I gave her the picture of Ruatha so we could go *between* there." She did not look at him, but her profile was outlined against the dark fur of the rug. "The Ruatha I knew so well—I accidentally sent myself backward in time to the day Fax invaded."

Her shock was now comprehensible to him.

"And . . ." he prompted her, his voice carefully neutral.

"And I saw myself—" Her voice broke off. With an effort she continued. "I had visualized for Ramoth the designs of the firepits and the angle of the Hold if one looked down from the pits into the Inner Court. That was where we emerged. It was just dawn"—she lifted her chin with a nervous jerk—"and there was no Red Star in the sky." She gave him a quick, defensive look as if she expected him to contest this detail. "And I saw men creeping over the firepits, lowering rope ladders to the top windows of the Hold. I saw the Tower guard watching. Just watching." She clenched her teeth at such treach-

ery, and her eyes gleamed malevolently. "And I saw
myself run from the Hall into the watch-wher's lair. And
do you know why"——her voice lowered to a bitter whisper
——"the watch-wher did not alarm the Hold?"

"Why?"

"Because there was a dragon in the sky, and *I*, Lessa
of Ruatha, was on her." She flung the mug from her as
if she wished she could reject the knowledge, too. "Because *I* was there, the watch-wher did not alarm the
Hold, thinking the intrusion legitimate, with one of the
Blood on a dragon in the sky. So I"——her body grew
rigid, her hands clasped so tightly that the knuckles were
white——"*I* was the cause of my family's massacre. Not
Fax! If I had not acted the captious fool today, I would
not have been there with Ramoth and the watch-wher
would——"

Her voice had risen to an hysterical pitch of recrimi-
nation. He slapped her sharply across the cheeks, grabbing her, robe and all, to shake her.

The stunned look in her eyes and the tragedy in her
face alarmed him. His indignation over her willfulness
disappeared. Her unruly independence of mind and spirit
attracted him as much as her curious dark beauty. Infuriating as her fractious ways might be, they were too
vital a part of her integrity to be exorcised. Her indom-
itable will had taken a grievous shock today, and her
self-confidence had better be restored quickly.

"On the contrary, Lessa," he said sternly, "Fax would
still have murdered your family. He had planned it very
carefully, even to scheduling his attack on the morning
when the Tower guard was one who could be bribed. Remember, too, it was dawn and the watch-wher, being a
nocturnal beast, blind by daylight, is relieved of responsibility at dawn and knows it. Your presence, damnable
as it may appear to you, was not the deciding factor by
any means. It did, and I draw your attention to this very
important fact, cause you to save yourself, by warning
Lessa-the-child. Don't you see that?"

"I could have called out," she murmured, but the
frantic look had left her eyes and there was a faint hint
of normal color in her lips.

"If you wish to flail around in guilt, go right ahead,"
he said with deliberate callousness.

Ramoth interjected a thought that since the two of them had been there that previous time as Fax's men had prepared to invade, it had already happened, so how could it be changed? The act was inevitable both that day and today. For how else could Lessa have lived to come to the Weyr and impress Ramoth at the hatching?

Mnementh relayed Ramoth's message scrupulously, even to imitating Ramoth's egocentric nuances. F'lar looked sharply at Lessa to see the effect of Ramoth's astringent observation.

"Just like Ramoth to have the final word," she said with a hint of her former droll humor.

F'lar felt the muscles along his neck and shoulders begin to relax. She'd be all right, he decided, but it might be wiser to make her talk it all out now, to put the whole experience into proper perspective.

"You said you were there twice?" He leaned back on the couch, watching her closely. "When was the second time?"

"Can't you guess?" she asked sarcastically.

"No," he lied.

"When else but the dawn I was awakened, feeling the Red Star was a menace to me? . . . Three days before you and Fax came out of the northeast."

"It would seem," he remarked dryly, "that you were your own premonition both times."

She nodded.

"Have you had any more of these presentiments . . . or should I say reinforced warnings?"

She shuddered but answered him with more of her old spirit.

"No, but if I should, *you* go. I don't want to."

F'lar grinned maliciously.

"I would, however," she added, "like to know why and how it could happen."

"I've never run across a mention of it anywhere," he told her candidly. "Of course, if you have done it—and you undeniably have," he assured her hastily at her indignant protest, "it obviously can be done. You say you thought of Ruatha, but you thought of it as it was on that particular day. Certainly a day to be remembered. You thought of spring, before dawn, no Red Star—yes, I remember your mentioning that—so one would have to remember references peculiar to a significant day to return to *between* times to the past."

She nodded slowly, thoughtfully.

"You used the same method the second time, to get to the Ruatha of three Turns ago. Again, of course, it was spring."

He rubbed his palms together, then brought his hands down on his knees with an emphatic slap and rose to his feet.

"I'll be back," he said and strode from the room, ignoring her half-articulated cry of warning.

Ramoth was curling up in the weyr as he passed her. He noticed that her color remained good in spite of the drain on her energies by the morning's exercises. She glanced at him, her many-faceted eye already covered by the inner, protective lid.

Mnementh awaited his rider on the ledge, and the moment F'lar leaped to his neck, took off. He circled upward, hovering above the Star Stone.

You wish to try Lessa's trick, Mnementh said, unperturbed by the prospective experiment.

F'lar stroked the great curved neck affectionately. *You understand how it worked for Ramoth and Lessa?*

As well as anyone can, Mnementh replied with the approximation of a shrug. *When did you have in mind?*

Before that moment F'lar had had no idea. Now unerringly his thoughts drew him backward to the summer day R'gul's bronze Hath had flown to mate the grotesque Nemorth, and R'gul had become Weyrleader in place of his dead father, F'lon.

Only the cold of *between* gave them any indication that they had transferred; they were still hovering above the Star Stone. F'lar wondered if they had missed some essential part of the transfer. Then he realized that the sun was in another quarter of the sky and the air was warm and sweet with summer. The Weyr below was empty; there were no dragons sunning themselves on the ledges, no women busy at tasks in the Bowl. Noises impinged on his senses: raucous laughter, yells, shrieks, and a soft crooning noise that dominated the bedlam.

Then from the direction of the weyrling barracks in the Lower Caverns, two figures emerged—a stripling and a young bronze dragon. The boy's arm lay limply along the beast's neck. The impression that reached the hovering observers was one of utter dejection. The two halted by the lake, the boy peering into the unruffled blue waters, then glancing upward toward the queen's weyr.

F'lar knew the boy for himself, and compassion for that younger self filled him. If only he could reassure that boy so torn by grief, so filled with resentment that he would one day become Weyrleader. . . .

Abruptly, startled by his own thoughts, he ordered Mnementh to transfer back. The utter cold of *between* was like a slap in his face, replaced almost instantly as they broke out of *between* into the cold of normal winter.

Slowly Mnementh flew back down to the queen's weyr, as sobered as F'lar by what they had seen.

Rise high in glory,   Count three months and more,
Bronze and gold.   And five heated weeks,
Dive entwined,   A day of glory and
Enhance the Hold.   In a month, who seeks?

A strand of silver
In the sky . . .
With heat all quickened
And all times fly.

"I don't know why you insisted that F'nor unearth these ridiculous things from Ista Weyr," Lessa exclaimed in a tone of exasperation. "They consist of nothing but trivial notes on how many measures of grain were used to bake daily bread."

F'lar glanced up at her from the Records he was studying. He sighed, leaned back in his chair in a bone-popping stretch.

"And I used to think," Lessa said with a rueful expression on her vivid, narrow face, "that those venerable Records would hold the total sum of all dragonlore and human wisdom. Or so I was led to believe," she added pointedly.

F'lar chuckled. "They do, but you have to disinter it."

Lessa wrinkled her nose. "Phew. They smell as if we had . . . and the only decent thing to do would be to rebury them."

"Which is another item I'm hoping to find . . . the old

preservative technique that kept the skins from hardening and smelling."

"It's stupid anyhow, to use skins for recording. There ought to be something better. We have become, dear Weyrleader, entirely too hidebound."

While F'lar roared with appreciation of her pun, she regarded him impatiently. Suddenly she jumped up, fired by another of her mercurial moods.

"Well, you won't find it. You won't find the facts you're looking for. Because I know what you're really after, and it isn't recorded!"

"Explain yourself."

"It's time we stopped hiding a rather brutal truth from ourselves."

"Which is?"

"Our mutual feeling that the Red Star is a menace and that the Threads *will* come! *We* decided that out of pure conceit and then went back *between* times to particularly crucial points in our lives and strengthened that notion, in our earliest selves. And for you, it was when you decided you were destined"—her voice made the word mocking—"to become Weyrleader one day.

"Could it be," she went on scornfully, "that our ultra-conservative R'gul has the right of it? That there have been no Threads for four hundred Turns because there are no more? And that the reason we have so few dragons is because the dragons sense they are no longer essential to Pern? That we *are* anachronisms as well as parasites?"

F'lar did not know how long he sat looking up at her bitter face or how long it took him to find answers to her probing questions.

"Anything is possible, Weyrwoman," he heard his voice replying calmly. "Including the unlikely fact that an eleven-year-old child, scared stiff, could plot revenge on her family's murderer and—against all odds—succeed."

She took an involuntary step forward, struck by his unexpected rebuttal. She listened intently.

"I prefer to believe," he went on inexorably, "that there is more to life than raising dragons and playing spring games. That is not enough for me. And I have made others look further, beyond self-interest and comfort. I have given them a purpose, a discipline. Everyone, dragonfolk and Holder alike, profits.

"I am not looking in these Records for reassurance. I'm looking for solid facts.

"I can prove, Weyrwoman, that there have been Threads. I can prove that there have been Intervals during which the Weyrs have declined. I can prove that if you sight the Red Star directly bracketed by the Eye Rock at the moment of winter solstice, the Red Star will pass close enough to Pern to throw off Threads. Since I can prove these facts. I believe Pern is in danger. *I* believe . . . not the youngster of fifteen Turns ago. F'lar, the bronze rider, the Weyrleader, believes it!"

He saw her eyes reflecting shadowy doubts, but he sensed his arguments were beginning to reassure her.

"You felt constrained to believe in me once before," he went on in a milder voice, "when I suggested that you could be Weyrwoman. You believed me and . . ." He made a gesture around the weyr as substantiation.

She gave him a weak, humorless smile.

"That was because I had never planned what to do with my life once I did have Fax lying dead at my feet. Of course, being Ramoth's Weyrmate is wonderful, but" —she frowned slightly—"it isn't enough anymore, either. That's why I wanted so to learn to fly and . . ."

". . . that's how this argument started in the first place," F'lar finished for her with a sardonic smile.

He leaned across the table urgently.

"Believe with me, Lessa, until you have cause not to. I respect your doubts. There's nothing wrong in doubting. It sometimes leads to greater faith. But believe with me until spring. If the Threads have not fallen by then . . ." He shrugged fatalistically.

She looked at him for a long moment and then inclined her head slowly in agreement.

He tried to suppress the relief he felt at her decision. Lessa, as Fax had discovered, was a ruthless adversary and a canny advocate. Besides these, she was Weyrwoman: essential to his plans.

"Now let's get back to the contemplation of trivia. They do tell me, you know, time, place, and duration of Thread incursions," he grinned up at her reassuringly. "And those facts I must have to make up my timetable."

"Timetable? But you said you didn't know the time."

"Not the day to the second when the Threads may spin

down. For one thing, while the weather holds so unusually cold for this time of year, the Threads simply turn brittle and blow away like dust. They're harmless. However, when the air is warm, they are viable and . . . deadly." He made fists of both hands, placing one above and to one side of the other. "The Red Star is my right hand, my left is Pern. The Red Star turns very fast and in the opposite direction to us. It also wobbles erratically."

"How do you know that?"

"Diagram on the walls of the Fort Weyr Hatching Ground. That was the very first Weyr, you know."

Lessa smiled sourly. "I know."

"So when the Star makes a pass, the Threads spin off, down toward us, in attacks that last six hours and occur approximately fourteen hours apart."

"Attacks last six hours?"

He nodded gravely.

"When the Red Star is closest to us. Right now it is just beginning its Pass."

She frowned.

He rummaged among the skin sheets on the table, and an object dropped to the stone floor with a metallic clatter.

Curious, Lessa bent to pick it up, turning the thin sheet over in her hands.

"What's this?" She ran an exploratory finger lightly across the irregular design on one side.

"I don't know. F'nor brought it back from Fort Weyr. It was nailed to one of the chests in which the Records had been stored. He brought it along, thinking it might be important. Said there was a plate like it just under the Red Star diagram on the wall of the Hatching Ground."

"This first part is plain enough: 'Mother's father's father, who departed for all time *between*, said this was the key to the mystery, and it came to him while doodling. He said that he said: ARRHENIUS? EUREKA! MYCORRHIZA . . .' Of course, that part doesn't make any sense at all," Lessa snorted. "It isn't even Pernese—just babbling, those last three words."

"I've studied it, Lessa," F'lar replied, glancing at it again and tipping it toward him to reaffirm his conclusions. "The only way to depart for all time *between* is to die, right? People just don't fly away on their own obviously. So it is a death vision, dutifully recorded by a grandchild who couldn't spell very well either. 'Doodling' as the present tense of dying!" He smiled indulgently. "And as for the rest of it, after the nonsense—like most death visions—it 'explains' what everyone has always known. Read on."

" 'Flamethrowing fire lizards to wipe out the spores. Q.E.D.'?"

"No help there either. Obviously just a primitive rejoicing that he is a dragonman, who didn't even know the right word for Threads." F'lar's shrug was expressive.

Lessa wet one fingertip to see if the patterns were inked on. The metal was shiny enough for a good mirror if she could get rid of the designs. However, the patterns remained smooth and precise.

"Primitive or no, they had a more permanent way of recording their visions that is superior to even the well-preserved skins," she murmured.

"Well-preserved babblings," F'lar said, turning back to the skins he was checking for understandable data.

"A badly scored ballad?" Lessa wondered and then dismissed the whole thing. "The design isn't even pretty."

F'lar pulled forward a chart that showed overlapping horizontal bands imposed on the projection of Pern's continental mass.

"Here," he said, "this represents waves of attack, and this one"—he pulled forward the second map with vertical bandings—"shows time zones. So you can see that with a fourteen-hour break only certain parts of Pern are affected in each attack. One reason for spacing of the Weyrs."

"Six full Weyrs," she murmured, "close to three thousand dragons."

"I'm aware of the statistics," he replied in a voice devoid of expression. "It meant no one Weyr was overburdened during the height of the attacks, not that three thousand beasts must be available. However, with these timetables we can manage until Ramoth's first clutches have matured."

She turned a cynical look on him. "You've a lot of faith in one queen's capacity."

He waved that remark aside impatiently. "I've more

faith, no matter what your opinion is, in the startling repe-
titions of events in these Records."

"Ha!"

"I don't mean how many measures for daily bread,
Lessa," he retorted, his voice rising. "I mean such things
as the time such and such a wing was sent out on patrol,
how long the patrol lasted, how many riders were hurt.
The brooding capacities of queens during the fifty years a
Pass lasts, and the Intervals between such Passes. Yes, it
tells that. By all I've studied here," and he pounded emphatically on the nearest stack of dusty, smelly skins,
"Nemorth should have been mating twice a Turn for the
last ten. Had she even kept to her paltry twelve a clutch,
we'd have two hundred and forty more beasts . . . Don't
interrupt. But we had Jora as Weyrleader, and we had
fallen into planet-wide disfavor during a four hundred
Turn Interval. Well, Ramoth will brood over no measly
dozen, and she'll lay a queen egg, mark my words. She
will rise often to mate and lay generously. By the time the
Red Star is passing closest to us and the attacks become
frequent, we'll be ready."

She stared at him, her eyes wide with incredulity. "Out
of Ramoth?"

"Out of Ramoth and out of the queens she'll lay. Remember, there are Records of Faranth laying sixty eggs
at a time, including several queen eggs."

Lessa could only shake her head slowly in wonder.

" 'A strand of silver/In the sky . . . With heat, all
quickens/And all times fly,' " F'lar quoted to her.

"She's got weeks more to go before laying, and then the
eggs must hatch . . ."

"Been on the Hatching Ground recently? Wear your
boots. You'll be burned through sandals."

She dismissed that with a guttural noise. He sat back,
outwardly amused by her disbelief.

"And then you have to make Impression and wait till
the riders—" she went on.

"Why do you think I've insisted on older boys? The
dragons are mature long before their riders."

"Then the system is faulty."

He narrowed his eyes slightly, shaking the stylus at her.

"Dragon tradition started out as a guide . . . but there
comes a time when man becomes too traditional, too—

what was it you said?—too hidebound? Yes, it's traditional to use the weyrbred because it's been convenient.
And because this sensitivity to dragons strengthens where
both sire and dam are weyrbred. That doesn't mean
weyrbred is best. You, for example . . ."

"There's Weyrblood in the Ruathan line," she said
proudly.

"Granted. Take young Naton; he's craftbred from
Nabol, yet F'nor tells me he can make Canth understand
him."

"Oh, that's not hard to do," she interjected.

"What do you mean?" F'lar jumped on her statement.

They were both interrupted by a high-pitched, penetrating whine. F'lar listened intently for a moment and
then shrugged, grinning.

"Some green's getting herself chased again."

"And that's another item these so-called all-knowing
Records of yours never mention. Why it is that only the
gold dragon can reproduce?"

F'lar did not suppress a lascivious chuckle.

"Well, for one thing, firestone inhibits reproduction. If
they never chewed stone, a green could lay, but at best
they produce small beasts, and we need big ones. And for
another thing"—his chuckle rolled out as he went on deliberately, grinning mischievously—"if the greens could
reproduce, considering their amorousness and the numbers
we have of them, we'd be up to our ears in dragons in
next to no time."

The first whine was joined by another, and then a low
hum throbbed as if carried by the stones of the Weyr itself.

F'lar, his face changing rapidly from surprise to triumphant astonishment, dashed up the passage.

"What's the matter?" Lessa demanded, picking up her
skirts to run after him. "What does that mean?"

The hum, resonating everywhere, was deafening in the
echo-chamber of the queen's weyr. Lessa registered the
fact that Ramoth was gone. She heard F'lar's boots
pounding down the passage to the ledge, a sharp *ta-ta-tat*
over the kettledrum booming hum. The whine was so
high-pitched now that it was inaudible but still nerve-
racking. Disturbed, frightened, Lessa followed F'lar out.

By the time she reached the ledge, the Bowl was a-whir

with dragons on the wing, making for the high entrance to the Hatching Ground. Weyrfolk, riders, women, children, all screaming with excitement, were pouring across the Bowl to the lower entrance to the Ground.

She caught sight of F'lar, charging across to the entrance, and she shrieked at him to wait. He couldn't have heard her across the bedlam.

Fuming because she had the long stairs to descend, then must double back as the stairs faced the feeding grounds at the opposite end of the Bowl from the Hatching Ground, Lessa realized that she, the Weyrwoman, would be the last one there.

Why had Ramoth decided to be secretive about laying? Wasn't she close enough to her own weyrmate to want her with her?

A dragon knows what to do, Ramoth calmly informed her.

You could have told me, Lessa wailed, feeling much abused.

Why, at the time F'lar had been going on largely about huge clutches and three thousand beasts, that infuriating dragon-child had been doing it!

It didn't improve Lessa's temper to have to recall another remark of F'lar's—on the state of the Hatching Grounds. The moment she stepped into the mountain-high cavern, she felt the heat through the soles of her sandals. Everyone was crowded in a loose circle around the far end of the cavern. And everyone was swaying from foot to foot. As Lessa was short to begin with, this only decreased the likelihood of her ever seeing what Ramoth had done.

"Let me through!" she demanded imperiously, pounding on the wide backs of two tall riders.

An aisle was reluctantly opened for her, and she went through, looking neither to her right or left at the excited weyrfolk. She was furious, confused, hurt, and knew she looked ridiculous because the hot sand made her walk with a curious mincing quickstep.

She halted; stunned and wide-eyed at the mass of eggs, and forgot such trivial things as hot feet.

Ramoth was curled around the clutch, looking enormously pleased with herself. She, too, kept shifting, closing and opening a protective wing over her eggs so that it was difficult to count them.

No one will steal them, silly, so stop fluttering, Lessa advised as she tried to make a tally.

Obediently Ramoth folded her wings. To relieve her maternal anxiety, however, she snaked her head out across the circle of mottled, glowing eggs, looking all around the cavern, flicking her forked tongue in and out.

An immense sigh, like a gust of wind, swept through the cavern. For there, now that Ramoth's wings were furled, gleamed an egg of glowing gold among the mottled ones. A queen egg!

"A queen egg!" The cry went up simultaneously from half a hundred throats. The Hatching Ground rang with cheers, yells, screams, and howls of exultation.

Someone seized Lessa and swung her around in an excess of feeling. A kiss landed in the vicinity of her mouth. No sooner did she recover her footing than she was hugged by someone else—she thought it was Manora, and then pounded and buffeted around in congratulation until she was reeling in a kind of dance between avoiding the celebrants and easing the growing discomfort of her feet.

She broke from the milling revelers and ran across the Ground to Ramoth. Lessa came to a sudden stop before the eggs. They seemed to be pulsing. The shells looked flaccid. She could have sworn they were hard the day she Impressed Ramoth. She wanted to touch one, just to make sure, but dared not.

You may, Ramoth assured her condescendingly. She touched Lessa's shoulder gently with her tongue.

The egg was soft to touch, and Lessa drew her hand back quickly, afraid of doing injury.

The heat will harden it, Ramoth said.

"Ramoth, I'm so proud of you," Lessa sighed, looking adoringly up at the great eyes that shone in rainbows of pride. "You are the most marvelous queen ever. I do believe you will redragon all the Weyrs. I do believe you will."

Ramoth inclined her head regally, then began to sway it from side to side over the eggs protectingly. She began to hiss suddenly, raising from her crouch, beating the air

with her wings, before settling back into the sands to lay
yet another egg.

The weyrfolk, uncomfortable on the hot sands, were
beginning to leave the Hatching Ground now that they
had paid tribute to the arrival of the golden egg. A queen
took several days to complete her clutch so there was no
point to waiting. Seven eggs already lay beside the important golden one, and if there were seven already, this au-
gered well for the eventual total. Wagers were being made
and taken even as Ramoth produced her ninth mottled
egg.

"Just as I predicted, a queen egg, by the mother of us
all," F'lar's voice said in Lessa's ear. "And I'll wager
there'll be ten bronzes at least."

She looked up at him, completely in harmony with the
Weyrleader at this moment. She was conscious now of
Mnementh, crouching proudly on a ledge, gazing fondly
at his mate. Impulsively Lessa laid her hand on F'lar's
arm.

"F'lar, I do believe you."

"Only now?" F'lar teased her, but his smile was wide
and his eyes proud.

> Weyrman, watch; Weyrman, learn
> Something new in every Turn.
> Oldest may be coldest, too.
> Sense the right; find the true!

IF F'LAR'S orders over the next months caused no end
of discussion and muttering among the weyrfolk, they
seemed to Lessa to be only the logical outcomes of their
discussion after Ramoth had finished laying her gratifying
total of forty-one eggs.

F'lar discarded tradition right and left, treading on
more than R'gul's conservative toes.

Out of perverse distaste for outworn doctrines against
which she herself had chafed during R'gul's leadership,
and out of respect for F'lar's intelligence, Lessa backed
him completely. She might not have respected her earlier
promise to him that she would believe him until spring if
she had not seen his predictions come true, one after another. These were based, however, not on the premoni-

tions she no longer trusted after her experience *between* times, but on recorded facts.

As soon as the eggshells hardened and Ramoth had rolled her special queen egg to one side of the mottled clutch for attentive brooding, F'lar brought the prospective riders into the Hatching Ground. Traditionally the candidates saw the eggs for the first time on the day of Impression. To this precedent F'lar added others: very few of the sixty-odd were weyrbred, and most of them were in their late teens. The candidates were to get used to the eggs, touch them, caress them, be comfortable with the notion that out of these eggs young dragons would hatch, eager and waiting to be Impressed. F'lar felt that such a practice might cut down on casualties during Impression when the boys were simply too scared to move out of the way of the awkward dragonets.

F'lar also had Lessa persuade Ramoth to let Kylara near her precious golden egg. Kylara readily enough weaned her son and spent hours, with Lessa acting as her tutor, beside the golden egg. Despite Kylara's loose attachment to T'bor, she showed an open preference for F'lar's company. Therefore, Lessa took great pains to foster F'lar's plan for Kylara since it meant her removal with the new-hatched queen to Fort Weyr.

F'lar's use of the Hold-born as riders served an additional purpose. Shortly before the actual Hatching and Impression, Lytol, the Warder appointed at Ruath Hold, sent another message.

"The man positively delights in sending bad news," Lessa remarked as F'lar passed the message skin to her.

"He's gloomy," F'nor agreed. He had brought the message. "I feel sorry for that youngster cooped up with such a pessimist."

Lessa frowned at the brown rider. She still found distasteful any mention of Gemma's son, now Lord of her ancestral Hold. Yet . . . as she had inadvertently caused his mother's death and she could not be Weyrwoman and Lady Holder at the same time, it was fitting that Gemma's Jaxom be Lord at Ruatha.

"I, however," F'lar said, "am grateful for his warnings. I suspected Meron would cause trouble again."

"He has shifty eyes, like Fax's," Lessa remarked.

"Shifty-eyed or not, he's dangerous," F'lar answered.

"And I cannot have him spreading rumors that we are deliberately choosing men of the Blood to weaken Family Lines."

"There are more craftsmen's sons than Holders' boys, in any case," F'nor snorted.

"I don't like him questioning that the Threads have not appeared," Lessa said gloomily.

F'lar shrugged. "They'll appear in due time. Be thankful the weather has continued cold. When the weather warms up and still no Threads appear, then I will worry." He grinned at Lessa in an intimate reminder of her promise.

F'nor cleared his throat hastily and looked away.

"However," the Weyrleader went on briskly, "I can do something about the other accusation."

So, when it was apparent that the eggs were about to hatch, he broke another long-standing tradition and sent riders to fetch the fathers of the young candidates from craft and Hold.

The great Hatching Cavern gave the appearance of being almost full as Holder, and Weyrfolk watched from the tiers above the heated Ground. This time, Lessa observed, there was no aura of fear. The youthful candidates were tense, yes, but not frightened out of their wits by the rocking, shattering eggs. When the ill-coordinated dragonets awkwardly stumbled—it seemed to Lessa that they deliberately looked around at the eager faces as though pre-Impressed—the youths either stepped to one side or eagerly advanced as a crooning dragonet made his choice. The Impressions were made quickly and with no accidents. All too soon, Lessa thought, the triumphant procession of stumbling dragons and proud new riders moved erratically out of the Hatching Ground to the barracks.

The young queen burst from her shell and moved unerringly for Kylara, standing confidently on the hot sands. The watching beasts hummed their approval.

"It was over too soon," Lessa said in a disappointed voice that evening to F'lar.

He laughed indulgently, allowing himself a rare evening of relaxation now that another step had gone as planned. The Holder folk had been ridden home, stunned, dazed, and themselves impressed by the Weyr and the Weyrleader.

"That's because you were watching this time," he remarked, brushing a lock of her hair back. It obscured his view of her profile. He chuckled again. "You'll notice Naton . . ."

"N'ton," she corrected him.

"All right, N'ton—Impressed a bronze."

"Just as you predicted," she said with some asperity.

"And Kylara is Weyrwoman for Pridith."

Lessa did not comment on that, and she did her best to ignore his laughter.

"I wonder which bronze will fly her," he murmured softly.

"It had better be T'bor's Orth," Lessa said, bridling.

He answered her the only way a wise man could.

> Crack dust, blackdust,
> Turn in freezing air.
> Waste dust, spacedust,
> From Red Star bare.

LESSA WOKE abruptly, her head aching, her eyes blurred, her mouth dry. She had the immediate memory of a terrible nightmare that just as quickly escaped recall. She brushed her hair out of her face and was surprised to find that she had been sweating heavily.

"F'lar?" she called in an uncertain voice. He had evidently risen early. "F'lar," she called again louder.

He's coming, Mnementh informed her. Lessa sensed that the dragon was just landing on the ledge. She touched Ramoth and found that the queen, too, had been bothered by formless, frightening dreams. The dragon roused briefly and then fell back into deeper sleep.

Disturbed by her vague fears, Lessa rose and dressed, forgoing a bath for the first time since she had arrived at the Weyr.

She called down the shaft for breakfast, then plaited her hair with deft fingers as she waited.

The tray appeared on the shaft platform just as F'lar entered. He kept looking back over his shoulder at Ramoth.

"What's gotten into her?"

"Echoing my nightmare. I woke in a cold sweat."

"You were sleeping quietly enough when I left to assign

patrols. You know, at the rate those dragonets are growing, they're already capable of limited flight. All they do is eat and sleep, and that's . . ."

". . . what makes a dragon grow," Lessa finished for him and sipped thoughtfully at her steaming hot *klah.* "You are going to be extra-careful about their drill procedures, aren't you?"

"You mean to prevent an inadvertent flight *between* times? I certainly am," he assured her. "I don't want bored dragonriders irresponsibly popping in and out." He gave her a long, stern look.

"Well, it wasn't my fault no one taught me to fly early enough," she replied in the sweet tone she used when she was being especially malicious. "If I'd been drilled from the day of Impression to the day of my first flight, I'd never have discovered that trick."

"True enough," he said solemnly.

"You know, F'lar, if I discovered it, someone else must have, and someone else may. If they haven't already."

F'lar drank, making a face as the *klah* scalded his tongue. "I don't know how to find out discreetly. We would be foolish to think we were the first. It is, after all, an inherent ability in dragons, or you would never have been able to do it."

She frowned, took a quick breath, and then let it go, shrugging.

"Go on," he encouraged her.

"Well, isn't it possible that our conviction about the imminence of the Threads could stem from one of us coming back when the Threads are actually falling? I mean . . ."

"My dear girl, we have both analyzed every stray thought and action—even your dream this morning upset you, although it was no doubt due to all the wine you drank last night—until we wouldn't know an honest presentiment if it walked up and slapped us in the face."

"I can't dismiss the thought that this *between* times ability is of crucial value," she said emphatically.

"That, my dear Weyrwoman, *is* an honest presentiment."

"But why?"

"Not why," he corrected her cryptically. *"When."* An idea stirred vaguely in the back of his mind. He tried to nudge it out where he could mull it over. Mnementh announced that F'nor was entering the weyr.

"What's the matter with you?" F'lar demanded of his half brother, for F'nor was choking and sputtering, his face red with the paroxysm.

"Dust . . ." he coughed, slapping at his sleeves and chest with his riding gloves. "Plenty of dust, but no Threads," he said, describing a wide arc with one arm as he fluttered his fingers suggestively. He brushed his tight wher-hide pants, scowling as a fine black dust drifted off.

F'lar felt every muscle in his body tense as he watched the dust float to the floor.

"Where did you get so dusty?" he demanded.

F'nor regarded him with mild surprise. "Weather patrol in Tillek. Entire north has been plagued with dust storms lately. But what I came in for . . ." He broke off, alarmed by F'lar's taut immobility. "What's the matter with dust?" he asked in a baffled voice.

F'lar pivoted on his heel and raced for the stairs to the Record Room. Lessa was right behind him, F'nor belatedly trailing after.

"Tillek, you said?" F'lar barked at his wingsecond. He was clearing the table of stacks for the four charts he then laid out. "How long have these storms been going on? Why didn't you report them?"

"Report dust storms? You wanted to know about warm air masses."

"How long have these storms been going on?" F'lar's voice crackled.

"Close to a week."

"How close?"

"Six days ago the first storm was noticed in upper Tillek. They have been reported in Bitra, Upper Telgar, Crom, and the High Reaches," F'nor reported tersely.

He glanced hopefully at Lessa but saw she, too, was staring at the four unusual charts. He tried to see why the horizontal and vertical strips had been superimposed on Pern's land mass, but the reason was beyond him.

Flar was making hurried notations, pushing first one map and then another away from him.

"Too involved to think straight, to see clearly, to understand," the Weyrleader snarled to him, throwing down the stylus angrily.

"You did say only warm air masses," F'nor heard himself saying humbly, aware that he had somehow failed his Weyrleader.

F'lar shook his head impatiently.

"Not your fault, F'nor. Mine. I should have asked. I knew it was good luck that the weather held so cold." He put both hands on F'nor's shoulders, looking directly into his eyes. "The Threads have been falling," he announced gravely. "Falling into the cold air, freezing into bits to drift on the wind"—F'lar imitated F'nor's finger-fluttering—"as specks of black dust."

" 'Crack dust, blackdust,' " Lessa quoted. "In 'The Ballad of Moreta's Ride,' the chorus is all about black dust."

"I don't need to be reminded of Moreta right now," F'lar growled, bending to the maps. "She could talk to any dragon in the Weyrs."

"But I can do that!" Lessa protested.

Slowly, as if he didn't quite credit his ears, F'lar turned back to Lessa. "What did you just say?"

"I said I can talk to any dragon in the Weyr."

Still staring at her, blinking in utter astonishment, F'lar sank down to the tabletop.

"How long," he managed to say, "have you had *this* particular skill?"

Something in his tone, in his manner, caused Lessa to flush and stammer like an erring weyrling.

"I . . . I always could. Beginning with the watch-wher at Ruatha." She gestured indecisively in Ruatha's westerly direction. "And I talked to Mnementh at Ruatha. And . . . when I got here, I could . . ." Her voice faltered at the accusing look in F'lar's cold, hard eyes. Accusing and, worse, contemptuous.

"I thought you had agreed to help me, to believe in me."

"I'm truly sorry, F'lar. It never occurred to me it was of any use to anyone, but . . ."

F'lar exploded onto both feet, his eyes blazing with aggravation.

"The one thing I could not figure out was how to direct the wings and keep in contact with the Weyr during an attack, how I was going to get reinforcements and firestone in time. And you . . . you have been sitting there, spitefully hiding the . . ."

"I am *NOT* spiteful," she screamed at him. "I said I was sorry. I am. But you've a nasty, smug habit of keeping your own council. How was I to know you didn't have the same trick? You're F'lar, the Weyrleader, you can do *any*thing. Only you're just as bad as R'gul because you never *tell* me half the things I ought to know . . ."

F'lar reached out and shook her until her angry voice was stopped.

"Enough. We can't waste time arguing like children." Then his eyes widened, his jaw dropped. "Waste time? That's it."

"Go *between* times?" Lessa gasped.

"*Between* times!"

F'nor was totally confused. "What are you two talking about?"

"The Threads started falling at dawn in Nerat," F'lar said, his eyes bright, his manner decisive.

F'nor could feel his guts congealing with apprehension. At dawn in Nerat? Why, the rainforests would be demolished. He could feel a surge of adrenalin charging through his body at the thought of danger.

"So we're going *back* there, *between* times, and be there when the Threads started falling, two hours ago. F'nor, the dragons can go not only where we direct them but *when*."

"Where? When?" F'nor repeated, bewildered. "That could be dangerous."

"Yes, but today it will save Nerat. Now, Lessa," and F'lar gave her another shake, compounded of pride and affection, "order out all the dragons, young, old, any that can fly. Tell them to load themselves down with firestone sacks. I don't know if you can talk across time . . ."

"My dream this morning . . ."

"Perhaps. But right now rouse the Weyr." He pivoted to F'nor. "If Threads are falling . . . were falling . . . at Nerat at dawn, they'll be falling on Keroon and Ista right now because they are in that time pattern. Take two wings to Keroon. Arouse the plains. Get them to start the firepits blazing. Take some weyrlings with you and send them on to Igen and Ista. Those Holds are not in as immediate danger as Keroon. I'll reinforce you as soon as I can. And . . . keep Canth in touch with Lessa."

F'lar clapped his brother on the shoulder and sent him

off. The brown rider was too used to taking orders to argue.

"Mnementh says R'gul is duty officer, and R'gul wants to know——" Lessa began.

"C'mon, girl," F'lar said, his eyes brilliant with excitement. He grabbed up his maps and propelled her up the stairs.

They arrived in the weyr just as R'gul entered with T'sum. R'gul was muttering about this unusual summons.

"Hath told me to report," he complained. "Fine thing when your own dragon——"

"R'gul, T'sum, mount your wings. Arm them with all the firestone they can carry, and assemble above Star Stone. I'll join you in a few minutes. We go to Nerat at dawn."

"Nerat? I'm watch officer, not patrol——"

"This is no patrol," F'lar cut him off.

"But, sir," T'sum interrupted, his eyes wide. "Nerat's dawn was two hours ago, the same as ours."

"And that is *when* we are going to, brown rider. The dragons, we have discovered, can go *between* places temporally as well as geographically. At dawn Threads fell at Nerat. We're going back, *between* time, to sear them from the sky."

F'lar paid no attention to R'gul's stammered demand for explanation. T'sum, however, grabbed up firestone sacks and raced back to the ledge and his waiting Munth.

"Go on, you old fool," Lessa told R'gul irascibly. "The Threads are here. You were wrong. Now be a dragonman! Or go *between* and stay there!"

Ramoth, awakened by the alarms, poked at R'gul with her man-sized head, and the ex-Weyrleader came out of his momentary shock. Without a word he followed T'sum down the passageway.

F'lar had thrown on his heavy wher-hide tunic and shoved on his riding boots.

"Lessa, be sure to send messages to all the Holds. Now this attack will stop about four hours from now. So the farthest west it can reach will be Ista. But I want every Hold and craft warned."

She nodded, her eyes intent on his face lest she miss a word.

"Fortunately, the Star is just beginning its Pass, so we

won't have to worry about another attack for a few days.
I'll figure out the next one when I get back.

"Now, get Manora to organize her women. We'll need
pails of ointment. The dragons are going to be laced, and
that hurts. Most important, if something goes wrong,
you'll have to wait till a bronze is at least a year old to
fly Ramoth . . ."

"No one's flying Ramoth but Mnementh," she cried,
her eyes sparkling fiercely.

F'lar crushed her against him, his mouth bruising hers
as if all her sweetness and strength must come with him.
He released her so abruptly that she staggered back
against Ramoth's lowered head. She clung for a moment
to her dragon, as much for support as for reassurance.

That is, if Mnementh can catch me, Ramoth amended
smugly.

> Wheel and turn
> Or bleed and burn.
> Fly *between,*
> Blue and green.
> Soar, dive down,
> Bronze and brown
> Dragonmen must fly
> When Threads are in the sky.

As F'LAR raced down the passageway to the ledge, fire-
sacks bumping against his thighs, he was suddenly grateful for the tedious sweeping patrols over every Hold and
hollow of Pern. He could see Nerat clearly in his mind's
eye. He could see the many-petaled vineflowers which
were the distinguishing feature of the rainforests at this
time of year. Their ivory blossoms would be glowing in
the first beams of sunlight like dragon eyes among the
tall, wide-leaved plants.

Mnementh, his eyes flashing with excitement, hovered skittishly over the ledge. F'lar vaulted to the bronze
neck.

The Weyr was seething with wings of all colors, noisy
with shouts and countercommands. The atmosphere was
electric, but F'lar could sense no panic in that ordered
confusion. Dragon and human bodies oozed out of
openings around the Bowl walls. Women scurried across

the floor from one Lower Cavern to another. The children playing by the lake were sent to gather wood for a fire. The weyrlings, supervised by old C'gan, were forming outside their barracks. F'lar looked up to the Peak and approved the tight formation of the wings assembled there in close flying order. Another wing formed up as he watched. He recognized brown Canth, F'nor on his neck, just as the entire wing vanished.

He ordered Mnementh aloft. The wind was cold and carried a hint of moisture. A late snow? This was the time for it, if ever.

R'gul's wing and T'bor's fanned out on his left, T'sum and D'nol on his right. He noted each dragon was well-laden with sacks. Then he gave Mnementh the visualization of the early spring rainforest in Nerat, just before dawn, the vineflowers gleaming, the sea breaking against the rocks of the High Shoal. . . .

He felt the searing cold of *between*. And he felt a stab of doubt. Was he injudicious, sending them all possibly to their deaths *between* times in this effort to outtime the Threads at Nerat?

Then they were all there in the crepuscular light that promises day. The lush, fruity smells of the rainforest drifted up to them. Warm, too, and that was frightening. He looked up and slightly to the north. Pulsing with menace, the Red Star shone down.

The men had realized what had happened, their voices raised in astonishment. Mnementh told F'lar that the dragons were mildly surprised at their riders' fuss.

"Listen to me, dragonriders," F'lar called, his voice harsh and distorted in an effort to be heard by all. He waited till the men had moved as close as possible. He told Mnementh to pass the information on to each dragon. Then he explained what they had done and why. No one spoke, but there were many nervous looks exchanged across bright wings.

Crisply he ordered the dragonriders to fan out in a staggered formation, keeping a distance of five wings' spread up or down.

The sun came up.

Slanting across the sea, like an ever-thickening mist, Threads were falling, silent, beautiful, treacherous. Silvery gray were those space-transversing spores, spinning

from hard frozen ovals into coarse filaments as they
penetrated the warm atmospheric envelope of Pern. Less
than mindless, they had been ejected from their barren
planet toward Pern, a hideous rain that sought organic
matter to nourish it into growth. One Thread, sinking into
fertile soil, would burrow deep, propagating thousands in
the warm earth, rendering it into a black-dusted wasteland. The southern continent of Pern had already been
sucked dry. The true parasites of Pern were Threads.

A stifled roar from the throats of eighty men and dragons broke the dawn air above Nerat's green heights—as
if the Threads might hear this challenge, F'lar mused.

As one, dragons swiveled their wedge-shaped heads to
their riders for firestone. Great jaws macerated the
hunks. The fragments were swallowed and more firestone was demanded. Inside the beasts, acids churned and
the poisonous phosphines were readied. When the dragons belched forth the gas, it would ignite in the air into
ravening flame to sear the Threads from the sky. And
burn them from the soil.

Dragon instinct took over the moment the Threads began to fall above Nerat's shores.

As much admiration as F'lar had always held for his
bronze companion, it achieved newer heights in the next
hours. Beating the air in great strokes, Mnementh soared
with flaming breath to meet the down-rushing menace.
The fumes, swept back by the wind, choked F'lar until
he thought to crouch low on the lee side of the bronze
neck. The dragon squealed as a Thread flicked the tip of
one wing. Instantly F'lar and he ducked into *between,*
cold, calm, black. The frozen Thread cracked off. In the
flicker of an eye, they were back to face the reality of
Threads.

Around him F'lar saw dragons winking in and out of
between, flaming as they returned, diving, soaring. As the
attack continued and they drifted across Nerat, F'lar began to recognize the pattern in the dragons' instinctive
evasion-attack movements. And in the Threads. For contrary to what he had gathered from his study of the Records, the Threads fell in patches. Not as rain will, in
steady unbroken sheets, but like flurries of snow, here,
above, there, whipped to one side suddenly. Never
fluidly, despite the continuity their name implied.

You could see a patch above you. Flaming, your dragon would rise. You'd have the intense joy of seeing the clump shrivel from bottom to top. Sometimes a patch would fall between riders. One dragon would signal he would follow and, spouting flame, would dive and sear.

Gradually the dragonriders worked their way over the rainforests, so densely, so invitingly green. F'lar refused to dwell on what just one live Thread burrow would do to that lush land. He would send back a low-flying patrol to quarter every foot. One Thread, just one Thread, could put out the ivory eyes of every luminous vineflower.

A dragon screamed somewhere to his left. Before he could identify the beast, it had ducked *between.* F'lar heard other cries of pain, from men as well as dragons. He shut his ears and concentrated, as dragons did, on the here-and-now. Would Mnementh remember those piercing cries later? F'lar wished he could forget them now.

He, F'lar, the bronze rider, felt suddenly superfluous. It was the dragons who were fighting this engagement. You encouraged your beast, comforted him when the Threads burned, but you depended on his instinct and speed.

Hot fire dripped across F'lar's cheeks, burrowing like acid into his shoulder . . . a cry of surprised agony burst from F'lar's lips. Mnementh took them to merciful *between.* The dragonmen battled with frantic hands at the Threads, felt them crumble in the intense cold of *between* and break off. Revolted, he slapped at injuries still afire. Back in Nerat's humid air, the sting seemed to ease. Mnementh crooned comfortingly and then dove at a patch, breathing fire.

Shocked at self-consideration, F'lar hurriedly examined his mount's shoulder for telltale score marks.

I duck very quickly, Mnementh told him and veered away from a dangerously close clump of Threads. A brown dragon followed them down and burned them to ash.

It might have been moments, it might have been a hundred hours later when F'lar looked down in surprise at the sunlit sea. Threads now dropped harmlessly into the salty waters. Nerat was to the east of him on his right, the rock tip curling westward.

F'lar felt weariness in every muscle. In the excitement of frenzied battle, he had forgotten the bloody scores on cheek and shoulder. Now as he and Mnementh glided slowly, the injuries ached and stung.

He flew Mnementh high, and when they had achieved sufficient altitude, they hovered. He could see no Threads falling landward. Below him, the dragons ranged, high and low, searching for any sign of a burrow, alert for any suddenly toppling trees or disturbed vegetation.

"Back to the Weyr," he ordered Mnementh with a heavy sigh. He heard the bronze relay the command even as he himself was taken *between*. He was so tired he did not even visualize where—much less when—relying on Mnementh's instinct to bring him safely home through time and space.

> Honor those the dragons heed,
> In thought and favor, word and deed.
> Worlds are lost or worlds are saved
> From those dangers dragon-braved.

CRANING HER NECK toward the Star Stone at Benden Peak, Lessa watched from the ledge until she saw the four wings disappear from view.

Sighing deeply to quiet her inner fears, Lessa raced down the stairs to the floor of Benden Weyr. She noticed that someone was building a fire by the lake and that Manora was already ordering her women around, her voice clear but calm.

Old C'gan had the weyrlings lined up. She caught the envious eyes of the newest dragonriders at the barracks windows. They'd have time enough to fly a flaming dragon. From what F'lar had intimated, they'd have Turns.

She shuddered as she stepped up to the weyrlings but managed to smile at them. She gave them their orders and sent them off to warn the Holds, checking quickly with each dragon to be sure the rider had given clear references. The Holds would shortly be stirred up to a froth.

Canth told her that there were Threads at Keroon, falling on the Keroon side of Nerat Bay. He told her that F'nor did not think two wings were enough to protect the meadowlands.

Lessa stopped in her tracks, trying to think how many wings were already out.

K'net's wing is still here, Ramoth informed her. *On the Peak.*

Lessa glanced up and saw bronze Piyanth spread his wings in answer. She told him to get *between* to Keroon, close to Nerat Bay. Obediently the entire wing rose and then disappeared.

She turned with a sigh to say something to Manora when a rush of wind and a vile stench almost overpowered her. The air above the Weyr was full of dragons. She was about to demand of Piyanth why he hadn't gone to Keroon when she realized there were far more beasts a-wing than K'net's twenty.

But you just left, she cried as she recognized the unmistakable bulk of bronze Mnementh.

That was two hours ago for us, Mnementh said with such weariness in his tone that Lessa closed her eyes in sympathy.

Some dragons were gliding in fast. From their awkwardness it was evident that they were hurt.

As one, the women grabbed salve pots and clean rags and beckoned the injured down. The numbing ointment was smeared on score marks where wings resembled black and red lace.

No matter how badly injured he might be, every rider tended his beast first.

Lessa kept one eye on Mnementh, sure that F'lar would not keep the huge bronze hovering like that if he'd been hurt. She was helping T'sum with Munth's cruelly pierced right wing when she realized that the sky above the Star Stone was empty.

She forced herself to finish with Munth before she went to find the bronze and his rider. When she did locate them, she also saw Kylara smearing salve on F'lar's cheek and shoulder. She was advancing purposefully across the sands toward the pair when Canth's urgent plea reached her. She saw Mnementh's head swing upward as he, too, caught the brown's thought.

"F'lar, Canth says they need help," Lessa cried. She didn't notice then that Kylara slipped away into the busy crowd.

F'lar wasn't badly hurt. She reassured herself about

that. Kylara had treated the wicked burns that seemed to be shallow. Someone had found him another fur to re-place the tatters of the Thread-bared one. He frowned —and winced because the frown creased his burned cheek. He gulped hurriedly at his *klah.*

Mnementh, what's the tally of able-bodied? Oh, never mind, just get 'em aloft with a full load of firestone.

"You're all right?" Lessa asked, a detaining hand on his arm. He couldn't just go off like this, could he?

He smiled tiredly down at her, pressed his empty mug into her hands, giving them a quick squeeze. Then he vaulted to Mnementh's neck. Someone handed him a heavy load of sacks.

Blue, green, brown, and bronze dragons lifted from the Weyr Bowl in quick order. A trifle more than sixty drag-ons hovered briefly above the Weyr where eighty had lingered so few minutes before.

So few dragons. So few riders. How long could they take such toll?

Canth said F'nor needed more firestone.

She looked about anxiously. None of the weyrlings were back yet from their messenger rounds. A dragon was crooning plaintively, and she wheeled, but it was only young Pridith, stumbling across the Weyr to the feeding grounds, butting playfully at Kylara as they walked. The only other dragons were injured or—her eye fell on C'gan, emerging from the weyrling barracks.

"C'gan, can you and Tagath get more firestone to F'nor at Keroon?"

"Of course," the old blue rider assured her, his chest lifting with pride, his eyes flashing. She hadn't thought to send him anywhere, yet he had lived his life in training for this emergency. He shouldn't be deprived of a chance at it.

She smiled her approval at his eagerness as they piled heavy sacks on Tagath's neck. The old blue dragon snorted and danced as if he were young and strong again. She gave them the references Canth had visualized to her.

She watched as the two blinked out above the Star Stone.

It isn't fair. They have all the fun, said Ramoth peevishly. Lessa saw her sunning herself on the Weyr ledge, preening her enormous wings.

"You chew firestone and you're reduced to a silly green," Lessa told her Weyrmate sharply. She was inwardly amused by the queen's disgruntled complaint.

Lessa passed among the injured then. B'fol's dainty green beauty moaned and tossed her head, unable to bend one wing that had been threaded to bare cartilage. She'd be out for weeks, but she had the worst injury among the dragons. Lessa looked quickly away from the misery in B'fol's worried eyes.

As she did the rounds, she realized that more men were injured than beasts. Two in R'gul's wing had sustained serious head damages. One man might lose an eye completely. Manora had dosed him unconscious with numbweed. Another man's arm had been burned clear to the bone. Minor though most of the wounds were, the tally dismayed Lessa. How many more would be disabled at Keroon?

Out of one hundred and seventy-two dragons, fifteen already were out of action, some only for a day or two, however.

A thought struck Lessa. If N'ton had actually ridden Canth, maybe he could ride out on the next dragonade on an injured man's beast since there were more injured riders than dragons. F'lar broke traditions as he chose. Here was another one to set aside—if the dragon was agreeable.

Presuming N'ton was not the only new rider able to transfer to another beast, what good would such flexibility do in the long run? F'lar had definitely said the incursions would not be so frequent at first when the Red Star was just beginning its fifty-Turn long circling pass of Pern. How frequent was frequent? He would know, but he wasn't here.

Well, he *had* been right this morning about the appearance of Threads at Nerat, so his exhaustive study of those old Records had proved worthwhile.

No, that wasn't quite accurate. He had forgotten to have the men alert for signs of black dust as well as warming weather. As he had put the matter right by going *between* times, she would graciously allow him that minor error. But he did have an infuriating habit of guessing correctly. Lessa corrected herself again. He didn't guess. He studied. He planned. He thought and then he used common good sense. Like figuring out where and when Threads would strike according to entries in those smelly Records. Lessa began to feel better about their future.

Now if he would just make the riders learn to trust their dragons' sure instinct in battle, they would keep casualties down, too.

A shriek pierced air and ear as a blue dragon emerged above the Star Stone.

"Ramoth!" Lessa screamed in an instinctive reaction, hardly knowing why. The queen was a-wing before the echo of her command had died. For the careering blue was obviously in grave trouble. He was trying to brake his forward speed, yet one wing would not function. His rider had slipped forward over the great shoulder, precariously clinging to his dragon's neck with one hand.

Lessa, her hands clapped over her mouth, watched fearfully. There wasn't a sound in the Bowl but the flapping of Ramoth's immense wings. The queen rose swiftly to position herself against the desperate blue, lending him wing support on the crippled side.

The watchers gasped as the rider slipped, lost his hold, and fell—landing on Ramoth's wide shoulders.

The blue dropped like a stone. Ramoth came to a gentle stop near him, crouching low to allow the weyrfolk to remove her passenger.

It was C'gan.

Lessa felt her stomach heave as she saw the ruin the Threads had made of the old harper's face. She dropped beside him, pillowing his head in her lap. The weyrfolk gathered in a respectful, silent circle.

Manora, her face, as always, serene, had tears in her eyes. She knelt and placed her hand on the old rider's heart. Concern flicked in her eyes as she looked up at Lessa. Slowly she shook her head. Then, setting her lips in a thin line, she began to apply the numbing salve.

"Too toothless old to flame and too slow to get *between*," C'gan mumbled, rolling his head from side to side. "Too old. But 'Dragonmen must fly/When Threads are in the sky. . . .'" His voice trailed off into a sigh. His eyes closed.

Lessa and Manora looked at each other in anguish. A terrible, ear-shattering note cut the silence. Tagath sprang aloft in a tremendous leap. C'gan's eyes rolled slowly open, sightless. Lessa, breath suspended, watched the blue dragon, trying to deny the inevitable as Tagath disappeared in midair.

A low moan sprang up around the Weyr, like the torn, lonely cry of a keening wind. The dragons uttered tribute.

"Is he . . . gone?" Lessa asked, although she knew.

Manora nodded slowly, tears streaming down her cheeks as she reached over to close C'gan's dead eyes.

Lessa rose slowly to her feet, motioning to some of the women to remove the old rider's body. Absently she rubbed her bloody hands dry on her skirts, trying to concentrate on what might be needed next.

Yet her mind turned back to what had just happened. A dragonrider had died. His dragon, too. The Threads had claimed one pair already. How many more would die this cruel Turn? How long could the Weyr survive? Even after Ramoth's forty matured, and the ones she soon would conceive, and her queen-daughters, too?

Lessa walked apart to quiet her uncertainties and ease her grief. She saw Ramoth wheel and glide aloft to land on the Peak. One day soon would Lessa see those golden wings laced red and black from Thread marks? Would Ramoth . . . disappear?

No, Ramoth would not. Not while Lessa lived.

F'lar told her long ago that she must learn to look beyond the narrow confines of Hold Ruatha and mere revenge. He was, as usual, right. As Weyrwoman under his tutelage, she had further learned that living *was* more than raising dragons and Spring Games. Living was strugling to do something impossible—to succeed, or die knowing you had tried!

Lessa realized that she had, at last, fully accepted her role: as Weyrwoman and as mate, to help F'lar shape men and events for many Turns to come—to secure Pern against the Threads.

Lessa threw back her shoulders and lifted her chin high. Old C'gan had had the right of it.

> Dragonmen *must* fly
> When Threads are in the sky!

> Worlds are lost or worlds are saved
> By those dangers dragon-braved.

As F'LAR had predicted, the attack ended by high noon, and weary dragons and riders were welcomed by Ramoth's high-pitched trumpeting from the Peak.

Once Lessa assured herself that F'lar had taken no additional injury, that F'nor's were superficial, and that Manora was keeping Kylara busy in the kitchens, she applied herself to organizing the care of the injured and the comfort of the worried.

As dusk fell, an uneasy peace settled on the Weyr—the quiet of minds and bodies too tired or too hurtful to talk. Lessa's own words mocked her as she made out the list of wounded men and beasts. Twenty-eight men or dragons were out of the air for the next Thread battle. C'gan was the only fatality, but there had been four more seriously injured dragons at Keroon and seven badly scored men, out of action entirely for months to come.

Lessa crossed the Bowl to her Weyr, reluctant but resigned to giving F'lar this unsettling news.

She expected to find him in the sleeping room, but it was vacant. Ramoth was asleep already as Lessa passed her on the way to the Council Room—also empty. Puzzled and a little alarmed, Lessa half-ran down the steps to the Records Room to find F'lar, haggard of face, poring over musty skins.

"What are you doing here?" she demanded angrily. "You ought to be asleep."

"So should you," he drawled, amused.

"I was helping Manora settle the wounded . . ."

"Each to his own craft." But he did lean back from the table, rubbing his neck and rotating the uninjured shoulder to ease stiffened muscles.

"I couldn't sleep," he admitted, "so I thought I'd see what answers I might turn up in the Records."

"More answers? To what?" Lessa cried, exasperated with him. As if the Records ever answered anything. Obviously the tremendous responsibilities of Pern's defense against the Threads were beginning to tell on the Weyrleader. After all, there had been the stress of the first battle, not to mention the drain of the traveling *between* time itself to get to Nerat to forestall the Threads.

F'lar grinned and beckoned Lessa to sit beside him on the wall bench.

"I need the answer to the very pressing question of how one understrength Weyr can do the fighting of six."

Lessa fought the panic that rose, a cold flood, from her guts.

"Oh, your time schedules will take care of that," she replied gallantly. "You'll be able to conserve the dragon-power until the new forty can join the ranks."

F'lar raised a mocking eyebrow.

"Let us be honest between ourselves, Lessa."

"But there have been Long Intervals before," she argued, "and since Pern survived them, Pern can again."

"Before there were always six Weyrs. And twenty or so Turns before the Red Star was due to begin its Pass, the queens would start to produce enormous clutches. All the queens, not just one faithful golden Ramoth. Oh, how I curse Jora!" He slammed to his feet and started pacing, irritably brushing the lock of black hair that fell across his eyes.

Lessa was torn with the desire to comfort him and the sinking, choking fear in her belly that made it difficult to think at all.

"You were not so doubtful—"

He whirled back to her. "Not until I had actually had an encounter with the Threads and reckoned up the numbers of injuries. That sets the odds against us. Even supposing we can mount other riders to uninjured dragons, we will be hard put to keep a continuously effective force in the air and still maintain a ground guard." He caught her puzzled frown. "There's Nerat to be gone over on foot tomorrow. I'd be a fool indeed if I thought we'd caught and seared every Thread in mid-air."

"Get the Holders to do that. They can't just immure themselves safely in their inner Holds and let us do all. If they hadn't been so miserly and stupid—"

He cut off her complaint with an abrupt gesture. "They'll do their part all right," he assured her. "I'm sending for a full Council tomorrow, all Hold Lords and all Craftmasters. But there's more to it than just marking where Threads fall. How do you destroy a burrow that's gone deep under the surface? A dragon's breath is fine for the air and surface work but no good three feet down."

"Oh, I hadn't thought of that aspect. But the fire-pits . . ."

". . . are only on the heights and around human habitations, not on the meadowlands of Keroon or on Nerat's so green rainforests."

This consideration was daunting indeed. She gave a rueful little laugh.

"Shortsighted of me to suppose our dragons are all poor Pern needs to dispatch the Threads. Yet . . ." She shrugged expressively.

"There are other methods," F'lar said, "or there were. There must have been. I have run across frequent mention that the Holds were organizing ground groups and that they were armed with fire. What kind is never mentioned because it was so well-known." He threw up his hands in disgust and sagged back down on the bench. "Not even five hundred dragons could have seared all the Threads that fell today. Yet *they* managed to keep Pern Thread-free."

"Pern, yes, but wasn't the Southern Continent lost? Or did they just have their hands too full with Pern itself?"

"No one's bothered with the Southern Continent in a hundred thousand Turns," F'lar snorted.

"It's on the maps," Lessa reminded him.

He scowled disgustedly at the Records piled in uncommunicative stacks on the long table.

"The answer must be there. Somewhere."

There was an edge of desperation in his voice, the hint that he held himself to blame for not having discovered those elusive facts.

"Half those things couldn't be read by the man who wrote them," Lessa said tartly. "Besides that, it's been your *own* ideas that have helped us most so far. You compiled the time maps, and look how valuable they have been already."

"I'm getting too hidebound again, huh?" he asked, a half-smile tugging at one corner of his mouth.

"Undoubtedly," she assured him with more confidence than she felt. "We both know the Records are guilty of the most ridiculous omissions."

"Well said, Lessa. So let us forget these misguiding

and antiquated precepts and think up our own guides. First, we need more dragons. Second, we need them now. Third, we need something as effective as a flaming dragon to destroy Threads which have burrowed."

"Fourth, we need sleep or we won't be able to think of anything," she added with a touch of her usual asperity.

F'lar laughed outright, hugging her.

"You've got your mind on one thing, haven't you?" he teased, his hands caressing her eagerly.

She pushed ineffectually at him, trying to escape. For a wounded, tired man, he was remarkably amorous. One with that Kylara. Imagine that woman's presumption, dressing his wounds.

"My responsibility as Weyrwoman includes care of you, the Weyrleader."

"But you spend hours with blue dragonriders and leave me to Kylara's tender ministrations."

"You didn't look as if you objected."

F'lar threw back his head and roared. "Should I open Fort Weyr and send Kylara on?" he taunted her.

"I'd as soon Kylara were Turns as well as miles away from here," Lessa snapped, thoroughly irritated.

F'lar's jaw dropped, his eyes widened. He leaped to his feet with an astonished cry.

"You've said it!"

"Said what?"

"Turns away! That's it. We'll send Kylara back, *between* times, with her queen and the new dragonets." F'lar excitedly paced the room while Lessa tried to follow his reasoning. "No, I'd better send at least one of the older bronzes. F'nor, too . . . I'd rather have F'nor in charge . . . Discreetly, of course—"

"Send Kylara back . . . where to? When to?" Lessa interrupted him.

"Good point." F'lar dragged out the ubiquitous charts. "Very good point. Where can we send them around here without causing anomalies by being present at one of the other Weyrs? The High Reaches are remote. No, we've found remains of fires there, you know, still warm, and no inkling as to who built them or why. And if we had already sent them back, they'd've been ready for today, and they weren't. So they can't have been in two places already . . ." He shook his head, dazed by the paradoxes.

Lessa's eyes were drawn to the blank outline of the neglected Southern Continent.

"Send them there," she suggested sweetly, pointing.

"There's nothing there."

"Then bring in what they need. There must be water, for Threads can't devour that. We fly in whatever else is needed, fodder for the herdbeasts, grain . . ."

F'lar drew his brows together in concentration, his eyes sparkling with thought, the depression and defeat of a few moments ago forgotten.

"Threads wouldn't be there ten Turns ago. And haven't been there for close to four hundred. Ten Turns would give Pridith time to mature and have several clutches. Maybe more queens."

Then he frowned and shook his head dubiously. "No, there's no Weyr there. No Hatching Ground, no . . ."

"How do we know that?" Lessa caught him up sharply, too delighted with many aspects of this project to give it up easily. "The Records don't mention the Southern Continent, true, but they omit a great deal. How do we know it isn't green again in the four hundred Turns since the Threads last spun? We do know that Threads can't last long unless there is something organic on which to feed and that once they've devoured all, they dry up and blow away."

F'lar looked at her admiringly. "Now why hasn't someone wondered about that before?"

"Too hidebound." Lessa wagged her finger at him. "Besides, there's been no need to bother with it."

"Necessity—or is it jealousy?—hatches many a tough shell." There was a smile of pure malice on his face, and Lessa whirled away as he reached for her.

"The good of the Weyr," she retorted.

"Furthermore, I'll send you along with F'nor tomorrow to look. Only fair since it is your idea."

Lessa stood still. "You're not going?"

"I feel confident I can leave this project in your very capable, interested hands." He laughed and caught her against his uninjured side, smiling down at her, his eyes glowing. "I must play ruthless Weyrleader and keep the Hold Lords from slamming shut their Inner Doors. And

I'm hoping"—he raised his head, frowning slightly—
"one of the Craftmasters may know the solution to the
third problem—getting rid of Thread burrows."

"But . . ."

"The trip will give Ramoth something to stop her fuming." He pressed the girl's slender body more closely to
him, his full attention at last on her odd, delicate face.
"Lessa, you are my fourth problem." He bent to kiss her.

At the sound of hurried steps in the passageway, F'lar
scowled irritably, releasing her.

"At this hour?" he muttered, ready to reprove the in-
truder scathingly. "Who goes there?"

"F'lar?" It was F'nor's voice, anxious, hoarse.

The look on F'lar's face told Lessa that not even his
half brother would be spared a reprimand, and it pleased
her irrationally. But the moment F'nor burst into the
room, both Weyrleader and Weyrwoman were stunned
silent. There was something subtly wrong with the brown
rider. And as the man blurted out his incoherent message, the difference suddenly registered in Lessa's mind.
He was tanned! He wore no bandages and hadn't the
slightest trace of the Thread-mark along his cheek that
she had tended this evening!

"F'lar, it's not working out! You can't be alive in two
times at once!" F'nor was exclaiming distractedly. He
staggered against the wall, grabbing the sheer rock to
hold himself upright. There were deep circles under his
eyes, visible despite the tan. "I don't know how much
longer we can last like this. We're all affected. Some
days not as badly as others."

"I don't understand."

"Your dragons are all right," F'nor assured the Weyrleader with a bitter laugh. "It doesn't bother them. They
keep all their wits about them. But their riders . . . all
the weyrfolk . . . we're shadows, half-alive, like dragonless men, part of us gone forever. Except Kylara." His
face contorted with intense dislike. "All she wants to do
is go back and watch herself. The woman's egomania will
destroy us all, I'm afraid."

His eyes suddenly lost focus, and he swayed wildly.
His eyes widened, and his mouth fell open. "I can't stay.
I'm here already. Too close. Makes it twice as bad. But I
had to warn you. I promise, F'lar, we'll stay as long as

we can, but it won't be much longer . . . so it won't be long enough, but we tried. We tried!"

Before F'lar could move, the brown rider whirled and ran half-crouched from the room.

"But he hasn't gone yet!" Lessa gasped. "He hasn't even gone yet!"

F'lar stared after his half brother, his brows contracting with the keen anxiety he felt.

"What can have happened?" Lessa demanded of the Weyrleader. "We haven't even told F'nor. We ourselves just finished considering the idea." Her hand flew to her own cheek. "And the Thread-mark—I dressed it myself tonight—it's gone. Gone. So he's been gone a long while." She sank down to the bench.

"However, he has come back. So he did go," F'lar remarked slowly in a reflective tone of voice. Yet we now know the venture is not entirely successful even before it begins. And knowing this, we have sent him back ten Turns for whatever good it is doing." F'lar paused thoughtfully. "Consequently we have no alternative but to continue with the experiment."

"But what could be going wrong?"

"I think I know, and there is no remedy." He sat down beside her, his eyes intent on hers. "Lessa, you were very upset when you got back from going *between* to Ruatha that first time. But I think now it was more than just the shock of seeing Fax's men invading your own Hold or in thinking your return might have been responsible for that disaster. I think it has to do with being in two times at once." He hesitated again, trying to understand this immense new concept even as he voiced it.

Lessa regarded him with such awe that he found himself laughing with embarrassment.

"It's unnerving under any conditions," he went on, "to think of returning and seeing a younger self."

"That must be what he meant about Kylara," Lessa gasped, "about her wanting to go back and watch herself . . . as a child. Oh, that wretched girl!" Lessa was filled with anger for Kylara's self-absorption. "Wretched, selfish creature. She'll ruin everything."

"Not yet," F'lar reminded her. "Look, although F'nor warned us that the situation in his time is getting desperate, he didn't tell us how much he was able to accomplish. But you noticed that his scar had healed to invisibility—consequently some Turns must have elapsed. Even if Pridith lays one good-sized clutch, even if just the forty of Ramoth's are mature enough to fight in three days' time, we have accomplished something. Therefore, Weyr-woman," and he noticed how she straightened up at the sound of her title, "we must disregard F'nor's return. When you fly to the Southern Continent tomorrow, make no allusion to it. Do you understand?"

Lessa nodded gravely and then gave a little sigh. "I don't know if I'm happy or disappointed to realize, even before we get there tomorrow, that the Southern Continent obviously will support a Weyr," she said with dismay. "It was kind of exciting to wonder."

"Either way," F'lar told her with a sardonic smile, "we have found only part of the answers to problems one and two."

"Well, you'd better answer number four right now!" Lessa suggested. "Decisively!"

> Weaver, Miner, Harper, Smith,
> Tanner, Farmer, Herdsman, Lord,
> Gather, wingsped, listen well
> To the Weyrman's urgent word.

THEY BOTH managed to guard against any reference to his premature return when they spoke to F'nor the next morning. F'lar asked brown Canth to send his rider to the queen's weyr as soon as he awoke and was pleased to see F'nor almost immediately. If the brown rider noticed the curiously intent stare Lessa gave his bandaged face, he gave no sign of it. As a matter of fact, the moment F'lar outlined the bold venture of scouting the Southern Continent with the possibility of starting a Weyr ten Turns back in time, F'nor forgot all about his wounds.

"I'll go willingly only if you send T'bor along with Kylara. I'm not waiting till N'ton and his bronze are big enough to take her on. T'bor and she are as—" F'nor broke off with a grimace in Lessa's direction. "Well, they're as near a pair as can be. I don't object to being . . . importuned, but there are limits to what a man is willing to do out of loyalty to dragonkind."

F'lar barely managed to restrain the amusement he felt over F'nor's reluctance. Kylara tried her wiles on every rider, and because F'nor had not been amenable, she was determined to succeed with him.

"I hope two bronzes are enough. Pridith may have a mind of her own, come mating time."

"You can't turn a brown into a bronze!" F'nor exclaimed with such dismay that F'lar could no longer restrain himself.

"Oh, stop it!" And that touched off Lessa's laughter. "You're as bad a pair," F'nor snapped, getting to his feet. "If we're going south, Weyrwoman, we'd better get started. Particularly if we're going to give this laughing maniac a chance to compose himself before the solemn Lords descend. I'll get provisions from Manora. Well, Lessa? *Are* you coming with me?"

Muffling her laughter, Lessa grabbed up her furred flying cloak and followed him. At least the adventure was starting off well.

Carrying the pitcher of *klah* and his cup, F'lar adjourned to the Council Room, debating whether to tell the Lords and Craftmasters of this southern venture or not. The dragons' ability to fly *between* times as well as places was not yet well-known. The Lords might not realize it had been used the previous day to forestall the Threads. If F'lar could be sure that project was going to be successful—well, it would add an optimistic note to the meeting.

Let the charts, with the waves and times of the Thread attacks clearly visible, reassure the Lords.

The visitors were not long in assembling. Nor were they all successful in hiding their apprehension and the shock they had received now that Threads had again spun down from the Red Star to menace all life on Pern. This was going to be a difficult session, F'lar decided grimly. He had a fleeting wish, which he quickly suppressed, that he had gone with F'nor and Lessa to the Southern Continent. Instead, he bent with apparent industry to the charts before him.

Soon there were but two more to come, Meron of Nabol (whom he would have liked not to include for the man was a troublemaker) and Lytol of Ruatha. F'lar had sent for Lytol last because he did not wish Lessa to

encounter the man. She was still overly—and, to his
mind, foolishly—sensitive at having had to resign her
claim to Ruatha Hold for the Lady Gemma's posthumous
son. Lytol, as Warder of Ruatha, had a place in this conference. The man was also an ex-dragonman, and his return to the Weyr was painful enough without Lessa's
compounding it with her resentment. Lytol was, with the
exception of young Larad of Telgar, the Weyr's most valuable ally.

S'lel came in with Meron a step behind him. The
Holder was furious at this summons; it showed in his
walk, his eyes, in his haughty bearing. But he was also
as inquisitive as he was devious. He nodded only to Larad among the Lords and took the seat left vacant for
him by Larad's side. Meron's manner made it obvious
that that place was too close to F'lar by half a room.

The Weyrleader acknowledged S'lel's salute and indicated the bronze rider should be seated. F'lar had given
thought to the seating arrangements in the Council
Room, carefully interspersing brown and bronze dragonriders with Holders and Craftsmen. There was now
barely room to move in the generously proportioned
cavern, but there was also no room in which to draw
daggers if tempers got hot.

A hush fell on the gathering, and F'lar looked up to
see that the stocky, glowering ex-dragonman from Ruatha had stopped on the threshold of the Council. He
slowly brought his hand up in a respectful salute to the
Weyrleader. As F'lar returned the salute, he noticed that
the tic in Lytol's left cheek jumped almost continuously.

Lytol's eyes, dark with pain and inner unquiet, ranged
the room. He nodded to the members of his former wing,
to Larad and Zurg, head of his own weavers' craft. Stiff-
legged, he walked to the remaining seat, murmuring a
greeting to T'sum on his left.

F'lar rose.

"I appreciate your coming, good Lords and Craftmasters. The Threads spin once again. The first attack has
been met and seared from the sky. Lord Vincet," and
the worried Holder of Nerat looked up in alarm, "we
have dispatched a patrol to the rainforest to do a low-
flight sweep to make certain there are no burrows."

Vincet swallowed nervously, his face paling at the

thought of what Threads could do to his fertile, lush holdings.

"We shall need your best junglemen to help—"

"Help? But you said . . . the Threads were seared in the sky?"

"There is no point in taking the slightest chance," F'lar replied, implying that the patrol was only a precaution instead of the necessity he knew it would be.

Vincet gulped, glancing anxiously around the room for sympathy, and found none. Everyone would soon be in his position.

"There is a patrol due at Keroon and at Igen." F'lar looked first at Lord Corman, then at Lord Banger, who gravely nodded. "Let me say by way of reassurance that there will be no further attacks for three days and four hours." F'lar tapped the appropriate chart. "The Threads will begin approximately here on Telgar, drift westward through the southernmost portion of Crom, which is mountainous, and on through Ruatha and the southern end of Nabol."

"How can you be so certain of that?"

F'lar recognized the contemptuous voice of Meron of Nabol.

"The Threads do not fall like a child's jackstraws, Lord Meron," F'lar replied. "They fall in a definitely predictable pattern; the attacks last exactly six hours. The intervals between attacks will gradually shorten over the next few Turns as the Red Star draws closer. Then, for about forty full Turns, as the Red Star swings past and around us, the attacks occur every fourteen hours, marching across our world in a time-able fashion."

"So *you* say," Meron sneered, and there was a low mumble of support.

"So the Teaching Ballads say," Larad put in firmly.

Meron glanced at Telgar's lord and went on, "I recall another of your predictions about how the Threads were supposed to begin falling right after Solstice."

"Which they did," F'lar interrupted him. "As black dust in the Northern Holds. For the reprieve we've had, we can thank our lucky stars that we have had an unusually hard and long Cold Turn."

"Dust?" demanded Nessel of Crom. "That dust was Threads?" The man was one of Fax's blood connections

and under Meron's influence: an older man who had
learned lessons from his conquering relative's bloody
ways and had not the wit to improve or alter the original. "My Hold is still blowing with them. They're dangerous?"

F'lar shook his head emphatically. "How long has the
black dust been blowing in your Hold? Weeks? Done any
harm yet?"

Nessel frowned.

"I'm interested in your charts, Weyrleader," Larad of
Telgar said smoothly. "Will they give us an accurate idea
of how often we may expect Threads to fall in our own
Holds?"

"Yes. You may also anticipate that the dragonmen will
arrive shortly before the invasion is due," F'lar went on.
"However, additional measures of your own are necessary, and it is for this that I called the Council."

"Wait a minute," Corman of Keroon growled. "I want
a copy of those fancy charts of yours for my own. I want
to know what those bands and wavy lines really mean.
I want . . ."

"Naturally you'll have a timetable of your own. I mean
to impose on Masterharper Robinton"—F'lar nodded respectfully toward that Craftmaster—"to oversee the
copying and make sure everyone understands the timing
involved."

Robinton, a tall, gaunt man with a lined, saturnine
face, bowed deeply. A slight smile curved his wide lips
at the now hopeful glances favored him by the Hold
Lords. His craft, like that of the dragonmen, had been
much mocked, and this new respect amused him. He was
a man with a keen eye for the ridiculous, and an active
imagination. The circumstances in which doubting Pern
found itself were too ironic not to appeal to his innate
sense of justice. He now contented himself with a deep
bow and a mild phrase.

"Truly all shall pay heed to the master." His voice was
deep, his words enunciated with no provincial slurring.

F'lar, about to speak, looked sharply at Robinton as
he caught the double barb of that single line. Larad, too,
looked around at the Masterharper, clearing his throat
hastily.

"We shall have our charts," Larad said, forestalling

Meron, who had opened his mouth to speak. "We shall have the dragonmen when the Threads spin. What are these additional measures? And why are they necessary?"

All eyes were on F'lar again.

"We have one Weyr where six once flew."

"But word is that Ramoth has hatched over forty more," someone in the back of the room declared. "And why did you Search out still more of our young men?"

"Forty-one as yet unmatured dragons," F'lar said. Privately he hoped that this southern venture would still work out. There was real fear in that man's voice. "They grow well and quickly. Just at present, while the Threads do not strike with great frequency as the Red Star begins its Pass, our Weyr is sufficient . . . if we have your co-operation on the ground. Tradition is that"—he nodded tactfully toward Robinton, the dispenser of Traditional usage—"you Holders are responsible for only your dwellings, which of course are adequately protected by firepits and raw stone. However, it is spring, and our heights have been allowed to grow wild with vegetation. Arable land is blossoming with crops. This presents vast acreage vulnerable to the Threads, which one Weyr, at this time, is not able to patrol without severely draining the vitality of our dragons and riders."

At this candid admission, a frightened and angry mutter spread rapidly throughout the room.

"Ramoth rises to mate again soon," F'lar continued in a matter-of-fact way. "Of course, in other times the queens started producing heavy clutches many Turns before the critical solstice as well as more queens. Unfortunately Jora was ill and old, and Nemorth intractable. The matter—" He was interrupted.

"Your dragonmen with your high and mighty airs will bring destruction on us all!"

"You have yourselves to blame," Robinton's voice stabbed across the ensuing shouts. "Admit it, one and all. You've paid less honor to the Weyr than you would your watch-wher's kennel—and that not much! But now the thieves are on the heights, and you are screaming because the poor reptile is nigh to death from neglect. Beat him, will you? When you exiled him to his kennel because he tried to warn you? Tried to get you to prepare against the

invaders? It's on *your* conscience, not the Weyrleader's
or the dragonriders', who have honestly done their duty
these hundreds of Turns in keeping dragonkind alive . . .
against your protests. How many of you"—his tone was
scathing—"have been generous in thought and favor
toward dragonkind? Even since I became master of my
craft, how often have my harpers told me of being
beaten for singing the old song as is their duty? You earn
only the right, good Lords and Craftsmen, to squirm inside your stony Holds and writhe as your crops die
a-borning."

He rose.

" 'No Threads will fall. It's a harper's winter tale,' "
he whined, in faultless imitation of Nessel. " 'These dragonmen leech us of heir and harvest,' " and his voice took on
the constricted, insinuating tenor that could only be
Meron's "And now the truth is as bitter as a brave
man's fears and as difficult as mockweed to swallow. For
all the honor you've done them, the dragonmen should
leave you to be spun on the Threads' distaff."

"Bitra, Lemos, and I," spoke up Raid, the wiry Lord of
Benden, his blunt chin lifted belligerently, "have always
done our duty to the Weyr."

Robinton swung around to him, his eyes flashing as
he gave that speaker a long slow look.

"Aye, and you have. Of all the Great Holds, you three
have been loyal. But you others," and his voice rose indignantly, "as spokesman for my craft, I know, to the
last full stop in your score, your opinion of dragonkind. I
heard the first whisper of your attempt to ride out
against the Weyr." He laughed harshly and pointed a
long finger at Vincet. "Where would you be today, good
Lord Vincet, if the Weyr had *not* sent you packing back,
hoping your ladies would be returned you? All of you,"
and his accusing finger marked each of the Lords of the
abortive effort, "actually rode against the Weyr because . . .
'there . . . were . . . no . . . more . . . Threads!' "

He planted his fists on either hip and glared at the as-
sembly. F'lar wanted to cheer. It was easy to see why the
man was Masterharper, and he thanked circumstance
that such a man was the Weyr's partisan.

"And now, at this critical moment, you have the incredible presumption to protest aganst any measure the

Weyr suggests?" Robinton's supple voice oozed derision and amazement. "Attend what the Weyrleader says and spare him your petty carpings!" He snapped those words out as a father might enjoin an erring child. "You were," and he switched to the mildest of polite conversational tones as he addressed F'lar, "I believe, asking our cooperation, good F'lar? In what capacities?"

F'lar hastily cleared his throat.

"I shall require that the Holds police their own fields and woods, during the attacks if possible, definitely once the Threads have passed. All burrows which might land must be found, marked, and destroyed. The sooner they are located, the easier it is to be rid of them."

"There's no time to dig firepits through all the lands . . . we'll lose half our growing space," Nessel exclaimed.

"There were other ways, used in olden times, which I believe our Mastersmith might know." F'lar gestured politely toward Fandarel, the archetype of his profession if ever such existed.

The Smith Craftmaster was by several inches the tallest man in the Council Room, his massive shoulders and heavily muscled arms pressed against his nearest neighbors, although he had made an effort not to crowd against anyone. He rose, a giant tree-stump of a man, hooking thumbs like beast-horns in the thick belt that spanned his waistless midsection. His voice, by no means sweet after Turns of bellowing above roaring hearths and hammers, was, by comparison to Robinton's superb delivery, a diluted, unsupported light baritone.

"There were machines, that much is true," he allowed in deliberate, thoughtful tones. "My father, it was he, told me of them as a curiosity of the Craft. There may be sketches in the Hall. There may not. Such things do not keep on skins for long." He cast an oblique look under beetled brows at the Tanner Craftmaster.

"It is our own hides we must worry about preserving," F'lar remarked to forestall any intercraft disputes.

Fandarel grumbled in his throat in such a way that F'lar was not certain whether the sound was the man's laughter or a guttural agreement.

"I shall consider the matter. So shall all my fellow craftsmen," Fandarel assured the Weyrleader. "To sear Threads from the ground without damaging the soil may not be so easy. There are, it is true, fluids which burn and sear. We use an acid to etch design on daggers and ornamental metals. We of the Craft call it agenothree. There is also the black heavy-water that lies on the surface of pools in Igen and Boll. It burns hot and long. And if, as you say, the Cold Turn made the Threads break into dust, perhaps ice from the coldest northlands might freeze and break grounded Threads. However, the problem is to bring such to the Threads where they fall since they will not oblige us by falling where we want them . . ." He screwed up his face in a grimace.

F'lar stared at him, surprised. Did the man realize how humorous he was? No, he was speaking with sincere concern. Now the Mastersmith scratched his head, his tough fingers making audible grating sounds along his coarse hair and heat-toughened scalp.

"A nice problem. A nice problem," he mused, undaunted. "I shall give it every attention." He sat down, the heavy bench creaking under his weight.

The Masterfarmer raised his hand tentatively.

"When I became Craftmaster, I recall coming across a reference to the sandworms of Igen. They were once cultivated as a protective—"

"Never heard Igen produced anything useful except heat and sand," quipped someone.

"We need every suggestion," F'lar said sharply, trying to identify that heckler. "Please find that reference, Craftmaster. Lord Banger of Igen, find me some of those sandworms!"

Banger, equally surprised that his arid Hold had a hidden asset, nodded vigorously.

"Until we have more efficient ways of killing Threads, all Holders must be organized on the ground during attacks, to spot and mark burrows, to set firestone to burn in them. I do not wish any man to be scored, but we know how quickly Threads burrow deep, and no burrow can be left to multiply. You stand to lose more," and he gestured emphatically at the Holder Lords, "than any others. Guard not just yourselves, for a burrow on one man's border may grow across to his neighbor's. Mobilize every man, woman, and child, farm and crafthold. Do it now."

The Council Room was fraught with tension and

stunned reflection until Zurg, the Masterweaver, rose to speak.

"My craft, too, has something to offer . . . which is only fair since we deal with thread every day of our lives . . . in regard to the ancient methods." Zurg's voice was light and dry, and his eyes in their creases of spare, lined flesh, were busy, darting from one face in his audience to another. "In Ruath Hold I once saw upon the wall . . . where the tapestry now resides, who knows?" He slyly glanced at Meron of Nabol and then at Bargen of the High Reaches who had succeeded to Fax's title there. "The work was as old as dragonkind and showed, among other things, a man on foot, carrying upon his back a curious contraption. He held within his hand a rounded, sword-long object from which tongues of flame . . . magnificently woven in the orange-red dyes now lost to us . . . spouted toward the ground. Above, of course, were dragons in close formation, bronzes predominating . . . again we've lost that true dragon-bronze shade. Consequently I remember the work as much for what we now lack as for its subject matter."

"A flamethrower?" the Smith rumbled. "A flamethrower," he repeated with a falling inflection. "A flamethrower," he murmured thoughtfully, his heavy brows drawn into a titanic scowl. "A thrower of what sort of flame? It requires thought." He lowered his head and didn't speak, so engrossed in the required thought that he lost interest in the rest of the discussion.

"Yes, good Zurg, there have been many tricks of every trade lost in recent Turns," F'lar commented sardonically. "If we wish to continue living, such knowledge must be revived . . . fast. I would particularly like to recover the tapestry of which Master Zurg speaks."

F'lar looked significantly at those Lords who had quarreled over Fax's seven Holds after his death.

"It may save all of you much loss. I suggest that it appear at Ruatha. Or at Zurg's or at Fandarel's crafthall. Whichever is most convenient."

There was some shuffling of feet, but no one admitted ownership.

"It might then be returned to Fax's son, who is now Ruatha's Lord," F'lar added, wryly amused at such magnanimous justice.

Lytol snorted softly and glowered around the room. F'lar supposed Lytol to be amused and experienced a fleeting regret for the orphaned Jaxom, reared by such a cheerless if honest guardian.

"If I may, Lord Weyrleader," Robinton broke in, "we might all benefit, as your maps prove to us, from research in our own Records." He smiled suddenly, an unexpectedly embarrassed smile. "I own I find myself in some disgrace for we Harpers have let slip unpopular ballads and skimped on some of the longer Teaching Ballads and Sagas . . . for lack of listeners and occasionally in the interest of preserving our skins."

F'lar stifled a laugh with a cough. Robinton was a genius.

"I must see that Ruathan tapestry," Fandarel suddenly boomed out.

"I'm sure it will be in your hands very soon," F'lar assured him with more confidence than he dared feel. "My Lords, there is much to be done. Now that you understand what we all face, I leave it in your hands as leaders in your separate Holds and crafts how best to organize your own people. Craftsmen, turn your best minds to our special problems: review all Records that might turn up something to our purpose. Lords Telgar, Crom, Ruatha, and Nabol, I shall be with you in three days. Nerat, Keroon, and Igen, I am at your disposal to help destroy any burrow on your lands. While we have the Masterminer here, tell him your needs. How stands your craft?"

"Happy to be so busy at our trade, Weyrleader," piped up the Masterminer.

Just then F'lar caught sight of F'nor, hovering about in the shadows of the hallway, trying to catch his eye. The brown rider wore an exultant grin, and it was obvious he was bursting with news.

F'lar wondered how they could have returned so swiftly from the Southern Continent, and then he realized that F'nor—again—was tanned. He gave a jerk of his head, indicating that F'nor take himself off to the sleeping quarters and wait.

"Lords and Craftmasters, a dragonet will be at the disposal of each of you for messages and transportation. Now good morning."

He strode out of the Council Room, up the passageway into the queen's weyr, and parted the still swinging curtains into the sleeping room just as F'nor was pouring himself a cup of wine.

"Success!" F'nor cried as the Weyrleader entered. "Though how you knew to send just thirty-two candidates I'll never understand. I thought you were insulting our noble Pridith. But thirty-two eggs she laid in four days. It was all I could do to keep from riding out when the first appeared."

F'lar responded with hearty congratulations, relieved that there would be at least that much benefit from this apparently ill-fated venture. Now all he had to figure out was how much longer F'nor had stayed south until his frantic visit the night before. For there were no worry lines or strain in F'nor's grinning, well-tanned face.

"No queen egg?" asked F'lar hopefully. With thirty-two in the one experiment, perhaps they could send a second queen back and try again.

F'nor's face lengthened. "No, and I was sure there would be. But there are fourteen bronzes. Pridith outmatched Ramoth there," he added proudly.

"Indeed she did. How goes the Weyr otherwise?"

F'nor frowned, shaking his head against an inner bewilderment. "Kylara's . . . well, she's a problem. Stirs up trouble constantly. T'bor leads a sad time with her, and he's so touchy everyone keeps a distance from him." F'nor brightened a little. "Young N'ton is shaping up into a fine wingleader, and his bronze may outfly T'bor's Orth when Pridith flies to mate the next time. Not that I'd wish Kylara on N'ton . . . or anyone."

"No trouble then with supplies?"

F'nor laughed outright. "If you hadn't made it so plain we must not communicate with you here, we could supply you with fruits and fresh greens that are superior to anything in the north. We eat the way dragonmen should! F'lar, we must consider a supply Weyr down there. Then we shall never have to worry about tithing trains and . . ."

"In good time. Get back now. You know you must keep these visits short."

F'nor grimaced. "Oh, it's not so bad. I'm not here in this time anyway."

"True," F'lar agreed, "but don't mistake the time and come while you're still here."

"Hmmm? Oh, yes, that's right. I forget time is creeping for us and speeding for you. Well, I shan't be back again till Pridith lays the second clutch."

With a cheerful goodbye, F'nor strode out of the weyr. F'lar watched him thoughtfully as he slowly retraced his steps to the Council Room. Thirty-two new dragons, fourteen of them bronzes, was no small gain and seemed worth the hazard. Or would the hazard wax greater?

Someone cleared his throat deliberately. F'lar looked up to see Robinton standing in the archway that led to the Council Room.

"Before I can copy and instruct others about those maps, Weyrleader, I must myself understand them completely. I took the liberty of remaining behind."

"You make a good champion, Masterharper."

"You have a noble cause, Weyrleader," and then Robinton's eyes glinted maliciously. "I've been begging the Egg for an opportunity to speak out to so noble an audience."

"A cup of wine first?"

"Benden grapes are the envy of Pern."

"If one has the palate for such a delicate bouquet."

"It is carefully cultivated by the knowledgeable."

F'lar wondered when the man would stop playing with words. He had more on his mind than studying the timecharts.

"I have in mind a ballad which, for lack of explanation, I had set aside when I became the Master of my crafthall," he said judiciously after an appreciative savoring of his wine. "It is an uneasy song, both the tune and the words. One develops, as a harper must, a certain sensitivity for what will be received and what will be rejected . . . forcefully," and he winced in retrospect. "I found that this ballad unsettled singer as well as audience and retired it from use. Now like that tapestry, it bears rediscovery."

After his death C'gan's instrument had been hung on the Council Room wall till a new Weyrsinger could be chosen. The guitar was very old, its wood thin. Old C'gan had kept it well-tuned and covered. The Masterharper handled it now with reverence, lightly stroking the strings to hear the tone, raising his eyebrows at the fine voice of the instrument.

He plucked a chord, a dissonance. F'lar wondered if the instrument was out of tune or if the harper had, by some chance, struck the wrong string. But Robinton repeated the odd discord, then modulating into a weird minor that was somehow more disturbing than the first notes.

"I told you it was an uneasy song. And I wonder if you know the answers to the questions it asks. For I've turned the puzzle over in my mind many times of late."

Then abruptly he shifted from the spoken to the sung tone.

> Gone away, gone ahead,
> Echoes roll unansweréd.
> Empty, open, dusty, dead.
> Why have all the Weyrfolk fled?
>
> Where have dragons gone together?
> Leaving Weyrs to wind and weather?
> Setting herdbeasts free of tether?
> Gone, our safeguards, gone, but whither?
>
> Have they flown to some new Weyr
> Where cruel Threads some others fear?
> Are they worlds away from here?
> Why, oh, why, the empty Weyr?

The last plaintive chord reverberated.

"Of course, you realize that the song was first recorded in the craft annals some four hundred Turns ago," Robinton said lightly, cradling the guitar in both arms. "The Red Star had just passed beyond attack-proximity. The people had ample reason to be stunned and worried over the sudden loss of the populations of five Weyrs. Oh, I imagine at the time they had any one of a number of explanations, but none . . . not one explanation . . . is recorded." Robinton paused significantly.

"I have found none recorded either," F'lar replied. "As a matter of fact, I had all the Records brought here from the other Weyrs . . . in order to compile accurate attack timetables. And those other Weyr Records simply

end—" F'lar made a chopping gesture with one hand. "In
Benden's Records there is no mention of sickness, death,
fire, disaster—not one word of explanation for the sudden
lapse of the usual intercourse between the Weyrs. Benden's Records continue blithely, but only for Benden.
There is one entry that pertains to the mass disappearance . . . the initiation of a Pernwide patrol routing, not
just Benden's immediate responsibility. And that is all."

"Strange," Robinton mused. "Once the danger from
the Red Star was past, the dragons and riders may have
gone *between* to ease the drain on the Holds. But I simply cannot believe that. Our craft Records do mention
that harvests were bad and that there had been several
natural catastrophes . . . other than the Threads. Men
may be gallant and your breed the most gallant of all,
but mass suicide? I simply do not accept that explanation
. . . not for dragonmen."

"My thanks," F'lar said with mild irony.

"Don't mention it," Robinton replied with a gracious
nod.

F'lar chuckled appreciatively. "I see we have been
too weyrbound as well as too hidebound."

Robinton drained his cup and looked at it mournfully
until F'lar refilled it.

"Well, your isolation served some purpose, you know,
and you handled that uprising of the Lords magnificently. I nearly choked to death laughing," Robinton
remarked, grinning broadly. "Stealing their women in the
flash of a dragon's breath!" He chuckled again, then suddenly sobered, looking F'lar straight in the eye. "Accustomed as I am to hearing what a man does *not* say
aloud, I suspect there is much you glossed over in that
Council meeting. You may be sure of my discretion . . .
and . . . you may be sure of my wholehearted support
and that of my not ineffectual craft. To be blunt, how
may my harpers aid you?" and he strummed a vigorous
marching air. "Stir men's pulses with ballads of past
glories and success?" The tune, under his flashing fingers, changed abruptly to a stern but determined rhythm.
"Strengthen their mental and physical sinews for
hardship?"

"If all your harpers could stir men as you yourself do,

I should have no worries that five hundred or so additional dragons would not immediately end."

"Oh, then despite your brave words and marked charts, the situation is"—a dissonant twang on the guitar accented his final words—"more desperate than you carefully did not say."

"It may be."

"The flamethrowers old Zurg remembered and Fandarel must reconstruct—will they tip the scales?"

F'lar regarded this clever man thoughtfully and made a quick decision.

"Even Igen's sandworms will help, but as the world turns and the Red Star nears, the interval between daily attacks shortens and we have only seventy-two new dragons to add to those we had yesterday. One is now dead and several will not fly for several weeks."

"Seventy-two?" Robinton caught him up sharply. "Ramoth hatched but forty, and they are still too young to eat firestone."

F'lar outlined F'nor and Lessa's expedition, taking place at that moment. He went on to F'nor's reappearance and warning, as well as the fact that the experiment had been successful in part with the hatching of thirty-two new dragons from Pridith's first clutch. Robinton caught him up.

"How can F'nor already have returned when you haven't heard from Lessa and him that there is a breeding place on the Southern Continent?"

"Dragons can go *between* times as well as places. They go as easily to a *when* as to a *where*."

Robinton's eyes widened as he digested this astonishing news.

"That is how we forestalled the attack on Nerat yesterday morning. We jumped back two hours *between* time to meet the Threads as they fell."

"You can actually jump backward? How far back?"

"I don't know. Lessa, when I was teaching her to fly Ramoth, inadvertently returned to Ruath Hood, to the dawn thirteen Turns ago when Fax's men invaded from the heights. When she returned to the present, I attempted a *between* times jump of some ten Turns. To the dragons it is a simple matter to go *between* times or spaces, but there appears to be a terrific strain on the rider. Yesterday, by the time we returned from Nerat and had to go on to Keroon, I felt as though I had been pounded flat and left to dry for a summer on Igen Plain." F'lar shook his head. "We have obviously succeeded in sending Kylara, Pridith, and the others ten Turns *between* because F'nor has already reported to me that he has been there several Turns. The drain on humans, however, is becoming more and more marked. But even seventy-two more mature dragons will be a help."

"Send a rider ahead in time to see if it is sufficient," Robinton suggested helpfully. "Save you a few days' worrying."

"I don't know how to get to a *when* that has not yet happened. You must give your dragon reference points, you know. How can you refer him to times that have not yet occurred?"

"You've got an imagination. Project it."

"And perhaps lose a dragon when I have none to spare? No, I must continue . . . because obviously I have, judging by F'nor's returns . . . as I decided to start. Which reminds me, I must give orders to start packing. Then I shall go over the time-charts with you."

It wasn't until after the noon meal, which Robinton took with the Weyrleader, that the Masterharper was confident that he understood the charts and left to begin their copying.

> Across a waste of lonely tossing sea,
> Where no dragonwings had lately spread,
> Flew a gold and sturdy brown in spring,
> Searching if a land be dead.

As RAMOTH and Canth bore Lessa and F'nor up to the Star Stone, they saw the first of the Hold Lords and Craftmasters arriving for the Council.

In order to get back to the Southern Continent of ten Turns ago, Lessa and F'nor had decided it was easiest to transfer first *between* times to the Weyr of ten Turns back which F'nor remembered. Then they would go *between* places to a seapoint just off the coast of the neglected Southern Continent which was as close to it as the Records gave any references.

F'nor put Canth in mind of a particular day he remembered ten Turns back, and Ramoth picked up the references from the brown's mind. The awesome cold of *between* times took Lessa's breath away, and it was with intense relief that she caught a glimpse of the normal weyr activity before the dragons took them *between* places to hover over the turgid sea.

Beyond them, smudged purple on this overcast and gloomy day, lurked the Southern Continent. Lessa felt a new anxiety replace the uncertainty of the temporal displacement. Ramoth beat forward with great sweeps of her wings, making for the distant coast. Canth gallantly tried to maintain a matching speed.

He's only a brown, Lessa scolded her golden queen.

If he is flying with me, Ramoth replied coolly, *he must stretch his wings a little.*

Lessa grinned, thinking very privately that Ramoth was still piqued that she had not been able to fight with her weyrmates. All the males would have a hard time with her for a while.

They saw the flock of wherries first and realized that there would have to be some vegetation on the Continent. Wherries needed greens to live, although they could subsist on little else beside occasional grubs if necessary.

Lessa had Canth relay questions to his rider. *If the Southern Continent was rendered barren by the Threads, how did new growth start? Where did the wherries come from?*

Ever notice the seed pods split open and the flakes carried away by the winds? Ever notice that wherries fly south after the autumn solstice?

Yes, but . . .

Yes, but!

But the land was Thread-bared!

In less than four hundred Turns even the scorched hilltops of our Continent begin to sprout in the springtime, F'nor replied by way of Canth, *so it is easy to assume the Southern Continent could revive, too.*

Even at the pace Ramoth set, it took time to reach the jagged shoreline with its forbidding cliffs, stark stone in the sullen light. Lessa groaned inwardly but urged Ramoth higher to see over the masking highlands. All seemed gray and desolate from that altitude.

Suddenly the sun broke through the cloud cover and

the gray dissolved into dense greens and browns, living
colors, the live greens of lush tropical growth, the browns
of vigorous trees and vines. Lessa's cry of triumph was
echoed by F'nor's hurrah and the brass voices of the
dragons. Wherries, startled by the unusual sound, rose
in squeaking alarm from their perches.

Beyond the headland, the land sloped away to jungle
and grassy plateau, similar to mid-Boll. Though they
searched all morning, they found no hospitable cliffs
wherein to found a new Weyr. Was that a contributing
factor in the southern venture's failure, Lessa wondered.

Discouraged, they landed on a high plateau by a small
lake. The weather was warm but not oppressive, and
while F'nor and Lessa ate their noonday meal, the two
dragons wallowed in the water, refreshing themselves.

Lessa felt uneasy and had little appetite for the meat
and bread. She noticed that F'nor was restless, too, shooting surreptitious glances around the lake and the jungle
verge.

"What under the sun are we expecting? Wherries don't
change, and wild whers would come nowhere near a
dragon. We're ten Turns before the Red Star, so there
can't be any Threads."

F'nor shrugged, grimacing sheepishly as he tossed his
unfinished bread back into the food pouch.

"Place feels so empty, I guess," he tendered, glancing
around. He spotted ripe fruit hanging from a moonflower
vine. "Now that looks familiar and good enough to eat,
without tasting like dust in the mouth."

He climbed nimbly and snagged the orange-red fruit.

"Smells right, feels ripe, looks ripe," he announced and
deftly sliced the fruit open. Grinning, he landed Lessa
the first slice, carving another for himself. He lifted it
challengingly. "Let us eat and die together!"

She couldn't help but laugh and saluted him back.
They bit into the succulent flesh simultaneously. Sweet
juices dribbled from the corners of her mouth, and Lessa
hurriedly licked her lips to capture the least drop of the
delicious liquid.

"Die happy—I will," F'nor cried, cutting more fruit.

Both were subtly reassured by the experiment and
were able to discuss their discomposure.

"I think," F'nor suggested, "it is the lack of cliff and

cavern and the still, still quality of the place, the knowing that there are no other men or beasts about but us."

Lessa nodded her head in agreement. "Ramoth, Canth, would having no Weyr upset you?"

We didn't always live in caves, Ramoth replied, somewhat haughtily as she rolled over in the lake. Sizable waves rushed up the shore almost to where Lessa and F'nor were seated on a fallen tree trunk. *The sun here is warm and pleasant, the water cooling. I would enjoy it here, but I am not to come.*

"She is out of sorts," Lessa whispered to F'nor. "Let Pridith have it, dear one," she called soothingly to the golden queen. "You've the Weyr and all!"

Ramoth ducked under the water, blowing up a froth in disgruntled reply.

Canth admitted that he had no reservations at all about living Weyrless. The dry earth would be warmer than stone to sleep on, once a suitably comfortable hollow had been achieved. No, he couldn't object to the lack of the cave as long as there was enough to eat.

"We'll have to bring herdbeasts in," F'nor mused. "Enough to start a good-sized herd. Of course, the wherries here are huge. Come to think of it, I believe this plateau has no exits. We wouldn't need to pasture it off. I'd better check. Otherwise, this plateau with the lake and enough clear space for Holds seems ideal. Walk out and pick breakfast from the tree."

"It might be wise to choose those who were not Hold-reared," Lessa added. "They would not feel so uneasy away from protecting heights and stone-security." She gave a short laugh. "I'm more a creature of habit than I suspected. All these open spaces, untenanted and quiet, seem . . . indecent." She gave a delicate shudder, scanning the broad and open plain beyond the lake.

"Fruitful and lovely," F'nor amended, leaping up to secure more of the orange-red succulents. "This tastes uncommonly good to me. Can't remember anything this sweet and juicy from Nerat, and yet it's the same variety."

"Undeniably superior to what the Weyr gets. I suspect Nerat serves home first, Weyr last."

They both stuffed themselves greedily.

Further investigation proved that the plateau was isolated and ample to pasture a huge herd of foodbeasts for

the dragons. It ended in a sheer drop of several dragon-
lengths into denser jungle on one side, the sea-side escarp-
ment on the other. The timber stands would provide raw
material from which dwellings could be made for the
Weyrfolk. Ramoth and Canth stoutly agreed dragonkind
would be comfortable enough under the heavy foliage of
the dense jungle. As this part of the continent was similar,
weatherwise, to Upper Nerat, there would be neither intense heat nor cold to give distress.

However, if Lessa was glad enough to leave, F'nor
seemed reluctant to start back.

"We can go *between* time and place on the way back,"
Lessa insisted finally, "and be in the Weyr by late afternoon. The Lords will surely be gone by then."

F'nor concurred, and Lessa steeled herself for the trip
between. She wondered why the *when between* bothered
her more than the *where,* for it had no effect on the dragons at all. Ramoth, sensing Lessa's depression, crooned
encouragingly. The long, long black suspension of the utter cold of *between* where and when ended suddenly in
sunlight above the Weyr.

Somewhat startled, Lessa saw bundles and sacks spread
out before the Lower Caverns as dragonriders supervised
the loading of their beasts.

"What has been happening?" F'nor exclaimed.

"Oh, F'lar's been anticipating success," she assured him
glibly.

Mnementh, who was watching the bustle from the ledge
of the queen's weyr, sent a greeting to the travelers and
the information that F'lar wished them to join him in the
weyr as soon as they returned.

They found F'lar, as usual, bent over some of the oldest
and least legible Record skins that he had had brought to
the Council Room.

"And?" he asked, grinning a broad welcome at them.

"Green, lush, and livable," Lessa declared, watching
him intently. He knew something else, too. Well, she
hoped he'd watch his words. F'nor was no fool, and this
foreknowledge was dangerous.

"That is what I had so hoped to hear you say," F'lar
went on smoothly. "Come, tell me in detail what you observed and discovered. It'll be good to fill in the blank
spaces on the chart."

Lessa let F'nor give most of the account, to which F'lar listened with sincere attention, making notes.

"On the chance that it would be practical, I started packing supplies and alerting the riders to go with you," he told F'nor when the account was finished. "Remember, we've only three days in this time in which to start you back ten Turns ago. *We* have no moments to spare. And we must have many more mature dragons ready to fight at Telgar in three days time. So, though ten Turns will have passed for you, three days only will elapse here. Lessa, your thought that the farm-bred might do better is well-taken. We're lucky that our recent Search for rider candidates for the dragons Pridith will have come mainly from the crafts and farms. No problem there. And most of the thirty-two are in their early teens."

"Thirty-two?" F'nor exclaimed. "We should have fifty. The dragonets must have some choice, even if we get the candidates used to the dragonets before they're hatched."

F'lar shrugged negligently. "Send back for more. *You'll* have time, remember," and F'lar chuckled as though he had started to add something and decided against it.

F'nor had no time to debate with the Weyrleader for F'lar immediately launched on other rapid instructions.

F'nor was to take his own wingriders to help train the weyrlings. They would also take the forty young dragons of Ramoth's first clutch: Kylara with her queen Pridith, T'bor and his bronze Piyanth. N'ton's young bronze might also be ready to fly and mate by the time Pridith was, so that gave the young queen two bronzes at least.

"Suppose we'd found the continent barren?" F'nor asked, still puzzled by F'lar's assurance. "What then?"

"Oh, we'd've sent them back to, say, the High Reaches," F'lar replied far too glibly, but quickly went on. "I should send on other bronzes, but I'll need everyone else here to ride burrow-search on Keroon and Nerat. They've already unearthed several at Nerat. Vincet, I'm told, is close to heart attack from fright."

Lessa made a short comment on that Hold Lord.

"What of the meeting this morning?" F'nor asked, remembering.

"Never mind that now. You've got to start shifting *between* by evening, F'nor."

Lessa gave the Weyrleader a long hard look and decided she would have to find out what had happened in detail very soon.

"Sketch me some references, will you, Lessa?" F'lar asked.

There was a definite plea in his eyes as he drew clean hide and a stylus to her. He wanted no questions from her now that would alarm F'nor. She sighed and picked up the drawing tool.

She sketched quickly, with one or two details added by F'nor, until she had rendered a reasonable map of the plateau they had chosen. Then abruptly, she had trouble focusing her eyes. She felt light-headed.

"Lessa?" F'lar bent to her.

"Everything's . . . moving . . . circling . . ." and she collapsed backward into his arms.

As F'lar raised her slight body into his arms, he exchanged an alarmed look with his half brother.

"I'll call for Manora," F'nor suggested.

"How do you feel?" the Weyrleader called after his brother.

"Tired but no more than that," F'nor assured him as he shouted down the service shaft to the kitchens for Manora to come and for hot *klah*. He needed that, and no doubt of it.

F'lar laid the Weyrwoman on the sleeping couch, covering her gently.

"I don't like this," he muttered, rapidly recalling what F'nor had said of Kylara's decline, which F'nor could not know was yet to come in his future. Why should it start so swiftly with Lessa?

"Time-jumping makes one feel slightly . . ." F'nor paused, groping for the exact wording. "Not entirely . . . whole. You fought *between* times at Nerat yesterday . . ."

"I fought," F'lar reminded him, "but neither you nor Lessa battled anything today. There may be some inner . . . mental . . . stress simply to going *between* times. Look, F'nor, I'd rather only you came back once you reach the southern Weyr. I'll make it an order and get Ramoth to inhibit the dragons. That way no rider can take it into his head to come back even if he wants to. There is some factor that may be more serious than we can guess. Let's take no unnecessary risks."

"Agreed."

"One other detail, F'nor. Be very careful which times you pick to come back to see me. I wouldn't jump *between* too close to any time you were actually here. I can't imagine what would happen if you walked into your own self in the passageway, and I can't lose you."

With a rare demonstration of affection, F'lar gripped his half brother's shoulder tightly.

"Remember, F'nor. I was here all morning and you did not arrive back from the first trip till mid-afternoon. And remember, too, *we* have only three days. You have ten Turns."

F'nor left, passing Manora in the hall.

The woman could find nothing obviously the matter with Lessa, and they finally decided it might be simple fatigue; yesterday's strain when Lessa had to relay messages between dragons and fighters followed by the disjointing *between* times trip today.

When F'lar went to wish the southern ventures a good trip, Lessa was in a normal sleep, her face pale, but her breathing easy.

F'lar had Mnementh relay to Ramoth the prohibition he wished the queen to instill in all dragonkind assigned to the venture. Ramoth obliged, but added in an aside to bronze Mnementh, which he passed on to F'lar, that everyone else had adventures while she, the Weyr queen, was forced to stay behind.

No sooner had the laden dragons, one by one, winked out of the sky above the Star Stone than the young weyrling assigned to Nerat Hold as messenger came gliding down, his face white with fear.

"Weyrleader, many more burrows have been found, and they cannot be burned out with fire alone. Lord Vincet wants you."

F'lar could well imagine that Vincet did.

"Get yourself some dinner, boy, before you start back. I'll go shortly."

As he passed through to the sleeping quarters, he heard Ramoth rumbling in her throat. She had settled herself down to rest.

Lessa still slept, one hand curled under her cheek, her dark hair trailing over the edge of the bed. She looked fragile, childlike, and very precious to him. F'lar smiled to himself. So she was jealous of Kylara's attentions yesterday. He was pleased and flattered. Never would Lessa learn from him that Kylara, for all her bold beauty and sensuous nature, did not have one-tenth the attraction for him that the unpredictable, dark, and delicate Lessa held. Even her stubborn intractableness, her keen and malicious humor, added zest to their relationship. With a tenderness he could never show her awake, F'lar bent and kissed her lips. She stirred and smiled, sighing lightly in her sleep.

Reluctantly returning to what must be done, F'lar left her so. As he paused by the queen, Ramoth raised her great, wedge-shaped head; her many-faceted eyes gleamed with bright luminescence as she regarded the Weyrleader.

"Mnementh, please ask Ramoth to get in touch with the dragonet at Fandarel's crafthall. I'd like the Mastersmith to come with me to Nerat. I want to see what his agenothree does to Threads."

Ramoth nodded her head as the dragon relayed the message to her.

She has done so, and the green dragon comes as soon as he can. Mnementh reported to his rider. *It is easier to do, this talking about, when Lessa is awake,* he grumbled.

F'lar agreed heartily. It had been quite an advantage yesterday in the battle and would be more and more of an asset.

Maybe it would be better if she tried to speak across time to F'nor . . . but no, F'nor had come back.

F'lar strode into the Council Room, still hopeful that somewhere within the illegible portions of the old Records was the one clue he so desperately needed. There must be a way out of this impasse. If not the southern venture, then something else. Something!

Fandarel showed himself a man of iron will as well as sinew; he looked calmly at the exposed tangle of perceptibly growing Threads that writhed and intertwined obscenely.

"Hundreds and thousands in this one burrow," Lord Vincet of Nerat was exclaiming in a frantic tone of voice. He waved his hands distractedly around the plantation of young trees in which the burrow had been discovered. "These stalks are already withering even as you hesitate. Do something! How many more young trees will die in this one field alone? How many more burrows escaped dragon's breath yesterday? Where is a dragon to sear them? Why are you just standing there?"

F'lar and Fandarel paid no attention to the man's raving, both fascinated as well as revolted by their first sight of the burrowing stage of their ancient foe. Despite Vincet's panicky accusations, it was the only burrow on this particular slope. F'lar did not like to contemplate how many more might have slipped through the dragons' efforts and had reached Nerat's warm and fertile soil. If they had only had time enough to set out watchmen to track the fall of stray clumps. They could, at least, remedy that error in Telgar, Crom, and Ruatha in three days. But it was not enough. Not enough.

Fandarel motioned forward the two craftsmen who had accompanied him. They were burdened with an odd contraption: a large cylinder of metal to which was attached a wand with a wide nozzle. At the other end of the cylinder was another short pipe-length and then a short cylinder with an inner plunger. One craftsman worked the plunger vigorously, while the second, barely keeping his hands steady, pointed the nozzle end toward the Thread burrow. At a nod from this pumper, the man released a small knob on the nozzle, extending it carefully away from him and over the burrow. A thin spray danced from the nozzle and drifted down into the burrow. No sooner had the spray motes contacted the Thread tangles than steam hissed out of the burrow. Before long, all that remained of the pallid writhing tendrils was a smoking mass of blackened strands. Long after Fandarel had waved the craftsmen back, he stared at the grave. Finally he grunted and found himself a long stick with which he poked and prodded the remains. Not one Thread wriggled.

"Humph," he grunted with evident satisfaction. "However, we can scarcely go around digging up every burrow. I need another."

With Lord Vincet a hand-wringing moaner in their wake, they were escorted by the junglemen to another undisturbed burrow on the sea-side of the rainforest. The Threads had entered the earth by the side of a huge tree that was already drooping.

With his prodding stick, Fandarel made a tiny hole at the top of the burrow and then waved his craftsmen forward. The pumper made vigorous motions at his end, while the nozzle-holder adjusted his pipe before inserting it in the hole. Fandarel gave the sign to start and counted slowly before he waved a cutoff. Smoke oozed out of the tiny hole.

After a suitable lapse of time, Fandarel ordered the junglemen to dig, reminding them to be careful not to come in contact with the agenothree liquid. When the burrow was uncovered, the acid had done its work, leaving nothing but a thoroughly charred mass of tangles.

Fandarel grimaced, but this time scratched his head in dissatisfaction.

"Takes too much time either way. Best to get them still at the surface," the Mastersmith grumbled.

"Best to get them in the air," Lord Vincet chattered. "And what will that stuff do to my young orchards? What will it do?"

Fandarel swung around, apparently noticing the distressed Holder for the first time.

"Little man, agenothree in diluted form is what you use to fertilize your plants in the spring. True, this field has been burned out for a few years, but it is *not* Thread-full. It *would* be better if we could get the spray up high in the air. Then it would float down and dissipate harmlessly—fertilizing very evenly, too." He paused, scratched his head gratingly. "Young dragons could carry a team aloft . . . Hmmm. A possibility, but the apparatus is bulky yet." He turned his back on the surprised Hold Lord then and asked F'lar if the tapestry had been returned. "I cannot yet discover how to make a tube throw flame. I got this mechanism from what we make for the orchard farmers."

"I'm still waiting for word on the tapestry," F'lar replied, "but this spray of yours is effective. The Thread burrow is dead."

"The sandworms are effective, too, but not really efficient," Fandarel grunted in dissatisfaction. He beckoned abruptly to his assistants and stalked off into the increasing twilight to the dragons.

Robinton awaited their return at the Weyr, his outward calm barely masking his inner excitement. He inquired politely, however, of Fandarel's efforts. The Mastersmith grunted and shrugged.

"I have all my craft at work."

"The Mastersmith is entirely too modest," F'lar put in. "He has already put together an ingenious device that sprays agenothree into Thread burrows and sears them into a black pulp."

"Not efficient. *I* like the idea of flamethrowers," the smith said, his eyes gleaming in his expressionless face. "A thrower of flame," he repeated, his eyes unfocusing. He shook his heavy head with a bone-popping crack. "I go," and with a curt nod to the harper and the Weyrleader, he left.

"I like that man's dedication to an idea," Robinton observed. Despite his amusement with the man's eccentric behavior, there was a strong undercurrent of respect for the smith. "I must set my apprentices a task for an appropriate Saga on the Mastersmith. I understand," he said, turning to F'lar, "that the southern venture has been inaugurated."

F'lar nodded unhappily.

"Your doubts increase?"

"This *between* times travel takes its own toll," he admitted, glancing anxiously toward the sleeping room.

"The Weyrwoman is ill?"

"Sleeping, but today's journey affected her. We need another, less dangerous answer!" and F'lar slammed one fist into the other palm.

"I came with no real answer," Robinton said, then briskly, "but with what I believe to be another part of the puzzle. I have found an entry. Four hundred Turns ago the then Masterharper was called to Fort Weyr not long after the Red Star retreated away from Pern in the evening sky."

"An entry? What is it?"

"Mind you, the Thread attacks had just lifted, and the Masterharper was called one late evening to Fort Weyr. An unusual summons. However," and Robinton emphasized the distinction by pointing a long, callous-tipped finger at F'lar, "no further mention is ever made of that visit. There ought to have been, for all such summonses have a purpose. All such meetings are recorded, yet no explanation of this one is given. The record is taken up several weeks later by the Masterharper as though he had not left his crafthall at all. Some ten months afterward, the Question Song was added to compulsory Teaching Ballads."

"You believe the two are connected with the abandonment of the five Weyrs?"

"I do, but I could not say why. I only feel that the events, the visit, the disappearances, the Question Song, are connected."

F'lar poured them both cups of wine.

"I have checked back, too, seeking some indications." He shrugged. "All must have been normal right up to the point they disappeared. There are Records of tithing trains received, supplies stored, the list of injured dragons and men returning to active patrols. And then the Records cease at full Cold, leaving only Benden Weyr occupied."

"And why that one Weyr of the six to choose from?" Robinton demanded. "Island Ista would be a better choice if only one Weyr was to be left. Benden so far north is not a likely place to pass four hundred Turns."

"Benden is high and isolated. A disease that struck the others and was prevented from reaching Benden?"

"And no explanation of it? They can't all—dragons, riders, weyrfolk—have dropped dead on the same instant and left no carcasses rotting in the sun."

"Then let us ask ourselves, why was the harper called? Was he told to construct a Teaching Ballad covering this disappearance?"

"Well," Robinton snorted, "it certainly wasn't meant to reassure us, not with that tune—if one cares to call it a tune at all, and I don't—nor does it answer any questions! It poses them."

"For us to answer?" suggested F'lar softly.

"Aye." Robinton's eyes shone. "For us to answer, indeed, for it is a difficult song to forget. Which means it was meant to be remembered. Those questions are important, F'lar!"

"Which questions are important?" demanded Lessa, who had entered quietly.

Both men were on their feet. F'lar, with unusual attentiveness, held a chair for Lessa and poured her wine.

"I'm not going to break apart," she said tartly, almost annoyed at the excess of courtesy. Then she smiled up at F'lar to take the sting out of her words. "I slept and I feel much better. What were you two getting so intense about?"

F'lar quickly outlined what he and the Masterharper had been discussing. When he mentioned the Question Song, Lessa shuddered.

"That's one I can't forget either. Which, I've always been told," and she grimaced, remembering the hateful lessons with R'gul, "means it's important. But why? It only asked questions." Then she blinked, her eyes went wide with amazement.

" 'Gone away, gone . . . *ahead!*' " she cried, on her feet. "That's it! All five Weyrs went . . . *ahead*. But to when?"

F'lar turned to her, speechless.

"They came ahead to our time! Five Weyrs full of dragons," she repeated in an awed voice.

"No, that's impossible," F'lar contradicted.

"Why?" Robinton demanded excitedly. "Doesn't that solve the problem we're facing? The need for fighting dragons? Doesn't it explain why they left so suddenly with no explanation except that Question Song?"

F'lar brushed back the heavy lock of hair that overhung his eyes.

"It would explain their actions in leaving," he admitted, "because they couldn't leave any clues saying where they went, or it would cancel the whole thing. Just as I couldn't tell F'nor I knew the southern venture would have problems. But how do they get here—if here is *when* they came? They aren't here now. How would they have known they were needed—or *when* they were needed? And this is the real problem—how can you conceivably give a dragon references to a *when* that has not yet occured?"

"Someone here must go back to give them the proper references," Lessa replied in a very quiet voice.

"You're mad, Lessa," F'lar shouted at her, alarm written on his face. "You know what happened to you today. How can you consider going back to a *when* you can't remotely imagine? To a *when* four hundred Turns ago? Going back ten Turns left you fainting and half-ill."

"Wouldn't it be worth it?" she asked him, her eyes grave. "Isn't Pern worth it?"

F'lar grabbed her by the shoulders, shaking her, his eyes wild with fear.

"Not even Pern is worth losing you, or Ramoth. Lessa,

Lessa, don't you dare disobey me in this." His voice dropped to an intense, icy whisper, shaking with anger.

"Ah, there may be a way of effecting that solution, momentarily beyond us, Weyrwoman," Robinton put in adroitly. "Who knows what tomorrow holds? It certainly is not something one does without considering every angle."

Lessa did not shrug off F'lar's viselike grip on her shoulders as she gazed at Robinton.

"Wine?" the Masterharper suggested, pouring a mug for her. His diversionary action broke the tableau of Lessa and F'lar.

"Ramoth is not afraid to try," Lessa said, her mouth set in a determined line.

F'lar glared at the golden dragon who was regarding the humans, her neck curled around almost to the shoulder joint of her great wing.

"Ramoth is young," F'lar snapped and then caught Mnementh's wry thought even as Lessa did.

She threw her head back, her peal of laughter echoing in the vaulting chamber.

"I'm badly in need of a good joke myself," Robinton remarked pointedly.

"Mnementh told F'lar that he was neither young nor afraid to try, either. It was just a long step," Lessa explained, wiping tears from her eyes.

F'lar glanced dourly at the passageway, at the end of which Mnementh lounged on his customary ledge.

A laden dragon comes, the bronze warned those in the Weyr. *It is Lytol behind young B'rant on brown Fanth.*

"Now he brings his own bad news?" Lessa asked sourly.

"It is hard enough for Lytol to ride another's dragon or come here at all, Lessa of Ruatha. Do not increase his torment one jot with your childishness," F'lar said sternly.

Lessa dropped her eyes, furious with F'lar for speaking so to her in front of Robinton.

Lytol stumped into the queen's weyr, carrying one end of a large rolled rug. Young B'rant, struggling to uphold the other end, was sweating with the effort. Lytol bowed respectfully toward Ramoth and gestured the young brown rider to help him unroll their burden. As the immense tapestry uncoiled, F'lar could understand why

Masterweaver Zurg had remembered it. The colors, ancient though they undoubtedly were, remained vibrant and undimmed. The subject matter was even more interesting.

"Mnementh, send for Fandarel. Here's the model he needs for his flamethrower," F'lar said.

"That tapestry is Ruatha's," Lessa cried indignantly. "I remember it from my childhood. It hung in the Great Hall and was the most cherished of my Blood Line's possessions. Where has it been?" Her eyes were flashing.

"Lady, it is being returned to where it belongs," Lytol said stolidly, avoiding her gaze. "A masterweaver's work, this," he went on, touching the heavy fabric with reverent fingers. "Such colors, such patterning. It took a man's life to set up the loom, a craft's whole effort to complete, or I am no judge of true craftsmanship."

F'lar walked along the edge of the immense arras, wishing it could be hung to afford the proper perspective of the heroic scene. A flying formation of three wings of dragons dominated the upper portion of half the hanging. They were breathing flame as they dove upon gray, falling clumps of Threads in the brilliant sky. A sky just that perfect autumnal blue, F'lar decided, that cannot occur in warmer weather. Upon the lower slopes of the hills, foliage was depicted as turning yellow from chilly nights. The slatey rocks suggested Ruathan country. Was that why the tapestry had hung in Ruatha Hall? Below, men had left the protecting Hold, cut into the cliff itself. The men were burdened with the curious cylinders of which Zurg had spoken. The tubes in their hands belched brilliant tongues of flame in long streams, aimed at the writhing Threads that attempted to burrow in the ground.

Lessa gave a startled exclamation, walking right onto the tapestry, staring down at the woven outline of the Hold, its massive door ajar, the details of its bronze ornamentation painstakingly rendered in fine yarns.

"I believe that's the design on the Ruatha Hold door," F'lar remarked.

"It is . . . and it isn't," Lessa replied in a puzzled voice.

Lytol glowered at her and then at the woven door. "True. It isn't and yet it is, and I went through that door a scant hour ago." He scowled down at the door before his toes.

"Well, here are the designs Fandarel wants to study," F'lar said with relief as he peered at the flamethrowers.

Whether or not the smith could produce a working model from this woven one in time to help them three days hence F'lar couldn't guess. But if Fandarel could not, no man could.

The Mastersmith was, for him, jubilant over the presence of the tapestry. He lay upon the rug, his nose tickled by the nap as he studied the details. He grumbled, moaned, and muttered as he sat cross-legged to sketch and peer.

"Has been done. Can be done. Must be done," he was heard to rumble.

Lessa called for *klah,* bread, and meat when she learned from young B'rant that neither he nor Lytol had eaten yet. She served all the men, her manner gay and teasing. F'lar was relieved for Lytol's sake. Lessa even pressed food and *klah* on Fandarel, a tiny figure beside the mammoth man, insisting that he come away from the tapestry and eat and drink before he could return to his mumbling and drawing.

Fandarel finally decided that he had enough sketches and disappeared to be flown back to his crafthold.

"No point in asking him when he'll be back. He's too deep in thought to hear," F'lar remarked, amused.

"If you don't mind, I shall excuse myself as well," Lessa said, smiling graciously to the four remaining around the table. "Good Warder Lytol, young B'rant should soon be excused, too. He's half-asleep."

"I most certainly am not, Weyrlady," B'rant assured her hastily, widening his eyes with simulated alertness.

Lessa merely laughed as she retreated into the sleeping chamber. F'lar stared thoughtfully after her.

"I mistrust the Weyrwoman when she uses that particularly docile tone of voice," he said slowly.

"Well, we must all depart," Robinton suggested, rising.

"Ramoth is young but not that foolish," F'lar murmured after the others had left.

Ramoth slept, oblivious of his scrutiny. He reached for the consolation Mnementh could give him, without response. The big bronze was dozing on his ledge.

Black, blacker, blackest,
And cold beyond frozen things.
Where is *between* when there is naught
To Life but fragile dragon wings?

"I JUST want to see that tapestry back on the wall at Ruatha," Lessa insisted to F'lar the next day. "I want it where it belongs."

They had gone to check on the injured and had had one argument already over F'lar's having sent N'ton along with the southern venture. Lessa had wanted him to try riding another's dragon. F'lar had preferred for him to learn to lead a wing of his own in the south, given the Turns to mature in. He had reminded Lessa, in the hope that it might prove inhibiting to any ideas she had about going four hundred Turns back, about F'nor's return trips, and he had borne down hard on the difficulties she had already experienced.

She had become very thoughtful, although she had said nothing.

Therefore, when Fandarel sent word that he would like to show F'lar a new mechanism, the Weyrleader felt reasonably safe in allowing Lessa the triumph of returning the purloined tapestry to Ruatha. She went to have the arras rolled and strapped to Ramoth's back.

He watched Ramoth rise with great sweeps of her wide wings, up to the Star Stone before going *between* to Ruatha. R'gul appeared on the ledge just then, reporting that a huge train of firestone was entering the Tunnel. Consequently, busy with such details, it was midmorning before he could get to see Fandarel's crude and not yet effective flamethrower—the fire did not "throw" from the nozzle of the tube with any force at all. It was late afternoon before he reached the Weyr again.

R'gul announced sourly that F'nor had been looking for him—twice, in fact.

"Twice?"

"Twice, as I said. He would not leave a message with me for you." R'gul was clearly insulted by F'nor's refusal.

By the evening meal, when there was still no sign of Lessa, F'lar sent to Ruatha to learn that she had indeed brought the tapestry. She had badgered and bothered the entire Hold until the thing was properly hung. For upward of several hours she had sat and looked at it, pacing its length occasionally.

She and Ramoth had then taken to the sky above the Great Tower and disappeared. Lytol had assumed, as had everyone at Ruatha, that she had returned to Benden Weyr.

"Mnementh," F'lar bellowed when the messenger had finished. "Mnementh, where are they?"

Mnementh's answer was a long time in coming.

I cannot hear them, he said finally, his mental voice soft and as full of worry as a dragon's could be.

F'lar gripped the table with both hands, staring at the queen's empty weyr. He knew, in the anguished privacy of his mind, where Lessa had tried to go.

> Cold as death, death-bearing,
> Stay and die, unguided.
> Brave and braving, linger.
> This way was twice decided.

BELOW THEM was Ruatha's Great Tower. Lessa coaxed Ramoth slightly to the left, ignoring the dragon's acid comments, knowing that she was excited, too.

That's right, dear, this is exactly the angle at which the tapestry illustrates the Hold door. Only when that tapestry was designed, no one had carved the lintels or capped the door. And there was no Tower, no inner Court, no gate. She stroked the surprisingly soft skin of the curving neck, laughing to hide her own tense nervousness and apprehension at what she was about to attempt.

She told herself there were good reasons prompting her action in this matter. The ballad's opening phrase, "Gone away, gone ahead," was clearly a reference to *between* times. And the tapestry gave the required reference points for the jump *between* whens. Oh, how she thanked the Masterweaver who had woven that doorway. She must remember to tell him how well he had wrought. She hoped she'd be able to. Enough of that. Of course, she'd be able to. For hadn't the Weyrs disappeared? Knowing they had gone ahead, knowing how to go back to bring them ahead, it was she, obviously, who must go back and lead them. It was very simple, and only she and Ramoth could do it. Because they already had.

She laughed again, nervously, and took several deep, shuddering breaths.

"All right, my golden love," she murmured. "You have the reference. You know when I want to go. Take me *between*, Ramoth, *between* four hundred Turns."

The cold was intense, even more penetrating than she had imagined. Yet it was not a physical cold. It was the awareness of the absence of *everything*. No light. No sound. No touch. As they hovered, longer and longer, in this nothingness, Lessa recognized full-blown panic of a kind that threatened to overwhelm her reason. She knew she sat on Ramoth's neck, yet she could not feel the great beast under her thighs, under her hands. She tried to cry out inadvertently and opened her mouth to . . . nothing . . . no sound in her own ears. She could not even feel the hands that she knew she had raised to her own cheeks.

I am here, she heard Ramoth say in her mind. *We are together,* and this reassurance was all that kept her from losing her grasp on sanity in that terrifying aeon of un-passing, timeless nothingness.

Someone had sense enough to call for Robinton. The Masterharper found F'lar sitting at the table, his face deathly pale, his eyes staring at the empty weyr. The craftmaster's entrance, his calm voice, reached F'lar in his shocked numbness. He sent others out with a peremptory wave.

"She's gone. She tried to go back four hundred Turns," F'lar said in a tight, hard voice.

The Masterharper sank into the chair opposite the Weyrleader.

"She took the tapestry back to Ruatha," F'lar continued in that same choked voice. "I'd told her about F'nor's returns. I told her how dangerous this was. She didn't argue very much, and I know going *between* times had frightened her, if anything could frighten Lessa." He banged the table with an impotent fist. "I should have suspected her. When she thinks she's right, she doesn't stop to analyze, to consider. She just does it!"

"But she's not a foolish woman," Robinton reminded him slowly. "Not even she would jump *between* times without a reference point. Would she?"

"'Gone away, gone ahead'—that's the only clue we have!"

"Now wait a moment," Robinton cautioned him, then snapped his fingers. "Last night, when she walked upon the tapestry, she was uncommonly interested in the Hall door. Remember, she discussed it with Lytol."

F'lar was on his feet and halfway down the passageway.

"Come on, man, we've got to get to Ruatha."

Lytol lit every glow in the Hold for F'lar and Robinton to examine the tapestry clearly.

"She spent the afternoon just looking at it," the Warder said, shaking his head. "You're sure she has tried this incredible jump?"

"She must have. Mnementh can't hear either her or Ramoth anywhere. Yet he says he can get an echo from Canth many Turns away and in the Southern Continent." F'lar stalked past the tapestry. "What is it about the door, Lytol? Think, man!"

"It is much as it is now, save that there are no carved lintels, there is no outer Court or Tower . . ."

"That's it. Oh, by the first Egg, it is so simple. Zurg said this tapestry is old. Lessa must have decided it was four hundred Turns, and she has used it as the reference point to go back *between* times."

"Why, then, she's there and safe," Robinton cried, sinking with relief in a chair.

"Oh, no, harper. It is not as easy as that," F'lar murmured, and Robinton caught his stricken look and the despair echoed in Lytol's face.

"What's the matter?"

"There is nothing *between*," F'lar said in a dead voice. "To go *between* places takes only as much time as for a man to cough three times. *Between* four-hundred Turns . . ." His voice trailed off.

> Who wills,
> Can.
> Who tries,
> Does.
> Who loves,
> Lives.

THERE WERE voices that first were roars in her aching ears and then hushed beyond the threshold of sound. She gasped as the whirling, nauseating sensation apparently spun her and the bed which she felt beneath her around and around. She clung to the sides of the bed as pain jabbed through her head from somewhere directly in the middle of her skull. She screamed as much in protest at the pain as from the terrifying, rolling, whirling, dropping lack of a solid ground.

Yet some frightening necessity kept her trying to gabble out the message she had come to give. Sometimes she felt Ramoth trying to reach her in that vast swooping darkness that enveloped her. She would try to cling to Ramoth's mind, hoping the golden queen could lead her out of this torturing nowhere. Exhausted, she would sink down, down, only to be torn from oblivion by the desperate need to communicate.

She was finally aware of a soft, smooth hand upon her arm, of a liquid, warm and savory, in her mouth. She rolled it around her tongue, and it trickled down her sore throat. A fit of coughing left her gasping and weak. Then she experimentally opened her eyes, and the images before her did not lurch and spin.

"Who . . . are . . . you?" she managed to croak.

"Oh, my dear Lessa . . ."

"Is that who I am?" she asked, confused.

"So your Ramoth tells us," she was assured. "I am Mardra of Fort Weyr."

"Oh, F'lar will be so angry with me," Lessa moaned as her memory came rushing back. "He will shake me and shake me. He always shakes me when I disobey him. But I was right. I was right. Mardra? . . . Oh, that . . . awful . . . nothingness," and she felt herself drifting off into sleep, unable to resist that overwhelming urge. Comfortably, her bed no longer rocked beneath her.

The room, dimly lit by wallglows, was both like her own at Benden Weyr and subtly different. Lessa lay still, trying to isolate that difference. Ah, the weyr-walls were very smooth here. The room was larger, too, the ceiling higher and curving. The furnishings, now that her eyes were used to the dim light and she could distinguish details, were more finely crafted. She stirred restlessly.

"Ah, you're awake again, mystery lady," a man said.

Light beyond the parted curtain flooded in from the outer weyr. Lessa sensed rather than saw the presence of others in the room beyond.

A woman passed under the man's arm, moving swiftly to the bedside.

"I remember you. You're Mardra," Lessa said with surprise.

"Indeed I am, and here is T'ton, Weyrleader at Fort."

T'ton was tossing more glows into the wallbasket, peering over his shoulder at Lessa to see if the light bothered her.

"Ramoth!" Lessa exclaimed, sitting upright, aware for the first time that it was not Ramoth's mind she touched in the outer weyr.

"Oh, that one," Mardra laughed with amused dismay. "She'll eat us out of the Weyr, and even my Loranth has had to call the other queens to restrain her."

"She perches on the Star Stones as if she owned them and keens constantly," T'ton added less charitably. He cocked an ear. "Ha. She's stopped."

"You can come, can't you?" Lessa blurted out.

"Come? Come where, my dear?" Mardra asked, confused. "You've been going on and on about our 'coming,' and Threads approaching, and the Red Star bracketed in the Eye Rock, and . . . my dear, don't you realize the Red Star has been past Pern these two months?"

"No, no, they've started. That's why I came back *between* times . . ."

"Back? *Between* times?" T'ton exclaimed, striding over to the bed, eyeing Lessa intently.

"Could I have some *klah?* I know I'm not making much sense, and I'm not really awake yet. But I'm not mad or still sick, and this is rather complicated."

"Yes, it is," T'ton remarked with deceptive mildness. But he did call down the service shaft for *klah*. And he did drag a chair over to her bedside, settling himself to listen to her.

"Of course you're not mad," Mardra soothed her, glaring at her weyrmate. "Or she wouldn't ride a queen."

T'ton had to agree to that. Lessa waited for the *klah* to come; when it did, she sipped gratefully at its stimulating warmth.

Then she took a deep breath and began, telling them of

the Long Interval between the dangerous passes of the
Red Star; how the sole Weyr had fallen into disfavor and
contempt, how Jora had deteriorated and lost control over
her queen, Nemorth, so that as the Red Star neared, there
was no sudden increase in the size of clutches. How she
had Impressed Ramoth to become Benden's Weyrwoman.
How F'lar had outwitted the dissenting Hold Lords the
day after Ramoth's first mating flight and taken firm command of Weyr and Pern, preparing for the Threads he
knew were coming. She told her by now rapt audience of
her own first attempts to fly Ramoth and how she had inadvertently gone back *between* time to the day Fax had
invaded Ruath Hold.

"Invade . . . my family's Hold?" Mardra cried, aghast.

"Ruatha has given the Weyrs many famous Weyrwomen," Lessa said with a sly smile at which T'ton burst
out laughing.

"She's Ruathan, no question," he assured Mardra.

She told them of the situation in which dragonmen now
found themselves, with an insufficient force to meet the
Thread attacks. Of the Question Song and the great tapestry.

"A tapestry?" Mardra cried, her hand going to her
cheek in alarm. "Describe it to me!"

And when Lessa did, she saw—at last—belief in both
their faces.

"My father has just commissioned a tapestry with such
a scene. He told me of it the other day because the last
battle with the Threads was held over Ruatha." Incredulous, Mardra turned to T'ton who no longer looked
amused. "She must have done what she has said she'd
done. How could she possibly know about the tapestry?"

"You might also ask your queen dragon, and mine,"
Lessa suggested.

"My dear, we do not doubt you now," Mardra said sincerely, "but it is a most incredible feat."

"I don't think," Lessa said, "that I would ever try it
again, knowing what I do know."

"Yes, this shock makes a forward jump *between* times
quite a problem if your F'lar must have an effective fighting force," T'ton remarked.

"You will come? You will?"

"There is a distinct possibility we will," T'ton said

gravely, and his face broke into a lopsided grin. "You said we left the Weyrs . . . abandoned them, in fact, and left no explanation. We went somewhere . . . somewhen, that is, for we are still here now . . ."

They were all silent, for the same alternative occurred to them simultaneously. The Weyrs had been vacant, but Lessa had no way of proving that the five Weyrs reappeared in her time.

"There must be a way. There must be a way," Lessa cried distractedly. "And there's no time to waste. No time at all!"

T'ton gave a bark of laughter. "There's plenty of time at this end of history, my dear."

They made her rest then, more concerned than she was that she had been ill some weeks, deliriously screaming that she was falling and could not see, could not hear, could not touch. Ramoth, too, they told her, had suffered from the appalling nothingness of a protracted stay *between,* emerging above ancient Ruatha a pale yellow wraith of her former robust self.

The Lord of Ruatha Hold, Mardra's father, had been surprised out of his wits by the appearance of a staggering rider and a pallid queen on his stone verge. Naturally and luckily he had sent to his daughter at Fort Weyr for help. Lessa and Ramoth had been transported to the Weyr, and the Ruathan Lord kept silence on the matter.

When Lessa was strong enough, T'ton called a Council of Weyrleaders. Curiously, there was no opposition to going . . . provided they could solve the problem of time-shock and find reference points along the way. It did not take Lessa long to comprehend why the dragonriders were so eager to attempt the journey. Most of them had been born during the present Thread incursions. They had now had close to four months of unexciting routine patrols and were bored with monotony. Training Games were pallid substitutes for the real battles they had all fought. The Holds, which once could not do dragonmen favors enough, were beginning to be indifferent. The Weyrleaders could see these incidents increasing as Thread-generated fears receded. It was a morale decay as insidious as a wasting disease in Weyr and Hold. The alternative that Lessa's appeal offered was better than a slow decline in their own time.

Of Benden, only the Weyrleader himself was privy to these meetings. Because Benden was the only Weyr in Lessa's time, it must remain ignorant and intact, until her time. Nor could any mention be made of Lessa's presence, for that, too, was unknown in her Turn.

She insisted that they call in the Masterharper because her Records said he had been called. But when he asked her to tell him the Question Song, she smiled and demurred.

"You'll write it, or your successor will, when the Weyrs are found to be abandoned," she told him. "But it must be your doing, not my repeating."

"A difficult assignment to know one must write a song that four hundred Turns later gives a valuable clue."

"Only be sure," she cautioned him, "that it is a Teaching tune. It must *not* be forgotten, for it poses questions that I have to answer."

As he started to chuckle, she realized she had already given him a pointer.

The discussions—how to go so far safely with no sustained sense deprivations—grew heated. There were more constructive notions, however impractical, on how to find reference points along the way. The five Weyrs had not been ahead in time, and Lessa, in her one gigantic backward leap, had not stopped for intermediate time marks.

"You did say that a *between* times jump of ten years caused no hardship?" T'ton asked of Lessa as all the Weyrleaders and the Masterharper met to discuss this impasse.

"None. It takes . . . oh, twice as long as a *between* places jump."

"It is the four-hundred Turn leap that left you imbalanced. Hmmm. Maybe twenty or twenty-five Turn segments would be safe enough."

That suggestion found merit until Ista's cautious leader, D'ram, spoke up.

"I don't mean to be a Hold-hider, but there is one possibility we haven't mentioned. How do we know we made the jump *between* to Lessa's time? Going *between* is a chancy business. Men go missing often. And Lessa barely made it here alive."

"A good point, D'ram," T'ton concurred briskly, "but I feel there is more to prove that we do—did—will—go for-

ward. The clues, for one thing—they were aimed at
Lessa. The very emergency that left five Weyrs empty
sent her back to appeal for our help—"

"Agreed, agreed," D'ram interrupted earnestly, "but
what I mean is can you be sure we reached Lessa's time?
It hadn't happened yet. Do we know it can?"

T'ton was not the only one who searched his mind for
an answer to that. All of a sudden he slammed both
hands, palms down, on the table.

"By the Egg, it's die slow, doing nothing, or die quick
trying. I've had a surfeit of the quiet life we dragonmen
must lead after the Red Star passes till we go *between* in
old age. I confess I'm almost sorry to see the Red Star
dwindle farther from us in the evening sky. I say, grab the
risk with both hands and shake it till it's gone. We're dragonmen, aren't we, bred to fight the Threads? Let's go
hunting . . . four hundred Turns ahead!"

Lessa's drawn face relaxed. She had recognized the validity of D'ram's alternate possibility, and it had touched
off bitter fear in her heart. To risk herself was her own responsibility, but to risk these hundreds of men and dragons, the Weyrfolk who would accompany their men . . . ?

T'ton's ringing words for once and all dispensed with
that consideration.

"And I believe," the Masterharper's exultant voice cut
through the answering shouts of agreement, "I have your
reference points." A smile of surprised wonder illuminated
his face. "Twenty Turns or twenty hundred, you have a
guide! And T'ton said it. As the Red Star dwindles in the
evening sky . . ."

Later as they plotted the orbit of the Red Star, they
found how easy that solution actually was and chuckled
that their ancient foe should be their guide.

Atop Fort Weyr, as on all the Weyrs, were great stones.
They were so placed that at certain times of the year they
marked the approach and retreat of the Red Star as it or-
bited in its erratic two hundred Turn-long course around
their sun. By consulting the Records which, among other
morsels of information, included the Red Star's wanderings, it was not hard to plan jumps *between* of twenty-five
Turns for each Weyr. It had been decided that the com-
plement of each separate Weyr would jump *between*
above its own base, for there would unquestionably be ac-

cidents if close to eighteen-hundred laden beasts tried it at one point.

Each moment now was one too long away from her own time for Lessa. She had been a month away from F'lar and missed him more than she had thought possible. Also, she was worried that Ramoth would mate away from Mnementh. There were, to be sure, bronze dragons and bronze riders eager to do that service, but Lessa had no interest in them.

T'ton and Mardra occupied her with the many details in organizing the exodus so that no clues, past the tapestry and the Question Song that would be composed at a later date, remained in the Weyrs.

It was with a relief close to tears that Lessa urged Ramoth upward in the night sky to take her place near T'ton and Mardra above the Fort Weyr Star Stone. At five other Weyrs great wings were ranged in formation, ready to depart their own times.

As each Weyrleader's dragon reported to Lessa that all were ready, reference points determined by the Red Star's travels in mind, it was this traveler from the future who gave the command to jump *between*.

> The blackest night must end in dawn,
> The sun dispel the dreamer's fear:
> When shall my soul's black, hopeless pain
> Find solace in its darkening Weyr?

THEY HAD made eleven jumps *between*, the Weyrleaders' bronzes speaking to Lessa as they rested briefly between each jump. Of the eighteen-hundred-odd travelers, only four failed to come ahead, and they had been older beasts. All five sections agreed to pause for a quick meal and hot *klah* before the final jump, which would be but twelve Turns.

"It is easier," T'ton commented as Mardra served the *klah*, "to go twenty-five Turns than twelve." He glanced up at the Red Dawn Star, their winking and faithful guide. "It does not alter its position as much. I count on you, Lessa, to give us additional references."

"I want to get us back to Ruatha before F'lar discovers I have gone." She shivered as she looked up at the Red Star and sipped hastily at the hot *klah*. "I've seen the Star

just like that once . . . no, twice . . . before at Ruatha."
She stared at T'ton, her throat constricting as she remembered that morning: the time she had decided that the
Red Star was a menace to her, three days after which Fax
and F'lar had appeared at Ruatha Hold. Fax had died on
F'lar's dagger, and she had gone to Benden Weyr. She felt
suddenly dizzy, weak, strangely unsettled. She had not felt
this way as they paused between other jumps.

"Are you all right, Lessa?" Mardra asked with concern.
"You're so white. You're shaking." She put her arm
around Lessa, glancing, concerned, at her Weyrmate.

"Twelve Turns ago I was at Ruatha," Lessa murmured,
grasping Mardra's hand for support. "I was at Ruatha
twice. Let's go on quickly. I'm too many in this morning. I
must get back. I must get back to F'lar. He'll be so angry."

The note of hysteria in her voice alarmed both Mardra
and T'ton. Hastily the latter gave orders for the fires to be
extinguished, for the Weyrfolk to mount and prepare for
the final jump ahead.

Her mind in chaos, Lessa transmitted the references to
the other Weyrleaders' dragons: Ruatha in the evening
light, the Great Tower, the inner Court, the land at
springtime. . . .

> A fleck of red in a cold night sky,
> A drop of blood to guide them by,
> Turn away, Turn away, Turn, be gone.
> A Red Star beckons the travelers on.

BETWEEN THEM, Lytol and Robinton forced F'lar to
eat, deliberately plying them with wine. At the back of his
mind, F'lar knew he would have to keep on going, but the
effort was immense, the spirit gone from him. It was no
comfort that they still had Pridith and Kylara to continue
dragonkind, yet he delayed sending someone back for
F'nor, unable to face the reality of that admission: that in
sending for Pridith and Kylara, he had acknowledged the
fact that Lessa and Ramoth would not return.

Lessa, Lessa, his mind cried endlessly, damning her
one moment for her reckless, thoughtless daring, loving
her the next for attempting such an incredible feat.

"I said, F'lar, you need sleep now more than wine."
Robinton's voice penetrated his preoccupation.

F'lar looked at him, frowning in perplexity. He realized that he was trying to lift the wine jug that Robinton was holding firmly down.

"What did you say?"

"Come. I'll bear you company to Benden. Indeed, nothing could persuade me to leave your side. You have aged years, man, in the course of hours."

"And isn't it understandable?" F'lar shouted, rising to his feet, the impotent anger boiling out of him at the nearest target in the form of Robinton.

Robinton's eyes were full of compassion as he reached for F'lar's arm, gripping it tightly.

"Man, not even this Masterharper has words enough to express the sympathy and honor he has for you. But you must sleep; you have tomorrow to endure, and the tomorrow after that you have to fight. The dragonmen must have a leader . . ." His voice trailed off. "Tomorrow you must send for F'nor . . . and Pridith."

F'lar pivoted on his heel and strode toward the fateful door of Ruatha's great hall.

Oh, Tongue, give sound to joy and sing
Of hope and promise on dragonwing.

BEFORE THEM loomed Ruatha's Great Tower, the high walls of the Outer Court clearly visible in the fading light.

The claxon rang violent summons into the air, barely heard over the earsplitting thunder as hundreds of dragons appeared, ranging in full fighting array, wing upon wing, up and down the valley.

A shaft of light stained the flagstones of the Court as the Hold door opened.

Lessa ordered Ramoth down, close to the Tower, and dismounted, running eagerly forward to greet the men who piled out of the doors. She made out the stocky figure of Lytol, a handbasket of glows held high above his head. She was so relieved to see him that she forgot her previous antagonism to the Warder.

"You misjudged the last jump by two days, Lessa," he cried as soon as he was near enough for her to hear him over the noise of settling dragons.

"Misjudged? How could I?" she breathed.

T'ton and Mardra came up beside her.

"No need to worry," Lytol reassured her, gripping her
hands tightly in his, his eyes dancing. He was actually
smiling at her. "You overshot the day. Go back *between,*
return to Ruatha of two days ago. That's all." His grin
widened at her confusion. "It is all right," he repeated,
patting her hands. "Take this same hour, the Great Court,
everything, but visualize F'lar, Robinton, and myself here
on the flagstones. Place Mnementh on the Great Tower
and a blue dragon on the verge. Now go."

Mnementh? Ramoth queried Lessa, eager to see her
Weyrmate. She ducked her great head, and her huge eyes
gleamed with scintillating fire.

"I don't understand," Lessa wailed. Mardra slipped a
comforting arm around her shoulders.

"But I do, I do—trust me," Lytol pleaded, patting her
shoulder awkwardly and glancing at T'ton for support. "It
is as F'nor has said. You cannot be several places in time
without experiencing great distress, and when you stopped
twelve Turns back, it threw Lessa all to pieces."

"You know that?" T'ton cried.

"Of course. Just go back two days. You see, I *know* you
have. I shall, of course, be surprised then, but now, tonight, I know you reappeared two days earlier. Oh, go.
Don't argue. F'lar was half out of his mind with worry
for you."

"He'll shake me," Lessa cried, like a little girl.

"Lessa!" T'ton took her by the hand and led her back
to Ramoth, who crouched so her rider could mount.

T'ton took complete charge and had his Fidranth pass
the order to return to the references Lytol had given, adding by way of Ramoth, a description of the humans and
Mnementh.

The cold of *between* restored Lessa to herself, although
her error had badly jarred her confidence. But then there
was Ruatha again. The dragons happily arranged themselves in tremendous display. And there, silhouetted
against the light from the Hall, stood Lytol, Robinton's
tall figure, and . . . F'lar.

Mnementh's voice gave a brassy welcome, and Ramoth
could not land Lessa quickly enough to go and twine necks
with her mate.

Lessa stood where Ramoth had left her, unable to
move. She was aware that Mardra and T'ton were beside

her. She was conscious only of F'lar, racing across the
Court toward her. Yet she could not move.

He grabbed her in his arms, holding her so tightly to
him that she could not doubt the joy of his welcome.

"Lessa, Lessa," his voice raggedly chanted in her ear.
He pressed her face against his, crushing her to breath-
lessness, all his careful detachment abandoned. He kissed
her, hugged her, held her, and then kissed her with rough
urgency again. Then he suddenly set her on her feet and
gripped her shoulders. "Lessa, if you ever . . ." he said,
punctuating each word with a flexing of his fingers, then
stopped, aware of a grinning circle of strangers surrounding them.

"I told you he'd shake me," Lessa was saying, dashing
tears from her face. "But, F'lar, I brought them all . . . all
but Benden Weyr. And that is why the five Weyrs were
abandoned. I brought them."

F'lar looked around him, looked beyond the leaders to
the masses of dragons settling in the valley, on the
heights, everywhere he turned. There were dragons, blue,
green, bronze, brown, and a whole wingful of golden
queen dragons alone.

"You brought the Weyrs?" he echoed, stunned.

"Yes, this is Mardra and T'ton of Fort Weyr, D'ram
and . . ."

He stopped her with a little shake, pulling her to his side
so he could see and greet the newcomers.

"I am more grateful than you know," he said and could
not go on with all the many words he wanted to add.

T'ton stepped forward, holding out his hand, which
F'lar seized and held firmly.

"We bring eighteen-hundred dragons, seventeen queens,
and all that is necessary to implement our Weyrs."

"And they brought flamethrowers, too," Lessa put in
excitedly.

"But . . . to come . . . to attempt it . . ." F'lar murmured in admiring wonder.

T'ton and D'ram and the others laughed.

"Your Lessa showed the way—"

"—with the Red Star to guide us—" she said.

"We are dragonmen," T'ton continued solemnly, "as
you are yourself, F'lar of Benden. We were told there are

Threads here to fight, and that's work for dragonmen to do . . . in any time!"

> Drummer, beat, and piper, blow,
> Harper, strike, and soldier, go.
> Free the flame and sear the grasses
> Till the dawning Red Star passes.

EVEN AS the five Weyrs had been settling around Ruatha Valley, F'nor had been compelled to bring forward in time his southern Weyrfolk. They had all reached the end of endurance in double-time life, gratefully creeping back to quarters they had vacated two days and ten Turns ago.

R'gul, totally unaware of Lessa's backward plunge, greeted F'lar and his Weyrwoman on their return to the Weyr with the news of F'nor's appearance with seventy-two new dragons and the further word that he doubted any of the riders would be fit to fight.

"I've never seen such exhausted men in my life," R'gul rattled on, "can't imagine what could have gotten into them, with sun and plenty of food and all, and no responsibilities."

F'lar and Lessa exchanged glances.

"Well, the southern Weyr ought to be maintained, R'gul. Think it over."

"I'm a fighting dragonman, not a womanizer," the old dragonrider grunted. "It'd take more than a trip *between* times to reduce me like those others."

"Oh, they'll be themselves again in next to no time," Lessa said, and to R'gul's intense disapproval, she giggled.

"They'll have to be if we're to keep the skies Thread-free," R'gul snapped testily.

"No problem about that now," F'lar assured him easily.

"No problem? With only a hundred-and-forty-four dragons?"

"Two hundred and sixteen," Lessa corrected him firmly.

Ignoring her, R'gul asked, "Has that Mastersmith found a flamethrower that'll work?"

"Indeed he has," F'lar assured R'gul, grinning broadly.

The five Weyrs had also brought forward their equipment. Fandarel all but snatched examples from their backs, and undoubtedly every hearth and smithy through the continent would be ready to duplicate the design by morning. T'ton had told F'lar that in his time, each Hold had ample flamethrowers for every man on the ground. In the course of the Long Interval, however, the throwers must have been either smelted down or lost as incomprehensible devices. D'ram, particularly, was very much interested in Fandarel's agenothree sprayer, considering it better than thrown-flame since it would also act as a fertilizer.

"Well," R'gul admitted gloomily, "a flamethrower or two will be some help day after tomorrow."

"We have found something else that will help a lot more," Lessa remarked and then hastily excused herself, dashing into the sleeping quarters.

The sounds that drifted past the curtain were either laughter or sobs, and R'gul frowned on both. That girl was just too young to be Weyrwoman at such a time. No stability.

"Has she realized how critical our situation is? Even with F'nor's additions? That is, if they can fly?" R'gul demanded testily. "You oughtn't to let her leave the Weyr at all."

F'lar ignored that and began pouring himself a cup of wine.

"You once pointed out to me that the five empty Weyrs of Pern supported your theory that there would be no more Threads."

R'gul cleared his throat, thinking that apologies—even if they might be due from the Weyrleader—were scarcely effective against the Threads.

"Now there was merit in that theory," F'lar went on, filling a cup for R'gul. "Not, however, as you interpreted it. The five Weyrs were empty because they . . . they came here."

R'gul, his cup halfway to his lips, stared at F'lar. This man also was too young to bear his responsibilities. But . . . he seemed actually to believe what he was saying.

"Believe it or not, R'gul—and in a bare day's time you will—the five Weyrs are empty no longer. They're here, in the Weyrs, in this time. And they shall join us, eighteen hundred strong, the day after tomorrow at Telgar, with flamethrowers and with plenty of battle experience."

R'gul regarded the poor man stolidly for a long moment. Carefully he put his cup down and, turning on his heel, left the weyr. He refused to be an object of ridicule. He'd better plan to take over the leadership tomorrow if they were to fight Threads the day after.

The next morning, when he saw the clutch of great bronze dragons bearing the Weyrleaders and their wingleaders to the conference, R'gul got quietly drunk.

Lessa exchanged good mornings with her friends and then, smiling sweetly, left the weyr, saying she must feed Ramoth. F'lar stared after her thoughtfully, then went to greet Robinton and Fandarel, who had been asked to attend the meeting, too. Neither Craftmaster said much, but neither missed a word spoken. Fandarel's great head kept swiveling from speaker to speaker, his deep-set eyes blinking occasionally. Robinton sat with a bemused smile on his face, utterly delighted by ancestral visitors.

F'lar was quickly talked out of resigning his titular position as Weyrleader of Benden on the grounds that he was too inexperienced.

"You did well enough at Nerat and Keroon. Well indeed," T'ton said.

"You call twenty-eight men or dragons out of action good leadership?"

"For a first battle, with every dragonman green as a hatchling? No, man, you were on time at Nerat, however you got there," and T'ton grinned maliciously at F'lar, "which is what a dragonman must do. No, that was well-flown, I say. Well-flown." The other four Weyrleaders muttered complete agreement with that compliment. "Your Weyr is understrength, though, so we'll lend you enough odd-wing riders till you've gotten the Weyr up to full strength again. Oh, the queens love these times!" And his grin broadened to indicate that bronze riders did, too.

F'lar returned that smile, thinking that Ramoth was about ready for another mating flight, and this time Lessa . . . oh, that girl was being too deceptively docile. He'd better watch her closely.

"Now," T'ton was saying, "we left with Fandarel's crafthold all the flamethrowers we brought up so that the groundmen will be armed tomorrow."

"Aye, and my thanks," Fandarel grunted. "We'll turn out new ones in record time and return yours soon."

"Don't forget to adapt that agenothree for air spraying, too," D'ram put in.

"It is agreed," and T'ton glanced quickly around at the other riders, "that all the Weyrs will meet, full strength, three hours after dawn above Telgar to follow the Threads' attack across to Crom. By the way, F'lar, those charts of yours that Robinton showed me are superb. We never had them."

"How did you know when the attacks would come?"

T'ton shrugged. "They were coming so regularly even when I was a weyrling, you kind of knew when one was due. But this way is much, much better."

"More efficient," Fandarel added approvingly.

"After tomorrow when all the Weyrs show up at Telgar, we can request supplies we need to stock the empty Weyrs," T'ton grinned. "Like old times, squeezing extra tithes from the Holders." He rubbed his hands in anticipation. "Like old times."

"There's the southern Weyr," F'nor suggested. "We've been gone from there six Turns in this time, and the herd-beasts were left. They'll have multiplied, and there'll be all that fruit and grain."

"It would please me to see that southern venture continued," F'lar remarked, nodding encouragingly at F'nor.

"Yes, and continue Kylara down there, please, too," F'nor added urgently, his eyes sparkling with irritation.

They discussed sending for some immediate supplies to help out the newly occupied Weyrs and then adjourned the meeting.

"It is a trifle unsettling," T'ton said as he shared wine with Robinton, "to find that the Weyr you left the day before in good order has become a dusty hulk." He chuckled. "The women of the Lower Caverns were a bit upset."

"We cleaned up those kitchens," F'nor replied indignantly. A good night's rest in a fresh time had removed much of his fatigue.

T'ton cleared his throat. "According to Mardra, no man can *clean* anything."

"Do you think you'll be up to riding tomorrow, F'nor?" F'lar asked solicitously. He was keenly aware of the stress showing in his half brother's face, despite his improvement overnight. Yet those strenuous Turns had been nec-

essary, nor had they become futile even in hindsight with
the arrival of eighteen hundred dragons from past time.
When F'lar had ordered F'nor ten Turns backward to
breed the desperately needed replacements, they had not
yet brought to mind the Question Song or known of the
tapestry.

"I wouldn't miss that fight if I were dragonless," F'nor
declared stoutly.

"Which reminds me," F'lar remarked, "we'll need
Lessa at Telgar tomorrow. She can speak to any dragon,
you know," he explained almost apologetically to T'ton
and D'ram.

"Oh, we know," T'ton assured him. "And Mardra
doesn't mind." Seeing F'lar's blank expression, he added,
"As senior Weyrwoman, Mardra, of course, leads the
queens' wing."

F'lar's face grew blanker. "Queen's wing?"

"Certainly," and T'ton and D'ram exchanged questioning glances at F'lar's surprise. "You don't keep your
queens from fighting, do you?"

"*Our queens?* T'ton, we at Benden have had only *one*
queen dragon—at a time—for so many generations that
there are those who denounce the legends of queens in
battle as black heresy!"

T'ton looked rueful. "I had not truly realized till this
instant how small your numbers were." But his enthusi-
asms overtook him. "Just the same, queens are very useful
with flamethrowers. They get clumps other riders might
miss. They fly in low under the main wings. That's one
reason D'ram's so interested in the agenothree spray.
Doesn't singe the hair off the Holders' heads, so to speak,
and is far better over tilled fields."

"Do you mean to say that you allow your queens to fly
—against Threads?" F'lar ignored the fact that F'nor was
grinning, and T'ton, too.

"Allow?" D'ram bellowed. "You can't stop them. Don't
you know your Ballads?"

" 'Moreta's Ride'?"

"Exactly."

F'nor laughed aloud at the expression on F'lar's face as
he irritably pulled the hanging forelock from his eyes.
Then sheepishly, he began to grin.

"Thanks. That gives me an idea."

He saw his fellow Weyrleaders to their dragons, waved cheerfully to Robinton and Fandarel, more lighthearted than he would have thought he'd be the morning before the second battle. Then he asked Mnementh where Lessa might be.

Bathing, the bronze dragon replied.

F'lar glanced at the empty queen's weyr.

Oh, Ramoth is on the Peak, as usual. Mnementh sounded aggrieved.

F'lar heard the sound of splashing in the bathing room suddenly cease, so he called down for hot *klah.* He was going to enjoy this.

"Oh, did the meeting go well?" Lessa asked sweetly as she emerged from the bathing room, drying-cloth wrapped tightly around her slender figure.

"Extremely. You realize, of course, Lessa, that you'll be needed at Telgar?"

She looked at him intently for a moment before she smiled again.

"I *am* the only Weyrwoman who can speak to any dragon," she replied archly.

"True," F'lar admitted blithely. "And no longer the only queen's rider in Benden . . ."

"I hate you!" Lessa snapped, unable to evade F'lar as he pinned her cloth-swathed body to his.

"Even when I tell you that Fandarel has a flame-thrower for you so you can join the queens' wing?"

She stopped squirming in his arms and stared at him, disconcerted that he had outguessed her.

"And that Kylara will be installed as Weyrwoman in the south . . . in this time? As Weyrleader, I need my peace and quiet between battles . . ."

The cloth fell from her body to the floor as she responded to his kiss as ardently as if dragon-roused.

From the Weyr and from the Bowl,
Bronze and brown and blue and green,
Rise the dragonmen of Pern,
Aloft, on wing; seen, then unseen.

RANGED ABOVE the Peak of Benden Weyr, a scant three hours after dawn, two hundred and sixteen dragons held their formations as F'lar on bronze Mnementh inspected their ranks.

Below in the Bowl were gathered all the Weyrfolk and some of those injured in the first battle. All the Weyrfolk, that is, except Lessa and Ramoth. They had gone on to Fort Weyr where the queens' wing was assembling. F'lar could not quite suppress a twinge of concern that she and Ramoth would be fighting, too. A holdover, he knew, from the days when Pern had only one queen. If Lessa could jump four hundred Turns *between* and lead five Weyrs back, she could take care of herself and her dragon against Threads.

He checked to be sure that every man was well-loaded with firestone sacks, that each dragon was in good color, especially those in from the southern Weyr. Of course, the dragons were fit, but the faces of the men still showed evidences of the temporal strains they had endured. He was procrastinating, and the Threads would be dropping in the skies of Telgar.

He gave the order to go *between*. They reappeared above and to the south of Telgar Hold itself, and were not the first arrivals. To the west, to the north, and yes, to the east now, wings arrived until the horizon was patterned with the great Vs of several thousand dragon wings. Faintly he heard the claxon bell on Telgar Hold Tower as the unexpected dragon strength was acclaimed from the ground.

"Where is she?" F'lar demanded of Mnementh. "We'll need her presently to relay orders—"

She's coming, Mnementh interrupted him.

Right above Telgar Hold another wing appeared. Even at this distance, F'lar could see the difference: the golden dragons shone in the bright morning sunlight.

A hum of approval drifted down the dragon ranks, and despite his fleeting worry, F'lar grinned with proud indulgence at the glittering sight.

Just then the eastern wings soared straight upward in the sky as the dragons became instinctively aware of the presence of their ancient foe.

Mnementh raised his head, echoing back the brass thunder of the war cry. He turned his head, even as hundreds of other beasts turned to receive firestone from their riders. Hundreds of great jaws masticated the stone, swallowed it, their digestive acids transforming dry stone into flame-producing gases, igniting on contact with oxygen.

Threads! F'lar could see them clearly now against the spring sky. His pulses began to quicken, not with apprehension, but with a savage joy. His heart pounded unevenly. Mnementh demanded more stone and began to speed up the strokes of his wings in the air, gathering himself to leap upward when commanded.

The leading Weyr already belched gouts of orange-red flame into the pale blue sky. Dragons winked in and out, flamed and dove.

The great golden queens sped at cliff-skimming height to cover what might have been missed.

Then F'lar gave the command to gain altitude to meet the Threads halfway in their abortive descent. As Mnementh surged upward, F'lar shook his fist defiantly at the winking Red Eye of the Star.

"One day," he shouted, "we will not sit tamely here, awaiting your fall. We will fall on you, where you spin, and sear you on your own ground."

By the Egg, he told himself, if we can travel four hundred Turns backward and across seas and lands in the blink of an eye, what is travel from one world to another but a different kind of step?

F'lar grinned to himself. He'd better not mention that audacious notion in Lessa's presence.

Clumps ahead, Mnementh warned him.

As the bronze dragon charged, flaming, F'lar tightened his knees on the massive neck. Mother of us all, he was glad that now of all times conceivable, he, F'lar, rider of bronze Mnementh, was a dragonman of Pern!

1969

PASSENGERS

by Robert Silverberg

There are only fragments of me left now. Chunks of memory have broken free and drifted away like calved glaciers. It is always like that when a Passenger leaves us. We can never be sure of all the things our borrowed bodies did. We have only the lingering traces, the imprints.

Like sand clinging to an ocean-tossed bottle. Like the throbbings of amputated legs.

I rise. I collect myself. My hair is rumpled; I comb it. My face is creased from too little sleep. There is sourness in my mouth. Has my Passenger been eating dung with my mouth? They do that. They do anything.

It is morning.

A gray, uncertain morning. I stare at it a while, and then, shuddering, I opaque the window and confront instead the gray, uncertain surface of the inner panel. My room looks untidy. Did I have a woman here? There are ashes in the trays. Searching for butts, I find several with lipstick stains. Yes, a woman was here.

I touch the bedsheets. Still warm with shared warmth. Both pillows tousled. She has gone, though, and the Passenger is gone, and I am alone.

How long did it last this time?

I pick up the phone and ring Central. "What is the date?"

The computer's bland feminine voice replies, "Friday, December fourth, nineteen eighty-seven."

"The time?"

"Nine fifty-one, Eastern Standard Time."

"The weather forecast?"

"Predicted temperature, thirty-one. Wind from the north, sixteen miles an hour. Chances of precipitation slight."

"What do you recommend for a hangover?"

"Food or medication?"

"Anything you like," I say.

The computer mulls that one over for a while. Then it decides on both and activates my kitchen. The spigot yields cold tomato juice. Eggs begin to fry. From the medicine slot comes a purplish liquid. The Central Computer is always so thoughtful. Do the Passengers ever ride it, I wonder? What thrills could that hold for them? Surely it must be more exciting to borrow the million minds of Central than to live a while in the faulty short-circuited soul of a corroding human being!

December 4, Central said. Friday. So the Passenger had me for three nights.

I drink the purplish stuff and probe my memories in a gingerly way, as one might probe a festering sore.

I remember Tuesday morning. A bad time at work. None of the charts will come out right. The section manager is irritable; he has been taken by Passengers three times in five weeks, and his section is in disarray as a result, and his Christmas bonus is jeopardized. Even though it is customary not to penalize a person for lapses due to Passengers, according to the system, the section manager seems to feel he will be treated unfairly. So he treats us unfairly. We have a hard time. Revise the charts, fiddle with the program, check the fundamentals ten times over. Out they come: the detailed forecasts for price variations of public utility securities, February-April 1988. That afternoon we are to meet and discuss the charts and what they tell us.

I do not remember Tuesday afternoon.

That must have been when the Passenger took me. Perhaps at work; perhaps in the mahogany-paneled boardroom itself, during the conference. Pink concerned faces all about me; I cough, I lurch, I stumble from my seat. They shake their heads sadly. No one reaches for me. No one stops me. It is too dangerous to interfere with one who has a Passenger. The chances are great that a second Passenger lurks nearby in the discorporate state looking for a mount. So I am avoided. I leave the building.

After that, what?

Sitting in my room on bleak Friday morning, I eat my scrambled eggs and try to reconstruct the three lost nights.

Of course it is impossible. The conscious mind functions during the period of captivity, but upon withdrawal of the Passenger nearly every recollection goes, too. There is only a slight residue, a gritty film of faint and ghostly memories. The mount is never precisely the same person afterwards; though he cannot recall the details of his experience, he is subtly changed by it.

I try to recall.

A girl? Yes: lipstick on the butts. Sex, then, here in my room. Young? Old? Blond? Dark? Everything is hazy. How did my borrowed body behave? Was I a good lover? I try to be, when I am myself. I keep in shape. At 38, I can handle three sets of tennis on a summer afternoon without collapsing. I can make a woman glow as a woman is meant to glow. Not boasting: just categorizing. We have our skills. These are mine.

But Passengers, I am told, take wry amusement in controverting our skills. So would it have given my rider a kind of delight to find me a woman and force me to fail repeatedly with her?

I dislike that thought.

The fog is going from my mind now. The medicine prescribed by Central works rapidly. I eat, I shave, I stand under the vibrator until my skin is clean. I do my exercises. Did the Passenger exercise my body Wednesday and Thursday morning? Probably not. I must make up for that. I am close to middle age now; tonus lost is not easily regained.

I touch my toes twenty times, knees stiff.

I kick my legs in the air.

I lie flat and lift myself on pumping elbows.

The body responds, maltreated though it has been. It is the first bright moment of my awakening: to feel the inner tingling, to know that I still have vigor.

Fresh air is what I want next. Quickly I slip into my clothes and leave. There is no need for me to report to work today. They are aware that since Tuesday afternoon I have had a Passenger; they need not be aware that before dawn on Friday the Passenger departed. I will have a free day. I will walk the city's streets, stretching my limbs, repaying my body for the abuse it has suffered.

I enter the elevator. I drop fifty stories to the ground. I step out into the December dreariness.

The towers of New York rise about me.

In the street the cars stream forward. Drivers sit edgily at their wheels. One never knows when the driver of a nearby car will be borrowed, and there is always a moment of lapsed coordination as the Passenger takes over. Many lives are lost that way on our streets and highways; but never the life of a Passenger.

I begin to walk without purpose. I cross Fourteenth Street, heading north, listening to the soft violent purr of the electric engines. I see a boy jigging in the street and know he is being ridden. At Fifth and Twenty-second a prosperous-looking paunchy man approaches, his necktie askew, this morning's *Wall Street Journal* jutting from an overcoat pocket. He giggles. He thrusts out his tongue. Ridden. Ridden. I avoid him. Moving briskly, I come to the underpass that carries traffic below Thirty-fourth Street toward Queens, and pause for a moment to watch two adolescent girls quarreling at the rim of the pedestrian walk. One is a Negro. Her eyes are rolling in terror. The other pushes her closer to the railing. Ridden. But the Passenger does not have murder on its mind, merely pleasure. The Negro girl is released and falls in a huddled heap, trembling. Then she rises and runs. The other girl draws a long strand of gleaming hair into her mouth, chews on it, seems to awaken. She looks dazed.

I avert my eyes. One does not watch while a fellow sufferer is awakening. There is a morality of the ridden; we have so many new tribal mores in these dark days.

I hurry on.

Where am I going so hurriedly? Already I have walked more than a mile. I seem to be moving toward some goal, as though my Passenger still hunches in my skull, urging me about. But I know that is not so. For the moment, at least, I am free.

Can I be sure of that?

Cogito ergo sum no longer applies. We go on thinking even while we are ridden, and we live in quiet desperation, unable to halt our courses no matter how ghastly, no

matter how self-destructive. I am certain that I can distinguish between the condition of bearing a Passenger and
the condition of being free. But perhaps not. Perhaps I
bear a particularly devilish Passenger which has not quit
me at all, but which merely has receded to the cerebel-
lum, leaving me the illusion of freedom while all the time
surreptitiously driving me onward to some purpose of its
own.

Did we ever have more than that: the illusion of freedom?

But this is disturbing, the thought that I may be ridden
without realizing it. I burst out in heavy perspiration,
not merely from the exertion of walking. Stop. Stop here.
Why must you walk? You are at Forty-second Street.
There is the library. Nothing forces you onward. Stop a
while, I tell myself. Rest on the library steps.

I sit on the cold stone and tell myself that I have made
this decision for myself.

Have I? It is the old problem, free will versus determinism, translated into the foulest of forms. Determinism
is no longer a philosopher's abstraction; it is cold alien
tendrils sliding between the cranial sutures. The Passengers arrived three years ago. I have been ridden five
times since then. Our world is quite different now. But
we have adjusted even to this. We have adjusted. We
have our mores. Life goes on. Our governments rule, our
legislatures meet, our stock exchanges transact business as
usual, and we have methods for compensating for the
random havoc. It is the only way. What else can we do?
Shrivel in defeat? We have an enemy we cannot fight; at
best we can resist through endurance. So we endure.

The stone steps are cold against my body. In December few people sit here.

I tell myself that I made this long walk of my own free
will, that I halted of my own free will, that no Passenger
rides my brain now. Perhaps. Perhaps. I cannot let myself believe that I am not free.

Can it be, I wonder, that the Passenger left some lingering command in me? Walk to this place, halt at this
place? That is possible, too.

I look about me at the others on the library steps.

An old man, eyes vacant, sitting on newspaper. A boy
of thirteen or so with flaring nostrils. A plump woman.

Are all of them ridden? Passengers seem to cluster about me today. The more I study the ridden ones, the more convinced I become that I am, for the moment, free. The last time, I had three months of freedom between rides. Some people, they say, are scarcely ever free. Their bodies are in great demand, and they know only scattered bursts of freedom, a day here, a week there, an hour. We have never been able to determine how many Passengers infest our world. Millions, maybe. Or maybe five. Who can tell?

A wisp of snow curls down out of the gray sky. Central had said the chance of precipitation was slight. Are they riding Central this morning, too?

I see the girl.

She sits diagonally across from me, five steps up and a hundred feet away, her black skirt pulled up on her knees to reveal handsome legs. She is young. Her hair is deep, rich auburn. Her eyes are pale; at this distance, I cannot make out the precise color. She is dressed simply. She is younger than thirty. She wears a dark green coat, and her lipstick has a purplish tinge. Her lips are full, her nose slender, high-bridged, her eyebrows carefully plucked.

I know her.

I have spent the past three nights with her in my room. She is the one. Ridden, she came to me, and ridden, I slept with her. I am certain of this. The veil of memory opens, I see her slim body naked on my bed.

How can it be that I remember this?

It is too strong to be an illusion. Clearly this is something that I have been *permitted* to remember for reasons I cannot comprehend. And I remember more. I remember her soft gasping sounds of pleasure. I know that my own body did not betray me those three nights, nor did I fail her need.

And there is more. A memory of sinuous music; a scent of youth in her hair; the rustle of winter trees. Somehow she brings back to me a time of innocence, a time when I am young and girls are mysterious, a time of parties and dances and warmth and secrets.

I am drawn to her now.

There is an etiquette about such things, too. It is in poor taste to approach someone you have met while being ridden. Such an encounter gives you no privilege; a stranger remains a stranger, no matter what you and she may have done and said during your involuntary time together.

Yet I am drawn to her.

Why this violation of taboo? Why this raw breach of etiquette? I have never done this before. I have been scrupulous.

But I get to my feet and walk along the step on which I have been sitting, until I am below her, and I look up, and automatically she folds her ankles together and angles her knees as if in awareness that her position is not a modest one. I know from that gesture that she is not ridden now. My eyes meet hers. Her eyes are hazy green. She is beautiful, and I rack my memory for more details of our passion.

I climb step by step until I stand before her.

"Hello," I say.

She gives me a neutral look. She does not seem to recognize me. Her eyes are veiled, as one's eyes often are, just after the Passenger has gone. She purses her lips and appraises me in a distant way.

"Hello," she replies coolly. "I don't think I know you."

"No. You don't. But I have the feeling you don't want to be alone just now. And I know I don't." I try to persuade her with my eyes that my motives are decent. "There's snow in the air," I say. "We can find a warmer place. I'd like to talk to you."

"About what?"

"Let's go elsewhere, and I'll tell you. I'm Charles Roth."

"Helen Martin."

She gets to her feet. She still has not cast aside her cool neutrality; she is suspicious, ill at ease. But at least she is willing to go with me. A good sign.

"Is it too early in the day for a drink?" I ask.

"I'm not sure. I hardly know what time it is."

"Before noon."

"Let's have a drink anyway," she says, and we both smile.

We go to a cocktail lounge across the street. Sitting face to face in the darkness, we sip drinks, daiquiri for her, bloody mary for me. She relaxes a little. I ask myself what it is I want from her. The pleasure of her company, yes. Her company in bed? But I have already had that pleasure, three nights of it, though she does not know that. I want something more. Something more. What?

Her eyes are bloodshot. She has had little sleep these past three nights.

I say, "Was it very unpleasant for you?"

"What?"

"The Passenger."

A whiplash of reaction crosses her face. "How did you know I've had a Passenger?"

"I know."

"We aren't supposed to talk about it."

"I'm broadminded," I tell her. "My Passenger left me some time during the night. I was ridden since Tuesday afternoon."

"Mine left me about two hours ago, I think." Her cheeks color. She is doing something daring, talking like this. "I was ridden since Monday night. This was my fifth time."

"Mine also."

We toy with our drinks. Rapport is growing, almost without the need of words. Our recent experiences with Passengers give us something in common, although Helen does not realize how intimately we shared those experiences.

We talk. She is a designer of display windows. She has a small apartment several blocks from here. She lives alone. She asks me what I do. "Securities analyst," I tell her. She smiles. Her teeth are flawless. We have a second round of drinks. I am positive, now, that this is the girl who was in my room while I was ridden.

A seed of hope grows in me. It was a happy chance that brought us together again, so soon after we parted as dreamers. A happy chance, too, that some vestige of the dream lingered in my mind.

We have shared something, who knows what, and it must have been good to leave such a vivid imprint on me, and now I want to come to her conscious, aware, my own master, and renew that relationship, making it a real one this time. It is not proper, for I am trespassing on a privilege that is not mine except by virtue of our Passengers' brief presence in us. Yet I need her. I want her.

She seems to need me, too, without realizing who I am. But fear holds her back.

588   *Robert Silverberg*

I am frightened of frightening her, and I do not try to press my advantage too quickly. Perhaps she would take me to her apartment with her now, perhaps not, but I do not ask. We finish our drinks. We arrange to meet by the library steps again tomorrow. My hand momentarily brushes hers. Then she is gone.

I fill three ashtrays that night. Over and over I debate the wisdom of what I am doing. But why not leave her alone? I have no right to follow her. In the place our world has become, we are wisest to remain apart.

And yet—there is that stab of half-memory when I think of her. The blurred lights of lost chances behind the stairs, of girlish laughter in second-floor corridors, of stolen kisses, of tea and cake. I remember the girl with the orchid in her hair, and the one in the spangled dress, and the one with the child's face and the woman's eyes, all so long ago, all lost, all gone, and I tell myself that this one I will not lose, I will not permit her to be taken from me.

Morning comes, a quiet Saturday. I return to the library, hardly expecting to find her there, but she is there, on the steps, and the sight of her is like a reprieve. She looks wary, troubled; obviously she has done much thinking, little sleeping. Together we walk along Fifth Avenue. She is quite close to me, but she does not take my arm. Her steps are brisk, short, nervous.

I want to suggest that we go to her apartment instead of to the cocktail lounge. In these days we must move swiftly while we are free. But I know it would be a mistake to think of this as a matter of tactics. Coarse haste would be fatal, bringing me perhaps an ordinary victory, a numbing defeat within it. In any event her mood hardly seems promising. I look at her, thinking of string music and new snowfalls, and she looks toward the gray sky.

She says, "I can feel them watching me all the time. Like vultures swooping overhead, waiting, waiting. Ready to pounce."

"But there's a way of beating them. We can grab little scraps of life when they're not looking."

"They're *always* looking."

"No," I tell her. "There can't be enough of them for that. Sometimes they're looking the other way. And while they are, two people can come together and try to share warmth."

"But what's the use?"

"You're too pessimistic, Helen. They ignore us for months at a time. We have a chance. We have a chance."

But I cannot break through her shell of fear. She is paralyzed by the nearness of the Passengers, unwilling to begin anything for fear it will be snatched away by our tormentors. We reach the building where she lives, and I hope she will relent and invite me in. For an instant she wavers, but only for an instant: she takes my hand in both of hers, and smiles, and the smile fades, and she is gone, leaving me only with the words, "Let's meet at the library again tomorrow. Noon."

I make the long chilling walk home alone.

Some of her pessimism seeps into me that night. It seems futile for us to try to salvage anything. More than that: wicked for me to seek her out, shameful to offer a hesitant love when I am not free. In this world, I tell myself, we should keep well clear of others, so that we do not harm anyone when we are seized and ridden.

I do not go to meet her in the morning.

It is best this way, I insist, I have no business trifling with her. I imagine her at the library, wondering why I am late, growing tense, impatient, then annoyed. She will be angry with me for breaking our date, but her anger will ebb, and she will forget me quickly enough.

Monday comes. I return to work.

Naturally no one discusses my absence. It is as though I have never been away. The market is strong that morning. The work is challenging; it is mid-morning before I think of Helen at all. But once I think of her, I can think of nothing else. My cowardice in standing her up. The childishness of Saturday night's dark thoughts. Why accept fate so passively? Why give in? I want to fight, now, to carve out a pocket of security despite the odds. I feel a deep conviction that it can be done. The Passengers may never bother the two of us again, after all. And that flickering smile of hers outside her building Saturday, that momentary glow—it should have told me that behind her wall of fear she felt the same hopes. She was waiting for me to lead the way. And I stayed home instead.

At lunchtime I go to the library, convinced it is futile.

But she is there. She paces along the steps; the wind slices at her slender figure. I go to her.

She is silent a moment. "Hello," she says finally.

"I'm sorry about yesterday."

"I waited a long time for you."

I shrug. "I made up my mind that it was no use to come. But then I changed my mind again."

She tries to look angry. But I know she is pleased to see me again—why else did she come here today? She cannot hide her inner pleasure. Nor can I. I point across the street to the cocktail lounge.

"A daiquiri?" I say. "As a peace offering?"

"All right."

Today the lounge is crowded, but we find a booth somehow. There is a brightness in her eyes that I have not seen before. I sense that a barrier is crumbling within her.

"You're less afraid of me, Helen," I say.

"I've never been afraid of you. I'm afraid of what could happen if we take the risks."

"Don't be. Don't be."

"I'm trying not to be afraid. But sometimes it seems so hopeless. Since *they* came here—"

"We can still try to live our own lives."

"Maybe."

"We have to. Let's make a pact, Helen. No more gloom. No more worrying about the terrible things that might just maybe happen. All right?"

A pause. Then a cool hand against mine.

"All right."

We finish our drinks, and I present my Credit Central to pay for them, and we go outside. I want her to tell me to forget about this afternoon's work and come home with her. It is inevitable now that she will ask me, and better sooner than later.

We walk a block. She does not offer the invitation. I sense the struggle inside her, and I wait, letting that struggle reach its own resolution without interference from me. We walk a second block. Her arm is through mine, but she talks only of her work, of the weather, and it is a remote, arm's-length conversation. At the next corner she

swings around, away from her apartment, back toward
the cocktail lounge. I try to be patient with her.

I have no need to rush things now, I tell myself. Her
body is not a secret to me. We have begun our relationship topsy-turvy, with the physical part first; now it will
take time to work backward to the more difficult part
that some people call love.

But of course she is not aware that we have known
each other that way. The wind blows swirling snowflakes
in our faces, and somehow the cold sting awakens honesty
in me. I know what I must say. I must relinquish my unfair advantage.

I tell her, "While I was ridden last week, Helen, I had
a girl in my room."

"Why talk of such things now?"

"I have to, Helen. You were the girl."

She halts. She turns to me. People hurry past us in the
street. Her face is very pale with dark red spots growing
in her cheeks.

"That's not funny, Charles."

"It wasn't meant to be. You were with me from Tuesday night to early Friday morning."

"How can you possibly know that?"

"I do. I do. The memory is clear. Somehow it remains,
Helen. I see your whole body."

"Stop it, Charles."

"We were very good together," I say. "We must have
pleased our Passengers because we were so good. To see
you again—it was like waking from a dream, and finding
that the dream was real, the girl right there—"

"No!"

"Let's go to your apartment and begin again."

She says, "You're being deliberately filthy, and I don't
know why, but there wasn't any reason for you to spoil
things. Maybe I was with you and maybe I wasn't, but
you wouldn't know it, and if you did know it, you should
keep your mouth shut about it, and—"

"You have a birthmark the size of a dime," I say,
"about three inches below your left breast."

She sobs and hurls herself at me, there in the street.
Her long silvery nails assail me. No one pays attention;
those who pass by assume we are ridden, and turn their
heads. She is all fury, but I have my arms around hers

like metal bands, so that she can only stamp and snort, and her body is close against mine. She is rigid, anguished.

In a low, urgent voice, I say, "We'll defeat them, Helen. We'll finish what they started. Don't fight me. There's no reason to fight me. I know, it's a fluke that I remember you, but let me go with you and I'll prove that we belong together."

"Let—go—"

"Please. Please. Why should we be enemies? I don't mean you any harm. I love you, Helen. Do you remember, when we were kids, we could play at being in love? I did; you must have done it, too. Sixteen, seventeen years old. The whispers, the conspiracies—all a big game, and we knew it. But the game's over. We can't afford to tease and run. We have so little time when we're free—we have to trust, to open ourselves—"

"It's wrong."

"No. Just because it's the stupid custom for two people brought together by Passengers to avoid one another, that doesn't mean we have to follow it. Helen—Helen—"

Something in my tone registers with her. She ceases to struggle. Her rigid body softens. She looks up at me, her tear-streaked face thawing, her eyes blurred.

"Trust me," I say. "Trust me, Helen!"

She hesitates. Then she smiles.

In that moment I feel the chill at the back of my skull, the sensation as of a steel needle driven deep through bone. I stiffen. My arms drop away from her. For an instant, I lose touch, and when the mists clear all is different.

"Charles?" she says. *"Charles?"*

Her knuckles are against her teeth. I turn, ignoring her, and go back into the cocktail lounge. A young man sits in one of the front booths. His dark hair gleams with pomade; his cheeks are smooth. His eyes meet mine.

I sit down. He orders drinks. We do not talk.

My hand falls on his wrist, and remains there. The bartender, serving the drinks, scowls but says nothing. We sip our cocktails and put the drained glasses down.

"Let's go," the young man says.

I follow him out.

TIME CONSIDERED AS A HELIX OF SEMI-PRECIOUS STONES

by Samuel R. Delany

Lay ordinate and abscissa on the century. Now cut me a quadrant. Third quadrant if you please. I was born in 'fifty. Here it's 'seventy-five.

At sixteen they let me leave the orphange. Dragging the name they'd hung me with (Harold Clancy Everet, and me a mere lad—how many monickers have I had since; but don't worry, you'll recognize my smoke) over the hills of East Vermont, I came to a decision:

Me and Pa Michaels, who had belligerently given me a job at the request of *The Official* looking *Document* with which the orphanage sends you packing, were running Pa Michaels' dairy farm, i.e., thirteen thousand three hundred sixty-two piebald Guernseys all asleep in their stainless coffins, nourished and drugged by pink liquid flowing in clear plastic veins (stuff is sticky and messes up your hands), exercised with electric pulsers that make their muscles quiver, them not half-awake, and the milk just a-pouring down into stainless cisterns. Anyway. The Decision (as I stood there in the fields one afternoon like the Man with the Hoe, exhausted with three hard hours of physical labor, contemplating the machinery of the universe through the fog of fatigue): With all of Earth, and Mars, and the Outer Satellites filled up with people and what-all, there had to be something more than this. I decided to get some.

So I stole a couple of Pa's credit cards, one of his helicopters, and a bottle of white lightning the geezer made

593

himself, and took off. Ever try to land a stolen helicopter
on the roof of the Pan Am building, drunk? Jail, schmail,
and some hard knocks later I had attained to wisdom. But
remember this o best beloved: I have done three honest
hours on a dairy farm less than ten years back. And nobody has ever called me Harold Clancy Everet again.

Hank Culafroy Eckles (red-headed, a bit vague, six-foot-
two) strolled out of the baggage room at the spaceport,
carrying a lot of things that weren't his in a small briefcase.

Beside him the Business Man was saying, "You young
fellows today upset me. Go back to Bellona, I say. Just
because you got into trouble with that little blonde you
were telling me about is no reason to leap worlds, come
on all glum. Even quit your job!"

Hank stops and grins weakly: "Well . . ."

"Now I admit, you have your real needs, which maybe
we older folks don't understand, but you have to show
some responsibility toward . . ." He notices Hank has
stopped in front of a door marked MEN. "Oh. Well. Eh."
He grins strongly. "I've enjoyed meeting you, Hank. It's
always nice when you meet somebody worth talking to on
these damned crossings. So long."

Out same door, ten minutes later, comes Harmony C.
Eventide, six-foot even (one of the false heels was
cracked, so I stuck both of them under a lot of paper
towels), brown hair (not even my hairdresser knows for
sure), oh so dapper and of his time, attired in the bad
taste that is oh so tasteful, a sort of man with whom no
Business Men would start a conversation. Took the regu-
lation 'copter from the port over to the Pan Am building
(Yeah. Really. Drunk), came out of Grand Central Station, and strode along Forty-second towards Eighth Avenue, with a lot of things that weren't mine in a small
briefcase.

The evening is carved from light.

Crossed the plastiplex pavement of the Great White
Way—I think it makes people look weird, all that white
light under their chins—and skirted the crowds coming up
in elevators from the subway, the sub-sub-way, and the
sub-sub-sub (eighteen and first week out of jail, I hung
around here, snatching stuff from people—but daintily,

daintly, so they never knew they'd been snatched), bulled my way through a crowd of giggling, goo-chewing school girls with flashing lights in their hair, all very embarrassed at wearing transparent plastic blouses which had just been made legal again (I hear the breast has been scene [as opposed to obscene] on and off since the seventeenth century) so I stared appreciatively; they giggled some more. I thought, Christ, when I was that age, I was on a God-damn dairy farm, and took the thought no further.

The ribbon of news lights looping the triangular structure of Communication, Inc., explained in Basic English how Senator Regina Abolafia was preparing to begin her investigation of Organized Crime in the City. Days I'm so happy I'm disorganized I couldn't begin to tell.

Near Ninth Avenue I took my briefcase into a long, crowded bar. I hadn't been in New York for two years, but on my last trip through ofttimes a man used to hang out here who had real talent for getting rid of things that weren't mine profitably, safely, fast. No idea what the chances were I'd find him. I pushed among a lot of guys drinking beer. Here and there were a number of well-escorted old bags wearing last month's latest. Scarfs of smoke gentled through the noise. I don't like such places. Those there younger than me were all morphadine heads or feeble-minded. Those older only wished more younger ones would come. I pried my way to the bar and tried to get the attention of one of the little men in white coats.

The lack of noise behind me made me glance back.

She wore a sheath of veiling closed at the neck and wrists with huge brass pins (oh so tastefully on the border of taste); her left arm was bare, her right covered with chiffon like wine. She had it down a lot better than I did. But such an ostentatious demonstration of one's understanding of the fine points was absolutely out of place in a place like this. People were making a great show of not noticing.

She pointed to her wrist, blood-colored nail indexing a yellow-orange fragment in the brass claw of her wristlet. "Do you know what this is, Mr. Eldrich?" she asked; at the same time the veil across her face cleared, and her eyes were ice; her brows, black.

Three thoughts: (One) She is a lady of fashion, because coming in from Bellona I'd read the *Delta* coverage of the "fading fabrics" whose hue and opacity were controlled by cunning jewels at the wrist. (Two) During my last trip through, when I was younger and Harry Calamine Eldrich, I didn't do anything *too* illegal (though one loses track of these things); still I didn't believe I could be dragged off to the calaboose for anything more than thirty days under that name. (Three) The stone she pointed to. . . .

". . . Jasper?" I asked.

She waited for me to say more; I waited for her to give me reason to let on I knew what she was waiting for (when I was in jail, Henry James was my favorite author. He really was).

"Jasper," she confirmed.

"—Jasper . . ." I reopened the ambiguity she had tried so hard to dispel.

" . . . Jasper—" But she was already faltering, suspecting I suspected her certainty to be ill-founded.

"Okay. Jasper." But from her face I knew she had seen in my face a look that had finally revealed I knew she knew I knew.

"Just whom have you got me confused with, ma'am?"

Jasper, this month, is the Word.

Jasper is the pass/code/warning that the Singers of the Cities (who last month sang "Opal" from their divine injuries; and on Mars I'd heard the Word and used it thrice, along with devious imitations, to fix possession of what was not rightfully my own; and even there I pondered Singers and their wounds, relay by word of mouth for that loose and roguish fraternity with which I have been involved (in various guises) these nine years. It goes out new every thirty days; and within hours every brother knows it, throughout six worlds and worldlets. Usually it's grunted at you by some blood-soaked bastard staggering into your arms from a dark doorway; hissed at you as you pass a shadowed alley; scrawled on a paper scrap pressed into your palm by some nasty-grimy moving too fast through the crowd. And this month, it was: Jasper.

Here are some alternate translations:

Help!

or

I need help!

or

I can help you!
or
You are being watched!
or
They're not watching now, so *move!*

Final point of syntax: If the Word is used properly, you should never have to think twice about what it means in a given situation. Fine point of usage: Never trust anyone who uses it improperly.

I waited for her to finish waiting.

She opened a wallet in front of me. "Chief of Special Services Department Maudline Hinkle," she read without looking at what it said below the silver badge.

"You have that very well," I said, "Maud." Then I frowned. "Hinkle?"

"Me."

"I know you're not going to believe this, Maud. You look like a woman who has no patience with her mistakes. But my name is Eventide. Not Eldrich. Harmony C. Eventide. And isn't it lucky for all and sundry that the Word changes tonight?" Passed the way it is, the Word is no big secret to the cops. But I've met policemen up to a week after change date who were not privy.

"Well, then: Harmony. I want to talk to you."

I raised an eyebrow.

She raised one back and said, "Look, if you want to be called Henrietta, it's all right by me. But you listen."

"What do you want to talk about?"

"Crime, Mr. . . . ?"

"Eventide. I'm going to call you Maud, so you might as well call me Harmony. It really is my name."

Maud smiled. She wasn't a young woman. I think she even had a few years on Business Man. But she used make-up better than he did. "I probably know more about crime than you do," she said. "In fact I wouldn't be surprised if you hadn't even heard of my branch of the police department. What does Special Services mean to you?"

"That's right, I've never heard of it."

"You've been more or less avoiding the Regular Service with alacrity for the past seven years."

"Oh, Maud, really—"

"Special Services is reserved for people whose nuisance

value has suddenly taken a sharp rise . . . a sharp enough rise to make our little lights start blinking."

"Surely I haven't done anything so dreadful that—"

"We don't look at what you do. A computer does that for us. We simply keep checking the first derivative of the graphed-out curve that bears your number. Your slope is rising sharply."

"Not even the dignity of a name—"

"We're the most efficient department in the Police Organization. Take it as bragging if you wish. Or just a piece of information."

"Well, well, well," I said. "Have a drink?" The little man in the white coat left us two, looked puzzled at Maud's finery, then went to do something else.

"Thanks." She downed half her glass like someone stauncher than that wrist would indicate. "It doesn't pay to go after most criminals. Take your big-time racketeers, Farnesworth, The Hawk, Blavatskia. Take your little snatch-purses, small-time pushers, housebreakers, or vice-impresarios. Both at the top and the bottom of the scale, their incomes are pretty stable. They don't really upset the social boat. Regular Services handles them both. They think they do a good job. We're not going to argue. But say a little pusher starts to become a big-time pusher; a medium-sized vice-impresario sets his sights on becoming a full-fledged racketeer; that's when you get problems with socially unpleasant repercussions. That's when Special Services arrive. We have a couple of techniques that work remarkably well."

"You're going to tell me about them, aren't you."

"They work better that way," she said. "One of them is hologramic information storage. Do you know what happens when you cut a hologram plate in half?"

"The three dimensional image is . . . cut in half?"

She shook her head. "You get the whole image, only fuzzier, slightly out of focus."

"Now I didn't know that."

"And if you cut it in half again, it just gets fuzzier still. But even if you have a square centimeter of the original hologram, you still have the whole image—unrecognizable but complete."

I mumbled some appreciative *m*'s.

"Each pinpoint of photographic emulsion on a hologram plate, unlike a photograph, gives information about the entire scene being hologrammed. By analogy, hologramic information storage simply means that each bit of information we have—about you, let us say—relates to your entire career, your overall situation, the complete set of tensions between you and your environment. Specific facts about specific misdemeanors or felonies we leave to Regular Services. As soon as we have enough of our kind of data, our method is vastly more efficient for keeping track—even predicting—where you are or what you may be up to."

"Fascinating," I said. "One of the most amazing paranoid syndromes I've ever run up against. I mean just starting a conversation with someone in a bar. Often, in a hospital situation, I've encountered stranger—"

"In your past," she said matter-of-factly, "I see cows and helicopters. In your not too distant future, there are helicopters and hawks."

"And tell me, oh Good Witch of the West, just how—" Then I got all upset inside. Because nobody is supposed to know about that stint with Pa Michaels save thee and me. Even the Regular Service, who pulled me, out of my mind, from that whirlibird bouncing towards the edge of the Pan Am, never got that one from me. I'd eaten the credit cards when I saw them waiting, and the serial numbers had been filed off everything that could have had a serial number on it by someone more competent than I: good Mister Michaels had boasted to me, my first lonely, drunken night at the farm, how he'd gotten the thing in hot from New Hampshire.

"But why"—it appalls me the clichés to which anxiety will drive us—"are you telling me all this?"

She smiled, and her smile faded behind her veil. "Information is only meaningful when shared," said a voice that was hers from the place of her face.

"Hey, look, I—"

"You may be coming into quite a bit of money soon. If I can calculate right, I will have a helicopter full of the city's finest arriving to take you away as you accept it into your hot little hands. That is a piece of information . . ." She stepped back. Someone stepped between us.

"Hey, Maud—"

"You can do whatever you want with it."

The bar was crowded enough so that to move quickly was to make enemies. I don't know—I lost her and made enemies. Some weird characters there: with greasy hair that hung in spikes, and three of them had dragons tattooed on their scrawny shoulders, still another with an eye patch, and yet another raked nails black with pitch at my cheek (we're two minutes into a vicious free-for-all, case you missed the transition. I did) and some of the women were screaming. I hit and ducked, and then the tenor of the brouhaha changed. Somebody sang, "Jasper!" the way she is supposed to be sung. And it meant the heat (the ordinary, bungling Regular Service I had been eluding these seven years) were on their way. The brawl spilled into the street. I got between two nasty-grimies who were doing things appropriate with one another, but made the edge of the crowd with no more wounds than could be racked up to shaving. The fight had broken into sections. I left one and ran into another that, I realized a moment later, was merely a ring of people standing around somebody who had apparently gotten really messed.

Someone was holding people back.

Somebody else was turning him over.

Curled up in a puddle of blood was the little guy I hadn't seen in two years who used to be so good at getting rid of things not mine.

Trying not to hit people with my briefcase, I ducked between the hub and the bub. When I saw my first ordinary policeman, I tried very hard to look like somebody who had just stepped up to see what the rumpus was.

It worked.

I turned down Ninth Avenue and got three steps into an inconspicuous but rapid lope—

"Hey, wait! Wait up there . . ."

I recognized the voice (after two years, coming at me just like that, I recognized it) but kept going.

"Wait! It's me, Hawk!"

And I stopped.

You haven't heard his name before in this story; Maud mentioned *the* Hawk, who is a multi-millionaire racketeer basing his operations on a part of Mars I've never been (though he has his claws sunk to the spurs in illegalities throughout the system) and somebody else entirely.

I took three steps back towards the doorway.

A boy's laugh there: "Oh, man. You look like you just did something you shouldn't."

"Hawk?" I asked the shadow.

He was still the age when two years' absence means an inch or so taller.

"You're still hanging out around here?" I asked.

"Sometimes."

He was an amazing kid.

"Look, Hawk, I got to get out of here." I glanced back at the rumpus.

"Get." He stepped down. "Can I come, too?"

Funny. "Yeah." It makes me feel very funny, him asking that. "Come on."

By the street lamp half a block down, I saw his hair was still pale as split pine. He could have been a nasty-grimy: very dirty black denim jacket, no shirt beneath; very ripe pair of black-jeans—I mean in the dark you could tell. He went barefoot; and the only way you can tell on a dark street someone's been going barefoot for days in New York is to know already. As we reached the corner, he grinned up at me under the street lamp and shrugged his jacket together over the welts and furrows marring his chest and belly. His eyes were very green. Do you recognize him? If by some failure of information dispersal throughout the worlds and worldlets you haven't, walking beside me beside the Hudson was Hawk the Singer.

"Hey, how long have you been back?"

"A few hours," I told him.

"What'd you bring?"

"Really want to know?"

He shoved his hands into his pockets and cocked his head. "Sure."

I made the sound of an adult exasperated by a child. "All right." We had been walking the waterfront for a block now; there was nobody about. "Sit down." So he straddled the beam along the siding, one filthy foot dangling above the flashing black Hudson. I sat in front of him and ran my thumb around the edge of the briefcase.

Hawk hunched his shoulders and leaned. "Hey . . ." He flashed green questioning at me. "Can I touch?"

I shrugged. "Go ahead."

He grubbed among them with fingers that were all

knuckle and bitten nail. He picked two up, put them down, picked up three others. "Hey!" he whispered. "How much are all these worth?"

"About ten times more than I hope to get. I have to get rid of them fast."

He glanced down past his toes. "You could always throw them in the river."

"Don't be dense. I was looking for a guy who used to hang around that bar. He was pretty efficient." And half the Hudson away a water-bound foil skimmed above the foam. On her deck were parked a dozen helicopters—being ferried up to the Patrol Field near Verrazano, no doubt. But for moments I looked back and forth between the boy and the transport, getting all paranoid about Maud. But the boat *mmmm*ed into the darkness. "My man got a little cut up this evening."

Hawk put the tips of his fingers in his pockets and shifted his position.

"Which leaves me up tight. I didn't think he'd take them all, but at least he could have turned me on to some other people who might."

"I'm going to a party later on this evening—" he paused to gnaw on the wreck of his little fingernail—"where you might be able to sell them. Alexis Spinnel is having a party for Regina Abolafia at Tower Top."

"Tower Top . . . ?" It had been a while since I palled around with Hawk. Hell's Kitchen at ten; Tower Top at midnight—

"I'm just going because Edna Silem will be there."

Edna Silem is New York's eldest Singer.

Senator Abolafia's name had ribboned above me in lights once that evening. And somewhere among the endless magazines I'd perused coming in from Mars, I remember Alexis Spinnel's name sharing a paragraph with an awful lot of money.

"I'd like to see Edna again," I said offhandedly. "But she wouldn't remember me." Folk like Spinnel and his social ilk have a little game, I'd discovered during the first leg of my acquaintance with Hawk. He who can get the most Singers of the City under one roof wins. There are five Singers of New York (a tie for second place with Lux on Iapetus). Tokyo leads with seven. "It's a two Singer party?"

"More likely four . . . if I go."

The inaugural ball for the mayor gets four.

I raised the appropriate eyebrow.

"I have to pick up the Word from Edna. It changes tonight."

"All right," I said. "I don't know what you have in mind, but I'm game." I closed the case.

We walked back towards Times Square. When we got to Eighth Avenue and the first of the plastiplex, Hawk stopped. "Wait a minute," he said. Then he buttoned his jacket up to his neck. "Okay."

Strolling through the streets of New York with a Singer (two years back I'd spent much time wondering if that were wise for a man of my profession) is probably the best camouflage possible for a man of my profession. Think of the last time you glimpsed your favorite Tri-D star turning the corner of Fifty-seventh. Now be honest. Would you really recognize the little guy in the tweed jacket half a pace behind him?

Half the people we passed in Times Square recognized him. With his youth, funereal garb, black feet and ash pale hair, he was easily the most colorful of Singers. Smiles; narrowed eyes; very few actually pointed or stared.

"Just exactly who is going to be there who might be able to take this stuff off my hands?"

"Well, Alexis prides himself on being something of an adventurer. They might just take his fancy. And he can give you more than you can get peddling them in the street."

"You'll tell him they're all hot?"

"It will probably make the idea that much more intriguing. He's a creep."

"You say so, friend."

We went down into the sub-sub. The man at the change booth started to take Hawk's coin, then looked up. He began three or four words that were unintelligible through his grin, then just gestured us through.

"Oh," Hawk said, "thank you," with ingenuous surprise, as though this were the first, delightful time such a thing had happened. (Two years ago he had told me sagely, "As soon as I start looking like I expect it, it'll

stop happening." I was still impressed by the way he wore
his notoriety. The time I'd met Edna Silem, and I'd mentioned this, she said with the same ingenuousness, "But
that's what we're chosen for.")

In the bright car we sat on the long seat; Hawk's hands
were beside him, one foot rested on the other. Down from
us a gaggle of bright-bloused goo-chewers giggled and
pointed and tried not to be noticed at it. Hawk didn't
look at all, and I tried not to be noticed looking.

Dark patterns rushed the window.

Things below the gray floor hummed.

Once a lurch.

Leaning once, we came out of the ground.

Outside, the city tried on its thousand sequins, then
threw them away behind the trees of Ft. Tryon. Suddenly the windows across from us grew bright scales. Behind them girders reeled by. We got out on the platform
under a light rain. The sign said TWELVE TOWERS STATION.

By the time we reached the street, however, the shower
had stopped. Leaves above the wall shed water down the
brick. "If I'd known I was bringing someone, I'd have had
Alex send a car for us. I told him it was fifty-fifty I'd
come."

"Are you sure it's all right for me to tag along then?"

"Didn't you come up here with me once before?"

"I've even been up here once before that," I said. "Do
you still think it's . . ."

He gave me a withering look. Well; Spinnel would be
delighted to have Hawk even if he dragged along a whole
gang of real nasty-grimies—Singers are famous for that
sort of thing. With one more or less presentable thief,
Spinnel was getting off light. Beside us rocks broke away
into the city. Behind the gate to our left the gardens
rolled up towards the first of the towers. The twelve immense, luxury apartment buildings menaced the lower
clouds.

"Hawk the Singer," Hawk the Singer said into the
speaker at the side of the gate. *Clang* and tic-tic-tic and
Clang. We walked up the path to the doors and doors of
glass.

A cluster of men and women in evening dress were
coming out. Three tiers of doors away they saw us. You
could see them frowning at the guttersnipe who'd some-

how gotten into the lobby (for a moment I thought one of
them was Maud because she wore a sheath of the fading
fabric, but she turned; beneath her veil her face was dark
as roasted coffee); one of the men recognized him, said
something to the others. When they passed us, they were
smiling. Hawk paid about as much attention to them as
he had to the girls on the subway. But when they'd
passed, he said, "One of those guys was looking at you."

"Yeah. I saw."

"Do you know why?"

"He was trying to figure out whether we'd met before."

"Had you?"

I nodded. "Right about where I met you, only back
when I'd just gotten out of jail. I told you I'd been here
once before."

"Oh."

Blue carpet covered three-quarters of the lobby. A
great pool filled the rest in which a row of twelve foot
trellises stood, crowned with flaming braziers. The lobby
itself was three stories high, domed and mirror-tiled.

Twisting smoke curled towards the ornate grill. Broken
reflections sagged and recovered on the walls.

The elevator door folded about us its foil petals. There
was the distinct feeling of not moving while seventy-five
stories shucked down around us.

We got out on the landscaped roof garden. A very
tanned, very blond man wearing an apricot jump-suit,
from the collar of which emerged a black turtleneck
dicky, came down the rocks (artificial) between the ferns
(real) growing along the stream (real water; phony current).

"Hello! Hello!" Pause. "I'm terribly glad you decided
to come after all." Pause. "For a while I thought you
weren't going to make it." The Pauses were to allow Hawk
to introduce me. I was dressed so that Spinnel had no way
of telling whether I was a miscellaneous Nobel laureate
that Hawk happened to have been dining with, or a varlet
whose manners and morals were even lower than mine
happen to be.

"Shall I take your jacket?" Alexis offered.

Which meant he didn't know Hawk as well as he would
like people to think. But I guess he was sensitive enough

to realize from the little cold things that happened in the boy's face that he should forget his offer.

He nodded to me, smiling—about all he could do—and we strolled towards the gathering.

Edna Silem was sitting on a transparent inflated hassock. She leaned forward, holding her drink in both hands, arguing politics with the people sitting on the grass before her. She was the first person I recognized (hair of tarnished silver; voice of scrap brass). Jutting from the cuffs of her mannish suit, her wrinkled hands about her goblet, shaking with the intensity of her pronouncements, were heavy with stones and silver. As I ran my eyes back to Hawk, I saw half a dozen whose names/faces sold magazines, music, sent people to the theater (the drama critic for *Delta,* wouldn't you know), and even the mathematician from Princeton I'd read about a few months ago who'd come up with the "quasar/quark" explanation.

There was one woman my eyes kept returning to. On glance three I recognized her as the New Fascistas' most promising candidate for president, Senator Abolafia. Her arms were folded, and she was listening intently to the discussion that had narrowed to Edna and an overly gregarious younger man whose eyes were puffy from what could have been the recent acquisition of contact lenses.

"But don't you feel, Mrs. Silem, that—"

"You must remember when you make predictions like that—"

"Mrs. Silem, I've seen statistics that—"

"You *must* remember"—her voice tensed, lowered till the silence between the words was as rich as the voice was sparse and metallic—"that if everything, *everything* were known, statistical estimates would be unnecessary. The science of probability gives mathematical expression to our ignorance, not to our wisdom," which I was thinking was an interesting second installment to Maud's lecture when Edna looked up and exclaimed, "Why, Hawk!"

Everyone turned.

"I *am* glad to see you. Lewis, Ann," she called: there were two other Singers there already (he dark, she pale, both tree-slender; their faces made you think of pools without drain or tribute come upon in the forest, clear and very still; husband and wife, they had been made Singers together the day before their marriage seven years ago), "he hasn't deserted us after all!" Edna stood, extended her arm over the heads of the people sitting, and barked across her knuckles as though her voice were a pool cue. "Hawk, there are people here arguing with me who don't know nearly as much as you about the subject. You'd be on my side, now wouldn't you—"

"Mrs. Silem, I didn't mean to—" from the floor.

Then her arms swung six degrees, her fingers, eyes, and mouth opened. "You!" Me. "My dear, if there's anyone I never expected to see here! Why it's been almost two years, hasn't it?" Bless Edna; the place where she and Hawk and I had spent a long, beery evening together had more resembled that bar than Tower Top. "Where have you been keeping yourself?"

"Mars, mostly," I admitted. "Actually I just came back today." It's so much fun to be able to say things like that in a place like this.

"Hawk—both of you—" (which meant either she had forgotten my name, or she remembered me well enough not to abuse it) "come over here and help me drink up Alexis' good liquor." I tried not to grin as we walked towards her. If she remembered anything, she certainly recalled my line of business and must have been enjoying this as much as I was.

Relief spread Alexis' face: he knew now I was *someone* if not *which* someone I was.

As we passed Lewis and Ann, Hawk gave the two Singers one of his luminous grins. They returned shadowed smiles. Lewis nodded. Ann made a move to touch his arm, but left the motion unconcluded; and the company noted the interchange.

Having found out what we wanted, Alex was preparing large glasses of it over crushed ice when the puffy-eyed gentleman stepped up for a refill. "But, Mrs. Silem, then what do you feel validly opposes such political abuses?"

Regina Abolafia wore a white silk suit. Nails, lips and hair were one color; and on her breast was a worked copper pin. It's always fascinated me to watch people used to being the center thrust to the side. She swirled her glass, listening.

"I oppose them," Edna said. "Hawk opposes them. Lewis and Ann oppose them. We, ultimately, are what you have." And her voice had taken on that authoritative resonance only Singers can assume.

Then Hawk's laugh snarled through the conversational fabric.

We turned.

He'd sat cross-legged near the hedge. "Look . . ." he whispered.

Now people's gazes followed his. He was looking at Lewis and Ann. She, tall and blonde, he, dark and taller, were standing very quietly, a little nervously, eyes closed (Lewis' lips were apart).

"Oh," whispered someone who should have known better, "they're going to . . ."

I watched Hawk because I'd never had a chance to observe one Singer at another's performance. He put the soles of his feet together, grasped his toes, and leaned forward, veins making blue rivers on his neck. The top button of his jacket had come loose. Two scar ends showed over his collarbone. Maybe nobody noticed but me.

I saw Edna put her glass down with a look of beaming anticipatory pride. Alex, who had pressed the autobar (odd how automation has become the upper crust's way of flaunting the labor surplus) for more crushed ice, looked up, saw what was about to happen, and pushed the cut-off button. The autobar hummed to silence. A breeze (artificial or real, I couldn't tell you) came by, and the trees gave us a final *shush*.

One at a time, then in duet, then singly again, Lewis and Ann sang.

Singers are people who look at things, then go and tell people what they've seen. What makes them Singers is their ability to make people listen. That is the most magnificent over-simplification I can give. Eighty-six-year-old El Posado in Rio de Janeiro saw a block of tenements collapse, ran to the Avenida del Sol and began improvising, in rhyme and meter (not all that hard in rhyme-rich Portuguese), tears runneling his dusty cheeks, his voice clashing with the palm swards above the sunny street. Hundreds of people stopped to listen; a hundred more; and another hundred. And they told hundreds more what they had heard. Three hours later, hundreds from among them had arrived at the scene with blankets, food, money, shovels, and more incredibly, the willingness and ability to organize themselves and work within that organization. No Tri-D report of a disaster has ever produced that sort of reaction. El Posado is historically considered the first Singer. The second was Miriamne in the roofed city of Lux, who for thirty years walked through the metal street, singing the glories of the rings of Saturn—the colonists can't look at them without aid because of the ultraviolet the rings set up. But Miriamne, with her strange cataracts, each dawn walked to the edge of the city, looked, saw, and came back to sing of what she saw. All of which would have meant nothing except that during the days she did not sing—through illness, or once she was on a visit to another city to which her fame had spread—the Lux Stock Exchange would go down, the number of violent crimes rise. Nobody could explain it. All they could do was proclaim her Singer. Why did the institution of Singers come about, springing up in just about every urban center throughout the system? Some have speculated that it was a spontaneous reaction to the mass media which blanket our lives. While Tri-D and radio and news-tapes disperse information all over the worlds, they also spread a sense of alienation from first-hand experience. (How many people still go to sports events or a political rally with their little receivers plugged to their ears to let them know that what they see is really happening?) The first Singers were proclaimed by the people around them. Then, there was a period where anyone could proclaim himself who wanted to, and people either responded to him or laughed him into oblivion. But by the time I was left on the doostep of somebody who didn't want me, most cities had more or less established an unofficial quota. When a position is left open today, the remaining Singers choose who is going to fill it. The required talents are poetic, theatrical, as well as a certain charisma that is generated in the tensions between the personality and the publicity web a Singer is immediately snared in. Before he became a Singer, Hawk had gained something of a prodigious reputation with a book of poems published when he was fifteen. He was touring universities and giving readings, but the reputation was still small enough so that he was

amazed that I had ever heard of him, that evening we encountered in Central Park (I had just spent a pleasant
thirty days as a guest of the city and it's amazing what
you find in the Tombs Library). It was a few weeks after
his sixteenth birthday. His Singership was to be announced in four days, though he had been informed already. We sat by the lake till dawn while he weighed and
pondered and agonized over the coming responsibility.
Two years later, he's still the youngest Singer in six worlds
by half a dozen years. Before becoming a Singer, a person need not have been a poet, but most are either that or
actors. But the roster through the system includes a
longshoreman, two university professors, an heiress to the
Silitax millions (Tack it down with Silitax), and at
least two persons of such dubious background that the
ever-hungry-for-sensation Publicity Machine itself has
agreed not to let any of it past the copy editors. But
wherever their origins, these diverse and flamboyant living myths sang of love, of death, of the changing of seasons,
social classes, governments, and the palace guard. They
sang before large crowds, small ones, to an individual laborer coming home from the city's docks, on slum street
corners, in club cars of commuter trains, in the elegant
gardens atop Twelve Towers, to Alex Spinnel's select
soireé. But it has been illegal to reproduce the "Songs"
of the Singers by mechanical means (including publishing
the lyrics) since the institution arose, and I respect the
law, I do, as only a man in my profession can. I offer the
explanation then in place of Lewis' and Ann's song.

They finished, opened their eyes, stared about with expressions that could have been embarrassment, could
have been contempt.

Hawk was leaning forward with a look of rapt approval. Edna was smiling politely. I had the sort of grin
on my face that breaks out when you've been vastly
moved and vastly pleased. Lewis and Ann had sung su-
perbly.

Alex began to breathe again, glancing around to see
what state everybody else was in, saw, and pressed the
autobar, which began to hum and crush ice. No clap-
ping, but the appreciative sounds began; people were nodding, commenting, whispering. Regina Abolafia went over

to Lewis to say something. I tried to listen until Alex shoved a glass into my elbow.

"Oh, I'm sorry . . ."

I transferred my briefcase to the other hand and took the drink smiling. When Senator Abolafia left the two Singers, they were holding hands and looking at one another a little sheepishly. They sat down again.

The party drifted in conversational groups through the gardens, through the groves. Overhead clouds the color of old chamois folded and unfolded across the moon.

For a while I stood alone in a circle of trees, listening to the music: a de Lassus two-part canon programmed for audio-generators. Recalled: an article in one of last week's large-circulation literaries, stating that it was the only way to remove the feel of the bar lines imposed by five centuries of meter on modern musicians. For another two weeks this would be acceptable entertainment. The trees circled a rock pool; but no water. Below the plastic surface, abstract lights wove and threaded in a shifting lumia.

"Excuse me . . . ?"

I turned to see Alexis, who had no drink now or idea what to do with his hands. He *was* nervous.

". . . but our young friend has told me you have something I might be interested in."

I started to lift my briefcase, but Alex's hand came down from his ear (it had gone by belt to hair to collar already) to halt me. Nouveau riche.

"That's all right. I don't need to see them yet. In fact, I'd rather not. I have something to propose to you. I would certainly be interested in what you have if they are, indeed, as Hawk has described them. But I have a guest here who would be even more curious."

That sounded odd.

"I know that sounds odd," Alexis assessed, "but I thought you might be interested simply because of the finances involved. I am an eccentric collector who would offer you a price concomitant with what I would use them for: eccentric conversation pieces—and because of the nature of the purchase I would have to limit severely the people with whom I could converse."

I nodded.

"My guest, however, would have a great deal more use for them."

"Could you tell me who this guest is?"

"I asked Hawk, finally, who you were, and he led me to believe I was on the verge of a grave social indiscretion. It would be equally indiscreet to reveal my guest's name to you." He smiled. "But indiscretion is the better part of the fuel that keeps the social machine turning, Mr. Harvey Cadwaliter-Erickson . . ." He smiled knowingly.

I have *never* been Harvey Cadwaliter-Erickson, but then Hawk was always an inventive child. Then a second thought went by, viz., the tungsten magnates, the Cadwaliter-Ericksons of Tythis on Triton. Hawk was not only inventive, he was as brilliant as all the magazines and newspapers are always saying he is.

"I assume your second indiscretion will be to tell me who this mysterious guest is?"

"Well," Alex said with the smile of the canary-fattened cat, "Hawk agreed with me that *the* Hawk might well be curious as to what you have in there," (he pointed) "as indeed he is."

I frowned. Then I thought lots of small, rapid thoughts I'll articulate in due time. *"The* Hawk?"

Alex nodded.

I don't think I was actually scowling. "Would you send our young friend up here for a moment?"

"If you'd like." Alex bowed, turned. Perhaps a minute later, Hawk came up over the rocks and through the trees, grinning. When I didn't grin back, he stopped.

"Mmmm . . ." I began.

His head cocked.

I scratched my chin with a knuckle. ". . . Hawk," I said, "are you aware of a department of the police called Special Services?"

"I've heard of them."

"They've suddenly gotten very interested in me."

"Gee," he said with honest amazement. "They're supposed to be effective."

"Mmmm," I reiterated.

"Say," Hawk announced, "how do you like that? My namesake is here tonight. Wouldn't you know."

"Alex doesn't miss a trick. Have you any idea *why* he's here?"

"Probably trying to make some deal with Abolafia. Her investigation starts tomorrow."

"Oh." I thought over some of those things I had thought before. "Do you know a Maud Hinkle?"

His puzzled look said "no" pretty convincingly.

"She bills herself as one of the upper echelon in the arcane organization of which I spoke."

"Yeah?"

"She ended our interview earlier this evening with a little homily about hawks and helicopters. I took our sub-sequent encounter as a fillip of coincidence. But now I discover that the evening has confirmed her intimations of plurality." I shook my head. "Hawk, I am suddenly cata-pulted into a paranoid world where the walls not only have ears, but probably eyes and long, claw-tipped fin-gers. Anyone about me—yea, even very you—could turn out to be a spy. I suspect every sewer grating and second-story window conceals binoculars, a tommygun, or worse. What I just can't figure out is how these insidious forces, ubiquitous and omnipresent though they be, induced you to lure me into this intricate and diabolical—"

"Oh, cut it out!" He shook back his hair. "I didn't lure—"

"Perhaps not consciously, but Special Services has Ho-logramic Information Storage, and their methods are in-sidious and cruel—"

"I said cut it out!" And all sorts of hard little things happened again. "So you think I'd—" Then he realized how scared I was, I guess. "Look, the Hawk isn't some small-time snatch-purse. He lives in just as paranoid a world as you're in now, only all the time. If he's here, you can be sure there are just as many of his men—eyes and ears and fingers—as there are of Maud Hickenlooper."

"Hinkle."

"Anyway, it works both ways. No Singer's going to—Look, do you really think I would—"

And even though I knew all those hard little things were scabs over pain, I said, "Yes."

"You did something for me once, and I—"

"I gave you some more welts. That's all."

All the scabs pulled off.

"Hawk," I said. "Let me see."

He took a breath. Then he began to open the brass

buttons. The flaps of his jacket fell back. The lumia colored his chest with pastel shiftings.

I felt my face wrinkle. I didn't want to look away. I drew a hissing breath instead, which was just as bad.

He looked up. "There're a lot more than when you were here last, aren't there?"

"You're going to kill yourself, Hawk."

He shrugged.

"I can't even tell which are the ones I put there anymore."

He started to point them out.

"Oh, come on," I said too sharply. And for the length of three breaths, he grew more and more uncomfortable till I saw him start to reach for the bottom button. "Boy," I said, trying to keep despair out of my voice, "why do you do it?" and ended up keeping out everything. There is nothing more despairing than a voice empty.

He shrugged, saw I didn't want that, and for a moment anger flickered in his green eyes. I didn't want that either. So he said: "Look . . . you touch a person softly, gently, and maybe you even do it with love. And, well, I guess a piece of information goes on up to the brain where something interprets it as pleasure. Maybe something up there in my head interprets the information all wrong . . ."

I shook my head. "You're a Singer. Singers are supposed to be eccentric, sure; but—"

Now he was shaking his head. Then the anger opened up. And I saw an expression move from all those spots that had communicated pain through the rest of his features and vanish without ever becoming a word. Once more he looked down at the wounds that webbed his thin body.

"Button it up, boy. I'm sorry I said anything."

Halfway up the lapels, his hands stopped. "You really think I'd turn you in?"

"Button it up."

He did. Then he said, "Oh." And then, "You know, it's midnight."

"So?"

"Edna just gave me the Word."

"Which is?"

"Agate."

I nodded.

He finished closing his collar. "What are you thinking about?"

"Cows."

"Cows?" Hawk asked. "What about them?"

"You ever been on a dairy farm?"

He shook his head.

"To get the most milk, you keep the cows practically in suspended animation. They're fed intravenously from a big tank that pipes nutrients out and down, branching into smaller and smaller pipes until it gets to all those high-yield semi-corpses."

"I've seen pictures."

"People."

". . . and cows?"

"You've given me the Word. And now it begins to funnel down, branching out, with me telling others and them telling still others, till by midnight tomorrow . . ."

"I'll go get the—"

"Hawk?"

He turned back. "What?"

"You say you don't think I'm going to be the victim of any hanky-panky with the mysterious forces that know more than we. Okay, that's your opinion. But as soon as I get rid of this stuff, I'm going to make the most distracting exit you've ever seen."

Two little lines bit down Hawk's forehead. "Are you sure I haven't seen this one before?"

"As a matter of fact I think you have." Now I grinned.

"Oh," Hawk said, then made a sound that had the structure of laughter but was all breath. "I'll get the Hawk."

He ducked out between the trees.

I glanced up at the lozenges of moonlight in the leaves. I looked down at my briefcase.

Up between the rocks, stepping around the long grass, came the Hawk. He wore a gray evening suit; a gray silk turtleneck. Above his craggy face, his head was completely shaved.

"Mr. Cadwaliter-Erickson?" He held out his hand.

I shook: small sharp bones in loose skin. "Does one call you Mr. . . . ?"

"Arty."

"Arty the Hawk?" I tried to look like I wasn't giving his gray attire the once-over.

He smiled. "Arty the Hawk. Yeah. I picked that name up when I was younger than our friend down there. Alex says you got . . . well, some things that are not exactly yours. That don't belong to you."

I nodded.

"Show them to me."

"You were told what—"

He brushed away the end of my sentence. "Come on, let me see."

He extended his hand, smiling affably as a bank clerk. I ran my thumb around the pressure-zip. The cover went *tsk*. "Tell me," I said, looking up at his head still lowered to see what I had, "what does one do about Special Services? They seem to be after me."

The head came up. Surprise changed slowly to a craggy leer. "Why, Mr. Cadwaliter-Erickson!" He gave me the up and down openly. "Keep your income steady. Keep it steady, that's one thing you can do."

"If you buy these for anything like what they're worth, that's going to be a little difficult."

"I would imagine. I could always give you less money—"

The cover went *tsk* again.

"—or, barring that, you could try to use your head and outwit them."

"You must have outwitted them at one time or another. You may be on an even keel now, but you had to get there from somewhere else."

Arty the Hawk's nod was downright sly. "I guess you've had a run-in with Maud. Well, I suppose congratulations are in order. And condolences. I always like to do what's in order."

"You seem to know how to take care of yourself. I mean I notice you're not out there mingling with the guests."

"There are two parties going on here tonight," Arty said. "Where do you think Alex disappears off to every five minutes?"

I frowned.

"That lumia down in the rocks"—he pointed towards

my feet—"is a mandala of shifting hues on our ceiling. Alex," he chuckled, "goes scuttling off under the rocks where there is a pavilion of Oriental splendor—"

"—and a separate guest list at the door?"

"Regina is on both. I'm on both. So's the kid, Edna, Lewis, Ann—"

"Am I supposed to know all this?"

"Well, you came with a person on both lists. I just thought . . ." He paused.

I was coming on wrong. Well. A quick change artist learns fairly quick that the verisimilitude factor in imitating someone up the scale is your confidence in your unalienable right to come on wrong. "I'll tell you," I said. "How about exchanging these"—I held out the brief-case—"for some information."

"You want to know how to stay out of Maud's clutches?" He shook his head. "It would be pretty stupid of me to tell you, even if I could. Besides, you've got your family fortunes to fall back on." He beat the front of his shirt with his thumb. "Believe me, boy. Arty the Hawk didn't have that. I didn't have anything like that." His hands dropped into his pockets. "Let's see what you got."

I opened the case again.

The Hawk looked for a while. After a few moments he picked a couple up, turned them around, put them back down, put his hands back in his pockets. "I'll give you sixty thousand for them, approved credit tablets."

"What about the information I wanted?"

"I wouldn't tell you a thing." He smiled. "I wouldn't tell you the time of day."

There are very few successful thieves in this world. Still less on the other five. The will to steal is an impulse towards the absurd and the tasteless. (The talents are poetic, theatrical, a certain reverse charisma. . . .) But it is a will, as the will to order, power, love.

"All right," I said.

Somewhere overhead I heard a faint humming.

Arty looked at me fondly. He reached under the lapel of his jacket and took out a handful of credit tablets— the scarlet-banded tablets whose slips were ten thousand apiece. He pulled off one. Two. Three. Four.

"You can deposit this much safely—?"

"Why do you think Maud is after me?"

Five. six.

"Fine," I said.

"How about throwing in the briefcase?" Arty asked.

"Ask Alex for a paper bag. If you want, I can send them—"

"Give them here."

The humming was coming closer.

I held up the open case. Arty went in with both hands. He shoved them into his coat pockets, his pants pockets; the gray cloth was distended by angular bulges. He looked left, right. "Thanks," he said. "Thanks." Then he turned and hurried down the slope with all sorts of things in his pockets that weren't his now.

I looked up through the leaves for the noise, but I couldn't see anything.

I stooped down now and laid my case open. I pulled open the back compartment where I kept the things that did belong to me and rummaged hurriedly through.

Alex was just offering Puffy-eyes another Scotch, while the gentleman was saying, "Has anyone seen Mrs. Silem? What's that humming overhead—?" when a large woman wrapped in a veil of fading fabric tottered across the rocks, screaming.

Her hands were clawing at her covered face.

Alex sloshed soda over his sleeve, and the man said, "Oh, my God! Who's that?"

"No!" the woman shrieked. "Oh, no! Help me!" waving her wrinkled fingers, brilliant with rings.

"Don't you recognize her?" That was Hawk whispering confidentially to someone else. "It's Henrietta, Countess of Effingham."

And Alex, overhearing, went hurrying to her assistance. The Countess, however, ducked between two cacti and disappeared into the high grass. But the entire party followed. They were beating about the underbrush when a balding gentleman in a black tux, bow tie, and cummerbund coughed and said in a very worried voice, "Excuse me, Mr. Spinnel?"

Alex whirled.

"Mr. Spinnel, my mother . . ."

"Who are *you?*" The interruption upset Alex terribly. The gentleman drew himself up to announce: "The

Honorable Clement Effingham," and his pants leg shook for all the world as if he had started to click his heels. But articulation failed. The expression melted on his face. "Oh, I . . . my mother, Mr. Spinnel. We were downstairs at the other half of your party when she got very upset. She ran up here—oh, I told her not to! I knew you'd be upset. But you must help me!" and then looked up.

The others looked, too.

The helicopter blacked the moon, doffing and settling below its hazy twin parasols.

"Oh, please . . ." the gentleman said, "You look over there! Perhaps she's gone back down. I've got to"—looking quickly both ways—"find her." He hurried in one direction while everyone else hurried in others.

The humming was suddenly syncopated with a crash. Roaring now, as plastic fragments from the transparent roof clattered down through the branches, clattered on the rocks. . . .

I made it into the elevator and had already thumbed the edge of my briefcase clasp, when Hawk drove between the unfolding foils. The electric-eye began to swing them open. I hit DOOR CLOSE full fist.

The boy staggered, banged shoulders on two walls, then got back breath and balance. "Hey, there's police getting out of that helicopter!"

"Hand-picked by Maud Hinkle herself, no doubt." I pulled the other tuft of white hair from my temple. It went into the case on top of the plastiderm gloves (wrinkled, thick blue veins, long carnelian nails, that had been Henrietta's hands, lying in the chiffon folds of her sari.

Then there was the downward tug of stopping. The Honorable Clement was still half on my face when the door opened.

Gray and gray, with an absolutely dismal expression on his face, the Hawk swung through the doors. Behind him people were dancing in an elaborate pavilion festooned with Oriental magnificence (and a mandala of shifting hues on the ceiling). Arty beat me to DOOR CLOSE. Then he gave me an odd look.

I just sighed and finished peeling off Clem.

"The police are up there?" the Hawk reiterated.

"Arty," I said, buckling my pants, "it certainly looks that way." The car gained momentum. "You look almost as upset as Alex." I shrugged the tux jacket down my arms, turning the sleeves inside out, pulled one wrist free, and jerked off the white starched dicky with the black bow tie and stuffed it into the briefcase with all my other dickies; swung the coat around and slipped on Howard Calvin Evingston's good gray herringbone. Howard (like Hank) is a redhead (but not as curly).

The Hawk raised his bare brows when I peeled off Clement's bald pate and shook out my hair.

"I noticed you aren't carrying around all those bulky things in your pocket any more."

"Oh, those have been taken care of," he said gruffly. "They're all right."

"Arty," I said, adjusting my voice down to Howard's security-provoking, ingenuous baritone, "it must have been my unabashed conceit that made me think that those Regular Service police were here just for me——"

The Hawk actually snarled. "They wouldn't be that unhappy if they got me, too."

And from his corner Hawk demanded, "You've got security here with you, don't you, Arty?"

"So what?"

"There's one way you can get out of this," Hawk hissed at me. His jacket had come half-open down his wrecked chest. "That's if Arty takes you out with him."

"Brilliant idea," I concluded. "You want a couple of thousand back for the service?"

The idea didn't amuse him. "I don't want anything from you." He turned to Hawk. "I need something from you, kid. Not him. Look, I wasn't prepared for Maud. If you want me to get your friend out, then you've got to do something for me."

The boy looked confused.

I thought I saw smugness on Arty's face, but the expression resolved into concern. "You've got to figure out some way to fill the lobby up with people, and fast."

I was going to ask why, but then I didn't know the extent of Arty's security. I was going to ask how, but the floor pushed up at my feet and the doors swung open. "If you can't do it," the Hawk growled to Hawk, "none of us will get out of here. None of us!"

I had no idea what the kid was going to do, but when I started to follow him out into the lobby, the Hawk grabbed my arm and hissed, "Stay here, you idiot!"

I stepped back. Arty was leaning on DOOR OPEN.

Hawk sprinted towards the pool. And splashed in.

He reached the braziers on their twelve-foot tripods and began to climb.

"He's going to hurt himself!" the Hawk whispered.

"Yeah," I said, but I don't think my cynicism got through. Below the great dish of fire, Hawk was fiddling. Then something under there came loose. Something else went *Clang!* And something else spurted out across the water. The fire raced along it and hit the pool, churning and roaring like hell.

A black arrow with a golden head: Hawk dove.

I bit the inside of my cheek as the alarm sounded. Four people in uniforms were coming across the blue carpet. Another group were crossing in the other direction, saw the flames, and one of the women screamed. I let out my breath, thinking carpet and walls and ceiling would be flame-proof. But I kept losing focus on the idea before the sixty-odd infernal feet.

Hawk surfaced on the edge of the pool in the only clear spot left, rolled over on to the carpet, clutching his face. And rolled. And rolled. Then, came to his feet.

Another elevator spilled out a load of passengers who gaped and gasped. A crew came through the doors now with fire-fighting equipment. The alarm was still sounding.

Hawk turned to look at the dozen-odd people in the lobby. Water puddled the carpet about his drenched and shiny pants legs. Flame turned the drops on his cheek and hair to flickering copper and blood.

He banged his fists against his wet thighs, took a deep breath, and against the roar and the bells and the whispering, he Sang.

Two people ducked back into two elevators. From a doorway half a dozen more emerged. The elevators returned half a minute later with a dozen people each. I realized the message was going through the building, there's a Singer Singing in the lobby.

The lobby filled. The flames growled, the fire fighters stood around shuffling, and Hawk, feet apart on the blue rug by the burning pool, Sang, and Sang of a bar off

Times Square full of thieves, morphadine-heads, brawl-
ers, drunkards, women too old to trade what they still
held out for barter, and trade just too nasty-grimy; where
earlier in the evening, a brawl had broken out, and an old
man had been critically hurt in the fray.

Arty tugged at my sleeve.

"What . . . ?"

"Come on," he hissed.

The elevator door closed behind us.

We ambled through the attentive listeners, stopping to
watch, stopping to hear. I couldn't really do Hawk justice.
A lot of that slow amble I spent wondering what sort of
security Arty had:

Standing behind a couple in a bathrobe who were
squinting into the heat, I decided it was all very simple.
Arty wanted simply to drift away through a crowd, so he'd
conveniently gotten Hawk to manufacture one.

To get to the door we had to pass through practically a
cordon of Regular Service policemen, who I don't think
had anything to do with what might have been going on
in the roof garden; they'd simply collected to see the fire
and stayed for the Song. When Arty tapped one on the
shoulder—"Excuse me please—" to get by, the policeman
glanced at him, glanced away, then did a Mack Sennet
double-take. But another policeman caught the whole
interchange, touched the first on the arm, and gave
him a frantic little headshake. Then both men turned
very deliberately back to watch the Singer. While the
earthquake in my chest stilled, I decided that the Hawk's
security complex of agents and counter-agents, maneuver-
ing and machinating through the flaming lobby, must be
of such finesse and intricacy that to attempt understanding was to condemn oneself to total paranoia.

Arty opened the final door.

I stepped from the last of the air-conditioning into the
night.

We hurried down the ramp.

"Hey, Arty . . . ?"

"You go that way." He pointed down the street. "I go
this way."

"Eh . . . what's that way?" I pointed in my direction.

"Twelve Towers sub-sub-subway station. Look. I've
got you out of there. Believe me, you're safe for the time

being. Now go take a train someplace interesting. Good-bye. Go on now." Then Arty the Hawk put his fists in his pockets and hurried up the street.

I started down, keeping near the wall, expecting some-one to get me with a blow-dart from a passing car, a deathray from the shrubbery.

I reached the sub.

And still nothing had happened.

Agate gave way to Malachite:

Tourmaline:

Beryl (during which month I turned twenty-six):

Porphyry:

Sapphire (that month I took the ten thousand I hadn't frittered away and invested it in The Glacier, a perfectly legitimate ice cream palace on Triton—the first and only ice cream palace on Triton—which took off like fire-works; all investors were returned eight-hundred percent, no kidding. Two weeks later I'd lost half of those earn-ings on another set of preposterous illegalities and was feeling quite depressed, but The Glacier kept pulling them in. The new Word came by):

Cinnabar:

Turquoise:

Tiger's Eye:

Hector Calhoun Eisenhower finally buckled down and spent three months learning how to be a respectable member of the upper middle class underworld. That is a long novel in itself. High finance; corporate law; how to hire help: Whew! But the complexities of life have al-ways intrigued me. I got through it. The basic rule is still the same: observe carefully, imitate effectively.

Garnet:

Topaz (I whispered that word on the roof of the Trans-Satellite Power Station, and caused my hirelings to commit two murders. And you know? I didn't feel a thing):

Taafite:

We were nearing the end of Taafite. I'd come back to Triton on strictly Glacial business. A bright pleasant morning it was: the business went fine. I decided to take off the afternoon and go sight-seeing in the Torrents.

". . . two hundred and thirty yards high," the guide announced, and everyone around me leaned on the rail and gazed up through the plastic corridor at the cliffs of frozen methane that soared through Neptune's cold green glare.

"Just a few yards down the catwalk, ladies and gentlemen, you can catch your first glimpse of the Well of This World, where over a million years ago, a mysterious force science still cannot explain caused twenty-five square miles of frozen methane to liquefy for no more than a few hours during which time a whirlpool twice the depth of Earth's Grand Canyon was caught for the ages when the temperature dropped once more to . . ."

People were moving down the corridor when I saw her smiling. My hair was black and nappy, and my skin was chestnut dark today.

I was just feeling overconfident, I guess, so I kept standing around next to her. I even contemplated coming on. Then she broke the whole thing up by suddenly turning to me and saying perfectly deadpan: "Why, if it isn't Hamlet Caliban Enobarbus!"

Old reflexes realigned my features to couple the frown of confusion with the smile of indulgence. *Pardon me, but I think you must have mistaken . . .* No, I didn't say it. "Maud," I said, "have you come here to tell me that my time has come?"

She wore several shades of blue with a large blue brooch at her shoulder, obviously glass. Still, I realized as I looked about the other tourists, she was more inconspicuous amidst their finery than I was. "No," she said. "Actually I'm on vacation. Just like you."

"No kidding?" We had dropped behind the crowd. "You are kidding."

"Special Services of Earth, while we cooperate with Special Services on other worlds, has no official jurisdiction on Triton. And since you came here with money, and most of your recorded gain in income has been through The Glacier, while Regular Services on Triton might be glad to get you, Special Services is not after you as yet." She smiled. "I haven't been to The Glacier. It would really be nice to say I'd been taken there by one of the owners. Could we go for a soda, do you think?"

The swirled sides of the Well of This World dropped away in opalescent grandeur. Tourists gazed, and the

guide went on about indices of refraction, angles of in-
cline.

"I don't think you trust me," Maud said.

My look said she was right.

"Have you ever been involved with narcotics?" she
asked suddenly.

I frowned.

"No, I'm serious. I want to try and explain something . . . a point of information that may make both
our lives easier."

"Peripherally," I said. "I'm sure you've got down all
the information in your dossiers."

"I was involved with them a good deal more than peripherally for several years," Maud said. "Before I got into
Special Services, I was in the Narcotics Division of the
regular force. And the people we dealt with twenty-four
hours a day were drug users, drug pushers. To catch the
big ones we had to make friends with the little ones. To
catch the bigger ones, we had to make friends with the
big. We had to keep the same hours they kept, talk the
same language, for months at a time live on the same
streets, in the same buildings." She stepped back from the
rail to let a youngster ahead. "I had to be sent away to
take the morphadine de-toxification cure twice while I
was on the narco squad. And I had a better record than
most."

"What's your point?"

"Just this. You and I are traveling in the same circles
now, if only because of our respective chosen professions.
You'd be surprised how many people we already know
in common. Don't be shocked when we run into each
other crossing Sovereign Plaza in Bellona one day, then
two weeks later wind up at the same restaurant for lunch
at Lux on Iapetus. Though the circles we move in cover
worlds, they *are* the same, and not that big."

"Come on." I don't think I sounded happy. "Let me
treat you to that ice cream." We started back down the
walkway.

"You know," Maud said, "if you do stay out of Special
Services' hands here and on Earth long enough, eventually you'll be up there with a huge income growing on a
steady slope. It might be a few years, but it's possible.
There's no reason now for us to be *personal* enemies.

You just may, someday, reach that point where Special Services loses interest in you as quarry. Oh, we'd still see each other, run into each other. We get a great deal of our information from people up there. We're in a position to help you, too, you see."

"You've been casting holograms again."

She shrugged. Her face looked positively ghostly under the pale planet. She said, when we reached the artificial lights of the city, "I did meet two friends of yours recently, Lewis and Ann."

"The Singers?"

She nodded.

"Oh, I don't really know them well."

"They seem to know a lot about you. Perhaps through that other Singer, Hawk."

"Oh," I said again. "Did they say how he was?"

"I read that he was recovering about two months back. But nothing since then."

"That's about all I know, too," I said.

"The only time I've ever seen him," Maud said, "was right after I pulled him out."

Arty and I had gotten out of the lobby before Hawk actually finished. The next day on the news-tapes I learned that when his Song was over, he shrugged out of his jacket, dropped his pants, and walked back into the pool.

The fire-fighter crew suddenly woke up; people began running around and screaming: he'd been rescued, seventy percent of his body covered with second- and third-degree burns. I'd been industriously trying not to think about it.

"*You* pulled him out?"

"Yes. I was in the helicopter that landed on the roof," Maud said. "I thought you'd be impressed to see me."

"Oh," I said. "How did you get to pull him out?"

"Once you got going, Arty's security managed to jam the elevator service above the seventy-first floor, so we didn't get to the lobby till after you were out of the building. That's when Hawk tried to—"

"But it was you who actually saved him, though?"

"The firemen in that neighborhood hadn't had a fire in twelve years! I don't think they even knew how to operate the equipment. I had my boys foam the pool, then I waded in and dragged him—"

"Oh," I said again. I had been trying hard, almost succeeding, these eleven months. I wasn't there when it happened. It wasn't my affair. Maud was saying:

"We thought we might have gotten a lead on you from him, but when I got him to the shore, he was completely out, just a mass of open, running—"

"I should have known the Special Services uses Singers, too," I said. "Everyone else does. The Word changes today, doesn't it? Lewis and Ann didn't pass on what the new one is?"

"I saw them yesterday, and the Word doesn't change for another eight hours. Besides, they wouldn't tell me, anyway." She glanced at me and frowned. "They really wouldn't."

"Let's go have some sodas," I said. "We'll make small talk and listen carefully to each other while we affect an air of nonchalance; you will try to pick up things that will make it easier to catch me; I will listen for things you let slip that might make it easier for me to avoid you."

"Um-hm." She nodded.

"Why did you contact me in that bar, anyway?"

Eyes of ice: "I told you, we simply travel in the same circles. We're quite likely to be in the same bar on the same night."

"I guess that's just one of the things I'm not supposed to understand, huh?"

Her smile was appropriately ambiguous. I didn't push it.

It was a very dull afternoon. I couldn't repeat one exchange from the nonsense we babbled over the cherry-peaked mountains of whipped cream. We both exerted so much energy to keep up the appearance of being amused, I doubt either one of us could see our way to picking up anything meaningful; if anything meaningful was said.

She left. I brooded some more on the charred phoenix.

The Steward of The Glacier called me into the kitchen to ask about a shipment of contraband milk (The Glacier

makes all its own ice cream) that I had been able to
wangle on my last trip to Earth (it's amazing how little
progress there has been in dairy farming over the last ten
years; it was depressingly easy to hornswoggle that bum-
bling Vermonter) and under the white lights and great
plastic churning vats, while I tried to get things straightened out, he made some comment about the Heist Cream
Emperor; that didn't do *any* good.

By the time the evening crowd got there, and the moog
was making music, and the crystal walls were blazing;
and the floor show—a new addition that week—had
been cajoled into going on anyway (a trunk of costumes
had gotten lost in shipment [or swiped, but I wasn't
about to tell them that]), and wandering through the tables I, personally, had caught a very grimy little girl,
obviously out of her head on morph, trying to pick up a
customer's pocketbook from the back of a chair—I just
caught her by the wrist, made her let go, and led her to
the door daintily, while she blinked at me with dilated
eyes and the customer never even knew—and the
floor show, having decided what the hell, were doing
their act *au naturel,* and everyone was having just a high
old time, I was feeling really bad.

I went outside, sat on the wide steps, and growled
when I had to move aside to let people in or out. About
the seventy-fifth growl, the person I growled at stopped
and boomed down at me, "I thought I'd find you, if I
looked hard enough! I mean if I really looked."

I looked at the hand that was flapping at my shoulder,
followed the arm up to a black turtleneck where there
was a beefy, bald, grinning head. "Arty," I said, "what
are . . . ?" But he was still flapping and laughing with
impervious *gemütlicheit.*

"You wouldn't believe the time I had getting a picture
of you, boy. Had to bribe one out of the Triton Special
Services Department. That quick change bit. Great gim-
mick. Just great!" The Hawk sat down next to me and
dropped his hand on my knee. "Wonderful place you got
here. I like it, like it a lot." Small bones in veined dough.
"But not enough to make you an offer on it yet. You're
learning fast there, though. I can tell you're learning fast.
I'm going to be proud to be able to say I was the one
who gave you your first big break." His hand came away,

and he began to knead it into the other. "If you're going to move into the big time, you have to have at least one foot planted firmly on the right side of the law. The whole idea is to make yourself indispensable to the good people; once that's done, a good crook has the keys to all the treasure houses in the system. But I'm not telling you anything you don't already know."

"Arty," I said, "do you think the two of us should be seen together here . . . ?"

The Hawk held his hand above his lap and joggled it with a deprecating motion. "Nobody can get a picture of us. I got my men all around. I never go anywhere in public without my security. Heard you've been looking into the security business yourself," which was true. "Good idea. Very good. I like the way you're handling yourself."

"Thanks. Arty, I'm not feeling too hot this evening. I came out here to get some air . . ."

Arty's hand fluttered again. "Don't worry, I won't hang around. You're right. We shouldn't be seen. Just passing by and wanted to say hello. Just hello." He got up. "That's all." He started down the steps.

"Arty?"

He looked back.

"Sometime soon you will come back; and that time you will want to buy out my share of The Glacier, because I'll have gotten too big; and I won't want to sell because I'll think I'm big enough to fight you. So we'll be enemies for a while. You'll try to kill me. I'll try to kill you."

On his face, first the frown of confusion; then the indulgent smile. "I see you've caught on to the idea of hologramic information. Very good. Good. It's the only way to outwit Maud. Make sure all your information relates to the whole scope of the situation. It's the only way to outwit me, too." He smiled, started to turn, but thought of something else. "If you can fight me off long enough and keep growing, keep your security in tiptop shape, eventually, we'll get to the point where it'll be worth both our whiles to work together again. If you can just hold out, we'll be friends again. Someday. You just watch. Just wait."

"Thanks for telling me."

The Hawk looked at his watch. "Well. Goodbye." I thought he was going to leave finally. But he glanced up again. "Have you got the new Word?"

"That's right," I said. "It went out tonight. What is it?"

The Hawk waited till the people coming down the steps were gone. He looked hastily about, then leaned towards me with hands cupped at his mouth, rasped, "Pyrite," and winked hugely. "I just got it from a gal who got it direct from Colette," (one of the three Singers of Triton). Then he turned, jounced down the steps, and shouldered his way into the crowds passing on the strip.

I sat there mulling through the year till I had to get up and walk. All walking does to my depressive moods is add the reinforcing rhythm of paranoia. By the time I was coming back, I had worked out a dilly of a delusional system: The Hawk had already begun to weave some security ridden plot about me, which ended when we were all trapped in some dead end alley, and trying to get aid I called out, "Pyrite!" which turned out not to be the Word at all but served to identify me for the man in the dark gloves with the gun/grenade/gas.

There was a cafeteria on the corner. In the light from the window, clustered over the wreck by the curb was a bunch of nasty-grimies (á la Triton: chains around the wrist, bumblebee tattoo on cheek, high-heel boots on those who could afford them). Straddling the smashed headlight was the little morph-head I had ejected earlier from The Glacier.

On a whim I went up to her. "Hey?"

She looked at me from under hair like trampled hay, eyes all pupil.

"You get the new Word yet?"

She rubbed her nose, already scratch red. "Pyrite," she said. "It just came down about an hour ago."

"Who told you?"

She considered my question. "I got it from a guy, who says he got it from a guy, who came in this evening from New York, who picked it up there from a Singer named Hawk."

The three grimies nearest made a point of not looking at me. Those further away let themselves glance.

"Oh," I said. "Oh. Thanks."

Occam's Razor, along with any real information on how security works, hones away most such paranoia. Pyrite. At a certain level in my line of work, paranoia's just an occupational disease. At least I was certain that Arty (and Maud) probably suffered from it as much as I did.

The lights were out on The Glacier's marquee. Then I remembered what I had left inside and ran up the stairs.

The door was locked. I pounded on the glass a couple of times, but everyone had gone home. And the thing that made it worse was that I could see it sitting on the counter of the coatcheck alcove under the orange bulb. The steward had probably put it there, thinking I might arrive before everybody left. Tomorrow at noon Ho Chi Eng had to pick up his reservation for the Marigold Suite on the Interplanetary Liner *The Platinum Swan,* which left at one-thirty for Bellona. And there behind the glass doors of The Glacier, it waited with the proper wig, as well as the epicanthic folds that would halve Mr. Eng's sloe eyes of jet.

I actually thought of breaking in. But the more practical solution was to get the hotel to wake me at nine and come in with the cleaning man. I turned around and started down the steps; and the thought struck me, and made me terribly sad, so that I blinked and smiled just from reflex; it was probably just as well to leave it there till morning because there was nothing in it that wasn't mine anyway.

A BOY AND HIS DOG

by Harlan Ellison

I

I was out with Blood, my dog. It was his week for annoying me; he kept calling me Albert. He thought that was pretty damned funny. Payson Terhune: ha ha.

I'd caught a couple of water rats for him, the big green and ochre ones, and someone's manicured poodle, lost off a leash in one of the downunders.

He'd eaten pretty good, but he was cranky. "Come on, son of a bitch," I demanded, "find me a piece of ass."

Blood just chuckled, deep in his dog-throat. "You're funny when you get horny," he said.

Maybe funny enough to kick him upside his sphincter asshole. that refugee from a dingo-heap.

"Find! I ain't kidding!"

"For shame, Albert. After all I've taught you. Not 'I *ain't* kidding.' I'm *not* kidding."

He knew I'd reached the edge of my patience. Sullenly, he started casting. He sat down on the crumbled remains of the curb, and his eyelids flickered and closed, and his hairy body tensed. After a while he settled down on his front paws, and scraped them forward till he was lying flat, his shaggy head on the outstretched paws. The tenseness left him and he began trembling, almost the way he trembled just preparatory to scratching a flea. It went on that way for almost a quarter of an hour, and finally he rolled over and lay on his back, his naked belly toward the night sky, his front paws folded man-

632

tislike, his hind legs extended and open. "I'm sorry," he said. "There's nothing."

I could have gotten mad and booted him, but I knew he had tried. I wasn't happy about it, I really wanted to get laid, but what could I do? "Okay," I said, with resignation, "forget it."

He kicked himself onto his side and quickly got up.

"What do you want to do?" he asked.

"Not much we *can* do, is there?" I was more than a little sarcastic. He sat down again, at my feet, insolently humble.

I leaned against the melted stub of a lamppost, and thought about girls. It was painful. "We can always go to a show," I said. Blood looked around the street, at the pools of shadow lying in the weed-overgrown craters, and didn't say anything. The whelp was waiting for me to say okay, let's go. He liked movies as much as I did.

"Okay, let's go."

He got up and followed me, his tongue hanging, panting with happiness. Go ahead and laugh, you eggsucker. No popcorn for *you!*

Our Gang was a roverpak that had never been able to cut it simply foraging, so they'd opted for comfort and gone a smart way to getting it. They were movie-oriented kids, and they'd taken over the turf where the Metropole Theater was located. No one tried to bust their turf, because we all needed the movies, and as long as Our Gang had access to films, and did a better job of keeping the films going, they provided a service, even for solos like me and Blood. *Especially* for solos like us.

They made me check my .45 and the Browning .22 long at the door. There was a little alcove right beside the ticket booth. I bought my tickets first; it cost me a can of Oscar Meyer Philadelphia Scrapple for me, and a tin of sardines for Blood. Then the Our Gang guards with the bren guns motioned me over to the alcove and I checked my heat. I saw water leaking from a broken pipe in the ceiling and I told the checker, a kid with big leathery warts all over his face and lips, to move my weapons where it was dry. He ignored me. "Hey you! Motherfuckin' toad, move my stuff over the other side

. . . it goes to rust fast . . . **an'** it picks up any spots, man, I'll break your bones!"

He started to give me jaw about it, looked at the guards with the brens, knew if they tossed me out I'd lose my price of admission whether I went in or not, but they weren't looking for any action, probably under-strength, and gave him the nod to let it pass, to do what I said. So the toad moved my Browning to the other end of the gun rack, and pegged my .45 under it.

Blood and me went into the theater.

"I want popcorn."

"Forget it."

"Come on, Albert. Buy me popcorn."

"I'm tapped out. You can live without popcorn."

"You're just being a shit."

I shrugged: sue me.

We went in. The place was jammed. I was glad the guards hadn't tried to take anything but guns. My spike and knife felt reassuring, lying-up in their oiled sheaths at the back of my neck. Blood found two together, and we moved into the row, stepping on feet. Someone cursed and I ignored him. A Doberman growled. Blood's fur stirred, but he let it pass. There was always *some* hard-case on the muscle, even in neutral ground like the Met-ropole.

(I heard once about a get-it-on they'd had at the old Loew's Granada, on the South Side. Wound up with ten or twelve rovers and their mutts dead, the theater burned down and a couple of good Cagney films lost in the fire. After that was when the roverpaks had got up the agreement that movie houses were sanctuaries. It was better now, but there was always somebody too messed in the mind to come soft.)

It was a triple feature. "Raw Deal" with Dennis O'Keefe, Claire Trevor, Raymond Burr and Marsha Hunt was the oldest of the three. It'd been made in 1948, eighty-six years ago; god only knows how the damn thing'd hung together all that time; it slipped sprockets and they had to stop the movie all the time to re-thread it. But it was a good movie. About this solo who'd been japped by his roverpak and was out to get revenge. Gangsters, mobs, a lot of punching and fighting. Real good.

The middle flick was a thing made during the Third

War, in '92, twenty-seven years before I was even born, thing called "Smell of a Chink." It was mostly gut-spilling and some nice hand-to-hand. Beautiful scene of skirmisher greyhounds equipped with napalm throwers, jellyburning a Chink town. Blood dug it, even though we'd seen this flick before. He had some kind of phony shuck going that these were ancestors of his, and *he* knew and *I* knew he was making it up.

"Wanna burn a baby, hero?" I whispered to him. He got the barb and just shifted in his seat, didn't say a thing, kept looking pleased as the dogs worked their way through the town. I was bored stiff.

I was waiting for the main feature.

Finally it came on. It was a beauty, a beaver flick made in the late 1970s. It was called "Big Black Leather Splits." Started right out very good. These two blondes in black leather corsets and boots laced all the way up to their crotches, with whips and masks, got this skinny guy down and one of the chicks sat on his face while the other one went down with him. It got really hairy after that.

All around me there were solos playing with themselves. I was about to jog it a little myself when Blood leaned across and said, real soft, the way he does when he's onto something unusually smelly, "There's a chick in here."

"You're nuts," I said.

"I tell you I smell her. She's in here, man."

Without being conspicuous, I looked around. Almost every seat in the theater was taken with solos or their dogs. If a chick had slipped in there'd have been a riot. She'd have been ripped to pieces before any single guy could have gotten into her. "Where?" I asked, softly. All around me, the solos were beating-off, moaning as the blondes took off their masks and one of them worked the skinny guy with a big wooden ram strapped around her hips.

"Give me a minute," Blood said. He was really concentrating. His body was tense as a wire. His eyes were closed, his muzzle quivering. I let him work.

It was possible. Just maybe possible. I knew that they made really dumb flicks in the downunders, the kind of crap they'd made back in the 1930s and '40s, real clean

stuff with even married people sleeping in twin beds.
Myrna Loy and George Brent kind of flicks. And I knew
that once in a while a chick from one of the really strict
middle-class downunders would cumup, to see what a
hairy flick was like. I'd heard about it, but it'd never
happened in any theater *I'd* ever been in.

And the chances of it happening in the Metropole, particularly, were slim. There was a lot of twisty trade came
to the Metropole. Now, understand, I'm not specially
prejudiced against guys corning one another . . . hell, I
can understand it. There just aren't enough chicks anywhere. But I can't cut the jockey-and-boxer scene because it gets some weak little boxer hanging on you,
getting jealous, you have to hunt for him and all he
thinks he has to do is bare his ass to get all the work
done for him. It's as bad as having a chick dragging
along behind. Made for a lot of bad blood and fights in
the bigger roverpaks, too. So I just never swung that way.
Well, not *never,* but not for a long time.

So with all the twisties in the Metropole, I didn't think
a chick would chance it. Be a toss-up who'd tear her
apart first: the boxers or the straights.

And if she *was* here, why couldn't any of the other
dogs smell her . . . ?

"Third row in front of us," Blood said. "Aisle seat.
Dressed like a solo."

"How's come *you* can whiff her and no other dog's
caught her?"

"You forget who I am, Albert."

"I didn't forget, I just don't believe it."

Actually, bottom-line, I guess I *did* believe it. When
you'd been as dumb as I'd been and a dog like Blood'd
taught me so much, a guy came to believe *everything* he
said. You don't argue with your teacher.

Not when he'd taught you how to read and write
and add and subtract and everything else they used to
know that meant you were smart (but doesn't mean much
of anything now, except it's good to know it, I guess).

(The reading's a pretty good thing. It comes in handy
when you can find some canned goods someplace, like in
a bombed-out supermarket; makes it easier to pick out
stuff you like when the pictures are gone off the labels.

Couple of times the reading stopped me from taking canned beets. Shit, I *hate* beets!)

So I guess I *did* believe why he could whiff a maybe chick in there, and no other mutt could. He'd told me all about *that* a million times. It was his favorite story. History he called it. Christ, I'm not *that* dumb! I knew what history was. That was all the stuff that happened before now.

But I liked hearing history straight from Blood, instead of him making me read one of those crummy books he was always dragging in. And *that* particular history was all about him, so he laid it on me over and over, till I knew it by heart . . . no, the word was *rote*. Not *wrote*, like writing, that was something else. I knew it by rote, like it means you got it word-for-word.

And when a mutt teaches you everything you know, and he tells you something rote, I guess finally you *do* believe it. Except I'd never let that leg-lifter know it.

II

What he'd told me rote was:

Over sixty-five years ago, in Los Angeles, before the Third War even got going completely, there was a man named Buesing who lived in Cerritos. He raised dogs as watchmen and sentries and attackers. Dobermans, Danes, schnauzers and Japanese akitas. He had one four-year-old German shepherd bitch named Ginger. She worked for the Los Angeles Police Department's narcotics division. She could smell out marijuana. No matter how well it was hidden. They ran a test on her: there were 25,000 boxes in an auto parts warehouse. Five of them had been planted with marijuana sealed in cellophane, wrapped in tin foil and heavy brown paper, and finally hidden in three separate sealed cartons. Within seven minutes Ginger found all five packages. At the same time that Ginger was working, ninety-two miles further north, in Santa Barbara, cetologists had drawn and amplified dolphin spinal fluid and injected it into Chacma baboons and dogs. Altering surgery and grafting had been done. The first successful product of this cetacean experimentation had been a two-year-old male Puli named Ahbhu, who had communicated sense-impressions telepathically. Cross-breeding and continued experimentation had produced the first skirmisher dogs, just in time for the Third War. Telepathic over short distances, easily trained, able to track gasoline or troops or poison gas or radiation when linked with their human controllers, they had become the shock commandos of a new kind of war. The selective traits had bred true. Dobermans, greyhounds, akitas, pulis and schnauzers had steadily become more telepathic.

Ginger and Ahbhu had been Blood's ancestors.

He had told me so, a thousand times. Had told me the story just that way, in just those words, a thousand times, as it had been told to him. I'd never believed him till now.

Maybe the little bastard *was* special.

I checked out the solo scrunched down in the aisle seat three rows ahead of me. I couldn't tell a damned thing. The solo had his (her?) cap pulled way down, fleece jacket pulled way up.

"Are you sure?"

"As sure as I can be. It's a girl."

"If it is, she's playing with herself just like a guy."

Blood snickered. "Surprise," he said sarcastically.

The mystery solo sat through "Raw Deal" again. It made sense, if that was a girl. Most of the solos and all of the members of roverpaks left after the beaver flick. The theater didn't fill up much more, it gave the streets time to empty, he/she could make his/her way back to wherever he/she had come from. I sat through "Raw Deal" again myself. Blood went to sleep.

When the mystery solo got up, I gave him/her time to get weapons if any'd been checked, and start away. Then I pulled Blood's big shaggy ear and said, "Let's do it." He slouched after me, up the aisle.

I got my guns and checked the street. Empty.

"Okay, nose," I said, "where'd he go?"

"Her. To the right."

I started off, loading the Browning from my bandolier. I still didn't see anyone moving among the bombed-out shells of the buildings. This section of the city was crummy, really bad shape. But then, with Our Gang running the Metropole, they didn't have to repair anything else to get their livelihood. It was ironic; the Dragons had to keep an entire power plant going to get tribute from the other roverpaks; Ted's Bunch had to mind the reservoir; the Bastinados worked like fieldhands in the marijuana gardens; the Barbados Blacks lost a couple of dozen members every year cleaning out the radiation pits all over the city; and Our Gang only had to run that movie house.

Whoever their leader had been, however many years ago it had been that the roverpaks had started forming out of foraging solos, I had to give it to him: he'd been a flinty sharp mother. He knew what services to deal in.

"She turned off here," Blood said.

I followed him as he began loping, toward the edge of the city and the bluish-green radiation that still flickered from the hills. I knew he was right, then. The only things out here were screamers and the access dropshaft to the downunder. It was a girl, all right.

The cheeks of my ass tightened as I thought about it. I was going to get laid. It had been almost a month, since Blood had whiffed that solo chick in the basement of the Market Basket. She'd been filthy, and I'd gotten the crabs from her, but she'd been a woman, all right, and once I'd tied her down and clubbed her a couple of times she'd been pretty good. She'd liked it, too, even if she did spit on me and tell me she'd kill me if she ever got loose. I left her tied up, just to be sure. She wasn't there when I went back to look, week before last.

"Watch out," Blood said, dodging around a crater almost invisible against the surrounding shadows. Something stirred in the crater.

Trekking across the nomansland I realized why it was that all but a handful of solos or members of roverpaks were guys. The War had killed off most of the girls, and that was the way it always was in wars . . . at least that's what Blood told me. The things getting born were seldom male *or* female, and had to be smashed against a wall as soon as they were pulled out of the mother.

The few chicks who hadn't gone downunder with the middle—classers were hard, solitary bitches like the one in the Market Basket; tough and stringy and just as likely to cut off your meat with a razor blade once they let you get in. Scuffling for a piece of ass had gotten harder and harder, the older I'd gotten.

But every once in a while a chick got tired of being roverpak property, or a raid was got-up by five or six roverpaks and some unsuspecting downunder was taken, or—like this time, yeah—some middle-class chick from a downunder got hot pants to find out what a beaver flick looked like, and cumup.

I was going to get laid. Oh boy, I couldn't wait!

III

Out here it was nothing but empty corpses of blasted buildings. One entire block had been stomped flat, like a steel press had come down from Heaven and given one solid wham! and everything was powder under it. The chick was scared and skittish, I could see that. She moved erratically, looking back over her shoulder and to either side. She knew she was in dangerous country. Man, if she'd only known *how* dangerous.

There was one building standing all alone at the end of the smash-flat block, like it had been missed and chance let it stay. She ducked inside, and a minute later I saw a bobbing light. Flashlight? Maybe.

Blood and I crossed the street and came up into the blackness surrounding the building. It was what was left of a YMCA.

That meant "Young Men's Christian Association." Blood taught me to read.

So what the hell was a young men's christian association? Some times being able to read makes more questions than if you were stupid.

I didn't want her getting out; inside there was as good a place to screw her as any, so I put Blood on guard right beside the steps leading up into the shell, and I went around the back. All the doors and windows had been blown out, of course. It wasn't no big trick getting in. I pulled myself up to the ledge of a window, and dropped down inside. Dark inside. No noise, except the sound of her, moving around on the other side of the old YMCA. I didn't know if she was heeled or not, and I wasn't about to take any chances. I bowslung the Browning and took out the .45 automatic. I didn't have to snap back the action—there was always a slug in the chamber.

I started moving carefully through the room. It was a locker room of some kind. There was glass and debris all over the floor, and one entire row of metal lockers had the paint blistered off their surfaces; the flash blast had caught them through the windows, a lot of years ago. My sneakers didn't make a sound coming through the room.

The door was hanging on one hinge, and I stepped over—through the inverted triangle. I was in the swimming pool area. The big pool was empty, with tiles buckled down at the shallow end. It stunk bad in there; no wonder, there were dead guys, or what was left of them, along one wall. Some lousy cleaner-up had stacked them, but hadn't buried them. I pulled my bandana up around my nose and mouth and kept moving.

Out the other side of the pool place, and through a little passage with popped light bulbs in the ceiling. I didn't have any trouble seeing. There was moonlight coming through busted windows and a chunk was out of the ceiling. I could hear her real plain now, just on the other side of the door at the end of the passage. I hung close to the wall, and stepped down to the door. It was open a crack, but blocked by a fall of lath and plaster from the wall. It would make noise when I went to pull it open, that was for certain. I had to wait for the right moment.

Flattened against the wall, I checked out what she was doing in there. It was a gymnasium, big one, with climbing ropes hanging down from the ceiilng. She had a squat, square, eight-cell flashlight sitting up on the croup of a vaulting horse. There were parallel bars and a horizontal bar about eight feet high, the tempered steel all rusty now. There were swinging rings and a trampoline and a big wooden balancing beam. Over to one side there were wall-bars and balancing benches, horizontal and oblique ladders, and a couple of stacks of vaulting boxes. I made a note to remember this joint. It was better for working-out than the jerry-rigged gym I'd set up in an old auto wrecking yard. A guy has to keep in shape, if he's going to be a solo.

She was out of her disguise. Standing there in the skin, shivering. Yeah, it was chilly, and I could see a pattern of chicken-skin all over her. She was maybe five—six or seven, with nice tits and kind of skinny legs.

She was brushing out her hair. It hung way down the back. The flashlight didn't make it clear enough to tell if she had red hair or chestnut, but it wasn't blonde, which was good, and that was because I dug redheads. She had nice tits, though. I couldn't see her face, the hair was hanging down all smooth and wavy and cut off her profile.

The crap she'd been wearing was thrown around on the floor, and what she was going to put on was up on the vaulting horse. She was standing in little shoes with a kind of a funny heel on them.

I couldn't move. I suddenly realized I couldn't move. She was nice, really nice. I was getting a real big kick out of just standing there and seeing the way her waist fell inward and her hips fell outward, the way the muscles at the side of her tits pulled up when she reached to the top of her head to brush all that hair down. It was really weird the kick I was getting out of standing and just staring at a chick do that. Kind of very, well, woman stuff. I liked it a lot.

I'd never ever stopped and just looked at a chick like that. All the ones I'd ever seen had been scumbags that Blood had smelled out for me, and I'd snatchn'grabbed them. Or the big chicks in the beaver flicks. Not like this one, kind of soft and very smooth, even with the goose bumps. I could of watched her all night.

She put down the brush, and reached over and took a pair of panties off the pile of clothes and wriggled into them. Then she got her bra and put it on. I never knew the way chicks did it. She put it on backwards, around her waist, and it had a hook on it. Then she slid it around till the cups were in front, and kind of pulled it up under and scooped herself into it, first one, then the other; then she pulled the straps over her shoulder. She reached for her dress, and I nudged some of the lath and plaster aside, and grabbed the door to give it a yank.

She had the dress up over her head, and her arms up inside the material, and when she stuck her head in, and was all tangled there for a second, I yanked the door and there was a crash as chunks of wood and plaster fell out of the way, and a heavy scraping, and I jumped inside and was on her before she could get out of the dress.

She started to scream, and I pulled the dress off her

with a ripping sound, and it all happened for her before she knew what that crash and scrape was all about.

Her face was wild. Just wild. Big eyes: I couldn't tell what color they were because they were in shadow. Real fine features, a wide mouth, little nose, cheekbones just like mine, real high and prominent, and a dimple in her right cheek. She stared at me really scared.

And then . . . and this is really weird . . . I felt like I should *say* something to her. I don't know what. Just something. It made me uncomfortable, to see her scared, but what the hell could I do about *that,* I mean, I was going to rape her, after all, and I couldn't very well tell her not to be shrinky about it. She was the one cumup, after all. But even so, I wanted to say hey, don't be scared, I just want to lay you. (That never happened before. I never wanted to *say* anything to a chick, just get in, and that was that.)

But it passed, and I put my leg behind hers and tripped her back, and she went down in a pile. I leveled the .45 at her, and her mouth kind of opened in a little o shape. "Now I'm gonna go over there and get one of them wrestling mats, so it'll be better, comfortable, uh-huh? You make a move off that floor and I shoot a leg out from under you, and you'll get screwed just the same, except you'll be without a leg." I waited for her to let me know she was onto what I was saying, and she finally nodded real slow, so I kept the automatic on her, and went over to the big dusty stack of mats, and pulled one off.

I dragged it over to her, and flipped it so the cleaner side was up, and used the muzzle of the .45 to maneuver her onto it. She just sat there on the mat, with her hands behind her, and her knees bent, and stared at me.

I unzipped my pants and started pulling them down off one side when I caught her looking at me real funny. I stopped with the jeans. "What're *you* lookin' at?"

I was mad. I didn't know why I was mad, but I was.

"What's your name?" she asked. Her voice was very soft, and kind of furry, like it came up through her throat that was all lined with fur or something.

She kept looking at me, waiting for me to answer.

"Vic," I said. She looked like she was waiting for more.

"Vic what?"

I didn't know what she meant for a minute, then I did. "Vic. Just Vic. That's all."

"Well, what're your mother and father's names?"

Then I started laughing, and working my jeans down again. "Boy, are you a dumb bitch," I said, and laughed some more. She looked hurt. It made me mad again. "Stop lookin' like that, or I'll bust out your teeth!"

She folded her hands in her lap.

I got the pants down around my ankles. They wouldn't come off over the sneakers. I had to balance on one foot and scuff the sneaker off the other foot. It was tricky, keeping the .45 on her and getting the sneaker off at the same time. But I did it.

I was standing there buck-naked from the waist down and she had sat forward a little, her legs crossed, hands still in her lap. "Get that stuff off," I said.

She didn't move for a second, and I thought she was going to give me trouble. But then she reached around behind and undid the bra. Then she tipped back and slid the panties off her ass.

Suddenly, she didn't look scared any more. She was watching me very close and I could see her eyes were blue now. Now this is the really weird thing. . . .

I couldn't do it. I mean, not exactly. I mean, I *wanted* to fuck her, see, but she was all soft and pretty and she kept *looking* at me, and no solo I ever met would believe me, but I heard myself *talking* to her, still standing there like some kind of wetbrain, one sneaker off and jeans down around my ankle. "What's *your* name?"

"Quilla June Holmes."

"That's a weird name."

"My mother says it's not that uncommon, back in Oklahoma."

"That where your folks come from?"

She nodded. "Before the Third War."

"They must be pretty old by now."

"They are, but they're okay. I guess."

We were just frozen there, talking to each other. I could tell she was cold, because she was shivering. "Well," I said, sort of getting ready to drop down beside her, "I guess we better—"

Damn it! That damned Blood! Right at that moment he came crashing in from outside. Came skidding through the lath, and plaster, raising dust, slid along on his ass till he got to us. *"Now* what?" I demanded.

"Who're you talking to?" the girl asked.

"Him. Blood."

"The dog!?!"

Blood stared at her and then ignored her. He started to say something, but the girl interrupted him. "Then it's true what they say . . . you can all talk to animals . . ."

"You going to listen to her all night, or do you want to hear why I came in?"

"Okay, why're you here?"

"You're in trouble, Albert."

"Come *on,* forget the mickeymouse. What's up?"

Blood twisted his head toward the front door of the YMCA. "Roverpak. Got the building surrounded. I make it fifteen or twenty, maybe more."

"How the hell'd they know we was here?"

Blood looked chagrined. He drooped his head.

"Well?"

"Some other mutt must've smelled her in the theater."

"Great."

"Now what?"

"Now we stand 'em off, that's what. You got any better suggestions?"

"Just one."

I waited. He grinned.

"Pull your pants up."

IV

The girl, this Quilla June, was pretty safe. I made her a kind of a shelter out of wrestling mats, maybe a dozen of them. She wouldn't get hit by a stray bullet, and if they didn't go right for her, they wouldn't find her. I climbed one of the ropes hanging down from the girders and laid out up there with the Browning and a couple of handfuls of reloads. I wished to God I'd had an automatic, a bren or a Thompson. I checked the .45, made sure it was full, with one in the chamber, and set the extra clips down on the girder. I had a clear line-of-fire all around the gym.

Blood was lying in shadow right near the front door.

He'd suggested I try and pick off any dogs with the rover-pak first, if I could. That would allow him to operate freely.

That was the least of my worries.

I'd wanted to hole up in another room, one with only a single entrance, but I had no way of knowing if the rovers were already in the building, so I did the best I could with what I had.

Everything was quiet. Even that Quilla June. It'd taken me valuable minutes to convince her she'd damned well better hole up and not make any noise; she was better off with me than with twenty of *them.* "If you ever wanna see your mommy and daddy again," I warned her. After that she didn't give me no trouble, packing her in with mats.

Quiet.

Then I heard two things, both at the same time. From back in the swimming pool I heard boots crunching plaster. Very soft. And from one side of the front door, I heard a tinkle of metal striking wood. So they were going to try a yoke. Well, I was ready.

Quiet again.

I sighted the Browning on the door to the pool room. It was still open from when I'd come through. Figure him at maybe five-ten, and drop the sights a foot and a half, and I'd catch him in the chest. I'd learned long ago you don't try for the head. Go for the widest part of the body: the chest and stomach. The trunk.

Suddenly, outside, I heard a dog bark, and part of the darkness near the front door detached itself and moved inside the gym. Directly opposite Blood. I didn't move the Browning.

The rover at the front door moved a step along the wall, away from Blood. Then he cocked back his arm and threw something—a rock, a piece of metal, something —across the room, to draw fire. I didn't move the Browning.

When the thing he'd thrown hit the floor, two rovers jumped out of the swimming pool door, one on either side of it, rifles down, ready to spray. Before they could open up, I'd squeezed off the first shot, tracked across and put a second shot into the other one. They both went down. Dead hits, right in the heart. Bang, they were down, neither one moved.

The mother by the door turned to split, and Blood was on him. Just like that, out of the darkness, riiiip!

Blood leaped, right over the crossbar of the guy's rifle held at ready, and sank his fangs into the rover's throat. The guy screamed, and Blood dropped, carrying a piece of the guy with him. The guy was making awful bubbling sounds and went down on one knee. I put a slug into his head, and he fell forward.

It went quiet again.

Not bad. Not bad atall atall. Three takeouts and they still didn't know our positions. Blood had fallen back into the murk by the entrance. He didn't say a thing, but I knew what he was thinking: maybe that was three out of seventeen, or three out of twenty, or twenty-two. No way of knowing; we could be faced-off in here for a week and never know if we'd gotten them all, or some, or none. They could go and get poured full again, and I'd find myself run out of slugs and no food and that girl, that Quilla June, crying and making me divide my attention, and daylight—and they'd be still laying out there, waiting till we got hungry enough to do something dumb, or till we ran out of slugs; and then they'd cloud up and rain all over us.

A rover came dashing straight through the front door at top speed, took a leap, hit on his shoulders, rolled, came up going in a different direction, and snapped off three rounds into different corners of the room before I could track him with the Browning. By that time he was close enough under me where I didn't have to waste a .22 slug. I picked up the .45 without a sound and blew the back off his head. Slug went in neat, came out and took most of his hair with it. He fell right down.

"Blood! The rifle!"

Came out of the shadows, grabbed it up in his mouth and dragged it over to the pile of wrestling mats in the far corner. I saw an arm poke out from the mass of mats, and a hand grabbed the rifle, dragged it inside. Well, it was at least safe there, till I needed it. Brave little bastard: he scuttled over to the dead rover and started worrying the ammo bandolier off his body. It took him a while; he could have been picked off from the doorway or outside one of the windows, but he did it. Brave little bastard. I had to remember to get him something good to eat when we got out of this. I smiled, up there in the darkness: *if* we get out of this, I wouldn't have to worry about getting him something tender.. It was lying all over the floor of that gymnasium.

Just as Blood was dragging the bandolier back into the shadows, two of them tried it with their dogs. They came through a ground floor window, one after another, hitting and rolling and going in opposite directions, as the dogs—a mother-ugly akita, big as a house, and a Doberman bitch the color of a turd—shot through the front door and split in the unoccupied two directions. I caught one of the dogs, the akita, with the .45, and it went down thrashing. The Doberman was all over Blood.

But firing, I'd given away my position. One of the rovers fired from the hip and .30–06 soft-nosed slugs spanged off the girders around me. I dropped the automatic, and it started to slip off the girder as I reached for the Browning. I made a grab for the .45 and that was the only thing saved me. I fell forward to clutch at it, it slipped away and hit the gym floor with a crash, and the rover fired at where I'd been. But I was flat on the girder, arm dangling, and the crash startled him. He fired at the sound, and right at that instant I heard another shot, from a Winchester, and the other rover, who'd made it safe into the shadows, fell forward holding a big pumping hole in his chest. That Quilla June had shot him, from behind the mats.

I didn't even have time to figure out what the fuck was happening . . . Blood was rolling around with the Doberman and the sounds they were making were awful . . . the rover with the .30–06 chipped off another shot and hit the muzzle of the Browning, protruding over the side of the girder, and wham it was gone, falling down. I was naked up there without clout, and the sonofabitch was hanging back in shadow waiting for me.

Another shot from the Winchester, and the rover fired right into the mats. She ducked back behind, and I knew I couldn't count on her for anything more. But I didn't need it; in that second, while he was focused on her, I grabbed the climbing rope, flipped myself over the girder, and howling like a burnpit-screamer, went sliding down, feeling the rope cutting my palms. I got down far enough to swing, and kicked off. I swung back and forth,

whipping my body three different ways each time, swinging out and over, way over, each time. The sonofabitch
kept firing, trying to track a trajectory, but I kept spinning
out of his line of fire. Then he was empty, and I kicked
back as hard as I could, and came zooming in toward his
corner of shadows, and let loose all at once and went ass-
over-end into the corner, and there he was, and I went
right into him and he spanged off the wall, and I was
on top of him, digging my thumbs into his eye-sockets.
He was screaming and the dogs were screaming and that
girl was screaming, and I pounded the motherfucker's
head against the floor till he stopped moving, then I
grabbed up the empty .30–06 and whipped his head till I
knew he wasn't gonna give me no more aggravation.

Then I found the .45 and shot the Doberman.

Blood got up and shook himself off. He was cut up
bad. "Thanks," he mumbled, and went over and lay down
in the shadows to lick himself off.

I went and found that Quilla June, and she was crying.
About all the guys we'd killed. Mostly about the one *she'd*
killed. I couldn't get her to stop bawling so I cracked her
across the face and told her she'd saved my life, and
that helped some.

Blood came dragassing over. "How're we going to get
out of this, Albert?"

"Let me think."

I thought and knew it was hopeless. No matter how
many we got, there'd be more. And it was a matter of
macho now. Their honor.

"How about a fire?" Blood suggested.

"Get away while it's burning?" I shook my head.
"They'll have the place staked-out all around. No
good."

"What if we don't leave? What if we burn up with it?"
I looked at him. Brave . . . and smart as hell.

V

We gathered all the lumber and mats and scaling ladders
and vaulting boxes and benches and anything else that
would burn, and piled the garbage against a wooden di-
vider at one end of the gym. Quilla June found a can of

kerosene in a storeroom, and we set fire to the whole damn pile. Then we followed Blood to the place he'd found for us. The boiler room way down under the YMCA. We all climbed into the empty boiler, and dogged down the door, leaving a release vent open for air. We had one mat in there with us, and all the ammo we could carry, and the extra rifles and sidearms the rovers'd had on them.

"Can you catch anything?" I asked Blood.

"A little. Not much. I'm reading one guy. The building's burning good."

"You be able to tell when they split?"

"Maybe. *If* they split."

I settled back. Quilla June was shaking from all that had happened. "Just take it easy," I told her. "By morning the place'll be down around our ears, and they'll go through the rubble and find a lot of dead meat, and maybe they won't look too hard for a chick's body. And everything'll be all right . . . if we don't get choked off in here."

She smiled, very thin, and tried to look brave. She was okay, that one. She closed her eyes and settled back on the mat and tried to sleep. I was beat. I closed my eyes, too.

"Can you handle it?" I asked Blood.

"I suppose. You better sleep."

I nodded, eyes still closed, and fell on my side. I was out before I could think about it.

When I came back, I found the girl, that Quilla June, snuggled up under my armpit, her arm around my waist, dead asleep. I could hardly breathe. It was like a furnace; hell, it *was* a furnace. I reached out a hand and the wall of the boiler was so damned hot I couldn't touch it. Blood was up on the mattress with us. That mat had been the only thing'd kept us from being singed good. He was asleep, head buried in his paws. She was asleep, still naked.

I put a hand on her tit. It was warm. She stirred and cuddled into me closer. I got a hard-on.

Managed to get my pants off, and rolled on top of her. She woke up fast when she felt me pry her legs apart, but it was too late by then. "Don't . . . *stop* . . . what are you doing . . . no, don't . . ."

But she was half-asleep, and weak, and I don't think she really wanted to fight me anyhow.

She cried when I broke her, of course, but after that it was okay. There was blood all over the wrestling mat. And Blood just kept sleeping.

It was really different. Usually, when I'd get Blood to track something down for me, it'd be grab it and punch it and pork it and get away fast before something bad could happen. But when she came, she rose up off the mat, and hugged me around the back so hard I thought she'd crack my ribs, and then she settled back down slow slow slow, like I do when I'm doing leg-lifts in the makeshift gym I rigged in the auto wrecking yard. And her eyes were closed, and she was relaxed looking. And happy. I could tell.

We did it a lot of times, and after a while it was her idea, but I didn't say so. And then we lay out side-by-side and talked.

She asked me about how it was with Blood, and I told her how the skirmisher dogs had gotten telepathic, and how they'd lost the ability to hunt food for themselves, so the solos and roverpaks had to do it for them, and how dogs like Blood were good at finding chicks for solos like me. She didn't say anything to that.

I asked her about what it was like where she lived, in one of the downunders.

"It's nice. But it's always very quiet. Everyone is very polite to everyone else. It's just a small town."

"Which one you live in?"

"Topeka. It's real close to here."

"Yeah. I know. The access dropshaft is only about half a mile from here. I went out there once, to take a look around."

"Have you ever been in a downunder?"

"No. But I don't guess I want to be, either."

"Why? It's very nice. You'd like it."

"Shit."

"That's very crude."

"*I'm* very crude."

"Not all the time."

I was getting mad. "Listen, you ass, what's the matter with you? I grabbed you and pushed you around, I raped you half a dozen times, so what's so good about me, huh?

What's the matter with you, don't you even have enough smarts to know when somebody's—"

She was smiling at me. "I didn't mind. I liked doing it. Want to do it again?"

I was really shocked. I moved away from her. "What the hell is wrong with you? Don't you know that a chick from a downunder like you can be really mauled by solos? Don't you know chicks get warnings from their parents in the downunders, 'Don't cumup, you'll get snagged by them dirty, hairy, slobbering solos!' Don't you know that?"

She put her hand on my leg and started moving it up, the fingertips just brushing my thigh. I got another hard-on. "My parents never said that about solos," she said. Then she pulled me over her again, and kissed me, and I couldn't stop from getting in her again.

God, it just went on like that for hours. After a while Blood turned around and said, "I'm not going to keep pretending I'm asleep. I'm hungry. And I'm hurt."

I tossed her off me—she was on top by this time—and examined him. The Doberman had taken a good chunk out of his right ear, and there was a rip right down his muzzle, and blood-matted fur on one side. He was a mess. "Jesus, man, you're a mess," I said.

"You're no savory rose garden yourself, Albert!" he snapped. I pulled my hand back.

"Can we get out of here?" I asked him.

He cast around, and then shook his head. "I can't get any readings. Must be a pile of rubble on top of this boiler. I'll have to go out and scout."

We kicked that around for a while, and finally decided if the building was razed, and had cooled a little, the rover-pak would have gone through the ashes by now. The fact that they hadn't tried the boiler indicated that we were probably buried pretty good. Either that, or the building was still smoldering overhead. In which case, they'd still be out there, waiting to sift the remains.

"Think you can handle it, the condition you're in?"

"I guess I'll *have* to, won't I?" Blood said. He was really surly. "I mean, what with you busy coitusing your brains out, there won't be much left for staying alive, will there?"

I sensed real trouble with him. He didn't like Quilla

June. I moved around him and undogged the boiler hatch. It wouldn't open. So I braced my back against the side, and jacked my legs up, and gave it a slow, steady shove.

Whatever had fallen against it from outside resisted for a minute, then started to give, then tumbled away with a crash. I pushed the door open all the way, and looked out. The upper floors had fallen in on the basement, but by the time they'd given, they'd been mostly cinder and lightweight rubble. Everything was smoking out there. I could see daylight through the smoke.

I slipped out, burning my hands on the outside lip of the hatch. Blood followed. He started to pick his way through the debris. I could see that the boiler had been almost completely covered by the gunk that had dropped from above. Chances were good the roverpak had taken a fast look, figured we'd been fried, and moved on. But I wanted Blood to run a recon anyway. He started off, but I called him back. He came.

"What is it?"

I looked down at him. "I'll tell you what it is, man. You're acting very shitty."

"Sue me."

"Goddamit, dog, what's got your ass up?"

"Her. That nit chick you've got in there."

"So what? Big deal . . . I've had chicks before."

"Yeah, but never any that hung on like this one. I warn you, Albert, she's going to make trouble."

"Don't be dumb!" He didn't reply. Just looked at me with anger, and then limped off to check out the scene. I crawled back inside and dogged the hatch. She wanted to make it again. I said I didn't want to; Blood had brought me down. I was bugged. And I didn't know which one to be pissed off at.

But God she was pretty.

She kind of pouted and settled back with her arms wrapped around her. "Tell me some more about the downunder," I said.

At first she was cranky, wouldn't say much, but after a while she opened up and started talking freely. I was learning a lot. I figured I could use it some time, maybe.

There were only a couple of hundred downunders in what was left of the United States and Canada. They'd been sunk on the sites of wells or mines or other kinds of deep holes. Some of them, out in the west, were in natural cave formations. They went way down, maybe two to five miles. They were like big caissons, stood on end. And the people who'd settled them were squares of the worst kind. Southern Baptists, Fundamentalists, lawan-order goofs, real middle-class squares with no taste for the wild life. And they'd gone back to a kind of life that hadn't existed for a hundred and fifty years. They'd got-ten the last of the scientists to do the work, invent the how and why, and then they'd run them out. They didn't want any progress, they didn't want any dissent, they didn't want anything that would make waves. They'd had enough of that. The best time in the world had been just before the First War, and they figured if they could keep it like that, they could live quiet lives and survive. Shit! I'd go nuts in one of the downunders.

Quilla June smiled, and snuggled up again, and this time I didn't turn her off. She started touching me again, down there and all over, and then she said, "Vic?"

"Uh-huh."

"Have you ever been in love?"

"What?"

"In love. Have you ever been in love with a girl?"

"Well, I damn well guess I haven't!"

"Do you know what love is?"

"Sure. I guess I do."

"But if you've never been in love . . . ?"

"Don't be dumb. I mean, I've never had a bullet in the head, and I know I wouldn't like it."

"You don't know what love is, I'll bet."

"Well, if it means living in a downunder, I guess I just don't wanna find out." We didn't go on with the conversa-tion much after that. She pulled me down and we did it again. And when it was over, I heard Blood scratching at the boiler. I opened the hatch, and he was standing out there. "All clear," he said.

"You sure?"

"Yeah, yeah, I'm sure. Put your pants on," he said it with a sneer in the tone, "and come on out here. We have to talk some stuff."

I looked at him, and he wasn't kidding. I got my

jeans and sneakers on, and climbed down out of the boiler.

He trotted ahead of me, away from the boiler over some blacksoot beams, and outside the gym. It was down. Looked like a rotted stump tooth.

"Now what's lumbering you?" I asked him.

He scampered up on a chunk of concrete till he was almost nose-level with me.

"You're going dumb on me, Vic."

I knew he was serious. No Albert shit, straight Vic. "How so?"

"Last night, man. We could have cut out of there and left her for them. *That* would have been smart."

"I wanted her."

"Yeah, I know. That's what I'm talking about. It's to-day now, not last night. You've had her about a half a hundred times. Why're we hanging around?"

"I want her some more."

Then he got angry. "Yeah, well, listen, chum . . . *I* want a few things myself. I want something to eat, and I want to get rid of this pain in my side, and I want away from this turf. Maybe they *don't* give up this easily."

"Take it easy. We can handle all that. Don't mean she can't go with us."

"*Doesn't* mean," he corrected me. "And so *that's* the new story. Now we travel three, is that right?"

I was getting really uptight myself. "You're starting to sound like a damn poodle!"

"And you're starting to sound like a boxer."

I hauled back to crack him one. He didn't move. I dropped the hand. I'd never hit Blood. I didn't want to start now.

"Sorry," he said softly.

"That's okay."

But we weren't looking at each other.

"Vic, man, you've got a responsibility to me, you know."

"You don't have to tell me that."

"Well, I guess maybe I do. Maybe I have to remind you of some stuff. Like the time that burnpit-screamer came up out of the street and made a grab for you."

I shuddered. The motherfucker'd been green. Right-eous stone green, glowing like fungus. My gut heaved, just thinking.

"And I went for him, right?"

I nodded. Right, mutt, right.

"And I could have been burned bad, and died, and that would've been all of it for me, right or wrong, isn't that true?" I nodded again. I was getting pissed off proper. I didn't like being made to feel guilty. It was a fifty-fifty with Blood and me. He knew that. "But I did it, right?" I remembered the way the green thing had screamed. Christ, it was all ooze and eyelashes.

"Okay, okay, don't hanger me."

"Harangue, not hanger."

"Well, WHATEVER!" I shouted, "Just knock off the crap, or we can forget the whole fucking arrangement!"

Then Blood blew. "Well, maybe we *should,* you simple *dumb putz!"*

"What's a *putz,* you little turd . . . is that something bad . . . yeah, it must be . . . you watch your fucking mouth, son of a bitch or I'll kick your ass!"

We sat there and didn't talk for fifteen minutes. Neither one of us knew which way to go.

Finally, I backed off a little. I talked soft and I talked slow. I was about up to here with him, but told him I was going to do right by him, like I always had, and he threatened me, saying I'd damned well better because there were a couple of very hip solos making it around the city, and they'd be delighted to have a sharp tail-scent like him. I told him I didn't like being threatened, and he'd better watch his fucking step or I'd break his leg. He got furious and stalked off. I said screw you and went back to the boiler to take it out on that Quilla June again.

But when I stuck my head inside the boiler, she was waiting, with a pistol one of the dead rovers had supplied. She hit me good and solid over the right eye with it, and I fell straight forward across the hatch, and was out cold.

VI

"I told you she was no good." He watched me as I swabbed out the cut with disinfectant from my kit, and painted the gash with iodine. He smirked when I flinched.

I put away the stuff, and rummaged around in the boiler, gathering up all the spare ammo I could carry, ditching the Browning in favor of the heavier .30–06. Then I found something that must've slipped out of her clothes.

It was a little metal plate, about three inches long and an inch-and-a-half high. It had a whole string of numbers on it, and there were holes in it, in random patterns. "What's this?" I asked Blood.

He looked at it, sniffed it.

"Must be an identity card of some kind. Maybe it's what she used to get out of the downunder."

That made up my mind.

I jammed it in a pocket and started out. Toward the access dropshaft.

"Where the hell are you going?" Blood yelled after me.

"Come on back, you'll get killed out there!

"I'm hungry, dammit! I'm wounded!

"Albert, you simpleton! Come back here!"

I kept right on walking. I was gonna find that bitch and brain her. Even if I had to go downunder to find her.

It took me an hour to walk to the access dropshaft leading down to Topeka. I thought I saw Blood following, but hanging back a ways. I didn't give a damn. I was mad.

Then there it was. A tall, straight, featureless pillar of shining black metal. It was maybe twenty feet in diameter, perfectly flat on top, disappearing straight into the ground. It was a cap, that was all. I walked straight up to it, and fished around in the pocket for that metal card. Then something was tugging at my right pants leg.

"Listen, you moron, you can't go down there!"

I kicked him off, but he came right back.

"Listen to me!"

I turned around and stared at him.

Blood sat down; the powder puffed up around him. "Albert . . ."

"My name is Vic, you little egg sucker."

"Okay, okay, no fooling around. Vic." His tone softened. "Vic. Come on, man." He was trying to get through to me. I was really boiling, but he was trying to make sense. I shrugged, and crouched down beside him.

"Listen, man," Blood said, "this chick has bent you

way out of shape. You *know* you can't go down there. It's all square and settled, and they know everyone; they hate solos. Enough roverpaks have raided downunder and raped their women, and stolen their food, they'll have defenses set up. They'll *kill* you, Vic!"

"What the hell do you care? You're always saying you'd be better off without me." He sagged at that.

"Vic, we've been together almost three years. Good and bad. But this can be the worst. I'm scared, man. Scared you won't come back. And I'm hungry, and I'll have to go find some dude who'll take me on . . . and you know most solos are in paks now, I'll be low mutt. I'm not that young anymore. And I'm hurt pretty bad."

I could dig it. He was talking sense. But all I could think of was how that bitch, that Quilla June, had rapped me. And then there were images of her soft tits, and the way she made little sounds when I was in her, and I shook my head, and knew I had to go get even.

"I got to do it, Blood. *I got to.*"

He breathed deep and sagged a little more. He knew it was useless. "You don't even see what she's done to you, Vic. That metal card, it's too easy, as if she *wanted* you to follow."

I got up. "I'll try to get back quick. Will you wait . . . ?"

He was silent a long while, and I waited. Finally, he said, "For a while. Maybe I'll be here, maybe not."

I understood. I turned and started walking around the pillar of black metal. Finally I found a slot in the pillar, and slipped the metal card into it. There was a soft humming sound, then a section of the pillar dilated. I hadn't even seen the lines of the sections. A circle opened and I took a step through. I turned and there was Blood, watching me. We looked at each other, all the while that pillar was humming.

"So long, Vic."

"Take care of yourself, Blood."

"Hurry back."

"Do my best."

"Yeah. Right."

Then I turned around and stepped inside. The access portal irised closed behind me.

VII

I should have known. I should have suspected. Sure, every once in a while a chick came up to see what it was like on the surface, what had happened to the cities; sure, it happened. Why, I'd believed her when she'd told me, cuddled up beside me in that steaming boiler, that she'd wanted to see what it was like when a girl did it with a guy, that all the flicks she'd seen in Topeka were sweet and solid and dull, and the girls in her school'd talked about beaver flicks, and one of them had a little eight-page comic book and she'd read it with wide eyes . . . sure, I'd believed her. It was logical. I should have suspected something when she left that metal i.d. plate behind. It was too easy. Blood'd tried to tell me. Dumb? Yeah!

The second that access iris swirled closed behind me, the humming got louder, and some cool light grew in the walls. Wall. It was a circular compartment with only two sides to the wall: *in*side and *out*side. The wall pulsed up light and the humming got louder, and the deckplate I was standing on dilated just the way the outside port had done. But I was standing there, like a mouse in a cartoon, and as long as I didn't look down I was cool, I wouldn't fall.

Then I started settling. Dropped through the floor, the iris closed overhead, I was dropping down the tube, picking up speed but not too much, just dropping steadily. Now I knew what a dropshaft was.

Down and down I went and every once in a while I'd see something like 10 LEV or ANTIPOLL 55 or BREEDER-CON or PUMP SE 6 on the wall, faintly I could make out the sectioning of an iris . . . but I never stopped dropping.

Finally, I dropped all the way to the bottom, and there was TOPEKA CITY LIMITS POP. 22,860 on the wall, and I settled down without any strain, bending a little from the knees to cushion the impact, but even that wasn't much.

I used the metal plate again, and the iris—a much bigger one this time—swirled open, and I got my first look at a downunder.

It stretched away in front of me, twenty miles to the dim shining horizon of tin can metal where the wall behind me curved and curved and curved till it made one smooth, encircling circuit and came back around around around to where I stood, staring at it. I was down at the bottom of a big metal tube that stretched up to a ceiling an eighth of a mile overhead, twenty miles across. And in the bottom of that tin can, someone had built a town that looked for all the world like a photo out of one of the water-logged books in the library on the surface. I'd seen a town like this in the books. Just like this. Neat little houses, and curvy little streets, and trimmed lawns, and a business section and everything else that a Topeka would have.

Except a sun, except birds, except clouds, except rain, except snow, except cold, except wind, except ants, except dirt, except mountains, except oceans, except big fields of grain, except stars, except the moon, except forests, except animals running wild, except. . . .

Except freedom.

They were canned down here, like dead fish. Canned. I felt my throat tighten up. I wanted to get out. Out! I started to tremble, my hands were cold and there was sweat on my forehead. This had been insane, coming down here. I had to get out. *Out!*

I turned around to get back in the dropshaft, and then it grabbed me.

That bitch Quilla June! I shoulda suspected!

The thing was low, and green, and boxlike, and had cables with mittens on the ends instead of arms, and it rolled on tracks, and it grabbed me.

It hoisted me up on its square flat top, holding me with them mittens on the cables, and I couldn't move, except to try kicking at the big glass eye in the front, but it didn't do any good. It didn't bust. The thing was only about four feet high, and my sneakers almost reached the ground, but not quite, and it started moving off into Topeka, hauling me along with it.

People were all over the place. Sitting in rockers on their front porches, raking their lawns, hanging around the gas station, sticking pennies in gumball machines, painting a white stripe down the middle of the road, selling newspapers on a corner, listening to an oompah band in a shell in a park, playing hopscotch and pussy-in-the-corner, polishing a fire engine, sitting on benches, washing windows, pruning bushes, tipping hats to ladies, collecting milk bottles in wire carrying racks, grooming horses, throwing a stick for a dog to retrieve, diving into a communal swimming pool, chalking vegetable prices on a slate outside a grocery, walking hand-in-hand with a girl, all of them watching me go past on that metal motherfucker.

I could hear Blood speaking, saying just what he'd said before I'd entered the dropshaft: *It's all square and settled and they know everyone; they hate solos. Enough roverpaks have raided downunders, and raped their women, and stolen their food, they'll have defenses set up. They'll kill you, man!*

Thanks, mutt.

Goodbye.

VIII

The green box tracked through the business section and turned in at a shopfront with the words BETTER BUSINESS BUREAU on the window. It rolled right inside the open door, and there were half a dozen men and old men and very old men in there, waiting for me. Also a couple of women. The green box stopped.

One of them came over and took the metal plate out of my hand. He looked at it, then turned around and gave it to the oldest of the old men, a withered toad wearing baggy pants and a green eyeshade and garters that held up the sleeves of his striped shirt. "Quilla June, Lew," the guy said to the old man. Lew took the metal plate and put it in the top left drawer of a rolltop desk. "Better take his guns, Aaron," the old coot said. And the guy who'd taken the plate cleaned me.

"Let him loose, Aaron," Lew said.

Aaron stepped around the back of the green box and something clicked, and the cable-mittens sucked back inside the box, and I got down off the thing. My arms were numb where the box had held me. I rubbed one, then the other, and I glared at them.

"Now, boy . . ." Lew started.

"Suck wind, asshole!"

The women blanched. The men tightened their faces.

"I told you it wouldn't work," another of the old men said to Lew.

"Bad business, this," said one of the younger ones.

Lew leaned forward in his straight-back chair and pointed a crumbled finger at me. "Boy, you better be nice."

"I hope all your fuckin' children are hare-lipped!"

"This is no good, Lew!" another man said.

"Guttersnipe," a woman with a beak snapped.

Lew stared at me. His mouth was a nasty little black line. I knew the sonofabitch didn't have a tooth in his crummy head that wasn't rotten and smelly. He stared at me with vicious little eyes. God, he was ugly, like a toad ready to snaffle a fly off the wall with his tongue. He was getting set to say something I wouldn't like. "Aaron, maybe you'd better put the sentry back on him." Aaron moved to the green box.

"Okay, hold it," I said, holding up my hand.

Aaron stopped, looked at Lew, who nodded. Then Lew leaned real far forward again, and aimed that bird-claw at me. "You ready to behave yourself, son?"

"Yeah, I guess."

"You'd better be dang sure."

"Okay. I'm *dang* sure. Also *fuckin'* sure!"

"And you'll watch your mouth."

I didn't reply. Old coot.

"You're a bit of an experiment for us, boy. We tried to get one of you down here other ways. Sent up some good folks to capture one of you little scuts, but they never came back. Figgered it was best to lure you down to us."

I sneered. That Quilla June. I'd take care of her!

One of the women, a little younger than Bird-Beak, came forward and looked into my face. "Lew, you'll never get this one to cow-tow. He's a filthy little killer. Look at those eyes."

"How'd you like the barrel of a rifle jammed up your ass, bitch?" She jumped back. Lew was angry again. "Sorry," I said real quickly, "I don't like bein' called names. *Macho,* y'know?"

He settled back and snapped at the woman, "Mez,

leave him alone. I'm tryin' to talk a bit of sense here. You're only making it worse."

Mez went back and sat with the others. Some Better Business Bureau these creeps were!

"As I was saying, boy: you're an experiment for us. We've been down here in Topeka close to thirty years. It's nice down here. Quiet, orderly, nice people, who respect each other, no crime, respect for the elders, and just all around a good place to live. We're growin' and we're prosperin'."

I waited.

"But, well, we find now that some of our folks can't have no more babies, and the women that do, they have mostly girls. We need some men. Certain special kind of men."

I started laughing. This was too good to be true. They wanted me for stud service. I couldn't stop laughing.

"Crude!" one of the women said, scowling.

"This's awkward enough for us, boy, don't make it no harder." Lew was embarrassed.

Here I'd spent most of Blood's and my time above-ground hunting up tail, and down here they wanted me to service the local ladyfolk. I sat down on the floor and laughed till tears ran down my cheeks.

Finally, I got up and said, "Sure. Okay. But if I do, there's a couple of things *I* want."

Lew looked at me close.

"The first thing I want is that Quilla June. I'm gonna fuck her blind, and then I'm gonna bang her on the head the way she did me!"

They huddled for a while, then came out and Lew said, "We can't tolerate any violence down here, but I s'pose Quilla June's as good a place to start as any. She's capable, isn't she, Ira?"

A skinny, yellow-skinned man nodded. He didn't look happy about it. Quilla June's old man, I bet.

"Well, let's get started," I said. "Line 'em up." I started to unzip my jeans.

The women screamed, the men grabbed me, and they hustled me off to a boarding house where they gave me a room, and they said I should get to know Topeka a little bit before I went to work because it was, uh, er, well, awkward, and they had to get the folks in town to

accept what was going to have to be done . . . on the
assumption, I suppose, that if I worked out okay, they'd
import a few more young bulls from aboveground and
turn us loose.

So I spent some time in Topeka, getting to know the
folks, seeing what they did, how they lived.

It was nice, real nice.

They rocked in rockers on the front porches, they
raked their lawns, they hung around the gas station,
they stuck pennies in gumball machines, they painted
white stripes down the middle of the road, they sold
newspapers on the corners, they listened to oompah
bands in a shell in the park, they played hopscotch and
pussy-in-the-corner, they polished fire engines, they sat
on benches reading, they washed windows and pruned
bushes, they tipped their hats to ladies, they collected
milk bottles in wire carrying racks, they groomed horses
and threw sticks for their dogs to retrieve, they dove
into the communal swimming pool, they chalked vegetable prices on a slate outside the grocery, they walked
hand-in-hand with some of the ugliest chicks I've ever
seen, *and they bored the ass off me.*

Inside a week I was ready to scream.

I could feel that tin can closing in on me.

I could feel the weight of the earth over me.

They ate artificial shit: artificial peas and fake meat
and make-believe chicken and ersatz corn and bogus
bread. and it all tasted like chalk and dust to me.

Polite? Christ, you could puke from the lying, hypocrit-
ical crap they called civility. Hello Mr. This and Hello
Mrs. That. And how are you? And how is little Janie?
And how is business? And are you going to the sodality
meeting Thursday? And I started gibbering in my room at
the boarding house.

The clean, sweet, neat, lovely way they lived was
enough to kill a guy. No wonder the men couldn't get it up
and make babies that had balls instead of slots.

The first few days, everyone watched me like I was
about to explode and cover their nice whitewashed fences
with shit. But after a while, they got used to seeing me.
Lew took me over to the Mercantile, and got me fitted out
with a pair of bib overalls and a shirt that any solo
could've spotted a mile away. That Mez, that dippy bitch

who'd called me a killer, she started hanging around, finally said she wanted to cut my hair, make me look civilized. But I was hip to where she was at. Wasn't a bit of the mother in her.

"What'sa'matter, cunt," I pinned her. "Your old man isn't taking care of you?"

She tried to stick her fist in her mouth, and I laughed like a loon. "Go chop off *his* balls, baby. My hair stays the way it is." She cut and run. Went like she had a diesel tail-pipe.

It went on like that for a while. Me just walking around, them coming and feeding me, keeping all their young meat out of my way till they got the town stacked-away for what was coming with me.

Jugged like that, my mind wasn't right for a while. I got all claustrophobed, clutched, went and sat under the porch in the dark at the rooming house. Then that passed, and I got piss-mean, snapped at them, then surly, then quiet, then just mud dull. Quiet.

Finally, I started getting hip to the possibilities of getting out of there. It began with me remembering the poodle I'd fed Blood one time. It had to come from a downunder. And it couldn't of got up through the dropshaft. So that meant there were other ways out.

They gave me pretty much the run of the town, as long as I kept my manners around me and didn't try anything sudden. That green sentry box was always somewhere nearby.

So I found the way out. Nothing so spectacular; it just had to be there, and I found it.

Then I found out where they kept my weapons, and I was ready. Almost.

IX

It was a week to the day when Aaron and Lew and Ira came to get me. I was pretty goofy by that time. I was sitting out on the back porch of the boarding house, smoking a corncob pipe with my shirt off, catching some sun. Except there wasn't no sun. Goofy.

They came around the house. "Morning, Vic," Lew greeted me. He was hobbling along with a cane, the old fart. Aaron gave me a big smile. The kind you'd give a big black bull about to stuff his meat into a good breed cow. Ira had a look that you could chip off and use in your furnace.

"Well, howdy, Lew. Mornin' Aaron, Ira."

Lew seemed right pleased by that.

Oh, you lousy bastards, just you wait!

"You 'bout ready to go meet your first lady?"

"Ready as I'll ever be, Lew," I said, and got up.

"Cool smoke, ain't it?" Aaron said.

I took the corncob out of my mouth. "Pure dee-light." I smiled. I hadn't even lit the fucking thing.

They walked me over to Marigold Street and as we came up on a little house with yellow shutters and a white picket fence, Lew said, "This's Ira's house. Quilla June is his daughter."

"Well, land sakes," I said, wide-eyed.

Ira's lean jaw muscles jumped.

We went inside.

Quilla June was sitting on the settee with her mother, an older version of her, pulled thin as a withered muscle. "Miz Holmes," I said and made a little curtsy. She smiled. Strained, but smiled.

Quilla June sat with her feet right together, and her hands folded in her lap. There was a ribbon in her hair. It was blue.

Matched her eyes.

Something went thump in my gut.

"Quilla June," I said.

She looked up. "Mornin', Vic."

Then everyone sort of stood around looking awkward, and finally Ira began yapping and yipping about get in the bedroom and get this unnatural filth over with so they could go to Church and pray the Good Lord wouldn't Strike All Of Them Dead with a bolt of lightning in the ass, or some crap like that.

So I put out my hand, and Quilla June reached for it without looking up, and we went in the back, into a small bedroom, and she stood there with her head down.

"You didn't tell 'em, did you?" I asked.

She shook her head.

And suddenly, I didn't want to kill her at all. I wanted to hold her. Very tight. So I did. And she was crying into my chest, and making little fists beating on my back, and then she was looking up at me and running her words all together: "Oh, Vic, I'm sorry, so sorry, I didn't mean to, I had to, I was sent out to, I was so scared, and I love you, and now they've got you down here, and it isn't dirty, is it, it isn't the way my Poppa says it is, is it?"

I held her and kissed her and told her it was okay, and then I asked her if she wanted to come away with me, and she said yes yes yes she really did. So I told her I might have to hurt her Poppa to get away, and she got a look in her eyes that I knew real well.

For all her propriety, Quilla June Holmes didn't much like her prayer-shouting Poppa.

I asked her if she had anything heavy, like a candlestick or a club, and she said no. So I went rummaging around in that back bedroom and found a pair of her Poppa's socks in a bureau drawer. I pulled the big brass balls off the headboard of the bed and dropped them into the sock. I hefted it. Oh. Yeah.

She stared at me with big eyes. "What're you going to do?"

"You want to get out of here?"

She nodded.

"Then just stand back behind the door. No, wait a minute, I got a better idea. Get on the bed."

She lay down on the bed. "Okay," I said, "now pull up your skirt, pull off your pants, and spread out." She gave me a look of pure horror. "Do it," I said. "If you want out."

So she did it, and I rearranged her so her knees were bent and her legs open at the thighs, and I stood to one side of the door and whispered to her, "Call your Poppa. Just him."

She hesitated a long moment, then she called out in a voice she didn't have to fake, "Poppa! Poppa, come here, please!" Then she clammed her eyes shut tight.

Ira Holmes came through the door, took one look at his secret desire, his mouth dropped open, I kicked the door closed behind him and walloped him as hard as I could. He squished a little, and spattered the bedspread, and went very down.

She opened her eyes when she heard the thunk! and when the stuff spattered her legs, she leaned over and puked on the floor. I knew she wouldn't be much good to me in getting Aaron into the room, so I opened the door, stuck my head around, looked worried, and said, "Aaron, would you come here a minute, please?" He looked at Lew, who was rapping with Mrs. Holmes about what was going on in the back bedroom, and when Lew nodded him on, he came into the room. He took a look at Quilla June's naked bush, at the blood on the wall and bedspread, at Ira on the floor, and opened his mouth to yell just as I whacked him. It took two more to get him down, and then I had to kick him in the chest to put him away. Quilla June was still puking.

I grabbed her by the arm and swung her up off the bed. At least she was being quiet about it, but man, did she stink.

"Come on!"

She tried to pull back, but I held on and opened the bedroom door. As I pulled her out, Lew stood up, leaning on his cane. I kicked the cane out from under the old fart and down he went in a heap. Mrs. Holmes was staring at us, wondering where her old man was. "He's back in there," I said, heading for the front door. "The Good Lord got him in the head."

Then we were out in the street, Quilla June stinking along behind me, dry-heaving and bawling and probably wondering what had happened to her underpants.

They kept my weapons in a locked case at the Better Business Bureau, and we detoured around by my boarding house where I pulled the crowbar I'd swiped from the gas station out from under the back porch. Then we cut across behind the Grange and into the business section, and straight into the BBB. There was a clerk who tried to stop me, and I split his gourd with the crowbar. Then I pried the latch off the cabinet in Lew's office and got the .30–06 and my .45 and all the ammo, and my spike and my knife and my kit, and loaded up. By that time Quilla June was able to make some sense.

"Where we gonna go, where we gonna go, oh, Poppa Poppa Poppa . . . !"

"Hey, listen, Quilla June, Poppa me no Poppas. You said you wanted to be with me . . . well, I'm goin'! *Up,* baby, and if you wanna go with me, you better stick ~~se."

She was too scared to object.

I stepped out the front of the shopfront, and there was that green box sentry, coming on like a whippet. It had its cables out, and the mittens were gone. It had hooks.

I dropped to one knee, wrapped the sling of the .30–06 around my forearm, sighted clean, and fired dead at the big eye in the front. One shot, spang!

Hit that eye, the thing exploded in a shower of sparks, and the green box swerved and went through the front window of The Mill End Shoppe, screeching and crying and showering the place with flames and sparks. Nice.

I turned around to grab Quilla June, but she was gone. I looked off down the street, and here came all the vigilantes, Lew hobbling along with his cane like some kind of weird grasshopper.

And right then the shots started. Big, booming sounds. The .45 I'd given Quilla June. I looked up, and on the porch around the second floor, there she was, the automatic down on the railing like a pro, sighting into that mob and snapping off shots like maybe Wild Bill Elliott in a '40s Republic flick.

But dumb! Mother, dumb! Wasting time on that, when we had to get away.

I found the outside staircase going up there, and took it three steps at a time. She was smiling and laughing, and every time she'd pick one of those boobs out of the pack her little tonguetip would peek out of the corner of her mouth, and her eyes would get all slick and wet and wham! down the boob would go.

She was really into it.

Just as I reached her, she sighted down on her scrawny mother. I slammed the back of her head, and she missed the shot, and the old lady did a little dance-step and kept coming. Quilla June whipped her head around at me, and there was kill in her eyes. "You made me miss." The voice gave me a chill.

I took the .45 away from her. Dumb. Wasting ammunition like that.

Dragging her behind me, I circled the building, found a shed out back, dropped down onto it, and had her follow. She was scared at first, but I said, "Chick can shoot her old lady as easy as you do shouldn't be worried about a drop this small." She got out on the ledge, other side of the railing and held on. "Don't worry," I said, "you won't wet your pants. You haven't got any."

She laughed, like a bird, and dropped. I caught her, we slid down the shed door, and took a second to see if that mob was hard on us. Nowhere in sight.

I grabbed Quilla June by the arm and started off toward the south end of Topeka. It was the closest exit I'd found in my wandering, and we made it in about fifteen minutes, panting and weak as kittens.

And there it was.

A big air-intake duct.

I pried off the clamps with the crowbar, and we climbed up inside. There were ladders going up. There had to be. It figured. Repairs. Keep it clean. Had to be. We started climbing.

It took a long, long time.

Quilla June kept asking me from down behind me, whenever she got too tired to climb, "Vic, do you love me?" I kept saying yes. Not only because I meant it. It helped her keep climbing.

X

We came up a mile from the access dropshaft. I shot off the filter covers and the hatch bolts, and we climbed out. They should have known better down there. You don't fuck around with Jimmy Cagney.

They never had a chance.

Quilla June was exhausted. I didn't blame her. But I didn't want to spend the night out in the open; there were things out there I didn't like to think about meeting even in daylight. It was getting on toward dusk.

We walked toward the access dropshaft.

Blood was waiting.

He looked weak. But he'd waited.

I stooped down and lifted his head. He opened his eyes, and very softly he said, "Hey."

I smiled at him. Jesus, it was good to see him. "We ᵃade it back, man."

ᵉe tried to get up, but he couldn't. The wounds on him ᵃ ugly shape. "Have you eaten?" I asked.

"No. Grabbed a lizard yesterday . . . or maybe it was day before. I'm hungry, Vic."

Quilla June came up then, and Blood saw her. He closed his eyes. "We'd better hurry, Vic," she said. "Please. They might come up from the dropshaft."

I tried to lift Blood. He was dead weight. "Listen, Blood, I'll leg it into the city and get some food. I'll come back quick. You just wait here."

"Don't go in there, Vic," he said. "I did a recon the day after you went down. They found out we weren't fried in that gym. I don't know how. Maybe mutts smelled our track. I've been keeping watch, and they haven't tried to come out after us. I don't blame them. You don't know what it's like out here at night, man . . . you don't know . . ."

He shivered.

"Take it easy, Blood."

"But they've got us marked lousy in the city, Vic. We can't go back there. We'll have to make it someplace else."

That put it on a different stick. We couldn't go back, and with Blood in that condition we couldn't go forward. And I knew, as good a solo as I was, I couldn't make it without him. And there wasn't anything out here to eat. He had to have some food at once, and some medical care. I had to do something. Something good, something fast.

"Vic," Quilla June's voice was high and whining, "come *on!* Leave him. He'll be all right. We have to hurry."

I looked up at her. The sun was going down. Blood trembled in my arms.

She got a pouty look on her face. "If you love me, you'll come *on!*"

I couldn't make it alone out there without him. I knew it. If I loved her. She asked me, in the boiler, do you know what love is?

It was a small fire, not nearly big enough for any rover-pak to spot from the outskirts of the city. No smoke. And after Blood had eaten his fill, I carried him to the air-duct a mile away, and we spent the night inside on a little ledge. I held him all night. He slept good. In the morning, I fixed him up pretty good. He'd make it; he was strong.

He ate again. There was plenty left from the night before. I didn't eat. I wasn't hungry.

We started off across the blast wasteland that morning. We'd find another city, and make it.

We had to move slow because Blood was still limping. It took a long time before I stopped hearing her calling in my head. Asking me, asking me: *do you know what love is?*

Sure I know.

A boy loves his dog.